GUN OF GOD

A NOVEL

by

David R. Cudlip

Pen & Pencil Press ✦ Tryon, North Carolina
www.penandpencilpress.com

Interior Book Design: Kimberly Martin
Book Cover: Christina Carden

For Georgia Lee
Sine Qua Non
in so many ways

Author's Note

A work of fiction, this story is wholly woven from this writer's imagination. While references are made to public figures of the past, this is done strictly for verisimilitude. Otherwise, the characters portrayed are not meant to resemble, or in any way depict, living persons.

The outcomes of bioscience, as told in this story, are events and doings that are entirely possible. Here, an example:

A piece headed as Human Artificial Chromosome Created appeared on April 5, 1997 in Science News Online, accompanied by a statement which told us, *"Some researchers envision a day when they can slip into a person's cells synthetic chromosomes containing genes that correct a disease."*

Here's another. Twelve years later, yet another article dated August 31, 2009 in USA TODAY, reported this: *Scientists aim to cook up new medicines…but fears of abuse simmer…referring to "synthetic biology", a hot buzzword in the biomedical field, strongly suggesting that those who know how to do it are busy concocting a future unknown for all.*

Translate both articles as meaning—making life from scratch.

Boggling questions intrude. One, for example, is if we are to assume for ourselves the tasks of Nature's handiwork, then who among us decides who can do it better? And do *what* better? Another brain-stroker is: if we set about creating new forms of life, exactly what should they be? And why? Leading, at the very least, to a fourth inquiry: What if we guess wrongly about modifying humans, or pre-programming them before conception takes place? Is this paragraph one in the writing of our own obituary *en mass*?

One can look up transhumanism on the internet to gain a fuller picture of what some pundits have in mind for our future. Maybe they're right, but what if they aren't?

The riddle of reliable gene therapy will surely be resolved at some point; after which it's a safe bet that life, as we know it, will alter profoundly. How? Illnesses, for one, will be cut sharply; life will easily last for 200 or 300 years; marriages for, say, 100 years or for the duration of love feelings, which, by themselves are unlikely to be enhanced by gene therapy. Working careers, well, who knows? Say 150 years till you can retire affordably. Besides, someone has to earn bread for the billions who chose to live to the age of Methuselah, the famed Hebrew patriarch of Genesis 5:25-27.

Never passing up an opportunity to be heard when science and religion are poised for a tangle, the Pope, while addressing the faithful on Palm Sunday of 2011, had this to say: "While great advances of technology have improved life for man…they have also increased possibilities for evil and recent natural disasters were a reminder, if any were needed, that mankind is not all-powerful."

One, of course, might say the same of religion. Or of anything else, man-made…

In science, may I submit this: that the Law of Unintended Consequences is forever in play; fate's dice, once rolled in the endeavor to genetically manipulate ourselves, can easily come up snake eyes.

To compete in society, even survive its rigors, humans may one day be forced to become another species. Quasi-humans. Some of this, some of that—a change to the genetic recipe. Nothing is unusual in evolution about that outcome, since all species evolve over time, and, at some point, come to their end. Yet, if a new species of humans is contrived, and unnaturally so, who is to say if it's for better or for worse. Exactly who, and why them?

After all, dice rolls are dice rolls. You win, you lose. You adapt, you don't.

In his seminal book, *The End of History and the Last Man*, Francis Fukuyama argues we are at "*…the end point of mankind's ideological evolution and the universalization of Western liberal democracy as the final form of human government.*" Here we go, he suggests, heading off for an irreversible tipping point from which no return is possible. Why? Bioscience will remake us, that's why. For all we know, posthumans will re-enter the Dark Ages, or perhaps it will be an Age beyond our comprehension, a sort of void that we cannot grasp till it's too late.

In this story, you can weigh what happens to one man, Thomas Courmaine, who figured out how to make gene therapy work, thereby changing our planet's everyday life. Then, seeing what he'd done, seeing how his life's endeavor was corrupted, he felt compelled to wage a fight for humans to remain as humans. In his shoes, what would you do?

Tryon, North Carolina, 2011

PART I

To risk nothing is to risk everything
—Plato

Or, if you're leaving home, switch on a new
Four-pointed star in Heaven as you do,
To light a vacant world with steady blaze
And follow you forever with its gaze.
—Joseph Brodsky

The Naruma Territory, Africa

Nearing the women's dome-shaped hut, Thomas Courmaine whistled a tune to signal his approach. Already they knew of his arrival, ever since the drum-talk had begun when first he had set foot in the village.

Va-dom-va-va-baroom-boom, a staccato beat rising in various crescendos. Meant to rattle his nerves and it always did. He had entered the far end of the Mzura village without permission, with the incursion duly noted by the sinister sounds of those beats: *va-va-baroom-boom.* He walked a well-worn path, almost a mile of it, not too hurriedly yet at a pace driven by a jumpy spine. One change in those drum beats, especially the wrong change, and spears would quickly fly.

Rounding a bend, there it was—the hut, home to three Mzura women: his Eves, his creations. Hearing the drums quicken, Courmaine, his nerves rattled, scurried the last twenty yards to his destination.

Sweeping aside a curtain of blue-and-yellow beaded strings, he stepped across the threshold, almost bumping into two of the women. Giggling, their hands fluttering about like startled doves struggling for altitude, they swayed nakedly before a full-length mirror that he had finagled from a caravan of Indian traders. The three women prized the looking-glass, taking turns to rag it—two, sometimes three times daily, till it glittered like sunrays on flat water.

With much affection, he had begun to think of them as his Eves. They were the first on earth who had ever reversed their physical appearance via gene transplants. In their seventies now, but looking as if they only in their mid-to-late thirties. Gone were the sags, gone were most of the wrinkles; their skins, at least for two of them, smooth looking as polished ebony.

Years had seemingly melted away, and when they had pestered him to know the trick, he had truthfully said it was due to an exudate—an enzyme—derived from the root of a native plant called *semba.*

In disbelief, they had scoffed. Like all Mzura, they knew a good deal about *semba*, a millennia-old healing plant used throughout the tribe for healing.

Nothing in *semba's* lore could explain how they had so mysteriously returned to youth.

Two of the women had begun to gyrate their hips, an act meant to reassure them that the images they saw in the mirror were alive, were the new truth of themselves, and the gift of returned youth was truly refilling them with its urges. A third woman, also disrobed, stood apart. A bashful look masked her face, smiling an inward smile, her mood rarely easy to read.

Collectively, they only recalled the slight prick of a needle and a clear fluid vanishing into an arm. Not caring a whit about anything so inconsequential; nor had they even the thinnest notion they were the centerpiece of a transforming moment, done by this man whom the Mzura called Eanu.

Still, he had not invested them with new bodies, but only new skins; three layers of dermal tissue, the same as any normal human. Other changes might've happened. He thought so because, surprisingly, much of their body shells had tightened, firmed—as if some invisible net had drawn tight around their muscles. Something unusual was going on under those skin layers. He'd give plenty to know what it was, but only an autopsy could tell that story.

Still, a problem faced them and it faced him. The mirror fibbed. The women were not in their thirties, they were in their seventies. Despite the mirror's illusions, they contended with the ailments and sufferings as would any person at that time of life.

He had saved their lives when wagering with Swiali, the Mzura chieftain who had ordered the women killed for no reason other than their age. Thomas had won the wager, as he knew he would win, when saying to Swiali, an oaf of a higher sort, that he could return youth to the women, and if he did, they'd be spared a stoning.

Saving them from one fate, he had brought them yet another; for all their remaining years they'd be living with a false sense of themselves. One day a reckoning would arrive, and they'd realize they were not who that mirror said they were. That they'd been tricked somehow. What would they think of him then? That he had made them freakish? Made them into a sort of joke? It worried him, as it should, but he had done what he had done so he could save them. And there was no way of reversing the woman's appearance, or denying the fact of what he'd done.

Setting down a black medical bag, he bantered with them, attempting to put them at ease. Himself, too, for he verged on anxiety; first, from the nerve-bending drum-talk and its ominous messages, and then thinking he might never see the Eves again. He was off for Europe in two days. Turning his back on the Eves, even for a short stretch of a week or two, might tempt Swiali to turn them into bone-bricks, his favorite method of riddance.

Beckoning then to K'masa-ne. From hints she had dropped, he had guessed her age at seventy-two, give or take a year. She came to him, smiling her wide toothy smile, with amazingly perfect teeth. Smelling of cinnamon oil, her skin glistening, she shifted her hips suggestively. Coming so near to him that he moved back a step. Haughty, high-rumped, with a saucy-face, she stood nearly six feet, her legs endless. She wore anklets of strung giraffe teeth, thick as thumbs, that rattled with her every step. Fractious, aggressive, she was unlike the other two who were usually as peaceable as the swing of a pendulum.

In his halting Mzura, he joked with her, then, pulling out a magnifying glass, examined her for changes of skin texture, pliability, smoothness, signs of new hair growth, other attributes.

Tracing his fingers along the shoulder blades, then down her spine, looking and looking, then adjusting her stance for better light, he toured her buttocks, her thighs, calves, feet. Opening both his hands he spread her breasts, searching for anything hidden in the cleavage. In their lower spheres, both breasts had been pierced by thin snout-bones of warthogs, making his inspection slightly complicated. When touching her this way, K'masa-ne always dropped her left hand, groping him, the sexual invitation unmistakable to him, especially, a m'frada, a white man whom everyone in the tribe called Eanu, meaning a man who had no use for women.

K'masa-ne handled him intimately, believing she was young again, that she had the powers to arouse a man. Men from the village, who had known her for decades, would never show the slightest interest in her. Not in that way.

For Thomas, a simple thing to let her take liberties. Small recompense for the bio-proof she had provided him—that a human could accept the genes of another mammal, manifesting them, seemingly without harm.

K'masa-ne had been the only one to be implanted with the skin genes of a chimp. Amity, the name of the chimp, was kept at a lab at University of Witwatersrand in Johannesburg. K'masa-ne's appearance, though markedly better than before, revealed a rougher skin than the other two who'd been altered with the skin genes of younger Mzura women. Never had he let her know she was a necessary side of the experiment to determine if a strip of animal DNA could take hold in a human, and make changes. She, his guinea pig, but at least she'd been spared an agonizing death. To a very minor extent, she was now mutated into something of a new species. Perhaps, in a sense, she was the true Eve of the three.

4

K'masa-ne fondled him again, boldly. Pleasantly, and with a smile, he subtly backed away.

Unlatching his medical bag, he withdrew a syringe, took a blood sample, and then, with a glass-slide he scooped skin cells off her arm. Easing the pouting K'masa- ne aside, he beckoned to Chikeezie, the laugher of the trio, an outgoing woman of much kindness. Nodding his head respectfully, he touched her shoulder briefly with three fingers, the customary Mzura greeting of friends. He took more blood and skin cell samples. Then, motioned to M'brama, the third woman. Of the three, M'brama had responded to his experiments with the greatest success. She gave the appearance of someone who might even be in her late twenties. She almost looked nubile, persuading Thomas, that, as expected, everyone's body is its own unique temple. No two alike and now two reacted exactly alike.

Before treating her with Zyme-One, which was derived from the *semba* root, her cheeks had sagged like jowls on a bulldog. Much of that sag had disappeared. The smoothing of her skin he could account for, but the disappearance of the sagging stood as a mystery.

His exams done with, he stood apart from the women, who were over by the hut's single window where a wide bar of sunlight caught them, making them dazzle like polished alabaster. Four months ago, they had looked their age. Now, this—a makeover no cosmetic surgeon in the world could replicate.

Looking at them, he was convinced he was very close to solving the ever-elusive riddle of gene therapy. Biologists had been tracking after an answer for decades, but it was here in this backwater, this wild and lawless nowhere that he had discovered how it could be done.

Amazing him. Thrilling him.

In a few days, he'd be reporting on it to other biologists, gathering in Cambridge at the university from all corners of the world. He'd not tell all, not reveal the technique until he was sure of his ground; and, similarly, could figure out how to bar the great drug combines from poaching his discovery, claiming it as their own.

And then to Rome for a face-off with Augustin deMehlo, who had sent him here to Africa, saving him from other wounds by the sharp claws of the Vatican. Owing deMehlo more than he could ever repay, he nonetheless knew it was time to lay down his cards, knowing a very tough day awaited him at number 4 Borgo S. Spirito, there in the Eternal City that had become his eternal nemesis.

That was his life, he supposed: *pay, pay, pay*. One's price for doing as one wished in this world.

Rome, Italy

Leaning forward, Thomas Courmaine told the cab driver, "Drop me at the gate to St. Peter's. If you'd be so kind, take my bags to Borgo S. number 4 and leave them with the receptionist. That's the Curia."

"Si, signor. Anything else I may do for you."

"Thanks, that'll be fine. Just the bags."

He dug into his pocket for Euros, startled at the cost of the ride from Leonardo da Vinci Airport. He'd have to watch his outlays. With time to kill before the meeting with deMehlo, he decided to have a look at the scene of his garroting. Get his thinking geared up, shape his mood for a showdown that must happen, however excruciating.

Walking through the gate into St. Peter's Square, he mingled with hundreds of visitors, easily passing himself off as one of them. He wore his dressiest outfit, consisted of slightly baggy gray flannels, a herringbone tweed jacket, a faded blue denim shirt with a black knit tie, its knot hanging and tied loosely. The same get-up he had worn yesterday in Cambridge at the Sigma of Science meeting, where he'd made the biggest pitch of his life to 94 of the world's ranked biologists, hoping they'd invite him back for a finale. He had told them roughly half the story about his chance discovery in Africa, that he was convinced it was the long-awaited solution to gene therapy…and if he was right, then Eureka…and then *everything imaginable…*

Thinking of it, he tingled but then a red bolt of anger stopped his movements; standing motionless, then as he reacquainted himself with that day he preferred to forget but could never forget.

Three years ago, when Maistinger, a Bishop out of Mainz in Germany, had laid waste to him, set on making an example of any miscreant who defied Vatican dogma, no matter how lacking, outdated, illogical. The Bishop, a cold, calculating battering ram, forever poised to crush any dissenter who appeared to be gathering acclaim among Catholics and non-Catholics alike. At the six-week trial before a Canonical Tribunal, Maistinger, with his kangaroo court, had triumphed, swinging the axe that had severed Thomas from his teaching days.

He had had it good till then. A Visiting Lecturer at Cambridge, and the co-host of a BBC Saturday morning broadcast called The Human Condition. Very popular, very penetrating at times, and he had on one episode debunked the myth-making of religions, all religions, going back to Zeus and before. That religion was contrived by mythology of miracle-conjuring, wild notions like virgin births. Simple enough: in the Back Ages people needed explanations, reasons to hope, to believe. Nothing particularly wrong with it and neither was there anything wrong with a Grimm's fairytale.

A squall of complaints became a tsunami of protest, led by the Archbishop of Canterbury, and summarily he'd been ordered back to Rome to face his foes. Refusing to recant, he soon felt the slicing power of the Vatican's long knives.

Bitter days, bitter everything.

It all raced through his mind now, almost as if it had occurred in the past week. They had slathered him with lies, with half-truths, with innuendo. It still stung, always would.

His eyes came to rest now on the dome of the great basilica. He walked to his left about forty paces, catching a fuller view of the Palace of Justice. Standing very still now, rigid, he summoned himself, retrieving the words of the Writ of Censure levied against him.

> "...Whereas, in your committing of Most Grievous Offense against Holy Mother Church, it is the judgment of this Tribunal, now proclaimed, that you, Thomas Ignatius Courmaine, of Society of Jesus, shall henceforth be voided of any permissions, of any kind and any nature whatsoever, to teach, profess, or in any way instruct in institutions of learning. Per curiam, this Tribunal, by grace of God Himself, finds the falsity of your assailments against Holy Scripture, and your unfounded and offensive claims uttered in public statements, attested to by credible witnesses, that, and as you have many times claimed and stated, "Nature itself is the mattering Divinity." All, each and every one of your utterances is anathema to Holy Mother Church...

A hundred words or so, crippling him. Defying the ban, he had written anyway, a dozen or so articles, needing the money. He had waited, though, till he was well clear of Rome, for deMehlo's sake and making sure no new round of criticism was heaped on the Society for his defiance.

Once or twice yearly his pieces appeared in such heralded journals as *Nature* and *Science*, also *Cell*, all three widely read in the bioscience community. In one article, he had gone so far as to chide the Pontifical Science Academy for its hostility to stem cell research, using fetal tissue. Uncommonly, the Vatican had not rebuked him for it, and he had always wondered why.

Backtracking through the Square, he legged the three blocks to the Curia on Borgo S. Spirito. At the reception desk, he greeted a young novice, a cheerful-faced fellow in his late twenties or so, who had been reading Gibbon's *Decline and Fall of the Roman Empire*.

Identifying himself, he told the novice that Father-General deMehlo expected him. The novice, his face straining with doubt, made a brief call to the upstairs while Thomas signed the visitor's register.

Hanging up, the novice apologized for his hesitancy and Thomas said, "I wouldn't blame you in the least. It's been a while since I've been in a cassock."

"That is your luggage, is it?" The novice pointed to Thomas's duffels, piled in a corner that the cab driver had dropped off.

"Yep, mine. I'll get them out of your way shortly."

"Have you come far?"

"Africa, way down. I came by way of the U.K. I used to live here in Rome but now it's Africa."

"I think I know who you are."

Thomas smiled. "Well, don't mention my name or they'll add another year to your novitiate. How much longer before your ordination?"

"Two years more, Father."

Father. Trying to recall, then, when last he had been addressed as *Father*? Thomas smiled again, saying, "You'll be glad of it. Never forget that."

"They'd never let me forget."

Thomas laughed to himself, and headed down a long hallway, its floor laid with polished, timeworn, umber-colored tiles. Hearing his footfalls, as if he were inside an echo chamber, his gut began to knot, tensed now at meeting with the grand maestro, Augustin deMehlo, his friend and the *numero uno* of the Society of Jesus and overseer of its twenty-odd thousand priests.

It wouldn't last long. deMehlo's time was rationed as if each minute were gold-plated. He had worked closely with the General for almost a year, subsequent to his censure, at a time when deMehlo was safeguarding him against his assailants over the Wall at the Vatican. He learned at first-hand deMehlo's astonishing pace and the man's skill at running the world's largest education establishment as well as the hundred or so Jesuitical provinces that spanned the globe. Chief advisor to the pope, he met and conferred constantly with power brokers throughout the world seeking his counsel. As usual, he cut deals of such secrecy that none were ever committed to paper; and, as usual, deMehlo kept a jealous Vatican bureaucracy at bay so they would not meddle on Jesuit turf.

Arguably, deMehlo was the single most influential man in the entire Church. Like all of his predecessors, he was known as the Black Pope. That, because he always was attired in black as opposed to the white worn by the one sitting on the Vatican throne.

Sui generis—one of a kind: that was deMehlo.

Thomas tarried for a time in one of the larger first-floor rooms.

Twenty-eight portraits stared down at him. Stern, with military visages, they were the Black Popes of other eras—for over four centuries they had counted as some of the most noteworthy men of their times. Collectively, they had rolled up more history than Christ and Genghis Khan combined. Some of them had commanded upwards of twenty-thousand scholars, worldwide, men who served as the fishers of souls belonging to emperors, kings, farmers, doctors, engineers, and everything in between.

A Man for Others, that was what it meant to be a Jevvie. A dictum, an article of faith, and Thomas had earnestly tried never to forget it.

Up a flight of stairs, Thomas turned to the right, went by a trickling fountain, and then down a hallway under a vaulted ceiling until he reached a suite of offices.

Suddenly, a noisy commotion. Word of his arrival had made it down the corridors. Old friends were streaming out of their offices. Handshakes, desultory hugs traded with four secretaries, exuberant smiles and greetings, newer faces gawking, curious about the eruption of a sudden clamor in the otherwise hushed atmospherics of the Curia. He had come home, in a very true sense, and his earlier feelings of trepidation vanished in the warmth of the moment.

Unable to speak, so great was his emotion, until deMehlo's gatekeeper rescued him from the cage of bouncy chatter. The gatekeeper turned out to be a Lebanese, a short and balding Jesuit, with a jaw blanketed by a square-shaped beard black as charcoal. He drew Thomas away, escorting him to a small anteroom.

"Just fifteen minutes, if you please, Father Courmaine," the Lebanese cautioned him. "The schedule is maddening today."

"I know what you mean. Fifteen it is, I'll be sure to watch it."

"The General knows that you've arrived. He is most anxious to see you."

"And I, him."

"May we send in something? Tea? Coffee?"

"Thanks, no."

Excusing himself, the Lebanese spun neatly on one heel, heading off to the day's undone errands. Thomas reached for a copy of the morning paper, *La Republica*, scanned the headlines and thumbed through the sheets to the sports section. An office woman brought in an espresso, nodding with appreciation, he left it untouched.

Soon, the reunion and the hard news. deMehlo was a man that one must prepare for. He was the top honcho in the Society, renowned where it really counted, a classicist of the highest rank, fluent in many languages, including Ancient Greek and Aramaic, and the heralded translator of Sophocles's *Antigone*. Also, a superb gent and from all angles.

Shortly, the Lebanese poked his head through the doorway. "Your turn, Father Courmaine."

Thomas crossed the hall to the spacious room that, at its far end, led to Augustin deMehlo's office. His feet fell on the familiar Aubusson, a slightly worn and faded rug; the same Monet hung on one wall, the painting a gift of a Chilean family. Two very old and illegally kept Etruscan urns stood on marble pedestals in the corners. The walls seemed slightly brighter, probably from a recent visit of the paintbrush. He went right by the smaller office where he had once sat, worked and wondered what new and mysterious nuggets lay on that desk calling for immediate action.

Pausing before the wide mahogany door, he inhaled twice. Opening it, he was slightly startled to see Augustin deMehlo in the middle of the room, waiting for him.

Arms wide, they advanced on each other, clasping each other's forearms. Like two veterans of other wars, they stood there, surveying each other. Eyes against eyes, moist with the pleasure.

deMehlo looked much the same as he had two years earlier. Sixtyish—still hard, neat, and masculine. A Moor's nose, and gleaming dark eyes; the face of an eagle. His speech was the speech of a Basque, always distinct, always courteous. With the build of a middleweight, and the hands of a plowman, he stood straight as a grenadier. His face was slightly florid, as if, perhaps, he had just heard something displeasing.

"Thomas, Thomas"—the embrace enthusiastic—"so very kind of you to come, my son. What a pleasure, this day's best pleasure."

"Wonderful to see you, too. You look better than ever."

"As do you, as do you. A Riviera tan. Africa agrees, I see."

Thomas was motioned over to a group of chairs flanking a sofa. Sturdy, quietly appointed, the drapery faintly regal, not a Spartan room yet neither did it shout with the gilt and pomp of the Vatican. A long credenza held silver-framed photos of several heads of state; one of Garcia-Morga, the Spanish poet; another of the famed Greek historian Costas-Mestos; and one down at the end of deMehlo standing side-by-side with the U.S. president, also Vladimir Putin of Russia, and the pope. An unlikely quartet, thought Thomas. With deMehlo, one never knew; for, the man was his own universe. A dozen other photos, studio-like portraits, were autographed by the Queen of England, Sophia of Belgium, Ibn Saud and King Faisal, then, startlingly, one of Katherine Hepburn sitting with deMehlo as they were being poled in a Venetian gondola.

"My gallery," deMehlo observed, amused, then adding, "hardly a convert in the bunch." Heading off on another track, he said, "You're living still in Narum-er-a? That's not right, is it?"

"Na-room-ah. Loosely translated it means the Plain of Honey."

"Is that so? The Plain of Honey. Never heard of that one before, Thomas. Tell me, are you satisfied? Is there a place for us in that country?"

"Missionaries are forbidden. They do away with them on sight. Not so long ago, an itinerant preacher was clubbed to death. He arrived in a truck one day, set up shop, and handed out bags of beans and rice. He was a real pulpit-pounder and selling Jesus, Baptist-style, and…well… they clubbed him to death. I'm told they fed his brains to a pack of feral dogs and I firmly believe it."

"You can't mean this," said deMehlo, stunned and looking it.

"I do, very much so. The Mzura tribe has dozens of their own god-images. Spirits. Which spirit they call upon depends on the season of the year. They'd never grasp our beliefs and would never care to either. If they knew who I really was, they'd get pretty nasty about it. I'm sure of that."

"*Nasty*, you say? What does that mean—pretty nasty?"

"They were deceived as to my actual identity as a priest when I first arrived there. Doing away with me would mean nothing to them. Nothing at all."

"Killing, you say? You're saying that might kill you?"

Thomas nodded. "Possibly."

"You're to leave there instantly. I insist you do. I'll brook no argument, none."

"I've already made plans to leave,"

deMehlo's face lighted up, crinkling with a grin. "We've our own plans for you. You'll like what you're about to hear. I'm most pleased I'm the one to tell you…indeed, I am," deMehlo continued, as his eyes traveled to something on his desk; then, looking up, he added, "you've perhaps heard Maistinger was elected to the College of Cardinals some months ago."

"Did he buy the votes, or was it an accident?"

"Now, now…"

"Sorry, but I'm not raising my cup in a toast."

"Enough, Thomas. Quite enough of that talk. Well, you wouldn't know about Maistinger, would you, being so far from Rome? He's been complaining about your violations of the Writ. Your magazine articles. Expressly forbidden. You'll have to make amends, of course. See him, show some respect, make a contrite apology. And I'll do him a favor or two and that ought to clear the air. You will, won't you?"

"I don't think I could withstand that moral squint of his again."

"May I also remind that it was you who provoked this situation."

And with that remark, the moment showed itself. He could never be rude, not to deMehlo, but knew he must now be candid. "May I speak to this?"

"I urge you to."

"I'm not going to apologize to Maistinger or the Vatican, or, for that matter, to anyone else. I've had enough of that shark tank over the Wall. Sorry, but there it is. Either I speak whatever I wish to speak about in this life, think as I choose to think, write on what aspects of science I find of interest, or I may as well be a dead man." Choosing a newer tack, he continued, "I—well—what I want to say is that you've meant everything to me. Protecting me, and I surely know what I owe this Society. Whoever I am, I am because of the Jesuits. I can never repay it all."

"No one asks you to repay anything, other than to give service to the Society's mission."

"That's done with, I'm breaking ranks, General. I must resign."

Lifting an ivory-tipped baton that lay on his desk, deMehlo looked away; the baton a gift from Merz Swelmeir, a former conductor of the Berlin Philharmonic. deMehlo tapped the instrument on the desktop, an old habit signaling a flurry of thought.

The silence was slow and it was awkward. It seemed as if an electrical current was buzzing around the room.

"You are not permitted to resign," deMehlo declared in a flattish tone, turning flatter when saying, "you'd need my consent and I won't give it. The

Pope must also approve. You're a pledged Pope's Man and that will bring Maistinger back into it—very poor tactics on your part." deMehlo's eyes rolled as he uttered, "Resign! You've obviously been away too long."

"Will you hear me out?"

"Have I not always done so?"

"This is somewhat different."

"It usually is. Proceed."

"I believe I'm close to a scientific breakthrough and it involves gene manipulation. It's the kind of genetic manipulation that can save lives, give children to barren couples, give the hope of health to millions and millions who've got nothing but misery facing them. I might be able to help change all that, and I'd like to try. I intend to try. The deeper I go into my work, the greater irritant I'll become to Maistinger and the Vatican, and, much more importantly, to you. I'd never expect you to stage another brawl with the Vatican on my behalf. Once was too much. Not again. When I resign, you'll be free of me."

"We don't choose to be free of you."

"Maistinger is Vatican to the hilt. They've never been fond of scientists, no matter what they say. And that's what I am, bottom to top. A scientist."

"One can always make a few compromises."

"I tried. It's been my largest mistake to date."

"Pride, you suppose? It sounds like all-out pride to me."

"Yes, I take pride in what I'm trying to do. I'm not looking for anything personal out of it." Then, taking in deMehlo's dispraising look, Thomas went on, "I've loved you, General, and I always shall. My resignation stands. I need a free mind and no religion ever permits that. And I will never forget that you got me out of Rome when they were after my scalp and then introducing me to Baster. Wonderful of you...it's made a considerable difference in my life. I'd never have known him were it not for you, General."

"I wish I hadn't done it." deMehlo's thick fingers were postured in a steeple, then he twisted one hand twice across his mouth as if he were gagging. After a pause, he said, "Tell me about this thing you say you must do."

Thomas told all. About Zyme-One, the potent enzyme milked from a shrub-root called *semba* by the Mzura tribe of Naruma; about transforming the skin of three aging women, making them look two generations younger in many respects. He'd done it by infusing them with the skin genes of tribal women in their thirties; done it also on a wager with an oaf named Swiali, the Mzura chieftain who had ordered the three women's death on account of age and uselessness; then went on, reporting yesterday's revelations before SOS, trying to get the members to approve of his return to offer the required Proof of Concept on his idea for gene therapy technology to be shared by all nations. No royalties, no profits, just a pure sharing for the benefit of all; then more, everything he could think of that could be crammed into four minutes.

"If we can gene switch and rejuvenate skin, we can do it elsewhere. Heart, eyes, kidneys, whatever and wherever. It'll take time but it's now possible."

"And you're the only one who can do this?"

"So far as I know. But that'll change, I'm sure. If I'm right, you'll be living for another hundred years. Probably more."

"I may not wish to."

"Maybe the Vatican-*ers* won't give you a choice. You're so valuable."

"We needn't bring them into this…"

"They're in it already and so am I, or I will be. When you add a couple of hundred years on to everyone's life, then the world will be forced to enforce birth control. Like China. Then what? The Vatican will take five seconds to figure that out, and they'll jump out of their trees. Jump on me and jump on you. No thanks. I'm a prime liability, General. I'm your house-leper."

deMehlo, pondering, waited a time before speaking. "What or who is this SOS business?"

"It's an acronym that stands for Sigma of Science. The British founded it after World War II. Sir Arthur Fleming, the man who discovered penicillin, he was the main organizer. It's all biologists, who meet quarterly at Cambridge. It's a very important group representing fifty-odd nations. Baster Muldaur had me appointed as the rep from South Africa. Me being an American, it was somewhat controversial. It's quite an honor."

"Controversial, eh? I'm not surprised, especially you. Baster, you say."

"Right."

"How very very worrisome. Did the Vatican give you permission to involve yourself?"

"I didn't ask."

"No surprise there, either. Is teaching involved?"

"There're over twenty Nobel laureates who're members of SOS. No, no teaching. They all teach each other, I suppose."

"How old are you? Thirty-five—"

"—six."

"Six? A tenderfoot. You've a penchant, it would seem, for exciting the Vatican's central nervous system."

"That's why I'm quitting. It'll never change."

Another stress-filled silence as deMehlo stared across the desk, a blank-white look on his face. *Quitting!* It was as if deMehlo was attempting to grasp the meaning of a new word. The rapping of the baton again, with deMehlo evading Thomas's pleading look. The general's head went from side to side, his shoulders lifting slightly as he spoke. "I trust that Baster Muldaur isn't behind this? Your quitting idea."

"He knows nothing of it, not so much as a comma. I'll tell him, I'll have to." Thomas refrained from adding that Baster Muldaur had offered to fund a laboratory, knowing deMehlo would see it as an inducement to leave the Society.

"You're not mixed up with a woman?"

"No, it's not about a woman. I'm surprised you'd say that."

"I'm liable to say anything. I'm in such shock, you coming here and saying this."

The general grimaced, leaning back in his chair as a tiny amber light flashed on the top of a small wooden panel at one end of the desk.

"Hell has no fire brighter than that insufferable light. Like a whip on my back," deMehlo said, staring at the blinking light. "A peril to a man's peace." He picked up the phone. From the conversation, Thomas inferred that other visitors were impatiently cooling their heels as the clock ticked. He had overstayed his fifteen minutes.

deMehlo, talking into the receiver, offering an apology, giving instructions to make the visitors comfortable. He hung up, rubbed his blade of a nose, picked up the baton and immediately laid it down on his desk.

"What a terrible blunder I made, sending you to Africa. Who else knows about this? The details? The methods of your, uh, experiments?"

"You're looking at him. Only me."

deMehlo raised a sovereign hand, as if to hold back anything more from Thomas. "It's got all the makings of disaster, what you're talking about. You seem so interested in thinking up some process that could lead humanity to a living Hell. I cannot believe or accept that you'd want to be involved in something like this. Fighting your Church. Disturbing the natural law. Undoing or threatening to undo the civilized things we've done for over two-thousand years."

"If not me, someone else will," Thomas returned, then hearing a low groan from deMehlo.

"Hardly making it right."

"Or wrong, either," said Thomas. "I've been lucky to get something discovered. Mainly by chance, but it works, or at least I'm quite sure it does. It can possibly lead to a new era of curing diseases. Especially pandemic disease."

"Is this—you say it has to do with the manipulation of genes?"

"Essentially."

"Seems to me it's like one of those American-made stealth weapons. No one really knows what will come out of the end of the barrel of all this—this confounded genetic engineering. One reads and I find it terrorizing. And what gives you any right? Mark my words, Thomas, if you meddle with natural law, punishment comes next. You'll start something pernicious. You're fooling with a—with—it's like a gun with a u-turn in its barrel. That's what it is, God's gun, and it will backfire one day."

God's gun, mused Thomas. An odd way of putting it, he thought as he filed it away.

"I ask you to review your thinking for a month or two," deMehlo suggested. "Scientists seem to run around looking for trouble, don't they? You're a good example, Thomas. A futurist, aren't you?"

"Christ was a futurist."

"That'll be quite enough of that, if you please…you do go to perilous lengths and you'll regret it one day."

The light on the desk blinked excitedly. deMehlo stood, so did Thomas. The general's smile was faintly paternal, but so quick it moved only one side of his face. "When you walked in here, I was about to tell you you might get a chance to teach again. At Sofia University in Tokyo. I was there once myself."

"I know you were, and also its president if I recall. But I'll not be teaching for a time and maybe never again."

A pinched frown showed up on deMehlo disapproving face, revealing his exasperation. "How long are you in Rome?"

"I was planning on three days, but I'll probably fly out tonight or tomorrow."

"I'll want to know where you'll be keeping yourself. Have you money? Other things you need?" A sweep of bonhomie now, ready to empty his pockets and then some.

"I'm all set in that department. Thanks very much anyway."

"Are you paid a salary of some sort?"

"I am." He gave the amount to deMehlo. "It's paid by African Heritage…a Muldaur project."

"Everything down that way seems a Muldaur project of one sort or another."

"Lots are."

"I needn't remind you, Thomas. In the past, you've seen things and done things here, with me, that are to remain forever inside the Curia. That's understood, I'm sure?"

"I can keep my mouth shut."

"Can you? How gratifying. I'll pass the word to the Vatican, and you can pass it on to BBC."

At that, they laughed. Thomas's face warmed to a noticeable flush. He was glad to end the meeting this way, layered with an uplifting feeling.

"Con Dios, Thomas, con Dios."

"There is no daylight between us, General. I stand with you forever as your friend."

Without another word, deMehlo wheeled, his black cassock swirling like a matador's cape. He lurched slightly when he walked, as if carrying a hidden weight on one side. It was the walk of a mailman, thought Thomas, and indeed Augustin deMehlo carried a good many of the world's prime messages in that most able of minds.

Fifty like you, Thomas thought, and there'll always be a civilization.

In the hallway, Thomas encountered the Lebanese priest bobbing out of a side-room. "Join us for supper, Father?" he asked.

"I really can't. I've had a change of plans and I'm off for the airport if I can get myself a flight."

"But your friends—"

"Next time, I promise." Thomas paid him a placating smile.

But there would not be a next time. He never expected to return to the Curia and yet he hadn't the heart to admit it. Instead, he asked, "Could I use a phone? I've a card I can charge the calls to."

"You won't be needing that, Father. Come along to my office and use it for as long as you wish."

He found a seat available on an all-night flight to Jo-burg. He next placed a call to Cyro in Switzerland, informing the facilities-manager he'd be canceling out on the visit to inspect the *semba* roots he had had previously shipped up for cold storage. He'd never before visited Cyro, was curious, and had proprietary feelings about the precious rootstock and its safety.

His final call went to the Muldaur head offices in South Africa, where he spoke to Baster's senior assistant. Would she find out if he could fix an appointment with the mogul himself, and then to leave word at the Alitalia counter at Jan Smuts Airport? He expected to arrive on Flight 4042 around nine the next morning. If possible, and if Baster would be accessible, he also needed a bed for a night or two at the Muldaur estate.

A pattering sound at the window, and he turned to see the drooling beads of a springtime drizzle coursing down the pane. He hadn't brought rain-gear with him and didn't relish an eleven-hour sopping wet trip down to the African land-tip. He'd wait a while; see if the weather cleared before returning to the street.

He'd have to go on without this formidable brotherhood that had saved him from a life of waste and indirection, perhaps even heavy trouble with the law. A life of a Baltimore street kid, an orphan, who'd been bounced from one foster home to another, until old enough and strong enough to fend for himself at seventeen. He'd gone to the streets where he had found camaraderie in a gang, and eventually had knocked up Marianne Danavan, from an eastside Irish-Catholic family. Two years older, hair the color of flame, a body engineered for mortal sin, a laugh heard a block away, frisky as a month-old filly.

A sepsis from a botched abortion at the hands of a medical student—solicited by her eldest brother, a cop—had killed Marianne. The abortion had been procured for five-hundred dollars, the money bled from a hapless dope peddler shaken down by Marianne's two police-force brothers.

Catching him alone one day in south Baltimore, the brothers muscled him into a van, driving him to the police firing range, well away from the city.

It began with the slam of a crowbar to his back, igniting a red fury in him. Turning on them, wild as a cornered animal, he broke their ribs, dislocated shoulders, smashed noses, used breath-stopping chokeholds, closing their eyes with ripping jabs and bloodletting hooks. He fractured the right kneecap of one brother, using a rock he picked up when he'd been toppled to the ground. He left them there, both brothers only semi-conscious. He returned the van to Baltimore, remembering how he had been tempted to sell it for salvage to a chop-shop. Wisely he had relented, calling a random police station, telling of the van's whereabouts. He had said nothing as to where the brothers might be found.

Charges of assault and battery were levied against him. The usual lies were told in superior court. Sworn statements were twisted out of all recognition as to actual events and what caused them. The judge, a Catholic himself, took a little pity and the story soon outed about Marianne—their affair, the abortion, her tragic death. And the fight.

Marianne's elder brother was charged with manslaughter as an accessory to Marianne's death. Thomas, himself, was to face a lesser offense than assault and battery, but the fact remained that he had waylaid two officers of the law, hospitalizing them.

A social worker's report to the judge estimated that while Thomas had no police record, he was from off the streets, consorted with petty criminals, was likely bound for a life behind bars if he didn't get straightened out.

But how? Held by whose grip?

His choice, the judge ruled, was either a stint in the U.S. Army or more schooling under the no-nonsense Jesuits at Loyola.

The Jesuits accepted him and his re-shaping began. A better education than he had ever had a right to expect was knocked into him. Ethics. Understanding. Knowledge of dozens of subjects, not least of them the classics. Support, tough love, hardening his backbone. Brotherhood. Care, respect. He had come far with them until today, when, for a yet unproven piece of biology, he had only a few moments ago thrown away the only family he could claim.

They had given him the whole plate, including the chance to earn his doctorate at Johns Hopkins. In return, he had given them nothing but problems and trouble, the most bitter of them being his clash with Maistinger.

In a day or two, he'd have to lay it out again with Baster Muldaur; the genetic magic he'd used to make the Mzura women, his three Eves, appear forty years younger. They weren't but they surely looked it and would till they died. Hearing of it, what would Baster do, or think? deMehlo hadn't liked any of it, and deMehlo would likely be in Baster's ear soon, grumbling. It would all be news to South Africa's leading rainmaker and Thomas knew Baster Muldaur would not like hearing it second-hand.

You never get free of paying, Thomas thought. *Never.*

Johannesburg, South Africa

At the Alitalia counter, Thomas asked if a message awaited him. A pert attendant, wearing the light blue colors of the airline, handed him a monogrammed envelope. The scrawl on the page inside read: *Outside, so get a move on—Jaggy*

Still sleepy-eyed after the all-night flight out of Rome, Thomas heard his name shouted as he emerged from the terminal. Down the way, a yellow-and-black Daimler was parked curbside and there beside it stood Jaggy Muldaur. Dropping his bags, pleased and excited, he hurried to her.

"Been months, you stranger," she said, her elbows resting on the ledge of the door. "Well, a hug hello, a peck? Something, I hope." She owned a smile that belonged in a toothpaste ad.

What began as a brother and sister embrace, soon changed when she adjusted herself to him. He backed away. "I hadn't expected anyone to meet me," Thomas said, "and here you are, complete with this magnifico machine...I thought you were out in the Far East somewhere."

"I was, then I cut it short."

He looked at her. Her eyes almost seemed to be in shadow, darker underneath than he recalled. Otherwise, she was the picture of health and vitality. A strong, strong woman, careful of her body, and half-wild in all she did with it.

"Baster would've come, too," Jaggy was saying, "but he's up half the night with those DuPont people. They sent the big drinkers this time."

"A bad time for me to arrive?"

"No, not really."

"I can go on up to Naruma and come back next week."

"Uh-uh. Baster is anxious to see you. So am I and here you are. Behold!"

"Here, let me take care of this and off we'll go."

He retrieved his bags, loading them into the Daimler, climbing in beside her. She was on the gas pedal before he could buckle the safety belt.

Inspecting her again, appraisingly, searching for changes. A few silvery strands in her hair, but nothing else other than the shadowy eyes. She was a handsome Afrikaner, a touch wide-beamed, with a horsewoman's thighs, and eyes that lit up with blue fire at times. But then, if provoked, the eyes turned flat and hard as razor-steel. Coal black hair fell in thick waves around a rose-tinted face needing little in the way of feminine war paint, which is what made him wonder about her eyes. She was five-feet-nine of collected woman, with the fluid movements of an athlete and blessed with obvious natural strength. Breasts that were high, large. Thomas had once heard a Muldaur family friend describe Jaggy as a woman built for the night. Probably so, he silently agreed—exuding, as she did, a vivid sexuality. Just the way she looked at you, if she felt like it, could be engulfing.

"Been on the horses, I see."

"Do I stink that much?" Smiling as she said it.

"Your jodhpurs, I meant."

"Been out every morning since I've been here. Baster brought in three new mares from Kentucky. Beauties."

"I tried to hunt you up in London by phone. That's how I found out you were in Asia. I'd been in Cambridge for a meeting and had hopes I could buy you dinner and catch up. So now you'll have to fill me in on all your news."

"Having a smashing year at the firm. My side of it, anyway"—she blew on her fingertips and dusted them on her pink jersey—"and of course we all know who's responsible for that." He had watched her hand move over the heavy breasts, their nipples protruding like fingertips. "You should see our London numbers," Jaggy said. Looking straight at him now as if they were seated in a room, and with time to look at each other; yet she was tracking down the highway at eighty or so, unconcerned.

"No sane woman or man ever denied your father's talents," Thomas teased her.

"Listen you"—she shook a fist—"let a girl brag once in a while."

"Fear not, I happen to know Baster thinks you personally raise the moon every evening."

"That's more like it."

Effortlessly, she wheeled the Daimler through winding curves as if it were suspended on air cushions. A coachworks in Milan had removed the top of what originally had been a sedan, changing it into a four-door convertible. A custom suspension system made the car ride like a feather, and its power came from a dual-carburetor Offenhauser engine. The dashboard was carved from

Circassian walnut and Zebrano, and the baby-smooth calf-leather seats had been chrome-dyed to a sea-green color by a tannery outside Paris. A Dubai sheik had made a gift of the car to Baster in appreciation for services unknown. Unknown, at least, to Thomas.

They covered another mile or so, in quiet, Thomas observing other drivers gawking at the Daimler as it sped by. Then he asked, before he was told, "Got a new man in your life, Jaggy? A Duke? The Count of somewhere-or-other? Maybe another racer? Anyone I ought to know about before I see it in the newspapers?"

"Do you have to make it sound as if I'm trolling? Actually, I'm in state of in-between. Celibacy, that sort of mush. Exceedingly boring it is, too, I must say."

"Your divorce come through yet?"

"Quite a while ago. He was a nuisance about none of it. Quite dear of him, really, being such a good chap. It descended to money, as usual."

"I won't ask."

"It wasn't really so bad. He was too proud to push. We settled everything in the Connaught Grill one afternoon. I insisted on some public place so we wouldn't start yelling. We did the money on the back of a napkin, and I bobbed it right over to the solicitor, quick as you please. Always have a good solicitor, a blowtorch, behind you. Don't get a smart one, just fast, so he can do all the paperwork before anyone changes their mind." Looking over at him again, an amused glint in her bluish eyes. "You don't approve, do you?"

"Not for me to say, is it?"

"I asked you."

"Doesn't mean I have to answer, madam."

"Say exactly what you think, then I shall know what amends I must make."

"No amends to me. What I can't figure out is how you can do all the adjusting, one to the next. Three husbands. Three personalities, quirks, this's and that's, must be sort of confusing, breaking in three men."

A muddled reply, yet he was hardly in a position to give her a clear, straight answer. She was fishing. He didn't know for what, but she was. For him, though, commenting on the sanctity of the given word would be hypocritical. He'd just renounced his own vows in Rome without so much as a handshake. How could he judge her, or anyone?

Enough, he thought.

The morning bloomed, the views glorious, the air as effervescent as champagne bubbles. He ought to be supremely thankful for that, and not worry overly much about the marital affairs of a Midas-rich woman. Except, and as he reminded himself again, this was her third walkout and she was only thirty-five.

"I had to get out of it," she said after a while. "We both did. He was different, a little too different for me." Without him asking, she told Thomas what she paid to get rid of Hawkes-Powell, a well-known Harley Street British gynecologist. "A good and decent settlement," she went on, "and much easier than some dragged-out court battle."

"If you're happy, then so is the world," he said casually, hoping the topic would dissolve itself.

"And you, you're still of my world?"

"Eternally and always," he assured. Thomas said nothing more. Staggered by the sum—five-million pounds—it had cost to remove Dr. Asquith Hawkes-Powell from her life, he sat and watched the morning go by at speed.

"I didn't mean to send you into silence," she said.

"Long flight."

"Oh, stop. Don't be a horsecock, Thomas! You're just being Catholic-blind about divorce."

"Am I? Probably I am. Old habits are hard to break. Where would you be at Muldaur's if you backed out of every deal you didn't like?" A defensive remark, and he knew it instantly.

"You're putting me down, aren't you?" she said.

"Nope."

"Yes, you are."

"I am practically dead certain no one's ever done that to you."

She sent him another smile. "I'd let you, dearie, in a manner of speaking."

There she goes again, he thought, slightly alarmed. But she was already off on another slant, asking, "Be a love, and dial the house on the dash-phone." He did and then handed the phone to her.

She talked rapidly with someone on the house-staff about a dinner, a big dinner it sounded like, though it was nothing unusual, as an event, for Jacgelét Margit Josephus Muldaur, or her stepfather, for whom she often acted as hostess. She was good at it. Profound, even. People loved Muldaur parties and she and Baster went to extremes to keep the soirees out of the news, for fear of offending people who hadn't been invited.

When she hung the phone on its cradle, Thomas said. "Sounds to me like you're pretty busy. Nice of you to come to the airport, I really appreciate that."

"You said so already, and you're welcome. How else would you get to us?"

"A taxi, I guess."

"Taxi! It's miles. Charge you a fortune for it."

Not anything like five-million pounds of get-lost divorce money, he thought.

"Are you staying long? A week or so?"

"More like a day or two," he said. "I've got to get back up to Naruma. I just came by to see your father."

"And not me?"

"And you. You're the bonus. Every man's dream for a chauffeur. But then I didn't know you'd be here."

"But then why hurry off to Naruma?"

"They're things to take care of up there and other things to set up. I'm going to try and rescue that big forest elephant. Then I'm closing up the Station unless African Heritage sends me a replacement before I leave."

"You may have company, too, on the elephant hunt."

"I hope that means you," he said, though was of two minds about it. She was superb out in the bush, but could get too rambunctious at times. She was born with no evident sense of fear, and it told when she went hunting in places Thomas refused to follow.

"All depends. Baster seems terribly keen to go up to the farm. Oh, the other night he was telling me about your experiments with the N'jorro cattle, saying that it's all quite the marvel what you've done. Like a ten-year old getting a new pony, when he talks about it."

"We need at least another breeding season, maybe two. It's getting interesting, I'll admit."

"He thinks so," said Jaggy.

"A favor?"

"Gladly."

"I've got a present for Baster. It's been ready for pick-up for a month or more, but I haven't had a chance to get it. I'd like to give it to him while I'm here."

"Am I to know?"

"You're to see it after Baster does. I can't have you talking me out of it."

"One of those, eh?" She smiled, ingratiatingly. "Oh, Thomas, Thomas. I could do things with you."

"You have, you are...Pilaster Street, next stop, if you'd be so good."

The street was in the outskirts of Johannesburg, an older section of the city. They were headed to the shop of a well-known ivory carver. An Indian from Goa, nearly blind from a lifetime of etching bone so intricately that parts of the scrimshaw could be appreciated only by viewing them with a magnifying glass. The carver was much in demand; Thomas had gotten him to take on the job only after telling him who it was for.

Off the highway, now, Jaggy drove to the shop located in a ramshackle street, black children scooting around everywhere, many young and many naked, some of them urinating in the garbage-strewn gutters. He shooed a few of the boys away from the Daimler; a car like this was unlikely to have ever rolled through this section of the city. Pulling out a crumpled wad, he handed a ten-rand note to an older lad, telling him to mind the other boys or they'd all be seeing the police.

Knowing that Jaggy would be intensely uncomfortable, remaining outside and by herself, he made quick work of getting in and out of the blue-boarded house, so old it was tilting to one side, with three of its shutters hanging askew. A haggard, hard-luck section of the city. He had no idea why the Indian lived there, for surely he was well enough off to afford better quarters.

Minutes later he returned, lugging a package under one arm. Off they went, Jaggy curious as to whether Thomas was returning any time soon to London. Why not stay with her in Belgravia, she suggested, even when she was away from London. "I've oodles of room, as you know." And what was this about a lab, she wanted to know, telling him she expected to be one of the backers. News to him, that she'd be a party to the arrangement, making him instantly wary.

"It's all in the talking stage," he said. "Baster and I've been discussing it for a time and I submitted some estimates and his number-crunchers did up some spreadsheets and so on."

"Baster had an attack of mental scarlet fever this morning. Your headman in Rome rang him up. No end of brash talk. All about you, I gather."

"Augustin deMehlo, you mean?"

"Baster didn't say. He was roundly peeved, I can tell you that much."

"They're old friends, you know. Very old friends. It was Augustin deMehlo who introduced me to Baster, if you recall. That's how I came to South Africa."

"What is deMehlo? The nationality? It sounds like a sorbet or something."

"A Basque. Beautiful, beautiful guy."

"Literally so."

"To my way of looking at him."

"Ah, a monk. Tonsured hair and a hair-shirt, one of those white ropes around the waist?"

"Anything but. He paints on a canvas nearly as big as Baster's. Even bigger when it comes to education. You'd like him, I'm sure of it. He's what I call a summa."

"Perhaps," she said. "At any rate, you, my dear, were the topic of a stiff conversation and I'm telling you this so you don't bring it up unless Baster does."

"A quarrel, was it?"

She nodded twice.

"I see, or maybe I don't see. That's not like deMehlo, or Baster either. Were you in on it?"

"Not even a teensy, but Baster tells me just about everything. He was told you had threatened to resign."

"It was no threat. I was quite definite about it."

"So, you're not any longer a priest, I assume?"

"I'm trying to get a yard of paperwork started through the Vatican, but they're a few pillars there who intensely dislike yours truly. So, it may be a while. Possibly never."

"Ridiculous."

"It's the way of their world."

Her jaw jutted the way it always did when she was perturbed. He decided not to tell her of the niceties of priesthood, that, once a priest, always a priest. Even if you were released from your vows, you were tattooed with priesthood for eternity, or for life, anyway. No point in explaining any of it, because she'd lose interest within ten seconds. She would catalogue it as stupid for any man to condemn himself to promises of that sort, and for a lifetime, at that.

Jaggy downshifted, climbing now up a graded mountain half-owned by the Muldaurs, the rest of it by the city government. She was busy moving the Daimler on a stretch of road that narrowed in places where it hugged the steeper ridges of the mountainside.

Leaving her to her driving, he glanced out the windshield at the magnificent lay of countryside, then looked down at the city, then up into the blues of the morning sky, and over at her again, that tanned, intent face with its rosy cheeks, her competent hands swinging the wheel as she expertly accelerated into a curve. Wonderfully coordinated, she had once been regarded as the finest woman big-game hunter in South Africa. She was a jet-qualified pilot and in her late teens had been an Olympic-class equestrienne.

"You never said how long you'll be here," he said as the road began to straighten out.

"Another couple of weeks, I hope. I may have to go up to London for a meeting. But I've been bashed silly with work. I'm dragging, so I thought what the hells-bells, why not take some time off and get myself back to the mark."

"You don't look very Jaggy-draggy to me."

"A Muldaur, you know." She whacked the side of her rump in one of her free-spirited gestures. "A hard-assed lot, we are."

"Is that so?"

"You know how to find out?" She turned to him, winking.

"One day I'm going to wash out that mouth of yours." Half jesting, half not.

"Why stop there?" she retorted. "You can do me all over, and check under the hood while you're at it."

He knew her, or knew her well enough anyway. Whim moved her to test his resilience to her off-hand, double-edged remarks. Jaggy Muldaur was a changeable, willful type: she could be any of several women, depending on the hour and her moods of the day. He was about to be the houseguest of her stepfather, and, he supposed, the guest of herself now that she was back in town. So, he'd tread with care, keeping his remarks to a guestly level. She wasn't saying anything at the moment, and he didn't want her starting up again when she was in one of her sex-scouting moods.

The Daimler's engine purred quietly as a contented cat, and up they went, the last incline on the part of the ride he most enjoyed. The view spread for miles across land that bent down to eventually become the Cape of South Africa. Colors rarely seen around any big city—blues of every shade, gas-greens and the fleshy greens of the forest. When spring returned, the colors would resonate against a carpet of South Africa's national flower, the king protea. In the falling distance, lakes, grayish now, would brighten by noontime till sparkling like sapphires. For now, against the honey-hued sky, all looked soft and idyllic.

One more turn and they sped through high iron-gates and under a canopy of verdant foliage arching like the upper half of a vast Christmas wreath over a mile-long driveway. To one side was a long pond flocked with stilt-legged flamingos, standing as close together as books on a shelf. Some of the house-staff's children were running about with a pack of red-coated Irish setters on the far-off lawns. Under a huge-spread oak, a groom held the bridles of a black horse, a white, and another that was roan-colored. Someone must be going for a ride on the estate's twenty-one miles of trails.

Ahead, the main house. White stucco, cross-timbered every ten yards; the residence was deceiving in appearance, as though it were a low-slung building, but all sides had soaring two-story windows to draw the outside views into the vast rooms, halls and circular stairwells. The roof was plated with silvery-gray Belgian slate. Ivy crept to the eaves, every leaf looking as though it were oiled. Forty-one rooms of splendor. Thomas had counted them once out of sheer curiosity. Other than the house staff and the outside grounds-keepers, only Baster lived here now, for Jaggy kept her principal residence in London.

Shutting off the engine, she glanced over, passing him a cryptic smile. "Welcome, and I'm ecstatic you're here. You may not see Baster today. He's trying to finish up with those cod-headed Americans."

"Careful, if you please—my countrymen, my countrymen."

"Well, if I were you I wouldn't be too quick to claim this lot."

A house-steward bounded down the steps, a wizened black man, green-coated, wearing patent-leather boots and black jodhpurs: the man in charge of the front entrance. He raised a hand at Thomas in a familiar greeting. Everyone coming here was treated like some rajah, and the pure magic of it was you soon began to think you really were one.

"Like to go out with the horses later?"

"Sure, if you can keep it to a canter. What's a good time?"

"After luncheon. Say, three. Then it'll be dinner with the DuPont-ers, I suppose, then we'll see what else. Some bridge perhaps. Have you dinner clothes for tomorrow?"

"Black tie?" Thomas laughed. "You're kidding. Dinner clothes? Never in my life."

"We'll have someone come round and doll you up."

"Very many thanks, but I don't want anyone to—"

"It's a must-do, Tommy. Don't get stubborn on me. None of your twaddle now. You cannot be the only one here wearing a potato sack or something ludicrous. We're turning on all the chandeliers. The President is coming, along with the rest of his goons, and we must look our part. If you argue with me, I'll cry and then I'll be so cross I'll shoot a cannon your way."

She might, too, he decided. She was a crack shot. Her keen gun-eye had won her shelves of trophies, testifying to her prowess. He'd been on safari with her three times; she never missed her prey.

He followed his bags up ten granite steps to the front doors, wondering why the DuPont people were here; wondering, too, what he'd feel like in a bow tie, stiffened shirt and black dinner clothes. A popinjay. But knew he'd better acquiesce.

Next afternoon, Baster Muldaur, finally free of his DuPont guests, met with Thomas. For most of a week Baster had been closeted with DuPont executives trying to button up the details of a deal that had brought them scurrying to Jo-burg from Delaware. Muldaur Ltd. wanted to buy out DuPont's share of a jointly owned chemical plant that employed 2,000 blacks and sundry African immigrants, along with 300 whites, who held the best jobs and had always held them. A wearying negotiation, apparently, with the Americans hemming and hawing. Jaggy had filled him in.

Thomas was sitting across from Baster, each occupying a high-backed wicker chair; they were inside a screened-in gazebo that looked out to the estate's sweeping lawns and the farther vista of blue-hued mountains.

"So, you said you had something I'd better know about," Baster was saying.

"I do. Probably deMehlo beat me to the punch. Jaggy said he called."

"deMehlo did call yesterday. An extremely fretful hornet, putting it mildly. I had a time quieting him. He says that you're thinking of leaving him. Surely he can spare us one priest, can he not?"

"I'm done with it. I laid it out very flat for him."

"You're sure, are you?"

"Completely."

"That makes a difference and I shall shortly tell you why. We'll let him stew a few days and then I'll build him a new church or something. Been a good man to have in business with us. Augustin deMehlo can extract gold out of your teeth before you can open your mouth."

Thomas laughed. "He's something else. But then so are you."

"Well, let's march onward. What happened with those women? How many were there?"

"Three."

Taking the better part of five minutes, Thomas told his tale, front to back. The part he hadn't admitted to deMehlo had involved one of the women. In her case, Thomas told Baster how he had infused a chimp's skin genes instead of human genes, and that woman's skin had changed as dramatically as the others, only it was noticeably coarser. The idea, in that case, was to test whether the Zyme-One enzyme worked as well trans-genetically: animal genes to a human, and, when there, did their job.

While listening, Baster handed Thomas a Cohiba, a Cuban cigar much favored by his host. The older man lit up, and passed to Thomas a gold table lighter mounted on a lion's head of jade.

"That's the entire picture?" Baster asked when Thomas finished.

"Everything that counts."

"Christ's nuts, if this isn't something. You realize if this gets out, there'll be a firestorm. A white man using black natives as guinea pigs."

"It's good science, Baster. It's plenty real, believe me. We've done more or less the same thing to your N'jorro cattle."

"That makes it worse. Cattle. Black women. Chimps. What'll come next? I'm getting an ache in my own balls."

"In Naruma, it was legal. No laws against it, and I was trying to save the lives of three old women and I did save them."

"If it's blasted about, many won't see it that way."

"It's what happened, though."

"People'll want to know how."

"I won't say, not yet anyway."

"You mean I'm not to know?"

"Certainly, you can. It's the *semba* root. I can't explain why it does what it does. And one or two successes mean something, but to really know I'd have to learn all about the root's insides and then repeat experiments fifty times. On humans, preferably. I can only do it legally in Naruma."

"Completely forget that notion. That murdering fool Swiali will come up with some way, some lie, to tell the government and then they'll be asking questions of African Heritage. That will involve me, or course, or my name." He shook his head. "At all costs I want African Heritage left out of this. We've built up a fine reputation and I won't have it smudged."

"Okay, I'll keep my silence."

A curt nod. "It's a delicate, touchy time. I'll let you in on something. I've made a highly confidential arrangement with the government so they'll keep their hands off our South African mining interests for the next ten years. If your experiment were to be known to those who stand against us, then they'd use it, I'm sure, to create a blowback. Create unrest and anger among the blacks and that'd result in very unfavorable repercussions."

"I understand."

"What's done is done and now it's time for discretion. I need time to add this all up before it causes a collapse in my groin. New topic. I've been wanting to talk to you about the farm at N'jorro. And then another item or two that—"

The screen-door swung open.

A servant, his face black as a domino, entered the gazebo and placed on the table a tray holding a silver pitcher of iced-tea, leaded-crystal mugs packed with shaved ice, topped with mint and lime peel. The tea (harvested from tall tea trees by trained monkeys on leashes) came from an Indonesian plantation owned by Baster. A gift on his twenty-first birthday from his father, and now something of an heirloom, to end up as Jaggy's one day. The tea, dolloped with Barbados rum, was a standard libation around the Muldaur home, served at all hours. Baster imbibed three or four daily, calling the drink his *adjutant*.

When they were alone again, Baster took up the farm. "The N'jorro farmlands are about to be turned over to the Mzura. It won't make that much difference, they graze the land anyway, and I don't have the heart to shoo them off. Five years from now, they'll no doubt have ruined the place."

"Why would you ever give it to them?"

"That's part of an understanding I have with the South African government. Taxes, for one thing. I'm deeding N'jorro to our government and they'll turn it over to the Mzura, no doubt in exchange for some new border understandings. A cheap way to bribe the Mzura, and keep them quiet up there. Jaggy's riled about N'jorro, of course. But we can't keep holding on forever. She rarely goes up anymore, and I'm getting too long in the tooth. So, along with a couple of other arrangements, we'll get more use out of it by giving it back to the natives. Damn shame, I suppose. I get so sick of the politics, sick to death of it. We've owned that land for over 200 years. Piet Friejjarr-Muldaur the third, no, he was the fourth, bought it for a thousand bails of ostrich feathers and two oxcarts of salt. Think of it. Those fellows knew how to trade. You couldn't buy N'jorro today for 400-million rand." He swallowed more of his adjutant, then went on, "Now, Tommy, you left me a message about that elephant up there. Fill me in on this, and we'll see what other trouble you've got in store for us."

This was the huge forest elephant—called Tunda by the Mzura—that he and Ghibwa, the shaman who'd taught him about *semba*, had tracked; at times. They baited Tunda with bushels of sweet grain, enticing him to safer areas, away from poachers. The tusks were at least twelve-footers, worth a ransom in the illicit ivory market. Tunda, a giant, was an animal-god to the Mzura who had given him his name. Thomas intended to preserve its DNA, and had never had the right set-up to manage a rescue. He intended it as his last gesture for his employer, African Heritage.

"Baster, if we can move the elephant, say, to Kruger Park, we'd of course need Mzura trackers. Three or four, anyway. Let me tell Swiali that if he'll help us with the elephant, provide us the trackers, it will assist him in getting his hands on the farm. Might as well get all you can for N'jorro."

"Excellent. Good idea. Elephant-napping...my, my...one scheme after the other."

"It's worth it. I can do it by myself with some good trackers. And Ghib-wa."

"You let me think on this. A day or so. Let's move on to this laboratory of yours. Then I've something else. On the lab, have you looked at the memo they put together at the office?"

"Yes, it's great. It's far more than I can ever thank you for. A dream come true."

"I'd not want you to skimp. Two-million is enough to start off with?"

"I'm sure it'll be plenty."

"I'd be most pleased if we could take a good crack at this AIDS business that is ravaging so much of Africa. The figures take your breath away."

"I hope we can contribute, Baster. But I can't promise anything soon."

"I do realize, Tommy. I want to be clear that we're setting up the lab for profit"—Baster waved a heavy-boned hand—"I know what you're going to say. But we're not exploiting the poor and the homeless, mind you. It's got to be self-sustaining, Tommy. Grow its revenues, meet its costs. Otherwise, it'll be a sinkhole and we can't have that, can we? Not our style. If we have to invest and lose for a few years, that's not bothersome. I'm used to that. But, in the end, we're looking for a money-maker."

"I'm not a socialist, Baster."

"When I'm through with you, you'll be an ardent capitalist."

"Not that, either, I'm afraid."

"You don't mind if Jaggy takes half of my half, do you?"

"I'd be very pleased." Saying it because he knew it to be the politic thing to do, and that he had better say it.

"We often go shares."

"I'm fine with it, if she is."

"Oh, she most assuredly is. She insists."

Baster leaned back in the wicker chair. After a prodigious swallow of his adjutant, he stood and excused himself, then went out the screened door of the gazebo. Built square as a brick, with a broad square face, square footballer's shoulders—solid as a vault, all the way through. First, when meeting him, you noticed his silver-blondish hair, cut pioneer-style, drawn at the back into a short pigtail held by a gold ringlet. A well lived-in face showed his full age one day, yet on the next, he seemed barely more than fifty. Perhaps, the changes were from the daily excitement or the ongoing burdens of his expansive life.

Someone once remarked that Baster Muldaur was double-headed, one working its way in the western hemisphere, while the other dealt with the eastern. A friendly exaggeration, of course, yet the point of the remark spoke for itself, perpetuating the tycoon's legend. Africa's Croesus and a world-class rainmaker; of this, never a doubt.

Baster returned, zipping his fly. Sitting, he treated himself to another wallop of the adjutant, then wiped his mouth on the back of a sleeve. "I'm about to tell you several things in deepest confidence," he began. "Strictly between us. You follow me?"

"Yes."

"Not even to Jaggy, and there isn't much I keep from that rather plentiful woman."

"I understand."

"A tricky situation is at stake here. It affects all of Muldaur's future interests. And it'll impact Jaggy, too. She's a stepdaughter, as you know, but most think of her as a full-blooded Muldaur and that I'm her actual father. Makes sense, I suppose, she's been around here for twenty-five years. Fifteen of them since her mother passed away."

"Well, it's true. I'd never have known she wasn't a true Muldaur unless you had told me. I think of her as one, like everyone else."

"Part of the problem…where should I start? You're likely to find this quite strange. I do, when I think of it and I think about it every day. I must create an heir. And you'll have to help me in this."

"An heir?"

Baster nodded.

"How can I—an heir?"

"You wouldn't know anything about The Muldaur Trust. We refer to it simply as The Trust. Very, very few people are aware of it. Jaggy knows but only vaguely. She isn't aware of its intricacies. Nor its size, either. If I may say so, it's on the order of what can fairly be called stupendous. The Trust is managed by three overseers or trustees. We recently lost one of them to a heart attack. A first-pew fellow, Hanta-hong Zheng of Singapore. The best trader in Asia, a comprador of the old school. Are you with me so far?"

"To an extent, I am."

"I'm diverting...we'll get back to the heir business in a moment...I want you to take old Zheng's place. Become the third trustee..."

Blinking from surprise, he looked across to Baster whose face had assumed an unreadable poker-table look, a look that appeared to be contemplating a new tactic. The older man sipped on his silver tea-straw, then extracted a lime peel from the crystal mug, munching on it.

"I'd flub it. I'd only disappoint you. I have no experience whatsoever with trusts and estates, that kind of thing."

"You're right for The Trust," Baster insisted, "and that's why I want you installed. Sit back, let me give you a better idea of what we're discussing."

Baster broke it down.

How four-hundred years ago, Piet Friejjarr-Muldaur I, a Flemish-Belgian had landed in a trading schooner on the barren shores of what is now Cape Town in South Africa. He came looking for a way-station to service the Dutch trading fleet that plied between Europe and the Far East. Piet Friejjarr-Muldaur I had been designated as the African agent of the fabled Dutch East Indies Company—their man on the scene, empowered to stake out a surpassing position for the Company on the African continent while abetting the hugely profitable flow of goods between Europe and Asia, and, in the course of it, break the stranglehold of the Portuguese. A swashbuckler straight out of a Hollywood film, his impact had been immediate, lasting. He exacted his allowed commissions on the east-west trade that multiplied mightily under his protection, with Muldaur riches spreading like algae. Later, a grandson, Piet III, established The Muldaur Trust in Switzerland at Braunsweig und Sohn, private bankers of Geneva. Piet III had married a Braunsweig daughter, thus cementing a centuries-old bond between the bank and the Muldaur family. Braunsweig, itself, as a permanent trustee of Muldaur Trust, acted as sole custodian of its immense assets.

The Trust covenants stipulated that the eldest son of each Muldaur generation, unless incapacitated, would automatically be named as sole beneficiary, within his life, of all the Trust's income and its assets. If no son, then the eldest daughter came next in line. The formula for succession was modeled after the primogeniture laws of England, in much the same way as the inheritor of the British Crown is chosen. The method was adopted so that this part of the family wealth could be consolidated and controlled; more, by domiciling The Trust secretly in Switzerland; the tax levies had been minimized.

"That's the essence," Baster explained. "Today, as we sit here, that income is well over two billion Euros annually. Strictly the income, mind you. I've never touched a penny of it. Never needed to. It keeps ballooning. Four-hundred years of balloons, compounding and compounding, adds up. I'm told The Trust is the largest single stockholder in many of Switzerland's most prominent companies. Quite a few in the States, as well. Mainly pharmaceuticals and banks and real estate holdings all over the earth. Jaggy cannot succeed to The Trust because, as you well know, she's a stepdaughter and not in the direct bloodline. If we tried to amend The Trust to put her in the picture, we'd have to consult with the government here, since they're the contingent beneficiary if ever there are no blood heirs to take over. That would open up a bag of wildcats none of us want to deal with. I certainly don't, nor do I ever intend to."

"Is that because of The Trust's size?" Thomas asked.

"Precisely. It's too much to transfer to our blacks here. Yet they will stand to have it all if I haven't an heir. That's not an acceptable outcome to me. Though Jaggy has nothing to say about it, it makes her fur fly in ten directions. She wants to be the new trustee, but I can't allow it. She's far too antagonistic to the blacks and especially this government. Picks fights unnecessarily. She's liable to say the wrong thing, or do the wrong thing and the government could easily retaliate"—he shook his head, his eyes narrowing—"she's simply not a good choice. We've troubles enough already and I'm not cruising in search of a frantic mess to deal with. As it is, there is rumbling about nationalizing our most profitable mines. Were that to occur, it would be the requiem for Muldaur operations in all Africa. All the others would do the same, I'm sure. You see, don't you, that if Muldaur Ltd. loses its African interests, then it would be reduced to its overseas real estate holdings. So, The Trust itself may become paramount to the future of our operations, whereas before it never was…and there you have it…and that's why I'm forced to produce an heir."

"Shouldn't you be the trustee?"

"I'm looking downstream. It calls for someone younger. You're ideal. An academic man and you're well acquainted with African Heritage. If there's no heir then I want someone who'll dispose of The Trust in the appropriate way. Someone who can convince the other two trustees of the right thing to do in Africa."

"What's that to be?"

"I want the exact language of The Trust skirted. Not its main purpose, the public good, but that the Trust's resources, when disbursed, as it stands now, and as I've mentioned will go directly to our government here. Instead, I want the money to come directly to the colleges and universities of South Africa, and also to African Heritage. It's billions, mind."

"Yes, but would the government go along?"

"They'll need bribing, of course. A few million rands should take care of the only people that matter."

"Bribes?"

"I'm bribing them now. That's why the DuPont-ers are here. That's why we're letting this government crowd have N'jorro, which they'll use to bribe the Mzura. Baksheesh is how business is sometimes done in part of the world. The blacks understand it as well as the Arabs."

"The government here, did you say, knows nothing about The Trust?"

"Probably they do and probably they don't. It's on record somewhere in the archives. Gathering dust, I suspect. The testaments are hundreds of years old. Ancient. Written in Latin, not a forte of the black bureaucrats. That has advantages and disadvantages. The government likely doesn't pay any attention, I suppose, because they've forgotten all about it after several centuries have passed. Nor would they have the foggiest as to what's in The Trust's asset structure. As of now, they aren't entitled to know. When it was set up centuries ago, the presumption was there'd always be an all-white government here in South Africa. For all these years, until a couple of decades ago, it was the only way of life here."

"And Jaggy, is she...well, can I say is she a detriment somehow? Other than her attitude, I mean?"

"Vesuvial is what she is. Raving, when she thinks the blacks might walk off with everything. I remind her she's so well off she needn't have a worry. A very rich woman in her own right. She inherited ten-percent of Muldaur Ltd. that I'd given her mother when we married. When they lay me out in a blue suit, she'll get all the rest, less the pounds of flesh the government whittles out of her. A quite extraordinary amount of wealth. Even so, she's made it coarsely clear she wants her place in the affairs of The Trust. Maybe one day she'll have a family. But it makes no difference as to The Trust if she does, since no child of hers would be a lawful Muldaur descendent. It's become a bugger's muddle and I should've done something about it after Jaggy's mother passed. I didn't, though. A gross error on my ledger, I suppose. Now I've no choice but to act. Either a blood heir or we lose out. It's rather dire, that's what it is."

"I'm sure you know how to make heirs, Baster."

"It's not what I'd term a humorous matter."

"I didn't mean to make light of it. What can I do?"

"We're providing you a laboratory. One of your projects will be to make me an heir. A legitimate descendent. That'll settle the issue of what happens to The Trust."

"And who's to be the other half, the lucky lady?"

"Not another wife, not at my time of life. I've had a wife. I revered her and there'll never be another like Margit. I need a midwife and the midwife is you, Tommy. We'll need a surrogate, one of those female incubators we hear about. But I don't want her to know I'm the one who's the other half of the loaf. I mustn't have my name involved. The lawyers are adamant and I tend to agree."

"I'm afraid, I don't follow."

"The lawyers tell me that any woman I impregnate might be in a position to enter claims, serious claims at that, against Muldaur interests. Interfering on behalf of the child, for example, and calling for audits and identifying indirect interests such as The Trust. On and on. Of course, they might not prevail, but then again they might. Our courts have black judges now. If they were to pry their way in, force us to open The Trust's holdings and unveil the trust instrument itself, we'd only whet the appetite of the government here. Some hell of a pickle, I assure you. A ruckus the *Daily Mail and Guardian* or *Sunday Times* would revel in. We cannot take that risk of a public airing, or we're back to square one. That's also why I'm somewhat unsettled about what you did with the three Mzura women. The right thing, perhaps, what you did, but the wrong time for it."

"I begin to see. The picture clears. Well, somehow we need a surrogate mother. Who's that to be?"

"There isn't any."

"No one?"

"Jaggy's offered herself. I don't mean that the way it sounds. What I'm saying is she offered to become the carrier of a child made by an *in vitro* procedure. My juices, some woman's egg, and Jaggy's womb. It's a poor idea on its face but it offers the supreme advantage of secrecy."

"Be pretty awkward, too, wouldn't it? Her being your stepdaughter and with most people thinking she really is your natural daughter."

"And if she were the surrogate she'd be arguing all over again, pushing her way into the trusteeship. Besides, she has some sort of female plumbing problems and so it might not work at all. No, not Jaggy, she's to be kept out of the equation altogether."

"Have you a timeline on all this, Baster?"

"I've got to know we've a solution in hand. As soon as you get your laboratory up and running, I'd like you to start in. Within a month, say. You won't have a lab by then, but a plan can be organized."

"A couple of other things. We still need an egg or eggs to do this. An Afrikaner woman, I presume?"

"Decidedly an Afrikaner. Muldaurs, men and women have almost always been Afrikaners. Last I was told, there are the eggs of ten-thousand or more Afrikaner women on deposit at Cyro in Switzerland."

"You'd need permission from the egg donor. The donor would then know what's behind this, or who's behind it. There goes the secrecy angle, possibly."

"We'll simply take one. No one will miss an egg or two."

A baleful look from Thomas as he observed, "That's neither easy nor legal, Baster."

"Many things aren't. I've an extremely severe problem to contend with. It's safer all the way round, to obtain an egg with no one the wiser."

"Swiping one? That's, well"—shrugging abjectly—"it's a crime. I can create an *in vitro* embryo, that's easy enough. But I prefer not to be involved in a felony."

"An egg? An egg shouldn't matter. You took that chimp's genes, the DNA, didn't you? Why is this any different?"

"It's quite different. You know it is."

"I leave it to you, my friend. If you don't want to purloin an egg or two, then hire a surrogate. But she's never to know whom she's transporting. You'll take care of that, too. As said already, I cannot afford to get my name involved. Just *in vitro* her and tell her you're the father."

"The child would never know its real mother."

"Can't be helped."

"A hired womb. It's been done. I suppose it can be worked out."

"I hire and pay over a hundred-thousand people as it is, so why not a wet nurse? Or why not a healthy womb?"

"No reason, I was just musing aloud. But it's usually the case that the surrogate knows everything about the biological parents. Not so, in this situation. We'll have to figure something out. One other thing, if you don't mind. Who'll raise the child? Will you?"

"You and Jaggy can do it."

"*Me?* You couldn't really mean me."

"Why not, Tommy? She's free of that fop doctor of hers up in London. She needs a chap like you, someone who doesn't kiss her bottom whenever she crooks her finger. You can stand up to her. It'll be worth your while, you know. I'll see to it, Tommy."

"I couldn't. I really couldn't do anything like that. I'm a bench-scientist flailing around for a job, hardly ready for fatherhood. She's…well,"—laughing quickly, nervously—"I don't have to explain to you who she is."

"Give it a thought, why not? Two or three thoughts, while you're at it. Fair, isn't it"—the voice now like a sergeant's—"you're getting a lab and I get an heir." Baster stood. "I'm off to take care of a few last details with the Americans. See you at the dinner tonight. Thank you for managing this for me. Spare nothing, Tommy. May I remind, there's not a breath of this to anyone. And in case you're ever wondering, the doctors say I've got plenty of juice left in my balls to pop open that egg. Do two eggs, Tommy, just in case. Hell, make it three, and pick the one that'll be my good son."

Baster headed for the door, leaving Thomas to fly his way through a cloud of perplexity. A complex scheme, no princely heir, then a kingdom lost, end of the bloodline for a historically fascinating family. Down the drain, just like that: a disappearing dynasty.

Just thinking about the task—saving a famed family from extinction—was daunting enough. Doing it by thievery chilled his innards. Or doing it by tricking a surrogate also was yet another recipe for trouble. So much was at stake. Some gigantic trust, Baster's progeny, the lab.

Baster as much as suggested the lab was his, pending a few formalities. Yet there was an implied price. Always a price, it seemed. He'd paid one in Rome, now he must fork over another outlay here in Africa. It wasn't money, it was what he stood for, his beliefs. The right, the wrong.

In the loud silence, his mind stopping and starting, he began to see himself in an entirely new light. He wanted that lab, his constant waking dream. But stealing human eggs? Or deceiving some unsuspecting woman to get the use of her womb; and what if she were to rebel once a child was born, then refused to give it up?

What then? He couldn't do it. But how to refuse Baster, after rebuffing deMehlo only two days earlier; the two most important, most cherished people he had ever known. Friends. Mentors. Men who had been everything to him.

And the lab might well be at stake. If so, the findings he had made in Naruma would slip into never-land. Three changed women were nothing but a start, hardly incontrovertible proof that would stand hard scrutiny. What could he say? What could he show? He had made a heavy pitch to the SOS biologists, promising them half the moon, and the prospect of eating crow now loomed.

Become a thief? Was that what it took?

Hours later.

Thomas stood at the edge of a milling crowd, there in the great foyer of the mansion, chatter and movement all about him, teams of waitresses bearing trays of canapés and cocktails. Amused, he observed Jaggy greeting the guests. She stood directly underneath an enormous crystal chandelier, her shoulders and head bathed by its spears of dazzling downlight; she glowed as surely if she had swallowed a lump of radium.

Wearing a gown of shimmering white and green silk, her hair swept up in a black crown, a rope of heavy emerald-cut diamonds circling her strong neck, falling just short of her deep cleavage—"the twins" as Jaggy mischievously called her regal bosom. The centerpiece of the necklace shone brilliantly with the famed and eye-catching Verde Cyclops, 87 carats, green-hued, rarest of all diamonds.

Like some adept stage actress, she handled two conversations simultaneously, while shaking hands with yet another guest. Smiling, laughing, she stood alongside Baster, a head taller than he, processing the parade as it traipsed across the marble floors.

Noting the Verde Cyclops again, he recalled a past remark of Jaggy's, "I never wear diamonds before six," to which he had parried: "Some women never wear them at all," and to that she had tartly retorted: "But you see, don't you, I am not *some* women."

Not tonight, she wasn't. She seemed like Aphrodite resurrected.

Never a constant drinker, nor given to small talk, and not a ready mixer with strangers, he glanced about looking for anyone he knew. In his black dinner clothes, with bow tie and starched white shirt, a set of studs borrowed from Baster, he felt awkward as some teenager at a first dance. Still, he'd be completely out of place if wearing other garb, which, in his case, amounted to sparse pickings at best.

Tall, hard-muscled, his head thatched with sun-bleached blond hair and a deeply weathered face, he drew looks from several women when passing them on his way to a mahogany drum table, where he picked out a card with his name on it. Number 3 was embossed in royal blue on the rectangular card, instructing him where to find his seat at the grand dinner to come.

Later, gongs reverberated from afar, summoning the guests who moved in a swarming body for the dining room, a towering, wood-beamed hall that could easily seat eighty people; and more if side tables were set up.

Surprised, Thomas found himself seated on Jaggy's immediate left. Sitting on her other side was one of the Americans, a smooth urbane type from DuPont named Forrest Payton who, non-stop, was bending her ear.

As many times as he'd stayed at the residence, he'd never eaten at the massive dining table. Not an empty chair tonight, he noted while gazing down its length. A long run of wood sawn from a giant Angola mahogany tree, hewn and smooth-planed a century earlier, and tonight softly lighted by eight massive silver candelabra. Scarlet roses floated in Baccarat crystal bowls. Hand-rolled linens from Belgium, embroidered on their corners with the letter *M* were at each place setting. Two dozen green-coated footmen were arrayed on both sides of the table, serving, taking away, and serving again. Standing at intervals were six wine stewards, three to a side, manning their wheeled-carts that held rows of South African wines, all from Muldaur vineyards in the Stellenbosch region near Cape Town.

No Sultan ever lived in more opulence, thought Thomas.

Almost to the minute, one hour after the five-course dinner had begun, Baster arose and the room settled into a hush. His eyes seemed glitteringly bright, even at a distance, as that leonine head surveyed the two columns of faces seated before him. `

Praising the ladies, he went on to salute the twenty black guests, saying how honored he was to dine with them. Conviction rang in his words as he came to the part soon to ignite a buzz throughout the huge room.

"Tonight, we're about to inaugurate change," Baster began. "For fifty-three years we've been partners with our American friends from the famed DuPont company. About four hours ago, that came to an end. We bought them out. They took too much of our money in the process, but that's what friends are for. We have money, what we lack is progress. We face a most serious problem in South Africa, and for one I'm ashamed to say it has to do with color. Skin color. We have a new government, led by the estimable Robert Mastambwe, here on my right as you see. Like Mr. Mastambwe, I concern myself with the tomorrows we face. What we're celebrating tonight is the fact that we are handing over the Muldaur-DuPont Chemical Works to Mr. Mastambwe's government. By this, I hope we can demonstrate to ourselves, to the world at large, what South Africans can do for our brothers...for we are all brothers...sisters and brothers. Allow me to clarify a point. I don't care about a man's color, unless he cares about mine. In which case he has a problem, not me," Baster paused, gathering himself. "That is this evening's report. Jaggy and I thank you for coming, and we extend particular thanks to our friends at DuPont. Now, if I may, I suggest we withdraw and free the ladies from all the boredom they've endured, while the rest of us see to cigars and cognac."

He sat.

His words hung in the air, unclaimed, almost no applause except for a scatter of clapping from the black guests. Silence. It was as though the speech had frozen the organs of everyone present, numbing them into thinking that the great House of Muldaur was bowing to the blacks, subsidizing them for some arcane reason.

Mastambwe rose, his arms outstretched as if welcoming a throng of well-wishers on the campaign trail. In a rich, sonorous voice he accepted the part of the gift bequeathed to his government, then added a remark meant as a joke but it thudded like a dropped bowling ball..."I shall see to it that this brother" pointing a thumb at himself, "will take enough of the shares to assure my retirement."

Thomas spotted more than a few brows rising. A high-voiced sob from down the table. Others stared blankly. Heads turned. Whisperings behind cupped hands. Next to him Jaggy muttered, "The fucking sodders. Bloody hell!" A crescent of red revealed itself on her cheek nearest to him.

The sumptuous dinner had ended on this bleak note.

Chair legs scraped. Footmen assisted the elderly. Guests moved off to the twin drawing rooms for coffee and liqueurs, cigars if they wanted them, and then dancing to violin and piano music from the foyer-area. He was no dancer and didn't feel like small talk.

Out on the terrace he looked up to a night vivid with its vast expanse of sparkling starlight. The music played on. Laughter erupting and the noises of congregated people drifted out into the night. At odds now, and uncertain of what to do with himself.

Sleep, why not some sleep? A long day of it and he was tiring.

Female eggs still hung perilously on his mind. So did thievery. How to get his arms around that dilemma?

Why wasn't it much simpler to dicker anonymously with a woman to sell her eggs, and somehow let her or someone else carry a Muldaur heir unknowingly? Must be an Afrikaner woman somewhere who would agree to part with a few eggs, or be the incubator for nine months…and meanwhile ignore the anxieties of the lawyers for once. Why bring them into it? The child, and its Muldaur transmitted DNA, was all that really counted.

Then thinking the money at stake in that Trust must be in the tonnages. And what of the lab? Did its destiny hang in the balance, if he didn't play ball. He suspected it might, as Baster had not so subtly inferred.

All right, then. He would have to manufacture a legitimate heir somehow, and in secrecy.

With that thought bobbing and weaving inside his troubled head, he ambled the length of the terrace, fifty yards or so in length, then legged it across a lawn to the service-entrance at the rear of the cosmic-sized residence.

Threading his way through the immense kitchens, startling several of the scullery maids, he climbed the back staircase and went down a long L-shaped hallway to his bedroom. Relieved to be through with the night, he would find out soon enough the night was not yet through with him.

Waking to a stray fingertip tracing his spine and then a waft of perfume: Joy—knowing the fragrance because once he'd asked her its name. Nor had he been in bed with that bouquet before, alternately tingling his nerves and then icing them. He never forgot a smell and he wasn't forgetting hers. He felt a toe caressing his calf, as his nerves jumped everywhere.

"Ah, old sleepy-head himself. Finally up and at 'em."

"I thought I was in a dream."

"You soon will be."

"Lost our way, have we?"

"Not at all. If I'm to be your business partner, I thought it a fine idea to drop by and get acquainted."

"Now that you have, and we've become more fully introduced, it's time for good-bye and good night. Except it's morning."

Her taunt abundantly clear, she returned, "I've never been in this particular bed. It's exceedingly comfortable but colder than it should be. On my side, that is."

A suggestive inference, *your business partner?* Meaning what? That he'd best cooperate with her whims of this night? Thinking, but not very quickly, he said, "We have a company rule that applies to all stockholders. No mixing of the coffee and the tea, in a manner of speaking, and I'm sure you get the manner I mean."

"But, you see, ducks, I'm not here to mix coffee with tea. Far from it. Come closer and I'll show you the best little mixing machine you've seen in quite some time."

"Jaggy, if Baster walked in here, he'd go justifiably insane."

She laughed too loudly. "Dear boy, don't concern yourself so. Baster is a good hundred yards from here. Besides, in bed two's company and three's against our family custom. So, we shan't want him. He'd love it, though. He'd call the band back and applaud us, and you know it. You're a heavy sleeper, Thomas. Like the dead."

"To a point, I'm finding out."

"Yes, lovey, and I found the point. I think I'm about to find another one. I hope so."

"You're making this complicated."

"How can there be anything complicated? Silly you. We have the rest of the night, do we not? We're young, more or less. Healthy. Free as birds. What else do we need? It's the ideal recipe, and I'm ready for a feast. Am I shocking you?"

"I passed the shock test five minutes ago. What I want, and all I want, is for you to put one foot in front of the other and lay a straight course for your own room."

"Lay, yes, that's just what I had in mind, too, Tommy. Don't be an old goofus. I want to be shagged, darling man. Hear me, do you?"

Her voice had hardened a touch, and maybe, he thought, he was getting somewhere. He knew how rashly determined she could get. A willful, granitic woman at times. But how to get rid of her without injuring her feelings?

"You've got to vamoose. I'm asking you as a friend."

"I am your friend. I stopped by to prove it. Don't be an old poop, you poop. My, what a nice hard bum you have. Like marble. Ohhh—ah-la-la."

"Scram." He rocked her away with a shove of his arm.

"Hey! Don't, that's horribly impolite."

"Go, please. You must be exhausted."

"I'm lonely, Thomas. Lonely as a sleepwalker but I wasn't walking in my sleep when I came through your door. Whatever happened to you at the party? There you were and then there you weren't. Were you bored? I thought it a rather interesting crowd. Some of the ladies hoped to have a twirl with you."

"I dance about the way a kangaroo swims. I'll tell you where I was, if you'll put your hand back in its holster."

The bedside light suddenly flashed on, startling him. He moved reactively, and, facing the wall, was glad he didn't have to look at her. One cushiony breast had fused itself to his shoulder blade. Her bared thighs had joined to the backs of his own.

"Let's talk a little," he suggested. "You're going through a patch. The divorce blues, perhaps. Everyone gets lonely at one time or another. I do, all the time. I'm still a priest. Haven't even sent in my resignation yet. I'm bound to my vows. You've got to respect that—"

"Oh, fuck-all to your vows. It's all so insane anyway. Vows for what!"

"It's out of the question," he retorted. "O-U-T. I'm hugely flattered, but it's not in our crystal ball. You're being mule-headed, Jaggy, and making this awkward, even if you're trying not to."

"It's sex, that's what it is and all that it is. Friendly sex. You have no one, I have no one. I want it, and you must. Here you are. Five inches away and it may as well be a mile."

She moved again, first her legs and then her arms. He no longer felt her pressed against him, tightly as a second skin. Then, he felt her fingers resting on his wrist, lynching any hope that she would be leaving soon. She touched him intimately. The bedcovers moved, slipping away. Damage, if not disaster, was begging to happen.

"I'll do it...I can do it for us. Let me. It's all right, it's fan-tas..."

Pushing him down, straddling his hips, on top of him now, she pinned him with a quick scissors-like move of her powerful legs. The bedside lamp bathed them with its shallow beam, her heavy breasts swaying over him, the nipples the size of raspberries. Thighs, flat hard, gripped him. She was amazingly strong, and then, coming down on him, she almost connected.

"Give me...give..."

In that one suspended instant, as she widened herself and as he lay motionless but erect where she had made him erect, and now, overtaken, blood rushing behind his ears, deafeningly; tumid, his nerves racing everywhere, he sensed the relaxing of her thigh-grip as she aimed him. She was on one knee, slightly off balance now and he lurched upward, grabbing her shoulders and tumbling her over on her side.

Her face a mask of different pinks as he told her, "Nothing I say is going to sound right, not even to me."

Heaving as if winded, she scoffed, "How about Jesus Christ! Start with that, why don't you?"

"Don't get sore."

He took her hand in his, a tense moment went by, then another, before she shifted their clasped hands to her bosom. Closing her eyes, she said, "I could make you a thankful man. I'm a damn good ride in bed. I went to a school for it, a sort of school." She turned her head toward him, her ebony hair spilling over one eye, and then she moved the back of his hand to her thigh, pressing it there. "Here, this is me. I'm a woman, remember. I like to feel like one. Be held, be caressed. I thought you might like a night on the nest, my nest, and I want you terribly. I have for so long. I was all built up inside for you tonight. Why is it so awful for you, when it can be so beautiful for both of us?"

He wanted this night, every hour of it, to disappear to the center of the earth itself. Be forgotten, too, but it would never be forgotten. And he knew their friendship would never retreat to what it had once been, brotherly, fun and warming, even confiding at times.

Her breathing waned. She was on the verge of dozing but abruptly her eyes opened and she said to him, "I'll trim the light. I need some night on me now." Her voice a hurt-child voice. "It's all right if I stay with you, isn't it? Let me do that. I must be with someone tonight, even if it's you."

She edged closer, naked and warm-feeling, her hand where it shouldn't be. She kept it there, he guessed, because she wanted him knowing she was still in charge, could not be so easily dismissed. At dawn, waking, he found that Jaggy had left. He thought he'd truly been through a dream but then caught sight of a poppy-red kimono hanging limply on a bedpost. He knew the night, then, for what it had been.

Stirring himself, he removed the kimono from the bedpost, folded it, placing it in a dresser drawer. She must've returned to her bedroom in the nude. Zany of her, but she had her own rules, a mind of her own, and woe to whomever got in her way.

He called the kitchen, asking for a pot coffee and then sat at a secretary with a folding desktop. Get it over with, he told himself, and set about composing a formal letter of resignation to the Society. Even if rejected by the Vatican, as deMehlo had predicted, he decided it best to go on record. Twice he started, twice he tossed it away.

At ten-thirty, he went downstairs, lugging the gift he had picked up for Baster: the picture with the bone-frame etched by the Indian artisan.

Outside, the gold-hued morning was autumn in its unshucked glory. He hoped Jaggy might be out with the horses but she was there with Baster in the morning room. As he entered, they both looked up, all conversation coming to a halt. "I've barged in," Thomas said. "I'll come back."

"Just blathering away about the party," said Baster. "What is it you're carrying there?"

"Jaggy and I picked this up on the trip in from the airport. He handed the carton to Baster. "That's the big boy I've been talking about. Have a look, it's for you."

The older man opened a loose flap, dug his hand in, and lifted. "Quite heavy, why, look there—it's all ivory, no, oh, horns. Well…now…Tommy, let's have a look at this"—agape with surprise—"my boy, what a splendid—you must see this, Jaggy. Look at him!"

Jaggy stood over Baster's shoulder, gazing down at the photo Thomas had taken months before in the Naruma Territory. The picture had been enlarged to the size of 24″x18″, was now framed with bleached ibex horns found on the savannahs of Naruma, the horns intricately scrimshawed with designs of animals, mostly from the antelope family, ibex, impala, bongo, kudu and klipspringer.

A clear blue African sky served as backdrop to two geysers of sun-speckled water bursting everywhere as the great elephant charged out of a watering hole, ears as outstretched as lateen sails. One ear had a curious white splotch that ran top to bottom, like some huge birthmark. Enormous tusks, easily a hundred-pounds each, curved upward below the flying trunk. A majestic sight of a majestic and rare animal. In a rage at being disturbed when the picture was taken, the bull seemed ready to lunge out of the frame. An animal this size needed many trees of foliage daily to survive.

To Thomas's knowledge, not another forest elephant like him existed anywhere in southern-most Africa.

"I'll have this beauty sent over to the offices," Baster said. "On second thought, no, let's hang it over the fireplace right here. Tommy, I cannot tell you of my joy…why it's absolutely stunning. Takes me back, it does. Look at that sky, African blue. Like none other anywhere. That one eye there, see that, Jaggy? You can tell he's hot, he'll be bent on ripping up something." Baster stared at the picture, looked up, "You think he's still mating, Tommy?"

"Mating? I dunno, maybe. Old but I suppose he could. That's one reason I want to corral him. I've never seen a swamp elephant that large."

Jaggy said, "I'd say he's likely got quite a member on him," with a taunting look at Thomas.

Baster laughed. "This is the one, then, you want driven down to Kruger Park?"

"Yep."

"It's exciting...it is," and Baster looked up to Jaggy, still at his side.

"Tommy, you make the arrangements. We'll all take a run at him."

"If you'll permit me to use N'jorro as a bargaining chip, it'll all go better," said Thomas, thinking he might come up with a lever to gain better cooperation from Swiali. "Swiali wouldn't know off-hand that he's in line to get it anyway."

"Good thought. Yes, go right ahead with that idea," exhorted Baster, obviously pleased at the suggestion. "Tell that fat fool Swiali we want the best trackers he's got or no farm for him. Speak for me. Put it right to him, but get those trackers. Ghibwa will know the best of them."

"Shall we bring him with us?"

"Too old. A mighty nose on him, but he's in his sundown days." Taking a taste of his morning adjutant, Baster said, "You can fly tomorrow and get a fix on the trek. That fit your book, does it?"

"Fine by me."

"We'll overnight at N'jorro, and then go out to the bush. Make a list of everything we should bring and radio it to the office."

"Will do," Thomas replied.

At the mention again of N'jorro, Jaggy, simmering, got a little curt with Baster. "Why do this to N'jorro. It's an heirloom. I told you I'll gladly buy it."

"It's worth far more to us as a gift to the government."

"It's stupid."

Baster glowered, and then passed her an indulgent smile before his voice rumbled with warning.

"You do very well, daughter, as a tactician. You're a day-to-day person and have done so brilliantly for Muldaur's trading operations. I note that we paid you a bonus of over forty-millions last year. You think you can kick the blacks in their balls and get away with it. Those days are long gone. Long, long gone. You *must* adjust or we'll be run over. Flattened. I'm trying to buy time and maneuvering room for Muldaur, it's something we sorely need. We've got contracts to fulfill all over the world and we may be unable to fulfill them. Up and down Africa, in Gabon, the Congo, Zimbabwe, Namibia, right here in our back yard of South Africa our interests are exposed. They want our mines, our metals, our strategic materials. Illegal strikes. Threats of confiscation. We need allies—black, yellow or whatever color—I do not care about color and you'd better not either." A blue vein pulsed in his upper forehead. His face seemed to flatten as he asked, "What is your current net worth? How's the count of it these days?"

"My—what! I can't—Thomas is here."

"I can see for myself he's here. Thomas is family. Thomas is the son I never had. Did you think I was stuttering? What is your net worth?"

"I'm not—"

"What!"

"Somewhat less than three-billion in pounds sterling."

"Is it that you lack for anything?"

Stiff-jawed, she shook her head. "I remind, that last night we turned over a valuable chemical works and that two-shilling cockhead of a president almost thought it a joke."

"He is the president...*the* president and is owed your respect."

"A gangster. As if he were doing *us* the favor."

"Quiet now—"

"Just the job, aren't they? Aren't they and—"

"I said quiet, daughter."

Glowering, her jaw stretching forward like a small plow, she stood and then strode through the open door.

Baster drank, shook his head as if puzzled, then reminisced about his younger days, of the older Africa, the princely hunts at N'jorro, the royalty visiting from everywhere, streams of them. Statesmen, too, of the first pew—Churchill, Eden, Eisenhower, Schumann, Gandhi. Platoons of them—who came for safari, sometimes meeting in secret at the House of Muldaur, sometimes bringing their wives, other times their mistresses. Maharajahs, too, of India, desperate for loans, even the Chinese bosses of the old Shanghai opium cartel—and industrialists like Henry Ford II, Thomas Watson of IBM, Alfred Krupp of Germany, Gianni Agnelli of Fiat in Italy, the heads of the big Hong Kong trading houses, Hutcheson and Jardine Mathieson, the biggest of all.

A sweeping experience for a young man in his twenties—Baster's age then—as he stood at the side of the father for whom he was named; and as they hunted all of South Africa; a time when, as a young man, he had sometimes been permitted to overhear things, impending deals, insider gossip. He was being shaped, his self-confidence and know-how tuned up, lessons handed down for future times.

"I apologize for Jaggy," he said at last. "She's something of a lioness these days. Likes to get control, you know?"

"She doesn't always," Thomas answered, thinking of the night just past. "But who can blame her about the farm. N'jorro is a one of a kind paradise."

Baster raised from his chair. "I'll see you up in Naruma in a few days. I'll be running off myself very early tomorrow. Up to Cairo. When we get back from our jaunt, you can start up your lab. What're you calling it, by the way?"

"What about something like this…Muldaur-Courmaine Laboratory?"

"Suits me. And don't forget that egg business, Tommy. Time gallops on us, you know."

And with a slightly lopsided smile, off he went, with Thomas left alone to figure out how to handle Swiali. Whether he'd see the Eves again, whether they could find and secure the elephant, whether Jaggy was about to turn into a nagging, permanent problem? She might if she were a partner in the lab. A very good thing Baster was around to chain her down, as he just had done.

Jaggy had gone down the hall to the billiards room. She yanked a cue off its rack, and began banking balls off the rails, the balls making loud clicking noises as they careened off one another.

Fretting, furious.

Thomas Courmaine, the proclaimed celibate, had rejected her hours earlier. No man had ever before refused her advances. Baster, her lodestar and ally, had minutes ago said that *Thomas is family. Thomas, the son I never had.*

He is, is he?

What were they up to?

Baster had always trusted her, so why the brush-off now? He was planning to cut Thomas in on the business of The Trust? Thomas could not inherit, any more than she could inherit, but he could receive a great hulking gift if Baster were so inclined.

Baster had done so for her mother, and even herself.

Short of handcuffing her, they'd not keep her away from the proposed trek in Naruma. Up there, she could patrol things more closely, perhaps even set things right. Unthinkable, grossly so, to appoint Thomas as an overseer of a trust so secretive Baster wouldn't discuss its value even with her, though he hadn't minded asking her to disclose her own private wealth, and right in front of Thomas Courmaine.

She rammed the tip of the cue along the green baize cover of the table, making a thin rip a yard long in the cloth. So there, she thought. So, *goddamn there!*

Bethesda, Maryland

The news of Thomas Courmaine's revelations at the recent SOS meeting in Cambridge had crossed the Atlantic at speed. Its messenger sat across a conference table in the offices of Murray Raab, Director of Special Research Projects at The National Institutes of Health. Raab was also point-man in the U. S. government, who liaised with its two representatives at SOS, since everything at SOS was a futuristic proposition.

The messenger on this day was the loud-mouthed, contentious Milton Drossberg, a Nobel Laureate and chairman of the Life Sciences Department at University of Texas. Raab had disliked the *faux* Texan ever since their first meeting more than a decade ago, yet grudgingly admitted that Drossberg had his uses.

Less than a week ago, Drossberg, ranting and raving, had called from London demanding a get-together to relay the results of the recent SOS symposium at Cambridge, most notably the outlandish claims of Thomas Courmaine.

His tone disparaging, his words bitter and sarcastic, Drossberg had rammed insult after insult at Courmaine's talk before the SOS scientists. Somewhere during the trans-Atlantic tirade, Raab's sense of curiosity had peaked. It was though a separate message was being tapped out in Morse code. Every week, he listened to a spate of ideas; he had to; it was his job. NIH was widely accepted as the most respected, most capable biomedical research operation on the globe. Raab had a lot of say-so over what ideas made it from the mouth, or paper, to the drawing boards; and from there, just possibly, to the next step—a thorough screening.

If passing through those wickets, then the fortunate few survivors must still dodge the budget guillotine.

Comparatively few met with success.

Murray Raab had the power to make dreams happen. Equally and frequently, he killed them before they saw the light of day. Possibly, just possibly,

Courmaine might've stumbled into something—it was known to happen. Science was like that, half the time you were in a land of Oz.

At NIH, Raab was known as "the beaver", a dubious sobriquet gained by a countenance that was never easily forgotten. A waxed-tipped moustache drew attention to a face that would startle the most loving of mothers: pouchy cheeks, slightly protruding front teeth, and the cap of dark brown hair, wet-looking from gel, and giving the appearance of a pelt of small triangles pointing rearward—like a beaver's, when alighting from water.

Raab resented the tag, of course, the more so because he found it impossible to shake.

Wearying of the story that Drossberg was spinning today, he was about to shut it off, when Drossberg let out another burst "I mean here he comes, no one's heard of any of his work for years and all of a sudden *bingo*...he claims he's found a plausible answer to gene therapy. Merck didn't. Pfizer didn't. Eli Lilly can't, either...but Courmaine says he can. It's all so fantastic, what he's saying. Shit on a stick is what it is," Drossberg yelled in a spray of spittle, "and we'll only look idiotic ourselves if we get involved...you see that, don't you? I've told you nothing that is untrue. Remember, I was there and you weren't, so you ought to give me the benefit. I've been clear about that, I expect..."

"Supremely clear, Milt."

"Then you agree we should squash this nonsense, vote it right into the trash basket?"

"I've agreed to nothing of the kind."

"You've said nothing to the contrary."

"Only because you've sucked all the oxygen from the room. I haven't had a chance to utter a word. You ought to read the newspapers once in a while. Apparently, you don't know the way the wind is blowing in Congress and over at the White House, so I'll enlighten you."

In a flat minute Raab put Drossberg squarely in the frame of events. The government, he emphasized, staggered under the runaway costs of healthcare. Costs climbing off the charts. Costs that put overwhelming pressures on federal and state and corporate budgets. Insurance headaches by the tons. Doctors unable to stay on top of their patient loads. Premiums too high. Nightmare politics and meanwhile no solutions that met with wide support or agreement.

"Therefore," Raab pointed out, "no idea, no matter how remote, no matter who comes up with it, is off the table. We're looking at everything, Milt. This should come as no surprise to you, after all. What's more, I read Courmaine's recent piece on telomeres in *Nature,* and we're not about to reject a concept before we know what else he's got."

Drossberg, almost puffing, replied, "Why immerse ourselves in what'll prove to be trouble. Courmaine all but admitted that human guinea pigs were involved. Not outright, he didn't say it outright but a strong hint was there…you bet it was there. He was holding back and I know why. So he could entice us to hear the whole story. We'd be sued silly if we tried anything like that here in America without first getting ourselves ten pages of permissions. Shut down, too, that's what would happen here."

"You worried about the media or are you worried about your pals at Pfizer and Merck?"

"Partly, sure I am. Why shouldn't I be?"

Raab was mildly amused at Drossberg's discomfort. He had a busy calendar and the time had arrived to usher the Texan to the door.

"Milt, I'm volunteering as the chief worrier on this one. What I'm saying to you is that we're interested in hearing more. *Very in-ter-es-ted.*" Leaning back, lacing hands behind his odd-shaped head, Raab attempted an air of casualness. "You see, don't you, that it costs us nothing to listen to Courmaine? Give him his day. His showtime. He'll have to lay out his facts, whatever they are or aren't, and you will know, as will the others, what he's keeping in that kit-bag of his."

Drossberg shook his head angrily. "But we'll look like fools. He's down there in some place no one ever heard of and you think he can pull this off? Absurd. The best drug companies in the world can't solve it. Every top university works on it—"

"Believe it, Milt. Take it on faith. We're interested in what he's got in his little black bag. Starting tomorrow you'll need to begin lassoing enough SOS votes to get Courmaine up on the stage and singing like two cockatoos. He'll have to make good on his Proof of Concept and we'll take it from there." Raab shifted himself forward, his hands gripping the edge of the table as if he were about to rise. "Funny thing, I haven't heard much about Courmaine lately. You know, he interned here six or seven years ago. One summer. Maybe it was two summers, I forget. Smart boy. Got the Waterman Prize, if I remember and now I do remember. He did. The fair-haired boy over at Johns Hopkins. Who knows, maybe he caught some lightning in his bottle. It's happened, even to you, eh?"

"That idiot says he'd give his data and knowhow away for free. Even give it to SOS, who could take all the royalties."

"Did he? How nice of him. Free, you say?"

"You're a Jew, Murray. So am I. There is no free, not nowhere, not no how, not no way. Bastard's up to something. A fuckin' Jesuit, isn't he? That says enough, I'd say."

"You get those votes rounded up and leave the rest to us."

"I'm not stooping to pandering around for votes." Drossberg said. "If that's what you mean, I won't do it."

"You've done it before."

"Not for this crap. Not for a blowhard down in Africa chasing gazelles. I don't care to be classed with him. I'll quit first, Murray."

"I doubt you'll quit, Milt. I really seriously do."

"By Christ, I will. You'll see and—"

Suddenly Raab shot both hands in the air, palms outward, a gesture that halted the Texan's tirade. "You know how much grant funding we've approved for your lab down there in Austin? *Your lab*, Milton. Over the past five years, you've received upwards of thirty big ones. Those are thirty millions that others were applying for. Lots of moola, right? I trust I make myself abundantly clear to you. Quitting isn't in your Tarot cards, Milt. You're our designated pipeline to SOS, so let's keep it that way, huh? *Compre?* Now, off you go, Tex. I've got me a very rough day ahead. Your day is reserved for vote counting, and you had best get to it or we'll be stuffing your next grant application in the nearest trash bucket. You'd not want that to happen, Milt."

Drossberg's face quivered, turning crimson. The thick lips sputtered a hoarse-sounding groan; utterly deflated, so it seemed. Raab had never seen him at such a prime loss for words, and was grateful for it.

After escorting Drossberg to the door, he stood by watching the slump-shouldered biologist fade away down the corridor. Returning to his desk, he began to weigh the situation with an earnest caution, and in more quiet without the Drossberg's interfering theatrics. Raab dwelled on what he'd just heard. Courmaine was respected in his field, so why would he risk making outlandish claims to a room filled with eminent scientists, who could easily refute spurious claims. Courmaine hadn't the slightest thing to gain, shooting dice with his name at stake.

Drossberg had mentioned human experiments. Not likely, but then who knew?

He debated if he should advise his contact at The League, or await further developments. After all, Drossberg's version of Courmaine's proposition to SOS was pure hearsay at this point. Nothing hard and fast to go on, or to remit to his contact at The League, his other and largest paymaster.

Tell now or wait—a quandary.

The League would ask for details, even if only rumors, that touched upon the vast interests of Pharmus. Gene therapy, Murray Raab well knew, was far more than a detail just as he also knew that, in science, no matter what Drossberg argued, odd and curious things happened all the time, and in the strangest places.

Had Courmaine locked on to a winner? The great elusive fount of bioscience?

Free gene therapy? *Free*, Drossberg had said. Worrisome, thought Murray Raab. But then The League would stop that one in its tracks. He wondered if he should make an inquiry or two on his own, find Courmaine's whereabouts, hear the man out.

But how to find him? And what would Courmaine be willing to reveal anyway, off the record?

The Naruma Territory, Africa

Engines whined to a high pitch as the Dehavilland pivoted neatly at one end of the packed-dirt strip on the southerly end of N'jorro. Taxiing halfway back up the strip, the aircraft braked near the dented gray Land Rover parked near a thick patch of sword grass.

Outside, leaning against the Land Rover, stood Kanu, Thomas's assistant at the Station. Kanu's arms were folded across his naked muscle-packed chest. Watching intently, he flashed his chalk-white teeth as Thomas descended the aircraft's steps. When face-to face, both men raised hands and touched each other's shoulders, a traditional Mzura greeting.

"Kanu, my friend..."

"Friend, to you, To-mas...I take bags..."

A crewmember had set Thomas's duffels down at the foot of the steps. Kanu picked both up in one hand and steps away pitched them into the rear of the Rover, then went around and settled himself behind the steering wheel. Extremely pleased that Thomas had returned, he felt exultant and showed it with a constant ivory-white grin.

When Thomas had first come to The Territory, negotiations with Swiali had ensued, with goods paid over for the use of a small stone cottage and an outbuilding serving as a makeshift lab. In all, it was to become the Naruma Station of African Heritage's operations, small as they were, in the Naruma Territory. Swiali was provided with five bolts of posh Italian silk, eventually to make their way into his repertoire of ceremonial costumes. Kanu had been chosen as Courmaine's live-in assistant because the tribe had little use for him. Half Mzura-half Arab, he was all but an outcast. Yet a fine -looking man of twenty-three, as buffed up as a weight-lifter, a distance runner without equal in Naruma, and an indefatigable helper. The relationship had bloomed, and the two had become brothers at heart.

Thomas spent an hour or so each day teaching the younger man biology along with English, how to speak it, how to write it. Kanu, in return, gave over yet another hour to teaching Thomas the Mzura tongue, while indoctrinating him in various tribal customs and beliefs. A satisfactory arrangement, bonding them over and over.

They headed up a sun-hardened rutted road, skillet-hard, in olden days used by ox teams for hauling supplies. Kanu angled the Rover between two deep water holes, dry after a rain-starved summer. Thomas suspected that Tunda, the big tusker, would be somewhere in the Territory where it was possible to easily find forage, and, as importantly, ample water supplies. Still, he was a rover and he could be anywhere.

Down below, on a shallow valley floor, a herd of N'jorro cattle grazed. These were a new breed, one, as yet, without a name; half Angus, half antelope, and odd looking if you were not used to them—fat-barreled, sturdy-legged, with deer-like heads. Surprisingly fast-gaited, too. They were the same new breed he had described at the SOS meeting in Cambridge, a crossing of bovine and antelope genes made possible by *semba* and its exudate: Zyme-One. Less feed was needed to sustain the crossbred herd and much less water—a real break in animal husbandry for protein-starved Africa. One day, animals like these could account for a significant share of the Sub-Sahara tribal diets.

"Pull into Ghibwa's, Kanu."

"We stop?"

"Just for a few minutes. I need to see him."

A mile later, Kanu stopped before a large hut that, over years and years, had been added to until it was now the old hut with three extensions. Getting out, Thomas knocked loudly on a thick-planked door. He kept knocking until hearing the scuffle of slow-moving feet. The door parted and one dim eye peered at Thomas, then out came the rest of Ghibwa, piece by piece. The tattered white shirt frayed at the elbows and neck showed first; next fingers, gripping the door that were scarred from a lifetime of digging roots; a fairly clean Ace bandage was wrapped neatly around one elbow, the spiraled wraps covering layers of moistened herbs. No one was ever told what sort of herbs they were, nor what cures they performed. The arm had always seemed to work perfectly but the elbow and its Ace wrap-around had practically become one thing by now. Ghibwa's left foot was buried inside an old field boot; half ripped, with the other foot showing the flat splayed toes of an ageless man, who could still walk for miles, living off the land and his wits. His trousers, belted by a strip of rhino-hide, hung loosely around a reed-thin boney waist. A large tear in the trouser-fly revealed Ghibwa's privates. In most countries, he would've been hauled in for indecent exposure.

In the tribe Ghibwa would be called a *sangoma,* a man with a vast knowledge of bush medicine, especially the ancient ways of curing common ills. In the West, he'd be known as an ethno-botanist though without the usual academic credentials.

"Lo! to you, Thom-ass-a. You die, I be thinking."

"Lo, to you, Ghibwa. I am returned from dying."

"You happy? I happy see you."

"I'm ecstatic, my friend. Did I wake you?"

"Nevah wake-a. Sleep in dis month one-a day only, one-a night only. That all," Ghibwa boasted, a master exaggerator of his quite considerable feats, true or otherwise. "You go for long dis' time. Think you be dead for this life. Cry for you. Cry two night mebbe. Here come you be. All same-a."

"Let me in and I'll dry your tears for you."

Nimble, still supple as a ballet slipper, Ghibwa did a quick foot-jig. He swung the door wide as he danced, and Thomas entered a low-ceilinged, half-lit room rank with kerosene odors from a series of battered Arabian Sea lamps that Ghibwa burned night and day. For as long as anyone could remember, Ghibwa had lived here, and his father and mother before him. Twice he had refused a pension, enough to make him rich by Naruma standards. Outraged at the offer, he dismissed the thought out of hand, believing it was meant as his grave-money.

"How be dat Basta-man?" he asked as he always did when Thomas arrived from Jo-burg.

"Sends you his heart, Ghibwa."

"I not need a heart from dat Baster. Why no he send me wimmins?" cackling through his gapped teeth.

"You are too young, he thinks. Next year possibly."

"Nudda year, nevah 'dis one. Me, I shake he's head so he learn theengs. When the Basta-man evah come here?"

"In a week or so, Ghibwa. Maybe a week and some days." Thomas held up one finger, and bent the one next to it at the joint, indicating a measure of time. "Maybe the Missy, too."

"Dat woman, she many wimmins. I lika four, five, same-a likka her."

"Four or five, is it? You'd never be the same."

"Thom-ass wanna flower-drink? You be have one with Ghibwa?"

"Go ahead, please. I'm not thirsty right now."

On legs so loose they seemed boneless; the old man shuffled to an adjoining room where he cooked, and where he slept on a straw floor mat, with a huge giraffe skin as his blanket. He was about to fix one of his leaf-doctor brews from herbs, roots, tree bark, and wildflowers. Awful tasting, bitter as week-old coffee. Yet his elixirs had powers to heal beyond anything else Thomas was aware of.

He looked at the retreating stringy wise old owl, this superb man who'd taken him under wing, teaching him how to live on Naruma's plains, and the essence of so many other things in Nature. He loved Ghibwa. A man matchless as a mentor of the outdoors, and a man born for teaching.

The old relic could walk along, spy something, telling the age of a plant, herb, a root and why it was that the Spirit allowed us to have it; what it was good for, and not. He understood how these things had made their journey to wherever he found them, from seeds carried in bird droppings, special birds that flew only at night. All this he could tell you, or not, depending on whether he thought you were worthy enough to know. He did not grasp the concept of the atom or a molecule, for he had no need of knowing it. But he knew, anyway, that inside all living things a billion parts bustled in a sort of melody, each in harmony with the other.

Ghibwa returned, handing Thomas a battered tin cup. Deaf in the left ear, either Ghibwa hadn't heard his earlier refusal or chose to ignore it as he did so many things. Bracing himself, Thomas swallowed the peppery brew, the fluid souring his throat and sending a shudder down his spine.

The cackle again. "Dis-a soup maka you likka rocks here-a," Ghibwa said, clasping his crotch with fingers long and thin as vanilla beans. He jumped twice on his booted foot.

"You'll need a lot of that if you get your five wimmins."

"One-two cuppa dis soups, plenty for do all dem wimmins," Ghibwa boasted, though holding up only three fingers. On that hand were actually six fingers, one a stub that grew to the side of his little finger. His devil's teat (*kwela*), he called it. In reality, a genetic mutation.

"Let's sit," Thomas suggested.

Ghibwa squatted, sitting on his haunches, his fingers locked around the cup. His eyes, red-rimmed from all the smoke, showed like two glowing marbles in the vapory shadows.

It made no sense to tell him that N'jorro was to be transferred to the Mzura (meaning to their chief-king Swiali), for Ghibwa had no concept of private land ownership. He had all his life roamed Naruma Territory as though he owned it all. All of the tribe felt that way, and all knew that, as their king,

Swiali, if he so chose, could put any of the land off-limits. He'd never do it, but could.

Thomas spoke slowly. "We are going to take Tunda to a safe place. More food, more water. We need trackers, the best of the Mzura. I want you to choose them, three or four. Then tell Swiali who they are and that I'll be—I'll make talk with him soon. Tomorrow or next day after tomorrow. You must tell Swiali I want to see him. I will make him rich."

"Swiali no likk-a you. Hated you. Frighted you. You take Tunda, he kill. Kill me mebbe…mebbe." The grizzled head wagged back and forth, the face compressing with gravest doubt.

"No, he won't kill anyone," Thomas replied.

"He mad at you. Dem wimmins you do make young." Nodding in agreement with himself. "He theenk-a kill you. Make bricks of you."

Ghibwa's red-veined eyes fell away, rolling into whiteness as if besieged by a sudden fainting attack. A self-induced trance. He chanted unintelligibly, was off to a place where he was unreachable, falling into a brief dream perhaps. Something Thomas grasped, for he was something of a dream-spinner himself.

Thomas waited, but nothing. Waited longer, still nothing. Ghibwa breathed well enough but he had assuredly gone elsewhere.

Outside, he heard the sputter of the Rover's engine that needed a tune-up, and that Kanu was wasting scarce gas. He left the hut, not knowing if he could rely on this old magician to connect him up with that buffoon, the imbecilic Swiali, who nonetheless was key to the trek to find Tunda. He had to know, either to call it off or signal Baster that the trackers could be had, that the hunt was laid on.

N'jorro, where Ghibwa lived, lay almost forty miles to the west of the Mzura tribal village. Ghibwa had passed Thomas's message to Swiali through drum messages relayed one to the next, and just after dawn a runner arrived at Thomas's stone cottage with instructions from Swiali for Thomas to present himself no later than mid-morning.

He drove there by himself, a heavy pull over bumpy land. Parking the Rover at the east side of the village, he observed a line of fifty or sixty women parading by, on their way back from harvesting the meager pickings in the crop-fields. Men loitered under shade trees, smoking thin homemade cheroots, joking, trading gossip, planning their next hunt. An elder stood apart, a bent wizen-faced man who counted the women. As they sang the Song of Life, laughing gaily and innocently, passing him by, he smacked many of them on their calves with a stout stick.

Thomas sat there, watching, as one woman received a double whacking. Never even flinching. No Mzura women ever showed pain, even if blood were drawn.

Why the beatings, Thomas never had figured out. He suspected it was merely to remind the women the males of the Mzura reigned supreme.

Aged women, unable to pull their full weight for the tribe, were killed off, as had been intended for the three Eves. Waiting. Watching. He fixed the image carefully in his mind, for he never expected to see this scene again. When the trek to find Tunda ended, his days of residence in Naruma would end, sadly so and yet he was pleased at the prospect. The lab, finally his own lab!

Everything in his newer life had begun here in The Territory and so he dallied now, sowing memories for harvesting on unknown days and times to come.

Leaving the Rover, he walked toward the twelve-foot high ramparts erected as a fence around the tribal village, roughly some two square miles in its expanse. The fence-line was eight feet in thickness, constructed of flesh-ripping thornbush backed by acacia logs. Women, purposefully blinded at birth, braided the fencing every day, doing it all by touch alone. Any man attempting a breech had no chance; trapped in the snarls, he'd meet a slow agonizing death, which is how the Mzura rid themselves of the unwanted.

Thomas's back stiffened as he strode through a tall rounded opening in the fence, past four sleek-muscled, spear-carrying guards eyeing him with no more concern than if he were a stray goat sauntering by. He knew by their oblivious airs that he was safe. He had been *non-grata* for months, ever since transforming the Eves, raising concerns that he possessed a fright-making magic no Mzura could match or even grasp. More, others of the elder women, some fearing their own death, wanted him to make them appear youthful again. He had refused. Enmity followed; enmity and lasting resentment.

Halfway up a lane, Thomas turned right and saw a woman crouched under a low-hanging tree, hissing at him as he approached. She was one of the fifty or so of Swiali's wives whose names he could never keep straight and never tried to.

"*Ea-nu*," she called out in a singsong voice. *Eanu,* in the Mzura tongue meant 'man who had no use of women'.

Thomas stopped. "I see Swiali." he said in the Mzura tongue.

"They be washing him."

"I wait."

"You go to him, *Eanu*. He be there-a for you. Send for you."

"I know, mother. But I will wait." He bowed respectfully, though with an uneasy feeling the woman had known he was expected for some time, and that something unpleasant might be in the offing.

She shook her head. "Go, *Eanu*. Quick-a now-a. He know you be here." She put a forefinger to her lips, then bobbed her head toward an opening in a high stone wall, whitewashed with a paste made from crushed bones.

Thomas reluctantly moved on.

"You make me like three wimmins?" she called out.

"Someday, mother...some other day."

He legged it through a long twisting maze of woven branches, eventually stepping into a large four-sided enclosure. Autumnal flowers of every color were banked against the whitewashed walls, the ground dirt-packed hard as asphalt, the air a mélange of sometimes fragrant, sometimes confusing smells.

Two heavy-rumped women stirred a porridge in an iron cauldron: goat's blood cooked with wild herbs, radish leaves, and *tiishe*, a tuber root the Mzura believed to be a powerful aphrodisiac. Out of curiosity, Thomas had tried it once, and his bowels had gone loose for a week.

Scurrying about, or directly attending Swiali, were a dozen or so of his wives. None wore anything, not even breechcloths. It was bathing day, with Swiali going first.

The obese chief stood in a large oval tin tub, its sides reaching almost to his football-sized knees. Two of his wives scrubbed his blubbery rolls with soft tree-bark, and a young girl, no more than ten or twelve, stood inside the tub with him, washing his genitals and buttocks. Two other women were poised nearby, shading him with black umbrellas whose carved handles were made from the femurs of human females.

Swiali ignored everyone, putting on airs as he often did, indicating that no one else mattered, even if they existed.

An unlit briar pipe tilted from his thick-lipped mouth, and with both hands he held a tattered issue of *The Guardian* of Manchester, England. The pipe and newspaper were an act, a pose to impress Thomas, for Swiali couldn't read English—though spoke it passably.

Nearby stood a battered, rusted cement mixer, a stark reminder to the women. It had been placed there, apparently, from the time of Swiali's father who used it to permanently dispose of the skeletons of wives he no longer had any use for. Ground to dust, the wives' bones were then mixed with clay and made into bricks used for crude firewalls of the cooking ovens or hearths. The spirits of discarded women were, in this way, purified by everlasting heat and fire.

"*Eanu,*" said Swiali finally, peering over the newspaper. Nodding to himself, then, he returned to his reading, grunting at something he feigned seeing on one of the pages.

Swiali intended a game, a contest. Sometimes they were so childishly idiotic, they amused Thomas.

Today, though, business had to be transacted and done swiftly. Though Thomas had a fair grasp of the Mzura tongue, he found it an elliptical language and so given over to symbolisms that it sometimes took minutes to express a simple idea. A language created out of many shades, many nuances, embellished with many expansive concepts—almost like speaking with an artist's brush.

"H'lo, majesty of Naruma," Thomas replied formally in Mzura. "You send for me?"

"No, I command you come to me."

"Yes, command. Excuse me."

"You want bath?"

"I already had mine, but thanks to you for asking."

"I smell you, you come here. All this morning, I smell you. Many time I tell you, you stupid, stupid. Use this-a." Swiali grabbed a piece of the tree-bark from one of the wife-scrubbers and flung it at him. "You away somewhere, long time? When finish with this bath, we talk. You smell, *Eanu.* Bad smell. Where you go, and you not tell Swiali."

"I had no time to ask for your leave, Majesty. Baster-man send white sky-machine to fetch me. I was in a great hurry, and you, Majesty, you are so very...always so busy," Thomas was saying as he retrieved the tree-bark from the ground, adding, "I'll get myself a supply of this bark you use, Majesty of All." Thomas paused, then affably asked. "We talk now, maybe? You'll want to hear me. I have much for your ears today."

In a mood to impose himself, Swiali replied, "These wimmins be slow. Lazy like you. All things bad, they be. You stay here this night with me, we talk. Talk of your long journey."

Thomas looked helplessly at this ludicrous sight. Swiali, his middle like a stack of tires, one piled on the next, all of them protruding askew, leaving Thomas wondering if the day could be far off when Swiali's arteries would blow to smithereens. A miracle it hadn't happened already.

"Why you say nothing to me, *Eanu?*" Swiali demanded. "Tonight you stay?"

"Another time."

"I give you wimmins, you stay." Mocking Thomas now, wrongly believing him to be homosexual, an error so useful that Thomas had never bothered to correct it.

"They are your wimmins, not mine," he replied, smiling.

"*Ha-hahaha-uhha.*" Swiali guffawed, with his blubber jiggling, almost as if an electrical jolt had just passed through him. "*Eanu* be strange, stupid man. Never wimmins for *Eanu. Haruh-ha-ha-hah.*"

The young girl in the metal tub knelt and begat to mouth Swiali's genitals. The act itself didn't repel Thomas so much as seeing the girl, barely pubescent, being forced into it. Earning her future now. In two years, if she pleased Swiali, she'd become a concubine-wife. Yet if Swiali found fault, then one day she would simply be another victim of the bone-prayer, ending her youthful days as a brick somewhere in this kingly compound.

Thomas stood there, acting as if everything were normal, expected. Serenity itself.

Were he to show his disdain in the slightest, he'd never be allowed to set foot again in the village—nor, likely, would Swiali provide the trackers he sought.

Thomas asked, "Swiali, Majesty, we must talk now. I have things to say. It cannot wait."

Swiali burst out, "What you do, you make thes-a trouble? Now all old wimmins wants same new skin. New robes. New-a, new-a everything." Swiali repeated with rancor, his droopy jowls shaking like jelly. "Make sick, those three women. Soon die away, I think."

"They're not sick. Do not pretend they are. You and I had an understanding. All kings honor their understandings." Before Swiali could retort with some trumped-up angle, Thomas plunged ahead, "Today I come with a message from Muldaur of N'jorro, the king of you and me and all Mzura." Thomas nearly quaked as the words, now said, now in the open, widened Swiali's already enormous eye-sockets. The mouth going in three or four directions at once.

Thomas told him that when Baster Muldaur came to N'jorro soon they expected to hunt for a week or more on the plains. For this, they needed top trackers. Names he knew Ghibwa had mentioned somehow when sending the drum messages. Thomas demanded six, hoping for three or four.

Cajoling Swiali now, he said N'jorro was about to be given to Swiali, but only if Thomas gave approval, as Baster-man Muldaur, whom Swiali despised, had no use for the land anymore. As bold a lie as Thomas had ever told, and he went on, "If I, instead of you, become king-man of N'jorro, I may no longer allow the Mzura to graze the lands, free. Heavy payment must be made for the use of N'jorro, starting on the next moon."

"You get nothing."

"I will pay for Cubans in Bajjia, and they will guard N'jorro," Thomas said, running his bluff hard now, watching closely, as Swiali violently batted one of the wives away.

"N'jorro belong me, always belong me."

"Now it is you who lie."

"Mzura take you, Courmin. Kill you, cut your throat, empty all your pocket. And kill you two time, three time."

"No farm then, no N'jorro for you."

"Swiali take N'jorro. N'jorro belong to me."

"You'll have to take N'jorro from my Cubans," adding, "the Cubans will bring guns here, and I do not want to say what they will do with your wives. It will be your fault, of course. But you always know what is wisest, Majesty."

Cuban mercenaries hung out in Bajjia, Naruma's only town and it was a hell-pit nonpareil. The Cubans used it as a refuge in between engagements in Africa's numerous pocket wars. Well-trained, battle-hardened, the Cubans and a band of Nicaraguans were always for hire. Hard, tough types, giving no quarter, nor asking for any.

The lava-hot scowl on Swiali's face told he had digested Thomas's bamboozling, if not wholly falling for it. The blubber shaking again, the reddish eyes glazing over, perhaps from some tormented vision of what might befall him at the hands of those desperados that terrorized Bajjia, with nothing more than their cold-eyed, unwavering stares and the playing of mumbly-peg with bolo knives.

Things could tip either way now. Thomas clenched his hands, waiting, though inside he slumped a little, hoping he hadn't pressed too hard, or revealed some other sign of weakness. One never knew for certain with Swiali; he had moments of lucidity clear as fresh rainwater. Occasionally, he even owned a thought or two that approached an unlettered brilliance. Still, as a leader he was a parody; badly tilted, demented at times. At this instant, Thomas did not like the look on that fat-filled, snouty face, with its thick purplish tongue darting in and out of the half-opened mouth.

The wives had begun their one-sided struggle with Swiali's massive bulk, precariously guiding him out of his tin tub. They moved him as if they were handling an enormous black melon that might easily fall, splitting apart. They carefully, slowly sat him on a polished wooden log, naked and looking absurd, most of his stomach sitting on his lap. The women fussed over him, warily so, murmuring compliments and sweet consolations as they dried him and then wrapped him in robes of leopard and cheetah skins. A strip of zebra hide was folded around his head, there, to secure a two-foot crane feather of blue that seemed to grow directly out of his forehead.

Exerting himself like this, in the simple act of being dressed, Swiali's bluish tongue fell out like a panting dog's. He began to mop the corners of his mouth with his thick tongue made blue from chewing on indigo-colored *ol'pabo* nuts.

Aware of Thomas once more, "Ha, you again. I see a honey-bird some-time, that bird leave honey in yo' mouth. See him one time go buzz-zz in yo' mouth, and you talk trick, man-ny-y trick. Be bad for us. Bad for those wimmins."

"Wrong. Good for those wimmins."

Swiali roared, "No trackers."

"We intend to find that Tunda and save him if we can," said Thomas, so suddenly, so firmly that Swiali's eyes went dull with disbelief, as if he were drugged. A finger-thick artery pulsed under one ear. The nearby women froze in place, dead silent and obviously frightened.

"You take Tunda!"

"To a safe place so poachers cannot kill him."

Swiali demanded, "You tell me how you do wimmins."

"You must believe it would take a very long time to tell you and then show you. But I will always say to the Mzura that it could not be done without you, Majesty." A promise Thomas would long regret.

"I be thinking...I be think," said Swiali, his head falling a little to one side.

"You be thinking and I'll be sitting. Five minutes or no N'jorro for you, and I go away."

"Who you be, tell me? I king. I Swiali. You like Muldaur. You white man. You nothing." Then, in words that surprised Thomas, Swiali continued, "You come-a with what is impossible. Unbee-leef-able. Unmercee-iful to me, Swiali. What I do you? Never nothing. Go! You go, ever go away. You lie."

Lie, it was now the word of choice on this day.

"*Nwambe* (meaning final), our agreement must be made and made now. No exceptions, no conditions."

Swiali did not know the meaning of words like exceptions and conditions. His word was final to the Mzura. Incensed at Thomas's demands, especially in front of his gossipy wives, his facial features seemed to grow inward as if some invisible pressure were squeezing against the massive head. Yet he too was fright-ridden. He envied Thomas's odd, magical and obvious powers to rejuvenate the bodies of those three old women.

Thomas knew that one chopping motion from one of those suety arms, and by tomorrow or the next day, he'd be reduced to bone-brick. A dice-roll, using the N'jorro farm as a bribe, then standing firm, running the bluff. His feet felt as if they had turned to stone. Anything could happen. Sizing each other up in this face-off, each appraising the other, estimating what was to be gained, and what lost? Who the winner, who the loser? Or could they even the playing field somehow?

"You dead, Cour-min."

Thomas said, "We die together, Swiali."

"You bow to Swiali."

"I bow to no one, not even you."

Swiali's eyes, always red-rimmed, turned a vein-breaking scarlet. He shook almost convulsively and Thomas saw the wives and the young girl scamper into a passageway. "You not go those wimmins, Cour-min. I kill you, you go."

"I leave now. I will see the three women."

"What be in black bag?" Swiali pointed a trembling hand at the medicine kit Thomas carried.

"Nothing for you. After I see the women, I will go into Bajjia and arrange Cubans."

Swiali snorted. "If you not die, I send trackers."

"How very wise you are, majesty."

With that, he left and went off to visit his Eves. He'd won. Whatever he had won was speculative at best, but he knew he'd have his trackers to go searching for Tunda.

Johannesburg, South Africa

With bull-headed persistence, Jaggy kept on arguing, "He's simply not right for it, Baster. Knows nothing whatsoever of business, so how could you possibly appoint him?"

"I beg to differ, my dear, for he is precisely the right person. This money—it's huge—and if it comes to Africa one day, Thomas will know the right side of things and the wrong. He'll have first-rate legal help and, besides, he's only one of three trustees. There's Braunsweig und Sohn, and how can you get better? There's Claude-Paul Lavalier, a damn fine attorney. All in all, it ought to be a superior arrangement."

"I'd still be the better choice to fill that vacancy," Jaggy contended.

"But you are not the choice and you will not be the choice. This is not of concern to you, Jaggy."

"You adopted me, Baster. I've legal rights."

"Not to Compactus Muldaurus you don't. That's been told to you several times."

"A technicality."

"It is, I remind, a covenant. Blood means blood, and you are not of the bloodline. Nothing to be done about it, daughter."

"You could always marry me, there's nothing illegal about that."

"Not a joking matter, Jaggy, if you please."

"I don't mean it as a joke. We could marry and I could try an *in vitro*. We'd not have to have sex; I didn't mean that…if that's what's ripping at you."

His mouth compressed as he replied in a growling voice. "Sheer nonsense. I'm astonished you'd bring up an idea like that."

"I'm trying to be a help."

"Help like that…that'd be the end of us all, if others heard of it and they most obviously would do so."

"Well, just forget I brought it up. You've never said what is in The Trust. How much is it?"

"A confidential much, that is how much."

"Billions?"

"Too many billions."

"I'm asking you, Baster, asking you to let me fill the vacancy."

"Final is final and we'll speak no more of it. It is done business."

He had said it, knowing it wasn't so. Thomas had yet to consent to fill the empty trusteeship. But on no account would he risk naming Jaggy to that position. Her lust for power and wealth was ungovernable. With the weight of her ambition and cunning ways, she could be a menace to his strategy for safeguarding Muldaur's interests in sub-Sahara Africa. Despising the blacks as she did, and with her outspoken, headstrong ways, she needed a strong hand and a stronger bridle, or she could cause calamity. He even toyed with the idea of parking her out in the Far East, while he carried out his plans to erect a political moat around Muldaur Ltd. to protect its interests over the next several years. Africa, or much of it, was becoming despotic and if not that, then socialistic. If he could buy enough time, he could unload Muldaur's sprawling network of mines to the Chinese, who prowled the globe looking for deals that could supply their industries with the vital feedstock of strategic ores and minerals, without which they couldn't make so much as a washing machine.

He could swing those arrangements, or was fairly sure he could, but not if she was ruffling the waters every month or so, making foes needlessly in lower Africa, the sites of most Muldaur's mines.

Marry his own stepdaughter? God forbid! What was happening in her mind? Obviously, The Trust. She wanted a limitless war chest if she could get her hands on it, but what else?

He loved Jaggy dearly…but there were times…

Bethesda, Maryland

Murray Raab took the early morning call from Miles Bascomb of Boston, Massachusetts, Raab's contact with The League—the *eminence gris* behind Pharmus. Bascomb was the person he'd called when in doubt as to how he should process Milt Drossberg's recital of the proceedings at SOS, where Thomas Courmaine had unveiled his somewhat startling proposal.

They talked for a time, not very long but long enough, with Raab on the listening side of the conversation.

"...so, Murray," Bascomb prattled, "we want an assessment. We're lookin' to know what he has or hasn't. For real, is it, or a carton of horseshit? Tell Drossberg we want a full report. Very full. He's to brief you, first, then we'll decide the next step. Now, son, you have any opinion on any of this?"

"Not even the slightest," said Murray. "It's bizarre, or surely sounds it. Yet we've always been pretty impressed with Courmaine."

"At any rate, we're together...in synch, are we?"

"Completely."

"You know where Drossberg stands on pullin' those votes together?"

"He says he's been working on it."

"Tell 'em to work faster."

The line went dead, the honeyed accent gone, the instruction unmistakable.

Raab put in a call to Milt Drossberg in Austin, Texas. The whole business was interesting but nonetheless a nuisance. Soon enough he would learn that the so-called nuisance would become a fixation on several fronts, with himself at the epicenter.

The Naruma Territory, Africa

On the fourth day of the trek, across the camp clearing, Jaggy was sunning herself on a field-cot. She wore nothing but black briefs, oblivious to the camp-boys, to himself, to Baster, to the entire world. Her bared breasts were so perfectly set Thomas barely could avert his eyes. She had caught him glancing over at her a couple of times and smiled piquantly.

Suddenly, came the sound of an engine changing into lower gear, and he could tell it was the Rover. Going right by the cook-tent, then through a small copse of trees, he came out the other side to see Kanu stepping out of the vehicle, denoted as the lead-tracker by a yellow and red pennant attached to its radio aerial. One of the other Mzura trackers accompanied him, a spoke-thin man, wearing rope-soled shoes and a wash-blue loincloth. So thin you could count his ribs. A long-distance runner. One of those Mzura who ran ten miles, hardly working up a sweat.

Excitement loaded Kanu's face, who rambled through what he had seen, heard, then did; nearly out of words, he finished with, "He not far, To-mas. Five mile, mebbe six mile."

"You're sure it's him?"

"I know heem."

"Beautiful work. Perfect. C'mon with me."

Both boys followed Thomas back to where Baster and Jaggy were lounging. Instantly alert, Baster sat up. Puffed with pride, the orator of this hour, Kanu explained how they'd found another elephant herd—cows and calves traveling in a loose line to the west. Kanu had climbed a baobab tree and seen them, then spotted Tunda two miles or so east, moving in a parallel direction.

Thomas turned to Baster. "I'd like to have a look, are you game?"

"Now's the time. Let's not lose him."

"Jaggy?"

"You don't think you're going to leave me behind. Uh-uh, no thanks."

They stood talking, listening, asking—white and black men—and Kanu telling how they had found the big-padded foot marks, then finding steaming dung-balls big as melons, not more than four hours old. Five, at most. Smaller trees had been bowled over, leaves shorn, roots chewed for their moisture. When they had spotted Tunda, and slowly closing in, the elephant had moved to the other side of a ravine, losing himself in the heavy cover. Still, he must be in there somewhere. The trackers, Thomas knew, would not err.

"Thomas," said Kanu, "that one he eat seven, mebbe eight-hundred pounds."

"Probably." Thomas hung an arm across Kanu's back. "Nifty work, you really did something very special."

Teeth flashing, Kanu smiled bashfully.

"We'll split up. Kanu, you drive Missy and Baster-man in your Rover. I'll go with the truck, and bring up the grain and salt. We'll meet you there, close to the ravine."

"I'll get dressed," Baster said, looking down at his slippers, still wearing what he'd worn at breakfast, a silk robe with brocaded collar.

Kanu motioned to the other tracker, who stood there wordlessly, and off they went to bring up the truck with salt, and a ton of millet and maize—bait they would deploy to entice the animal closer to the South African border, then urge him to cross if they could manage an act of seduction.

Thomas left with the truck shortly. An hour later Baster and Jaggy followed, with Kanu driving them. They had gone a slow two miles over bumpy, slanted, hilly land. Baster, in a cheerful mood, rode up in front next to Kanu.

An up-and-down ride, until they reached one stretch of land, and Kanu, at Baster's suggestion, turned toward the middle of it. In moments, they'd entered a part of Naruma where Baster had hunted first with his father, sixty years before, on his tenth birthday.

"This is worth a detour," he said to Jaggy. "You remember this? Been years. The Mzura call it, Land of the First King. Isn't that so, Kanu?"

"Be so, sir-rr. Very much so."

Birdsong then, twittering, cawing, squawking, other noises not often heard of disturbed smaller animals..

As they slugged along in what was semi-swamp, they were met by smells as old as the world. Fetid at times, nature's rotted leavings; then a seepage of methane, then something like peat, or decayed moss, and in one area the scent of fresh flowers, meaty, as if they had just entered a flower shop where a hundred aromas soaked the air.

Chains of wild orchids fell from tree limbs, and a species of a huge violet grew profusely in the crotches of smaller trees. Near the center of the forest was another lake, sacred to the Mzura, running about three miles in length, still low and dry from the drought. Herons, and a bird like a flamingo but not a flamingo, pecked for food along the shoreline. A small island lay at the lake-center with huge old trees that were the only ones of their kind in the region. The Mzura knew them as gifts from secret spirits, and believed anyone venturing out to touch them would be killed by having their intestines gored out by the slow-eating *kdwala*—a mystical lizard, huge, six-legged.

Emerging on the far side of the swamp-forest, they came into the day's full light again; the sun bright as a new brass ball, sliding westward and signaling that in a few hours twilight would arrive.

Two miles farther on, Jaggy saw the other Rover and another scout-truck.

They hauled up a few yards away from where Thomas stood. Jaggy had never seen this stretch of the Territory. An eerie place, like an ancient cave turned inside out, bare, dry, hard, and with no visible life. The land itself was as yellow as old buried bones.

Thomas was saying something to the other trackers, who all had their competing expressions, smiling, solemn, attentive, aloof, feigning calm, but two of them tensed like gun dogs on point.

Thomas came over as Baster swung open the door. "He's over there on the other side of that deep ravine. I saw him near a ledge about ten minutes ago. He disappeared into the trees. Smelled us probably." He pointed. "That's like an island over there. Ravines seem to be all around it. With his color and the shadows, all that gray rock, he's perfectly camouflaged."

"How'd he ever get over there, I wonder?" asked Baster.

"Probably crossed over on that land bridge. There must be an escape trail over there. An elephant wouldn't choose a blind alley, not by choice anyway. With binoculars you might be able to get a good look." He handed the glasses to Baster.

Kanu, Jaggy and Thomas mingled together; a few yards away Baster stood with two of the trackers. Everyone kept looking across the ravine for the giant. But the elephant remained well back in the dense growth, feeding or resting.

Most of an hour went by and a restlessness set in. Would he show, or not? Jaggy kept looking through a range finder, then fiddling with the lens settings of her Nikon.

"I've another idea," offered Thomas. "I'll go across on the land-bridge. You all wait here, and if I see him, I'll signal you. Kanu, you go around the other way to the far side. Take the trackers. If he's in there, get upwind and let him get a good whiff of you, and maybe he'll come this way. See if there's an exit trail. Send one man out with the truck and have him start to lay out the salt and grain. Okay?"

Kanu nodded.

"I'm coming, too," Jaggy volunteered.

"No," said Thomas. Stay here with the Rover. Climb up on the hood. Keep an eye out for the elephant on this side. I've never seen this place. There could be other trails he could use for an escape. We need you right here. If you see him just shoot off a round. Skyward, if you don't mind." He grinned.

"But why do you get all the fun?"

"I've no idea what's over there. When I find out, I'll be back. Let's move," he instructed Kanu.

"Well, the hell, me too," Baster joined in. "I'm coming with you, Tommy. He's not liable to come running over that bridge toward us."

They went on ahead. Jaggy leaned against the Rover's fender, feeling left out, her face ablaze with frustration. Kanu sent two trackers off to the far side of the land-island, as agreed with Thomas, then took two others over to the truck filled with the feed and salt blocks.

An ancient land arch, nothing but air underneath it, crossed the serpentine ravine that had been gouged out by a river thousands of years before. Erosion had sliced the ravine sides to a depth of seventy feet or so, and the dried, cracked riverbed snaked along directly underneath them.

Thomas crossed first.

Once across the land-bridge, he stopped to listen for any sounds of movement. Unable to see much of anything through the dense high grasses, he waved at Baster that it seemed safe enough to cross.

For several minutes, Thomas moved—heel and toe as he'd been taught by Ghibwa—taking a few steps and then halting, listening.

Then a tell-tale sound. Branches thick as wrists were snapping as if they were mere twigs. Suddenly, the ground underneath Thomas seemed to tremble, then all breath locked inside him as he saw the massive gray front of the elephant crash through a tree-line only thirty-yards away. Ears flat, tusks raised, the thudding tons of elephant stamped the ground till it shook and shook. A trumpet-cry split the air.

"Jesus!" shouted Baster, from somewhere behind, the older man closer now than Thomas had thought.

Stone-faced and stone-footed, Thomas stood rooted to the earth itself. His senses reeling, the ground still quaking. Cut off now. With no time to look about, he yelled out to Baster but the yell was a mere gurgle from his fear-constricted throat. Suffering white-fright at the sight of the up-thrown trunk hammering at the air. Unable to think, to choose or decide, Thomas was unable to move.

"Tommy! To—"

Hearing Baster shout but still too petrified to turn. Suddenly, his legs responded and he dodged, spun one way and then pivoted the other way. No way out, he thought, desperate, befuddled.

Dashing a few yards, he stopped; crouching, confused. Tunda loomed like a ground-level thunder-cloud. Forcing himself to keep moving, Thomas skidded on a pile of flint-like shards, losing his balance, scrambling and slipping again as the elephant reared up once more on his rear legs. Tunda had stalked him into a vee-shaped, head-high rock formation, bottling him up there.

I'm to die here, he thought, cold with fear.

Again, Tunda swung his trunk, bellowing; alarm deluged Thomas as he saw the opened mouth, a gaping black and red hole. Mindlessly, he bolted straight for the front legs, hoping to confound Tunda, somehow dodge around the massive shaking body and make a dash for safety.

But before he could, the moving gray mass lunged at him, its great white prongs lowering, the trunk twisting high before lashing downward—swiping him solidly under the heart. His vision turned to a pool of twisting red pinwheels as the tusk-prongs shoveled under him, pitching him skyward and over the side of a ledge.

Like a just-shot duck, he tumbled into a dazed roll that stopped with a bone-splitting numbness as he slammed and slammed against the side of the ravine, cartwheeling helplessly through the rock-strewn thick scrub.

And he lay inert, unseeable in heavily tangled growth.

Johannesburg, South Africa

Gauzy images, garbled noises. With what seemed like a last possible effort in this life, the separate images fused into one, but were still a blur.

"Thomas, can you hear me?"

Blinking, trying to focus, he could hear but would he ever see again? He felt as if he were under water, everything milky, swirling.

Then, with miraculous relief, he did see. "H'lo," he said weakly.

"Hello yourself," Jaggy answered.

Lifting his hands to rub his eyes, a sharp pain tore through his chest. The smells, the whiteness of everything, his physical immobility, an imprisoning cage on his leg, hoses snaking ominously from an upside-down bottle—all told of his whereabouts. Dressed in a thigh-length gown completely open at its front, with a catheter inserted in his penis. He hadn't the energy to cover himself, and Jaggy made no effort to assuage his modesty.

Seeing her more vividly now. Her eyes puffed, reddish, bluish half-circles underneath, all telling of a worn, exhausted woman. Seeing a familiar face offered small comfort, as pain racked him everywhere.

"Am I—how bad am I?"

"Badly concussed. A few other things as well. You've been in and out of the known world for two days, and one very long night."

"Where are we?"

"Jo-burg. At the Park Lane Clinic."

"Oh? Was I"—his mind halted, a warning—"awake at all?"

"For a while, yesterday. You don't remember?"

Recalling something he didn't want to recall. Swallowing, and it felt as if a ball had stuck in his throat, his mouth cottony and dry. "Where's Baster?"

No reply, so he asked again. Pillows elevated his right leg, and the knee was wrapped as if ready for shipment. The edge of his vision caught a thickness of gauze along his left cheekbone.

"I won't ask you how you feel, but you look much like a blood clot," Jaggy quipped.

"Help me up."

"You're not getting up. You're damn lucky to be lying down."

"What's going on?" he asked Jaggy again. "Where's Baster?"

"He was killed. He was trying to rescue you, I suspect." The words said calmly, also frigidly.

His innards drained, spilling in every direction, out of his balls, out of his head, out the bottom of his feet. Shutting his eyes, he stared into oblivion, hearing a great crashing of brush, the trees shaking, the ground quaking, the massive elephant lifting in rage.

"You really don't remember, do you?"

"Now I do—the elephant wasn't it? That elephant. Baster dead? And Kanu, where's Kanu?"

"Kanu is at N'jorro, or he was...I'm terribly, terribly sorry to tell you like this, Thomas." Thinking he was about to weep, she added, "Don't say anything."

"I can't."

"Lie still or you'll hurt yourself."

"Talk to me. Tell me everything." A dry cough, then, and his rib cage felt as if struck by a bullet. "Is there something to drink?" He shut his eyes against the pain in his chest, not realizing it was a blessing that it was releasing him from the greater pain in his heart.

She hadn't seen any of it, she said, from where she'd been standing across the ravine. She had heard Thomas yell, the elephant roar and a great deal of crashing about. Then she repeated what Kanu and the other boys had told her; and what a chief investigator of South Africa's national police, who, accompanied by four other policemen from Pretoria, had relayed the day after statements were taken from Kanu and the trackers. The police had gone straight into Naruma, without permission, violating its territorial sovereignty. Working through the night to sift the facts, the police had learned that Kanu and two of the Mzura trackers had lugged Thomas out of a deep chasm. Within hours, he had been flown down to Johannesburg on a MedEvac aircraft and brought here to the Park Lane.

Jaggy, later, had identified the remains of her father. He'd been trampled into a mush of bones and bloody flesh-pulp. She recognized him from the shredded clothes he'd been wearing and a gold belt buckle embedded with a bean-sized ruby.

"Almighty God," Thomas said. "I'm so very sorry."

"Quite hard. Exceedingly hard."

"Jaggy, I—"

"Some other time. You're not yourself at the moment," said Jaggy, plumping his pillow, smoothing his white-blond hair with her fingers.

"We should never have gone that close to...never have tried it," Thomas said aimlessly. "I made a terrible mistake. Terrible. When will they...the services for Baster?"

"You'll not be going to the services or anywhere else. Not for a while. That's final." She fussed over him a little more, promised to come back, soon, but said to him she really must run off now. And in parting, she advised, "They're screening incoming calls for you. I instructed them to make a log. The newspapers are thick as dung-flies on this, and they'll not let up. I'm blockading them."

"Are the police in this? You said—"

She shook her head. "They say they have all they need. At any rate, I'll be handling them."

His head ached. It felt as if a wall had fallen on it. "Aren't you going to cry, Jaggy? You can in front of me, you know..."

She stood at the foot of the bed, silently. Her head lifted as she said, "I'll be crying for the rest of my life. Just one other thing. Pierre St. Germain flew in last night. He'd like to say hello to you, when you're feeling up to it."

"Who is he?"

It all came clear as she connected St. Germain to Braunsweig und Sohn of Geneva. St. Germain, she reminded, was one of the trustees of The Muldaur Trust. "No, not now," he begged off. "My apologies. But I can't even think about any of that now."

"You're not to worry about anything at all. I'll pop in whenever I can, and they have orders at the nurses' desk to keep me informed. You'll be having the best care. Be up in no time, let's hope."

Today, she was a nightingale. He was as helpless as he'd ever been in life, and he knew he had plenty to answer for. Orders. Never requests, not from Jaggy Muldaur. Only orders, whenever she was in charge of the moment. But he knew how lucky he was, having her at his side.

"Thanks," he said. Closing his eyes, hoping she'd leave. When finally he opened them, he had nothing more to say.

Neither did she. She was still standing near the door, her face in havoc, eyes still misted. He wanted to say something priestly, something that might offer a touch of solace. Even if able to think straight, he had nothing to say that could conceivably make a difference to her, or even to himself. The world and its present meanings had sunk out of view and he had not the slightest notion of how to remake her part of it, or even his own.

And why, he wondered, was this St. Germain so eager to talk with him? That Trust of course, but who cared now?

He's dead, I'm alive. The entire story in four words. And no Muldaur-Courmaine lab, he supposed, a fresh thought that speared him to his depths.

At the Muldaur estate, Jaggy sat with her guest Pierre St. Germain, who had been heaping commiseration upon her. Never had she seen him so stiff, so tight-strung, and their conversation seemed to stutter, whenever the topics turned away from Baster.

As now.

An affable man, often appearing to be smiling, when he wasn't, due to the natural formation of his lips. Fast-brained, fast to see through artifices, and faster yet to see the possibilities of a promising situation. He was fifty-six, somewhat portly, with reddish hair, and a strong Gallic nose. Widely regarded as one of Europe's front-line bankers, he was a senior partner of Braunsweig und Sohn, one of Switzerland's more famous private banking houses. He sat on the board of Muldaur Ltd., was one of three trustees of The Muldaur Trust, and had enjoyed the closest confidences with Baster. For the best part of three centuries, Braunsweig had banked the Muldaur interests, knowing most everything of the family's financial affairs. Over centuries past, Braunsweig had arranged credits exceeding a trillion-dollars in support of various Muldaur operations. The bank's files, if ever laid end-to-end, would reveal an avalanche of loan transactions evidenced by most every financing instrument in the arsenal of the banking industry: letters of credit issued against bills of lading, discounted bills of exchange, term loans, revolving credits, overnight repos, in short the whole gamut to keep liquid the family's far-flung mining, real estate and trading activities.

The relationship—brick-tight—had always been as unshakeable as the Alps.

St. Germain had known Jaggy for twenty-five years, from the time her widowed mother had wed Baster. He understood her, the highs and lows, the good and the not so good. At the moment, he was dueling as gracefully as he could with her, who, today and on many days, could be mule-stubborn when digging in her heels. Having heard *no* twice now, her mood had moved to her face: petulant, even sniffy, sometimes war-like. Her jaw now as hard-looking as the casing on a steam boiler.

Pitching once again, verging on argument, she was covering what by now was old ground. "It was all an exceedingly grievous mistake, Pierre," she was insisting once again. "Baster had a weak moment about Thomas Courmaine and we must mend it. You must do it. I'm counting on you, Pierre. Thomas Courmaine is a lordly chap, but he'd be a charade as a trustee."

"As I've been trying to tell you, my dear Jaggy, it is too late for anything like that. Voted on already and unanimously approved. I had the agreement-of-appointment notarized several days ago. That's exactly the way Baster wanted it, and that is the way it must stand. No one can undo it."

"But how could you ever have known what to do? Tom Courmaine never agreed to anything as far as I know. He'd have to agree, wouldn't he, to make it binding?"

"Quite so. Have you any proof he didn't agree?"

"Of course, I don't. Stop that!"

"There you are, then. Besides, you know Baster. He's always been a step ahead of us mortals. He sent us the instructions soon after Hanta-hong Zheng passed away. That was several weeks ago. Six, I think."

"Just reverse it. You must…*just must*, goddammit all."

Hands rising in resignation, Pierre St, Germain quietly replied, "I cannot oblige you, Jaggy," to which she swiftly retorted, "He knows nothing. Nothing at all about investments."

"At Braunsweig we think we know a great deal about investing The Trust's assets. We don't need his skills for any of that. He must be quite a chap. Baster said as much, even more…"

"Pierre, do it. Please, please do it! Don't you think we've done enough for Africa? Baster left over a billion rands just for black scholarships. We gave them the Muldaur-DuPont Works, then N'jorro is gone or soon will be. We've given endlessly to Witwatersrand and African Heritage and Christ knows what else. It's been endless. A list long as both your arms, Pierre."

"Commendable. It changes nothing, however. Unless Mr. Courmaine resigns, he stands as third trustee. I've papers with me I had hoped to have him sign. I suppose they'll have to wait."

"How much is The Trust valued at?"

"That is confidential."

"Baster said it was billions."

"It's confidential, Jaggy."

"This is me, Pierre. I'm family."

"But that's one of the problems, don't you see? You're family all right but not of the *blood of the family*. Quite a distinction there, legally speaking. You're not entitled to any information, whatsoever. That, Jaggy, is the controlling law of the matter. You are not an heir, and you must accept that well-defined fact."

"Why make this so complicated? I'm in charge of the House of Muldaur now and I'm entitled to know anything that affects our businesses."

"The Trust has nothing to do with your business interests at Muldaur Limited. It's wholly separate as I'm certain you've been informed."

Stiffening, she cut in, "We shall see, wont we? Ah, yes..." And looking directly at St. Germain's perplexed face, she calmly offered, "Care for a champagne? Roederer Cristal, it's nicely chilled. I'll fetch it myself. Four maids and that fucking day-butler are calling it quits. I suspect they're not all that fond of me."

"Thanks all the same, but I've calls to make." He arose as she was saying, "You can use one of the lines in Baster's library."

"Thanks, but I brought along a satellite-phone. Gimmicky thing but I can reach anyone in the world without being overheard. Handy at times, you know. Handy for us bankers."

Unsmiling, he left her. Unsmiling, she fumed.

St. Germain thought of himself as a good-hearted, understanding and helpful ally and friend to all he cared to befriend. Many times he had been complimented by others on his warmness and his helpful ways; even, in some cases, where he was not all that well-acquainted with the recipient of his generosity. It was, in a real sense, his personal style and hallmark; not a man, once met, easily forgotten. Yet he was Swiss in his every corpuscle and of the view that good sense and respect for the wishes of her stepfather would be sufficient to let matters stand exactly as Baster Muldaur desired that they stand. Jaggy, always a handful, cunning as a fox, and with a wolf-like behavior when failing to get her way.

Much as he had lavished his affections upon her, Baster had always pegged her for what she was: a fighter who believed in the back-alley rules of engagement, using that doubtful sobriquet to intimidate her foes.

Wealth-wise, what more could anyone want? Expect? Well-larded financially, even without the remaining stock in Muldaur Ltd. Baster had left her, she lacked for nothing; nor had she ever, not in his memory.

Aside from all else, she kept a stock of gold bullion—in Braunsweig's vaults—valued at some fifty-eight million Euros. She'd inherited five homes to go with two duplex apartments; together, the various residences housed a trove of extremely valuable art, spread across three continents for the sake of safety.

Contention, if not confrontation, was afoot. Pierre felt cold and felt very leery, wondering how Thomas Courmaine would fare against Jaggy's wiles and her subtle and not so subtle pressures. If able to find a chink, she'd pump him till he was drier than a Sahara dune. The man must be cautioned to tell her nothing of The Trust, nary a syllable. Still, Courmaine likely was a good bet at keeping a secret a secret. Baster had imparted that the man was Jesuit-trained; therefore, as one bound by the Seal of Confession he would know the value of keeping his mouth zipped.

All to the good, for Courmaine was about to become privy to the confession of his life; revelations knitted, one to the other, by sin, by treachery, by deceit, by copious acts of plunder—centuries of smaller and greater crimes. A few, when the main chance was to be had, that were on the order of the colossal.

Which, of course, was how all massive fortunes were aggregated, always so, and done so from time out of mind. The Trust, allegedly Europe's largest, was of the same ilk, its history a regular mind-stopper.

Sitting at a desk in the spacious bedroom, he spun the combination lock on a black leather case, then extracted a red phone. Flipping two battery-powered switches, he punched in the numbers for his private line at Braunsweig und Sohn in Geneva.

"Oh, Marissa, hello. Take a letter, please…then sign it for me and put my seal on it…address it to a Mr. Thomas I. Courmaine…yes. yes, that's correct…send it in care of the Park Lane Clinic and…."

Voices of the night; voices all day. Voices belonging to those who controlled all details of his life. Checking and re-checking him at all hours to see if he, their prisoner, was behaving; on his side of it, he was miserable from their attentions. Intravenous bottles, tubes, pills, the urinal, with its funny neck, emptied and replaced, the nurses' hands all over him as if they were natural appendages to his body. He was all but trussed to the bed, nearly immobile, with his back feeling as though a sledgehammer had struck it, a deep thudding pain ensuing. The knee, too, throbbing incessantly. He was wary of pain medication. Choosing to ache instead of coping with a fuzzy head, for he needed his wits.

The future stared at him, an unblinking, unremitting stare. It was a look that begged for answers about the future. He had no answers. What he had was a few thousand in savings, some clothes, and the brain he was born with. All else was lost somewhere inside the vapors of his dreams and hopes, largely dashed at present.

One morning, to his surprise, he awoke to a stalwart erection, sorely tempted to ring for a nurse just to witness her reaction. For the first time in his recent memory, he felt powerless to do or act for himself—being the next thing, he thought, to an infant without an infant's penchant for squalling when things went awry.

The Naruma Territory, Africa

Bajjia didn't look like much of anything nor was it much of anything other than an out-of-way crossroads for trouble in wholesale quantities. It stood as the black swollen heart of Naruma, a heart beating for no one. A century earlier, Bajjia, located on an estuary off the Indian Ocean, gave up on its future. It stopped trying to become a port-city. Ever after, it seemed content with its busted boardwalks, weather-rusted tin roofs, streets covered with a slurry of red dust, dog droppings every twenty-feet and the sour smells of sunbaked urine. Mercenaries slept the day through after a night of drinking, whoring and gambling. Within this god-forgotten outpost were a few ramshackle boarding houses, stores that rarely opened, an overgrown market square that doubled as a bazaar on Sundays, two restaurants with Arabic signs, and one abandoned Chinese eatery that had long since shuttered—this, then, was its main street, its only street, and it was a street without a name. In its center, one could find Darby Dawlin's bar and bordello, as close as anything to being the town hall, the hell-pit for criminal deals of every sort and scale, especially illicit ivory transactions, bribe giving and taking, for incoming and outgoing mail (at a price), all the women a man could stand, around the clock bar and card or faro gambling added in for good measure. Cubans hung out in droves, awaiting their next soldiering contracts to go killing in Africa's incessant pocket wars. Bajjia, always short on paint, was shorter yet on anything resembling law. None whatsoever existed, other than the law of the roughest men in town on any given day.

Into this iniquity came reporters from the international wire services and other media outlets large enough to maintain bureaus in nearby South Africa. Photo coverage of the death-site was wanted, along with any and all accounts from the Mzura trackers who had first spotted the killer-elephant and had witnessed subsequent events.

The list of news topics and related opportunities for inquiry was lengthy. Who, for example, had taken part in the trekking party? Why that specific elephant? Jaggy Muldaur was present, was she? How did this injured man, Courmaine, fit in? How many Mzura tribesmen accompanied the safari? What was the tribe's history? No hotel? No plug-in outlets for laptops. Who ran the town? Who, indeed, knew anything and where were they to be found? The prevailing attitude circulating among the gaggle of journalists was: who the fuck ever dreamed up this rat's nest?

The reporters quickly learned the "go-to" man was an ex-pat Brit named Darby Dawlin, who trafficked in anything and everything, but best known as a broker of illicit rhino horn and elephant tusks for the Asian market. With his impressive pedigree of racketeering, he knew every angle to be calculated, worked and reworked, in this southern tributary off the Indian Ocean. He had, at one time, been sentenced to three years in a U.K. clink for larceny, having filched the jewels of a highborn in Copenhagen, while visiting Bournemouth with her man-servant. Who was none other than Dawlin himself.

He had beat the rap by escaping beyond reach of almost anyone here to the sump. He loved it in Bajjia. No police to pay off. He reigned as a minor white prince. He had no announced enemies. It was, all in all, an illusory paradise: plenty of loose money, an ample flow of women, passable liquor, and utter freedom.

Havoc soon reigned for the incoming reporters. Prices spiraled for beer, or even or a simple sandwich of stale bread. Using a bathroom in privacy was priced at fifty South African rands. Otherwise, male or female, you went out to the alley, side by side, men and women alike.

Red-rimmed anger soon emerged. These were experienced men and women, who had had seen it all in most every corner of earth—twice, three times, even more; but Bajjia, they soon learned, fell into a slot of its own. No other Christian word existed for it, except *appalling*.

Vigorous protests against all-out extortion for every day necessities went unheeded. Dawlin merely shrugged off the yellers, replying with his crooked-mouthed, tobacco-stained smile: "Fuck off, mate," his standard reply to the incessant gripes. He had them by the shorts; they knew it, and he knew they knew it.

To one mark, Simon Ballester of the *London Times*, he let it be known that the many rumors running amuck were sometimes true. Over a hefty pour of White Label—at the equivalent of twenty-dollars a shot—Dawlin boasted to Ballester of two inside, ear-filling stories. He could get these intruders on the trail of at least one of them for, say, a sum of ten-thousand dollars. Numbed by the sum, Ballester, normally a smooth talker and calm as you please, turned red with outrage.

"Steady on, mate," Dawlin suggested. "This ain't a free country, like some places. You want, you pay."

Ballester's temperature dropped a degree or two, when hearing that the Mzura called Courmaine, an otherwise fine chap, as *Eanu*. Tribal argot for faggot. "And bye-the- bye, Thomas Courmaine had somehow pulled off the Second Coming or near to it, mate. Vouched for many times, you see. Three Mzura women in the village, that's thirty-odd miles west by north, they'd actually been rejuvenated, see. Not seen them myself, but I believe it. I knowed who had seen them, and more than once. All shit's been goin' on, you see, for the others in the tribe, the crones, they wants their lift-up, too."

"This Courmaine is gay, you said that?"

"Not by the looks of 'im, but they say he had his innings with the big man."

"What big man?"

"Why, it's old man Muldaur, of course. Why you're here in Naruma, ain't it so?"

"You're certain of this?"

"Matey, I wasn't there, see. Make a good story, I'd wager. Sell you some papers, heh? Get your money up and go see for yourself. I'll guarantee a return of it, if it ain't so, and all to your satisfaction. Want another drop? It's on me, this one is." Dawlin reached for the bottle.

"Ten-thousand, well, you're looney."

"Am I now? Am I, indeedy? What'd you come here for, a cuppa tea?"

"It's by far too much."

"Half goes to the Mzura chief, you see, then there's the transportation to be arranged, other favors. Protection, too. You can get yourself good and reamed if you ain't prepared like. You come all the way here, Mr. Simon B, and you'll leave empty as your old granny's cunny."

Ballester shot a reproachful look at Dawlin, then made a quick turn and beckoned several of his cohorts to follow him outside. Dawlin knew his man. An hour later Ballester returned, handing to the bordello-minder several wads of currency: pounds sterling, rands, Euros, U.S. dollars and yen. Added to this small treasury were a gold bracelet and two Rolex Oyster Perpetuals. A neat haul. Dawlin had no intention of sharing his loot with Swiali, yet he still had the back end of his hustle to arrange. Next day he canceled the bar bills of three Cubans, who, in exchange, painted a serviceable but aging Renault van so many colors it looked like an aggrieved Jackson Pollock done by the blind. He knew the Mzura chieftain would worship the chariot, as if a gift of the last Caesar, and likely would wreck it, if able to force his vast bulk into the front seat.

In a small bema-like setting, the full complement of eighteen onlookers sat, as bidden, on tamped-down ground. Their eyes were riveted to a spectacle that seemed like an outtake from a film of another era.

Dressed in soft buff-colored impala hides, with a fan of flamingo feathers around his neck, his suet-ringed arms were encircled with thick gold bangles and ivory bracelets that clattered against each other with his every ponderous move. Swiali glared fiercely at the assembled, fascinated faces. Milking the moment to its fullest, he waited theatrically for a hush to settle upon his audience, not one of whom had permission to be in Naruma and any of whom he could've ordered killed had whim so moved him.

Confusion reigned at first. In a voice soaked with disgust, Swiali broke the news about the three women of his tribe, implying that while he had been the one who warned Cour-min to leave the women be, he had nonetheless been disobeyed. The women had resisted, had begged to be let alone, but with stealth and cunningness, *Eanu* had poisoned his victims and they were now outcasts, to be forever separated from the tribe.

The massive jiggling face had spoken, revealing what his sinister view this foreigner, Cour-min, the friend to Muldaur-of-N'jorro; "...this *Eanu* who live among Mzura...turn old wimmins into young wimmins. *Eanu* a sick-a man. Keep no wimmins, and is no man himself but a blue spirit...he like mens more than wimmins. Carry sickness-a in hees-a pockets. That be *Eanu*. That be Cour-min. You must find 'em. He tell you. Make you sick-a."

Then Swiali pointed to his crotch. Cour-min and that Baster-man do this thing, one man to other man. They sick-a. Now you go...you find Cour-min. He kill 'dat Mul-door. I Swiali, I be king and king know truth, for to say to you...I bring you wimmins..."

On they came, buck-naked, filing in their small procession into the midst of the gape-jawed onlookers. The women stood shoulder to shoulder, displaying themselves, pleased and with sheepish smiles on their soon to be celebrated faces. Oiled with pig fat renderings, the Eves gleamed like black crystal, newly buffed. Swiali had them parade back and forth as if they were star attractions in a local peep show. Thrilled by all the fuss and attention, the three women beamed, postured, posed as if they were models on a photo shoot for a girlie magazine.

Reporters jotted furiously as two shoulder-mounted TV cameras whirred almost soundlessly.

Swiali, at his most cunning, attempted to dispel any lingering doubts about the women. At a clap of his hands, three other women suddenly appeared. They were of the same general age, looking it too. Prune-ish skins. Sags. Doubts could've been raised that it was all some sort of theatrical bush-stunt, but the doubts, if any existed, never were uttered. The scene was accepted for what it was: strange, a little too mysterious, the showmanship a little too circus-like.

Still, the onlookers saw, and they believed.

After a flurry of questions the situation began to emerge, a bit fuzzily to start with, but its essence largely intact; this two-act staging wasn't a ruse—the transformed trio had, in actual years, reached their mid-to-late seventies. But then what was it that accounted for their amazingly young, taut skins. They weren't young. By no means. Yet when compared to the other three women, they seemed as if they had erased thirty or more years in age.

Ageless wonders now, and how could that be?

Clearly, something was up. More clearly, a story was to be had—a gift after the dismal sojourn in this hell-pit, which had set the visitors' collective teeth on edge.

The story of the Eves was now about to be outed. No means of quick communication with their various news bureaus existed in this forgotten land known as Naruma. Yet within forty-eight hours, or as soon as they could return to Jo-burg, the accounts would be filed, written up, and thereafter blasted to the far regions of the earth. Re-write desks would compare and distill various renditions, telling of this odd, out-of-the-way place where Baster Muldaur spent part of his youth and all of his final hours. At the very least, these scenes of color could be added to the final days of the Midas of Africa.

And what of the other titillating buzz—had Muldaur and this Cour-min been lovers? Indeed, who was this Cour-min? And how could that scandalous tidbit of unconfirmed gossip be verified?

Johannesburg, South Africa

N ear one-o'clock on a cool autumnal afternoon, amidst half-lowered flags snapping in the afternoon breeze, marching bands supplied by three branches of the armed services, a formation of white cavalry horses, six-hundred hand-picked uniformed school children—a cortege of seventeen black limousines and a flower-bedecked hearse—all began their funereal voyage beginning at the steps of the Supreme Court on Pritchard Street, onward through Simmonds Street, through Braamfontein, ending its solemn journey at the foot of Pieter Roos Park.

An Elder of the Dutch Reformed Church gave the first of the eulogies, followed by the High Chief Justice, the President of the Republic, and then, as the last, Jaggy herself. She summoned herself, performing in queenly mode, her voice carrying across the assembled crowd paying a last tribute to a man like few others before him. Or afterward.

She spoke in Afrikaner, then in English; eloquently so.

A pivotal opportunity for a bereaved daughter—which she was—ensuring that all there, as well as the T-V spectators, knew the bright flaming torch of Muldaur was now hers to carry.

While the London Press often tagged her as the Stiletto: here, in her home country, she assumed almost a royal standing. No other South African family ranked close to the Muldaur name when *noblesse oblige* and generosity were mentioned in the same breath.

Possessing a keen sense of the power of public perception, of how others would see her now as titular head of the fading Muldaur family, she held herself as if posing for a monument. Still, her mood was inward, and she omitted thanking the government for declaring a national day of mourning, closing the schools, the banks and businesses. The omission, flagrantly rude, did not go unnoticed.

Thomas watched the proceeding on an elevated T-V from his bed. A commentator droned, heralding the life of a man who had actually fulfilled his own legend. Variously he was described as the richest man in Africa, or allegedly so; his years of open-handed but often secretive munificence had brought him highest esteem. Then, "Africa is the poorer at the loss of its illustrious and generous son," adding, "some said he was so far-seeing and prescient it was as if he observed the world from a space-satellite. In all events, a world-class influencer, and, reputedly, long a member of the secretive Shang Magan, a tight fraternity of top traders and business icons, controlling a huge fraction of East-West commodity flows."

Nation after nation, mostly Europe and Asia, had sent messages of sympathy, speaking to the memory of the man. In Jo-burg, T-V stations used the assorted tributes as fillers while the cortege rode its way to the cemetery, where Baster was to be interred with his deceased wife in a mausoleum faced with massive bronzed doors cast in Damascus.

Thomas was about to click the off-button when the commentator announced a three-minute break for commercials, then faded away with this remark: "When we return, we'll tell you news of a startling development in Naruma involving three women and a person named Thomas Courmaine, an American geneticist, who, we're told, is employed by African Heritage, a Muldaur charitable project. It is said that this Courmaine, also believed to be a close friend of the Muldaurs, somehow succeeded in wiping away decades, yes, decades, from the appearance of three Mzura women...we shall return shortly, ladies and gentlemen..."

Minutes later, agog, Thomas saw the Eves, naked from the waist up, broad smiles, prancing about and obviously enjoying themselves. In the background of the clip, he could see white people; reporters, he guessed. How had they found the Eves? The video-clip played on, accompanied by a voice-over with a British accent, and then he saw Swiali with his ponderous arms raised; festooned in full regalia—ostrich feathers, beads, gold arm bracelets, lion skins—as if expecting to greet the Mzura Green Spirit descending from a nearby star.

Watching it all, thinking that even if he performed handstands at SOS he'd never begin to approach this blown-up publicity, with his name mentioned several times. He, the alleged perpetrator of the *miraculous change* (the media's phrase) who had transformed three aged women.

Next day he asked the nurse on duty, who eyed him with a more considered look, to fetch copies of as many different newspapers as she could find. Hours later, poring over that day's editions, he saw his past being dug up.

Johannesburg's *The Daily Mail & Guardian* ran an article appearing below the fold that showed a photo of himself seated in the T-V studio at Cambridge four years earlier. Remarkable! How had they laid hands on it? He was written up as a Jesuit, an American biologist listed in *Who's Who in Science*, a new member of the National Academy of Sciences (U.S.), a member of the Royal Academy of Science (U.K.), and a senior field-biologist for African Heritage.

It was the Eves, of course, who earned the most space, and he was glad of it. Now that they were a known quantity, it was less likely Swiali would butcher them.

Reading on, he noted that the article cut back to him, and was at a loss to figure out how the media could excavate his history so swiftly. Embedded in the article was this:

Courmaine attracted attention before when igniting the fury of the Vatican for espousing beliefs that contradicted deep-seated dogma of the Roman Catholic Church and other faiths as well.

A Pretoria resident, formerly a student of Thomas Courmaine's at Cambridge where the biologist-priest had once taught as a Visiting Lecturer, provided access to tapes she had recorded at a series of his classes. They depict, among other views, the gospel as revised, according to Courmaine.

Quoting directly from those tapes, "New species require a big effort to establish themselves, and millions of species certainly preceded humans on earth. We can easily prove we were well down the line on Nature's list of favorites. We humans think we're the final word, that we're pretty snazzy but evolution tells us an altogether different story. Humans are decidedly an afterthought in evolution's long run; and possibly we're really nothing else but a random mutation that somehow has succeeded in surviving. Consider this: biologically speaking, when WoMan first appeared, as descended from our cousins, the apes, we could only, as a species, propagate by means of incest. Copulation, in order to kick-start the human species, had to take place among several so-called Eves with their sons and nephews. In turn, those sons and nephews, the sires of the herd, impregnated their sisters and cousins.

"If not," Courmaine argues, "the human race would have stopped dead in its tracks before it had any real chance to flower.

"Woman, we may be sure, arrived before man. It is an irrefutable fact that the male of our species is incapable of giving birth to an infant. Thus, there was no Adam, at least none who began us. The Eves, whoever they were, came first, no matter what they teach us in Bible class about transferring ribs and other hocus-pocus. That's wrong teaching, because it is an impossible way for beginning our species.

It all begins with the female and that ought to be plain as sunshine to anyone."

The article ran more grainy photos of the Eves, and he was childishly tempted to send a copy of it to Maistinger. But wouldn't and didn't, for he was certain enough the Jo-burg archdiocese would see to it and send it on to Rome.

In the week to follow:

He received a get-well letter from Augustin deMehlo, which also confirmed the news of the Mzura women, and all else, had reached the Vatican. Cards came from four of his old friends at Borgo S. in Rome.

When informed by the administrator's office that Rhoades McBride, his editor and friend at *NATURE*, Britain's top scientific journal, had tried to reach him several times, Thomas called McBride back. They conversed for almost half an hour, with Thomas much relieved to hear the voice of an old friend.

Two calls from Jaggy, her worries high, her spirits sagging, yet sounding pleased he was on the mend. She was leaving for London, she told him, and he must feel free to contact her at any time.

Resisting more appeals for interviews by the media, he walled them off once more. They didn't give up; he wouldn't give in. The clinic's chief administrator relayed on the phone to Thomas that Jo-burg's metro-police would like a word; they were held off pending a medical clearance that he was fit for an interview. Jaggy had already told him the police had no interest in a statement from him after Baster's death; so, he surmised this latest query concerned the Eves. Too bad. The Eves were well out of South Africa's jurisdiction.

Besides, what was there to say that hadn't been said already? The more said, the more there was to parse and to explain. And, then, likely to regret.

On a morning when his breakfast tray was delivered, he found a sealed envelope tucked inside the napkin. Opening it, he read: *"Allegations are made that you and Baster Muldaur were lovers. Care to comment?"*

Staggered by the insinuation, thinking it a ploy to get him talking, he debated if he should refer it to Jaggy. Instead, he tore up the note. Probably an enterprising reporter who had bribed someone on the kitchen staff, Thomas hazarded.

He intended, as before, to lie low. Yet where to go next? What to do with his life, when he got there? The kindnesses of a Baster Muldaur who would have bankrolled a lab or an Augustin deMehlo who had run interference when life got gnarly—they stood as relics of the past. His strongest struts had been replaced by a single, lonely, almost bereft person: himself. And while he knew what to do with himself, he wasn't at all sure how.

Or, as importantly, where?

He needed a lab, that much was not in question. He knew, or thought he knew, the promise of Zyme-One, and making it his life's work was highly appealing. He also must sustain himself, and, at that moment, lying on his bed, with mountains of time on his hands, he made a life-altering decision: he would accept the offer to join the other overseers of The Muldaur Trust.

What choice was there? He needed the fees.

Lost in this chain of accidents, random acts of fate, or simply the course of zigzagging events was a blatant subterfuge. Jaggy had pulled off a switch that would've blazed fresh headlines had anyone found out and squealed.

Two days before the funeral, she had arranged to collect Baster's remains from a government medical facility, then had them taken to the estate. Hours prior to the memorial services, what purported to be the remains were delivered to the mortuary in a sealed ceramic canister, and transferred under her watchful eyes to a mahogany casket inlaid with rare woods from three continents. The casket was then securely locked, with Jaggy retaining its only key.

No standard procedure, to be sure; yet, the maneuver was done so smoothly that no suspicions were aroused.

After a suitable interval of a few days, she ordered up a flight on a Muldaur jet to Zurich, where the canister with Baster's real remains was handed over to a senior representative of Cyro. Thereafter, Baster Muldaur's mushed flesh and bones were lodged in a nitrogen-cooled tank at Cyro's mountain redoubt in Winterthur, where previously deposited samples of his sperm had been stored for several years.

Nothing illegal about it, not so far anyway. Still, the spurious act had fooled everyone; even the citizens of South Africa who assumed, and rightly so, that their "good father" was buried at the iron-fenced, marble-infested, two-acre plot where twenty generations of the family slept for eternity.

Jaggy, however, had her own plans. She was trawling through her general thoughts on the matter while journeying up to London on the same B-737 that had previously made the flight to Zurich with the canister. Plans dovetailed into other plans; soon enough, the one moving to the top rung was The Trust;

and, now that she was ranked a non-starter, relegated to the sidelines, she was wondering how best to use Thomas Courmaine as her long-reaching paw.

A viable possibility badgered her thoughts. Marriage. She'd already tracked through three husbands, and number four might be the final and luckiest draw. Still, he'd need god-knows how much breaking in, but no matter—for they all needed reworking once you had them leashed.

Boston, Massachusetts
Bethesda, Maryland

The phone call was the fourth within two weeks between Murray Raab and Miles Bascomb, the retired medical doctor to whom Raab reported on matters affecting the interests of The League. Today's exchange dealt with the recent splurge of coverage about the three Naruma women, and the activities of Milton Drossberg in securing votes at SOS so Thomas Courmaine could offer his Proof of Concept at the next SOS quarterly meeting in Cambridge, England.

"…Whaddya make of those pictures of the women?" Bascomb was asking, early on.

"I can't really say. They're on the grainy side. The T-V clips are interesting. Unless it's some kind of ruse, I'd suppose Tom Courmaine has succeeded in some way just as he indicated at SOS. I had no idea that three women were involved in this incident, though Milt Drossberg, when he was here, said something or other about human experiments. The media that were there, they seem to be vouching for it. We'd need a helluva lot more than that, I know, but it gets more intriguing, doesn't it?"

"Ah'd say so. We're wantin' to know of all developments, Murray. Can you send over some investigatuhs? Check things out?"

"I needed three different maps just to see where Naruma is. No airport there, apparently, but there is a small seaport I'm told. How you get people there, I don't know. The State Department says it doesn't maintain a mission there. I don't think we can ask any NIH researchers to take that on."

"Better we do somethin' and soon."

"What do you suggest?"

"I just did my suggestin'."

"I see. I'll look into it."

"You do that. What's Drossberg have to say for himself? You still sqeezin' that sonofabitch, ah trust?"

"He says he's contacted about thirty members. He's unhappy about it. Thinks it's undignified."

"Tough titty…all right now, we'll be talkin'again soon. Get some people ovah there. Don't let that good brain of yuh's go to sleep, hear?"

In the next several days of digging and asking, all that Murray Raab could find out through the U.S. embassy in South Africa was that Courmaine himself was apparently recovering in a hospital, was unreachable, and that Naruma itself was not to be thought of as a tourist destination. There were no flights. The drive from Johannesburg required at least two days, and, once there, hostilities could be expected. Even when South Africa sent any sort of delegation to Naruma, it was always accompanied by a detail of armed soldiers.

Murray conveyed the information to Bascomb, who, after grunting, said, "Let's get this Courmaine tracked down, see what it is we can do with him. Find out everything yuh can, Murray Raab. Push hard on your gas pedal, son. Not an hour to waste, know what ah mean?"

No pedal and no gas that Raab knew of would allow him access to the hospitalized Thomas Courmaine. Still, a command was a command. Frustration rose. He had no one he could appeal to at The League. They were as compartmentalized as an intelligence agency. Ever since surreptitiously agreeing to "consult" for them—six years now—he had been assigned a single contact, who was, and probably always would be, Miles Bascomb. Months would go by with no conversations then something like this situation came along and pressure built, never relenting until all was judged safe and sound. He had no choice but to keep on trying, go through the motions, act alert and offer suggestions, deliver solutions, cover his tracks, plead, cajole.

He was The League's listening-post inside the American government's topmost medical research body. The League had found him, and he, after listening to the usual blandishments, had allowed himself to be bought and paid for, having collected over two-million in fees so far for his illicit services. A hooked fish. Somewhere they'd have a record of the payments.

If at times he resented the connection, he nonetheless had no recourse, knowing that if his deal-in-the-dark with The League were uncovered, he'd face ruin and quite possibly prison.

Only Courmaine knew the ins-and-outs of what had happened in Naruma, and, if it indeed had truly happened, then how? Would he talk? Press reports out of Africa indicated he had been uncommunicative. Likely, he'd have some tall explaining to do about experimenting on humans without the necessary approvals (Raab having no idea that Naruma had no law to prevent it).

Mulling, he came up empty of any idea for coping with the situation. Strongly, he suspected the women had been treated genetically, that indeed they had undergone a change of some sort, and the essence of all this had led Courmaine to lay out his argument before the SOS crowd.

Changing the DNA makeup of humans was always of highest interest; and if it were anything like a permanent change, then it was of colossal interest to NIH, The League itself, and the entire world of medicine. A watershed event. Everyone in the life sciences had awaited the breakthrough on gene therapy, haplessly and almost hopelessly, for at least the past half-century.

Was this it, finally? The lodestar discovery? Or just another red herring?

Johannesburg, South Africa

Mail, what there was of it, had been kept for him at African Heritage's offices in Muldaur Tower in downtown Johannesburg. A parcel of envelopes arrived late one afternoon, and, upon sorting it, he found one letter from SOS in an air-express packet.

Reading it, he then stared dumbly into space. By a vote of 72-28, he had been selected to make a formal presentation at SOS on New Methodology & Gene Therapy Applications. One passage instructed that he communicate with SOS's director (called the "captain" by the members) at the earliest opportunity to arrange details.

Fantastic, he thought.

He had to retrieve his lab journals, the photos and vials. They were at the Station in Naruma. How to get them? He had no way of returning there. Baster had insisted at their meeting in the gazebo at the estate —that "day of the eggs"—that the name of African Heritage be kept far distant from anything involving the Eves. He dare not ask them, but did anyway, placing a call to the Executive Director. No, the Station had already been closed. Nothing was known of any of his personal possessions, nor of Heritage's equipment, which would be abandoned.

Arguing with the director, he got nowhere.

And there, he supposed, in that stone hut lay some of the most valuable medical data on earth. Irreplaceable until, one day, enough convincing advances were made so that other humans could be treated, tested, and similar findings gotten.

Stymied, depressed, he lapsed into a funk.

The following day he placed a call to Jaggy who had returned two weeks earlier to London. Finally connecting with her in mid-afternoon, insisting to her he was getting along fine, but imploring her to get him out of this sanitized prison. If Muldaur Ltd. would handle the hospital bill, he'd remit repayment soon as he could obtain a new checkbook.

Air tickets for London, he needed those too, but Jaggy one-upped him with an offer of a Muldaur plane. He accepted so fast he shamed himself. Another hurdle, however, as he explained that, by himself, he could not manage a getaway out of South Africa. The police were asking for a visit and he feared his movements might be restricted and that he might be kept under their observation. Perhaps not, but perhaps so. Why risk it?

Could someone hustle him out of the Park Lane Clinic, with no one the wiser? He had left some clothes in the closet of the bedroom he used when staying at the estate. Could they be retrieved?

"Yes, and yes," she said to everything. "Oh, darling, won't it be wonderful? Exceedingly wonderful…"

A jostling of his shoulder, then another one, more vigorous. Thomas awoke to a dark silhouette at his bedside. Another nurse with her thermometer?

"Who're you?"

"We're here to take you out, sir."

"Now, you mean now?"

"Th'hell you think, my man? Of course, now. We're here, right? Get up, if you please. Be needing a hand, will you?"

"No, I can make it? You're from Muldaur?"

"You're looking for some identification, are you?"

"No, that's all right. I was startled, that's all."

One of the men switched on a light. Thomas looked at the clock on the bedside table, the hour was 12:08 a.m. Handed a blue suit-bag, he unzipped it and saw his own belongings, a jacket, shirt, the knit tie, and his baggy gray flannels. A small leather valise held toilet articles, socks, underwear, another shirt.

He began dressing, a somewhat slow process when pulling on his pants. Favoring the knee, he tried to be careful.

"In the small bag there," said the man who had wakened him, "there's a bank envelope. Ten-thousand pounds British. They said you were to make a receipt for it."

It was not posed as a question, and Thomas nodded, then asked, "Did you happen to find a trunk?" he asked. "Olive-drab, a military foot-locker." It contained folders upon folders of his own lab notes. It had been left behind with his other possessions at N'jorro, and he had planned to bring it down to Jo-burg after the elephant hunt. African Heritage had said they didn't know of its whereabouts, but he thought he better keep inquiring.

"It's not here with us."

"Check around for it, can you? I've got to have it."

"Not tonight, friend. We're under orders. Let's be movin' forward, eh?"

"What about those reporters in the lobby?"

"There's two chaps only. Won't be meetin' any of them tonight. Need help, d'ya? You're too big to carry. Can you make it down the fire escape? You requiring that fancy cane there?"

"Yep, I do require it. I can't get down a fire escape. Why so much money, why ten-thousand?"

"S'orders, you know. I don' ask many questions, if you get the meanin'."

The two men conferred again. They faced each other and Thomas couldn't make out what they were saying. Burly fellows; wearing thick-soled camou-flaged boots; ex-commandos, he guessed. One of them, the talker, had hands the size of boxing gloves.

He worked his feet into a pair of moccasins, tidied up the bags, stuffed the bank envelope into his jacket pocket, signaling he was ready.

At a bedside table, he opened the drawer and withdrew the recent letter from SOS. Also another one from the banker, Pierre St. Germain. When he turned around, he saw a hand holding a piece of paper. The receipt for the cash and he signed it.

They would have to carry the bags he told them; he needed one free hand for the cane, the other to keep his balance. Down the hall they went, and he saw the nurse was absent from her desk. Where was she? He didn't ask.

An elderly woman, wrapped in a terry-cloth robe, appeared at the doorway to her room. She gaped in surprise; she uttered a little gasp and swiftly disappeared. Nonetheless, a witness.

Someone, somehow, would be braced for an explanation as to his where-abouts. He had been brought to the clinic covered with a sheet—no clothes, no possessions. He had even lost his steel-plated pocket-watch. Someone in authority would know an escape had been adroitly executed, and how would they calm the impatient, long-waiting reporters? Or the police.

Within an hour, he found himself strapped to a leather couch in the cabin of a Gulfstream VI jet: destination London. In minutes, the wheels were up, the aircraft angling for altitude.

Here he was, a private jet, not even a passport in his possession, spirited out of Africa in the dead of a night that smacked of influence—in the form of one Jaggy Muldaur.

Thumping its way through an air pocket, the Gulfstream bounced heavily, almost as heavily as Thomas's crisscrossing thoughts. One, now that he was headed for Jaggy's home grounds, was his recollection of Baster's intimation that Jaggy and he ought to tie a marital knot..."and leave the Vatican to me"...words that still rang as if they were ten bells loud and he himself were the bell-ringer. Laughable almost, being married to a woman like her, three times divorced, so rich she could never track it all, so willful you'd need a whip to make her right.

Still, he was safe, relatively so, and it was she who was owed his thanks.

London, England

A place of infinite luxury, and he knew it well from his previous trips to Cambridge, and afterward staying a night or two here at her home in Belgravia, London's creamy residential sector. The home was Muldaur to the third power, he thought—everything in this room costing the earth and then some. He noted a few changes; different furniture or perhaps it was the same furniture with different upholstery. Expensive looking rugs he didn't recall and paintings that were hung in new places. She liked moving her art around, one year to the next.

And she ought to move it all to a museum, he thought, so others could enjoy it.

He moved, the cane making a soft tapping on the inlaid parquet floor. He gazed about at the art. Adorning one wall were three Whistlers and a Gilbert Stuart, and next to those a pair of Winslow Homer's quite remarkable seascapes, dramatic strokes depicting a turmoil of water that seemed poised to jump off the canvas. He remembered that at one time the Homers had hung in an upstairs drawing room, and wondering what treasures were there now. On an adjoining wall was a palace-sized Rubens, a horse scene, then two Constables—English pastorals—and underneath a row of works by Stubbs, famous for his portraits of horses. He had seen others by Stubbs in Baster's home in Johannesburg, some worth over a million dollars. On the far wall hung a collection of four Durers; next to those, a huge scene of horses by Donatello. Two Picasso's, three Utrillo's, one Cézanne.

Staggering, the art, in this one room alone.

In the center of the room, a long oaken refectory table held silver-framed pictures and a set of cut-crystal bowls with floating white lilies. Magazines were neatly nested at one end of the table.

Bending, he inspected the picture frames. Some he had seen before, so was checking out of curiosity for any new arrivals. It seemed a fuller gallery than the one kept by deMehlo, leaving Thomas to wonder if this were a hobby of the power-brokering elite.

One photo showed Baster, with Jaggy at its center, then Margaret Thatcher, the Prime Minister of another time, at her side. Others were studio portraits of film and stage actors, all signed with flourishing signatures. Another of the Duke and Duchess of Kent at Wimbledon, with Jaggy in between them. Princess Anne, at a party (in this house), and on and on.

At measured intervals along the refectory table stood three gold candelabra, each four feet tall at least and mounted on massive bases of gold and what might be layers of platinum. He had never seen them before. Leaning closer, he read the plaque at the base of one of them, Jacgelét Field, Shaft 2, 24 November, 1967.

A door closed and he heard, "Ostentatious, aren't they?"

"Are they what I think? Solid gold?"

"They've been in a vault for years at Barclay's. I finally decided it was such a waste, so I had them brought over here. Baster gave them to my mother and she bequeathed them to me. The ore was mined in the gold field named after her. They're solid as solid can be, all right. It's all one man can do to carry even one of them."

Jaggy was very close now. "You look so utterly new and divine. All mended, eh? Not a bandage anywhere. Rationing our arms, are we? Wherever the hell is my hug hello?"

She removed the cane from his hand, and they held, her arms encircling his neck, the rest of her wearing him as close as if he were her skirt.

"Are you all well, feeling right again?" Jaggy asked as they parted.

"I'm not trying out for the Olympics anytime soon. My knee is still sore. All the other departments are pretty much the way they're supposed to be. Thanks to you. Very many thanks to you."

"That cane of yours is on the ratty side. We'll get you another."

"I like this one. Lots of patina. It was loaned to me by a nurse's assistant and I'll have to send it back somehow."

Her eyes swam again. "So wonderful to see you, Thomas. And here you are in London, finally, finally. I'm not letting you out of my sight. I'm so happy...I am...and after all that's happened to us."

"Yes. Too much."

"We won't talk of it."

"I agree, let's let it rest."

"It's just us now, isn't it?"

"I guess it is," he said, "or will be. And you, are you all right?"

"No. No, I'm not. But I shall be now you're here with me. What fun!"

"Thanks for asking me. Double thanks for getting me out of Africa."

"I should say. It's no place for any of us now. God knows with Baster gone what they'll be doing to us. Ruination, I suppose. Cretins. Sodding nignogs, making a hash of everything. It won't be too jolly, I'll wager. Oh, Tommy...sorry, sorry, Thomas, it's Thomas, I know...we'll be happy...I know we'll be so good for each other, won't we? It's our turn after this ghastly month."

"I have something to return." He handed her the bank envelope. "I didn't need this, but one more round of thanks."

"Oh, is it—what—?"

"Ten-thousand pounds."

"Oh, was it a tenner?—oh, no, no, you keep it, just keep it."

"Thank you, but no I won't."

"You're to keep it, I *said*. Please don't argue; it's a bore, exceedingly boring." She averted his eyes when he went ahead and placed the thick money-envelope on the refectory table anyway. "Let's go to the greenhouse and we can talk. Come along," she insisted. "It's my flower-hour."

A smile reset her lips. A wonderful, kind-giving smile, the beacon telling of another of her instant mood swings. She could dazzle when she wanted and it made him mildly uncomfortable, wondering what wheels were spinning in that head.

They went down a long hallway lighted by overhead cone-lights that illuminated two Cluny tapestries, sixteenth century, covering spacious sections of wall. Like the art in the library, the tapestries were museum pieces. He remembered asking her once how she had acquired them and she told him they were given over to discharge a loan made to a titled English couple, fallen on grimmer days.

Then, onward through a glassed-in terrace and they stepped outside, heading to the greenhouse connected to the back side of the large garage. Inside, what seemed like a thousand scents drifted through the air. He could not distinguish one from another. Hothouse smells, ambrosial, the fragrances were almost too much for the senses. As he went down one wooden walkway, he passed bench after bench of orchids, then finally into an area of thick-leafed, meaty green plants, jungle-like, some with pearly blossoms.

Supported by the cane, he tagged behind her, watching as she snipped away at burgundy roses and milk-white chrysanthemums. She scissored meticulously, inspecting the nodes on the stems before she bladed them, then arranged the flowers in a plastic-lined wicker basket Thomas was carrying with his free hand.

"I've a message for you from Pierre St. Germain," Jaggy said. "He hopes he can persuade you to visit Geneva soon."

"He sent a letter. I have it with me."

"Are you going to go?"

"I think I must. How did he know I'd be here?"

"I talk to him at least twice in the week. More, sometimes. I told him we'd be fetching you."

"I'll get in touch with him. No rush is there?"

"He seems to think so."

"Yes, well…I will. Is this going to be a sore subject between us?"

"Frankly, I don't think you're qualified for it and I told Baster as much."

"Frankly, I heartily agree with you. I'll go to Geneva, check in, have a talk and we'll see what we'll see. I've no intention of getting on board if I'm an impediment of some sort. I know I should go out of courtesy. I'll call him tomorrow or the next day. I will admit I can use the money."

"You may do all that pleases you, and it would please me if we could get ourselves straight on this laboratory project. Baster wanted you to have it, and so do I. I believe he mentioned a credit for the equivalent of two-million Euros. Was that your understanding?"

"Yes, it was to be as much as five million, if needed. But that was before…"

"Before what? Oh, I catch you. Before he died, you mean. Well, he did die, but the lab has yet to be born. He would've wanted it so, so I'll take over his share of it and—"

"No, no. Not that, that wasn't what we agreed to. Not at all. It was to be Baster and myself, and you were in it because he asked that you take half of his share."

Her brow arched, along with her voice. "There's something the matter with my money? Has it a disease of some sort?"

"You know what I meant, Jaggy. I'm not holding anyone to anything. That was then, and it was a very different situation. An entirely different situation."

He didn't care to tell her that if the chips were down and counted, Baster, in the end, might not have agreed to back the lab; not when he learned that Thomas, outright, would refuse to steal eggs to beget an heir.

"As far as I'm concerned a bargain is a bargain," Jaggy replied. "He was to have thirty-percent, I was to have thirty, and you the remaining forty, which makes the full hundred, what? All right, then. I shall take on his thirty. Up to you, but after a time I'll agree to sell the whole boodle to you if you like. It's not but a few million. You'll likely need more before you're through, and I'll see to it that you receive whatever it is you need. Fair, Thomas?"

"Too fair."

"I must teach you how to be less ethical."

She winked, stroking his arm in a pass of her hand that ended at his wrist. "Don't let's argue about it," she went on. "What I'd like to know is how it all goes from here. What happens when we get our trolley on the track? More of those miracles? The Mzura miracles? This is the U.K. They've rules here. We might have to watch our step, what?" Jaggy put down her pruning shears, slipping off her gloves. "Tell me more," she said, running a hand through her thick dark hair. "You know the newspapers talked about those Mzura women, and I must say I was ready to file the whole thing under the category of horseshit. That's what Baster said. His words. Then, they—well, you know, and with what they wrote, I became absolutely convinced. I know Baster was unnerved for political reasons but I'm not. I want to know everything." She laughed from down deep, her eyes moistening. "You should've taken me to see them when we were in Naruma. I never saw Baster as antsy as he was about those women. If you're not too tired, we'll go out for dinner. The chef has come down with gout, it seems."

"Sure."

"You see all these orchids. They're all hybrids. That's something like gene-crossing isn't it?"

"Absolutely, it is."

"I'm wanting to learn about DNA." Pensive then, her jaw firming, "If I wanted to make an exact copy of a plant, could your Zyme-thing help me?"

"Probably."

"What if I tried to graft two plants from two different species? Ordinarily, that's impossible...they're not alike..."

"Off hand, I think it'd be quite possible," he said. "You'd have to do some experimenting. It's all genes and cells, anyway that you dice it."

"So, does that also mean you can invent people? Cloning them, like that sheep, Dolly, that one in Scotland that died. That's dangerous, isn't it? With humans, I mean?"

"You can clone anything, or try, if you have the DNA to work from. Cloning humans is extremely difficult and never has been done successfully. It's illegal in most places. Why're you asking all this?"

"Wondering, that's all. I must call Hong Kong, then later we'll go out for dinner. Can you find your way about? "

"Sure, I can."

Crossing the back lawn, they passed through the French doors into a hallway, and she relieved him of the flower baskets, placing them on a table. Blowing him a kiss, she went off to somewhere, disappearing through one of the hall doors. Going toward the front of the house, he encountered Mercer MacLeod, the butler, coming through an archway, wheeling a cart with a full tea service of finger sandwiches, scones, and a bowl of lustrous fruits.

"Tea, Mr. Thomas, will you?"

"Yes, I will. For you, too?"

"Not here, sir." Mercer chuckled. "Wouldn't do at all. Just you have yours and we'll be along right away and show you up to your rooms."

He sat for a time drinking tea and munching a cucumber sandwich, while weighing the conversation with Jaggy. Arrogant, willful, commanding, hot, cold, calculating, officious, generous. And she still wanted to back the lab, the money it cost meaning nothing to her. He'd need more than money to launch Zyme-One. Big players, non-profit types, they would be the right recipe for Zyme-One to succeed. By anyone's estimate Jaggy was a large-scale player on any scene she stepped into, anywhere, at any time. Still, she didn't carry clout in the world of bioscience where he most needed allies. Muscular, prestigious allies who knew how to influence the medical establishment, get things moving by endorsing a full-out project. Yet he knew the major foundations and institutions would likely be resistant to his discovery done in a makeshift lab, in a makeshift territory run by African natives. Besides, all the documentation was missing; he'd have to start from scratch. How, though?

Baster could make things happen with a phone call or two. He knew all the mighty button-pressers on both sides of the equator. Had past favors to call in. All the front-runners seemed to know one another, just as in the case of Baster and Augustin deMehlo. They talked, they dealt, they hob-nobbed; in some instances they even divorced and remarried the wives or husbands of their business friends. Titans made their own rules, or, if need be, followed no rules.

Himself, he couldn't make anything happen, not even with a hundred calls. Nor, he wagered, could Jaggy, or not on a par with Baster.

A fortnight passed and they were dining again at Petrossian's, her favorite, and where they had gone on the evening of his arrival when spirited out of Jo-burg. Stepping through the front portal of the restaurant, Jaggy made another of her public statements, doing it without uttering a single word. Under her unnecessary chinchilla, she wore a black sheath, and double strand of opera-length pearls that glowed softly around her strong neck; on her right hand a stamp-sized emerald sparkled, and, for the display on her wrist, a bracelet of matching emeralds, at one time owned by Elisabeth of Russia, Czarina in the mid-1700s.

The maître'd made his dutiful bow, two waiters hovered anxiously, and diners at every table she passed gave her the twice-over.

Already awaiting her was the same appetizer and wine they'd had on Thomas's first visit to the famed eatery, a tin of Beluga caviar nested in a silver bowl filled with cracked ice, and, to wash down the eggs, a chilled bottle of Roederer Cristal, a champagne no throat, once blessed by it, quickly forgot.

Thomas was telling her he had gone to Cambridge to resign as a member of SOS, instead of sending the letter he had intended. While there, he made his lame excuses, that, because of the upheaval caused by the incident in Naruma and the ensuing turmoil, much of the evidence he had assembled for his Proof-of-Concept presentation had been lost. He didn't know how. He'd therefore withdraw, refusing a much sought invitation to make his arguments. More, as he no longer resided in South Africa (and never had technically) the SOS by-laws required that he withdraw. He had expressed his deepest thanks for the members' vote, offering to write notes of apology to every one of them. Which the "permanent captain" of SOS said would be a wholly unnecessary act.

"Well," said Thomas, a little wearily as he finished updating Jaggy, "it's an end of another era in the life and times of T. Courmaine at Cambridge University. I really do enjoy it there. But for some reason it's been nothing but complications for me. I wonder why? Cut of the cards, I guess."

"You're sad about it? Leaving SOS?"

"I am. It's quite a group. Not easy to get asked to join it, either. Baster swung that one for me."

"Anything I can do?"

"Afraid not."

"Then what happened, did you come right back to London?"

"Not right away. After I said my goodbyes and amens, I walked over to the Eagle. That's a famous local pub in Cambridge, known far and wide in the town, and smoked a cigar and drank a tall glass of porter. The barkeep there is an old-Joe friend of mine from my teaching days. His boy is dying from some incurable disease. He's only twelve. A kid, just a kid. My troubles seemed quite petite. Therein, you have the folio of my great and lesser events for the past days. Oh, I had lunch with Rhoades McBride, my editor friend at *Nature*. He took me to White's, the mens' club—"

"Yes, I know all about White's."

"You do? I thought they didn't admit women."

"They don't. But I've many male friends who belong."

"I wonder about the next week or so, especially Geneva when I meet your friend St. Germain. That ought to be interesting. Any messages?"

"I'll be anxious to hear how it goes for you," Jaggy said, then added, "wouldn't those scientists take your word at SOS? Quite a crowd of the reporters and photographers vouched for some sort of happenings in Naruma."

"Remember, the SOS members are scientists, through and through. You need hard proof to attest to whatever it is you're claiming. Very hard proof and I've lost mine. It's in Naruma, whatever's left of it. "

"Well, I say balls to them."

"In the game of biology they're the big players. I have to think about what they think of me."

"I think a lot of you."

"Thanks."

"I mean it."

"Thanks twice, then. You haven't said much about Oslo. How did that go?"

"I'm trying to erase Oslo. I'd erase it from mother-earth if I had the chance. Not that I have anything against the Norwegians." Eyes ablaze, jaw jutting, her teeth seemed to grind behind the set of her mouth. "I went to Oslo to preside over a conference of our senior men, only to find out several of them may walk out on their employment contracts, wanting no part of my regime. Christ, I've hardly had time to take over...but there it is, the ingrates...they're all paid a bloody fortune..."

The message had been neither restrained nor veiled: the executives had let it be known that mining was a man's business, that Baster had appointed them to run their various fiefdoms, letting them have their own ways as long as they kept the profits rolling in. It was a system they understood, and not at all prepared to take orders from a woman, who could not possibly step into the shoes of a Baster Muldaur. Nor were they sanguine over the outlook in African countries where Muldaur's vast mining operations were vulnerable to sporadic political upheaval or even outright confiscation. Havoc in Africa would impact almost every part of the company save for its world-girdling real estate holdings, and the Hong Kong, London and North American trading operations, all solid cash cows.

"Some of them don't think I'm up to it, Jaggy asserted at one point. Well, I am. They're trying to gain the overall operating control, that's what they're up to, wanting a management committee and so on."

Her temper on the verge of erupting now and Thomas listened sympathetically. He knew what lay at the bottom of her grumbling. Her dream was not only to succeed to Baster's limelight but indeed to surpass it. A dream now flirting with defeat. Without top-hands to help run Muldaur, descent was all but assured in the days ahead.

He could interpret her thoughts without her explaining much more: the business of extracting the earth's treasures had always been a man's game, with rare exceptions. Indeed, as much a male bastion as a Prussian army. She had succeeded to a throne long the domain of Muldaur men, and the jury was out as to whether she was up to the mark. Thomas needed no help whatsoever in piecing together the jig-saw of her womanly reactions; for, Baster had many times outlined his worries about Jaggy, adding that Jaggy had little in the way of *give* in her makeup, especially where the male of the species was involved— or blacks.

She was invested with an arrogance, though, like Baster himself, she could be generous as a monsoon.

Leaving his ponderings, rejoining her, he heard her say in a severely wounded tone: "Sodders," and was about to feel wounded himself as she motioned for another bottle of Roederer. The first, down to its dregs, had evaporated in the wake of his smallish news and her tirade, and as he had left the conversation while appraising her fret.

An owner, one of the Petrossian brothers, had been keeping half an eye on them. A waiter appeared, to Thomas's dismay, with a fresh bottle, popped the cork, poured, and then gave the bottle its ice-bath in the wine cooler. On three occasions, the maître had stopped by, anxious to satisfy the slightest whim. More of the caviar, Madame? Extolling on the fish they were to be served shortly, then, pronouncing on the chef's prize-winning desserts, a dish Thomas rarely ate.

"Did we actually order?" Thomas asked. "Or is the maitre'd reading our minds for us?"

"I ordered ahead. I hope you like plaice. My favorite fish. Comes from Iceland. Can I say something reprehensible?"

"Sure."

"You won't get upset with me, you promise?"

"If it's very reprehensible, I might. Otherwise, feel free to shoot."

"You need new clothes. You have one tie that I know of, and one jacket, the one you have on. Those moldy shoes. Sorry, but they are and you look like a grown waif. And your shirt, with that button-down collar, it's dreadful, and it's missing a button at the collar point."

"The laundry does that and I never notice till I put the shirt on."

"We're going shopping. Not tomorrow, I can't tomorrow. But the day after."

"Actually, I'm allowed to shop by myself these days, but thanks."

"You wouldn't know where to go. I know you wouldn't. Do you know of Turnbull & Asser's?"

"Assers? You say that's a store? I'll skip that one. What do they sell or should I ask?"

"Or New and Lingwood?"

"That sounds better."

"It's not but it's quite good. You can't go around London looking like that."

"I like things that I'm used to. Besides, it takes me a long time to break in a shirt."

"We're going, Thomas. It's my gift."

"Thank you, but I don't want a gift. Then I'd be giving you a gift, then you'd be giving me one back. On and on."

She sent him a look. "You've a head hard as a cement block."

"So I'm told."

"You've talked further with Pierre?"

"He's going abroad on a business trip and so we agreed to meet in Geneva after he gets back. Meanwhile, I'll stay in London with you, if that's okay. My knee is a hundred-percent better, thanks to that therapist you found for me. I'll keep out of your way."

"I don't want you out of my way. But I must leave for a meeting in Bermuda on Tuesday next, and I can't have you at loose ends."

"Actually, I was thinking of going a few days early, spend some time at Cyro—"

Her voice, turning suddenly brittle, as she pressed with, "Cyro! Why there? What're you doing there?"

"I sent a shipment of *semba* up to Cyro some months ago. I want to check on it. It's fundamental to the making of Zyme-One…"

"Oh, that."

She smiled the way she smiled when something was going on in the back of that head of hers, as if some little theater-cast up there were putting on a private playlet. "I was thinking about asking you a favor," she said. "A Paris favor."

"Paris, well, okay. If I can," he said, amused and showing it. "Mystery number one is how could I possibly do you a favor in Paris?"

"I've a horse running at Longchamps, Saturday after next. We're flying over, some friends of mine, and maybe we'll win a pot. Will you come? You should meet some of these people."

"I'd be an eleventh toe at a horse race. I've never been to one, not even near one."

"We'll have fun if the weather's nice, and we'll be back in London for dinner. Or we can stay there the night, why not? You've never seen the house there."

"Not the house, not Paris, not the races. A strike-out."

"I'd appreciate it, really I would."

"You think they'll let me into the track with a button-down shirt?"

"You won't be wearing one by then. You'll love it. And when you come back from Geneva, we'll go to Wales, to my home at St Curig's Fields. I'm thinking of having a few people up, but not the same ones as Paris. We can't shoot yet, not at this time of year. It's most relaxing. Lovely grounds, you'd like Wales."

"Shoot what?"

"Birds. We have ducks, pheasants, geese, woodcock, wood pigeon."

He liked that idea even less than Paris. "I'm on my way to New York. Pretty soon, I think, and I've got to get myself prepared. The best place to do it is at Cambridge. They've got very good people there and it helps me to toss ideas around. You go to Paris and I'll go back to Cambridge."

"Thomas, a few days, that's all. Paris is for fun. Wales is business. Please come, do, my love. Please."

"I'll sleep on it."

"Pul-*leasee*." An imploring look, almost a look of canine trust.

"Fine...we'll go, we'll go."

"Thanks, really." Her eyes shone. "New York, when is that? What's in New York?"

"I've yet to find out. There're several foundations I want to see, if I can make dates with them. Some're there and others are in other cities. I hope to see if I can enlist support."

Dinner arrived and for a time conversation lapsed. After finishing the entrée, he looked keenly at Jaggy, thinking to himself the time is here and he told her for the second time he could not accept her offer to back a lab by herself alone. He wouldn't risk spending millions of anyone's money simply to prove a point. Baster, he told her, hadn't cared about that side of it, because Baster's main interest had been in finding quicker, cheaper cures for the ever-spreading AIDS pandemic in sub-Sahara Africa. Zyme-One might conceivably be part of the answer. He went on, reminding her how drug companies sweated for ten years while waiting to get new products approved; then, if approved, more years trying to get them launched and accepted by the medical profession. For him to win, it would take more than money; even Muldaur money, or Gates money, or Queen Elizabeth's reputed stash.

Influence was called for: in academia, in the world science community, in governments, and eventually with the public.

"You need to understand something, Jaggy. I could be dead right and still lose. For lots of reasons, too."

"Meaning what?"

"You know business and I don't. I'm setting out on something that's tectonic in its scope. I'm a one-man band. I dream a lot. It's my nature, I suppose. But I'm not dreaming when I say this is a hard uphill haul. I keep thinking of Mister Edison and his light bulb and having to beat back every whaler and candle maker on earth."

"I take your point, Thomas. I'm simply trying to help you."

"And you always do, and I thank you. You've been splendid. Getting me out of Africa for starters. I could still be there right now under the thumb of the police."

Thanking her sincerely but not quite thanking her completely. He had said not a syllable about Baster's designs to use the lab to create an heir. Afraid to mention it, fearing it might raise her ire over a touchy, almost flammable topic: The Muldaur Trust.

Looking a long way off, then, Jaggy, eventually returned to him, saying, "I don't know what constitutes acceptable proof in science. Don't tell me you expect to find more women to experiment on?"

"That was a one-in-a-million situation. No, no women, no men. But I'll find something. I must."

"What sort of something?"

"I don't know. Not yet. I depend on my dreams and my hopes. I figure if I rub the dreams and hopes together long enough, I can inveigle my genie to pop out of the bottle. If ever I find the right bottle."

"Am I in those dreams of yours?"

"I'm reserving a special one for you."

"Really, well, tell me when it happens and what it's about. You men. I try to help and you brush me off as though I were dandruff or something worse. You're almost as bad as that bunch in Oslo who told me where to get off. I won't get off...why should I?"

"Possibly, I misspoke. I appreciate all your generosity, I do."

But she hadn't heard him, or didn't choose to; she was aggravated about the brouhaha in Norway with her sub-chieftains who were unwilling to submit to her authority till they were convinced she understood what they were up against. Thomas was bearing the brunt of her annoyance.

"And don't tell me about your problems unless you want to hear about mine. That's what couples do sometimes, they commiserate." Dead quiet now. A cloud hovered over their table, pregnant with misunderstandings. "I think I've had enough of Petrossian's for tonight," she suggested. "Let's brave the street, shall we?"

No bill was presented. No matter where he went with her, it was always the same. Never a chit for anything. Instead, any charges for their outings made their way to her office. Nice, he supposed. He helped her on with the chinchilla. Even on the brink of summer, she chose luxuriant furs to be seen in. Nevertheless, she knew her town, for once outside they were greeted by a curling fog slithering along the street, damping everything and wetting the cobblestones to a sheen. Farther down, the lampposts, the curbsides, and parked cars were all but erased from view. Dim shafts of light from the storefronts guided them as they ambled along, saying little. A comment or two about the fog, the night, the dinner. She was still edgy, and he avoided any talk that might misfire again.

Jack, her chauffer, followed along in the blue and silver Bentley, keeping a half block distant, giving them plenty of space.

Stopping, stopping again, Jaggy window-shopped as she moseyed along. He had no idea of what she might be looking for, guessing that she didn't either. Jaggy owned ten of everything there was, or she seemed to.

She walked ahead, setting a pace. He caught up, stood beside her, listening to her comments about the window displays, then not listening, as he piped himself into his own world.

It was one thing to be a guest passing through, either here or Johannesburg; now Paris loomed, an afternoon with the horses, no less, then up to Wales. Thinking of it all, his heart moved a mile and not with any joy.

At yet another store window they halted, and the reflecting light made a wreath around her uptilted face.

"Kiss me," she said. "Do it while the night is still young."

"How shameless of you," he joked. "Especially when there isn't anyone around to watch."

"I am rather shameless, at that. I was a decent girl until I was fifteen. Then my hormones won the war and I found out what I'd been missing."

"Fifteen. The year of your great revelation?"

"Um-hmm. I'll tell you sometime. Perhaps, I'd better not. You might find it shocking."

"I'm immune to your shocks."

"You could love me, Thomas. You'll see, I know you will and you'll be better for it."

She had turned away from the storefront. Though he could not see her face clearly, he knew it held a sly smile. Her voice told that her mood was up again. She didn't press for the kiss, and if she had, he'd likely have succumbed after their slight and sudden tiff in the restaurant. But it wouldn't end with a kiss, and, wary of involvement, he wanted to give her not the slightest hint of encouragement.

Jaggy tucked an arm under his as they moved along in the dense fog. Was that a breast nudging his upper arm? Whispering something, too, but he didn't catch it. A block or so later, she complained of the night's damp, shivering slightly, and he stood out on the street, waving at Jack to bring up the Bentley.

At the house, after a chaste, speedy goodnight, up he went to his rooms on the third floor. She had made no more overtures about casual kisses, leaving him much relieved. How complicated she could be, so willful and making things doubly difficult as he always seemed in her debt for one thing or another, For a long time he searched the dark for the blessing of sleep. Questions pelting him; no answers graced the night, however.

She was up to something, he was sure of it. She had asked again one afternoon, when home early from her office, about DNA, about cloning technology. She seemed so intent on the lab. How come? Getting up, he latched both doors to the hallway, one opening to the bedroom, the other to the adjoining sitting room. Ridiculous, he supposed, but somehow it felt better. Beholden to Jaggy, he couldn't keep saying no to her advances without giving offense. Still, if she came prowling again, locked doors were as *no* of a message as he could imagine.

What then? Another fray? It was probably time to leave, but then he'd have to make excuses; excuses that would hold little water, so, he supposed, he was stuck until he could get himself to the States.

One floor down, Jaggy smoked a pipe of opium pellets; in part it quieted her anxiety and in other part because pain gripped her; little and sporadic daggers down her arms and legs. When standing, her legs would hurt and hurt worse after taking a few steps. She refused to admit it to others, was damned if she was letting anyone say she was sick, and on the path to being an invalid.

It was likely, nonetheless; she knew it, a tight circle of doctors knew it and she couldn't afford to have it talked about.

After a ten-minute struggle with her daggers, she finally felt a let up. A wisp of euphoria settled in, as she wondered for the tenth time what the hell was the matter with that man? Before leaving for Oslo, she had offered him funding for the lab again, and even more—he could own it all if that's what it took. He hadn't so much as twitched an eyelid. Granite-brained. A pauper, so why wouldn't he take a windfall? He hadn't anything: clothes, money, not many friends. He practically ran for cover whenever she offered her bed. Nothing there, either; nothing anywhere. What an utter, unspeakable waste, making her speculate if he might be asexual, or was mind-blocked due to some Jesuit-installed guilt trip.

She meant to find out. If he was gay, she promised herself a long crying jag. Months had drifted by since she'd been with a man, and it was telling. She wasn't right with herself, so how could she be right with anyone else?

Lingering on that thought as she drew heavily on the opium pipe. Her euphoria had begun its ascent as she saw the night in a different way now, its heavens parting, the galaxies spinning about as if they were multi-colored whirlpools.

A loose thought invaded her. If she couldn't find a way to clone Baster, or if his sperm didn't take, she'd require an option. An option named Thomas I. Courmaine, and he had damn well better deliver.

London, England
Geneva, Switzerland

"Pierre, you darling man, he's soon on his way to you. Look after him, he'll need it. I'd very much like him to succeed. He has no money, you see. He hates money, I think. I never met anyone like that, have you?"

"Not in Switzerland, I assure you. We have no dissidents where money is concerned."

She laughed. "I know he gets some sort of fee for being a trustee. I want you to double it, and charge the difference to me. He's not to know, not for any reason."

"I couldn't imagine how to explain such a thing. He already knows what the standard fees are."

"Change them."

"We'll not be party to that, Jaggy."

"It's my money."

"It's our bank, my friend, and we do not engage in deceptions. This fellow is about to be doing business with us, and with me personally."

"Spare us from the bankers of this world...."

"Just so, that is, until you come to us for loans. Are the two of you, uh, involved, or should I be asking?"

"I would say yes, but not in the customary way. Too complicated to explain. He thinks he's still a Jesuit priest. He trying to resign or the equivalent, and they won't let him. That's another facet I don't quite comprehend. I'm always at bay over how the Vatican functions. They take life-long prisoners, it appears. But I want him to succeed or at least to think he's succeeding. It's quite, quite important to me. Exceedingly so. Oh, and see what you can find out about this damn laboratory he wants. I've offered him the whole show and you'd think I was inoculating him with diphtheria. Odd, isn't it? I don't understand any of it. He wants the Americans, he says. Not me, but the Americans."

"Is he to be husband number...what is it? Number four, would that be right?"

An ensuing pause, heavy and slow.

"I hear a reproving tone and find it regrettable," Jaggy finally retorted. "Not a goddamn bit funny, it's not, Pierre."

"Now...now, easy, Jaggy. By the way, I've heard rumblings. A sore subject, I suspect, but as one of your directors I feel compelled to speak. Is it so that five of your senior managers are about to quit you?"

"Things have been said, yes."

"My advice is to increase their compensation. Keep them at all costs. They'd be difficult to replace, especially with the mounting difficulties we face in Africa. No time to be caught short-handed, you know."

"Is this a lecture?"

"A suggestion. A strong suggestion."

"Sounds more like the start of a sermon."

"What's happening down in Africa is grim news for Muldaur Ltd. We receive special reports here at Braunsweig and they're gloomy to say the least. We've other clients with operations there and they're affected as well."

"Bye, Pierre. Nice chatting with you. Look after my chap, please..."

Perplexed, St. Germain asked himself why would that woman ask him to pull some stunt about the trustees' fees? He contemplated for extended moments, then firmly made up his mind: Jaggy Muldaur must be roped off.

Meanwhile, what of this Courmaine? Was he coming to Geneva wearing two hats, with one belonging to Jaggy Muldaur? Or would he be an ally of The Trust and its growing complications. The Swiss banking bureaucrats had, as required by law, been notified when key Swiss assets were about to fall into foreign hands. They were not only chagrined at the size of The Trust, they were appalled, had let their feeling be known in stressful, almost fist-shaking language.

Geneva, Switzerland

Rain had washed the city's face for all of that morning. The sky hanging low with an armada of water-logged clouds sailing out of the Jura Mountains toward Geneva. Thomas had checked into the Hotel Richelieu, had his bags sent to the suite reserved for him, then taken a taxi to his next destination—Braunsweig und Sohn. Snaking its way in and out of tight, rain-slowed traffic, the taxi rounded a corner, suddenly swerving to the curb and stopping.

"This is it?" Thomas asked in French.

"Oui, m'sieur, this is Braunsweig."

"Merci."

Thomas took the granite steps two at a time, until he stood under an overhang, brushing raindrops off his sleeves. The building, dark as the day itself, was of dressed limestone and gave the impression of a medieval fortress, as it was probably meant to. One pillar displayed a small brass plate—bearing the number '101' and with no other indication of what might transpire behind the towering brass-bound doors.

Well, he thought, they hadn't a sign at Borgo Spirito 4 in Rome at the Jesuit Curia, either. Nor, as he remembered, was there one at St. Pierre's Basilica. Either you knew where you were, or you didn't.

A stick-thin gent in a black suit, black tie, and dove-gray gloves stepped out of nowhere. Thomas introduced himself, was then led up a circular marble staircase, past three statues set into niches of the curving wall. A house flag of two golden eagles, facing each other on a field of green, was displayed against a high wall. He entered a large room filled with executive-sized desks, more men sitting at them than women. Guided through a serpentine-shaped hallway, he found himself in a subdued, tastefully appointed room. Neither small nor large, the room was sided in polished mahogany; leather sofas and two Eames chairs made a very loose circle. An antique desk, with a sheaf of bluish notepaper centered on its blotter, stood in one corner.

Thomas stood there, passing a few moments as he scanned a set of leather-bound books on a wall shelf. He turned when hearing the snick of a door-latch behind him.

"Not a very cheerful day to welcome you, M'sieu Courmaine." Thomas turned. A smile saturated a friendly, slightly freckled face as a hand was extended. "Pierre St. Germain. Welcome to Braunsweig und Sohn."

Thomas took the hand. "A pleasure. Jaggy Muldaur sends you her regards."

"How very kind of her. In good form, is she?"

"I'd say so. Pretty good, considering."

"Hard to believe he's gone. I—well—what does one say. Baster was a good friend of ours. The most singular man I've ever dealt with. I'm glad to see you're on the mend yourself. I had hoped to meet you when I was in South Africa, but then Jaggy told me you were pretty well banged up. We got banged up, too, as it turned out. The day after Baster died our South African holdings decreased in value by sixteen-percent. I suppose that's as good a measure as any of a man's importance. Have a seat. May I address you as Thomas?"

"Certainly. Please do."

"Good. Pierre, as you know, is mine. I've made inquiries about you, as you might expect. Baster's word would be enough, of course. But we're Swiss and we're too cautious for our own good sometimes. All is well, however. You've quite a fan club in some quarters. While you're with us...uh, how many days can you stay?"

"Many as are needed, I suppose. I hadn't really thought about it."

"Fine. We'll get you schooled on the details of The Muldaur Trust. It'll require some reading, quite a haul of it, and you'll be asked to sign a confidentiality agreement. That comes first, by the way. When last I talked to Baster, he mentioned that you and he had an enterprise in mind. He was to supply a credit in your favor. Rather, we were to supply the credit and he was to guarantee its repayment. Perhaps we can cover that subject, as well, and any assistance we can give is, of course, yours for the asking." St. Germain all so smoothly, the credit, the proposed lab, as if it had all been rehearsed the day before.

"I'm terribly grateful. Thank you. Quite a place, your bank. I've known of it, even dealt with it, but never before stepped inside the gates."

"We're a touch over five-hundred years. In age, that is. You take on the appearance of a forgotten museum after all that time. Do you know much about us?"

"Well, some, yes. You maintain accounts here for the Society of Jesus. At one time I was handling those in Rome for about a year or so."

"Were you, indeed? Interesting."

"I think I still remember the account-codes. Probably you've changed them."

Ducking the comment, Germain replied, "Then you do know about us."

"Not all that much. I was only an errand boy."

"One of Augustin deMehlo's men?"

"You know him?"

"Several times, we've met. Not recently, however. He reports to a higher level than I do. Different circles of interest, you might say."

Thomas chuckled, again feeling the warmth of his host. "If you've any literature on Braunsweig, I'd be glad to read it."

"We have the usual propaganda, brochures and so forth. I'll find you a copy of one if you're interested. In the essentials, we're like other private banks in Switzerland." Smiling, as he added, "Better, of course, if that doesn't sound too ungallant. We don't deal with the general public. There's nothing wrong with the public, God knows, but we're not structured to give that sort of service. Our clients are corporations or institutions such as hospitals or universities, trade unions, governments. We bank for a good number of governments, and do our best to advise them. Seems as if they have all the money these days, so we dig our hands inside their pockets wherever we see an opportunity...now, what else...Braunsweig invests for its own account and manages money for others—pension funds, and high net-worth individuals. And, there you are. In a nutshell, that's Braunsweig. We've twenty-five partners, of which I'm one, and at present, we operate out of eight offices. Six of them are abroad. Now you won't need that brochure. I've said everything of any import."

"And said it very well. I know very little about the operations of banks."

"Simplest thing in the world. We buy money at one price and lend it out at a higher one, and try not to make too many mistakes in the process."

"And probably don't, not after five hundred years of doing it."

"We have our grim days and when we do we bury them as fast as possible. I hope you'll consider this bank as yours, if we can ever be of personal assistance," said St. Germain through another of his quick smiles.

"I'm sure you can be of assistance. But, frankly, I don't know where to begin. I was very surprised that Baster wanted me involved in this Muldaur

Trust. So, it's all quite murky to me. I'm what you might accurately call as eminently unqualified."

"*Au contraire.* Not in his view, at least."

"He was always exceptionally generous with his compliments," Thomas replied, slightly uncomfortable when noting St. Germain's intense scrutiny. His gaze never seemed to shift an inch.

"Yes, with one caveat. If he thought highly of someone or some particular thing, he would inevitably say so. And he knew how to pick his people. In this case, he picked you and reported commendable things about you. We took those to heart. Here, I mean. Braunsweig is the single permanent trustee of The Muldaur Trust, and the bank has appointed me to act as its proxy for the past seventeen or eighteen years. The Trust is in a new phase of life as you'll soon learn. Life, in the sense, that it is facing its death and we'll go into all that business while you're here."

"I gather it's extensive, the resources of The Trust."

"On the books, it's something on the order of thirty-seven billion Euros as of last Monday, I believe. The original cost of the assets was on the order of a billion or so in today's money. No liabilities of any consequence. If we were to price The Trust's assets at market, their value might be triple the number I just spoke of."

Stunned, Thomas believed it but then didn't believe it. "How can that be?" he asked, somewhat warily.

"Light taxes, old-fashioned investment policies. The Swiss way, and at Braunsweig we're as Swiss as Swiss chocolate. I would suppose it's the largest private trust in Europe. If there were one bigger on the continent, I'd imagine we'd have heard of it by now. And, of course, these holdings go back four centuries. Not the same holdings naturally, but the corpus of The Trust is always at work. Correctly and profitably, we hope."

"I'm astounded at the amount, the size."

"Sometimes, so am I." A wall clock chimed and St. Germain engagingly asked, "If you've no plans for lunch, we set a better than average table here. Perhaps you'd like to meet one or two of my partners."

"I'd be delighted, though I don't want to use up your day."

"You won't. Stay, and we'll find out together what the chef has created for us on such a gloomy day. Come along, and we'll have a look around." Smiling with an amiable ever-present smile, St. Germain extended his hand toward the door.

At 8:30 the next morning, he returned to Braunsweig and went directly to the room where he met with Pierre St. Germain on the day before. As instructed, Thomas made a call to the vault, a hundred-and-twenty feet below street level. Minutes later a gray-suited, cricket-like man with a face like a tomb-keeper, pinched and cadaverish-white, entered and deposited two black auditor's cases on the floor near the desk. Thomas signed a logbook, with the man then entering his own initials in an adjoining column, along with the date and time, before departing without a word.

A robotic moment.

Unlatching the brass locks, he eyed slews of papers, files, faded photos, aged parchments with crumbling red wax seals, and a quantity of manila folders.

Folder one held a certified copy of the primary trust document.

COMPACTUSMULDAURUS

Incabula per Fiducia

A.D. 1671

Written, as would be the custom hundreds of years earlier in Latin, a language in which he was well schooled. Hour blended into hour while he pored over the Trust's history, its burgeoning growth over the centuries, its enormous holdings, its carefully crafted investment policies.

Like reading a history book, one begun by a consummately successful robber on the high seas—Piet Friejjar-Muldaur I.

Politely advised to refrain from any note-taking, Thomas abided. Still, he possessed a retentive memory and filed away what he desired knowing, as he went along. He began to see why The Trust was such a massive secret, and thus massively concealed. He marveled at the pages and pages of covert maneuvers, and the role of The Trust in funding a good many monarchies of Europe in centuries past.

Came the second day and he started on the second case of documents. In its first folder, labeled No. 14, he found a monograph summing up the man who had begun it all, early in the seventeenth-century. Nearly it was in the same era when Ignatius Loyola, the Basque gentry-man, had founded the Society of Jesus. A rarity by itself: two more unlikely earth-shakers had entered the world-scene, forever changing it, or at least important aspects of how the future would unfold for centuries yet to come. One had founded a teaching empire, the other an empire whose only god was the one of wealth-making.

Piet Friejjar Muldaur. Born 1620 in the former Jutland principality. Of Dutch –Flemish parentage, he died in 1692 in what is now Cape Town, South Africa. Described by contemporaries as a ruthless, hard-driving seaman-merchant who had captained his first trading schooner at twenty-three, owning it a year later after marrying the daughter of the ship's previous owner, who Muldaur reportedly had killed in a dispute over voyage-profits. He sailed on commission for various merchants of the Hanseatic League, gradually acquiring a small fleet, then opening a trading house of his own with offices in Rotterdam and Hamburg. Five years later, he was elected as the youngest High Mightiness of the Dutch East Indies Company, and was soon posted to Africa, there to establish a maritime provisioning station in what was later to become Cape Town. He soon extended operations to Gao in India, then to Rangoon in Burma, and onward to the east China coast, gaining considerable prestige as one of the leading Asiatic purveyors in opium, silk, camphor, teak, tea (believed to be the first sea-trader to open up a regular tea-route between India and Europe), concubines, hemp, spices and fragrances, and caulking resins for ships.

Muldaur dueled with the British for control of the Malabar Coast (West India), and, though the Londoners were allied with the Sultan of Mysore, they were nonetheless forced to capitulate.

Thereafter, making plans to outflank other British interests, Muldaur established several trading ports on the Malacca Straights, forcing the archrival British East India Company to pay tribute for all of its shipping activities in the region. Somewhere near this time, Piet I took on the Portuguese sea-traders who were competing vigorously for the hugely profitable spice trade between Asia and Europe. Muldaur vanquished the Portuguese so roundly they were forced to either scuttle their caravels or charter them out to Muldaur, which, ultimately, was the decision they took, one that Muldaur used to great advantage.

Under the various auspices of Muldaur trading ventures, he supplied the Netherlands with untold access to rubber, tea, camphor, silk, ivory, gold, Burmese rubies, exotic woods and, later, oil used for petroleum products.

An old saying, dating from the 13th century, stated that whoever is Lord of the Straits of Malacca has his hands around the throat of Venice, at that time being Europe's most influential city-state. By his fortieth year, Piet Friejjar Muldaur was destined to become that lord. Vaulting so speedily up the ladder of Asiatic commerce, he made the name of Muldaur feared throughout the region, and it remained so for three centuries up until the time of The Great War when other forces made their presence felt, largely the lengthening reach of America interests. Diversifying its operations, in the late 1800s and early in the 1900s, Muldaur lands in the Dutch East Indies, mostly obtained by fraud, or sometimes by use of force, held huge petroleum deposits, discovered in 1913.These oil-bearing lands, at the request of the Netherlands government, were sold to (Royal Dutch) Shell Trading Company for sums aggregating four-hundred and twenty million in pounds Sterling. At the time, massive wealth, greatly adding to the Muldaur fortune.

Weary and a little dumb-eyed, Thomas put the document aside. An intriguing breed—tough, tenacious, far-seeing, who, combined, had gathered their riches in the dark, and sometimes at gunpoint. The Piets, one through six—had named themselves, one after another, like popes. All of the Piets, however, were sired at the onset by that original swashbuckler and sea-robber who had killed his father-in-law over money-splits.

Jaggy would likely, deify him. She had never said if she knew anything about the clan founder.

Needing fresh air, he left the bank. Nearly it was noon when he found Davidoff's, the famed tobacconist, where he bought seven Cohibas, a week's supply if he kept to his ration.

He legged it down to the lake, sat on a bench, lit up, and watched the noontime strollers. The Swiss, well fed, rosy cheeked, solid-looking, the women in their sensible shoes, the men in boxy suits, their world at peace, their lives comforted by abundance.

He observed them in their immense safety as he thought of The Trust…The Trust, and The Trust.

The enormity, the labyrinth of it all, boxes within boxes, like some impenetrable Chinese puzzle. Now taking on a life of its own, and now financially obese. Great good could be done in the feeding of Africa, in sending medical help to tribes that literally were starving, or, in some places, rotting away from disease. He had seen misery too despicable to repeat, not in Naruma but in lands to its north and west. Sickening, appalling, frightening.

Letting the sun warm him, he blew slow tendrils of smoke, savoring the taste of his much valued vice. He had given up cigars when hospitalized, but had recently succumbed again. Jaggy had bought him an extravagant humidor—inlaid with six exotic woods—from Dunhill's and had it filled with Cohibas, Partagas, and Montecristos. After that, he was sunk, a slave to the pleasure.

Back at Braunsweig, he delved deeper, learning of the exploits of Baster's ancestors. Folder to folder, reading along, pausing at times to reflect, Thomas discovered another world from a bygone time. Riches to more riches, and no rags in between. Crooks, builders, far-seers, gross sinners, and makers of benevolent works.

The Trust, he saw in one four-page spreadsheet, currently owned awesome chunks of Swiss industries. Chemicals. Pharmaceuticals. Textiles. Banks. An impressive list, its staggering value largely the work of Braunsweig's sound stewardship, keeping a solid percentage of the assets over the centuries in safe, solid Swiss investments. Yet, not entirely so, the Americas, Asia, and Europe were all amply represented in the Trust's portfolio.

A truly brilliant run of investment prowess, sprinkled with luck certainly, but transparently with much astute thinking.

No wonder, he thought, it was kept so confidential; what would the Swiss people think of all this concentration of ownership in their prime industries? Owned by one family, effectively, who were foreigners to boot.

Only three men were privy to the fullness of it. And, as there was no heir— a saga had now ended, and by an elephant, no less. Thomas looked away from the pages, pausing, while recalling that conversation out in the gazebo, with Baster, and Baster's plan to father a child with his own sperm and eggs filched from Cyro.

Everything pivoted on that—an heir—like the principalities of old, like the Monaco of today. Why had Baster not seen to an heir long ago? Lord knows he kept enough women and on more than one continent.

A puzzling affair. Political, too, now that the South African government stood to make a whopping gain out of it. A money fight loomed, if Jaggy had her way.

For the first time in his thirty-six years, he was relieved of worries about money. His annual trustee fees amounted to nothing less than a bonanza. Four-hundred-thousand in Euros. Nearly floored, hearing the number repeated when Pierre St. Germain had asked him if he wanted his fees transferred to a bank outside of Switzerland, or to remain here at Braunsweig. What could be better than here? He arranged for a quarter of his fees to be transferred to the Curia at Borgo S., in care of the *economico generale*. Done anonymously.

Gazing across the room, he felt a warmth blanketing him. Perhaps it was the soft sheen of the paneled walls, lighted subtly by a green shaded banker's lamp on the satinwood desk where he had been sitting, reading. Or perhaps it was because he was being accepted as a colleague, trusted to keep his mouth shut, and to help wherever he could. Something felt good, felt better, and he felt freer and less dependent, less like a fawning gigolo when with Jaggy. By his standards, he was rich. Manna had come his way.

Something clicked, then, and he picked up a pen and slid a sheet of pale blue stationery off a neat stack at the side of the desk blotter. At the sheet's top the name BRAUNSWEIG und SOHN appeared in raised blue letters. No address. Classy, in its understated way and so was much else in this temple of wizardry.

Dating the stationery, he began:

My dear Father-General,

An overdue note to advise that I'm quite alive, almost repaired, and grateful for the card you sent while I was out of commission. I am in Geneva at present, doing some homework on a project given me by Baster before he met his end so uselessly and tragically. For which, in part, I blame myself; it was I who had inveigled him on a safari to save a rare elephant. How devastatingly ironic that that very animal did him in, and nearly myself.

It indeed is a small world, as they say, and one of disarming coincidences. Here I sit, writing you, in this place to where I once sent account instructions for the Society from Borgo S. Not so long ago the simple notion that I'd be here in person would've seemed quite improbable, and yet so much has happened since last we saw each other in Rome that nothing seems either improbable or even impossible.

Pierre St. Germain says he's met with you before on two or three occasions. He reminds me of you in that he knows everyone everywhere. He is arranging meetings for me with several prominent foundations in America, with whom I intend to discuss funding for my "little pursuit". I say "little", for that is what it is, at present, an infant-sized dream needing a high-octane boost along with a great deal of work and some uncommon luck...

A knock on the door, and the keeper-of-the-cases entered. Thomas smiled back at what had to be the fastest, thinnest, frostiest smile in all Europe. Signing the log again, he watched as the man added his own initials, the time correctly entered, and he held the door as the phantom of few words departed for the bowels of Braunsweig.

Finish up with deMehlo—he told himself. Then call Jaggy. Yet, what could he say that he was permitted to say? Banalities, perhaps, but nothing else. She'd not settle for that, so the answer to that dilemma was not to call her at all.

His next to last evening he dined with the St. Germain's, father and son, the boy an engaging twelve-year old, and a smiler like his father. When coffee was served, St. Germain excused his boy and turned the conversation to biotechnology and Thomas's expectations of it.

As they talked, Thomas saw Pierre occasionally eye a half-length portrait of an auburn haired, distinguished-looking woman. She wore an aquamarine gown, with an ermine stole floating off one arm, then winding behind her and appearing on her other side.

"Join me in a cognac? A friend of mine in Provence sends me a case on every birthday. I suspect he does it to remind me of the finer French creations that we Swiss shall never equal. He's quite accurate when it comes to cognac." Then, the appealing smile again. "Noble of year, good nose, and what all. Have one?"

"The wine was plenty for me. Excellent, too."

"A Petrus. Poetry in a bottle and one of my favorites and it takes my mind off this damnable weather. Enough of a reason for me to swallow the entire bottle. A terrible summer so far. I don't think I recall a worse one. Won't change your mind? I'll vouch for its credentials. My friend knows his product."

"I pass."

Coming back from a sideboard at the end of the room, his hand gyrating a balloon-snifter, Pierre stopped on a square of blue marble floor in front of the fireplace. Flames danced behind his legs as the banker took a slug from the snifter, rolled his mouth and kept to a brief silence, as if wrestling with a passing thought.

"I invited you for dinner to bid you good-bye and to sound you out on something," said Pierre after a long moment. "Have a seat, please. I've a proposal some of my partners asked me to try out. We'd, like you to mull over an idea."

"All right."

"We've been looking for someone like you."

"Whatever for, may I ask?"

"Technical advice mainly. Insights we don't possess sufficiently at the bank. The big-think aspects, if I may put it that way."

"Seems to me you have a full corral of bright people. Loaded with them, I'd say."

"I agree, we do, but not always have the specialties we require. People tend to think banks deal only in money. That's half of it, that's the raw-material side. We have to know what we're doing, what we're backing, and to do that, or have any chance of doing it correctly, consistently, we must pick the right people to loan money to or invest in our money. To do that, we often rely on outside appraisals of new technology. What its chances are, what its drawbacks might be. These situations call for a feel, an intuitive sense of what the odds might be that a new product or service will sell, gain a regular market. We can take care of the money side. That's relatively simple. But are we betting the right way? A misnomer, for we never bet. We're not card players. We analyze and re-analyze until we understand a proposition, and then we move or we pass. But you always need access to the best advice available and that, often, and in certain fields, can only come from knowledgeable scientists such as yourself. Before I go to my main question may I ask something that has me a bit off center?"

"Anything you like."

"Are you still a Jesuit? Do I have that right? Some of my partners are Catholics, which is why I'm asking. They're curious."

"Yes and no. I'm waiting for my walking papers. I don't know if or when that'll be happening. Possibly never."

"Are you faced with any legal problems? Anything serious?"

"No. May I ask why you ask?"

"Checking facts."

"I'm clean. There's been some nonsense in the papers from time to time."

St. Germain nodded. "Well, newspapers never let facts stand in the way of good stories and improved circulation possibilities. You were a recipient of the

Waterman Award, and, I believe, at one time you were associated with the Pontifical Academy of Sciences at the Vatican."

"I was, yes, but only for a few months and then I was allowed to take a post at Cambridge."

"And I believe you're a member of the National Academy of Sciences in the U.S., is that right?"

"A recent member."

"I'm told you're quite young to be a member of the Academy."

"Somewhat so. But there are others my age."

"At thirty-six? Not many. I'd wager."

"People forget I had Victor McGlashen at Johns Hopkins and some other influential sponsors. People in the scientific community who aren't often refused. I got shoehorned in on the early side because I was working in areas that kept getting good publicity. And I happened to do a couple of things the United States Army liked, and the Army has money, and scientists are always anxious to get funding and, well...so forth and so on..."

Lowering his brandy snifter, St. Germain looked at it, pursing his lips appreciatively. "You make my point for me. You had top-rate endorsers who vouched for you. Your loudspeaker system."

"I'm not trying to be modest, but none of it is anything a banker would take as collateral."

"But a banker would take something else—he'd have a good look at what those memberships of yours represent, for example. The work involved, the achievement, the respect of one's colleagues. At Braunsweig we place more weight on performance than we do on a person's net worth. Sooner or later, we all run into some bad luck. Mistakes are made. We try to minimize them, naturally. You aren't a manager, a business manager. Your abilities lie in another direction apparently. We know you're well thought of by African Heritage. And you were highly regarded by Baster Muldaur, as I've said before. That you also belong to SOS is a statement in itself...oh, did I say something I shouldn't have?"

"I resigned recently from SOS," said Thomas, then told Pierre why, and ended with, "my sincere thanks to you. I'm flattered, but I'd never make it as a banker. I'm what they call a test-tube jockey. A bench man. And I like teaching. That's me and that's pretty much all of me."

"That's what appeals to us."

"Thank you, but I fail to see what I can do that'd make any difference. I'm committed to my own project. I could make some suggestions. There're good people in England. Germany and Japan, too. Mostly they're in America; the best of them are still there. Getting someone good...well, I dunno. If it's of any help, I can inquire around."

"You could never inquire the way Braunsweig can."

"I couldn't, could I?" Thomas smiled, amused. "There goes that idea."

"Think it over, why not?" Pierre urged, then said, "What's next on my list, oh yes, those foundations. I've made some calls and sent letters of introduction to several in America, as you asked. Copies of the letters you'll find on your desk in the morning. I think you'll get into see whomever you wish to."

"I can't thank you enough. Really, it's extremely kind of you."

"Easily done, I assure you."

St. Germain went back to the sideboard where he poured the other half of his nightcap. They talked for another half hour, mostly about Thomas's interests, the plan he was forming, the help he would need to get a lab underway, the possibilities of Zyme-One that had so excited him. That he lived it, dreamed it, hoped to line up a non-profit medical ally.

Thomas talked freely. He liked Pierre, was confident he could rely on his probity; that whatever was said tonight would go no further than the Braunsweig partners.

"At one point, St. Germain broke in, "I'd be glad to have you meet with companies here in Switzerland, if you'd like. I'm a director of MarocheChem, so I'm quite sure they'll see you."

"But they'd want what I don't want, a big profit out of it." Thomas raised both hands. "No, don't tell me, I know, I know. They're entitled to it. Probably they are, probably everyone is. But once, just once, I'd like to try it the other way and I don't want profit philosophies to get in the way."

"Business is profit, Thomas. Profit is what makes the tires turn."

"My business is healthcare at dirt cheap prices, and I'm going to go for it. I've seen awful, awful conditions in Africa. Terrible things. We can do better...we have to...and if I linked up with one of the big pharmaceutical outfits, I'd jinx my chances to succeed. They'd take what I had, or at least what I think I have, and run me out the back window."

He stopped there as a feeling of idiocy swept him. He sounded like someone on a soapbox, preaching. Who was he to remind the Vice-chairman of the International Red Cross about mass illness and catastrophe?

"Sorry," he said. "I get carried away at times."

"It's good that you do. It takes a plugger to make things change. Let's hope they don't change too fast, too soon. I saw you looking at my wife's portrait during dinner."

"I was, yes. I can see she is lovely."

"Yes, once she was stunning. That's how we like to remember her. Luisa-Marie. She's been ill these past five years."

"I've made a gaffe."

"No reason why you should know, Thomas." Pierre's mouth quivered slightly. "We had twins, girls. They were off skiing with their mother in Zermatt, and the girls tumbled into an unmarked fissure, perishing. Luisa never got over it. Wasn't anything sudden. But she simply descended into her own hell over time...we've gotten used to it, or I have, as much as you ever get used to something like that."

"I hope she'll come home to you one day."

"Not a chance of that, sorry to say. She's legally insane, and well—it's better for her to be somewhere where she can be looked after. Better for all of us."

"I can hope for her, anyway." He might've said pray for her, but he had surrendered that franchise, so he didn't say it.

As they moved from the room Thomas heard a piano from somewhere above the circular stairwell. The melody was *Satin Doll*, and he immediately recalled the Johnny Mercer lyric.

"My son," said Pierre, beaming. "He's quite taken by American music. Jazz particularly."

"Me, too. He certainly plays well, doesn't he?"

"Gets that from his mother," said Pierre. "She was a concert pianist. Superb hands. She taught him from an early age."

The memories must be devastating, thought Thomas, the past, and all its sweet beauty.

"Say good-bye to your boy. I can see how he'll turn out. You won't be disappointed. Well, Pierre, three words—thanks for everything."

"My pleasure. I'm off to Prague in the morning and won't be returning for several days. My secretary always knows where I can be reached. I'll leave word with her to find me if you call. Don't become a stranger and simply wait for one of our Trust meetings. I'd like to be of help." Smiling again. "There's no charge, not for a new friend. And do think of our offer, Thomas. There're worse things than having Braunsweig on your c.v."

Shaking hands near the front door, St. Germain seemed hesitant, holding on to Thomas's right hand as if trying to restrain him from leaving. Suavely, diplomatically, the banker said, "I quite realize you've signed your confidentiality agreement. Nonetheless, I feel it my duty to caution you…I've known Jaggy Muldaur from the time she was in her years as a teenager. I never underestimate her and trust you won't either. Bear it in mind."

Thomas nodded twice. "Say no more, Pierre."

"I speak of The Trust, primarily."

"I speak as someone who knows what it is to be bound to secrecy by the Seal of Confession. You needn't worry, ever."

Out he went into the ink of the night. A bank chauffeur clicked on a light in a Mercedes sedan, got out and opened the door. The sedan sped off and Thomas, settled in the rear seat, began to wonder if he'd spilled too much. In his enthusiasm, he had told St. Germain aplenty about the mystifying powers of Zyme-One. But then the banker had arranged those introductions to the American foundations, so was entitled to know some things, wasn't he?

Lights winked along the far shore of Lac Leman, as if they were sending Morse code through the night mist slithering across blackened waters. Back to London soon. Back to Jaggy, too. She'd be full of questions about The Trust, but he'd head her off, heeding St. Germain's cautioning words.

Before London, he had another stop to make, a necessary diversion to Cyro in Winterthur, a three-hour train ride to the other end of Switzerland. He had to bake up a batch of Zyme-One and take it to the States for demo purposes. Getting it through customs without a hitch. Like most countries, they would take a dim view of bringing in undeclared agricultural products; and *semba* was nothing less.

Yet plenty more, too.

With Thomas out of the way, St. Germain had returned to the fireplace, where he sat to measure the evening's outcome. The chessboard he presided over seemed to be enlarging, though something of a setback occurred when the American had refused the bait of a consulting arrangement with Braunsweig. It might've made things considerably easier. Too bad, that; in fact, it created yet another problem.

Trust business had brought Courmaine to Geneva, but other facets of his usefulness were now under the looking glass.

At a recent board meeting of MarocheChem, Switzerland's largest pharmaceutical company, interest had been expressed in Courmaine's alleged discovery. More, both Swiss delegates to SOS had jointly signed off on a report to the Swiss government, stating, in so many words, that Courmaine's concept, though baseless at this time other than all the media trumpeting, argued for more investigation.

Nothing to be lost, thought St. Germain, seeing advantages in making Thomas Courmaine a Swiss asset, though keeping him unawares. Even if the offer of a consultancy had been a flunk, things often had a way of changing. And, as Jaggy Muldaur had remarked, the man had no resources other than his trustee's fees.

Winterthur, Switzerland

Thirty-six...thirty-five...thirty-four...

At Cyro, Thomas's eyes awaited the second-hand as it swept toward the zero-point and he'd hear the timer's ping. Being excruciatingly careful with this batch of Zyme-One, in Africa he had used nothing more than a wood-fired stove and a sterilized copper cooking pot to extract from the boiling *semba* roots a slurry that, when treated, would eventually yield the enzyme—Zyme-One—after a series of warmings and coolings. A gob was all he needed; a gob went a long way.

He did all this in the way Ghibwa had once shown him, dicing the *semba* root into cubes, soaking them in water, boiling them, adding the boiled down reduction to a tincture of a plant belonging to the hazel family.

Spooning up a twist of the substance, kneading it into a ball, he smelled it; a smell like rotted milk. Smearing a bead of it on the back of his hand, he tasted it. It was exactly the process used by Ghibwa when first introducing Thomas to various exudates of *semba*.

Yesterday he had arrived in this small town of Winterthur, nestled against a curl of the River Töss, a short distance northeast from the outskirts of Zurich. Here lay the center of operations for Cyro, a leader in the field of cryogenics, the science of changing structures, or preserving most anything, at temperatures far below sub-zero. A year ago, he had arranged for a shipment to Cyro of the *semba* root, freighted to Switzerland via a Muldaur airplane. The gnarly roots were stored here under low-temperatures, along with the vast and growing collection of animal and human DNA, tissue of every description, blood scrums, sperm and ova collected by African Heritage. In time, and with a great deal more know-how, you could re-make the vanishing herds and, quite likely, and if necessary the humans who were decimating the great animal populations.

A goodly part of the Afrikaner race's genetic makeup was safeguarded here; and. added in, a wide catalogue of DNA belonging to two African native tribes of the southern region. It was precisely here at Cyro where Baster Muldaur had suggested that Thomas could harvest eggs of unknowing Afrikaner donors so as to create an heir.

By his hand, or someone else's, it might well have happened.

He could do it here and now. Baster had sperm stored here. All it would take was an egg or two, a dab of sperm, a petri dish and presto! Anything was possible in a world where discovery was so breathtakingly fast, just as St. Germain had noted two nights earlier.

At Harvard, they were growing human heart tissue out of cell cultures. Many mistakes, yes, but ere long they'd have it licked. At Stanford University, a top bioscience center, they were inserting human brain cells into embryonic mice—this, to study the workings of the human mind.

He wasn't so sure he liked that idea.

But it did intrigue him to think what would happen if a hundred of the dead here were brought to life again, years after they'd been cooled and preserved, and they were then to tell the rest of the world there was no hereafter. Heaven and Hell, all along, had been a farce. Not a one of the resurrected had found God or Satan anywhere.

How would Rome deal with that one?

Crossing the laboratory, he checked a temperature gauge, then laid out a couple of pipettes in a glass tray, and looked over at the timer again. Jelling nicely. Another thirty minutes and the gob of extract ought to be ready for its journey to America.

At a metal desk in the corner of the lab, he picked up the phone and talked to the Cyro operator, asking that a call be put through and to please track the charges. Three attempts later, he found Jaggy.

"But where are you, darling? I thought last night you'd call me. I did wait...you know…"

"I'm in Winterthur—"

"But I thought you were leaving Switzerland?"

"I'm here at Cyro. Clearing up a little chore."

"Cyro!"

"Cyro, yes."

"I've never been. What's it like? Cold, I suppose. Rather metallic, I also suppose." She was suddenly chuckling, whether at him or from some amusement, he hadn't any idea. Though he was aware a supply of Baster's sperm was frozen and stored at Cyro, he had not the slightest clue, not yet, that Cyro was a Muldaur holding, nor that the bone and mush of Baster's remains were frozen inside a nitrogen-filled steel cylinder not more than a hundred yards from where he stood.

"…It's very Swiss," he went on, "practical and efficient. You're right. It has a feel to it, like an intensive-care unit. Guess what I saw this morning? I was looking out a window and a Swiss military jet zoomed right out of the side of a mountain. Bang! There it was…then I found out they cut runways into the mountains and hide their air force in there. I'm getting a full schooling on air operations."

"You're there for that?"

"It's a bonus they throw in for the tourists. Very folkloric. Chocolate candy, private banks for the oil pashas, very expensive wristwatches, and stunt fliers that come out of the mouths of mountains. How can you beat a country like that, and they yodel. I might take that up—"

"Shush, when are you coming home?"

"Tonight, possibly tomorrow. I'll have to look up the flight schedules."

"I'll send a plane. Zurich, that's your nearest airport."

"Please don't bother. I'll fly—"

"Listen to me. L-i-s-t-e-n. We've planes…we use them…oh, oh I just had a smashing thought, Thomas. I'll fly down to Zurich, and then we'll fly to Paris. We've not been in an age—"

"Last month—"

"You're interrupting again…where was I, oh, there…I've a couple of things that need doing. I'd like a couple of things done to me, too. Perhaps by you." She slipped that in without so much as a lost breath. "Shall we?"

"Shall we what?"

"Paris, you booby. Let's do, darling. It'll be such fun."

"Jaggy, I've got a handful of letters Pierre's done up for me. I've got to get over to America and get going."

"My dear, my sweet. You were supposedly coming to London, remember? We'll switch things to Paris, and I'll bring all your new booties and undies. Boxes of them. I ordered you some luggage from Asprey's, and that'll come with me too. Leather and canvas. Your suits and blazers are ready. Exceedingly spiffy. I'll have Mercer pack everything…good, eh…all settled, yes?" And I must tell you about Poppi and Si…"

"Who're are they?"

"Si Nestor is in charge of Muldaur's North American operations. His wife is a dear, dear friend…Poppi…that's her name…Poppi. They'll look after you in New York. An office, that sort of thing. My apartment…oops, oh, a call is coming from Jakarta. I must run. I'll call back within the hour."

When the call ended—almost by itself, Thomas knew he had planted both feet on a banana peel again.

London, England
Geneva, Switzerland

An hour fled before Jaggy finally got through to Pierre St. Germain who had been tied up in the weekly partner's meeting at Braunsweig. Returning to his office, a sheaf of papers in his hand, ready to hand them to his secretary, he saw her raised eyebrows. Pointing at the phone, saying, "The Commandant awaits you." An old joke between them.

He took the call in his office. "Jaggy, sorry, I just walked in."

"Whatever is Thomas doing over there at Cyro?"

"I haven't any idea. I thought he was off to London. By the way, I tried to call you from Prague yesterday."

"I know. I'm returning your call. What do you make of my friend?"

"Attractive chap. Bright. A man with a quest. We were impressed enough to offer him a consultancy, which he declined. Politely."

"He is polite. What was your call about, Pierre?"

"We've fresh reports that Muldaur Ltd.'s interests in Zimbabwe are seriously threatened by the unrest down there. If they take over your Berkalite properties, this loan your people are requesting will be refused—"

"Then we'll go to Morgan or Deutchebank."

"You'll not do any better. We'd expected them to be in the proposed lending syndicate. Four billion-two in sterling is more than we can do by ourselves. There'll be four banks, if it can be done at all. I think we'll all have to wait and see what events dictate. Sorry, but there it is. And under the circumstances, you'll have to pledge real estate assets to collateralize the loan. No other way to do it."

"I disagree. Muldaur has never defaulted a loan."

"Muldaur was never under this sort of onslaught, my dear woman. You could lose much of everything you own in Africa. The banks won't touch those operations as collateral."

"Those bastard wogs. Every one of them ought to be nailed to a tree. It's thievery. Nothing else! They think they can get away with it now that Baster is gone. Well, Baster may not be completely gone and that's the next thing I'd like to discuss. I'm putting you on notice, Pierre, that one way or another I intend to have a bona-fide Muldaur heir. So don't you get any ideas about breaking up that family trust or hell will fling open its doors—"

"We've been all through this."

"I do not care to be interrupted, not even by you. This whole fuss is over an heir, or the lack thereof. It's always been about Baster's heir, but I need my own heir too. That's the crux of it, isn't it? No heirs for any of us. I'd advise you to listen. If you do anything to disburse the assets of The Trust, I'll go after you. I own Cyro, or I will when Baster's estate is settled. I can obtain Baster's sperm merely by signing a piece of paper and no one can stop me. Baster was thinking about an heir, and I'm doing the same. No one can stop me on that, either. In case you've mislaid your memory, Pierre, perpetuation is what we founded African Heritage for, and Cyro with it. And I'm perpetuating myself …"

Dead air. St. Germain held himself.

She sortied on. "If a child is made from Baster's leavings, we solve two problems. The Trust's and mine. One child answers for both. I'm set on it."

Thinking fast, St. Germain saw a glimmer of a chance; in an uncustomary sharp voice, he retorted. "This is your way of controlling The Trust?"

"One way. I've got another in mind."

"Which is?"

"None of your affair, Pierre. You all block me out when I ask my questions, and I'm choosing to do the same."

"This is hardly a way to encourage us to rustle up a multi-billion dollar loan."

"If you don't make it, someone will."

Leaning on her again, he went backward to the earlier topic. "If you—if you impregnate yourself, using Baster's sperm, and it gets around as those things often do, it'll make you look incestual. And tag you with all sorts of terrible publicity. Where is your judgment, woman?"

"In my head. You'd better ponder the situation. La-la…ta-ta and so forth." Words that weren't words but words that ended the conversation.

Baster, he thought. A corpse still with a pulse. St. Germain tried to gauge if her notion smacked of an attempt at fraud. Perhaps not. He ardently hoped not. If Jaggy could manage a birth whose child was provably Baster's offspring, much trouble could be sidelined. He knew her too well, and likely knew her better than she guessed. She kowtowed to no man. Pushing against her, as he had, would stiffen her resolve to produce an heir. She was headstrong enough to try, anyway. Indeed, there was nothing he could do to prevent her.

He was coping with other problems, as it was.

By law, when significant Swiss assets were slated to pass into foreign hands, the situation must be reported to the government. Blood had boiled as soon as he had advised the government Brahmins of Bern that South Africa was the sole residual beneficiary of The Trust. The trustees could dally no longer, a few months at best, before advising the South Africans of their stupendous good fortune. Otherwise, delays could occasion a possible blowback. Or ugly lawsuits, with Braunsweig in the middle of it all.

The Swiss technocrats wanted a better solution; and wanted those assets kept safe under Swiss control.

An heir solved everything if Baster were the other half. Whether by hook or crook—done in the dark, done any way imaginable. Just done!

Jaggy owned leverage and she knew it. If no heir, then she could always tell the South Africans, for a price and a heavy price at that, that Switzerland sat on a bonanza to which South Africa was entitled. Down there she was accepted as a Muldaur, had access to the top, knew enough about The Trust to induce that government to begin inquiries.

Genuine risk was afoot. A free-fall mess, with highly embarrassing implications and the specter of mammoth legal damages levied upon Braunsweig.

St. Germain felt as if his balls were in the grip of a nutcracker. Noticeably, he trembled. Noticeably, his face moistened. Noticeably, his head began to throb.

And now that Courmaine was in the fold, could he be relied upon? Talked to, persuaded? The man owed no allegiance to the Swiss, and neither did Jaggy Muldaur.

New York, New York

P aris never happened.

Instead, they had flown directly to Deauville, there to watch a weekend of polo matches. He had felt the burning itch of Braunsweig's letters of introduction, tucked away in a brief case. He wanted New York to begin, and he wanted to begin himself, too. All he could think about was making presentations to eager-faced foundation executives. In Deauville, barely had he withstood the flying hooves of polo ponies or the rounds of parties and receptions, champagne by the bucket, strawberries with *cream frasche* by the keg, omelets filled with caviar, raucous dinners lasting till midnight. The goings-on were wasted on him. He did his best, wore smile after tired smile, trading in trivia. On their last day, Jaggy unboxed and re-packed in four suitcases a small mountain of new clothes. Bespoke suits he had been fitted for in London, blazers, Sea Island cotton underwear, custom-made shirts, a dozen silk Charvet ties, monogrammed silk pajamas (which he never wore) and sundry accessories. A full-fledged popinjay. He could not say no to her. The only *no* in him was to decline to accompany her back to London; a weeklong stay, she had suggested, and a dinner she had in mind for three new members of Parliament.

Breaking loose, he had flown to New York.

In the States, his first several weeks had passed in a blur: Los Angeles, San Francisco, Houston, Chicago, Miami, Boston. Back and forth, thousands of miles of zigzagging flights. Lost sleep, lost appetite, serial turndowns. The foundations he met with were backers of medical research, their stated missions. Yet it seemed any projects not already ordained by the medical establishment were dead on arrival. A myopic outlook. Never in all his door-knocking was he given a straight answer as to why his idea didn't merit a tryout. Not a single foundation offered to sponsor a trial experiment.

Nothing for it, except to plod onward, and keep rekindling his hopes as he awaited a break. It seemed as if Zyme-One was hexed, that it was never meant to find its place, nor excite the same interest if held for him. Like selling a horse that had no teeth, he had begun to think.

After his road trips he'd return to New York, his base of operations where he was allowed use of an office at Muldaur—North America.

On an afternoon, having just returned from Chicago, a call came. He was asked to return to Boston for a second visit with a Dr. Miles Bascomb, head of Forbian Foundation, known for its grant-giving to medical and healthcare causes within the New England region.

A second shot, things might be looking up. Excitement churned; optimism glimmered; and he drew a deep breath.

Boston, Massachusetts

Miles Bascomb's secretary had instructed Thomas to join the doctor at The Somerset Club, a sanctuary of the city's social elite, located on Beacon Street directly across from Boston Common.

Thomas, admitted to the premises by a porter, found his host up on the second-floor observing a backgammon match.

The game suddenly ended with a round of whoops, excited chatter, and some currency changing hands. The onlookers turned toward the bar, and, Thomas, who had been standing off to the side, caught Bascomb's eye.

A friendly wave by the doctor, smiling, as he came over. He extended a bony hand that trembled its way through the space separating them. "Standin' there all by yourself. Why'nt you come over and watch with us?"

"It looked much too solemn for any interference. Solemn until the cheering began."

"Boys are warmin' up for the club championship," Bascomb replied in his front-porch, Louisiana manner. "Everyone gets a real punch out of it. Let's find you a drink of somethin' or other. What'll be yuh pleasure this evening?"

"A Coke would be fine. Lots of ice, please."

"I keep a stock of valid bourbon here. Twenty-five years in the cask before they allow it any circulation. Smoother'n that glass bottle it comes in. You don't imbibe, I take it?" Bascomb asked, looking at Thomas as though he needed counseling on life's other delights.

"Sometimes. Not tonight, though."

Bascomb nodded twice to himself as if making up his mind about something. "Coke, it'll be. Twenty-five years is a long time," he said reverently. "You won't mind if I partake?"

"Not at all, no."

Thomas drank thirstily as he watched the bartender measure out Bascomb's drink. Two slugs of bourbon, straight, then a sprinkle of sugar, a dash of crushed mint, with a Maraschino cherry added at the end. A southerner's drink. The doctor himself was monkey-thin, making his tired out face look out of proportion. A face worn beyond endurance. Its protruding lower lip was scoop-like, fleshy, decadent-looking. Riveting dark eyes that always seemed glassy as those of a sunning iguana.

Casual talk ensued, about the pleasant weather blanketing New England for the past weeks, the coming winter and Bascomb's intentions of spending his in Bermuda where he kept a second home. Standing apart from the others, the idle conversation took on a different meaning as Bascomb probed Thomas about the years in Africa. From there, talk swung to the three Mzura women with Bascomb peppering away with his queries.

"I sound like a police office, I s'pose," Miles Bascomb said at one point.

"Almost." Saying it, Thomas smiled. But the drift of the conversation was not what he had expected.

"Hungry yet?"

"Whenever you are. I'm in no particular hurry," Thomas replied, smiling again, looking about, absorbing the Federal-period ambience of The Somerset. High ceilings, beautiful trey paneling, groups of leather furniture, framed copies of important Massachusetts public documents fixed to the stark white walls: one, a centuries-old copy of the Mayflower Compact. The club was Boston at its upper-end of male life.

"They're fixin' clams and halibut off the grill tonight. Please yourself, though. The food is good as clubs go. I'll just have another little tail of that bourbon and we'll find us a quiet table. Have another cola?"

"No thanks, I'd be floating."

"S'alright," said Bascomb, approvingly. "You have friendly manners and I'm disposed toward any man with manners."

Midway through dinner Bascomb laid out his reasons for asking Thomas to return to Boston. Bascomb coughed twice, fidgeting, his hand trembling again before divulging that Forbian Foundation must regretfully decline Thomas's request for funding and a working alliance. They had, however, appreciated Thomas's candor when advising them of his turndowns from Rockefeller, Ford, Howard Hughes Medical, Sloan-Kettering, and three smaller foundations.

Forbian voted to pass on the project for three reasons; one, they didn't fund overseas projects, and Thomas had indicated he had planned to do his work somewhere in Europe; two, his proposal—in their view—was something that ought to be tackled by the government, or a large drug company; three, they felt his resistance to patenting any discovery was a counter-productive idea.

"No one does that, not ever," Bascomb insisted. "Not even the universities."

A disheartening summary, jarring Thomas. Even for a slow-talker like Bascomb, the words had come in an uninterrupted spurt. Rehearsed, Thomas thought: all this could've fit into a succinct e-mail. A waste of his time. But he was soon to find out that, if the dinner was in many ways a disagreeable hour, it would turn out as one of the most instructive interludes of his entire life, then and forevermore. He, a single entity, was up against a fortress-like phalanx; and, as a card-carrying idealist, was arrayed against hardened profiteers.

A feather in a windstorm.

"Course you can always ask for reconsideration," Bascomb was still explaining, "but I don't think it'd help too awfully much. I suppose you're upset'n'all at having to come all the way up here from New Yawk just to be told we can't see a clear way at Forbian to help you along."

"It's not a long trip here from New York but why not a phone call or a letter?"

"I might have somethin' else to interest you."

"Would it make any difference to Forbian, if we did our work here? Somewhere in New England? I'm flexible on that point. I'd chosen Europe first since it's closer to another responsibility of mine."

"No sir, I don't think it would help." Bascomb forked in a morsel of halibut, then continued, "I'm curious about what you're going to do with this idea of yours. But what's this other responsibility you mention?"

"I've been appointed to help oversee a family trust. One of three overseers."

"What trust is that, if I may ask?"

"A trust I don't discuss with anyone, doctor."

"Al'right. What do you do next if the foundations won't back you up?"

"If I can't get it on stream somehow, I suppose I'll be sending out for the hemlock bottle," Thomas replied, half-laughing, half not. "To be frank, I don't know exactly. What I need is traction and the right way to get started. I can't do what it is I want to do by myself."

"Few could, and I don't know any of them. You don't think your plan is somewhat radical? Inventin' some way to give gene therapy to millions of people free of charge? That's near too radical as it ever gets."

"Different, yes. Radical, well, maybe to you it is. Everything is different than it was even five years ago. Even last year or last month. In science, it is. You would know certainly."

"Ever cross your mind that the foundations who specialize in medical research might not like your idea because downstream it could threaten other work they support?"

"I've been heartily warned to expect resistance. I've been trying to overcome it, without success as you can tell."

"But you keep asking away."

"Of course."

"I see. How much money can you lay yuh hands on"—the Louisiana accent coming on stronger as the whiskey worked its way—"that is, if you don't mind my askin' so personal?"

"A few million perhaps."

"It's not yuh money, I assume?" Bascomb prodded.

"Not mine, no. I'm not wealthy, I'm a church mouse or I was until recently. But I cannot back this idea personally."

"Yet you have access to funds."

"If I want them, yes. But as I've said I need an alliance that can command attention with the National Institutes of Health, World Health Organization, and so on."

"These funds you mention, are they from the Muldaur people?"

Surprised, Thomas answered, "That's really not your business, doctor."

"Don't be abrupt with your elders. It's not seemly."

"Don't ask that kind of question and I won't be so abrupt."

"And yuh wanting to do all this work of yours on some pro-bono basis, or other? No patents? No licensing? No profit-making?"

"Correct. Nothing has changed. I mean to be able to provide the genetic remedies free of charge. Free is important, to me it is. Free or as close as I can get to it being free. I say it over and over. What else can it be? The part of the world that needs what I hope to develop is painfully short on doctors and drugs and everything else that we take for granted here and in Europe. They haven't any way to pay for it except with goats or maize. Not much of that, either, as I'm sure Forbian knows."

A nerve jangled, warning Thomas. Why the questions, the sharpened interest, he wondered, when Forbian had already rejected his proposal?

"Well, son, no one can say you haven't worked up a head of steam." His droopy-lipped mouth twisted into a sideways smile.

"Me, I like things that're new, doctor. People laugh but I'm reasonably sure that one day you can fix most illnesses for about two-hundred dollars a person, and you'll be fixing them for life. Maybe less than two-hundred. It'll take time, of course, to bring that about but I think I can shorten that time. The right team and we'll pull it off. I've done it already or something like it, as you know. And now...well, now...the next step. That's where I'm tracking anyway."

He stopped. An old refrain by now, in his head anyway, a belief so solid in him it was as reflexive as a parrot reciting a learned passage of words.

"Care for a lick of coffee? Some brandy?"

"I would, please. Only the coffee, no brandy for me."

Bascomb waved to a nearby waiter, ordering coffee and a double brandy for himself. Fixing Thomas with another granitic look, he started in, "I'm in a mind to do you a favor."

"Thank you. What favor is that if I may ask?"

"Explainin' to you how the scorecard gets marked. You might've forgotten, then again maybe no one ever told you. You did your studyin' under Victuh McGlashen at Hopkins, I understand?"

"I did, much of it anyway."

"Victuh, now there's a prince of the profession."

"The best."

"Maybe he ought to sit you down again, Thomas Courmaine. You're talking about curing any number of diseases, hundreds, thousands, and circumventing the medical profession in the process. Mebbe you're not actually talkin' about it, and yet it sounds as if it could turn out that way. Yessir. You can imagine what that'd do to the medical folks, if you succeeded. Closing hospitals right and left, closin' medical schools, you'd be ruining the lives of thousands of folks. Well-off folks, too, or many of them...those doctuhs are. So you're asking us at Forbian to work up what amounts to a threat to the medical community. We support them. We nevah pick wars with them. We're not out to break their rice bowls. Why, son, how'd you feel if you were one of them?"

Bascomb waved a forefinger around like a street-evangelist trying to save the world from itself. Louisiana oozed out of every pore as the face stiffened, reddened; whether from the alcohol or irritation, Thomas couldn't tell.

"I'm not out to injure anyone," Thomas argued. "That isn't my intention at all. It never was, never will be."

"Doesn't amount to a tinker's damn, if it was or wasn't your en-ten-shun. The short of it is plain enough for a blind man. Exasperated, Bascomb then asked, "You heard of The League, have you?"

"Baseball, you mean, or football?"

Bascomb delivered a pitying, patronizing gaze. "Medicine. I mean. That League. The biggest League. The capital L-league."

"I've never heard of that one."

"I'm goin' to do some speakin' now. Best you listen, and you might help yourself."

With gathering fascination, he did listen as Bascomb ladled out the background on how The League had been stroked into life in 1910 by the Rockefellers and Andrew Carnegie, heavily aided by the seminal work of the Kentuckian Abraham Flexner, another Johns Hopkins man, who was a groundbreaker in medical education, also a noted co-founder of the Institute of Advanced Study at Princeton. The depthless wallets of the very rich, together with Flexner's nimble brain had acted as midwives easing the birth of the new era of American medicine, and taking the long view of how it was to develop. They could afford to take their time, solidify each step of the strategy, ensuring its success, and guaranteeing huge profits for the approved participants. In so doing, they had changed the makeup of the entire profession, accrediting the medical schools, fixing the curriculums, limiting the number of degrees handed out, ensuring that the "right" laws were enacted in every state, and with the necessary regulations to enforce them.

An industry was thus spawned by two powerful, super-rich families—the largest, most profitable industry ever conceived of: Pharmus, as it came to be called. And The League, its hidden guardian, was still in existence, even if little known.

A flawless plan flawlessly executed.

Bascomb halted, licked his lower lip, then sipped from his refilled coffee cup after dosing it with a jigger of brandy. "See how it was set up, how it all works?"

"Somewhat. Is this league connected to the AMA?"

"Indirectly, you could say." Bascomb's eyes hardened as he said, "You may have somethin' and you may not. Let me fix you up with Merck or some other company. You'll be glad of it. I hope yuh understan' what ah is sayin'."

"I'm beginning to wish I didn't, and I can reliably inform you I won't be joining the cheering section any time soon," said Thomas, then pressing his host, "has someone asked you to speak to me?"

Bascomb wiped his mouth, looked away a moment before shifting his attention to Thomas. "You might say I took it upon myself to bring some enlightenment to you, son. I hope I did."

"Very charitable of you. What you're suggesting is if I cooperate, then all will become a walk in the rose garden. But if I refuse, I get spiked. Am I on the mark, Bascomb? Doctor to doctor?"

"I'd say yuh' a quick enough study of matters."

"I think I better say thanks for a very good dinner and a very disturbing education if that's what it was meant to be...no, please don't get up, I'll find my way out."

Bascomb nodded. Even with the liquor he'd taken in, his eyes were unwavering, and durably agate -looking. "Sorry you don't like the music, but ah'm tellin' you the truth. Nothin' personal, you look like a fine young fella. Yuh lookin' a little discouraged, too."

"Believe me, I am. Several weeks of it."

"Tomorrow, this'll all look different. We'll talk more. Yuh got a fine, fine future, so hold on to it. Never regret it, yuh won't, I can assure yuh."

"But, you see, I would regret it. Very much, I would."

"Ah can also see yuh'll never go down in history as a man famous for taking good advice. Here's some more. Go down to Bethesda and talk to the NIH and see what they make of it. If they get interested, then Forbian might have another look."

"I've been planning a trip there. Maybe I'll jump it ahead on my schedule."

"Talk to a fella there with the name of Raab. Murray Raab."

"Yes, I already know Murray. I was an intern there when working on my doctorate."

"Ah know you know Murray."

Thomas surveyed his host for a time, then said, "You or someone must spend a great deal of time checking up on me."

"Yuh a person of considerable interest, as they say," said Bascomb in a raised voice.

Thomas stood finally. "Good bye, Dr. Bascomb. I ought to thank you for telling me who not to climb into bed with. But I'm not thanking you except for the dinner, as I said. Probably the last one you and I will ever have together. Good-night to you."

Outside, he tarried while taking in the evening air and he began to assemble his reactions to the past two hours. What was this League business all about? Really about? What was Bascomb up to, other than issuing veiled threats to expect difficulties and snags and outright opposition? That seemed to be the nitty-gritty of the evening's fare.

A fresh notion cropped up as he reached one corner of Beacon Street, searching for a taxi.

They must think I have something, or why waste the time, and why all these scare tactics? They must want the Zyme-One know-how. How strange, too, Bascomb had him linked with Muldaur and why had Bascomb made efforts to find out he was already acquainted with Raab, whom he intended to be seeing shortly? He crossed off the witch-eyed Miles Bascomb on one list and added him to another, the one that told of people he didn't care to see again.

Well, he thought, I did some checking of my own. Had learned that Bascomb had racked up a commendable record himself. A professor at Tufts Medical School, and who had had, before retiring, surgical privileges at Mass General. Bascomb had once served as vice-chair of the Massachusetts Medical Society. He was among the top dogs at Forbian, its chairman emeritus. Thus, Establishment, up to his ears and then some. Nosy, too. Also filled with self-importance. And, generally, a pain in the canetta. Bascomb, however, had to be in the know about a great deal in the medical world, but why take the trouble to warn a bench scientist lurching from one ditch to the next?

Had he chosen to, Miles Bascomb could've supplied Thomas with many more facts about The League and even a glimmer of what the future held. For years, he had served as The League's "point man" in New England. As such, he wielded considerable influence in various legislative and professional matters affecting medical activities in northeastern America. In the pecking order, he stood well above Raab but not as high as others.

From its inception, The League had designs to remain off-stage, be intricate, be final and powerful and far-reaching. The League, as the igniter, had spawned Pharmus over decades from a cluster of small companies to the largest industry in the world, bar none. It did for Pharmus what Pharmus could not do for itself; it kept a useful rein on the U.S. Congress and in many state legislatures by adroitly peddling fear, dispensing bribes via jobs for family members of elected officials, as well as providing election support for the chosen, and, finally juicy retirement packages to suborned government employees.

Operating barely within the law and sometimes skirting it, The League's actions went unchecked; this, aided by a battery of well-connected lawyers including two of the best known criminal mouthpieces in Washington. Hired, among other reasons, to keep the prying eyes of the Justice Department at bay; other protection came from powerful committee chairmen in the Congress, also on the "sweet payroll."

The League had locked up the votes of 17 U.S. senators, together with a bloc of 76 representatives in the House. These legislators came from states or districts where, vote-wise, they faced election troubles. The betting was they'd not be in Washington had it not been for The League intervening with media experts, poll-takers, and top speechwriters who could sculpt issues out of thinnest air, embroidering them with era-catching phrases that sounded wonderful but could never stand much in the way of scrutiny. When needed, which was with discouraging frequency, investigators were hired to expose the peccadilloes of rival candidates...as often as not leading to marital breakups.

The League had also built a cleverly veiled recruiting operation, ferreting out key players in the federal bureaucracy. Two-hundred and thirty-nine mid-level and senior bureaucrats, bought and paid for, were sprinkled throughout the Federal Drug Administration, National Institutes of Health, Health and Human Services, Department of Agriculture and other Washington realms.

Leaving government, these loyalists saw their pensions tripled and a home bought in their own name in any place of their choosing. An act wholly illegal but as unreservedly effective as it was hard to discover, given that all transactions were funded through a League-controlled bank in Liechtenstein.

On other fronts, The League bulged its muscles through a wholly-owned Milwaukee publishing company that put out thirty-one monthly medical and pharmaceutical trade journals, buttressed by the slick efforts of a p. r. firm that doled out press releases and feature articles on behalf of doctors, nurses' associations, hospital workers, and, of course, Pharmus itself.

A greenhorn, Thomas Courmaine had been advised where and how to align himself; make the smart play, and where to find the lanes to speedy success. What he knew nothing of whatsoever was what to expect from a secretive juggernaut, if he desisted and refused to play ball.

Thomasville, Georgia

Waiting two full days, and part of the next, Miles Bascomb had hoped Thomas would bend to the winds of reality. Not so, it seemed. Bascomb made a call, rather excitedly, and on day four after the dinner with Thomas, he was in Georgia as a guest of Boyd Tarrant at Tarrant's 2,000-acre quail plantation. Long famed for its mild winters and superb hunting, Thomasville was Tarrant's winter retreat.

Tarrant, a retired drug company chieftain, had long been an industry leader and spokesman. To his credit, he had authored the plan for member companies of Pharmus to give free products to the needy, who would otherwise go without. It earned the industry a good many huzzahs, and Tarrant rode a wave of personal popularity for his brainchild.

He had journeyed far in life. Born in western Nebraska, the son of a railroad brakeman, he had attended a pharmacy college on a partial scholarship, supplying the rest of his needs by working odd jobs. Graduating near the top of his class, he had since never looked back. He had had his share of luck, to be sure. Still, his rocket-like advances were characterized by hard work, unbending perseverance, all fueled by a winning sales personality. His career had taken a sudden leap when he married the daughter of a vice-president of Eli Lilly, a known and respected drug company. Thenceforth, the stars seemed to shower him with their illuminating dust; thusly, he was marked for the top rungs of the pharmaceutical industry.

Upon his retirement Tarrant had been persuaded by his peers to lead the five-man "working group" that made industry-wide policy decisions, soon to wend their way into the ears of those who bossed the American pharmaceutical industry—Pharmus. The League, in this capacity, served as a conduit. Old competitors, well known to one another, off on fishing and hunting trips, golfing, sailing as they exchanged the usual political stories, traded jokes, tidbits of the industry's gossip, launched ideas, contrived plots out of earshot of unwanted listeners. One way or another, it presented a convenient, workable way of dodging anti-trust and restraint of trade allegations from the SEC, FTC, and the Justice Department.

On this particular Thursday morning, the sun beaming though the breeze-swayed pines, the ambient air feather-soft, Boyd Tarrant and Miles Bascomb sat on a flagstone terrace drinking coffee.

Tarrant, having digested Bascomb's sum-up of the dinner with Thomas Courmaine asked, "Is this fellow a socialist? Something on that order?"

"Sumbitch's is a do-gooder, is what he is. We can be damn sure of that, Boyd. Got those stripes all ovuh him. Real fervent, you might say."

"You say he won't deal with any of our members? You'd think he'd jump the moon to have their help," Tarrant observed. "I find that odd. Very odd. Unnerving, too." His head suddenly went backward as if he'd just been rocked by a punch. "Well, we've dealt with a few of those before."

"Doin' it all for free. Or the next thing to it. That's what he said to me. Be some helluva fix if the government ever gets behind this. Be everywhere before yuh know it. They might, the way Washington is fustigatin' over the health reform and all."

Tarrant rubbed a tender spot near his hairline, the vestige of recent cosmetic surgery for sun damage from long days on the golf links and in the shooting fields. Wondering, he said, "And he's in with that Muldaur crowd? The old man's dead."

"I'm told he's connected somehow. Lot of money there, they say."

"We're missing something here. We don't really know if he really has what he says. Apparently, he withdrew from an SOS invitation to speak again. Maybe he got ahead of his headlights, and it's all a lot of hooey."

"Could be. Surely could. But he doesn't strike me as that sort."

In quiet they sat until Tarrant decided to speak. "Well, Miles, I'd say we keep our ears glued to the ground. You say he's pretty well soaked up his prospects with the foundations. For certain, he has at Ford. Yet they were interested, I'll concede that. A lot more impressed than I hoped they'd be. I find that to be of some concern, too. Drossberg's SOS report is worth reading, if you haven't already. I'm told by Ford Foundation's Director of Science that Courmaine's claims are possible...actually more than possible, especially if one credits the story of those African women. Drossberg endorses that motion. So do two of Merck's microbiologists. We cannot ignore the possibility that he has what he says he has. I suppose that leaves us with the Muldaur people. Why do you suppose Courmaine is hustling his story in the U.S. when he has friends like them?"

"Can't help you there. One bright mark is he thinks he might head down to NIH one day soon. He worked there once in some capacity. Intern, I think. I urged him to make the trip."

"You didn't mention the NIH angle."

"Hadn't quite gotten 'round to it. You movin' pretty fast for me, Boyd. Yuh always do."

"Who's that fellow there? Our man?"

"Raab. Murray Raab's his name. I talked with him over a month ago, telling him to keep his eye on this situation. We got ourselves a lucky draw on that one. He knows Courmaine."

"Oh, right. Yes, Raab. Odd duck, I heard."

"Competent. Slow as a week in jail about some things but he generally knows what he's about."

"How do we know he'll go to Raab and not some other place in that colossus?"

"It figures he would. One thing is he already knows him. The other is that Raab's the one who directs all the special research projects at NIH. The new ideas and so on. It's logical."

"All right, Miles, talk to him. If Courmaine contacts him, tell this Raab to set up a meeting. To play along, but not too anxiously. Lay out the bait and see if our fish bites."

"I'll pass the instructions," Bascomb agreed. "Anything else?"

"Tell that fellow Raab to find out everything he can. Everything, and to the last period and comma. But to be careful about how he goes about it. He ought not to be too anxious to appease Courmaine. Put a boulder rock or two in the road."

"Ah'll make sure he understands."

And for a long and considering moment the men looked at each other. Judgment had been pronounced, its finality, if unspoken, grasped by both men. Bascomb would handle Raab, ensnare Courmaine, see what he had to offer the world. The short of it all was simple enough—milk him dry of what he knew, done. Tarrant would accept nothing less, if any chance existed for The League's interests to be challenged. Yet it was early. The budding affair, for the time being, was disposed of as far as he was concerned. He wanted Bascomb's thoughts on candidates for the number-two slot at the Department of Health and Human Services.

A prime opportunity had come to the fore to position another League *aficionado;* and Tarrant, who took his job most seriously, meant to begin the steps for choosing a man or woman in tune with The League's aspirations.

Tarrant was nothing, if not expedient. Courmaine was in his pigeon-hole till further notice; now, it the moment had arrived to set the gears in motion for infiltrating anew the higher ether of Washington decision-making: where the money was doled out, and to whom, and the action or inaction was resolved.

Tarrant was a master at gaming the system in Washington. He knew who controlled which buttons, and how to push them.

"Have a look at this list, Miles. Three Harvards are proposed, you know any of them?" Tarrant handed over a scrap of paper, sat back, and swirled his coffee with a monogrammed silver spoon. One of his prized English setters came up, nuzzling Tarrant's free hand; within the hour the dog would be larking about in the fields, scouring up for coveys of unlucky birds.

Not a good day for certain unsuspecting quail; nor for Thomas Courmaine, either.

Boston, Massachusetts
Bethesda, Maryland

"What ah can impart to yuh is this," said Miles Bascomb on the phone to Murray Raab. "Our man with all the fire in his belly, yuh hear anything more?"

"We will, I assure you. He called and said he'd call back for a date to fly down from New York."

"Treat him with courtesy, Murray. But don't appear to be too anxious. Hook him up and play him along, you see. You grasp that, Murray, I'm sure you do?"

"Totally, I do."

Putting down the phone, Raab doodled a note to himself, a reminder to have the Courmaine file sent over from *NIH*'s massive archives. There'd be the articles he'd had published from earlier times, plus the nearly eye-popping reports datelined from South Africa, and possibly added data about the enzyme theory Courmaine had been touting in *Nature*. The Milt Drossberg memo was also in there, summarizing Courmaine's remarks before SOS.

Pondering a moment, Raab then picked up the phone again.

"Alexis, it's Murray Raab here. Fine, fine...and you? How're you fixed for lunch tomorrow or the next day? You are, eh? All right, Thursday it is. Plan on a couple of hours...oh...I, see. Well, then an hour or a little more. I'll come by to get you, and we'll go off-site somewhere..."

And so it began, the crosshairs now shifting ever so slightly, in search of the target. Ever so swiftly, too.

Alexis Anne Hazlett sat at her metal desk two buildings distant from the administrative offices where Raab hung his hat, though she'd never seen him wear a hat. To her, Raab was an everlasting comedic sight, with those yellowish beaver-like teeth protruding whenever he opened his mouth. It simply tickled

157

her whenever she saw him, inducing her to wonder, if, like a beaver, he'd do a dive if she tossed a minnow at him. If the idea seemed ridiculous, so also did her encounters with the man, which, more and more, verged on the ridiculous.

Curiosity itched at her. Raab mentioned lunch—what was that all about? An off-site lunch, at that, the notion of it twitching at her nervous system. Another attempt to hit on her, was it? If Raab only knew her situation, maybe he'd mind his p's and q's and go away.

Two levels up the line, Murray Raab was her boss; indeed, her uppermost authority. In her wild hopes, she thought that possibly he was going to say he'd give her back the investigators he'd robbed her of, bringing her work to a near halt.

Two months ago, Raab had had her two assistants reassigned. Temporarily, she'd been told, well, what a laugh. A dismal, contemptible laugh. Temporarily could mean for the rest of the year or even forever. So short-handed now she was forced to shelve her main research projects, which, in any event, were drawing to an end, unless her grant was renewed. But it was Raab who was in charge of that turnstile. She had learned about the loss of her investigators when returning from a five-day break at Rehoboth Beach, over in Delaware, and finding her lab deserted. Until then, she had led a three-person team engaged in advanced studies of restriction enzymes. Restriction enzymes were the be-all when manipulating genes: with restriction enzymes, you could cut and paste genetic material endlessly. Keeping the changes in place was another proposition, but the cut and paste capability was vital to genetic engineering. The team had been making strides down a promising path till Raab had yanked the carpet and cut her small staff. Ever since, she'd been limping along, her hands tied, worried silly her grant would not be renewed.

No grant, no lab; and possibly no job.

Raab's game was easy to compute: either she gave in to his pathetic advances, or she faced the possibility of being dumped. She felt her eyes well up. Good at her work, very good, but he had stopped it cold, without notice, without mercy.

Over the past three years, Murray Raab had hit on her at least ten times. Evading him politely, making tut-tutting smiles, offering little jokes, reminding him once or twice that he was married. Saying she was already involved with someone. An affair with the beaver was so dreadful a notion, it made her gag. Still, he kept accosting her, insinuating, none too slyly either, that, if she were to come across, her life could be jump-started again at NIH.

Several times, she'd been tempted to file a harassment complaint yet where was her proof? Who'd stand as a witness? There were none, *dammit all!*

As flared as she got about Raab, she kept her own counsel. Patience, she told herself whenever her spirits sank, and patience was about to repay her. In the next two months, her world would swing on a star, brought about by a bedazzling revelation.

What had happened to *K'masa-ne,* in Naruma, the Eve who'd been injected with a chimp's skin genes, was very close now to being reversed. A case of the right time and right place, and now fate's needle was pointing toward Alexis Anne Hazlett. This time, it would be her own skin genes acting to modify certain skin genes of a mouse, which would bear the name Peter. One day, albeit in the future, Alexis Hazlett's name would become something akin to a rock star in the world of bio-engineering, appearing, as she would, in a cascade of science articles. She hadn't a vapor of a clue, naturally, that her days of stardom were yet to be counted—in 2014—when her *mojo* would sail skyward.

Still sitting there at her metal desk in that lonely, forlorn lab, caught up in momentary dreams, she nonetheless pined over her plight. Was deeply pissed. Alexis had no idea her bell was just about to be swung by a man she had heard of, yet never met. The exquisite irony of it all was that the beaver, for whom she knew limitless wrath, was the one who would be introducing her to her liberator.

New York, New York

Entering the building on Hanover Square, Thomas, in hurry, made for the elevators, nearly colliding with Si Nestor. Nestor ran Muldaur Ltd.'s operations on the North American continent. Mainly they consisted of mining activities in Canada and the western U.S., coupled with large-scale commodity trading operations dealing chiefly in strategic and precious metals. Trading-wise, Muldaur ranked as the number-one market-maker in the Americas, possibly as second or third in Europe and Asia. Nestor, a garrulous warm-hearted man, had taken an avuncular interest in Thomas ever since Thomas had first arrived in New York, providing him with endless courtesies and a pleasant patter of Jewish humor if their paths crossed during the day, or at their twice-weekly luncheons whenever Thomas returned from his junkets.

Nestor had arranged for Thomas to rent a four-room apartment in Grammercy Park vacated by a Muldaur executive temporarily assigned to Hong Kong. The apartment, a steal at two-thousand a month, was, for Thomas, a more acceptable arrangement than taking up Jaggy's offer of her duplex at the Waldorf Towers.

Si was conversing with someone Thomas didn't know, and, awaiting the elevator, he kept to a respectful distance. Finished, Si came over, pounding Thomas on the arm with a sledge-like blow.

"You got the best shirts I ever saw. Who stitches those for you?"

"Some shop in London. One of Jaggy's places. How're you today?"

"Never worse. So, you got news for me? Anything break, yet?"

"Well, I was in Boston a week ago. Another swift kick in the rompers, and then I was dutifully sent on my way. Then at the Pew Foundation in Philadelphia, a couple of days there and another third-degree, and got back late yesterday afternoon.

"So, any luck?"

"Strike outs.

"You know how it goes"—Nestor shrugged—"takes at least ten years to become an overnight success. So, now what?"

"I dunno. A kick and a kiss, that's life." Laughing thinly.

He was unconsciously absorbing Si Nestor, who was laughing that braying laugh of his, almost the sound of a mule. Short, but barrel-chested, Si had a wrestler's build. His broad smooth brow capped by wiry steel-gray hair. He had a paralyzing grip, even with one thumb missing. Legendary for his energy, he worked a killing schedule even after two bypasses for a heart condition. With a mind that worked with the precision of a diamond-cutter, Nestor was a prime force among the leading traders anywhere, and in his specialty—precious and strategic metals—he was celebrated with awe.

"I got a ring-a-ling-ding about you," Nestor offered as they entered the elevator door.

"Oh?"

"From the Chair herself. She was down to Jo-burg a few days ago. Flits around like a butterfly, that woman. Asks me how you're behaving, wants to know if you're learning anything, wants to know if you'd rather use her place at the Waldorf, and if not then why not. Wants to know if you know how to tie your shoes. You're a boychik. You know what that means?"

"Roughly."

"About forty different questions, I get. Maybe I missed somewhere that she's your nursemaid. Call her. Today, call her. If you please, that is. A note was placed on your desk yesterday to call her before she calls me again. Got time for a coffee? Guatemalan, pretty good." Si asked him as they got off the elevator at the eleventh floor.

"You bet."

He walked along beside Nestor on a thick hallway carpet woven in Portugal. They went past the word-processing pool, past the offices of other Muldaur executives, past the small dining room reserved for the higher-ups. They came to Si's corner office, glassed on two sides with views out to the harbor, Staten Island, and the great seaport known as New York, though rarely was it thought of as a port. Polished teak wainscoting wrapped the lower walls on the other two sides of the spacious office; maritime art filled one teal-painted wall; the fourth wall held a lighted, half-length portrait of his wife, Poppi, a one-time comedy actress on Broadway.

Si Nestor crossed directly to his desk. Slipping on a pair of reading glasses, he picked up a folder, flipping pages quickly, perusing the trading report from the close of business at midnight past.

"Not so bad yesterday. Not so bad," muttered Si, putting down the folder. "Poppi wants you over to dinner. She told me to tell you. She's got a friend coming over, a nice girl. She's my friend, too. A very deluxe bubee, I'm nuts for her. Poppi's little sister almost. What's Tuesday like for you?"

"That's a law class night for me."

"Forget the class. One night, you can forget the class. You'll like her. She walks in the room and all the air is sucked out. One of those. She's like that Italian, Loren, only without the cantaloupes." He lifted his cupped hands to his chest, eyed them, shaking his head. "A handful is enough. She doesn't even have that. Takes to blond guys, so you'll fit like a glove. The perfect goy."

"I'm supposed to be attending those classes. They're doing me a favor as it is."

"You're not gonna make me tell my Poppi that you refuse? Not coming? It'll rock her. I'll fire you," he said to Thomas who began to laugh.

His wife, Poppi, a close friend of Jaggy's, was a mothering jewel of a woman. She and Si had one child, a daughter out in Hollywood trying to make her mark as a television producer. So far, tough sledding. That the daughter was out west, instead of in New York, was a sore point with Si who didn't like the idea of his little *shatz* too close to what he thought of as an out-and-out racket. A wilderness of feeble-mindedness is how Si viewed Hollywood.

"This friend of ours, the dinner-lady, she's in p.r. You got any idea what they charge you to get your name in the paper? You know anyone nuts enough to want that? Poppi's in there. All those charities of hers, and I'm in the poorhouse half the time. I'm starting the Si Nestor Charity next month and get some of it back. We accept money in any form."

"I'll contribute. This lady, has she a name?"

"I didn't say? I didn't, did I? Two names. First, is Shandar, the second is Bazak. Iraqi. A Jew, like us. Her father was a famous doctor, very famous. Her mother a Sassoon, you know who they are? Big. They made Shanghai happen out of a goddam fishing village. Originally from Baghdad, that Bazak family. The Sassoon's, too. Merchant bankers. Smart. You're gonna like her. Lovely kid. What about Poppi's dinner?"

"Say no more."

"You want the coffee?"

"I'm okay, really."

"I can't drink it anymore, the caffeine. But they bring that thermos every morning. Wanting to tempt me, I guess. Tempt me, catch me and tell Poppi.

Never trust anyone, kid. Never. That coffee comes from Indonesia somewhere. A Muldaur plantation. I'll have some sent over to your place."

"That's all right, Si. I eat out mostly."

"Don't say I never made the offer. I always offer."

"And I appreciate it."

"One more thing about dinner. Very important. Ever since the last time my heart quit ticking right, Poppi's making me sick with this starvation program of hers. Like I'm on prison rations. I'm in big luck if I get birdseed and skim milk for breakfast."

"You look fine."

"That's on the outside. Inside, I'm a graveyard. Inside, I'm like cracked glass. I'm telling her you want a standing rib roast. Right? Those women think all you got inside you is a heart. The roast and we'll have everything else with it. The Yorkshire. Mashed Yukons. I'll tell her you want it. A special request."

"If you say that to her, and I'll sound like the rudest guest in town."

Si grimaced. "You won't do favors for your pal?"

"Anything Poppi wants is fine. The chicken was superb last time."

"Chicken, he says'—a theatrical roll of the eyes—"Chicken. You sound like my mother. She's gone a long time. No chicken, if you please. Any more chicken and I'll cluck."

"I think I'd better stay out of this."

Si laughed again. "You got makings in you, kid. That's what I tell Poppi. She's lulu about you, you know that? I'm keeping my eyes on you two."

Age-wise, Poppi Nestor could technically qualify as Thomas's grandmother. Thomas laughed and Si laughed with him.

"Your friend. You said she's from the public relations field?"

"Meric and Morris. Selling illusions, wha'd'ya think of that? Magicians with words. The bullshit's higher than Mount Rushmore. Higher even. Meric's one of the biggest. So dinner Tuesday, am I right?"

"What time?"

"Seven. Six-thirty if you're drinking anything. You're not a drinking man as I remember?"

"Seven or before. I'll be there. Poppi won't mind if I send over flowers?"

"Mind? Mind what? She'll adopt you."

"I'm switching signals. How would I find out about something called the League? Capital L. It's some sort of organization and it's possibly connected to the American Medical Association. Or connected to the large drug companies. A political arm, or maybe something more."

"Never heard of it. I'll ask Shandar."

"Who?"

"The morning-glory who's coming for the meal Tuesday. I just handed her to you, I thought. Are you listening?"

"How would she know?"

"I haven't any idea. She'll dig it up, believe me. She shudda been a private dick, except, well, we won't go into that. You want I should ask my doctor about it?"

"If you would, thanks."

"You're welcome. The roast, right?"

"The roast it is, Si."

"And don't forget to call Her Highness. Get the hell outta here. I gotta get my day started."

One floor down, entering the trading room, Thomas waved at a few faces as he crossed the floor to the small office he occupied. The room clamored like the controlled howl at a football game. Exciting, electric, and much like the trading room he'd seen at Braunsweig in Geneva, full of greenish computer screens, flashing lights on consoles, calls going out and coming in from all points on the globe.

At the front of the room, high enough so everyone could see it, was a long black electronic board. Liquid-crystal numbers of red flashed on and off like summer fireflies, as price quotes changed instantly for thirty metals and forty or so commodities, wheat, corn, soybeans.

The traders fascinated him.

Of another custom, they had their own special vocabulary, a high-spirited bunch and worked as though they'd all been raised in Siberian salt mines. Irish, other Anglos, Italians, a few blacks, many Jews, some women, mostly youngish men—in their late twenties and thirties. They swaggered. They boasted. They were tough as shock troops. They told jokes that might shock a dockworker.

He sat down, saw the note about Jaggy's call. He reached for the morning's copies of *Barron's* and *The Wall Street Journal*. He read an article on how the U.S. Patent and Trademark Office was announcing new rules making it more difficult to obtain patents on human and non-human genes in the face of 30,000 new patent applications on genes alone in the previous year. Recently, he had seen another article in *The New York Times* on the search for genes that controlled aging, something he knew that Zyme-One could contribute to, in lengthening life. Then, a piece about a religious group, the Raelians, who were attempting to clone a dead girl; possible, he supposed, if you tried it enough times, and were hugely lucky. He was again reminded of Jaggy's persistent questions about cloning: her many, many questions.

He flicked a button and the monitor screen on his desk lit up. Tapping in a PIN-number, he could see details of his trading account flash into view. Already, he showed a profit of $106,345.91 for his forty-eight days of active trading. Like a winning lottery ticket, he thought.

Si advised him. So did two of the traders Si put him onto, men in their mid-thirties, who, sixty or seventy-percent of the time, seemed uncanny in their ability to call the upticks or downticks of various strategic metals. They'd put Thomas's account in play, sometimes for only a few hours, and in that short space he might rack up a profit of almost $10,000 and losses on other transactions of, say, $6,000 or $7,000. Never consistent, day-to-day. On most days he came out ahead. He entered another access code on the computer, permitting him to engage in actual trades, and bought two palladium contracts on margin.

Consulting his new nickel-plated pocket watch, noting the hour, he dialed London. He spoke to a receptionist, then to Jaggy's assistant, then waited, waited more.

Thomas was about to hang up after five straight minutes of holding on to a voiceless phone.

"You're there, darling, are you"—Jaggy's voice breathy—"are you? Oh, I came as fast as I could, way down the hall. Trying to shoo a column of bankers out the door. Out the bore-door...are you all right? Are you? I miss you, Tommy...Thomas, I mean. Please speak."

"I'm listening to you."

"So you were, so you were. Now speak to me, my darling."

He did, giving her a rundown of the last week or so since last they had talked. Nothing new, he told her, and what was new was not very exciting. In fact, discouraging, "...but I'm doing gloriously in the market, thanks to Si and a few other fellows around here. You could probably spend it all in three days."

"Oh, shush. I'm on a strict economy drive. Dreary but necessary."

"What's the news out of Africa?"

"That they can go diddle themselves, those goddamn gangsters. It's what they are. Dirty black bastard villains. Ought to be shot out of hand."

"Sorry to hear it."

"Sorry isn't the word. Not by half. Shall I come to New York for a few days? Wouldn't you like me to?"

"Better not. I'm trying to set up a date with Bethesda—"

165

"Who is she? Beth? Who's Beth, Thomas?"

"Beth-es-da in Maryland. It's a town adjacent to Washington. That's where NIH is located."

"N-what? Never mind. I'm glad you're making a little money. Listen to Si, he's exceedingly smart about trades. Baster thought he was the best in the world."

"I'd bet on it. I *am* betting on it, aren't I?"

"Are you miserable without me?"

"Miserable isn't the word." There *isn't* a word, he thought.

I'll come over anyway. You can use the plane whenever you need it, to Beth...to, oh hell, you know where. I can do my work out of our NY office, I should think, what?"

"I just don't know if I'll be here. And I'm two nights a week at Fordham Law School."

"Nights are eight hours long, darling. I hope they don't keep you there until dawn."

He laughed, abruptly, nervously. "Then come, sure. Jaggy, I've been meaning to send a check for all these clothes. You've got to give me those bills."

"I've no idea where they are. They're paid, so why trouble your handsome head. Think of them as a birthday present for all the birthdays when I never gave you anything. You'll be here for Christmas? Still coming? I insist you do."

"I'm hoping so, Jaggy. Hoping."

"You're coming. No hoping about it. We'll go to Paris or Wales, one or the other or possibly the Seychelles. I've a superb beach house there, I rarely use. I'm counting on you. I'm not going to be alone. If you can't come over, then we'll have Christmas in New York. That's the plan, isn't it? *Isn't it?*"

"I've got to run, Jaggy—"

"Say it, say it, darling."

"Say what?"

"Say darling, say love, say honey-bell, say doodle-head, say something..."

"My dearest pet. My friend from all corners. My beacon on the stormy sea of life."

"Have to yank it out of you. A yank from a Yank, with a capital Y."

"Hugs to you, Jaggy. I'll be in touch. I'm to have dinner with Poppi and Si in a few days. Any messages?"

"No, thank you. I call Poppi every few days, as it is. I have to save my news or we end up repeating ourselves....bye, darling man, bye, double bye."

"Bye to you." And he looked for a long moment at the receiver before he hung it up.

Thomas busied himself reading reports on various strategic metals, then let himself get swallowed by his law textbook. As a favor to him, and his membership in the Society, Fordham, a Jesuit-run university, allowed him to attend a class at their law school. It was only one course and it dealt with patent law and licensing rights. He wanted only a feel for how it worked, how rights were established, the controlling case law, the principles underlying the existing laws. He kept a legal dictionary so he could look up the terms of reference he had never before had an opportunity to learn. The terms expressed in Latin were a snap and came easily. He had been well drilled, as a Jesuit, in that dead language. Even so, the reading of the law was a struggle, often dull going, but usually informative.

Hours passed.

At one point, he punched in his PIN number on the console's keyboard, checking the numbers in his account. He saw he had racked up $3,678.23 on this day's trades. A pittance by the standards of even an average Muldaur trader, but for him a bonanza.

A small lab was rarely out of his mind's eye; a million, the minimum to get one started. The thought, a magnet. He decided to stay on, work the markets, make a reach for his first ten-thousand dollar day.

Soon he'd try trades on his own, instead of taking the professional's guidance. A born chance-taker, he'd be happier on his own. He was getting fond, even addicted to the excitement of making bets all across the world. And if he could ever manage it, he would do his work here in New York, conduct nonhuman experiments, work up the proofs, get them checked out at Columbia or Rockefeller University, then write up an article for *Nature*. But he'd somehow have to retrieve that supply of *semba* stored at Cyro, then bring it into the States. A problem for another day. But that ought to do it; that, and a million dollars. He'd be on his own, wean himself from Jaggy, and establish a sensible life for himself.

Brooklyn Heights, New York

A brisk evening and Thomas rode a taxi to that far-land of Brooklyn Heights, facing lower Manhattan from across the East River. Si and Poppi Nestor's home. Si, able to afford whatever he felt like, chose the Heights because nearby, near Flatbush Avenue, was where he'd been born and raised; a cold-water tenement, his home till he entered the Navy at age seventeen.

Thomas pressed the bell at the side of etched-glass door front, and was greeted by a plump, smiling Hispanic maid. She relieved him of his Burberry and showed him up one flight to the living room. Si and Poppi sat on either side of a fireplace, laughing about something. A white-coated houseman passed a silver salver of canapés.

"Don't get up, Si. Hello Poppi."

Thomas went to them, nodding to Si who he'd seen that afternoon, and taking Poppi's hand, pressing it lightly.

She was as original as they ever came and Thomas had thought the same thing when first meeting her. Poppi Nestor had a look to her, had her own signature ways. Seventy, at least, and still she wore blood-red lipstick. Her shoulder-length hair was white as surgical cotton. The red fruity mouth, the platinum hair were set off by the black of her beautifully cut pants-suit and the patent leather pumps on her slender feet. A band of velvet wound its way around her fleshy throat; in the band's center, an impressive marquis-shaped diamond winked as if flirting with its spectator. She was quite different in her ways, too; her writings, letters, invitations were inked with a goose-quill pen, and in calligraphy. She would allow no one else to wash her undergarments— so Si had said—and when traveling over to Manhattan she engaged a rheumy-eyed old black man, for whom she had once bought an old-fashioned London cab. The chariot, Si called it.

Poppi Nestor talked like who she was—a straight, no nonsense Lithuanian-born but Brooklyn-raised woman of considerable moxie.

"You lovely man," she had said when he had taken her hand. "Orchids, he sends!"

"*Mon plaisair, madame*—orchids for an orchid, that's what the florist said."

"Listen to him. You could take a few lessons, Si, and I wish you would." And then to the houseman, "Ernesto, bring drinks for our guest. What can he fix, Thomas?"

"Fizz-water. Seltzer. Anything like that."

"And with what? Scotch?"

"With a lemon peel and lots of ice, please."

"He never drinks, either," Poppi said as though she were talking to someone invisible. An elegantly thin hand lifted, and, in a theatrical gesture, splayed itself across her bosom.

"I'm just thirsty, Poppi. Otherwise, I'd have a double Daniels."

Her head swung back and forth—"I know an abstemer when I see one. Is that a word, abstemer? It is now. A blessing, you don't drink. Si, here, he drinks triples. He says they're not but he's too far gone after eight o'clock to know what they are. Ever since he's a director of Seagram's, twenty years, more than twenty...God, *it is more*...and he drinks like we're having Prohibition next week again."

"And for a nasty crack like that," said Si, rising, "I'll have Thomas's share and my other share to go with his. I require an anesthetic. I was telling Poppi we went down almost twenty-million today, that's at five o'clock. I'm afraid to call in and find out what the book says now." Si glanced at his watch as he got out of his chair.

"Keep your seat," Poppi scolded.

"Quiet. A guest," Si noted, with a smile.

"A man your age. Why don't you retire, like you knew how sanity is spelled? Crazy! It is crazy, all that stress! Losing your hair, and twenty pounds overweight with those lunches and—such a *macher*, he thinks," Poppi allowed in mild despair. "A walking *vitz*, that's Si Nestor. Sit, Thomas, sit by me. Hold my hand again. You're always so warm. You know something about Si? His elevator doesn't go all the way up, and he doesn't know it...here, sit..." She tapped the adjoining seat cushion.

Thomas had dined here on two earlier occasions. He enjoyed the couple immensely, drawing deep comfort from their hospitality. He got a kick out of their bickering, always within bounds but sometimes nearing the edge. Si Nestor he knew as a rich man with a rich man's prerogatives, but without a rich man's profligacy. He did keep a sixty-foot cabin cruiser that he often used on weekends for fishing off Montauk Point on eastern Long Island. He golfed at his club in Lawrence out on Long Island's south shore. He avidly read mysteries. He supported the Metropolitan Opera, which he attended twice during the season, and was an ardent Yankee fan, keeping a season box in the first row behind the dugout. A generous patron of Jewish charities and to others that weren't Jewish. Other than his pastimes, and Poppi, he confined his active life to Wall Street trading, looking after Muldaur interests in North America, the occasional backing of Broadway theater productions, regular get-togethers with his friends at the Century, playing one set of gin rummy before lunch as long as the market was treating him right that day.

Si rejoined them, his freshened drink in hand. Ernesto returned with Thomas's iced water.

"You know what an avalanche is?" Si asked Thomas.

"Something I always stay out of the way of."

"For me, it's two avalanches today. Twice, not once, I get smothered."

"Oh? Serious?"

"Serious-serious. This nut-headed government in South Africa, they forget who they are. What they want is to ruin us. A no-good goddamn crowd of goniff socialists. Every time they open their mouths, a disaster for us."

"Jaggy says the same thing. More or less. Maybe more, now that I think of it. Can't someone reason with them?"

"You got a better chance of a blow-job by the Mona Lisa—"

"Simon Nestor! Listen to you, and I won't," Poppi protested. "Shame to you."

"How can anyone listen? You listen! Those people, fart-headed. Slow suicide, that's what—what it's doing to us, and the margins? Nothing left for us. They'd be looking up their black asses down there to find their brains and—"

"My God, Si!"

"Poppi, a grown man's with us. No children tonight. I gotta day here that's flattening me. I have to get this off my chest before dinner."

"Thomas is a priest! A priest, and you go on like that."

"A priest, you"—he looked over at Thomas—"I'm loving this. And we're fixing him up with my calendar girl. We're inventing a new sin or something. Thirty-million down in the market and we got a goy priest to take care of. You oughta go back on Broadway, Poppi. We could do a show on this..."

His face settled into a satisfied grin as he winked at Thomas who was watching Poppi vault out of her chair. "Oh, well, later," said Si. "But nudniks, and you watch what this'll cost," taking one last shot to relieve his anxiety. Exasperated though smiling, and seeming to be perversely enjoying himself.

Thomas felt Poppi go by him, making that rustling sound women make when hurrying somewhere. She headed toward the room's entrance, holding out her arms.

Si's nice girl had arrived.

Ten feet away…seven…and then about four as he took in her huge gypsy-dark eyes. Thinly hammered, gold hoops dangled from her ear-shells. Dusky skin, arched eyebrows, raven hair, Arabesque lips shaped so perfectly they seemed carved out of pink wax. She was lean as a gymnast. Thomas's eyes filled, his face as startled as if a leopard had just padded into the room.

"Shandar, darling, meet our new friend, Thomas. Thomas Courmaine."

He drew enough breath to make his voice heard. "They weren't kidding when they said you were right out of a seraph."

"Oh, boy," she replied, the smile faint but her eyes lighting up. "A seraph? I never hear that word anymore."

Noticing the puzzled look on Poppi's face, Thomas explained, "From a band of angels."

"A darling, isn't he?" Poppi vibrated in delight. "And so nicely mannered," she quickly added, sending Si an askance look.

Thomas could smell Shandar's aroma, fruity or flowery, yet was unable to place the fragrance wafting toward him. And then she said to Poppi, "I came straightaway from work. I haven't changed. Haven't stopped all day, haven't been out of meetings. I need the powder room and a vodka-rocks, in that order. I can't tell you what a day this has been, not in mixed company, anyway. I'll be right back…Si, are you all right?"

"I am now, chickie baby."

Smooth as a swan, Shandar faded from the room. What a particularly lucky night, he thought, anxious for her return.

Poppi had observed everything. "So?" she asked Thomas, her brow lifting.

"So lovely. So striking. Now, I'm out of so's."

Poppi chucked his chin. "And so you be a nice boy to her."

"Poppi, you're being a busybody," Si intervened. "I'm starving, so what's for dinner and when is it?" Goading her, smiling and happy with himself now, he said to Thomas, "Well, this part is complete. Everything is better in pairs. Especially with women…the tits, the round cheeks of their—"

"I'm asking, Si," said Poppi, plaintively. "No more, huh! Nothing more, Si Nestor, is what I'm meaning. Nothing!"

"I was only going to say I personally consider Miss Bazak the perfect Jewish holiday home companion." Si nudged him. "Did we do you right, kid?"

"A very pretty lady."

"That's all?"

"That's enough," Thomas replied, wondering about the scent she wore. Lavender? Rose? Something enticingly fragrant.

"And what a tail assembly...belongs in the Smithsonian, eh?" Si was saying.

Poppi shot her husband a sizzling look only a split second before the swan glided back into their midst.

"What am I missing?" Shandar asked, turning a little as Ernesto handed her the vodka-rocks.

"Nothing, poochie, not one bit of anything," Poppi trilled. "Here, sit here." Patting the sofa cushion as she had earlier for Thomas. "We'll have our own talk." Looking at Si, as she continued, "He's recovering. One of those days he's had and he says anything...very disturbing. A grown man, he thinks of himself."

At dinner, they sat on the glassed-in, heated terrace overlooking the East River. A breathtaking view and it carried across the light-flecked waters to the darkened towers and caverns of Manhattan's financial district. Wind gusted against the terrace glass, rattling it, and occasionally rain spattered. Si behaving with magnanimity. He got the dinner he wanted, Chateaubriand, cut thick; then a salad; two vegetables, cherries jubilee for dessert, followed by Jamaica-bean coffee served in cut-crystal tankards.

Idle, pleasant talk, sometimes hilarious. Other conversation touched on mutual friends of the Nestors and of this darkly lustrous vision, whose name—Shandar—sounded to Thomas like a brand of exotic aromatic oil. He was still trying to place that scent she wore. Jasmine, he decided.

At moments, they had avoided each other's eyes; and then, crossing glances an unspoken message was composed in mid-air.

Poppi kept eyeing him, smiling, knowingly tilting her head subtly toward Thomas whenever Shandar was engaged in talk with Si.

For a sociable hour after the meal, they chatted, and then Thomas stood and thanked his hosts.

"If you're leaving, then I better run along too," Shandar said.

"I've got an early morning, but I hate to be the one who breaks up the fun," Thomas said. "Thanks for including me. Double-thanks is more like it, the dinner and all else."

"We can share a taxi, if you're headed for Manhattan," Shandar suggested. She rose, patting Poppi's hands, then came over to buss Si. "Nifty time," she said to them. "I'll see you Sunday at the Mendelssohn's, won't I? Will I?"

"Poppi you'll see, not me," Si said. "I'm golfing."

"We'll both be seeing you at the Mendelssohn's," Poppi contradicted.

"For two minutes, and then I'm headed off for the first tee," Si countered.

Saying their goodnights, Shandar and Thomas gathered their coats downstairs, went out, and found a cab three blocks away.

"Get a feeling that you're being thrown at me?" Shandar said to him after they had arranged themselves in the backseat. She gave the driver her address.

"I've been wondering what the landing would be like...sorry, I suppose that's a smart-aleck crack. But, frankly, I never expected anyone like you. Si's got you on a moon-throne. You're at the front of the family scrapbook."

"Poppi's a dear. My matchmaker. It happens every few months. Are you embarrassed?"

"No, not a bit. Does it ever take, her match-making?"

"Not yet. But a girl can always hope."

"I wouldn't think you'd need much help in the hope department." Then a devil drove him to say, "Not many women can walk into a room and wreck it without touching anything."

She made a clucking sound. "That's as good as I've heard in weeks, and I'm in the message-making business."

"Si mentioned you're a public-relations whiz. Mer-what? Help me."

"Meric & Morris, of the chosen and champ-peen image-makers. We do saints, sinners, everything but politicos. There, we give up. Poppi said you're here only for a while. A few months or something."

"Going on three months. Longer than I had expected."

"Enjoying yourself?"

"I've been away from the States for several years, so it's a nice change getting back here. I'd never spent time in New York before. But otherwise I can't say it's been any smashing success. Long story with what promises to be a fast ending."

"Si said you'd been living in Africa?"

"I spent a couple of years in the southern part. A place called Naruma. Hardly anyone knows where it is, and even fewer go there. They don't encourage outsiders. I had to bribe my way in...well, not quite. Someone did the bribing for me."

"Are you going to be working with Muldaur in Europe?"

"Not at all. They're lending me an office and steering me around so I can find the more glorious landmarks of the city. You being a topmost example. Si's really been wonderful. Poppi too. I see a lot more of Si than I do her."

She looked over at him and once again he was struck by her face; even in the dim light he could see the arresting profile. "I've been asking you things I already know," Shandar said in a throaty voice. "Poppi told me you were coming to dinner and she is…well, she scouts the male population of New York and decides who I should get to know. It can be a little awkward. Forgive me, it's just that I didn't want to sound like I'd already asked a hundred questions about you before we even met. Actually, I know quite well who you are," she confessed, "Poppi sort of filled me in and, after that, I looked you up in Who's Who in Science. I also read about you in the newspapers a few months ago. Quite an impressive story."

"Parts of it are. Other parts I'd soon forget."

They had reached the Manhattan side of the river. The cab swung into the ribbon of late night traffic heading uptown on the East River Drive. Trying to sense her in the dark, concentrating on her voice and what the voice might reveal about the workings of her mind.

Shandar moved the conversation backwards." I read about ten newspapers every morning," she said. "Not cover to cover, but the main news stories and sometimes the features. The columns, too, of course. Five or six months ago, you were covered for about a week in some important metro papers. Others, only for a few days or so, did you know that? I suppose you must've known, so why do I ask?"

"Must've is the right word. Don't remind me. Once you're in the papers you think it'll never stop. It gets aggravating."

"Is it true? My curiosity is unquenchable."

"You're referring to the women?"

"The women and their skin, especially the skin. I'd love to get a piece done on that. In *Time* or *Newsweek*. I could too. Not the women, just their skin changing."

"Thanks anyway, but I'll pass."

"But it was true, am I right?"

"Yes."

"To you, how did it feel when it happened?"

Like I'd invented daylight, he thought. Slow to come up with a reply, he kept silent. For all he knew Swiali had utterly lost his mind again and put to death the three Mzura women after the press had created its ruckus in Naruma.

Swiali would have waited, bided his time, but he was as likely to eliminate them as not. Thinking about it, upset him.

"How did it feel?" he asked himself aloud, answering her. "Like I had discovered sugar or something like it. Mostly I amazed myself, and that's what I remember most. Like the first time you ride a bike all by yourself. You're shaky but you're thrilled...where do you live, did you say? I'll drop you off and then go on."

"Seventy-second. And you?"

"Gramercy Park."

"Then you will have to drop me off. We've already passed the turn-off for Gramercy."

"Good, I'm liking this. Does your firm represent Muldaur?"

"No. Muldaur doesn't deal with the public, per se. They're industrial and trading. Mining, too. But I personally help Poppi with her charities. She's a dynamo. She must run half the charities in the city, and Si, too, and of course he is Muldaur-connected. That's why I wondered if you were in the same line of work, so to speak."

"Nope, I'm free as a Montana eagle. And that's very nice of you, by the way."

"What's nice?"

"That you do all those charities with Poppi. It's really a nice thing to do."

"I meet a lot of people at those events. The mucky-mucks and some of them end up as clients. My efforts are not all for charity. We don't work for the Muldaur interests but we do work for the South Africa government, or their national tourism department. An account of ours. And Muldaur helped swing it for us. Si used his influence with Mr. Muldaur...oh, I remember that Si said you'd known him."

"Yes, I did. A great human and a great friend. May I ask what your perfume is, if that's all right to ask? I can't place the fragrance."

"Most men wouldn't ask."

"I like it."

"Comes from Baghdad. It's very inexpensive and made of jasmine and something else. They won't say what the something else is. Like lemon but it's not. It's two or three other things with the jasmine as the base."

"It's very, uh—fetching."

"Thanks, I'm glad you like it. Switching the subject, Si called me the other afternoon and mentioned you'd like some information on this...this group...the League. That's so, is it? Mind if I ask why?"

Thomas told her bits and pieces about his evening in Boston with Miles Bascomb, that he'd been on the receiving end of quite a story. Whether it held water was something he couldn't decide, nor had he the slightest idea of how to find out. Some of the history he was given might be verifiable. "Like some sort of Praetorian Guard," he added, "if that's not an exaggeration which it probably is."

"It's not as simple as I thought it would be, either," Shandar said. "I had supposed it was just another trade association and that Si hadn't given me the complete name of it. Left part of it out, you know. Anyway, we'll get something before long."

"How do you do that?"

"I called a consultant of ours in Washington, who knows everything that goes on down there. A former senator. You'd think I'd asked for the Pentagon's secret codes or something. Silencio! But he said he'd look into it."

"Whatever you find out, I'd appreciate knowing. Who runs it is what I'd like to know?"

"I'm pretty sure there's something to it. Our consultant left me with the impression I was treading on sacred turf. We'll see. I'm sort of intrigued myself. What it sounds like, if it exists, is another of those quiet little groups that never has a phone or an office. Washington revels in them. Must be dozens of them down there."

"Really."

"Umm-hmm."

"Is it rude to ask how you know all this?"

"*All?* Not all, by any means. I hear things. We're in the information business. It's our thing. They're strange, some of those organizations. Racial. Political. Rabble-rousers. Expatriates. Repatriates. They've got it all, that's Washington. Is there a particular reason you're interested in this League? I suppose it's the correct name. Maybe not."

"I'm trying to put a project on its tracks, if I can. I've been told this so-called League might have objections. I could care less, but it'd be useful to know who they are."

Crossing Madison Avenue, the cab headed west on Seventy-second as the driver rolled his head sideways and asked Shandar to point out her building.

"Up there," Shandar said. "On the right, the second canopy from the end." She turned to Thomas, "Will I see you again? Do we meet only in Brooklyn? Would you like to visit the Statue of Liberty? Watch the Rangers? The Knicks? We have tickets. Anything like that? Notice how aggressive we p.r. types are?"

"Sure, I'd love it. Dinner or something. In about two weeks. I'll call you."

"If it's going to be that indefinite, I'd better be the one to call you."

"Believe me, I will call. My calendar shifts around quite a bit. I have to go to Washington. Actually Maryland. On some nights I take a law course. Still a schoolboy, I guess."

"There's the laugh of this night...well, thank you for the lift."

The taxi pulled curbside. As she opened the door, the overhead light bloomed. In the pale light he could see her again, her Eastern face, her dark midnight eyes shining like something belonging on a necklace.

"You seem a pleasant man," she said. With those words and that possessing look she gave him, they became something other than just acquaintances. In all his life, he had never really asked a woman, or at least never formally, for a date. He'd be stumbling and fumbling like some teenager, he supposed. How to start? He was still thinking about it when, back at his apartment, he turned out the light, waiting a considerable time before he could exit his thoughts.

Three days later, Shandar called. Off and on, he'd been thinking about her, and now came this pleasant break in his morning.

"Some news." She was saying. "Not much but at least a little something."

"Ah, so soon."

"I tracked down a phone number for them, which is progress of a sort—it's unlisted. They keep up an office in Washington and one in Milwaukee. Staff people, I'd guess. A snooty bunch, really buttoned tight when it comes to information. They asked how I got a hold of their phone number. I could understand if they were one of those highfalutin security agencies. Anyway, this League definitely exists. And whoever they are, they've got to be pretty heavy if they're so secretive. I'm working on another contact as I told you before. That's it, I'm afraid. But they're alive and functioning. I thought you'd like to know that much, at least."

"Did this come from the ex-senator? The phone number?"

"It sure did. But he's asked to be left out of the loop."

"Did you hear anything about who runs it?"

"No dope on that, none whatsoever."

"Secretive bunch, sounds like."

"For sure."

"I owe you an extravagant lunch or something. Soon as I get back to New York, we'll go have a fling of it at your favorite restaurant."

"No, you needn't owe me a lunch, but that won't stop me from accepting. I have to run, Thomas. Have a good trip. Stay in touch, or I will send you a stiff consultant's bill. Bye now."

She hung up, and he let his hand linger on the receiver, as though he were holding on to her. Amiable, diligent too. He suspected Si Nestor had leaned on her for the favor, and he ought to thank Si and he would, when knowing more.

Returning to his work, he jotted a few notes and then sat back and began to memorize them. Columbia University had invited him to give a talk and he was excited, not nervous but an excitement born of expectancy. It was not the same as teaching, of having regular classes but it was as close as he could hope for. One of the microbiologists there had recently been nominated to SOS, had learned of Thomas's presence in New York, and had arranged the invitation. The talk, informal. With thirty or so to attend—he was advised—and one of the attendees, a renegade, born to a shining brilliance, would soon rearrange Thomas's life.

Early one morning, Thomas arose and pulled on his running togs. He took off on a medium-length run, jogging cross-town to the Hudson River, up the river toward mid-town, back through Seventh Avenue where lines of trucks, their motors puttering, waited to be loaded and unloaded with chromed-racks holding every imaginable sort of garment. In a burst, he ran hard all the way down to the Soho District. It was true that New York never really slept, and equally true that its first stirrings of the day were always an education.

Dawn had begun to spread its pewter light over the city, its first blade of light knifing through gaps between the towering buildings. Pushing himself in one last burst, he ran at speed for three blocks. Then slowed as he rounded the corner that led him into Gramercy Park. Walking now, his lungs heaving, he toweled his brow.

Not far, half a block away, Thomas saw someone sitting on the front-stoop of the town house where he temporarily rented an apartment. Whoever it was, a he or a she, looked like a balled-up circle, hunkered down, rocking back and forth as if keeping time to unhearable music.

Whoever it was sprang to life as Thomas warily placed a foot on the lowest step. A high-pitched, almost melodic voice asked, "You are the esteemed Doctor Courmaine, I think?"

No one called him Doctor except European scientists that he didn't know particularly well, or some of the SOS members, half of whom were European.

Thomas eyed his visitor. Chubby. Oriental. Wide-set chipmunk-like jaws, brown eyes steady as an owl's, crow-black hair standing up like the bristles of a brush. Separating the lips was a faintly insolent smile, leaving you to think this stranger knew something about you he could sell for money. On second glance, this intruder seemed triangular, with his narrow shoulders and wide hips, all of him bundled up in a multi-zippered black jumpsuit.

"I'm Thomas Courmaine, yes."

A hand leaped out. "Lin-pao, sincerely and completely at your service, Doctor. What a pleasure this is to meet a man of your hierarchy. Oh, and you've had morning exercise. I see. Excellent. Very good. You must drink hot lemon-tea. I arrive here at the suggestion of a mutual friend whose name I dare not mention except under duress. I've read some of your work, Doctor, and I have com—com—piled several considered suggestions to offer you at a time you are ready. I—good, oh, your talk at Columbia. Superb, sir. Very superb. At your discretion I will make known my suggestions, sir. Do I make marvelous impression? Hire me, sir. I work like ten dragons and I'm most intelligent. Catch on quick, very quickly indeed, sir."

"Is that so?"

"Absolutely so and dependably so."

"So I'm hearing."

"Oh, from whom, sir?"

"From you."

"You sound doubtful. Allow me, sir, to prove myself."

"Thanks, no. That's quite a monologue you do."

"I've been up all night, deciding what to say."

"A mouthful."

"I cook excellently. Shanghai-style, the very finest, sir. I am Lin-pao, by the way, sir. I already said that, I am so stress—stress—erd."

"Your name, again?"

"Lin-Pao. Separated by a hyphen. Two distinct-ly words."

The small hands danced in accompaniment to nearly every word. The sing-song voice never seemed to draw breath; like listening to radio, thought Thomas, who was caught entirely off guard by all this. Who sent him? What did he want?

Lin-pao answered for him, "Kind Doctor, do not make me start over."

"There's little chance of that, believe me. I'm off for the shower and then, uh, okay, twenty minutes. But not more."

"So few, Doctor? Some generosity, sir, if you will please be so kind."

179

"How do you know about me, or find me?"

"I attended your radiant talk at Columbia. As I said, sir. You must listen when I speak."

"Radiant, huh?"

"Very elegant, sir. Very."

"Thanks. You haven't answered how you found me."

"I have ways of making inquiries. I shall need a day or two to exhibit to you my—my acumen. No, sir, it is not possible in twenty impover-ish minutes."

"I've work to do today."

"Best then that I come upstairs with you. I can express myself while you shower and if you shave—sir, I can shave you, I'm quite expert—"

"Better not count on that, either."

"We can talk then while you bathe. Saves time, yes, it can, and yes it does. Time is so precious for a man of your stature. I will keep you famous, Doctor, if you will employ me. It is my promise. Would you like a massage? I give the best. After your exercise, it is best to massage the muscles and drain them of any lactic acid. I shall do it, sir."

A roly-poly little hustler with a staggering opinion of himself; he was beginning to make Thomas edgy. "You sit tight, Mr. Pao. I'll be back—"

"No, no, if it pleases. Please, Doctor, I am Lin-pao. *Two* words that are spoken as one word. Lin-pao. The Chinese have the most efficient names in the world. I am L-i-n-p-a-o." Spelling it out, letter by letter. "No deviations are necessary."

Thomas pulled a key from the pocket of his sweat suit, was about to proceed up the steps and then he relented. "C'mon in. Make yourself comfortable inside," then asked, "had your breakfast yet?"

A shake of the odd-shaped head and then, "On Thursdays I prefer bananas and green tea. I will pay for what I eat. Bananas yield phosphorous, which in combination with the tannic in tea is most beneficial to—"

"Tea, I have. No bananas today, I'm afraid."

"My English is excellent, yes? We can communicate easily. I write very excellent papers, Doctor. Concisely. To the point. In measured cadences. Ask anyone, sir. You and I will always know what to say to each other."

"Should I make an appointment to speak to you?" said Thomas, pointedly.

Lin-pao's face fell. It didn't have far to go, his neck being so short. Genuinely crestfallen, he spoke to his chest. "I am so anxious to make a fervent impression. Please excuse me."

"I'm being rude," said Thomas. "C'mon, let's go up."

Unlocking the door, he led the way, and they went up one floor. There, Thomas opened the door to his apartment and showed this newly found word-acrobat to a seat in the living room.

"I'll be right back. Ten minutes. There's yesterday's paper and help yourself to the magazines. You're a scientist? Or am I wrong?"

"A biochemist. The best in the world. I know no bounds, sir."

"Really, well. The honor is all mine then. Best in the world?"

"I am."

"Okay." Thomas smiled. This might be fun, he thought, and left for the bathroom.

Fifteen minutes later Thomas found Lin-pao just where he had left him. Seated on the sofa, his eyes shut, his lips moving but making no sound. Meditating, Thomas guessed. The hour was still early—7:22—and the north-facing windows just beginning to reflect the day's light. He was still curious as to how Lin-pao had found him.

Suddenly the eyes opened. "You exceeded my estimates. I didn't expect you so soon-ly."

"Soon."

"So soon. Yes, soon. Exactly so, sir. I was merely testing your command of the language so we could communicate with no misunderstanding."

Thomas almost laughed. But this man-boy was so serious, so earnest, and he didn't wish to offend him again. "Bananas are not on the menu, as I said. Cereal? Pears and apples, I think we have those. I'll listen to anything you have to say, and then I'll stand you to a breakfast."

"I will pay," he insisted.

"Not here, you won't. I'm not in the restaurant business. I want to know who sent you."

No one had sent him, not specifically. It turned out Lin-pao had been doing post-doctoral work at Columbia in the Microbiology Department. The work had been funded by a grant from Eli Lily. When the project was over, he had cast about for more work but, without a green card, and his visa about to expire, he was nearing the end of his stay in America. He'd been loitering around Columbia hoping against hope for some way to extend his visa, and had seen the posting about Thomas's talk. He had attended with about forty others and afterward had talked a sympathetic department secretary into retrieving Thomas's phone number. He had then asked another friend, a fellow postdoc, who worked part-time for the telephone company, to trace the number to an address.

They conferred about Thomas's talk at Columbia, with Thomas increasingly intrigued by Lin-pao's insights on gene manipulation. The odd-shaped man was bright as a low star. Thomas could tell. He could always tell, the good ones were like a good anything. They either had it or they didn't and always they seemed to fizz with sudden energy and fulsome thoughts over anything and everything.

"Have you got a c.v. or something about your work, your education?"

"On that coffee table, sir."

Thomas hadn't noticed it. Hadn't looked for it, either. He picked it up, counted out four-pages and asked, "Mind if I read this?"

"By all means do, sir."

"I'm not sir. Nor do I use the title of doctor. People call me Thomas mostly. You can too."

"Yes, sir. Thank you, with my profoundest pleasure, sir."

Thomas thumbed the pages, taking a minute or so for each, noting the information he wanted to read a second time. An outstanding summary of an outstanding career. The best Thomas had ever seen for a man of Lin-pao's age, which, according to the c.v., was twenty-seven.

"You sound like Leonardo DaVinci before there even was a Leonardo," he said, a note of respect in his voice; a note that was to remain there permanently. "Why are you in America? I should think China would name a province after you. I'm a little surprised I haven't heard of you before. But I see you've been moving around."

He had, too. Shanghai, then Singapore, then Sydney, followed by a stint at the Max Planck Institute in Berlin, then the University of Washington, and finally his last seven months at Columbia. An impressive march.

"Have you letters of recommendation?"

"Twenty-three of them. I will secure them and place them at your disposal this very afternoon."

"No, well—all right. Not this afternoon. Just drop them off sometime."

Then, he asked Lin-pao about various biologists who Thomas knew at several of the places where Lin-pao had studied or worked. Lin-pao knew them all, even supplied a few anecdotes, and knew what they looked like and a great deal about their specialties. There could be no mistake of it, Thomas thought; he wanted to see those letters, but what he had learned in the last ten minutes seemed a valid indication of the younger man's credentials.

"What're you trying to do?" asked Thomas. "Or become? How do I fit in, or do I?"

"I am a visionary, sir. Myself, of course, I still have many things to see and so I am not ready to return to China for a time." Lin-pao smiled faintly. "China is not ready for me, not exactly favorable to my interests. I am an orderly man. I am myself at that intersection in life where I am quite free to make choices, almost any choice. Various cautions suggest I be especially careful this particular year, select just the right opportunity. In China, you see, this is the year of the rooster. One must remain very alert, very, ah, controlled. Therefore, sir, this is my year to envision the whole of my future."

"Have you—are you considering other opportunities?"

"I do not feel at liberty to say, sir."

"Okay. Can you afford to go without work?"

"Is that not a deeply personal question, sir?"

"Don't sir me, or doctor me, either. We discussed that, I thought. Where do you live, if I may ask?"

"To conserve sums of money, I maintain my residence in a Chevrolet van, vintage of 1998. It suits admirably. I wash at my uncle's. He holds forth in Chinatown. I will take you to his restaurant for dinner. My mail, when I am graced with any, is kept for me at a post-office box, which you were supposed to have seen on my c.v. I have already submitted for your inspection. I think it very prestigious, to have a New York address, wouldn't you agree?" Lin-pao offered all this through another of his faint but knowing smiles. Then he added, "Now it is your turn to talk, sir."

"My turn to talk? Oh, I get it. Like getting that appointment to speak. You certainly sound like you're a low overhead operator. Very commendable."

"Chinese, we can survive an entire week on what an American consumes in a day."

"Again, what do you want of me?"

"In five years I expect to be rich. Very rich indeed. You can help me prepare for that specific and desired outcome just as I will help you with yours."

"That's a piece of your future I misplaced somewhere."

"It will happen. I am destined, you see."

"I haven't a doubt. Not a one. Where'd you learn to speak English?"

"Shanghai, my home. Then, of course, I improved my enunciation and syntax here in America. I keep audio tapes of all famous books. I watch Fox News for pronunciation techniques and opportunities for vocabulary improvement. One hour every day, improvement in English. I also speak

French, some German, and of course Mandarin and Shanghainese Cantonese, too, sir."

"No kidding?"

"Useful, don't you think? I do. And you, may I ask, you also speak languages?"

"A few, including American-ese. Unfortunately no Chinese, though."

"I will teach you my mother language."

"What do you know about genetics? How would you go about speculating on the likelihood of something in the absence of hard evidence? How far would you go on a blind search? How would you decide when to, how to, and where to head in a new direction? Then, in which direction would you go and why? What would be your indicators? Put that together for me, can you? Then tell me what you don't know, and why you think you don't know it. Genetics, I'm talking about genetics. Go ahead, sell me."

"Esteemed Doctor," Lin-pao began, with Thomas about to correct him again, but deciding otherwise when he heard, "listen carefully, sir, for I have been reviewing the problem you discussed at Columbia for the past several days. This idea you also exposed in *Nature*. A delicate, elegant idea yet perhaps a shade bizarre, I decided, but then I—I recanted." A great florid smile interrupted him, and then he went on, "I, sir, have many interesting things to share with others. Doctor…were I looking for what you are convinced exists, then I would choose between the male and female sex chromosomes. Perhaps, begin there on the short arm of the Y. Yes there, I can see it in my mind even, there in the vicinity of g221p, I think a hundred thousand base pairs to either side of it. Then, I would walk that chromosome until—"

"Hold it, hold on right there."

Thomas had been slightly expectant, but now something quite surprising flashed through him. How had this Shanghai dumpling figured that out? Someone was bound to come up with the same idea sooner or later, but this talk-machine out of China, how could he make all these guesses and be so close to the mark?

Slightly unnerved, Thomas asked, "What would you do about the female X chromosome?"

"Doctor, with respect, that was not your question."

"Indulge me, anyway."

They went on till late morning, the breakfast long forgotten. Words spewed forth from Lin-pao in a near torrent, threatening to use up all the available oxygen in the room. Thomas was undone at this stranger who came equipped with a mind resembling a fireworks display.

His earlier irritation at Lin-pao was softened by feelings of amusement, the amusement having converted to interest, and soon enough his interest turned into a blossoming admiration. Lin-pao seemed the real thing; a scientist with a full book of tickets. Big mind, big imagination.

Noon came. Noon passed.

As the sun tilted westerly, they went out for pizza and salad at a nearby Italian trattoria called Forsetta's. Thomas often ate early dinner there by himself, and they knew him and made a small fuss whenever he came in. It was only two blocks distant and, as they went, he noticed that Lin-pao walked on the balls of his feet. His heels never seemed to touch the pavement. He looked ridiculous in his jumpsuit, his shock of porcupine-like black hair, those wide cheeks always moving because the mouth they protected was incessantly at work.

As they neared the restaurant, incredibly, Lin-pao told him the number of windows they had passed on the right side of the street, 896. Thomas wanted to call him on it, but didn't, having gained a solid admiration for the dumpling's mind. A funny-talking, odd-looking little man had swung his world, making him thrum again.

The day went by fast as a stray bullet. When Lin-pao left, Thomas sat back and recounted some of their conversation. That mile-a-minute mouth was fed by an obviously fertile mind. Amused once more, and quite fascinated, Thomas began to think he'd been on an excursion with a clone of Sinbad. Wonders and more wonders to behold.

London, England

Fate, that leveler of all, had dug its claws into Jacgelét Margit Josephus Muldaur. For weeks she had lived in a cocoon of devastation, barely able at times to go through the motions of life. She was an Afrikaner, and, being one, she possessed a fraction of native black blood in her ancestral gene chain. This, from the mating of early European male settlers when no white women were available. Over centuries the Afrikaners had largely bred the tar out of their innate gene pool. But not all of it. Genes have a life of their own and a death of their own. Every human carries the genes of apes, of all hominids, of one's direct line of ancestors. Some genes, over eons, are parked, no longer needed. But that doesn't mean they don't still exist.

In the black race, a propensity exists for sickle cell anemia. Here, the human blood cells take on the shape of a tiny boomerang, eventually clogging arteries, joints, depriving the blood stream of oxygen, and death's early journey sets in.

Like everyone, at birth Jaggy's genome was set for her life. Somehow, the flawed genes that coded for sickle cells had squiggled their way into her makeup. For a time, they lay asleep. Then, awakening by some unknown series of body events, they readied themselves to make siege. That, more or less, is how genetic roulette did its thing. One unlucky spin when a sperm met an ovum, with life starting up, and five-hundred thousand years of genes mingling for better or worse.

Still, fate had rolled her dice: the outcome quite clear, about the same as a dagger striking in the night.

She hadn't been feeling up to par, chalking it off to nerves, the strain of Baster's death, overwork, over-worry about the pressures exerted against Muldaur, Ltd. And no heir. Where would it end, when the letup?

Damned if she would give up, and double-damned if she'd go down without an offspring, at least one. One, everyone was entitled to at least one, even in China. She needed it, she wanted it, and she was going to have it this time.

Tired so much of the time, wan, headaches, leg and arm pain—withstanding it for months. All of her life she'd been robust, athletic. Now, at times, she could barely drag herself out of bed.

She had consulted with her ex-husband, her third, the foppish Asquith Pawkes-Howell, a Harley Street gynecologist, treater of London's top tier of trend-setting women. He had sent her to blood specialists, one in Edinburg, a second in Dusseldorf. Swift, accurate, devastating, the diagnoses were the same—sickle cell anemia. No cure existed.

The news staggering, and it was news she couldn't afford to have traveling about.

She could count on a year; with luck and good care, possibly the better part of two years. She now owned a third interest in Klinik-Tönbrin-Foy in the town of St. Gallen, not far from Winterthur, the site of Cyro. The Klinik as private a place as she could hope for, and staffed with a top hematologist. And they could help on the other battle: getting her fertilized.

Wondering angrily to herself—why wasn't he here? Here beside her, helping, being supportive? What if he knew? Would he be even more diffident, more stand-offish that when she last spoke to him in New York, offering to fly there to be with him? Why had he put her off? Flitting around over there, and with no takers for his schemes, according to Si Nestor.

The sod, she thought. Were he in her bed, at least he'd be good for something.

Bethesda, Maryland

On the phone.

"…yes, Mr. Raab."

"I've told you a dozen times to call me Murray," he said to Alexis Hazlett.

"I prefer the professional level, as I've also told you a dozen times."

"It'd benefit you if you'd be, ah, more cooperative."

"I do my best." Smiling the smile she had practiced and practiced, trying to be civil to this buck-toothed insect.

"Anyway, at our lunch last week I told you we expected a visitor—"

"Yes, but you never gave me his name. I've been wondering why."

"I'm getting to that, so hold your boat. He'll be here tomorrow, so stand by. I haven't decided what's to happen as yet, but he may be coming your way. Keep a close watch on him, if I should send him over."

"Send who over and what for?"

"When the time comes, you'll be told."

"Why can't I know who it is, for godsakes?"

"His name is Thomas Courmaine. He interned here a few years back."

"Oh, him. Really! You're kidding. Hot diggety. I'd really like to meet him."

"We'll see."

"Even if you don't see, I'd still like to meet him. I think I know one of his secrets."

"Which is?"

"After I meet him, I'll tell you," Alexis Hazlett replied, impishly.

"If he does come your way, be cooperative but not overly so. Milk everything you can from him. *Everything.*"

"Milk as in cow or a goat?"

"Is that some sort of a joke, Hazlett?"

"I'll do whatever I can. It'd help mightily to know what you expect."

Raab went on, feeding her tidbits, feeding her curiosity. When his voice finally trailed off, Alexis hung up. She hadn't the vaguest idea of what secrets Thomas Courmaine possessed, or if he possessed any at all. She had read the news accounts of the Mzura women, but had her doubts. A hard-noser for facts, she ignored claims bereft of observable proof. To her, it was a story of another bio-Cinderella stunt, and with nothing to back it up.

Doubts about the expected visitor competed with her many other doubts about Raab. She suspected he was up to nothing good, as was usually the case, and so she took a heavenly joy at any opportunity to tweak him. He'd remember her flip replies, but she didn't particularly care. He'd done her enough harm, and, as she sat again at her desk, she thought that maybe—from the way Raab had talked—a smidgeon of intrigue was coming her way. Maybe more than a little, and if she could compute an opportunity to compromise that rotten bastard Raab, she'd leap at it.

Three days later.

Getting out of the cab, carrying an overnight valise, Thomas stood a moment, refreshing his memories as he gazed across the campus. Several years had passed since last he had set foot on these grounds. He scanned the buildings, viewed the bright blue sky, gandered at the grounds, and decided that not much had changed, or not outwardly.

Unrivaled as the citadel of health research centers, NIH, in the world of medical arts and sciences stood apart. Nothing else like it anywhere. Were it the art world, instead of the world of medical research, it would be tantamount to having the Metropolitan Museum, the Louvre, the British Museum all located on a single campus. Its twelve stood as a shining monument to the kind of thing Americans did better than anyone in the world. Home to the world's largest medical library, endless labs for investigating every imaginable disease, sweeping programs devoted to human health, NIH was the last stop for those with incurable ailments, and who had agreed to experimental treatments.

In the lobby, at a reception desk, Thomas signed the visitor's book, while a security guard examined a list, then scrutinized Thomas, who was quite aware a concealed ceiling camera was taking his picture.

He was directed to an office on the fourth floor, where he located the office suite he was looking for, went in, and saw an empty reception desk. He waited, waited more, then finally strode down a short hallway.

A man, bent over a pencil sharpener, turned as Thomas rapped on the door-jamb.

"Hello, I'm looking for a Murray Raab. He's the Director of—oh, my gosh, it's you Murray. How're you?"

Raab stood back. "Reduced to sharpening pencils as you can see. Tight budgets this year." He looked dispraisingly at Thomas. "You used to run around here in jeans and a Salvation Army sweatshirt. You look like the cover of GQ magazine. You win the lottery?"

Murray Raab smiled distantly. Not even a handshake. Thomas was surprised at the off-hand greeting.

"Well, it's been some years, hasn't it? It's good to see you again, Murray."

"Let's head for my office."

Raab had seen a lot of the sun lamp, his quick-eyed face looking as if had been painted with honey-amber dye. The shirt a spotless white, with bony wrists extending below the cuffs. Dark-jowled. A startling waxed mustache shot out like two black spikes on either side of his upper lip. There was nothing new in the face, the two slightly protruding teeth were still there, accounting for the nickname beaver. That was the reason for the outlandish moustache; Thomas supposed—to deflect attention from the teeth. It was a face you could feel sorry for, and the sobriquet—beaver—had stuck anyway.

The remote greeting when Thomas had arrived was bothersome and things seemed headed further south as Raab motioned Thomas to a chair, saying, "You've got half an hour at most. My schedule's gotten loused up."

About to protest, Thomas thought better of it. "All right, I'll start by asking if you had a chance to read the proposal I faxed you."

"It's being staffed. I haven't seen anything in detail on it yet."

"Does that mean you probably won't?"

"Could be," Raab agreed, disingenuously. "This is a busy beehive. We get a hundred proposals every week. More probably."

"I get you on a bad day?"

"We can't meander off and try every idea just for curiosity's sake."

"I happen to have a pretty good idea, Murray."

"Do you know anyone who doesn't have a good idea, especially around Washington? Down in the basement of this building are three corridors filled with cardboard boxes. Nothing but ideas and more ideas in those boxes. Boxes, in any color you want. You're probably wasting your time. We sound like we're almost through, are we?"

"Do I have enough of your time left to drop an unboxed idea in your lap?"

With an impatient look, Raab agreed, "Go right ahead."

Thomas laid out his case. On his own, he was prepared to put up the money to conduct a first-phase experiment. It could be done for no more than a thousand-dollars. From this, he argued, he could show that Zyme-One was just what he had said, and confirm that the stories out of Africa were true. Even if an experiment did not involve humans this time, he could get close enough so that fair conclusions could be reached.

"Look," Thomas earnestly proposed, "if I'm successful, I'm willing to deed any future patent rights to the U. S. government with one proviso, the government cannot license those particular patents to anyone wanting to make profits from the relevant technology. Otherwise, anyone else qualified would have complete access to the know-how for free. I made the same offer to SOS. How can you lose, with the offer I'm making you?"

"Go on," said Raab. "I think—yes, this was in your written proposal, wasn't it?"

"No." But now it occurred to Thomas that Raab, contrary to what he had said earlier, had indeed read the faxed three-page memo sent a week earlier. Why the deception? Thomas went ahead anyway, "I think I'm right. If I am, then everyone is ahead. Think of the medical costs the government could save. The whole business needs fresh thinking, fresh eyes, fresh everything."

"Maybe," interrupted Raab. "Also maybe you're wildcatting. Big-sky stuff. A man with your reputation ought to—"

"—ought to try and save America hundreds of billions in medical bills," Thomas interrupted, anxiously so, conscious of time.

"Tell it to Congress," Raab said sternly. "They take care of the money end."

"I want you to tell it to them after we get the facts settled. Or enough of them. I'm putting a lot on the table." Thomas moved forward in his chair. "In Wall Street and Chicago, they bet on futures every day, even government interest-rate futures. I'm not betting NIH money. I'll bet mine. All you have to do is protect the use of the patent if I'm right. What's so tough about that? I'm taking all the risk, not that it's very much."

No reaction. The buck teeth nibbling on the lower lip.

This is a deaf-chamber, thought Thomas, on edge, fearful of another turndown.

Not once had Thomas shifted his gaze from the tensely strung Raab, who was wringing Thomas dry, walking him along the plank, as instructed by Miles Bascomb.

"I can't bind the government to any such promise," Raab told him. "I don't even know how you'd go about it. Try the Justice Department, why don't you?"

"I'll take your word that you'll try to get my requirements worked out once any patents are filed. Find out who I have to speak with, and I'll help you get it done. I'll even engage a top public-relations firm to work with us," said Thomas, thinking of Shandar, promising the stars now, without the slightest idea where that money would come from.

"The government doesn't make deals like this. It's too complicated, too esoteric."

"Sure they do," Thomas rebutted. "They make them all the time." He'd give it a run, what was there to lose? "Look, I know for a fact that human skin can be regenerated by infusion of various skin genes. If you can do it with skin, you can probably do it with anything else. Heart, liver, whatever. Not the brain, too complex I imagine. Probably, in five years we can bring about medical revolution. I'm talking about watershed changes. I can show you, I'm sure of it, how a person's lifetime medical bill will never go over a few hundred dollars, unless they get hit by a truck or a train. Think of that, Murray. You can give the deaf back their hearing. You could even grow new eyes for the blind. Practically endless, the possibilities." Singing his aria, hard as he dared.

Thomas could see Raab's front teeth now, strangely wide, like two miniature dominoes. Genetic, he thought. Maybe new teeth, too—he almost added—and knew then that he needed sleep. He was talking too fast, betraying his angst.

His allotted time was running out just as Thomas felt he was finally cornering Raab's attention, a piece of it anyway. "In ten years, Zyme-One could help conquer hundreds of diseases," Thomas said, pushing relentlessly. "Even thousands. Get behind me, and I'll do it for you. Let NIH deliver perfect health, or nearly so, to the next generation. Why isn't that a worthy aim? Do it with me, and you can write your own ticket with Congress." Largely, his pitch echoed what he had offered SOS months ago in Cambridge. Without being aware, however, that on this occasion he was playing himself into Raab's snare.

Raab asked outright for a copy of Thomas's papers, journals, notes—everything that shed any light whatsoever on Zyme-One.

"Everything that I had has been lost in Africa. Don't ask me to explain, because I can't. I do have some of the enabling substance with me."

"Hand it over and we'll test it?"

"I'll test it and you can see the results."

"If there are any, you mean."

"Right."

"You're not an employee here. We can't turn facilities over to you, you know that."

"Let me work with a researcher. I'll be the unpaid consultant."

Raab hesitated, then asked, "Willing to sign a release?"

"Hand me one and it's done."

Raab—very coy, playing out Bascomb's hand—said, "Tell you what I'll do. Two buildings down there's a lab overseen by Alexis Hazlett, who has some time on her hands at the moment. Go on over there and make your sale. If she buys in, then we'll see. Otherwise, it was nice to see you, Thomas. We *are* through here now, aren't we?"

"How will she know I'm on my way over?"

"I'll let her know," said Raab. He wrote on a notepad, tore off the sheet, handing it to Thomas. "Alexis Hazlett. She's in the Basic Sciences, that's Building B, third floor."

Sitting with Alexis Hazlett, becoming acquainted, he was telling her the approximate history of Zyme-One. That, so far as he knew, it derived only from an African shrub-root, that a tribe had used it for centuries as a medication for ailments beyond count, yielding an amazing range of cures. It was one of those ethno-botany remedies, he told her, of the sort found in the Amazonia basin in South America; indeed, found by the hundreds there. And even if pooh-poohed by western medicine, the remedies work and work well. It was there in Africa, with help of a shaman, he had found a way to milk Zyme-One from an exudate of the shrub-root *semba*, using it to conduct the well-publicized gene experiment on the three Mzura tribeswomen.

"So, that's the rough background. As you see, I borrowed the basics from the Mzura to do what I did," Thomas explained.

"Odd, isn't it? I'm not versed in ethno-botany."

"Nor am I. But I've seen things not many white men ever see. We always think we're smarter than the rest of the world. I've become something of a recent convert to the ancient ways."

"You sound it."

"Remember, they've been at it for thousands of years. I walked their walk. You get out of the cocoon, and, like the butterfly, a whole world waits out there with things to learn about."

"Where can I get a sample of this—what is it again, the name?"

"Zyme-One."

Her brows lifted. "Does that stand for anything special?"

"Some postdocs in Johannesburg named it. You know, students and how they shorthand whatever they can. A good name for it, I think."

"You've got a sample for us?"

"I've got a sample with me and for my use. I'd like to set up an experiment and show you what it does."

Her brow arched. "What sort of experiment would that be?"

"I dunno. Let's figure one out." He knew what he wanted to do, and even could do; but was biding his moment, getting a sense of Alexis Hazlett.

"Give me a clue."

"I'm thinking…"

She seemed slightly agitated but he let it slide. Alexis Hazlett, he decided, must be a competent researcher. More than competent, possibly. Pretty, too. A mop of frizzy reddish-hair, green-eyed, trim, an expressive pixyish face. A shiny nose. On the front left of her neck appeared a reddish mark. From last night's lover, Thomas supposed, smiling a little, then explaining what he had in mind, ending with, "You and a couple of mice. In several weeks we'll see if one mouse roars and the other one whimpers."

"That's ridiculous. It sounds ridiculous to me anyway."

"When I was a kid, eleven or twelve, I read Jules Verne's *The Moon-Voyage*. I still remember most of it. It seemed ridiculous, too, when I read it. But then look what happened. Science fiction, I guess, at least back then, yet it all came to be. If you can tell me exactly, I repeat *exactly*, why my methods of gene manipulation won't work, then we'll forget the whole thing. I'll get out of your way. On the other hand, you might learn something and so might I."

"Well, I admit I can't tell you why it won't work. But you're asking me to prove a negative."

"Even if I am, what's to hold us back? Let's prove it the opposite way. There must be mice around here somewhere."

"Of all kinds."

She would know the genetic map of the mouse and the human are more similar than most people would suppose. Not as similar as a human and a chimp, but still similar enough. He used this fact persuasively, because most of the skin genes of humans and those of mice are located on chromosome-17 in the cells of each mammal. That helped greatly. He'd flood one mouse with Alexis Hazlett's skin genes after fortifying them with Zyme-One so that her skin genes, the many thousand copies of them, would overwhelm the target mouse's genome, eventually replacing its natural skin genes. Same for a second mouse, except, in that case, no Zyme-One would be mixed with Alexis's skin genes. By rights, the second mouse's immune system would reject the foreign skin genes, for there was no Zyme-One in play to keep the foreigners cemented in place.

That was the idea.

Another transgenic experiment, this time however he'd do the reverse of the experiment in Naruma; instead of putting chimp skin genes in a human, he'd put human skin genes into a mouse.

Because mice breed frequently, it would be relatively easy to see if succeeding generations carried Alexis's skin genes, assuming her genes took hold to begin with.

"You'd agree to the general concept, would you?" Thomas asked after he outlined his intentions. "You know all this stuff, but I'm trying to see if we're in sync."

Alexis knew Raab wanted a full assessment, up or down, plus or minus of whatever took place. Did it work, or didn't it? If she didn't appease that gizzard-head, she'd be on the outs with him permanently, never a hope of regaining her missing researchers.

Go with the flow, she told herself. Even so, another frown marred her face as she picked up the phone, spoke, spoke more, then hung up. "We can get two old-timers. Four years old, about. They're Monsanto mice that're engineered for lab work. Good enough, you think, for what you have in mind?"

"Not previously infected with anything, were they?"

"Absolutely pristine, they promised me. What else will you need besides a smock? You can't work in those clothes. You look like a banker."

Thomas gave her a list of items, asking, too, for a bench of his own. Working as fast as he could, he'd be out of her hair in a day or so. "If you'll scrape a few of your skin cells on to a glass, we'll be all set for a start. It would speed things if you could replicate your DNA. Say, ten-thousand copies. I'll set up the bench. If you'll lend me a pad of blue paper, I'll keep the protocol and notes. You can check it whenever you like. You can sign it, if you wish and I wish you would."

"I'll let you know after I read it."

"I need to identify which mouse is which. Let's name them. Any thoughts?"

"No. Nary a one. Have you?"

"Let's call the Zyme-One mouse, oh, I don't know, how about Peter? You name the other one."

"In that case, call it Paul. They're both male."

He grinned. "Peter and Paul, fair enough."

About to leave so she could scrounge up his requests, Alexis hesitated when he asked, "I forgot, I'll need a retrovirus. Any kind, as long as it's cleaned up and will do the carrier work. E coli or a flu virus, either is okay."

A retrovirus was a necessary delivery vehicle, sometimes called a vector, but all in all just another name for a virus that had been re-rigged to eliminate its toxic properties yet preserve its power to invade cells indiscriminately and unerringly. Infection was the primary business of any virus. They were innately, genetically powered like nothing else to bombard healthy cells, embedding disease—from something as common as flu to severe pneumonia, or even the body-twisting polio. When a virus was "retro-ed" it meant it had been stripped of its disease-making capability but retained its powers of cell-invasion. When the retrovirus was modified to carry Alexis's skin genes—323 of them, all performing different functions—it would carry her gene-cargo into nearly every cell in the mouse now named Peter. To that extent, if all worked as expected by Thomas, then Peter would become part human, with a major organ, the skin, as donated by Alexis. Quite possibly, the mouse's body-hair would also turn from rodent-gray to an auburn-color, like hers. He wasn't sure, but it might, and he hoped it would.

Twenty minutes or so later, as Thomas was ticking off the initial steps of how he intended to begin, and then he heard a noise. It was Alexis wheeling in a triple-shelved cart, piled with the items he had asked for. He helped her unload. About to sidle off, she asked, "You want how many copies of my DNA?"

"Ten- thousand, more or less."

"Be forty minutes or so."

"That'll be fine. I've got to set up shop."

Glass pipettes. Stainless steel trays. Gel sheets. Beakers and water baths. Near to him, within steps, was an Eppendorf centrifuge, a spectrophotometer, an inverted microscope. All he needed was here, more by far than he had had in his makeshift lab at the Naruma Station.

An hour went by. He now had Alexis's DNA copies and the two mice had arrived. Two white cotton-balls scampering about in their separate cages. Yet another hour fled as Thomas tinkered with various pieces of equipment, testing a few, situating them in the order of use. Making notes on a pad of blue paper as he went along.

Alexis hovered silently, her curiosity apparent. It didn't bother him. He wanted her involved, handy and observant.

Working away, using the scope as he teased out the hundreds of skin genes from the many thousands of genes in Alexis's DNA. These genes, once again, were then cloned by the thousands. Two hours later, he had what he needed to go forward.

He uncorked the vial of Zyme-One he'd derived from the *semba* roots stored at Cyro in Switzerland. The decoction smelled somewhat differently, something like an attic in the summer's dry heat. He wondered if the substance was still active; never having stored the exudate for this length of time.

Too late to worry now.

He was dwelling on skin. The largest of human organs, coded for and made daily from the finely orchestrated actions and reactions of 332 separate genes. One gene coded for skin color, another was responsible for texture, another for freckling, another for transparency, another for pore-density, another for follicles. On and on it went. Elasticity, acne, eczema, psoriasis, non-specific dermatitis, oiliness, whether you were prone to warts, wrinkles, fatty content, density, and thickness. Humans had three layers of skin or epidermal tissue. Bears had five. It was a highly complex organ because skin cells were lost by the millions each day; in flakes of dandruff, or skin that simply had gone dead, or was scrubbed away during a shower, or rubbed off during sleep.

Alexis, had returned to her desk, caught in an expanding web of her own thoughts.

She was feeling a little sick with herself, playing at Raab's game, whatever it was. This quite nice man, he seemed nice anyway, who had come here to run an experiment, stake out the meaning of a far-away discovery. And what it could mean? Here she was caught up in some idiotic, adolescent charade as required by Raab. Awful! Look at his hands, strong, supple, and he was so good-looking. Blonde. Sturdy. Very male, except those eyes that looked right through your organs. Lavender eyes, eyes for a woman and not a man. Never a man. *Men!* Who believed, quite incredibly, they knew all there was to know about everything. Linear-thinking beasts. She had sworn off men several years ago, but this…this Thomas Courmaine might be different. *A priest!* A Jevvie, no less.

Watching his proficient hands move across the bench top with the assurance of a surgeon, knowing where everything was exactly where he had placed it. Do it all in his sleep, probably. When Mr. Assenheimer-Raab had grudgingly revealed the name of Thomas Courmaine the other day, she had gone over to the main library and called for everything they had on Thomas Courmaine, geneticist, late of John Hopkins. A cart had arrived within an hour, loaded with cartons of files. Army work down in San Antonio, doing research there on skin. Burned skin. Article after article published in *Cell, Nature, Science*—the biggies—and she was envious now, for she had never had even one of hers accepted by any of them. She was good, but he was better. She wasn't about to tell him so; he had enough jewels in his crown.

Over at the library, she had also read nearly half of his doctoral thesis. Heady stuff. A *kahuna*, that's Courmaine, a man out of the front pew. He had to be good, maybe not Nobel-good, but, all the same, plenty damn good enough.

She had left her desk and taken up station at an adjoining bench. Look at him go, observing Thomas, feeling as if she were a twelve-year old gawking at the Hope diamond. Gawking so much she probably was giving the impression she was nosy. Couldn't really help herself, though. She was becoming intrigued now that she was part of a mouse and that mouse, in its own way, was part of her. At least, if this thing turned out as billed, the mouse Peter was expected to replicate a part of her. Doomed, to replicate…maybe…

Wishing dearly she hadn't raised a wall of doubts, when first he had ventured his idea for what was actually happening right now, only feet away from where she sat. She was amazed at herself; that she had changed her mind so swiftly. She was objective-minded, for she had to be, yet she had pooh-poohed him, just as Raab had instructed her. Raab was a nothing, yet he was a nothing with a noose around her neck.

Why had she succumbed to Raab's demands that she be a spy? She wasn't like that: not underhanded, not a snoop. Shame bolted through her. She hoped she wasn't blushing, wasn't looking senseless and silly or something.

Wondering what it would be like to sit on Thomas's lap, blow in his ear. Would he smile at her? Lick her? She'd never know because she wasn't cut that way. Not anymore. Still, stirring were stirrings. There was a time…once upon a time…possibly if Thomas Courmaine had come into her life back then; it all might've been another story, another song.

That horrid rape seven years ago had bollixed her. Changed her. Wrecked her for men, and for good and always

Another thing had dawned on her when she was traipsing about a little while ago on two different floors, scouting up things he'd asked her for. No scientist of his standing was coming down to NIH, asking for bench-time so he could prove a point, unless he already knew how the score would tally beforehand. It wasn't some idiotic, time-wasting joke; it wasn't some big fib; it wasn't that he wanted to make a fool of himself, either. Reputable and seemed like a straight shooter. She gauged him again for the fourth or fifth time since he'd come through the door to her lab, with a big fat friendly smile pasted on his tanned face. The real deal, is he? The bio-brain who may have pulled off in Africa what some of the biggest corporations in the world, with their crack research staffs, had failed at...leaving Merck and Pfizer in the dust. Leaving them all in the dust. How nifty would that be? Sensational—that's how nifty. The thought was ramping up her curiosity again. Her chair had small metal wheels on its legs, so she easily scooted herself a little closer to where Thomas was working, his head bent low. Another little push forward with her week-old Nike Air Zooms was all it took her. Zoom-e-de-zoom and she'd practically be able to breathe on the mice.

Oh, Joseph Christ! He must've caught my movements.

Looking up and directly at her with those laser eyes, making her a little terrified that he'd be upset over her intrusion into his private space. Earlier, he'd encouraged her to keep a close watch, but she hadn't felt all that comfortable about it. If Raab hadn't been so damn smug, so patronizing, so overbearing, then possibly she'd feel differently. But she didn't feel differently because she couldn't in a thousand years feel any different than how she felt at this precise, exact moment. She wasn't going to lower herself, and if Raab got her booted out of NIH, then so goddamn what? She wanted Thomas Courmaine to win, to do something immense, right here in her lab. And with her own cells mixed into the situation.

Startled, then, as he asked her: "Like to do the inoculating?"

"Oh, no. I wouldn't dare," Alexis answered, her voice sounding overly nervous to her own ears.

"It's pretty simple. After all, it's your cargo."

"No, no, it's your show. You're the one drivin' the white truck on this trip."

"You're sure?"

"I'm more than sure, believe me. I've never been so sure of anything, ever."

Thomas smiled, shrugged, and reached into Peter's cage. In a frenzy of fear the mouse jumped wildly, spurting through his clutching hand twice before finally being nabbed.

A pool of greenish light spread over his hands as he busied himself with a tiny surgical operation. He ingested Alexis's genes into a hypodermic syringe, plunging one set of them, treated with Zyme-One, into the haunches of the mouse Peter; repeating, then, with the untreated skin genes, as he poked yet another needle into the mouse Paul. Done, he leaned back in his chair. Looking at the mice, thinking about their futures, that it might well create the stir he so fervidly hoped for. He had artificially mutated life, taking Nature's job away from her, an act that one day he would ponder with unceasing regret and alarm.

6:20 p.m. A pivotal moment gained, and time, that incessant foe, had gone its own way. The windows had blackened. He leaned back in his bench chair, aches in his back, neck, and upper arms. Another couple of steps tomorrow, and he'd finish up. So he thought. Indeed, that afternoon he had begun a chain reaction that would follow him as if shadowing his every step. There was never going to be a finish. Not ever. A rustling noise made him turn his head.

"Planning to go through the night?" Alexis asked pleasantly.

"Completely lost track of the time. Another hour or so tomorrow and we'll be wrapped up." He stretched again. "Whew, my neck feels like I swallowed a rock and it's still in there somewhere."

"I'm not surprised. You've been doubled over for hours." Alexis smoothed her springy hair. "Have you a car or can I drop you somewhere?"

"At any hotel that's got a room. I'm starved, how about you?"

She placed a hand on her stomach. "I think it's inverted. I know it's growling."

"Have dinner with me, or are you, ah, spoken for?"

"I have a housemate. I'll have to let her know. I'd like having dinner with you, though. What I'd like even more is to know more about what you've done. The details I didn't or couldn't observe."

"It's all in the blue sheets or will be by tomorrow. Let me wash up, you make your call, and in five-minutes we're out the door. Have you a business card with your direct-dial number? Or a cell phone?"

"Sure do. My e-mail also. I'll write my home number on the back. You might want it, if you're six time zones somewhere else."

He stood, pocketed the vial with the remains of Zyme-One, taking note of Alexis's petulant grimace.

"It wouldn't do you much good," he told her. "You'd have to know where to find the source material and how to reduce it with reagents to make the active ingredients work right. Even if I told you, you couldn't get what you'd need. Is Raab wanting this?" Removing the vial from his pocket, he held it up.

"He will if your experiment works."

"Make book on it, amigo, it'll work just fine."

"Then that toad'll want it, you may be sure."

"He'd have to agree on a few things first. You can remind him. He'll know what you mean."

"I can't talk to him that way."

"I can, Alexis. I already have. And I will again once this work tells its story."

"Your enzyme, what's in it?"

"Two loads of dynamite. That's what's in it. One day I'll tell you all I know…for now, let's do our errands, end our hunger strike and go eat. Anywhere that's got good steaks and I'm buying."

"Bernstein's. They've the best anywhere. Terrific oysters, too, if you like those. The entire menu will make you salivate. I warn you, it's expensive."

"We earned it. Are they fussy about reservations?"

"I'll find out. I've things to tell you and they're things you'll not want to hear. But you ought to know, all the same."

"Such as?"

"My guess is someone's waiting in the high grass, ready to ambush you. Just a feeling but it won't go away."

Surprised, Thomas answered, "What makes you say a thing like that, Alexis?"

"You're not telling me very much, but I'm about to fly a very useful bug into your ear. Now, excuse me. I've got to make that call and then I've got to pee or those mice will drown."

He watched her glide away, quick and lithe. What was she telling him—a caveat of sorts? Strange, wasn't it? She'd been helpful, even if watching him at times like a circling hawk cruising for prey. Why believe her? But then, why not? Getting to like her, and Raab certainly had been none too friendly. Ice-cold, in fact, but why?

He'd had a good afternoon, doing his favorite thing—a bench project—and he wasn't going to let anything spoil it or undo the prospect of dinner with a pretty woman. He looked at the mice, both of them scampering about in their cages, oblivious to their futures. Which was how he felt about his own. He was a man in a hurry, but with no place to go. Not at the moment. NIH was likely his last stop in America, for he'd tried everything else he could think of. Maybe, after Si's help, he could ignite some interest at Rockefeller University. But here would be better; indeed, the best of all.

Taking another look at Peter, he was tempted to offer a prayer of hope. But considerable time had elapsed since he had sent any heaven-bound messages. He didn't think it especially kosher to start working those wires now.

Bernstein's had a clubby feel, paneled, with attentive white-jacketed waiters and bartenders who knew how to make excellent drinks. They split a 22-ounce porterhouse and gabbed like two old mates, who'd been long lost. The gabbing was about enzymes, her specialty. Listening to her, Thomas found another kindred soul; not with all the brain-flash of a Lin-pao, but someone who obviously knew how to conduct research at the prime level. Soon, he was to find out about her integrity.

After the meal, having an espresso, Alexis advanced her concerns with, "…Raab is *merde*. He's a hard-nosed infighter, and he's good at administration but it ends there. He's been trying me to bed him for two years and when I didn't play along, he gutted my little team. Two researchers reassigned. Either I give in, or I give out. It's very depressing. He's like a knife in my eye. If it's some leg he wants, he can go buy it on half the streets in downtown Bethesda. I cannot tell you how it ticks me off."

"I imagine so. It would anyone. Can't you go over his head?"

"I've no proof of anything. No witnesses, nothing like that…"

"I wish I could help."

"You better keep an eye on him, Thomas Courmaine. He's trying to trick you, I'm pretty sure of that."

"Trick me? About what?"

She told him of the lunch with Raab, then subsequent phone conversations with bald instructions to make it seem as if what Thomas had to offer was of little interest. To be standoffish, conduct a sham of indifference. "But that bastardo wants a report on what you did, and how you did it. Every move you made, every twitch."

"It's all there on the blue-pad, or will be by tomorrow."

"I'd not make another pencil mark, were I you."

"Sorry, I don't do business that way."

"You'd be wise to think it over. I mean it."

"Why're you telling me all this, Alexis? You don't know me at all."

"I'm telling you because I have to tell someone. You're a Jevvie, or I guess you are. Are you?"

Nodding slowly, he said, "Technically, yes. I'm still on the rolls but trying to get erased."

"I used to be a Catholic. I quit."

"Sorry to hear it."

"I'm not."

"What made you give up?"

"A Monsignor raped me one day. On Cape Cod. I was swimming in the ocean and it got windy and I went ashore and headed for the dunes, so I could dry off and change. There weren't any people around. Or I didn't see any, so I wasn't all that careful. Other than him, he was around all right. Was he *ever*! Must've followed me. He was a friend of the friends I was staying with, that's how I met him. They always think they can get away with it, the shitheads. And if make a complaint, they accuse you of being hysterical or something, lying and trying to make trouble for everyone. Or hit them up for a settlement. I did report it to the Archbishop's office in Boston and they sloughed me off, so I sloughed them off. I'm still sloughing them off. So he got away with it, the Monsignor. Just like Raab gets away with it...sorry, I'm running on like a loony..."

"Nothing to be sorry about. A terrible thing. Awful. You told the police?"

"A lawyer did. Most of the cops in Massachusetts are Irish Catholics, so you know what that means. The old cover up. Like that Kennedy incident at Chappaquiddick, when he drowned that staffer, Mary Jo Who*sis*. I forget her last name. Oh, I know, it's Kopechne...anyway, I mean they had that filthy lout dead to rights and Kennedy goes and beats it. Beats the whole rap. Beats it all. If you know how to put the fix in, you fly away for free...I mean *Jesus!* If all he wanted was some leg, why not go buy it? You can get tail anywhere. Almost anywhere, and he was rich enough."

"Story of history, I suppose. But I'm greatly sorry to hear of what happened to you. Are you with someone now? Someone who restores you, looks after you? Loves you?"

"I live with a woman I'm in love with. An artist. An artist in everything she does. *Everything*."

"Some good news after all. Happy to hear it."

"You're not shocked?"

"Shocked?" Thomas frowned. "Why would I be shocked?"

"The Church is against homosexuality. And me, I've become gay as three rainbows."

He smiled. "I'm not the Church, Alexis. Not anywhere close. They don't like what I say, either. Or what I do, or what I write. They're gonna drop straight out of their trees, when they find out what I'm really up to."

"Are you so sure of it? Of your—what shall I call it, your quest? A quest?"

"As good a word as any. Yes, I'm sure of it. I devote two-thirds of every day to it."

"What do you devote the rest of it to?"

"Sleep, if I can."

"How's it coming along? Your brainchild?"

It's a much harder idea to sell than I thought it'd ever be. My life's become a merry-go-round. Like everything ever attempted by anyone, it'll happen or it won't. But what we did today, that will stand. In a month or so, when Peter starts to change his looks, you'll see what it is that has me so revved up."

"Believe me, I'll be waiting. I told you about me. What about you? Have you someone in your life? A woman maybe?"

"Not in the way you mean, or probably mean."

"I don't like to sound nosy, but you ought to have someone. A man like you should."

"Well, the stars always have their ways, and I'll let you know if I get star-struck."

Ordering more coffee, he asked the waiter to bring him a Hennessy cognac, and a Drambuie for Alexis. She returned to her nemesis, Raab, angrily so, again warning Thomas to be wary. "He gives me the jumps", she said, her frown heavy.

For no special reason, other than taking her remarks to heart, he asked if she'd ever heard of anything called The League, giving her the few sparse details he knew.

Her reply: "Never heard of it. What is it?"

He had no answer for her, either. Now that he thought of it, he wished he had asked Shandar for the telephone number of the League's offices in Washington. Possibly, he could finagle a reason to stop by. Pester them a bit, see what he could see; having not the slightest hint he was already under their looking-glass.

Over France

In the air corridor over Lyon, the same aircraft that had spirited Thomas out of Johannesburg was now on a heading for St. Gallen in Switzerland. Jaggy lay on a divan in the cabin, eyes closed, her nerves stormy.

Struggles on all fronts. The Zimbabwe government had shut down two Muldaur mines, claiming they were unsafe. Extortion. The local Muldaur manager had reported an approach from a junior minister who had advised when Muldaur gave up its majority control, the mine would reopen. Not before.

But the key battle was the one inside her: her imperiled blood system, her barren womb.

Why is this so damnably hard? She had been asking herself that question since awakening three hours ago in her Belgravia home. So much fuss, the endless bother. She had sought and received periodic consultations with three fertility experts, one as far away at Duke Medical Center. She felt as if her innards belonged to everyone but herself.

Cyro had surrendered the last batches of Baster's sperm, initially deposited there when he had promoted the preservation of Afrikaners as a race worthy of perpetuating were it ever at risk of being diluted or disappearing. Her eggs had been extracted twice for attempted *in vitro* fertilizations. Then, three weeks ago, a degree of success when they'd implanted an embryo inside her but the triumph was short-lived, for shortly afterward she had expelled it. Tomorrow or the next day—a third try. The medical question was, if she could get with child, then would she possess the strength to carry a fetus to term? The legal question was, could anyone, anywhere, challenge that Baster Muldaur had left behind him a bona-fide child, that, even if not conceived in the usual manner, the child nonetheless carried a full set of Muldaur genes, sufficient to qualify it as a blooded heir?

She would keep trying till there was no more try left in her. But she was getting tired of putting her legs in stirrups, then all that fiddling with her privates, and then more failure. She'd been born—she thought bitterly—with a rebellious womb. The dish-dance of sperm-and-egg wasn't working as hoped. In a couple of hours she'd be locked in yet another consultation. And the consultation might end with her having to jet across the Atlantic to Duke, in North Carolina, to be pawed by other specialists who knew about other treatments.

Yet what if that failed?

Worry ran bone-deep. Worry kept leading to more worry, for the medics had cautioned her about the complications brought on by stress. And the Muldaur bankers and the Muldaur managers were adding to that stress daily, even by the hour sometimes.

New York, New York

November, with all its deadness, arrived; it's first day, a Monday. Thomas stepped into Si Nestor's office, noting the grizzled-haired head bent over the usual pile of reports. Nestor did not look up. Merely, he waved a hand to let Thomas know he'd been noticed, and to take a seat somewhere.

Moments later, Si said, "Didn't want to lose my place. I'm about to puke. Sons of bitches in Zimbabwe are nationalizing us." Wearily, shaking his head.

"What's Jaggy say?"

"Not talking, which means she's enraged. Markets are up shit's alley today, so give me what you got, but make it quick."

"I wanted to thank you again for setting things up at Rockefeller. It was a wonderful thing to do, Si."

"Poppi's idea. She's got that yen for you, kid."

"I'll thank her, then. But it was a very nice thing to do. I hadn't realized you'd been a trustee there."

"Was. They run your ass out at sixty-five."

"Beginning in a week or so, I'll be commuting in another direction. I probably won't be coming downtown at all, or rarely. So, thanks and double thanks for everything here, all you've done, and the others too."

"Yeh, sure. Nothing, kid, it's a nothing. What do we do about this account of yours? You want it closed or left open? These are tricky times."

"Leave it open. It's had its ups and downs, but mostly up. I can use the extra cash."

"The Chinaman, he costing you?"

"Right."

"Poppi loves 'em."

Thomas laughed. He had taken Lin-pao to the Nestors on a recent Sunday afternoon. Lin-pao had looked up and memorized all the Broadway productions Poppi had appeared in years gone by, his praise enthralling her.

She made a non-stop fuss over him, especially when he had taken her into the kitchen, showing her how to make Shanghai dim-sum.

"Seen Shandar?"

"No. Some phone calls. She travels around as if she's glued to a rocket."

"She's back in town. She and Poppi managed an hour on the phone last night. An hour! What the hell can anyone talk about for an hour?"

Thomas bid good-bye. He left the building, wanting fresh air and time to weigh some worries of his own. He hadn't an assured way to extend Lin-pao's visa, not without a formal offer of employment. That couldn't be done unless he were registered to do business in New York State, entailing a mound of paperwork, licenses, lawyer's fees, and compliance with dozens of laws and regulations. Artists didn't do it, so he had begun to think of himself in those terms; an artist with a helper, an artist sitting at the side of a Michelangelo, or the equivalent. He was plumb dazzled by the range of Lin-pao's capacities. A regular fireworks, always on display.

He ducked into a building near Fulton Street, placed a call to Shandar, and they connected. Two days later, the long-delayed get-together happened. Lunch, not dinner. Lunch, in turn, provided Shandar with the occasion to invite him to a new Broadway play enjoying good reviews, and made possible by unspoken for Meric & Morris tickets.

Then, it was his turn two evenings later. They dined at an Italian trattoria on 23rd Street. He had run across it one lonely night on his way to the Village Vanguard to listen to a jazz trio he'd once heard at Bricktops four or five years earlier in Rome.

After dinner Shandar wanted to go on, and they ended up at the Vanguard themselves.

Good at surprising him, she did so again, when he found out she knew twice what he did about jazz. Learnings she had acquired with no small effort in her weed blowing, Beaujolais-imbibing, cause-inspired days as a left-leaning activist student in Berlin, and later, at the Sorbonne.

Her parents, well off, had been generous with her allowances. Like her peers, she wore jeans and sloppy wool sweaters; little else in the way of clothing expenses dented her funds. She could, more or less, afford to be carefree, so had become the classic student-mongrel, joyfully engaging in militant pacifism, engaging in anti-war marching, attending peace vigils, shouldering protest-signs. Many moods, many fads, and she supported any popular student uprising of the hour. Free, alive, suffused with youth, and terrifically happy much of the time. Like her fellow students, she'd been strongly painted by American culture; unlike many of them, though, she had pursued the jazz idiom, forsaking the rock-scene. Jazz lifted her, rhythmically, even rested her. Nothing else had, and, being from a strict Jewish family, she had to use caution in her ways when back in Iraq with her parents.

Berlin and Paris, in her late teens and early twenties, had taught her what she had been sent to absorb. Studies, yes, of course, for she descended from a Jewish heritage of scholarship. But, as well, she was meant to open herself to a world greatly different from Baghdad, and the restrictions Iraq imposed on females of any age.

She had needed no urging.

She had wanted to write documentary films. Advertising, she had viewed as that path of artful deceit. Magazine work, or perhaps a job with *Agence France*, or perhaps the wire services.

All this, more even, she ladled out to Thomas on that evening. Inch by foot, they had begun themselves. For an unbroken stretch of nights and two weekends in a row, they seemed to ingest each other. He skipped three of his law classes at Fordham. She showed him New York, Bazak-style, an assortment of art galleries, the Metropolitan Museum, the Frick Museum, the ballet that he liked, two more Broadway shows, three cocktail receptions she dragged him to, dining at various neighborhood eateries, attending a Knicks game, and the Rangers. In their own ways, they were coming into their heart's sunlight, probing, diagnosing, learning the other's likes and dislikes. All of it very normal, abidingly pleasant, and for Thomas a feeling for another person like none he'd ever before known.

Was it love? He wasn't sure but didn't know what else it could be.

On a night before she had to leave town again, he'd come to her apartment and she'd asked, "What's on the menu for tonight?"

"Nothing special. Let's get lost somewhere. Destination moon."

"Perfect-o."

Up they went to Harlem to the Cotton Club, taking in the jazz and the revue of high-kicking dancers, some of the best Thomas had ever seen. She was making his stay in New York a joy, and getting his mind off his failure with the foundations. Alive, almost giddy at times, abuzz with enchantment. In his life, he'd never imagined this much fun, let alone having it with a woman.

Returning to New York late of an evening from St. Louis, after head-to-head workouts with Anheuser Busch who wanted more women drinking more beer, Shandar took a call from Poppi Nestor. They discussed a charity event for the

Boys Club of New York that Poppi was masterminding. As the details wound down, Poppi switched topics.

"Yesterday…yes, yesterday, I think it was, *Gott* my mind, my memory…I was working on lists and Jaggy Muldaur calls. She asks about that boy of yours."

"Boy, meaning Thomas, I suppose?"

"Who else? Things are friendly?"

"Pretty darn good. And please don't ask what I know you're about to ask."

"I'm not asking, I'm telling. Jaggy, you know what a dear friend she is. She calls and she makes these questions about him. The way she asks, though, so personal, it's maybe that they're better than friends. Mr. Thomas-the-divine, she thinks. Sometimes she gets that tone, and you know you shouldn't ask more. Si may, not me. No, thank you. She takes her milk with iron in it."

"And?"

"She's wanting to know if we're doing what she wants, looking after him. What can I say to that? I don't follow the man around, do I? He doesn't live with us, so what am I supposed to know?"

"And you're looking for a rundown from me?"

"Shandar, you give me something to tell her. Anything. This is Poppi asking you."

"Well, there is something you could say."

"Yes, and—"

"—that she can mind her own life and stay out of mine," Shandar asserted.

"You better listen, my precious. You don't want to get *meshugge* on that man. Lovely, oh yes. I'd have him for a son. I'd have him for anything. But Jaggy, she says—"

Two women, buddies, but one like a mother surveilling a much loved daughter on the brink of a blunder. They talked and talked, absorbing the slants of each other's thinking. On they went for the better part of ten minutes. Shandar had already acquired her lessons from the Nestors about the workings of the Muldaurs, and how, when wanting something, they almost always got it.

"I can make this go faster, Poppi. This is a nice, nice man. He's crazy about you and Si. I like him, what's not to like? That's all there is. You can make up something if you want. Tell her anything, I don't care."

"Come for lunch tomorrow."

"Tomorrow is a workday, how can I?"

"Listen, my lovely pet, you be careful…"

When the talk drew to its sluggish ending, she wasn't so sure of what Poppi had been driving at. Why would Jaggy Muldaur be nosing around about Thomas Courmaine and herself? He was likeable; he wasn't always on the make, like some men. She had even felt brief pangs of jealousy when other women trolled openly for his attentions at cocktail receptions she dragged him to. A sure sign of her feelings for him.

Looking out her office window at a vertical slice of Manhattan, she saw the pewter-colored sky was so low it had lost its line. A storm was heading in, probably. Suddenly, she stiffened, went very cold. Turmoil flooded her as she tried to rid herself of what was running loose inside her for the hundredth time.

Quarreling with herself now and losing again—forever believing she had put those horrifying days to rest, with a stern promise to herself never to unearth them again.

If he knew of her past, he'd never want her for his own. He might be magnanimous but magnanimity had its limits.

Staring dumbly at her reflection in the window, she suddenly became two people: the one whom she wanted to be but who was now receding; then, the other one—the slut—whom she so despised, avoided. Yet seemed unable to erase, no matter how fierce her attempts. Which one would triumph? She couldn't tell, she could never tell.

Taunting herself, then, judging and rejecting, raising the mask, lowering it, and then the remembering of what had befallen her.

Her family. All that weeping, gnashing, hand-wringing when she told them she was marrying the Lebanese civil engineer, a Marist Christian. Finally, she had had her way and the wedding vows were exchanged in a civil ceremony less than a year later. They had moved to Beirut, his place of birth and upbringing, the most majestic, romantic city of the Mid-east. One year later, she gave birth to a daughter, Jabella. Four incandescent years went by, when, one afternoon, husband and daughter were having ice cream at a sidewalk café. An explosion blew the street into rubble—a car bomb. Twenty-three people annihilated, another thirty-eight left maimed, many blinded for life. Her two loved ones among the dead. Grief-stricken, in a state of collapse, she had blanked out. Amnesia, or something close to it, set in. Escaping Beirut, she roamed blindly, alone and deadened inside. Her coat a camel's saddle blanket; on her feet, tattered sandals or sometimes nothing at all. She washed when she washed, in small streams, always at night. Often not knowing where she slept or what she fed on, her clothes in rags. Weeks went by. Dirty, her body a waif-like version of her former self. She had been wandering about up near the Syrian border, unsure of exactly where she was, and caring little. Every valley, every hill put a distance between her feet and Beirut. One day aimlessly crossing a vale, she was accosted by three terrorists masquerading as shepherds. They kept her in a cave, starving her whenever she resisted their molestings and outright assaults. Beaten with a hose, traded back and forth by the men, abused repeatedly, and then, when part of a flock wandered off in a storm, the men chasing after them, she managed her escape. Twenty or so kilometers to the south, she found a small monastery built on a mountainside. Eventually, the monks tracked her husband's family and she was returned to Beirut—as human wreckage.

Three months with those thugs had all but destroyed her.

Sent to Copenhagen, she was cared for by a psychotherapist and while there she slowly re-gathered her wits. Yet she still felt the touch of those grimy Arabs. Still felt the repulsion when they forced themselves inside her. Nothing had blotted the memory.

Recovered, or mainly so, at least thinking it, believing it, wanting it, she had landed in New York, determined to expel the past. Had found a job writing feature pieces for a Saudi-owned American periodical that summed the Middle East news, especially Saudi news. She went up the ladder in time, and eventually she was spotted by Abe Meric, head of Meric & Morris and a rainmaker in various Jewish causes. He had admired her choice of human-interest pieces, the way she did them up, the profiles and the color and background sketches.

For her, it was therapy—the writing. She wrote about Arabs, sometimes about Arabs who raised money for known terrorist groups. Forcing herself, in the process, to face her deep terrors. She looked at it as a sort of tonic that aided her in overcoming her hatred for Arabs, for every single Muslim extremist. To her, it was the same as taking small doses of poison to build one's immunity.

Still able as a Jew, and as a victim of Muslim-inspired atrocity, to write straight-ahead about a people sworn to annihilate her own kind. Day-to-day, her routine became her purgative. It worked, then for some reason it didn't work. The remedy wasn't enough.

Memory plagued her; a memory, at times, that seemed to haunt and devour.

How could she tell Thomas? What would he ever think about her? What would he think if she didn't tell him and somehow he found out? Who understood what two-hundred and eleven rapes were like, how they gouged at one's mind, how they splintered the soul? How the remembrance of it must be eternally fought against, repressed.

Harshly repressed, a never-ending effort exacting its own toll.

Still staring at the cold blankness of the window, her heart was stricken, a profound sadness sweeping through her. She had met someone she could care about, and care for, but what chance was there? In her mind, she was marked goods, steady in her belief she'd never again be right for a man.

Realizing suddenly one reason why Thomas had drawn her interest and affection. Safe, not platonic safe, but he had never pressed for sexual intimacy. She wasn't exactly sure why he hadn't, but in its way it was a relief; for, so far, she'd not been called upon to expose the darkest secret of her life.

Expose that secret by the act of refusing him intimacy, yet unable to explain why, unable even to give of herself: woman to man. How long could that last?

And if it couldn't last, then she had to accept what it meant: she wasn't leveling with him or with herself.

Having a day to himself at the Grammercy apartment, during one pause he glanced out the window and watched three cabs pull up in motorcade fashion in front of The Players Club across the park. He had been tempted to go over there one day, ask permission to go in and have a look around. As yet, he hadn't. He suspected they'd give him the bum's rush and yet he was still interested enough so that he toyed with the notion of asking Poppi Nestor, who seemed to know everyone in show business, to lasso an invite for him.

Mulling this, and missing Shandar, his mind drifted for a time. A reverie that was broken when the phone rang.

"Courmaine here."

"Hi. It is I, the doubting Thomasina from Bethesda."

"Alexis?"

"Yep, me."

"I thought I'd lost you."

"That's what I'm calling about. It worked. It did, it did, it did!" her voice rising almost to a shriek.

"Tell me. Give."

"Peter, our compliant little mouse, started to shed about two weeks ago. Vigorously shed. So I took him home, you know, to my own home so I could watch developments without any kibitzers. He shed all over his back, and there it was…a pinkish layer of skin. I scraped some cells, took it all back to my lab and ran a gel. The DNA, the part that matters, is mine. Can you believe it! Can you! You've got to tell me what's in that stuff of yours."

"In time, I promise. How much does Raab know?"

"Next to zero. I got a call a while back, but there was nothing to tell him then."

"Keep it that way for now, okay?"

"Hiding results like this, are you kidding? They'd ream me if they found out I concealed information like this."

"Well…yes, right. Sorry. I just wanted some time to piece things together."

"He'll go bananas, and I'll have to run the entire experiment by him and in full detail, using your notes. I can't hide anything, Thomas."

"I'd not want you to. Can you hold it up for three days or so? Something like that? When this gets out, it'll come back to me and I need to prepare for that. And I really do need advice about that aspect."

"Sure, three days. Four or five, even. I can stall that long easily. Will you let me know what's happening on your end?"

"You bet and by the way, congratulations, Alexis."

"You did it, not me. The whole thing was your idea. It's all I can think about. It's, well…I'm flying…"

"Thanks, thanks a million times. I'll be in touch soon. Take care of our friend Peter. What about the other mouse, Paul?"

"Nothing's happened, as you predicted it wouldn't."

"We're clicking. Our mouse roared, right? Give him a couple of extra pellets, compliments of T.I. Courmaine. Bye now and good going, Alexis."

Jackpot, he thought. Now, for a way to hang the news together, and maybe the foundations would take note, even if Raab and the NIH didn't bite.

At Rockefeller University, he reviewed a list with Lin-pao, delivered the weekly wad of cash to him, then poured the news from Alexis Hazlett. Pledging Lin-pao to silence, he then asked him to find another site where they could work in complete privacy. Thomas was concerned that if word leaked out at NIH, then half the researchers at Rockefeller would be crowding their office, with questions galore. Then, a cascade of publicity. He could imagine a headline: UNAUTHORIZED EXPERIMENT IN GOVERNMENT LAB.

"We may have to get out of here and find another place."

"This is ideal, is it not, sir? A famous institution…oh, indeed so, and I will be honored to list it prominently on my curriculum vitae."

"Don't even think about it. We're guests here, not employees. They can run us out any time that they need the space. Look around. See what you can find. Space will probably be too expensive here in Manhattan. Try over in Queens or possibly Brooklyn."

"I shall ask my uncle and auntie in Chinatown. They will apprehend space for us. Cheap. They never overpay, too sinful. You see—"

"Tell them not to apprehend it. If you get ideas from them, look at it and see what can be done. Something temporary, five-hundred feet or so. Enough to set up two benches and a couple of desks."

Lin-pao beamed. "From the very first, I classified you as a great genius. An American Confucius. A great wise man. I am right, am I not? Always right. I love myself for it."

Thomas didn't reply. He couldn't. When he made rejoining remarks to this talking machine, he often regretted his shortness. Lin-pao was a naturally exuberant type, packed full with energy, truly a priceless find. At times he had to contain himself, was learning how, mindful that once or twice he had trampled on his cohort's feelings.

His thoughts were stayed when the phone jangled. He had left a message with Shandar's office for her to call when she could. Two hours later, she did. "Where are you?" he asked.

"In Las Vegas."

"You mean seven-come-eleven, that Las Vegas?"

"The same but I'm not at the dice tables. We're thinking of representing the MGM group and I'm doing preliminary interviews. I wish I owned the power company out here, you should see the lights at night."

"I've got some interesting news," he told her. "I need a quarterback, and I'm choosing you. I'm up against a time-line, so if you can fit me in—"

"Fit you in! Are you all right, your mind? Of course, I always fit you in, as you put it. What's it all about?"

"I can't say at the moment. Good news, and I'll leave it there. Shall I come out and pick you up at the airport?"

"That'd be nice, very nice. Don't though. I have to drop by the office and chew the rag with Abe Meric for a while. I've no idea how long it'll take. He's in some flip-flop or other. Come by Saturday, in the morning, late morning."

"I'll call."

"Just come by. Ten, eleven, in there somewhere. I can't wait to hear. Can't wait to see you either. Oh, I know, would you be interested in a concert at Carnegie? It's next Wednesday."

"Whatever you say, I'm game."

"What I say is yes. It's Diana Krall, so I thought you'd like to go."

"Are you kidding? I'd be thrilled to go and thrilled to see you. Been a long week. Eight days of it."

"Saturday, then, that's for us. What fun."

Hanging up, she thought, I'm two people living two lives.

Jogging from Gramercy Park down to lower Manhattan, looping around Battery Park, he kept a steady pace most of the way up to Central Park. A seven-mile run. Walking for a while, the air frosty, the wind with a bite, he cut across Fifth Avenue, and ten minutes later rang the bell to Shandar's apartment.

Unshaven, his hair damp and his face splotched red from the whip of late autumn, he gave her a monstrous hug, as they clung. He sensed her eagerness, seeing the widening of her dark, depthless eyes as he put her down, their legs still pressed tight to each other.

"You're freezing," she said, seeing the cold pink in his cheeks and a dripping nose.

"Not anymore." A towel was curled around his neck, and he wore blue sweats with a white stripe blazed across the chest, encircling the arms.

"Tea? Hot tea? A bagel? I have lunch for us but it's a little early for that."

"Tea would be great. And wonderful to see you. A good trip?"

"Very good. I think MGM wants to sign with us. And you? You've got secrets you said, is that right? I'm practically down to the nub of my fingernails with curiosity."

"It isn't as big as it probably sounds but it's big enough," then telling her the essentials of what had been done at NIH. "It's no everyday thing. And it's enough to get all sorts of attention. That's where you come in, or I hope you do."

He was about to go on but she stopped him. "I want to know it all, Thomas. Let's go to the den, where we can be more comfortable."

There, in the den, she sat patiently while he stepped off the events at Bethesda. At interludes, Shandar posed questions, then more of them, as her foot beat a quiet tattoo against the floor, signaling she was engulfed by thought.

She said to him, "It's not so easy to see where this is headed, but you must feel absolutely on top of the moon."

"I do. This is central stuff. I've done it both ways: chimp to human and now human to rodent. And it worked...you see, Shandar, it really truly works. It predictably works." Beaming like a child with a first bicycle.

"I don't know the science part but you say it's big, so I say it's big. I'm astonished, I am. Aren't you?"

"To a degree. I've been through something like this before, remember."

"Africa is not the U.S., when it comes to news. We've battalions of media people here. They know every trick and they're relentless and even ruthless at times. Upset them and they'll also find ways to make you regret it. You're better off to meet with them, tell them the truth, and answer whatever it is they ask. Plenty, they'll be asking plenty. It sounds like plenty to me anyway."

"There're some things better left unanswered for now."

"Like?"

"The media will have questions about how this all works. I'm not sure how it does, frankly. The basics still must be worked out. The basis of it all is a shrub that grows in southern Africa, in Naruma. I don't want the source of Zyme-One revealed to anyone. It'll only encourage interlopers and the tribes-people there don't like interlopers. I want to stay well wide of that aspect."

"They may figure it out anyway. Just tell them that that's part of the background and for the time being, it's confidential. They'll keep at you, I'd guess, but they'll understand as long as you're truthful. She smiled, then, saying, "This one, really it's for the books. The skin angle, I find that incredible."

"I was thinking that there may be a delay after all. NIH will put a team on this, who'll study my notes and the protocol. Then they'll want to replicate the experiment with other mice. Measure, test, observe, quantify. But they can't, not without me they can't."

"What prevents them?"

"I've got the Zyme-One and they don't."

"Are you going to give it to them?"

"I will if they agree to my proposal. Agree if they take it over, the patents and everything else that's relevant, not to re-peddle it for profit. That it's open to anyone qualified in its use, free-of-charge. Otherwise, I'll not cooperate. There's an odd duck down there named Raab, a guy with a lot of power. They call him the beaver and he actually resembles one in a way. He's stump-shaped, with a funny head and his teeth are odd. I presented him with all this and he sort of shooed me off. But that's the only way I'll do it. No profit-making exclusives for the big drug outfits. That's iron-clad, and with no exceptions."

"Why're you so adamant on that point?"

"I grew up with nothing. Hardly a crust, you might say. I'd like to do something for the have-nothings of this world. For the most part, they get sicknesses at a larger and faster rate than the rest of us. They can't afford care, the treatments they need. I want to fix that and possibly I can."

"Noble of you."

"Not really. I'd get plenty of satisfaction just feeling that they're better off. I might even get my own statue in Khartoum one day. You can give a rousing speech and I'll take the pictures. I'm not a bad photographer, actually."

"You're not a bad anything. Tell you what, let's wait a week. If nothing happens on their end, I can call the NIH p.r. people and find out if they know anything or if they plan an announcement."

"And if they don't?"

"Well, then you have no worries on that front…oh, I see, I see…you mean if they decide to sit on it?"

"Right."

"Why would they?"

He shrugged. "I'm not sure why, except there's another side to this. The experiment was done, more or less, in conjunction with one of their research biologists. Alexis Hazlett. She donated her skin genes. Human genes, and when you do that, you're supposed to seek specific permission. That sort of thing. We didn't do that. It all happened pretty fast, but the omission could lead to problems. For her and for me. Another reason why I'm leery of the news people at this point."

"Will they do something to you? The government? Can they go after you?"

"I dunno. What would they gain? I took a chance because I got a chance. Besides, NIH, that's what it is primarily—one giant-sized experiment. Hundreds of them, probably thousands."

"But can they do anything to you?"

"If they want to they can. I somehow doubt they will. NIH likes break-throughs. Keeps em' in the limelight. Keeps Congress happy and that's what keeps the taxpayers' money coming in. I'll say this, if we'd moved the mouse's genes into Alexis Hazlett, instead of the other way around, there'd be a yell you could hear all the way to Zanzibar."

"You like walking the cliff's edge, don't you?"

"That's where the best views are."

Aiming a look of chagrin his way, she asked, "Is there more?"

"Really, a lot more. I'm pretty sure we can take human cells and trick them into thinking they're something different than what they started out to be. Here's what I mean. Supposing I had serious heart disease. Say, for example, my heart muscle was deteriorating. I think I could trick other cells into acting as if they're heart cells and thus rebuild the heart muscle. No surgery needed. They're doing something on that order at Harvard, as we speak. I think I know how to speed the process. How do you like that apple?"

"No surgery?"

"Nope."

"That'd be fantastic. What about a broken heart, can you fix that?"

"If it's the kind I think you mean, then the prescription for that problem is hugs and kisses."

"I suppose it is. Have you ever had your heart broken?"

"I grew up with one. No parents. No compass. No hugs or kisses that I remember."

"Never?"

"Not till I was seventeen, and I'd met a girl."

"Not so great. In fact, terrible. Not the girl but your childhood years."

"An emotional void, I'd say."

"So would I say."

"On the other hand, I was fortunate enough to have two fathers who were also close friends. Surrogates, but the best of the best. So, maybe I got the best end of it, after all."

"Perhaps."

And with that they kept to their own thoughts. He had stood and gone to the window, there to get a fix on the weather. He turned to her as she asked, "I guess all this razzle-dazzle gene fixing would go faster, wouldn't it, if one of the big drug companies stepped in?"

"No question there, yes it would," Thomas replied, recalling his evening in Boston with Miles Bascomb.

"That's a real hang-up, isn't it? Doing it all on your own?"

"A very high wall, I'm finding. Maybe too high in the end. I don't have the toolbox, not even the tools. Nonetheless, I like thinking about it. And I do think about it, especially when I'm not around you. Today is the exception. I'm here with you and I'm still thinking about it and pretty hard at the moment."

Her face blossomed. "Too hard, if it's taking away from your thoughts of me. Can we shift topics? Do you mind much?"

"I mind not at all. Shoot," he said, smiling his best.

"You might not like this and will think I'm prying. But I'd like to know something. It's about you and me."

"Go ahead, fire at will," he said, alerted by her tone, unsure of what to expect.

"Poppi talks to Jaggy Muldaur all the time and says that Her Highness constantly asks about you. Rivers of questions. Is there something between the two of you? A romance, say? An item we've neglected discussing."

"Jaggy? No, no. Jaggy and I are friends and have been for several years now. I was a closer friend of her stepfather's."

"You're sure?"

Looking straightly at her, he said, "Yes, very sure. Why?"

"Female curiosity on the rampage. I'd simply like to know the score."

"The score is zero to zero. A *nada*. Whatever brings this up?"

"I was just asking."

"You're asking for a reason. I don't mind you asking me anything at all. Jaggy and I are friends as I've told you and as Poppi surely knows. Until last year or so she's been married, mostly living in London. Married before that, too, twice, and living all over the world. When I resided in Naruma, the Muldaurs have a farm there, or did then, and we'd go on safari together a number of times. Always with her stepfather along. I saw her in London a three or four other times and, of course, at the big house in Jo-burg. That's ninety-percent of it. End of the Courmaine-Jaggy Muldaur connection in sketch form."

Knowing how easily Shandar could get the wrong idea, he redacted the parts about Jaggy sending a plane to fetch him out of harm's way when he needed to escape the hospital in Jo-burg. There was the junket to Paris to see her horse run; then, his prolonged stay at her home in Belgravia, the excursion to Deauville, and that night she came bedroom-prowling in Johannesburg; and, most damning of all, she had picked up the bill for his bespoke tailoring, custom shirts, the bench made shoes, and the promise he had made to spend the Christmas holidays with Jaggy. A promise he intended to somehow withdraw from.

Shandar suddenly, unbelievably blurted, "No sex?"

"That's no way to talk to me, Shandar."

"I'd like knowing. Please."

"Not with her. Frankly, not with anyone else, either."

"You're right, I shouldn't have asked that," said Shandar, quickly retracting when observing the grieved look on his face.

"I still don't understand how all this comes up."

"As I said, she calls Poppi all the time, and she says things and asks things. Missus Muldaur sounds suspiciously like a woman with very long arms."

"Ignore it. There's nothing there. A nice friend who's done me some really kind-hearted favors, but I'm not involved in the way you're suggesting."

"I'm not suggesting anything."

"But you are, you are indeed. Just so you know, and for future reference, her stepfather was one of the great friends I ever had. He'd thought I'd be a good influence over Jaggy, but that was all. Maybe it wouldn't've ended there but it did. And it has. And it will."

"I'm being nosy, aren't I? Subject closed. I have to make an appearance this evening at a cocktail shindig. I'd utterly, completely forgotten. But I must. Will you come?"

He groaned.

"You sound as if you're about to undergo an appendectomy. Please do, there'll be some fun people there."

"Of course, I'll go. I haven't seen you all week so I'd rather not share you with the public." He blew a theatrical sigh toward her. "Whatever the price, whatever the burden, whatever the cross to bear and the boredom that—I take that back, there's nothing, ever boring about you. What time do we run the gauntlet?"

"Seven."

"Whose party?"

"Sallie Ainge."

"Sallie Ainge, the columnist?"

"You don't know her, or do you?"

"Of her. In the newspapers, I've read her columns once or twice."

"She's the reason I have to go. She occasionally serves the great cause of one Shandar Bazak. Every so often, I have to get her to run an item for a client. So when the "voice" calls, I run right straight to the trough. You shouldn't mind a little party, Thomas. Half the women I introduce you to seem to snap their garters whenever you're around. I should think you'd love it. I ought to keep track of the ones I don't like and you can turn them into mice someday."

They laughed. "I'll be sure not to repeat any of that."

"It'll be dressy tonight."

"How dressy is dressy?"

"That divine blue suit will be per-*fect*-o. And my favorite shirt, the blue one with the pink stripes."

She had been sitting on one of the two white sofas in the den, and now she arose, tossing him a little wave of her hand and disappeared as if she'd never been there. She always seemed to move like air, invisibly. Instantly, he missed her and he gazed about quite absently. Though it was a spacious five-room apartment, they always seemed to end up here in the den. Fifteen-by-twelve square feet of stark whiteness, except for its hardwood floor that was partly covered with a colorful Navajo rug; the bright white walls held four brass-framed lithos by Miró and Chagall; pillows, all in jelly bean colors, were scattered haphazardly on the sofas and two beige-striped chairs. Everything else was white as a passing July cloud; against it, when Shandar, who was caramel-dark in color, entered the room, she became, oddly, its brightest part.

They ate a quick lunch at the kitchen counter; later, about to leave for his own apartment, he borrowed twenty-dollars for cab fare, having forgotten to bring cash when he had gone jogging that morning. At the door, Thomas reached for the handle, and Shandar let out a mild howl. "Hey, how 'bout me? Doesn't your p.r. advisor rate a Saturday afternoon kiss?"

They stood apart. Eyes searching, eyes filled with curiosity. Had she said something incurable? She had tried to be light and humorous, and now, Oh, God...*oh, God...*

But then their kiss, their first, loaded with commotion. When Thomas left, she leaned against the closed door. Time to let go, she thought, feeling like a virgin whose time had come—giddy with excitement yet uneasy. Knowing she must invoke the past, tell him all the things she wanted to forever hide.

On the way down to Grammercy, he remembered words he'd said at dinner with Alexis Hazlett that night in Bethesda: "I'll let you know if I get star-struck," he had told her, as she chided him about the lonely single life. Minutes ago, his parting from Shandar was a well-worn, pervading moment, happening countless times between couples everywhere. Yet never before by himself. In all his life, he never had ridden higher; finally her, finally a someone for him. Peter, Paul, the Eves, the fight with Maistinger that had driven him away from the Vatican, the loss of Baster, the semi-estrangement with deMehlo—none of it seemed to matter as he tripped off in a gauzy numbness.

He would be with her, make a life together. Marry one day, he hoped, and if he couldn't be released from his priestly vows, then marry anyway. If Shandar would agree, that is. And what to do about Jaggy and her Christmas plans? And why all those calls to Poppi Nestor?

Si Nestor arrived at the office early—5:36 a.m.—and there on the stack of urgent-messages, complied by a night-secretary, he saw a request to call Jaggy at Muldaur's London office.

Wishing later that he had never returned the call, one that he never mentioned to Poppi or to anyone. Alone, that lodged the episode, about to happen, deep in his memory.

"Jaggy, Si here."

"Yes, how're you?"

"Fine. I just plopped in my chair. A message here that you called."

"I did indeed…"

Wuddia mean *indeed*, he thought.

"Some questions, Si. First of them is, how is our friend Thomas progressing?"

"A regular prince, that boy. Poppi asks about him twice every day. Haven't seen as much of him lately."

"You remember that little arrangement we had of a few months ago. That you were to assign a few of the better traders to advise him, so he could build up some funds?"

"How could I forget that? Lately, he's been losing. I haven't said anything much because I don't want him getting suspicious. You know, Jaggy, it was working' just the way you wanted. Had a nice little run there, going very nicely, then he got kicked. Happens, of course. He started trading on his own…and took some losses…inevitable losses…"

"Si, the arrangement, it's canceled."

"All right, canceled. Anything else?"

"I want no other assistance given him from you or the other traders. Shut him off. Do it today."

Stunned, Si waited and then offered, "What for? Hell, Jaggy, he's a friend of ours. I can't do that. What'll I tell the traders? High-hat him? They like him. We all like him. I can't lay him out on the beach for the gulls to peck on."

"Is that so…fancy that? Oh, Simon Nestor, I find that exceedingly interesting. Are you saying you're not following what I'm asking of you? Or is it that you are following very closely what I'm asking but unwilling to follow my instructions? Which is it to be, Si?"

He heard Jaggy being Jaggy. Officious, overly deliberate, coercive. That dagger sharp voice, a hint of a red-toothed chewing-out from across the Atlantic. Taking a deep breath, he said, "Turn my back, is that it? I play dumb, is that it? You think he won't figure that out in an eighth-of-an-instant?"

"I don't particularly care what he figures out. Recess is over. He's taken his vacation. It's time he got himself back here. I presume he learned his lesson from those foundations that sent him packing. Didn't get anywhere, did he?"

"Why make it worse for him?"

"Worse, you say? Balls! I made a foolish mistake, thinking I might help him but you cannot help anyone by falsifying what's reality. I'm trying to be of help, be a friend…and he's seeing some woman? A friend of yours, I take it?"

A light blazed in Si's head. Of course, risen jealousy doing its vendetta. Poppi must've been sending woman-talk across the Atlantic. What the hell, he thought—a couple of kids having some fun, so what of it? He hoped they were enjoying themselves, and it sounded as if they were. Jaggy wants to break it up, does she?

"Yep, she is a friend of ours," Si confirmed. "Shandar Bazak. Nice woman, a best beloved."

"A Jew is she, Si?"

"An Iraqi Jew. Good family. I wished I were part of it. Sassoon, you know. Headliners, front of the synagogue and all that."

"I see."

"What's to see? A very special lady, and a big help to Poppi."

"How reassuring. You have my idea firmly in mind, do you? No more of anything. No cockups. I make myself exceedingly clear, I trust."

Christ, how she loved that word *exceedingly*. Si wished she'd choke on it, but said, "I got it all. Am I supposed to keep track, make reports?"

"I hardly think it'll be necessary. Ta-ta, I'll be in touch. Love to you, Si, and Poppi when you see her."

With that, the click. And with that, his heart revolted. He had become truly fond of Thomas who had become like a son. In a life of many gifts and successes, it was a gaping hole—that he and Poppi had never been blessed with a son.

The bitch. Baster would never pull a stunt like this, and yet Si knew he was in no position to countermand a clear order. The worst of it was, what if

Thomas's luck turned? What if he started to rake in trading profits again? Jaggy might never believe Thomas did it on his own.

London, England
New York, New York

Next day.

"Poppi...Jaggy here."

"Darling, darling, so early...uh"

"I'm due in Amsterdam and this is the only time I have. Who, pray, is this Bazak woman Thomas is seeing. Why haven't you been telling me?"

"I did, I remember I did."

"Not that he's with her so much of the time. How often do they go out? Are they sleeping? What's her claim? I want it all. Nothing left out, Poppi."

"How should I know all this? They're friends. That's what I know. Si...we...they came to dinner here...I told you this, Jaggy...I told you..."

"Is he shagging that woman?"

"Oh, oh, language, the language. I am not the mother. No talk like that, Jaggy, please."

"I want you to find out. Today find out and call me at noon your time."

"Jaggy, I cannot go to her and ask such things. I am not the police. I cannot do this."

On the other end of the line, Poppi heard an exasperated huffing sound, and then, "Poppi, is Si there?"

"He went to the office...he leaves at five-thirty...he's there if you want him."

"Have you any idea what we've paid to Si since he's been with us?"

"Some millions, I know. How many is it, do you know?"

"Three-hundred and twenty-four million. Somewhat more, actually. That's U.S. money and a tidy sum I'd say. Exceedingly tidy. And, of course, another seventeen million for your charities over the years."

"So much. I hope no more taxes on us." Poppi felt a thud in her stomach. Something was coming. "I never knew Si's income...he does the...looks after our money. He should tell me, that *naar*. I think he's off his diet again," Poppi

226

went on, trying to change the subject. "Men, you know them, never let them out of your sight is what I say to myself—huh—"

"I'll be in New York soon. Thomas is spending the holidays with me, so I'm coming over there to pick him up after a stop in North Carolina. Meanwhile, I want to know what I want to know. I think we've paid plenty for such a small favor. And another thing…are you listening…you are, aren't you?"

"With you talking like that, in that tone, I can't listen…I can't, I go deaf…I…this makes me in tears, Jaggy. Oh, please…please…two friends and you put me in the middle of…'

A sudden rush of tears. Poppi dropped the phone, lifting the corner of the bed sheet to dry her eyes. She felt plundered, all the while hearing a distant cackle from the phone, like some child's toy with a voice recorder sewn to its insides. The phone seemed to be shouting at her, "Find out! You hear me, Poppi? Are you there? I'll be over there, and you'd better have your friend straightened out by the time I…"

New York, New York

At Rockefeller University, several days later a call came as Thomas sat in the small office used by Lin-Pao and himself. Every part of the conversation packed with surprise.

"…Not so promising, I'm afraid," Shandar was cautioning him.

"Shoot."

"I talked to the public affairs people at NIH this morning. They seem to know nothing whatsoever about this mouse experiment of yours. I tend to believe them. So, you might want to check into it with your assistant, the researcher. I've forgotten her name."

"Alexis Hazlett."

"Yes."

"That's strange. She gave me what sounded like a straight-ahead report on what was going on. There'd be no point in fudging something like that, even if you could. And she wouldn't in any event."

"Are you all right with this?" Shandar asked. "Of course you aren't. Stupid of me, asking. It's distressing, isn't it?"

"Very odd. I wonder what Alexis Hazlett is thinking."

"Why not call her?"

"As soon as we hang up, I shall. I'll get back to you."

"Please do."

Out of ideas. Eight times he had been decked cold by eight foundations in America, now some terrible foul-up at NIH. Another fearful, fearful loss of time?

He phoned Alexis twice at her lab. No luck. In the evening, he tried her at her home. No answer there. He considered calling Raab, deciding against it. Had something happened to Alexis? An accident?

He called Shandar, telling her what he learned. Nothing. "I'll connect sooner or later."

"Strange. Two strange things in a row."

"What's the other one?"

"I had quite a chat with Poppi about an hour a go."

"Poppi's fine, is she?"

"Not really. Quite distraught, actually. You and I, it seems, must have a talk."

"Anytime. I'm spring-loaded in the listening position."

"Not now. Not on the phone. Keep Friday night open, Thomas. I'll be back from Pittsburgh and we can have dinner. Twenty-One, we'll go there."

"Twenty-one where? Twenty-one?"

"It's a restaurant located at Twenty-One West Fifty-Second Street. Everyone refers to it as Twenty-One. It's famous. Some people call it the 'numbers'."

"You sound serious."

"I am serious."

"You want to do a gallery in the afternoon? Then go for dinner afterward?"

"I'm drowned in wall-to-wall work. I have things to get ready for next week. Bye now…bye…"

Sounding offish, distant.

On a window-frosted morning at his apartment, awaiting Lin-pao, Thomas picked up the phone and heard Si Nestor's gravelly voice on the other end.

"That you, kid?"

"It's me. None else lives here. Morning, Si."

"Likewise. Got to make this snappy. Let's close up this trading account you opened. You got kicked in the ass yesterday and I've no extra time to look after you. You went down a little over forty fat ones at yesterday's close. You leave your position open overnight and it can bite your balls off. It's not a real breaker but you can lose all you got here with us."

"No one told me anything."

"Laddie, this is not a missing person's bureau. No one's got time to chase you down. You eat your loss and we stop the shenanigans."

"I thought the traders were looking after it."

"While you were here, mebbe. Look, a bath but not a big bath. I got to put some speed on my day. I'm calling to tell you we're closin' you out and we'll remit the balance in a check. Mail it to your apartment or come by and pick it up. Either."

"The mail will be fine, Si"

"Mail it is. Everything's jake then. You got the makins', kid, I keep telling you. Everyone knows that, huh? What a country! Lately not so good, but what the fuck, it's America. Who's got it any better? Gotta run. Jesus Maloney, what a morning. You give us a call and we do dinner. See ya', kid. In the mail today sometime, your check."

Bang! The click of the phone sounded like a forty-thousand dollar explosion, a sum that was most of what he had promised to pay Lin-pao for an entire year. Blank-eyed. Dumbfounded. His sporadic commodity trading, trying to cover the startup costs of a small makeshift lab in some low-rent district, was fully doomed. How could he be so stupid as to leave so much to chance, depending on the Muldaur traders to watch his trading positions? Why should they? He was penny-ante and they traded in the many millions within a given minute.

His head emptied of all thought, all feeling. Shaking it back and forth, he attempted to clear a buzzing nothingness in it.

At "21 they were waiting for a banquette. At the crowded bar she stood next to him; close, and she was sheathed in a moon-colored frock, backless, a single strand of pearls aglow against her almond-hued skin. Her black feathery hair was combed higher tonight. On its left side she had pinned a white camellia that reflected in the bar mirror, radiating like a single star, somehow enhancing the Oriental cast of her face.

As lovely as she looked, she seemed removed, a brittle tone creeping into her voice at times.

Bewildered, he had never seen her like this—so mechanical, and as if she'd just stepped out of cold storage. When he talked, she appeared indifferently glum. When he smiled, she smiled back; stiffly though, a lockjaw smile.

Bending forward, Thomas reached for his drink, and, with his free hand, laid his fingertips against the warm satiny texture of her bare back, Pliable, soft, smooth. Then a slight shudder—from her? Or was it his hand trembling?

Suddenly she went taut, moving away from his touch.

"Good drink, this," he said, unsure of what else to say. "What did you call it?"

"A Comstock. A vodka martini with two onions and dry sherry instead of vermouth."

"Annihilating, in other words."

"Here comes our table, I think."

A captain in a tuxedo showed them to a banquette in the front section of the room. When seated, Shandar said, "I'm going to have another annihilator. You, too?"

"If you say."

"I do say. For myself, anyway. You can do as you please."

"You should wear that rig of yours all the time," he said. "You've turned every head within sight."

"I'm so surprised you noticed."

"Sure, I noticed. But then you'd look great in a paper bag."

The waiter came over and greeted Shandar as if she were his long-missing cousin and she introduced him to Thomas. Luca, who hailed from the small town of Sofia outside of Rome, an area Thomas knew well. They reminisced a little in animated Italian. Then, taking their order, Luca departed and Shandar said, "Luca likes you."

"He likes you, too. For a moment there I thought he'd be sitting down with us."

"I've known him for years. I always sit in his area if I can. They look after me as if I'm in the family."

"Plenty of people would like to have you in their family."

"You, too?"

"Especially me. Only I am a family of one, as you well know."

"One is all it takes. Well, two. What're you looking at?"

"I'm looking at you, Shandar, and also a gent over there at the corner banquette. He's from DuPont. I met him in Johannesburg at a dinner given by the Muldaurs, a father and daughter affair. Quite a night. Big doings. The president of South Africa was there and some other high dignitaries."

"Is that his wife?"

"I don't know. Maybe she is. I think I'd remember, though, if she were with him in Jo-burg."

"Yes, I imagine any man would. Stunning, isn't she?"

"Very. They really pack them in here, don't they?"

"It's one of the better known restaurants in America. A lot of out-of-towners. Like a club, which is why they call it the "21 Club" or some people do. It's fun. We frequently bring clients here."

"*Macher.* Si Nestor would call the DuPont guy a *macher*."

She laughed for the first time that evening. "Yiddish."

"Means a big-shot, am I right?"

"A self-appointed big shot."

Shandar nibbled on her lower lip. She had a habit of doing it when carrying a heavy thought, and he was waiting on her to pick up the threads of what was biting her. Nothing though, not a single clue. To occupy himself, he gazed into the room, listening to the subdued hubbub, the gentle clink of glassware, observing the legion of waiters bustling about in their military-style red jackets and black trousers. An expensively cheerful and busy place, he thought.

"You're so quiet," he said.

"Cogitating, that's all. DuPont, gene fixes, mice, those things. Plus, some of the things you've been telling me. Interesting things but not half as interesting as things you've not been telling me. We need to talk, a real talk-talk."

"By all means, let's."

Looking away, she drew in an audible breath. "Something unexpected happened a couple of hours ago. Poppi called me. She'd mentioned the same things to me a few days ago and then again late this afternoon. And, well, I remember your saying you were supposed to go to Europe for Christmas but decided not to. But Poppi says you're going there anyway. She's heard it twice now, she says. I thought you might've said something to me."

"And I would have, too. But I'm not going to Europe. I'll be here with you, that's what I'd hoped for."

"Why would Poppi say that? She told me your Muldaur friend is due in New York and she's here to haul you off somewhere. You'd certainly know about that, wouldn't you?"

"In fact, I know nothing about her coming here. What brings all this up?"

"I just told you. That I heard you were off to Europe to be with her. Meanwhile, chapter two is that I've been reassigned by the firm and you'll never guess where. I'll save you the trouble and tell you."

"Reassigned to where?"

"I'm trying to tell you. Yesterday Abe Meric crooked his finger at me. We had an extremely dismal hour, with me being the dismal one. The short of it is I'm being sent to Australia for at least three months. Possibly longer. I hope not but it's always possible."

"Australia?"

"I'm being shipped out there until they can find a replacement. They fired the person who's there now. Losing too much money, I was told. The person running it"—she shrugged—"has drinking problems and the usual family troubles that go with it. That's bad enough but the Sydney office is hemorrhaging and Abe wants action. I'm not a manager. I create campaigns. I don't do numbers and fire and hire. But I'm still a hired hand and not an owner. So off I go…"

He moved his hand to his face, as if to clear his vision. "I'm temporarily out of oxygen. This is the second time in a couple of day I've been floored," thinking of Si Nestor's news about the trading losses.

"Me to Australia and you to Europe. Have you been playing me…some game or something? Trifling? Was I being gulled?"

"You know better than that, or I hope you do."

"It appears I don't know a thing and—"

"Yes, you do—"

"Will you stop interrupting?"

"As soon as you start making some sense, I will."

"Stop doing it."

"Doing what?"

"Interrupting."

"I'm not interrupting. You're sore about Jaggy. It wouldn't stop the world to hear a fact or two—"

"You and your facts—"

"Now who's interrupting?"

"You. And your friend Muldaur is in North Carolina or soon will be."

"What's she doing there?"

"You think I run her schedule?"

"You seem to know everything else."

"Oh, balls to you."

"No comment."

"I happen to have a few friends in the London press. You know what they call her? They call her the Stiletto and she sounds like one."

Smiling, he replied, "I suppose she can be. She's no daisy, I'll agree with that."

Shandar sat forward. "I want you to come with me. Just for a few weeks and we'll just have ourselves to ourselves. I'll be busy but—"

"All this comes out of thin air. Thin is hardly the word for it. I can't pack off for Australia," he said. "Pretty soon now I have to leave for Switzerland but only for a day or two. Three, at most."

"What's there that won't wait?"

"It's Muldaur family business. It has nothing whatsoever to do with Jaggy. It does have something to do with the South African government, however." Saying it without thinking and wishing he hadn't.

"Oh, is that so? Then there is something between the two of you, isn't there? She's coming here and you, you're going there and you make it sound as if it's nothing. Something you do every other week or so, like calling your mother—oh, I'm sorry, I didn't mean that. Thoughtless of me. Sorry."

"Lot's of this seems pretty thoughtless. None of my going to Geneva has to do with Jaggy Muldaur. The connection to her is mere. To say the least, it's mere."

"How strange. You just said it was Muldaur family business and then you say it has nothing to do with her. How can that be? Isn't she the only Muldaur left?"

"It's complex, Shandar, and I cannot easily explain it all. I'm sorry but—well, it's—it's a highly confidential situation and I've had to make my promises. They pay me handsomely and it's not milk money. I need it to live on, so I must honor my pledge. "

"Not the way you dress yourself, for sure it can't be milk money."

It wasn't possible to say it, or if he said it, then to explain it. He was about to squirm and he never squirmed. How had all this started? One call from Poppi Nestor and then this landfill of complications. He felt an urge to wring Poppi's neck, kibitzing and interfering like some nickel-and-dime matchmaker who didn't have the sense to butt out.

"We've gotten ourselves into a misunderstanding," Thomas suggested. "I'm sorry. Let's put it behind us, can we? Forget it, can we do that? Sorry about all the mix-ups and confusion but that really isn't my doing."

"Sorry, *you're* sorry. Sorry covers everything except what's really going on. That's all you can say…sorry?"

"At the moment, it is."

"Cancel Switzerland, can't you?"

"Impossible, really impossible. I missed the last meeting. Two in a row would be…I can't and that's all I can say about that…"

"They'll understand."

"No, they won't."

"Is that where she'll be? St. Moritz or Gstaad for the winter season?"

"I've no idea. I'll be in Geneva for one day of meetings and then back here."

"Come with me. Give them a rain check for when it rains again. Have you told her about us?"

"Hasn't been any need to. Why would I? We're us, not her. She has nothing to do with us."

"Tell her, why not? If she's any kind of a friend, she'll be delighted for you."

"Delighted? I don't know about delighted. Curious probably."

"You don't know women."

"Bingo."

"Thomas." The tone strident, the sounds of a woman not yet through with her kicking. "Tell her. Give her the big bulletin she hasn't been waiting for. And come with me. A month, that's all. Let's have a month straight and find out if we—if there's a future." She had said it, a straight clarified proposition.

"I have no month to give away. I'm trying to set something up with Lin-Pao. There's the NIH situation to deal with."

"I have to know, is she anything to you? I need the truth, and I need it now."

"You've had all the truth there is. Jaggy's an old friend, as I've said two or three times to you. That's it. Nothing more. *Nada*. Double *nada*."

"Does she mean more than I do?"

"No. Let's drop it. I can't say more because there isn't any more. And I can't go with you right now, either, to Australia or the Gobi Desert or anywhere but right here."

Shandar looked at him with her big luminous eyes. "Bull-balls!" she said flatly.

"Be reasonable, Shandar. I came to America to see about a project. Win or lose, I've got to see it through. I've no other choice. I'll be here, and I'll be waiting for you."

All sensibility had left them, their opposing attitudes having blocked any coherence or meeting of minds. It was as if they were practicing different foreign languages. At one point, she gored him, "I can't believe you're a rosebud. You're not wired that way, are you? *Are you?*"

"A which?"

"A virgin. A rosebud. You've been with women in bed, I presume?" She had stepped too far, and she knew it. "Oh, God, I apologize," Shandar blurted. "I'm just so damn upset. Look at me."

"I am," Thomas said.

"Harder, look at me."

"How `bout holstering your cannon?" Staring at her now, but his exasperation was rife.

"I have to know about us, about you. I—I had a real fantasy last night. You. I thought I'd—I was—never mind. And so even if I'm coming on to you like this, I hope you don't get the idea I'm an easy piece of trade. I'm not. I'm very fussy in that department." Not leveling with him, she was running her bluff, masking her neurosis, fear-ridden. Afraid of telling him about her past, afraid of losing him even if she did tell him. She was forcing herself now, unsure of her direction, her wants, her place. A muddle of feelings, all seeing to be at cross-purposes. She summoned all she had in her heart, saying: "Let's go, then, what're we waiting for?" Her eyes flashing, angrily or excitedly, even disdainfully—he couldn't tell, he was so fully at bay. "Let's go to my home like two adults and settle this. I'm all for initiating operations right now. All we've ever done is kiss twice. Two kisses in two months as though we're children. I'm not your sister, or am I?"

"You've been the bright spot in an otherwise crummy year. Yes, wouldn't it be wonderful, if we had more time to find out about each other in some far-off place? By ourselves. There isn't time right now. If we start up, right now, we'd have to stop as soon as you leave New York. I couldn't stand it. You're the kind of woman who ought to be celebrated to the fullest, but I can't do that in the next few days, not with any sincerity. What would sex mean, other than a sort of shacking up, then all the remorse and regretful good-byes? What would the rest of it mean? I may regret this for the rest of my life, but I can't go home with you for a one-night stand or even a three-night stand. Does that make sense to you?"

"Very gallant. But make sense? After two months I'd say it sounds ridiculous. I could've been one of the best people in your life."

"You already are."

"Was."

"You're here. We're together. We're not separated—"

"Yet."

A dead end. Her lips fluttered. Vexed about what her voice might do, she kept silent and then did the only thing she could, as she slid out of the banquette. Striding off then, the elegant legs moving her away as effortlessly as a wisp of smoke vanishing in thin air.

Digging into his pocket, he pulled out some bills, leaving fifty dollars on the table for their drinks. He walked toward the door, letting the room fade away, mentally placing it on the list of places he no longer wished to remember.

Catching up with her at the coatroom, he followed her outside where they waited wordlessly under the canopy. The night teemed with cold slushy wetness. He slung an arm over her shoulders, and, while she didn't shrug it off, she turned rigid, turning her head away. His eyes stung and it wasn't from the sleet-filled night. They lost any chance of privacy when another couple appeared, waiting in the small queue for taxis.

After a wait, one pulled up. The doorman handed Shandar into the back seat. Thomas was about to join her when she waved him off. The door slammed shut; her loud goodnight and what seemed an even louder goodbye.

Tires spun, kicking up the street-slush, soaking him from the knees down. He hardly felt it. Ten minutes later another taxi stopped at the curb, with the doorman holding an umbrella as he climbed in. In the stark, fluid night, an iron fist clenched his innards. He had thought he had found a friend, perhaps a lover, even one day a wife. How had it all shattered so suddenly?

Done in, Shandar leaned against the inside of her apartment door as soon she arrived home. Condemning herself, fully confused by what she had done. She had opened her seams, made a direct offer to have him with her for the night. As if a camera had clicked, and an instant of time was forever frozen, she summoned the image of this very door, when he had hugged her in those powerful arms, lifted her, and later kissed her. She could still taste that kiss.

Testing him, testing him, testing him.

No Australia, no sex, no anything; a stuporous ending to what had been a promising, fun-filled two months with a bright, somewhat priggish, attractive man.

How disingenuous. A big fat fakery, inviting him for the night. What if he had? What would it be like? What if she had frozen up as she had once before with another man, made a hash of it, humiliating herself to tears? She had not been with any man since her husband, not willingly anyway.

And here she was, limp as a rag-doll, astray in her wilderness of self-deception. Face it, she commanded herself for not less than the hundredth time, *you've erected a barrier against men*. So far, and no farther. Knowing she had behaved badly, even dishonestly, starting that quarrel. Giving him a dose of what-for, the full earful, all the while knowing she'd pull a deep-freeze act if they got anywhere near a bed. And then all but accusing him of being a traitor, a bounder, for having Jaggy Muldaur on the sly. A rosebud, even.

She had had two drinks at "21" and now felt like another. A third one and she'd be looped. Maybe not such a bad idea. Thinking all this as she dragged herself out of her clammy panty hose that had collected some of the night's wet from the street.

The hose lay on the floor. Two brown leg-shapes sprawled every which way.

She forgot the drink. It wasn't too late to call Brooklyn Heights. Worth a shot, wasn't it? Maybe she hadn't heard Poppi correctly; maybe she'd owe him a monstrous apology.

It was Si who answered. She asked for Poppi with speed that bordered on incivility.

Poppi, then: "Poochie, is that you, my darling?"

"Yes. Is it too late? I'm sorry."

"What's to be sorry for, and what is so troubling. Your voice. It's trouble, I can tell."

"I—I'd like to be sure of something. Do you know for certain that Thomas is leaving New York?"

"Uh-oh. You been cut in half, is it? By that *mench*? I told you, twice I told you. Oh, Shandar…"

"Are you sure of it?"

"It's what I was told. Jaggy, you know her…we'll, you don't know her. She says so and so I think it is a yes. Somehow he goes away. You know he's been looking everywhere. Those foundations, Si tells me. I will never understand. Gene things, something like that, and Si says no takers. But why does it matter? Jaggy says she'll take care of him. Planning to, all along. They will make the business somewhere in Wales, I think there…is what she said. I think so. I wasn't paying close attention to that part."

"She—she's buying him a laboratory?"

"Is what she says. Back they go to England and from there who knows?"

A breathless silence as Shandar inhaled this news.

"You there, poochie?"

"I'm here. I'm thinking up ways to butcher that slut."

"Ssshhh-ushy."

"Well, I would if I could."

"She's trying to have herself a baby. That's what she said also. She's here in America somewhere at a place they do those procedures."

"A baby? Whose baby? Not his?"

"Her own baby. Who else? She's needing an heir. She has no one."

"Who's the father?"

"Am I supposed to know the father? How should I know a thing like that?"

"Thomas, is that who it is? You don't mean that, you can't."

"Who can say? I can't. Didn't he go somewhere south for some days. Bethesda, I think. Near Washington. Maybe with her, who can tell anything?"

"You're saying he went away to have a child with her?"

"Poochie, all I tell you is she wants the baby. Also, him. He's got her coming here for him. Jaggy Muldaur says that to me explicitly."

An unfortunate mix-up of words by Poppi, causing Shandar to reach a mistaken conclusion. "I'll call tomorrow, Poppi. I—well—tomorrow okay?"

Soon as she set down the phone, the picture all but painted itself. He'd been gaming her, toying with her feelings. He'd lied, hadn't he? He'd trumped up the NIH story to keep her interested, impressed, stringing her along. That must be why the publicity people at NIH knew nothing about some fancy-assy experiment that supposedly would shake the world to pieces.

Even Africa, was that a lie too? Some ruse about those women, wasn't it, fooling the news media? Still steaming, her nerves tight as guy wires, she paced around her apartment, something she never had done before; then flummoxed, she went back to her bedroom, into the closet and began the process of packing for Australia. A week early but she had to get her mind off the evening's wreckage.

All of the following day Thomas kept to himself, aimlessly puttering around at his own apartment. He read, then he did not read. He thought, then he did not think. He dozed fitfully. When sunlight flowed, if it flowed at all, he daydreamed. All the while, wanting so desperately to see her. At least, hear her.

He left three calls for Shandar, no replies, making the day more regrettable. At a loss, yet he still did not call on Poppi to intercede, suspecting she may well have been the cause of the rupture with Shandar. Si? No, not Si, either. He hadn't spoken to Si since the close of his trading account. Besides, any call to Si would necessarily involve Poppi.

Where was she?

A long-awaited sound snapped him out of his reverie. The phone, ringing, twice or was it three times? Don't hang up, he implored to no one, racing across the room.

"Thomas…that you?"

"Yes."

"It's Alexis Hazlett—"

"—oh, Alexis, sorry, I thought it might be someone else. And here you are, and I've been phoning you for days."

"I know you have. I've gotten your messages. I've been away. All of a sudden I'd been offered five job interviews. One was in California, so it took almost three days for that one alone. Out and back."

"You're leaving NIH?"

"Yes, but not quite yet. It was a little strange getting all these interviews out of the blue. Stranger still, I was offered good jobs at three companies. The interviews were so transparently a set-up. Formalities. Offers to triple my salary. That kind of thing. I'm good, but no one's that good overnight."

"I see…maybe I don't see."

"I've got the worst news. It's awfully terrible."

"This is the week for it."

"Oh, is something wrong?"

"Go ahead with yours, please."

"I hope you're in your chair."

"I'm not, I'm standing."

"We've been robbed. Peter is gone and I don't know where. All of your lab notes, everything is missing…the shebang."

Not possible, he thought. Not again, not after losing his work concerning the Eves. "Start at the beginning," he said.

"I had made my preliminary report to Raab and he ordered me to bring Peter back to my lab. I was keeping him at home, so I could keep an eye on him. So I brought him back, I had to. I asked for a few days off so I could go on the interviews, though what I told Raab was that I needed a rest and would use the time to make a more thorough report. When I got back, Peter's cage was empty and someone had jimmied the lock on one of my file cabinets. Everything having to do with the experiment was missing…*kafooie*…gone, just like that. Everything! I called security and they sent someone over. He took my statement, shot a couple of photos and took off to see Raab. Apparently, Raab has denied just about everything…*everything*…except that he'd met with you in his office. Nothing about sending you over to my lab. He's lying and he's trying to make a liar out of me. I could strangle that shit-head, I really could."

"He'd have to admit I was there. I signed the visitor's log. Is that it? That's plenty, I admit. But is there anything more?

"There is, yes. Another call came from Raab and he said I was to say nothing to anyone until it was all sorted out. Nor was I to do anything else other than finish my report and forward it to him."

"Keep a copy."

"Definitely. It's all so crazy. It's scary. I can't verify or prove anything of what you did. Not without your notes. Sabotage, that's what I call it. Oh, there is something more, why did I forget?"

"Okay, shoot."

"Raab wants that material you used, that Zyme-One enzyme. I told him there wasn't any left. Or, if there was, it isn't here. He was furious I hadn't made you leave a specimen. No one can replicate the experiment without you. I don't think they want a repeat of it anyway, but he didn't say anything about that. Raab was up the wall like I've never seen him. He went nuts. Really ape."

"Good."

"I'm so pissed I can't even talk straight. Can you do it over again?"

"Not for a while. All the material needed to decoct another batch of Zyme-One is inaccessible at the moment. Thousands of miles away. The little I have left, well, I don't know if it's still active. "

"Where do you get it? Can't you say?"

"After this, I wouldn't tell anyone. No reflection, Alexis, just a precaution."

"What're we going to do?"

"I don't know. Something or other will turn up. I'm glad we had a chance to work together. You're high-hearted and that impresses me."

"That's nice of you, but I've let you down…oh, oh," her voice lowering, "here comes someone. I'm on my lab phone. Call me at home. I think I gave you the number. After eight…*Oh, yes, yes, great…California was fun…well, great…good, I'll meet you over at building six after five…yeh, yes, fine, everything's dandy-fine…no, I haven't decided yet…oh, hold it, I see I have a visitor, so I'll catch up with you later…*"

Not a bad actress, he thought, as he lay down the receiver quietly.

So Shandar had been right when she had told him the public affairs people at NIH knew nothing about any experiments involving a mouse and human skin genes, conducted in an NIH laboratory.

Walking to the window, he gazed at the iron-wrought fence that surrounded the park, then watched intently as snowflakes fell, fluttering through the air, daintily so. A long time since he had seen real snow, and for a time he stood there transfixed.

In the back of his mind a light flickered, and he knew that the mouse named Peter was clue enough that the era of regenerative medicine was nearing. You could do things to make new cells, new tissue, new bone even, and one day there would be little need for scalpels and thousands of drugs that often wrecked your body chemistry. You might not even need hospitals, or far fewer anyway.

Who owned Raab? Someone.

Two experiments had succeeded. He could always repeat one of them as long as he had a supply of *semba*. All of a sudden, he felt better.

Raab, in his way, had confirmed that someone, somewhere must be vitally interested and even worried about the future possibilities of Zyme-One. One doesn't demolish someone else's experiments conducted in a government-operated laboratory, without a compelling reason to undertake such a risk. Dwelling on it, he suspected that whoever it was had wanted to quash the news to the public, and to the Congress, where NIH got its funding, and where hearings took place about the runaway cost of medicine.

News of Peter and Alexis Hazlett would be prime fodder for a congressional hearing. A hearing quite possibly that could produce funding for what he wanted to do with his life.

All to the good in some ways, he thought, yet he would have thought differently had he known what was headed his way.

Thomasville, Georgia

Four men—all of them former chieftains of Pharmus companies—gathered on the side terrace of Boyd Tarrant's plantation home. While no longer active in the vast companies they once headed, nevertheless they still had reaching influence over the direction of Pharmus as an industry. Indeed, they acted as Pharmus's fist—its hidden *apparat*. They arbitrated disputes; masterminded the relationships with politicians and bureaucrats who safeguarded Pharmus's oligopoly, in part by erecting barriers difficult to surmount by those desiring admission to the industry; and—as today—worked out the sledgehammer tactics to thwart new technologies that could threaten Pharmus's market control, short-term or otherwise.

Control was the mantra of The League, where it was held in highest reverence.

Pharmus flourished because of innovation, then by imitation when paydirt was struck. In the wrong hands, innovation could be dire if not thwarted immediately. Every threat—no matter how innocuous appearing was viewed as insidious—never to be ignored. Pharmus, an oligopoly like Big Oil, had its own wise men to deal with the specter of menace, real or perceived as real.

Either the rules of the playing field were controlled, or the game could change under your nose, bringing disaster. Much was always at risk. Billions and billions in the research pipelines, and soaring profits that were assured by carefully calculated market shares of competing drugs, all of it done with artful legal tactics. Pharmus owed its existence to research and technology. Yet no oracle was handy to tell when and how technology would change, except all knew that when basic change came, and was accepted, if you weren't part of its vanguard, you lost out. Big enough loss, of ground or money, and you became a corporate carcass.

By their lights, Thomas Courmaine had been given ample opportunity in Boston, by Miles Bascomb, to line up his ducks, cooperate, and gain riches. Why wasn't that reasonable?

They knew, at least in summary form, of every instance where Courmaine had met with the foundations that were known for their grant-giving generosity to medical science endeavors; and that he'd been sent on his way by all of them.

At one point, Boyd Tarrant broke in, saying, "I'm a little tired of hearing about this sonofabitch. He's trying to slip between the cracks, it seems to me. A heart-bleeder, who thinks he's the double for the Dalai Lama. Probably has more up his sleeve than we're giving him credit for. If he's got Muldaur in his pocket, then I'd worry some. They could develop what he has, and push it to the British or even the fucking Chinese and Russians. I say let's lower the boom...let him find out what it's like to catch the falling knife..."

"You're right, Boyd," said another of the men. "Who've we got to sharpen the blade?"

"Bascomb," replied Tarrant. "He's already up to hips in this. Bascomb and that fellow Raab at NIH. They can get it kicked off and we'll keep a weather eye on it. I'll keep everyone of you informed." With that, he looked the other three men in the face, and those faces looked directly at him. Not a muscle twitched, and he took those stolid countenances as an all-out *carte blanche* to do as he thought best.

The meeting had closed, effectively; the hard-knuckle side of The League was now poised to punch away.

New York, New York

An incensed Lin-pao blew his jowls out and in, in and out, like a bellows bringing a campfire to life. "A dastardly act," he invoked, looking at Thomas. "Demonic. What one expects in China, not in America. How shall we deal with it, sir? Swords? Who is Hazlett? A woman, you said. Has she a high level of trustworth—trusti?"

"Trustworthiness," Thomas corrected, "I think so. She's been very cooperative. Believe me, she is not happy. She'd practically adopted that mouse."

"She is as Caesar's wife? Not embedded in a filthy underhanded cabal?'

"If you knew her, I think you'd agree with me that she's a safe bet."

"Destruction of private property, it is a crime, is that not so, sir?"

"Not so fast. It was their mouse, their lab, and their researcher. All of it government and none of it private."

"But it is your genius, sir. How dare they. I shall plot recompense. Is that the correct word?"

"Pretty close. And remember this, they've given us something. We demonstrated again that Zyme-One works and Alexis Hazlett herself now sees the possibilities. She's good, Lin-pao. She is an excellent witness to a fact and at NIH someone fears that fact. There's no other rhyme, reason or explanation. That tells us something and it's a good something. We're on the right road; we must be if they have to stoop to steal evidence. It is odd, very odd, and yet in another way it isn't so odd."

"But what of now? What next comes to us?"

"Keep learning all you can from the botanists. We'll need that, obviously, to start taking *semba* apart. I've got to get another supply of it soon. I'll be in Switzerland and I'll get it then, but that means smuggling it by customs again. I don't relish that."

"Hide it in your toothpaste tube. I'll show you the techniques."

"You can do that?"

"I have an extensive arsenal, sir. Oh, my visa, sir. It is of extreme-ly concern to myself."

"I'm aware. I have someone working on an extension. Can you make an honest case that you're a political refugee seeking asylum?"

"It would go hard on my family. Calamitously." Shaking his face rapidly. "The Chinese government would crucify them if I said that story."

"We'll find a way. Here, I almost forgot, and I wish it were ten times more."

Reaching into his pocket, Thomas pulled out a tissue-wrapped object, handing it to Lin-pao, watching as Lin-pao stripped off the flimsy red paper. A small, palm sized bar of gold bullion bearing the name of Braunsweig und Sohn on one face. Thomas had seen the small gold bricks offered for sale when visiting the New York branch office three days ago. Knowing of his colleague's abiding devotion to gold, he had bought one, and, seeing the blissful look before him, was glad he had.

"You are in my prayers, sir. Buddha will shower you with joy. It is written in my heart."

Just as Shandar—at "21"—had prophesied, it happened.

Late of a morning, reading a monograph on the cellular structure of plants, the buzz of the doorbell interrupted him. In the small foyer of his apartment, he thumbed the button that released the door lock at the street entrance of the townhouse; and then, after a climb of one flight, there she was, appearing like a spectral visage. Seeing her, unannounced and so suddenly, should not greatly surprise him and yet it had.

"Knock, knock. Hullo, hullo, here I am," Jaggy said brightly as he opened the door. In the thin light at the doorway she looked waxen, a little bluish, as if she'd gone without sleep for too long.

Seeing his perplexed look, not waiting for a reply, she smiled, then fell into him. "You've been some awful stranger," she murmured.

When she broke away, he said, "What a surprise. You didn't, well, you didn't do anything. Call ahead or let me know."

"Do I come in?"

He stepped aside. "Of course, of course. Please. Things are a little messy here."

"Things are a bit messy everywhere, I find," saying it as she moved forward. "You're nicely settled in. Found a new way of life in New York, eh?

Come closer so I can see you, darling. You've been quite the invisible object, avoiding me for months."

"Been a busy time, but it's good to see you, Jaggy. Here, have a seat. The sofa or anywhere."

"I shall, the sofa will do." Peeling off a calf-length sable before he could assist, she casually tossed it over a bench, the sleeves dragging on the floor.

"When did you arrive? You never said anything."

"Last night, latish. We had to go round and round before landing. I almost phoned you, then I was worried you might be somewhere you shouldn't be, or that you'd ignore me again. Went straight to the Waldorf. If you'd taken up my offer to use the apartment, you'd have been there, wouldn't you?"

He smiled. "Yep, but I wasn't. Where will we meet again? Africa, Paris, London. We've made it a third of the way around the globe. Like some tea or something? I can make a pot, if you like."

"No, love. No sit, tell me everything. Is that one of those divine shirts from New & Lingwood?"

"It is. I get compliments all the time."

He sat across from her, not nervous but somewhat anxious now that she was here, and not ready for a probing. Christmas was nearing and he knew what that meant, and poised himself for the shoe to drop.

"Si said you don't use the office anymore. What's been happening with you?"

"Oh, you wouldn't want to be bored with all my triumphs."

"Like that, is it?"

"Pretty much."

"Then, are you through here? This, um, New York escapade of yours?"

"I don't know. I've got to be in Geneva soon for a day or so. I shall be through with New York for that long anyway. Why didn't you tell me you were coming? I might've been out of town."

"The Nestors said you were in the city and gave me your address. I've a car and driver and it's not but twenty blocks or so from here to the Waldorf Towers. Here I am, here you are. Lovely, what? I've calls coming in from overseas. Come back to my apartment with me."

"Can't you route them here?"

"I do my phoning on a SAT-PHONE and it's back at the Waldorf, not here. Don't be prickly now, I've come a long way, and we've oodles to discuss."

Her SAT-PHONE was, as it sounded, a device that uplinked to a satellite, connecting her almost instantly to anywhere. A built-in voice-scrambler prevented eavesdropping. Very handy, and very expensive. Unable to think of any way to refuse her, off he went with her in her limousine.

Within the hour, they were sitting in her five-room apartment at the Waldorf Towers, a set of digs she used once yearly, at most twice. Seeing the layout, he almost wished he'd taken her up on her offer to use the apartment during his stay in the U.S. It was a slice of New York territory she was well familiar with, as Muldaur Ltd. owned two nearby skyscrapers, together with several ship-docks and a row of warehouses facing the city's Hudson River.

Jaggy had her feet tucked under her, sitting on a divan. Separated by a coffee table, he sat across from her in a matching divan.

She wasted no time in coming to the point of her visit. "Would you like to hear my proposition? Your lab project, that's what I'm referring to."

"Is it the same as before?"

"It is." Jaggy rearranged herself on the divan. Holding a nail-buffer in one hand, she inspected a finger, then buffed away.

"I'm prepared to make you a second offer, and it'll be the last I make. You'll have all the funds needed for your lab, and I know where you can put in all your hours, and have adequate facilities. I've just the place in mind. England. Wales, to be more exact. You can quit all this chasing about, like a hungry hen, and get down to what it is you want to do. If you've no better offer, and it most certainly sounds as if you don't, then why not take my life preserver? You can hardly lose, can you?"

"Probably not."

"Decidedly not."

She went on, outlining her commitment; much the same as she had before in London. He would not have *carte blanche* to spend at any clip he chose but would not lack for anything. Muldaur Ltd. in London would supply the accountants, the business planners, and perhaps a facilities manager. "Anyone you need," Jaggy promised, "to look after those details. I'll be giving the money to African Heritage and take a tax deduction, and they'll pass the funds on to you. If you agree, we'll discuss the ownership split. Think it over, ducks, I've got to go to the loo."

Her last offer, as she put it. The misery of hard choices, he thought. A heavy mix of events, and dynamics had descended in the past weeks. So many, many things had never been resolved, never would be, and the loss of what could have been, *might well have been*, drove a thrashing pain through him.

When Jaggy returned, he said, "I'm very grateful to you. I suppose you think I've wasted a lot of time over here. But it isn't so. I've had time to clarify my views. I think you ought to know that I'm still committed to my idea and doing it on a not-for-profit basis. That alone seems to poison the air here in America."

"Not only in America. But you're a long way from that decision. One step at a time. Now, what else?"

He told her of the NIH mouse experiment. They talked on, fencing; obviously, she was on to him and knew he had met with wholesale rejection of his ideas while in America, probably getting a full report from Poppi who'd, in turn, bled Si dry of everything that Si knew.

When Thomas paused at one point, Jaggy seized the moment, rehashing other points she had in mind. The name, she suggested, would be the same as Thomas had once agreed upon with Baster—Muldaur-Courmaine Laboratory Ltd.

Succinct, squared up, direct. That was Jaggy, always as direct as a laser beam.

Jaggy to own sixty-percent of the shares, Thomas the remaining forty. After five-years, he had the right to buy her out at a price determined by averaging the differences, if any, of the value of the enterprise as appraised by two investment banking houses, one to be named by her, the other by himself.

She acted graciously when refraining from reminding him that he could've had his lab months ago had he only agreed to what she had laid out the night they had dined at Petrossian's in London. She could've rubbed it in now.

"Your turn," she said. "Say whatever you like, love, and remember this is strictly business and nothing else."

"You're being overly generous, that's what I think. I feel like I'm looting you."

"I've always been generous. I also want this enterprise to succeed and my best insurance for that to happen is for you to profit by it."

"I can make the science succeed, I'm almost sure. But I can't say much about the business side of it."

"That's my side, so you leave that part of the equation to me."

With that, the conversation trailed elsewhere. He asked if she'd heard anything of Ghibwa, the three Mzura women, or if anyone had found his lost trunk with his personal papers and the Naruma lab notes.

No, no, and no.

She knew nothing at all. N'jorro had been transferred, as promised, to the Mzura and she desired forgetting about it. Her voice going low, going hard too. She was upset, he could see, and wished he hadn't brought Naruma up. She left the sofa and off she went again. Shortly, she appeared carrying her black ebony pipe. From a gold container the size of a lipstick case she shook out a few opium pellets, stuffing them into the bowl of the pipe.

A spicy sweet smell drifted through the room. Brazen of her, willful—her trademark behavior. He said nothing, neither did she. But then rarely did she explain herself, and never in the form of an apology.

Talk went on till the December sky darkened the city. He idly recounted the this's-and-that's of his stay in New York, telling her he had given a talk at Columbia, was generously provided temporary space at Rockefeller University due to Si Nestor, and, along the way, had crossed paths with an outrageously gifted biochemist. Reciting Lin-pao's talents, he sounded to himself like a flack trying to move tickets for an off-Broadway show as yet to open. "Prodigious," he mentioned, "you've never heard so many gears turning in one head and he's a glory to work with."

"How much for that one?"

"How much of what?"

"The money?"

"He's not exactly sold by the pound, you know."

"Oh, get stuffed, you loony. What is the price? The wage?"

He had already agreed to a sum of fifty-thousand dollars yearly with Lin-pao but instantly he reconsidered, replying, "Seventy-five or possibly eighty-thousand."

"Is this dollars?"

"Dollars, right."

"Per annum?"

"Right again."

"A fig. A pittance, what?"

"He's anything but a pittance, believe me."

"Oh, come off it. Get him. He'll need papers, won't he? I'll have a word with the Home Office when next I'm in London. A bit of arm-twisting is all. Pardon, I meant to say when *we're* in London. Oh, darling, I'm so happy to be here…and why not Petrossian's tonight? They've a good one in New York, though I've not been in an age. Bring your Chinese mastermind along and we'll have a good look at him. You said he comes from Shanghai. I know Shanghai quite well."

"This is a lot to absorb at one go. Maybe we ought to sleep on it some."

The jaw protruded a full inch or more. Obstinately, she let go in a bitten-off tone, "It's either a done thing between us or it's not. You're in or you're not in. I'll not bear the silver platter again, as I've told you already."

Nerve-dead from all the guessing, all the pavement pounding, the aimlessness of it all, and of his market losses, and of misplacing a woman he was intensely fond of. America had mostly been a failure, save for Lin-pao and his short-lived time with Alexis Hazlett and the Nestors. Here was Jaggy, generously offering to open her purse for the second time, and if it were not the purse he'd been hoping for, it nonetheless was his only and best prospect. And who else would fly across the Atlantic to wave a checkbook in front of his nose? Fly across a mud puddle, even? No one else had and no one else would, even though he had a prime discovery to shout about one day. But not yet. Not till the two experiments were replicated by others dozens of times. For that, they'd need Zyme-One, and for Zyme-One you needed *semba*. Artificially made *semba*. Gobs of it. And there was this to consider: hers was the best solution to resolve Lin-pao's visa woes.

He looked at her, then, for a long five seconds. Then, resigned, but smiling his widest, he surrendered. "Let's make it happen, Jaggy."

Her face instantly brightened as she clasped her hands, raising them in a cheering gesture. With his five words of assent, he had boarded the train to history, with all its blessings and all its heartbreaks. His naiveté would take its own time to diminish. He was about to take a firm step into a world he was well aware of, yet knew little of its more subtle customs, or where they would lead him. There was nothing to hold him in New York, by now a drear memory. He had chosen a fork in life's uncertain, illegible road. It was, at bottom, a compromise, neither his first one nor would it be his last. What else was there, at present? Nothing else, indeed, except to try whatever he could to move forward, see to the realization of Zyme-One.

Forward meant Wales; forward, likely, meant many things just then.

He most surely knew what it meant to be swallowed into Jaggy Muldaur's way of life. She'd be expecting far more than a simple business partnership, where she was the money and he was expected to be maker of a miracle•if a miracle was to be had at all.

She would clutch; she would control; she would demand.

Bleak, perhaps, but there it was; officially, on this day at the Waldorf Towers, he transferred himself into the ranks of the world's kept men.

Knew it, done it.

PART II

*All things must change to something new,
to something strange.*

—Henry Wadsworth Longfellow

St. Curig Fields, Isle of Anglesey, Wales

Minus the hours in the air on a Muldaur plane, and the ride from the island's RAF base to Jaggy's lodge in a Range Rover, he had hardly left her arms. Within minutes of their arrival, Jaggy had insisted he share her bedroom. With that single act, he grasped that the unsaid clauses of their agreement were now in play.

No repetition, *"if you please,"* she had conveyed, somewhat jokingly yet with an edge, of that night in Johannesburg when prowling into his room, looking for a romp but getting nowhere.

Radiant, beaming, she stood nude at a side of the massive canopied bed. Absorbing her, he was mesmerized by her inviting tone of voice. "And we'll break a few of your Commandments, darling, and I don't care which ones they are. You're nervous, aren't you? Yes, you are. Leave everything to me. I'll be your African honey-bird and show you how to sip the sweetness from life"— and laying down at his side, she began him.

Afterward, she told him, "Lovely for me...really topping..."

"Are we doomed to a life of ecstasy?"

"You'll never escape, so don't try."

"Escape? I just arrived. Haven't even unpacked, shaved, showered. Nothing, well...except this..."

"You're very good for me."

"Am I? It's nice to hear, thank you. It's also very nice for me down there at your headquarters."

"Head—oh, ha!—I never heard my kitty called that before."

"Neither have I, so now we've got a new word for an old word."

"New everything. I love it, oh how I do love it. And love you, too, darling." She snugged him to her breasts, their areolas large and the color of her unpainted lips.

Wales, for him, had begun in a medley of confusion, arriving here at St. Curig Fields early yesterday, dopey from lack of sleep, getting Lin-pao situated in the gatehouse, a quick meal, a sauna naked with Jaggy; a very, very long time since he had been naked with a woman. Rooms had been assigned him down the hall, though he had barely set foot in them. Two decades of celibacy had been shattered within an hour of their arrival, and very pleasurably so.

"Is anything the matter?" she asked, breaking into his thoughts.

"No, nothing at all. Why?"

"You've a surprised look on your face."

"I'm a surprised man."

"I love you, oh, I do. What are you thinking, darling?"

"Of sex. Of connecting with you. The glories of what I've been missing."

"You've been alone so many years. Now I'm alone and now we can be together. It's perfect, darling. Just heavenly perfect."

"Sometimes you'll be in London making the world of Muldaur jump over Saturn. I'll be here trying to dissect a mystery."

"But we shan't let it matter. Whenever we're separated, we'll still be one, my love, almost like the same person. You haven't an idea how exceedingly important lovemaking is to me. My well-being. My balance wheel. When I die, it better be in the middle of some marvelous sexual orgy."

She was serious, but he laughed. "You'll not know that for years and years. But I agree, a wonderful way to go when your number comes up."

If you but knew, she thought, then said, "I've an idea for you."

"I'm ready for one. I'm no good at suspense and never have been."

"I was thinking I might leave you a smaller plane and a pilot here in Wales. You could fly down to London every day after work, then fly back to St. Curig in the mornings. It's less than an hour by air."

"I don't think so. Often I work at night. I like the quiet. When it's happening for me and I'm cooking with gas and getting a lot done, I have to be here. On tap, so to speak. After last night, I'm beginning to wonder if I still have a head left. Anyway, it's complicated to explain, but it's true. When lightning strikes, I need to be there to catch it in the bottle. Most of what we'll be doing here is thinking, and more thinking. When I get the team put together, I can't be running off."

"That's enough thinking. I'm coming your way for another of those connections."

"I'm temporarily out of connectivity."

"Oh. Are you happy? Pleased with me? What I do?"

"I'm sailing."

"We're not really all that settled with each other. That usually takes a little time."

"What more could there ever be?"

"You'll see and you *will* see."

He looked right into those sapphire eyes. "I'm not a very good barometer," he said. "It's only the second time in my life, well, not the second time but you're the second person. Second woman. I'll get this right sooner or later. I'm feeling half nutty. Can't even speak straight."

"No one lasts for twenty years without sex."

"Well, then, I'm a no one."

"It's not believable. Not you, not the way you are. That's ridiculous."

"But it's true, and, yes, it is ridiculous."

"Who was she?"

"Only a memory."

"Well, who?"

"I think I won't say. It was a very long time ago and with a tragic ending. It started my life with the Jesuits, actually."

"I'm going to change your life, too."

"You already have."

"Dear me, I feel like I just deflowered a virgin. A first, well, for me anyway it's a first. Shall I tell you the history about me? My first journey through the orchard of sex? All the salacious sides of my life? Until I was fifteen, I was what Americans call a tomboy. Then I grew a foot, and ended up with these breasts and a yen for men, and everything went to hell. But I thought it all so wonderful."

"You don't have to tell me anything."

"Quite, but then I'm volunteering in this instance…it was in Jo-burg but not like being with you. Actually, darling, my first shag was rather humorous."

A most memorable confession, he thought later, and she was so youngish at the time. Not even legal. She led into it somewhat slowly, telling him she had attended Tamerloongg, where they knew all there was to know about sexual custom and practice, especially its Asian accents.

"How do you spell it? Tamer-what's-its-name?"

"Tam-er-loongg." Enunciating each syllable. "It means House of Wisdom."

"Really?"

A school, she had told him. More like a retreat, located in the mountains west of Djakarta, not so distant from three Muldaur tea plantations. At Tamerloongg, they taught the ancient sexual arts of Asia, from India, others derived from Japan and China, still others from Brunei and Indonesia and Tahiti. The full palette, use of exotic foods, the value of scents such as

Samarkand incenses, sexual positions, prolongation, anal stimulation, masturbation while clothed, the hotsie bath, forms of healthy contraception, the pleasures of pain, techniques for vaginal stimulation, tonguing the penis, rituals for the taking of lovers, incest, three-way copulation. Much study involved the limbic region of the brain, known as the "Seat of Emotions," the place responsible for passionate desire.

The tutelage lasted for a year but she had had her fill after a four-month sojourn. Sex had become a core belief for her, a way of life, daily whenever possible.

He was still absorbing her, her tale, her remarkable revelation as they lay in bed, sensing the newness of what had come his way.

"It'd be one of the understatements of my life to say I'm fascinated. How old were you?" he asked, "when you went to the, ah, school?"

"Sixteen, about. I traded in my purity when I was fifteen, as I said. That was with our stable-master in Jo-burg and when Baster found out he turned white, but he did the practical thing. Fired the stable-master and fired me off to Tamerloongg. He couldn't keep an eye on me, he was always everywhere. He kept a mistress in Paris and another one in Buenos Aries and spent a good deal of time in both places."

"You mean after your mother passed away?"

"Yes."

"Off you went for advanced graduate studies?"

"I've never regretted it."

"I can tell."

Punching him playfully, she said, "In a few weeks you'll be able to tell exceedingly well and you'll never regret it either."

"I never heard of a school—a retreat—like that one."

"There's another in Bombay. Well, Mumbai now. Used to be one there, anyway."

"How does one go about getting admitted?"

"Women only, so you can scotch that idea if that's what you're wonder-ing."

"I wasn't thinking of applying. Just wondering how. Must be costly, I suppose."

"A bomb."

They talked for a time, and then he dozed. Within the hour, he awoke to find her sitting across the room, speaking quietly into the phone. Seeing him stir, immediately she hung up.

"Are you famished?" she asked.

"I could eat my way through an ox."

"We'll have something sent up, or would you rather we go down?"

"Down. Eat, then take a good walk. I feel like a cigar."

"Do you? Jolly good. I'll meet you down in the hunt room. We can have breakfast there. Oh, I nearly forgot, I've had your things unpacked and had some others brought up from London—"

"What others?"

"Things I ordered for you, darling. You can't go round in Wales in city clothes. You need the right things. Jackets, boots. Outerwear. Sweaters."

"All right, but please save the bills this time."

"They're nothing."

"Not to me, they aren't."

"Have it your way. But it's a damn bother to find the bills. You're welcome to my bathroom but you might find the other down the hall more to your liking. Has a sauna, if you like saunas."

"I've had all the steam I can handle, thanks to you."

Getting up, he reached for a lavender gown, a Malian *bubu* Jaggy had given to him the evening before. He eyed the silver ice bucket, with its two upended and empty champagne bottles. All the makings of an orgy, he thought, waving to her as he departed the room. He tried walking quietly, hoping he wouldn't bump into the servants, but it was plain to him, they'd be fully aware of what was happening. Oddly, he felt right at home; more oddly, he felt a pungent desire for more of this wild, strong woman who had nearly devoured him, having decidedly returned sexual infatuation to his life.

Trying to know one woman, intimately, trying to forget another but couldn't.

They strolled the vast sea-bordered property, traipsed its sloping pastures, some with cattle, others with Belgian dray horses grazing alongside a small herd of flop-eared Nubian goats. Stone cottages with slate roofs appeared randomly along the roads, resided in by the head gamekeeper and his family, a forester and another larger one for an estate manager, then the last one which was occupied by her chef.

Thomas, delighted to be in the outdoors after months of city living, must've scaled a dozen or so dry-wall stone fences, centuries old, as he went along beside Jaggy. She was gotten up in a bottle-green, oiled-cotton coat, corded trousers, knee-high Wellingtons, and had tied a Hermès scarf around her wind-pink face. She was the image of privileged gentry gamboling about on her Welsh lands. Her black lab, Bicker, tail thumping and joyous, raced in and out of the gorse, the thick sedge, flushing pheasants, then bounding off in search of other frolics.

Walking ahead, then suddenly stooping to pick up a thin branch there. A little further on, Jaggy stopped and raised her hand, signaling for quiet. She took a deliberate careful step, then another, heel-and-toeing, before swiftly ramming the stick down into a clump of wet-grass. A squawk then, from a wildly thrashing bullfrog. Pulling it off the stick, she gave it a blow to its head, stilling it. Ripping off one of its legs, she examined it, then bit right into it, chewing, tearing off another chunk, the blood striping a line down her chin. She worked down the length of the bone, sucked it at one end, then threw the remains into a stand of tall grass. It seemed the most natural thing of all the world to her, and he recalled how once, on safari, she had had the camp chef fry a single testicle of a bull-cape buffalo, devouring it at lunch by herself.

"Want the other leg?" she offered, holding out the remains of the marsh frog.

"I'm still on my no-frog diet."

"It's fresh, delicious."

"I've eaten raw everything. Practically everything. Not frogs, though."

"Or women."

"Till you."

"Ha! Right. Tell me, are you mooning over that Jew?" Taunting him now. That Jew... that Jew!

"That Jew you refer to,"—speaking very evenly—"is quite a lady. A first-rate human," he added. "Don't slur her, not around me. The Nestors are Jewish. You like them well enough. So do I. I could care less if she's Jewish or Palestinian or Abyssinian or anything else."

His fists tightened.

"Apologies. I say things I don't really mean sometimes."

"You ought to watch it, Jaggy."

Regarding him frostily, she replied, "I did say I was sorry, Thomas."

"Yes, I heard. I cannot count the number of things I've said that've boomeranged on me. I lost my job at Cambridge for speaking my mind one morning on television. I never apologized and was never quite forgiven. You did apologize and so you are forgiven."

"I'll never bring it up again. But I'd wager you were sleeping together, were you?"

"I told you this morning there hasn't been anyone."

"And I told you that's not believable."

"Believe as you wish."

"How was she in bed? Better than I?"

"Cut it out."

"Touchy, touchy."

As they neared a pond, a great blue heron dawdled out of its ground-nest, flapping vigorously to make altitude, and Jaggy stopped to ask, "Would you like to look at the old manor house? We're not so very far. That'll be your quarters, your lab anyway. Or we can go to the gate-house and see how that roly-poly genius of yours is settling in."

They came upon the old manor. Gray-stoned, two storied, a slated fish-scale roof, and the windows and shutters trimmed out in fading white and black paint. They stood in the driveway, Thomas staring at the building, thinking it would be his now. It held fourteen rooms and only one bathroom.

Ideal, he thought. His.

"It is hell's own wicket to heat at this time of year. Fireplaces, the six of them, I think, and some electrical space heaters. That's all the heating. The manor is on the Historical List and you can't alter very much without a permit and they never issue permits, it seems. So there you are, a great old place but it's an ice tray in winter."

"We'll manage."

"I didn't think to bring a key. I'll give you one, if you remind me. You'll have plenty of space, you think?"

"More than enough. Just great. I have another favor, if you can."

"Of course."

"I want to bring Alexis Haslett over here, if she'll come. She is a vital witness to the experiment I mentioned at NIH and I want her on our side She's good. She's probably in complications over there at NIH. Maybe not, but I 'd like her on the team."

"Will there be more Americans?"

"No, that's it. Really only two of us, myself and Alexis. And her friend, another gal. I've never met her. They're, uh, involved."

"Are they now? Well...seems we'll have one of everything. Or two. Like Noah's Ark, what? This reminds me. I've not yet inquired for you or Lin-pao.

Your work permits. I must remind myself to do it. Amusing chap, your friend, isn't he?"

"He can be. I know he sounds like a one-man radio show, but I'm very fond of him. As to work permits, tell me where to get the forms and I'll get going on them."

When arriving from New York on a Muldaur jet, they had landed here on Anglesey, at a RAF fighter plane base where Jaggy, being Jaggy, had somehow obtained landing privileges. When disembarking upon arrival, a base officer greeted them, never asking for passports. No papers to show, no forms to sign, nothing but smiles and bonhomie. When Jaggy wasn't in residence, she allowed the base-commander and his guests the full use of St. Curig shooting fields. A mutually happy arrangement. But ever since arriving, Thomas had wondered if he were actually in the country illegally. The rich, he thought, do everything their way, cleaning up the mishaps later with phone calls to the well-placed Mandarins.

"Look, there to the west," she said, pointing. "It's making up into a squall."

A boneless finger of mist had slithered in from the sea, blocking out an entire line of the forest. It had all happened suddenly, quickly as a sneeze.

"Take me home, lover man." She was half-bent against the freshening wind. "I've been through these before. Inside five minutes we'll be drowned. Freeze the balls off you and we surely can't have that, can we?"

They trotted along on an old forest path, then stopped so Jaggy could catch her breath. Bicker, his pink tongue lolling, was still prancing, happy and oblivious to all. The wind laid its heavy arm against the trees, shoving them into contorted shapes. Branches cracking, breaking off. He led Jaggy into an open meadow, well away from the tree lines. First, the rain spit a little, then a driving drizzle chilled by the winter sea-wind. By the time they were in sight of the lodge, the rain lashed away in a stinging downpour.

Thomas was laughing, so was she—both drenched to the bone. She stopped, came to him, her eyes wet-happy, and she licked his cheek, making a purring sound.

They reached the lodge.

Dripping, Jaggy shucked her Barbour jacket, and, as he peeled off his turtleneck, she implored, "Hurry, darling. I'm nearly ice." She was down to her bra, then no bra at all, just the lavish damp breasts staring at him, with her unmindful of a servant suddenly appearing and then disappearing down the hallway. "Let's use your shower," Jaggy suggested. "It's larger than mine. I'll have dinner sent up to us later. Roast stag. You're my stag, aren't you?" Chucking him under his chin.

She smiled, taking his face in both hands and kissed him. A slightly salty taste. He wondered if he were tasting frog's blood.

Late into that night, she spoke to him of dinner gatherings and galas she would schedule; people he must meet, the well-wired of London, including bankers who were being such a bore for her lately. Members of Parliament, of course, at least the important ones. She reeled off names of permanent ministers, too. Then the titled-folk, and, perhaps, she suggested a sprinkling of London's stage personalities for idle amusement.

With much misgiving, he listened as she defined plans to launch him into her high-voltage world. Her London world, her Paris world, her Asiatic world. Yet he had come to Wales to work on the most important thing left in his life. As soon as that first deposit of a million pounds showed up to the credit of Muldaur-Courmaine Ltd., at Braunsweig's offices in London, he expected to be working a twelve-hour day.

"You'll see, darling," Jaggy was exclaiming, "how it makes such a true difference here. Knowing where the ivory gates are and who minds them. When we marry"—a quick aside—"we need to discuss that, don't we, love...not now, but soon, eh?" The words said in the deadly pitch of a woman who had already worked up a neatly measured blueprint for her future.

Marry!

Hearing it submerged him into a state of temporary deafness. Vacantly, he looked at her, seeing how expectantly she returned his gaze. Saying nothing, a silence that meant a different thing to her than to him. Tacitly, he supposed he had agreed to her palette of dinner engagements, not especially liking it, knowing it was bound to draw him away from Wales, yet he could do nothing to deter her. She held all the cards.

He'd had let himself be bought, and she was itemizing what she had paid for. All this and day three in Wales had yet to show itself. Unable to help himself, trying vigorously to prevent it, but losing out as remembrances of Shandar overtook him.

What had happened to them? What was happening to him?

Geneva, Switzerland

A Lucullan feast for the three trustees. Lamb Provencal, with all the trimmings; a wildly expensive Petrus claret, bananas flambé for dessert. When finished, a folio made its way around the table showing the latest round of Muldaur Trust investments, three billions of Euros recently deployed to North America, a smaller sum within Asia and Australia—a downtown skyscraper in Singapore and another one, smaller, in Sydney.

That was the sum of it for this go-around.

All told, the quarterly report showed the Trust's net assets to be so gigantic that Thomas still viewed it as a financial fairytale. With a certain temerity, he posed the question as to when the South African government might be advised of their colossal good fortune.

Pierre, smiling, merely said, "We've not decided, so far as I know, quite when to do it. A few matters yet to be sorted out with the Federal Department of Finance in Bern." Having disposed of that matter to his own satisfaction, St. Germain then asked, "Would you care to be the appointed messenger, Thomas? When you do, they're liable to name a boulevard after you down there in Pretoria."

A shadowy reply but Thomas, being the new boy at the table, didn't press the matter. More talk, then, about the state of the securities markets around the globe, and, due to price shifts in the Swiss markets, there was an over-weighted sum of the Trust's assets deployed in Swiss pharmaceuticals. He had been surprised to learn The Trust, over a century ago, had been an original backer of MarocheChem, the chemical and pharmaceutical giant, a crown jewel of the Swiss economy. The Trust held a whopping 27.6% of the outstanding shares, making it far and away the largest owner; the holding itself was sub-divided into smaller chunks, masked under a dozen shell companies.

A decision was taken to table the diversification issue for the next trustee's meeting.

Thomas was still in the absorbing, learning processes. He'd never be on a par with St. Germain or Claude-Paul Lavalier, when it came to grasping the intricacies of international finance; it was a chore just to learn the jargon. Yet what did it matter? The Trust, by its terms, was slated for dissolution within a year or thereabouts. Even so, he wanted to learn whatever he could, the ins–and-outs of managing all those billions.

Perturbed, Thomas could not help but quiz himself. Were Claude-Paul Lavalier and Pierre up to something? He was just getting to know the urbane Parisian, partner of a highly regarded firm of Pechiney & Barriquet, legal counselors. A bright man—Lavalier—also brittle, quick to take offense if argued with.

Why the put-off of advising the South Africans? Today marked the second time Thomas's questions had been all but shunted aside. He felt uncomfortable, sensing he was being left out of something important, something pivotal. Lavalier had to know what was legally called for, and the right thing to do. Why the hold up? Why hadn't they settled on a date for informing the South Africans?

It didn't add.

Bethesda, Maryland

Never had Raab suspected Alexis Hazlett would end up working with Courmaine, abroad now and out of reach. A scenario that seemed most improbable, but when submitting her resignation the previous week he had asked where she would be working, nearly recoiling at her reply, "I'm going to be with Thomas Courmaine. We expect to do our work in Wales."

Our work? Wales?

"Why Wales?"

"Why not? For one thing, it's a long way from you. I'll never forgive what you've done."

"Watch who you're talking to, miss."

"I am watching. You can piss up your sleeve for all I care. You're a thief. You used me, didn't you? When I have my exit interview, I'm going to sing like a dozen canaries."

"Who'll believe you?"

"I will."

"How far will that get you?"

"This far. If I asked Thomas Courmaine to make an affidavit, I think he would. He's respected. If I let the NIH Inspector-General know you'd been pestering me for sex, besides, they might not accept it, but, on the other hand, they just might. I do not mind at all telling the HR people that I'm a lesbian. Why would they care? I think it might start them thinking about you. The laugher of all time is that no one other than a blind person would try out a mattress with you. You're such a vile bastard, Raab, and I do think I'll tell them after all. I've got nothing to lose but you have"—taunting him further—"you're a fungus, a god-awful rotten fungus." Grimacing, shaking her head in disbelief and near tears, she turned and scurried for the door.

She'd been too quick for him to react with an insulting reply, yet he'd gleaned that Courmaine was now in Wales. News soon to find its way to Miles Bascomb. For now, other concerns were frying on his skillet of worries.

Bascomb had ordered him to get moving on a full-scale smear-job on Courmaine, who seemed so patently unable to understand the color of daylight. That it would go so much better for everyone if he would see the sense in sharing his work-product, sell the know-how, forget all this muck about the third world and its volumes of unceasing problems.

Bascomb, the apparent boss of this operation, had been checking in every few days by phone. Raab wished he knew if others were s involved, but The League, he knew, was as compartmentalized as a beehive.

To comply with Bascomb's order, he'd been culling a list of candidates, who had the competence to set up a back-alley campaign to make rubble of Courmaine. Maveen Cassidy topped the list. Cassidy, though a has-been, was well connected even if she'd been relegated to the sidelines of journalism. She'd be relatively cheap and Raab thought she was reliable enough and savvy enough to organize what was needed—a fatal wounding in print; fatal, that is, for Courmaine.

Things were getting tense, also a little too slippery. Several nights ago he had taken a phone call at his house, with the unnamed caller saying Raab would hear soon from someone named Charles Tavester, apparently a former field man for the Provisional Irish Army. Like Cassidy, Tavester was also free-lancing at present, and with a record for dealing with sticky situations.

Raab hadn't liked the sound of any of it and still didn't.

St. Curig Fields, Isle of Anglesey, Wales

Five weeks had melted into the past, since Thomas had returned from Geneva. By now the team had begun to settle in. Alexis Hazlett and her woman friend had taken one of the unoccupied stone cottages near the manor house. Two postdocs, both British, had been recruited; one a botanist named Timmothe Merrill from Cambridge, the other, a biostatistician, Joshua Noyes from the famed Sanger Centre, also at Cambridge. Both had chosen to live in the nearby village of Holyhead, biking every weekday morning to St. Curig Fields. Lin-pao had already appropriated the roomy, two story gatehouse for himself.

Today, a *tour d'horizon,* and the first time they had assembled as a team. Thomas, talking informally with them, as they drank coffee or tea in the manor's great room. A fire roared. All wore heavy sweaters against the island's bone-bending February chill.

"…We know a few things about Zyme-One," Thomas was saying, "and a glimmer of its potential. You've heard about the Mzura women or seen the news photos. Alexis Hazlett and I worked on an experiment in America whereby her skin genes were transferred to a mouse. It also succeeded, as Alexis can verify. We'll repeat that one before long, using it as something of a baseline. Today, I'd like to shape the next chapter of this investigation. We'll be working on cells, especially plant cells. We want to find out what it is that's inside the roots of the shrub known as *semba,* and how it goes about making the ingredients for Zyme-One. Then, what it is in Zyme-One that allows it to paste genetic material into foreign DNA, so that it isn't rejected by the new host's immune system. Later, we'll try to figure out other things. For example, can Zyme-One be used to make neurons faster? Can we make older cells become young again, thus healing traumatized tissue or even regenerating it. And how do we apply Zyme-One to an overall gene therapy regime? Your lab notes must be exact. No exceptions, if you please." He stopped, scanning their faces. "Timmothe is going to take the floor. He's our botany specialist and he may enlighten us on things that the rest of us don't know much about."

He nodded at Timmothe Merrill who pulled himself out of an over-stuffed chair. Rosy-cheeked, beanpole-thin, he wore his hair as might a woman; a dark blonde lock of it cutting a diagonal path across his narrow brow.

"We're to have great fun, what? A scavenger hunt among the thickets of our plant world. I should hazard that you'll find strong resemblances between human cells and those of plants. Likely as not, you know this. But may I remind that when we alter the chemistry of the human body, this, to remedy an ailment, we often use pharmaceuticals whose curative energies derive directly from the chemistry of plants found, for the most part, in jungles and rain forests. Here, you may find of interest some relevant numbers. In the Amazonia Basin, alone, grow an estimated 200,000 species of plants. Of that, only 5,000 do we use, or do the natives use, for healing purposes. You can see we've a long way to go and much to learn and discover. As to *semba*, it may be remarkable in what it can produce, but it is not remarkable at all that it makes whatever it makes from a single species within the plant family….and yet, very much like a human body, there are those thousands and thousands of infinitely small chemical factories that tell *semba* how to ultimately make Zyme-One. When we talk about the power of the plant world, it is useful to bear in mind that the most commonly used medicine anywhere is aspirin, and aspirin comes from the bark of a willow tree…and another one is what makes a birth control pill work. It's an ingredient of a Mexican yam. I can give you hundreds of similar examples, though we'll save that for another time."

When Merrill wrapped up his remarks, the way ahead was quite clear enough to all: find out what made *semba* tick, and the same for its derivative—Zyme-One.

After the others left the main room, Thomas remained behind writing up notes. What supplies of *semba* remained at Cyro were easily had, but there would be no more *semba* coming out of Naruma. They must detect how to artificially duplicate *semba's* chemistry, so that someday it would be possible to derive great quantities of Zyme-One from something other than *semba* itself More than anyone else, this was an issue of chemistry, and that was Lin-pao's province.

Things were tracking, He was excited. Also, his ire was up. Twice he'd had to be flown on fairly short notice to London to make appearances at Jaggy's dinners. Then, "after a night on the nest" as she put it, he returned the following dawn to St. Curig Fields, a trip that so sapped him that it took nearly a full day to get back in the groove.

Next week he was due back in London for a press conference Jaggy was staging. A real brouhaha, as it would turn out, making him even more wary of the media.

London, England

O n the fourth floor at Muldaur House, off Portland Place, Jaggy stood on a stage of a hundred-seat auditorium, a soft cone of down-light illuminating her as she stood at the podium. She had gone so far as to dab her eyes with glycerin, making them shine with a wet luminescence. A stage trick she'd learned years ago when taking acting and voice lessons. Wicked up now and in high form, she was deftly employing her five-feet eight-inches to tower above the front rows of her audience.

She deplored the press, and their meddling; and the press, in turn, was keenly aware of her feelings. Even so, an invitation from Muldaur House often led to news of some merit, occasionally a hearty laugh or two, and, with some frequency, a bone or two thrown to the gossip columnists she usually invited, who, in exchange for juicy tidbits, made mention in their writing of her charities or pet projects. She had nothing for them today—nothing titillating anyway—but had included them anyway so they wouldn't feel short-changed.

One disgruntled reporter had long-ago dubbed her the Stiletto; this, because she had arranged to have three reporters cashiered for cooking up a story that, though partly true, she thought unseemly and humiliating.

Like many a sobriquet, the name had stuck. A wag was known to put it bluntly at a pub-hangout of the press, "The royals may be in Buckingham Palace, and the angels in their Heaven, but the Stiletto is here. So let us all be entertained. Whose turn is it to give the bitch a touch of the stick?"

Today, the message to be delivered was nothing less than an outright grab for free publicity.

She let the press-guests graze for a time on a few warm-up lines, then let Thomas take over as she announced, "And now with immense pleasure I introduce my good friend and business partner in Muldaur-Courmaine Laboratory, Mr. Thomas I. Courmaine," then turning to him, sitting close by, she held out a heavily jeweled hand, a gesture indicating his moment to shine had arrived.

Thomas stood.

Moving to the podium, he drew unswerving attention from forty-four members of the London media. At her urging, he wore a tailored gray glen-plaid suit, a pale blue shirt of Sea Island cotton, and a dark blue tie. He appeared dashing, especially so when placing himself at the side of the dark-haired, formidable Jaggy Muldaur. With a piquant cat-smile, she looked straight into the waiting faces. Beaming, in sotto voce, she said to him, "Let's say nothing more than we have to," and then quickly admonished all those gathered, "nothing nasty, mind, in the way of questions or the security will have you out of here in a flash," nodding pleasantly then at the two uniformed guards, standing by each door.

Thomas opened with, "Let's start with your questions," pointing to a woman who identified herself as a reporter for the *Times*.

"Your press release refers to this Zyme-One, Mr. Courmaine—by the way, do you prefer to be addressed as doctor?"

"I don't, no."

"What is it? This Zyme-One? What's in it?"

"It's an enzyme. Enzymes, if you're not familiar with them, are critical catalysts in bio-chemical reactions that, for one thing, make all your cells function. You'd not survive without enzymes because you couldn't manufacture what your body needs in order to thrive. Proteins mainly. What's inside Zyme-One, you ask? We don't know, not exactly. We'll be making it our business to find out. My guess is that it's more than an enzyme. Maybe a lot more."

"How do you make it? In a laboratory?"

"Yes, but conceivably you could make it just about anywhere. You have to know how to do that, however, and we don't. Or not yet anyway."

A frown from the woman reporter. "I see and then I don't see. What is its origin? Some organic substance? An animal?"

"It derives from a shrub."

"The name for which is?"

"Not for publication at this time."

"A secret of some sort. Nonsense. Where do you find it?"

"Another secret, as you put it."

"Was this what was used on those African women? The ones of that tribe, they were in the news months ago?"

"Yes." Then, he amended, "Well, mostly so." Saying nothing about the chimp genes.

The newswoman sat down, her face skeptical, obviously displeased. Thomas signaled to another in the audience.

This one, a man, from the *Guardian-Herald*, asked, "In your own words, can you tell us exactly what it is you're up to. In words our readers can understand, please."

"Sure. The core of our work is to find ways to deliver cheap healthcare through gene therapy or a regenerative medium to the eighty-percent of the world that goes without any decent care at all. Famine, pestilence, in too many nations leads to disease, and to a staggering loss of life. Left unchecked, diseases migrate from continent to continent. AIDS, for example. It's a dangerous thing and it's very, very expensive for its victims. Low-cost care can be delivered without the aid or the interference of the present western medical establishment. Cheap means cheap"—Thomas emphasized —"but cheap doesn't exclude high quality…it is no secret that we live in world where the economics of medicine have made it prohibitively expensive for too many people, especially those in the poor nations. The entire unfair mess of modern medicine begs for change and we hope to help make that happen…what I'm conveying is a vision, and not a certainty…"

"Gene therapy for the misbegotten, am I right?"

"No one is misbegotten. Otherwise, yes, you're more correct than otherwise. We're trying to set the gears in motion for very low-cost health care. That's the nub of it."

"Eventually, are you saying that we'll be getting along with no medical people or even hospitals?"

"I'd say that's always a real possibility. One day in the future. Probably, the long future."

"You're digging for trouble, I'd hazard."

"We're all in trouble, as of this minute, as of last year, as of ten years hence if we don't do something. That's part of what we're trying to fix."

Waving both hands, another man stood, insisting on attention. Jaggy had pointed him out earlier, a double-gaiter, she had said, and mean-minded as a cobra. His face betrayed a sunlamp tan. His hair, dyed a reddish-brown, fell in cascading waves to his shoulders. Sharp, knowing eyes narrowed just before he peppered away.

"The name of your firm, Muldaur-Courmaine, does it signify anything else?"

"You'll have to parse that. I'm not sure I understand you."

"Have you some other relationship with Miss Muldaur? On, say, the friendly level?"

"We are friends. I was a friend of her late father's as well."

"Have it your way, then. I shall be more to the point. Are you and the Misses Muldaur in, um, a romantically involv—?"

"We're here to discuss a science project which Miss Muldaur has graciously agreed to back financially."

"We're quite aware, sir. What I'm asking is this, are the two of you, let us say, entwined?"

Thomas's hands opened and closed, as a burning sensation crept across the nape of his neck. He wondered how to cut the man off without making a ruckus out of it in front of the others, whom, he saw, were perked up, alert and waiting. Then, before he could divert the question, the next grenade was lobbed by the assailant.

"Mr. Courmaine, I've a reason for asking. Our readers will show more interest if you're making this a family triangle. A *ménage*, of you will. It is alleged by some in the media that a native chieftain in Africa stated publicly that you and Baster Muldaur were lovers. One of my colleagues from a sister paper was present at that, well, shall we call it a show—I guess you'd call it a show, the one where three African women were displayed in their nakedness. I believe this occurred several days after Mr. Baster Muldaur met his death. The African chieftain, I'm told, made that exact statement about you…and about Muldaur. Do you deny any of this?"

He remembered instantly how a note, alleging the same falsehood, appeared one morning on his breakfast tray at the Park Lane Clinic. He had dismissed it then but could not dismiss it now in front of forty-odd newshawks.

The accusation hung in the air, afloat like an ever-expanding balloon.

Before replying, he glimpsed Jaggy who was motioning to the security guards, then aiming a finger at the offender who was shortly hustled out of the auditorium. By then, hands had shot upwards. Voices cried out in a chaotic chorus. Jaggy grabbed Thomas's elbow and together they rushed off the stage.

After the press conference broke up, Thomas had taken the train up to Wales and Jaggy was driven to her home in Belgravia, exhausted. Nauseous again, she had gone straight to her bedroom. Lying on her bed, a forearm pressed to her brow, she had other things to duel with now.

The bell in her womb might finally chime.

Feurenreuth, her treating doctor at Klinik St. Foy-Tönbrin, had contacted her the day before. The last of Baster's sperm had been coaxed into one of her eggs; after a fourteen-day interlude another embryo had appeared. Special treatments applied to her uterus at Duke should have taken effect by now, and if she'd come to Switzerland soon they'd proceed at once with another implanting.

Go there, and with Thomas none the wiser. Taking no chances. If the uniting with Baster's sperm failed again, then there was always Thomas as a backup. He lived in her world now. She was freighting him, and when the right moment came, she'd clue him as to her plans. If there were to be a surrogate, he'd be it—to see to The Trust, that it would remain where it belonged, under her indirect control until a child came of age. Unconsciously, her fingers lingered on her belly, as if testing the area for safety.

Smiling, she recalled an old military adage: *When you've got them by the balls, their hearts and minds will follow.*

One more thing before her nap. She dialed her office, gave instructions and waited while she was patched through to the managing editor of *Mirage*, London's leading scandal sheet.

As the editor came on the line, she waded in, "That drifty faggot you sent over to the conference made a blithering fool of himself. If you print so much as a comma about Baster Muldaur and Thomas Courmaine, I'll break your ballocks into more pieces than an Einstein could count. Mind, I am dead serious…you people, you're despicable."

"But is it true, mam? Tell us, is it?"

"Baster Muldaur had more women than you can find hurrying along Bond Street at noon hour. And that's that. Get yourself ten barristers if you print something stupid. You'll need every one of them."

Hanging up, she fell back on her bed, taking deep breaths. Feurenreuth had insisted she keep herself in a calmed state; that it could make all the difference, even prevent another misfire. Paris, she needed Paris, and to hell with London.

Hell with everything, she was thinking, and with everyone.

On the morning after the aborted press conference, one tabloid led its coverage with, MULDAUR-COURMAINE TO BYPASS MEDICAL DOCTORS. Meant to kick sand into the gears, it succeeded, igniting a flurry of inquiries asking for clarification. Though Thomas's observations, brief as they were, had been taken out of context, the headline amounted to gold-plated news.

Almost overnight, a great many readers and viewers learned of the lab, thus becoming slightly more familiar with the name of Courmaine, and that it was somehow paired with that of Muldaur, a name widely known in the U.K. and elsewhere.

Within a span of three days, the telephone receptionists at Muldaur House fielded more than five-hundred calls, more than two-hundred originating from the Continent and as many from the Americas. The story, gradually withered, but not before due note was taken in a good many places, including Bethesda, Boston and Thomasville.

Washington, D.C.

Twice every month Murray Raab dropped by Milligan's, a saloon-grill in midtown Washington, just off K Street. He could not recall any visit when the popular watering hole was less than three-quarters filled, often staying that way well into the afternoon hours, as if the patrons had forgotten what they did for their daily keep.

The news crowd and an assortment of lobbyists had a sort of devotion to Milligan's, and some all but slept there, indeed, some of them had, if you could believe the stories. Every so often, a rumor was bandied about that trysts between well-known regulars were going on in an infamous if not historical bedroom, one floor up. Patrons were also accorded special privileges. Some had their private mail sent to Milligan's, preferring the saloon to their homes or offices. Messages could always be safely left for friends, from in-town or out. At the given word, the headwaiter would advise a phoning-in editor or distraught wife that a particular reporter hadn't been seen all day. Yet, another nicety was the management's willingness to carry bar and food bills, payday to payday.

Murray Raab chose Milligan's for his meeting with his prospective cat's-paw—a middle-aged reporter, Maveen Cassidy, a sidelined workhorse known for her outlandish dress, her waddling walk, and her complaisant attitude of cooperating with government officials in need of a pipeline for making leaks to the press.

Besides, as a longtime customer of Milligan's, when she could afford it, she and Murray Raab would arouse scant notice from others.

Cassidy, in her time, had been employed by a half-dozen major papers, two weekly periodicals, and had done a stint with the Associated Press a decade or so ago. Her raucous mouth, coupled with her drinking habits, had netted her a series of pink slips until a friend, high up in the pecking order of the Hearst chain, staked her to a dry-out at the Betty Ford Clinic in California. Of late, she was, so to speak, on the beach. No jobs, nor prospects. In the past, she had accommodated the intelligence agencies, when one or another of them asked that a certain piece be planted in the "right" news channels. Paid for this work by getting scoops that really mattered, she had subsisted on her free-lancing. But no more. The doors to the clandestine services were no longer opened to her. She'd been shunted to the bench of outcast, replaced by the younger, on-the-make writers who were faster to make friends their own age in Washington's countless bureaucracies.

Cassidy, it seemed, was as washed up as a dead cod. And Raab knew it and meant to take full advantage of the situation.

She sat directly across from him at one of the window tables. Halfway through lunch Raab was cautioning her, "I don't want our or my name anywhere near what we're talking about. If you screw up, it's on your head and no one else's. It's that or nothing."

"You don't have to treat me like I just graduated from kindergarten, godammit all."

"I hadn't meant to."

"Yes, you did. Go on, Mur, I'm still here, still with you. All ears."

"As I said earlier, you should read the coverage from that London press conference of Muldaur…Muldaur-Courmaine, no less. He's risen in the world. A handful of people over there doing some cockamamie research. All the hoopla, you'd think it was a mother having a kid at age one-hundred. Muldaur, is it? I'm trying to figure out how what's-her-name Muldaur got herself into the act and what's going on over there. I can't do that, but you can."

"She puts her name on it, and so she gives it a place in the sun. They got themselves a fortune worth of free advertising. Who wouldn't go for that kind of a deal?"

Even in mid-meal she smoked. Stubbing out her third cigarette, she lit another. She regarded Raab with colliding feelings of amusement and deepest suspicion. Then she went on, "Let's back-pedal a moment, so I can get all this into one lane."

Raab, his fork suspended halfway between mouth and plate, returned her look. The sight of her had nearly wrecked his appetite. A great sow of a woman, wearing the loose-hanging daisy-printed clothes of a fortune-teller, an iridescent yellow scarf attempting to hide a neck that likely measured a fleshy nineteen inches. Today, she accented her vast frontage with three strands of amber-colored, egg-sized beads. They made clicking sounds as they rolled to new places whenever she moved that hippo-like body.

Cassidy blew a neat circle of smoke that sailed over Raab's head. With her rasped voice, she said, "You're saying this guy thinks he's about to change the world. Like the hocus-pocus he supposedly did in Africa. Those women, the whatchamacallit tribe. Okay, I can find out what he's up to. And you say you're getting all this secondhand. That's a load of crap, Mur, and you know it is and you're not making me happy with all your bullshit. Now you tell me, what the hell's so wrong about what this dude is up to?"

"It's in the way he goes about it. You get the distinction, I'm sure."

"He may get the distinction of going into the Hall of Fame, if what you're suggesting rolls downhill in one piece. What the hell's got you in such a fret?"

"Maveen, you stand to do well on this project. Fifteen-thousand a month and your expenses. Do it right, and we can fix you up permanently. Not too many questions from you. Do what you're told to do. Top-grade work and lots of it. You want this assignment or do I offer it elsewhere?"

"Questions are my business, Mur, you know that, right? Don't be such a prick. I need background. I need motives. I need informants. I need to know why you, or the NIH is so piss-all worried. Then I can give this story a blowout like it was a tornado. Who's behind you, Murray? Is this one of those mirror tricks from Langley or someplace?"

"Nothing of the kind."

"Horse feathers. It's the drug companies, I bet. They and the NIH anyway. The FDA, they got a piece of this, too?"

"You want the assignment?"

"I think I do."

"Quiet down, then."

"Screw yourself. Now tell me more, Mur, honey-bunny. What's going on? What's this Courmaine really doing? Slicing up unborn babies or inventing Arctic virgins or something? I don't get it. Is one of those animal-torture crowds after him?"

Raab fiddled with his plate of haddock, thinking, weighing. Wondering how far he could go, and if she was truly worth it. Two forkfuls later, he replied, "He's using loopholes, foreign loopholes. In the U.K. for one, and who knows where else, if he has all the Muldaur operators to work with. He could hide anything, anywhere. He's not abiding by the rules of the road. There's a, uh, a set of precedents here, at NIH, the FDA, Congress, a slew of court judgments besides. Public policy is being flouted. He's thumbing his nose...a crackpot...an angle-player...hiding behind the skirts of that woman, who's too rich to fuck with..."

"Why should he care? He's got her. He's in Europe, not America."

"He *is* an American, for one thing. He's been trusted in the past, now he's going off on some half-cocked end run. There's a feeling he might be doing something off-beat and possibly dangerous. For certain, unregulated...and he's not the only one. Some of these self-styled scientists, you know, they get to be like those garage-biologists, and like those anthrax chefs."

"Pretty thin beer, Mur," she said. "Send in the FBI, why not? Has he swiped something?"

"No, not that I know of."

"Broken any laws?"

"That's under evaluation. And that's why we're looking for a good job of reporting and a few other things."

"What other things? I want to see a more complete picture here and with a lot of focus to it."

Raab told her as much as he safely could. He referred to an experiment at NIH supervised by Courmaine that had aroused interest, then mentioned it was still under wraps, confidential. Then, in a direct lie, stated that NIH was a natural partner for Courmaine, who had rejected the idea out of hand. "You're quite aware that The White House and Congress are hell-bent to lower health costs...will do about anything. Here comes Courmaine like some snake-oil peddler and if ever Congress buys it, then the spike goes right up our tailpipe. Months and months of hearings, and meanwhile Congress could derail billions in medical research funding. We can't have that, nor can the country be stalled while all this horseshit gets settled. Too much is at stake. University grants, National Science Foundation, NIH. It's billions. That ingrate has to be torpedoed, starting yesterday," said Raab, his voice trembling. "The way to handle it, is to mount a flame-throwing, attack-dog campaign that'll demolish the bastard."

"What else? Gimme the works, Mur."

"An entire strategy for protective patents—favoring the U.S.—could easily be forfeited if a new and uncontrolled technology springs up offshore. If he's on to something, suppose the Brits get it. They'd wring our butts. American jobs lost by the thousands. A massive science-based industry jeopardized. Our biggest industry, in fact. Doctors, thousands of them, maybe hundreds of thousands might lose out in the end. Health technology must be controlled. Fenced off. No fouling it up by Courmaine or anyone like him who tries to stray outside of our, uh, our national objectives. You get the idea, don't you? He has to be made an example of."

"Says who?"

"Says me."

"I see. Just you? And you think this one-man lead-head can topple the drug industry."

"Perhaps not. But why chance it? Just about every technical breakthrough that shook the earth was started in someone's basement somewhere."

"I'll grant you that. How high up does this go, Mur?"

"The highest, believe me."

"White House?"

"Not directly. But they'll be getting into it, if we ring their doorbell. You're to be the first bell-ringer."

Cassidy laughed nervously.

But Raab wasn't laughing as they played out their minuet; a verbal foot-dance of two Washington veterans well veneered by hard won experience in the trenches of politics. Cassidy probed with a reporter's inquisitiveness and Raab, like any schooled bureaucrat, said no more than he must. A quasi-agreement was reached after she set her conditions. She'd take a hard look at what she was up against before she committed any further, with Raab to be given her decision in several days. It was hatchet work, plainly, that Raab had in mind. Were she to take on the project then she was to be in charge, strictly in charge, of her end of the operation. Even one pound of interference from anyone and she'd quit. Letting out another flume of smoke, she went on, "Any cute stunts or Washington-style acrobatics at my expense and I'll blow the whistle so loud they'll hear it in the asylum for the deaf and the mute. Make book on that, Mur. I will, I promise you that, my friend."

Her ground rules, if not an outright threat, were a close bedfellow. Even her terms surprised Murray Raab.

"How much help can I hire?" Cassidy asked.

"Five, at tops. Free-lancers only, of course."

"Of course, yourself. You cluck-head, you'd think this is my first day on the Potomac."

Raab let her derision pass. He debated telling her about Tavester, the Irish head-knocker slated to come his way soon. Still queasy about it and thinking Cassidy, were she told of it, might wilt away.

Foul, dirty work—he had no one else to turn to. He sensed that she had sensed his predicament when giving her the invitation to have lunch.

Their session found its uncharted way to a cautious conclusion. Of the two, Murray was the one under pressure to find someone who knew how to smear foul ink by the pail. Cassidy, for her side of it, was in grimmest need of money. Like two magnets, they were about to enter each other's field of attraction. Cassidy was a street-savvy reporter, who took little guff from anyone. Still, she was no fool, and there were limits as to how far she'd go; those limits were about to be tested in ways her fertile brain had neither expected nor imagined.

Ten days after Maveen Cassidy accepted Murray Raab's offer, an anonymous caller reeled off a set of instructions: the first, was for Cassidy to remain at her home for all of the next day. A person would come calling to install an encryption program on her computer. More, she was instructed to busy herself with the hiring of a stable of writers. She would shortly receive a list of topics and she would parcel them out as she saw fit. Strict deadlines were to be observed. Anyone who was tardy would have his or her pay docked. Within a week, she'd receive an e-mail address to which she alone would forward all edited and encrypted material. Someone else, it seemed, would place the content in various publications.

Hoping to gather a hint as to whom was pulling the strings for this unholy yet profitable caper, she lobbed a couple of questions into the phone. Abruptly, she was advised to tend her own garden and never mind the diggings and plantings of others.

By that afternoon she received an envelope bearing a five-page list of twenty-four items meant as the thrust-points for editorial letters and possible articles.

Slash and burn, all of it aimed at Muldaur-Courmaine Laboratory, Ltd. She would fry some poor bastard hiding himself in Wales of all places.

Few things move faster than falsified rumor, and Cassidy had mastered the art of incubating them, knowing .how easy it was to dupe the public. As importantly, she knew the media was quite aware that rumors were not always wrong. She had had the best schooling. For three years, she had learned every chapter of the playbook when drumming up propaganda and disinformation pieces for the Mandarins at Langley. A great gig until she was let go after the inspector-general uncovered her lark; that she had taken up with two black men assigned to the agency's motor pool. Rightly, or not, she was considered a security risk, ending her days at Langley.

Cassidy put that thought in her forget-it-file as she lit up a toke: Ecuadorian, top quality weed. Slowly, and peaceably, she inhaled an ecstasy that soon untightened her.

The past couple of years had been thin, the cupboard always too bare. Now she envisioned some overdue goodies coming her way. She'd latched on to a good thing with Raab, pleasing her immensely.

In the coming dream-like, hazy minutes, she began to lay out her battle plans.

St. Curig Fields, Isle of Anglesey, Wales

Ms. Adele Quelmaithe Ponsoby, hired as office manager the previous month and serving as secretary to anyone on the team needing help, brought in the mail one morning, depositing the full stack on Thomas's desk. Ponsoby had been strongly endorsed by her cousin, the chief constable of Holyhead, a village a few miles distant from St. Curig Fields. With a twenty-five year stint as a librarian, she had put in for retirement at age forty-eight, was now ready for another go. Decent paying jobs on Anglesey were scarce, and she had leaped at the chance for this one that seemed to her as easy pickings.

The perfect fit for the lab: she was efficient as oxygen, punctual to a fault, diligent as a honeybee. In no time Thomas became a servant to her capacity for making order out of the ever growing piles of lab documents, incoming mail, accounting schedules and sundry junk mail. She soon evolved a logical filing system, turning all correspondence around in jig time, and compiled monthly lab expenses for Muldaur Ltd's London office.

When first interviewing her, Thomas had suggested a salary of twenty-five thousand pounds annually but she had declined, saying she already had a good pension, and that the sum he offered would raise her tax bracket. "Twenty will do ever so nicely," she had counter-offered, anxious for the work. Deal done, a friendship born, a treasure found.

On this morning, wearing a foreboding countenance, Ponsoby handed him the contents from a thick envelope, postmarked London, bearing the logo and name of Muldaur Ltd. He sat to read two clippings forwarded from the p.-r. department.

A columnist in Des Moines, Iowa, writing:

> Mr. Courmaine, one of science's latest fabulists, has seemingly aligned himself with the outlaw element of science, who insists they are halfway through the door of tomorrow, yet give us little or nothing to support their assertions. Some, like Courmaine elect to hide themselves in foreign countries; they find it simpler to dodge U.S. law enforcement agencies

and conduct their experiments. One of his so-called staff members is Alexis Hazlett, formerly a bio-investigator for the National Institutes of Health in Bethesda, Maryland, the leading medical research unit in the world. Hazlett, yet another renegade it seems, repeatedly infracted rules at NIH which lead to her dismissal.

Thus, we have a sort of cabal, or, one might say, "the wild, wild west" of bio-science devising its own laws and regulations as it masquerades under the guise of human research for our general betterment and well-being, but, and it is a behemoth of a *but*...

On the verge of picking up the phone to lodge a protest, he stopped his hand in midair. What good would that do? Play into their hands? Were they laying their bait, meaning to drag him into a melee?

Cooling, but only slightly, he turned his eyes to the second clipping. This from the *Albuquerque Morning Ledger*. Thomas saw his name only once, about halfway into the text. Someone at Muldaur had marked the passage with a red grease pencil.

...Courmaine, and others like him, hides behind the fig leaf of what they call advanced scientific research. It is balderdash. Like the rest of his fellow renegades, who write their own rules, go their own way, they are shunned by the more responsible members of the science community. Not long ago, Courmaine was forced to resign from the prestigious scientific organization, SOS, when he proposed some outlandish scheme that was soon quashed by wiser heads...

Further down, he noted:

...leading some, even in government, to harbor serious doubts about Courmaine, who at one time was a top staffer in the Jesuit Curia in Rome. Reportedly, he was banished from that religious order for espousing views that severely contradicted Roman Catholic dogma. A man who is viewed in science circles as a sort of maverick, Courmaine seems to take high delight in thumbing his nose at more responsible thinkers.

With a resounding thump, he smacked the clipping against the desktop. No one had bothered to ask for a clarifying reply. Why all this sudden notoriety? What would Jaggy think?—take a very dim view of it all is exactly what she'd think. He'd post the malicious clip on the hall bulletin board and do whatever he could to appease the team at next Monday morning's meeting.

Bad enough what they were saying about him, but why tear into Alexis with barefaced falsehoods. How could they do that, or any of it?

Was Bascomb somehow involved? Probably not, but Thomas, frantic, was trolling for every possibility. What of Raab? Was Raab serving up malicious lies about Alexis Hazlett? Somehow, somewhere Raab had to have had a hand in the theft and suppression of the Peter-Paul experiment. How to find out and where to start? He'd like a long, curt talk with Raab, but was in no mood to hike off to the States. Not now anyway. Too much was on the cusp of happening at the lab.

Bethesda, Maryland

Raab resented the intrusion the minute he laid eyes on Charles Tavester, the ex-IRA man who he'd been told to expect by an anonymous telephone caller. Tavester, it seemed, was to be some sort of on-the-spot lookout in Wales. Raab particularly disliked being dragged into any involvement with this strong-armer, who had arrived without any notice, and gave the impression he was doing Raab a favor just by being in the same room. With no choice other than have the stranger admitted, he gave his okay the security desk. Later, after Tavester left, he realized his own mistake of allowing the man in, in the first place.

At the lobby security desk a log-record existed now. Still, there or not, he was in no position to deny or defy The League. A throat-cutter, if he did.

An icy-looking customer, Tavester carried a fiercely coiled air about him, creating an instant tension; his low voice gave a taunting edge to his words. On one side of his face, a livid scar told its own story of violence. A killer? What else, if he were IRA? Certainly, no giver of tea parties.

Raab got rid of him as fast as he could, suggesting the Irishman do whatever he was told to do by others. That he, Raab, knew nothing about any of it and had nothing whatsoever to add.

With a flippant almost sneering smile, Tavester exited, leaving Raab on the verge of hot anger. He was being ensnared by The League, perhaps set up as the fall guy if things went haywire. Tavester, conceivably, could bring trouble and that trouble might trace its way to this very doorstep.

But how to get clear of it? He was into the Courmaine cabal up to his neck.

London, England

Thomas had been summoned to London for one of Jaggy's dinner parties, this one for the Secretary of State for Wales, a permanent member of the Cabinet. High time, Jaggy had advised, that he meet some of England's political brokers, starting with Edward Ballsrye, who massaged the special interests of Wales within the national government. Ballsrye had brought along his wife, and Jaggy had added four others, all prominent within the London theater. Ballsrye, an avid theater-goer, had been greatly amused by all the titillating thespian tittle-tattle. Still, he did not exclude Thomas, questioning him for a run of minutes on activities at St. Curig.

Next day, Jaggy and he had taken lunch at Blake's, another posh restaurant Jaggy favored in the West End. Fish today—more of the delicately textured Plaice from Iceland—accompanied by endive and a bottle of 1971 Sancerre. She toyed with her food, asking pointed questions, and once again mentioning her bio-tutor at London University. Several months earlier when she first raised the idea of learning something about genetics, he thought it a good suggestion. It ought to have made the activities at the lab easier for her to grasp. Lately, he had second thoughts.

"Tell me more about cloning," she urged at one point. "Human cloning."

"Right now, you mean?"

"Why not?"

"What is you'd like to know?"

"My prof at the university doesn't think it necessary that I know about it. Says I hired him to learn about genes and not biotechnology. So, how does one go about it. Hard to do, is it?"

"It's no cakewalk," Thomas answered. "The outcome is always in doubt, particularly with humans. One day that may change, but if I tried to clone you or the woman over there with the funny blue hat, the chances are good I'd get a freak of some kind. A fifty-fifty shot at best."

"But that says nothing about how one does it."

"It's done by remaking the nucleus of a human cell. Almost any cell that contains your genetic blueprint, your DNA. You start there. Step two, from one of your eggs, we remove its nucleus, its yoke if you will, which contains your heredity code. Next, we take that cell of yours that I just mentioned and we fuse it to the interior of your emptied egg. You okay with this, so far? Everything clear?" She nodded and he continued, "We give the newly loaded egg a dose of nutrients, then put the revised egg inside your womb and hope like Willy that it finds a nice friendly follicle to latch on to. If it all works right, and it probably won't, then we get an embryo, then a fetus, and finally out comes a little nine month old passenger, screaming at the world for having disturbed its peace and depriving it of that nice warm spa it's been living in."

"That's the whole of it?"

"More or less. But I repeat, cloned humans and cloned mammals of any type seem to inherit many problems and they're not just the genetic problems that are in the host cell. Cloning for some reason triggers a greater propensity to get colds, or measles, or liver problems, or dry rot—"

"What! Dry rot?"

"A figure of speech. The upshot is that a cloned-anything seems to get short-changed in its ability to normalize. It's risky. Cloned organisms die early. We know very little about how to do it successfully. Or what goes on at the molecular level, when we try to make copies of ourselves. Things can get very confused in the cells of any cloned object. Nature doing her thing. She spent millions of years figuring out how to make us into distinct beings. You've got to figure that if she wanted exact copies of anyone or anything, she'd make it happen herself. What she wants most of all is diversity, so cloning doesn't fit into her scheme of things. That's my guess, anyway."

"Well, twins. Identical twins."

"A misnomer. No twins are identical. Close, but never exactly identical."

"What about a partial copy?"

"We do that already. You're a partial copy of your mother and your father. In descending degrees, you're a copy of a copy of a copy of everyone in your ancestral chain."

"What if a third party was introduced into the equation?"

Where was she going with this, he asked himself? "I don't know," he replied. "That's another bag of apples. It's one thing to substitute a gene or a set of genes, but trying to do a three-way human being would be nutty. Why would anyone want to?"

"Are you capable of doing it?"

"I've no idea. It's against the law and it should be. Hybridizing the human race that way. Nature has already hybridized us a million-million times. I'm sure you know that from your school days."

"Not everywhere is it illegal, is it?"

"You can find places, I suppose. You're not getting any ideas about us trying something at the lab? You're not, are you?"

"Nothing illegal, no. But I have a home in the Seychelles and it's not illegal there to try it. I did some checking."

"Well, I can't imagine many people rushing off to the Seychelles for that kind of treatment. But in most places it is unlawful. It's nothing to meddle with, and I'm not going to if that's what you have in mind."

"Were I to offer you a million-pounds, would you?"

"Nope."

"Three-million?"

"Nope."

"You're an expensive chap."

"Sane, too, I hope."

He could tell she was warming up for a verbal swing at him. The hardening jaw teamed up with her snapping blue eyes as she took a cut. "I quite dislike it when you're so resistant, Thomas."

"I'm really not. But if you're suggesting I run illegal experiments, forget it. I know the top geneticists just about everywhere in the world, and none would give you ten seconds of their time, if they thought you wanted them to try anything like a human cloning. They might even report you. Probably they would. My upstairs light bulb just turned on. Let me ask you something. Have you access to any of Baster's DNA?"

"At Cyro, yes. I had it sent there, to be kept there with his sperm supply."

"I didn't know that. He's not in Jo-burg?"

"I just said he isn't."

Giving her a long look, he offered, "I'm surprised, that's all. Quite surprised."

"You are now enlightened."

"The Afrikaner DNA and all else stored there is under the auspices of African Heritage."

"Who do you think is the principal funder of African Heritage?"

"You are. But that wouldn't get you access to Cyro."

"It wouldn't, eh? Sometime if you're ever in the canton of Zug in Switzerland, have a look at the commercial registry. You'll see who owns Cyro."

"Muldaur?"

"None other."

"I'll be. Another surprise. I hope you're not getting wild ideas, Jaggy."

"Nothing wild about them. Necessary, perhaps, but not wild. You've got your lab, don't you? You can do more than one thing at a time, right?"

Déjà vu, he thought. She was plotting something. A version perhaps of what Baster had promoted that day in the gazebo in Jo-burg. The stolen eggs caper. Now her, and up to what? He could guess and he didn't like what his guessing was saying to him.

Saying nothing more, she rose to her feet and so did he. Again, no tab presented for the lunch. The maître bowed as they passed on their way to the waiting Bentley. Great for business, having Jaggy Muldaur drop in for lunch, the onlookers having their gander, the grist for a little midday tête-à-tête.

On the way to her home, she reminded him, "You've not forgotten Berlin, I trust?"

"How could I? This is the fourth time you've brought it up."

"I'll let you have a date soon. Oh, we'll have fun, darling. We will, you'll see. And I need some."

Fun? She had him worried. If ever a rumor circulated that she wanted to begin cloning experiments, he could expect more newspaper jabs. She flew about as if she were a migrating bird. Berlin. He was getting tired of her whims and the time he lost in satisfying them. Yet he was ever mindful of who stood behind the lab's monthly payroll.

St. Curig Fields, Isle of Anglesey, Wales

Atawdry piece in *Hamburg's Bild*, said to be the world's best-selling newspaper, its circulation constantly bolstered by write-ups on scandalous escapades of all sorts, interspersed with full-page photos of celebrities, who often sued on grounds of defamation.

The lead on the article read: THE BIO-BOY AND HIS RITZY MISTRESS.

It had to do with Jaggy, mostly, with himself as a sidebar. Midway down, two paragraphs disposed of him, telling of the fact that he lived and worked on her Wales estate, was seen frequently with her in London, adding that the name of the lab alone suggested the identity of the bankroller.

While nothing was untruthful in the article, he supposed Jaggy was raging. A paparazzi-type photo taken at an earlier time showed her on someone's yacht, sunbathing topless, wearing only a skimpy towel around her waist. Staring blankly at the revealing shot, he was somewhat stupefied Muldaur's p.r.-department had forwarded the article, wondering if Ponsoby had been addled when disgorging the envelope of its startling content.

A day later on the phone with Jaggy, he was asking, "Shouldn't we change the name of the lab, get you free of it? You can always be the silent partner."

"Stuff them, they're all sodders. You should know that by now. "

"But look what it's doing. Doing to you."

"I'd venture it's near time for a counter-attack."

"Except I don't know whom to attack or with what."

"Come up with something. Soon. By the way, I'm in Switzerland for the night. Give me a call. I adore you, Tom…and don't be working all the night….ta-ta, I've got to move my bum…"

She was off the line before he thought to ask her about calling her back that night. Switzerland, but where in Switzerland? No number as to where to reach her, and frankly he was happier for it. Likely he'd work well into the night, anyway, sleeping on a cot in one of the unused second-floor bedrooms.

An experiment was underway, something he and Lin-pao were pursuing and it was getting more interesting by the hour. In the process of cataloging the innards of *semba*, they'd been looking for the chemical combinations and sources that made Zyme-One tick. Everyone on the team was waltzing with excitement. On such occasions, Thomas often stood the night watch, sending the others home no later than seven in the evening. The hours were grueling, the pace unrelenting. Rest was vital, and he made sure they got it.

Tonight, he set aside work at his lab bench, his mind mired in thoughts about the attacks against Muldaur-Courmaine. It was scraping at the team's morale. Jaggy, too, was beginning to make noises; understandably so, for she was an extraordinarily image-conscious woman. Yet, Thomas felt powerless, out of his depth. It was like dueling with phantoms, and, besides, he hadn't any baseline or starting point. No targets to retaliate against; and, for that matter, as he'd said to Jaggy: retaliate with what?

Jaggy might have the right weapons at her command. But Jaggy's advisors had told her to keep out of the fray. Telling her she could only lose by going after these prevaricators, all of whom, in any event, were entitled to their opinions. More than half of what appeared in the newspapers was a rash of letters-to-the-editors. All around, for her it was a lose-lose situation were she to publicly react. She had mentioned to Thomas several times that she had talked to the authorities about the goings-on at St. Curig; that nothing illegal was afoot, nothing out of place, and they had accepted her word. And why not— she was Muldaur, had friends in the highest of places, and others belonging to the oldest of England's families, who, in near silence, and from high up in the nation's stratified society, waved mighty clubs. One carefully delivered murmur, a lifted eyebrow in the presence of the right Minister, and an ambitious technocrat could count on a ticket to the human scrap heap. And not be aware of it till others, junior in rank, passed him by. By then it was too late in one's career to do anything but wait out the endless gray days for a pension.

Alexis Hazlett was convinced Raab was mixed up in it. Yet she admitted to Thomas it was nothing but a hunch. "It's his style in spades, the shit-box," she had said, then said no more, nor did she need to. She was prone to occasional flashes of temper, a match perhaps with her reddish, Celtic like hair. He liked Alexis. One always knew where she stood, and where you stood with her.

And he harbored no misgivings about Jaggy herself. She'd dance on hot coals for only so long, and she'd not be inclined to over-use the welcome mat at Whitehall. What could he do? What could anyone do? And where were they?

Washington, D.C.

On the second and fourth Thursdays of each month, they met at the Washington Hilton at six or so in the lobby bar. Maveen Cassidy was already seated, having a cocktail, by the time Murray Raab arrived. She knew his tardiness for what it was: a calculated snub to impress upon her as to who ranked whom in their enlarging cabal.

Cassidy had never minded her quota of tail-licking at times, especially when Raab handed over the bank envelope made fat with crisp hundred dollar bills, her bi-weekly payment.

Today, he wanted her status report, and a little more besides.

A bureaucrat with a bureaucrat's mind, he relied on detail, always nosing around for the useful loophole, or any flaws in their campaign that might be exploited by Courmaine or Muldaur. The Muldaur angle had always disturbed him, the latent power there. His nervous system balked whenever he envisioned some smart-aleck private-eye poking around, someone with enough smarts to stumble on to the League's hatchet job. The right pro, with a bit of luck, could blow the lid off the assault against Courmaine. And Raab well knew he'd be in the lineup of the guilty. He was, after all, a paid Judas Goat singled out to lead Cassidy where he wanted her led, yet he'd be the one to take the fall if someone ever got wise to the smear tactics.

They sat there, barely noticed by passersby, as Cassidy updated her playbook for Raab. She was pleased with the campaign, employing, as it did, old-fashioned advertising tactics by reminding, and then reminding again, every possible reader that a dangerous subterfuge was underway, authored by a megalomaniacal scientist in the person of Thomas Courmaine. Soon, she explained, they'd kick it up a notch or two, "We'll scare the public. At the least, make them uneasy. Plus, I think the drug companies will get into this at some point," she said, fishing for a reaction and getting one.

"You may be sure of it."

"Is there anything I should know?"

"If there is, I'll let you in on it when the time comes."

"How do you suppose that some rich bitch gets herself tangled up with a priest and they go into biotechnology together? What're they up to? A secret lab hidden away, what's that all about? Is she looking for a new skin or something? Looking to go into the cosmetics racket? We can always connect it to those African women. Who're they anyway? Are they for real or did someone pull a cutey? That kind of thing. Sly sounding. Lots of questions. Enough to shove a sliver of fright into the British government, let's say. There's always that side of the street we can work, too."

"Yes, good. That's very good, I like that."

"We can twist that one eight ways from Sunday, if we want to. The Brits despise criticism. I favor the idea of pounding on the theme of something nefarious taking place under their own noses. Kick up the gravel, you know."

"When do you start launching again?" he asked.

"We've got five articles we sent in this week and they'll run over the next three weeks. Then we'll really lay down a killer of barrage. Courmaine won't know his own name, or he'll wish he had another one."

"You're sure, are you?"

"Of course, I'm sure, Mur. You can put that one where the monkey keeps its nuts."

On that perplexing note, Cassidy ordered another scotch-sour and advised Raab that she was planning a trip to Wales. She wanted *whoever it was* to shell out the funds for first-class passage, both ways. "I'm going to beard the lion, and I need some gas money."

"Ten-thousand do it?"

"Where's your heartbeat, Mur? It takes fifteen long ones for bingo to happen. It's time to shoot the moon."

"Fifteen-thousand? Who the hell—"

"The hell of it is this, that I'm the masher in this deal. You want the man fucked-over and I'm doing it for you. Any complaints?"

Scowling, Raab got up. "I'm leaving."

Instantly, she felt happier. "And the money?"

"Noon tomorrow," came the curt reply.

And off he went, vanishing amidst a crowd of conventioneers who had just flooded the lobby. After decades of jousting with politicians, corporate types, the general public, and unforgiving editors, Cassidy could ordinarily suffer the usual wounds of her trade. But Murray Raab was one of the rudest people she'd ever come across. Nothing redeemed the man. He must despise himself. What kind of wife, a paralytic apparently, would put up with a ham-hander like that jackass. Looking at him was like looking at a cartoon, and not a well-drawn cartoon. Must've broken his mother's heart, when realizing what she'd given birth to.

Well, the gig would end in a year or so. Probably less. Courmaine, if there was anything left of him, would be a twisted pretzel by then. And Cassidy knew she'd be out of work again, and with little chance of latching on to another fat, easy paycheck. She could hardly approach news editors, telling them she led the clique that had brought ruin to a scientist via a salvo of trumped up, almost libelous attacks. Taking that tack would make her the real story, instead of him.

Nursing her fresh drink for the next half-four, a bleak half-hour, she knew that she, too, was soiled goods. This would be her swan song. Unless, of course, she figured out some way to take the money and free herself from this operation at the right moment. Possible, she thought. Her involvement was known to Raab, naturally, also to five hired free-lancers. But who else? Not more than one or two, she gauged; upper echelon types, whoever they were. All right, okay, just maybe—*yes* and *yes*, she repeated to herself, hope rising in her heart. She'd size things up after she got to Wales, and had her own look at him. She'd make the sonofabitch jump a hoop or two, and see what he was made of.

St. Curig Fields, Isle of Anglesey, Wales

Increasingly, as time went onward, the team found themselves dazzled by Lin-pao, naturally gravitating to his innate prowess. No one ever seemed offended by the outlandish claims he made about himself; remarks that, if made by anyone else, would earn him little else but heavy scorn. He was a giver of prodigious help to all and any askers. Quicker yet to give credit to others, even when it hadn't been fully due them.

After the days he had spent in the Bronx at the Botanical Gardens, he had found his way into botany, getting the hang of the terminology, relating some of the specifics of that science to his own specialty of biochemistry.

He had not found it difficult to cross over, one science to the other. Having done it, and having probed into the living depths of *semba* as far as the past several months allowed, he had pursued several intriguing experiments with a variety of flora. Constantly raising the bar for the team, he strived for the new, the different, the unheard of. He excelled at designing ideas for investigations that intuitively demonstrated why they were on to a good thing, and maybe a great thing. A week earlier, Lin-pao had creased the brows of several botanists at Cambridge and, in glee, he was now about to upend his cohorts at St. Curig. When able to rivet an audience, small or large, he rose to his fullest moments.

Linking a bubble camera to a computer-aided projector that streamed a series of blown-up images to a wide screen, Lin-pao rigged up a picture show that revealed significant amounts of *semba*'s cell activity. All sorts of artificially color-tagged bits and pieces whirled around like spindrift, and yet what was visible on the screen was but a fraction of *semba*'s genes at pell-mell speed. Enough, however, to make the point visually: that the cell activity was profound.

On the screen a strip of *semba*'s DNA was unwinding, its genes poised to code for making specific proteins to replenish cells in *semba*'s roots.

Photos, dozens of them, showed this new life occurring in *semba*. But where, where—were the sets of genes that made Zyme-One possible? And how many of those genes did it take?

All this must be figured out just to draw up a scheme to isolate the genes, copy them, discern how they regulated themselves, and what the precise firing-order was for the creating of Zyme-One. Then, after learning the chemical and mineral combinations that built Zyme-One, they could launch the next and biggest step—make what they needed from *semba* artificially, and, once done, produce Zyme-One.

Not from scratch, but almost. That was the sought-after breakthrough.

Berlin, Germany

Everlasting days—four of them—and the nights, too, were exhausting. Jaggy had told him it was a trip for slumming around and he never knew what to expect, hour to hour.

They had prowled a dozen cabarets, many only risqué but one so lascivious—*Komödie Planet X*—he suspected the pay-offs to the police must be extravagant. Wild, raucous, abandoned behavior. Drugs everywhere. Eerie-looking Expressionist murals, painted by students, covering the walls. Puke splashed on the floor of the men's room. Gaudy purplish lighting, smoke-hazed air, pierced by ear-numbing music. At one stop, a young frizzy-haired woman wearing a lampshade, but not a stitch underneath, and with silvered pasties over her nipples, came over and sat on Thomas's lap, mussing his hair; then giving out with a taunting laugh before groping him.

He deposited her on the floor where, geyser-like, she spouted vicious curses yelling that he owed her the twenty-five Euros she'd come looking for.

Jaggy had gone to this nether world, taking Thomas along for the ride. One of those interludes where she could masquerade, do pretty much as she pleased, persuading herself that she could live like ordinary *volk*.

On an afternoon, they toured the Museen zu Berlin, viewing a retrospective of Durer, Brueghel and Hals. Jaggy had not been overly impressed. But she had been taken by an 18th-century painter, Caspar Friedrich, and made an inquiry of the curator, asking if he knew of anyone in Berlin who dealt in the artist's work. Too, there was yet another artist from Estonia, of the Renaissance Period, who had worked in egg tempura and that had also caught her eye. Lingering for a full hour, sitting and standing, letting the Estonian "flow into her"—as she imparted to Thomas.

Her dress expressed her moods. In the daylight she wore field khakis with buttoned cargo-pockets, a faded blue Safari shirt with shoulder straps, a black pea jacket. She altered her appearance, or thought she did, with aviator-style sunglasses. A Hermès scarf worn around head, wholly out of place, threw off a dash of color. At night she changed into black leather pants, lizard boots, a scoop-front silk blouse exposing a canyon of cleavage. Over this, she draped herself in a calf-length fur made of dyed Persian cat pelts conjured by a furrier in Barcelona.

No jewelry, though. Not so much as a single diamond ear stud. Very rare for her, even in bed she often wore earrings, losing them in the swirl of sheets after their sexual exertions.

She looked vampish, even slightly dangerous. Yet, and ironically so, she somehow seemed like a page out of *Elle*—expensive, chic, untouchable.

Ever the rule breaker, in a small handbag she kept what she called her protector; an unregistered Beretta .25 caliber, eight-shot semi-automatic. She showed Thomas how the serial number of the weapon had been filed into invisibility, raising his worries even higher. If caught with a firearm like that, they'd be arrested on the spot. She had no police permit to carry in Germany or in England either; the omission failed to perturb her in the slightest.

"I'm my own security, have always been," said in a way that suggested it was not a topic up for review.

Ignoring her tone, he responded, "I know you're a real two-gun Pete-the-pistol with firearms but why flout the law?"

"I grew up with guns. Guns instead of dolls. Should've been a boy, eh?"

"Thank God, not."

She laughed. Happy, carefree. Grabbing his arm, she pulled tighter to him. "Where are we headed?" he asked.

"I'm not sure. Come with me, sugar boy, and I'll show you how to get lost in the night."

"You're really fun, you are."

"Wait'll I get going. I'm fueled up. Hundred octane."

"How 'bout if we keep that Beretta at the Kemenski?"

"Are you balmy? This is Berlin."

At the Alexanderplatz, they engaged a horse-drawn carriage for a trip through the Tiergarten, the city's charming park. She smiled more, laughed, the air agreed with her but he'd detected a heavier use of face powder. He was grateful that she seemed relaxed, that she wasn't goading him for yet another trip to some faraway place, and that he'd not have to risk a confrontation. He steered wide of any mention of Muldaur's setbacks in Africa, and, thankfully, neither did she.

Back at the Grand Kempenski, their hotel, Jaggy ensured the concierge came one step closer to his retirement. She always tipped on the scale of a rajah, and this was no exception. Thomas did the actual tipping but she kept jamming wads of Euros into his hands, insisting he do the duty, keeping the staff always primed in the ready position. "Do it for me, please," she begged, or almost begged. "Baster was a strong tipper," she said and once again Thomas was reminded of how Baster still remained in her marrow. She copied most every habit of his she could manage as a female.

Late of a morning, paging through the hotel's guest magazine, she came across an advertisement. She did not speak German so Thomas translated for her; afterward, she had him phone a gallery to inquire about the artists on exhibit. At the mention of two Renaissance painters, she brightened, and they were on their way.

When there, she made her inspection and then cajoled a reluctant Thomas to dicker with the gallery owner for a work by a Belgian who impressed her. Speaking in German, he purposefully botched the negotiations by questioning the painting's authenticity. The gallery owner, reddening, foot-pawed the floor, turned his back in disgust and then turned again, demanding they leave the premises.

"Whatever's rubbing his tail." Jaggy wanted to know.

"He doesn't like Americans much."

"I'm not a Yank."

"He doesn't know who you are. I reminded him that Americans had saved his city from the Russians."

"Is he one of those leftover Communists?"

"Not likely, though, not if he owns this place. Let's get out of here while we're still solvent."

"I want that painting, ducks. I really must. Get it for me and I'll be yours forever."

"Not this painting, and not here."

"Hell you say."

"The owner's in a swivet. You can always calm him down with that popgun you carry around."

"You'd better shut up, too."

"How many paintings do you own?"

"I've not the slightest…"

And he let her answer hang by its neck.

Boorish of him to torpedo the purchase and he knew it, of course. He could have retrieved the situation simply by telling the owner who Jaggy was, and that he, a neophyte, was translating for her. A misunderstanding, nothing personal intended, *mien herr*, in a tone of deepest servility. Begging a bit of forgiveness, as he wrote himself off as another ugly-mannered American, not quite up to snuff on his use of the German tongue. He could've intoned that it was not really a sale, but an acquisition by an admirer from afar with surpassing interest in preserving Europe's best. No haggling on the price, *mien herr*, not an ounce of fuss either. Merely a wrap-up job, the usual exchange of legal tender so the gallery could book a slamming profit without so much as a crook of a finger or negotiations over the dreadful subject of cost.

Over a million Euros, at that, and the sum sickening him. Two or three years' worth of payroll for the lab.

Leaving the gallery, done with it all, barely had they covered a block when suddenly she pulled up. "I want it, and godammit and we're going back and get it."

Yanking at his arm, she reversed their direction back to the scene of his deceptions. She moved fast, her dark thick hair flying at times. Entering, she marched right up to the owner who blinked, looking befuddled, then suddenly wheeled as if to find the nearest sanctuary. She kept right on his tail. "Stop, you blockheaded Kraut," she hollered. "Get back here or I'll clobber you one."

She hadn't any idea of what Thomas had done to kill the sale, taking it out on the owner now, believing that earlier she had been dismissed as some no-account street tourist. Dressed as she was, she could not be mistaken as Jaggy Muldaur, woman of the continent, woman of so many news accounts and endless gossiping.

On she went, right after him, till he halted in his tracks. "Now then, Skippy, let's have you a little closer up so I can get a look at you. Thomas, tell this sodder he's got a sale in the wind. A sale he doesn't deserve. Find out what he wants on the price. I can see he'll be a crook, but we'll pay his extortion anyway. I'm used to it. Here, love, you'll need this" and she slipped a hand in her pocket and withdrew a wad of Euros and a gold-edged Braunsweig und Sohn debit card, forcibly adding, "have him do his robbing of us with this, and have the painting crated and sent on to Paris. Tell him to hop right to it or I'll have a hundred cats in here pissing on the walls. Tell him I'm out of sorts today and all other days as far as he's concerned." Her face rigid now, the cords of her neck like clay pipes. She is an assembled force—Thomas was thinking—an iron ball ready to leave its cannon. "Let's have the name of his solicitor," Jaggy demanded, "and the provenance had better be up to scratch. If there's even the faintest falsification I'll have his balls hung on top of the Bundestag. And I don't want ever to be hearing any whimpers from Jews who insist they owned it a hundred years back before the Nazis stole it. Not so much as a fucking whisper…mind."

At the expletive Nazi, the owner blanched.

Thomas edited and then translated this rash of war-making instructions. Jaggy had gone to a desk where she picked up a crystal paperweight. Her face cool, eyes darting and sharply appraising the situation. She wore the look of an African stick-fighter. Winding her arm like a windmill's blades, she threw the crystal oval with main force against the floor. An explosion then, shards of the crystal flying everywhere, bright and glittering as a sudden splash of sunlit water.

"Add that to my account, you little cocker," Jaggy roared at the owner, and then to Thomas, "And tell him that's exactly what'll happen to his miserable fucking head if he doesn't put a shoulder to it and get done with it. We're not waiting for the Second Coming here."

She moved on the owner again. Immediately, he threw up an arm in defense, half-squatting as he did, then righting himself, he hurried off somewhere.

"Have you lost your senses?" Thomas said, appalled.

"Lost it? Lost what?"

"Your mind, that's what. He'll have the police on us."

"He'll be looking at the business end of my Beretta, too. I ought to shoot the communistic sodder. Fetch him for me and I shall."

"I'm getting out of here."

"Coward."

Thomas restrained her as she went for her other pocket. He didn't know if the gun was there, but was taking no chances. "Leave, Jaggy, right now," he scolded. "Go back to the hotel and let me handle this."

"What does that suffering cockhead want for it?"

"Leave."

"I asked you a question, godammit all."

"1,089,000 Euros, not including insurance or shipping."

"You think it a fair price?"

"I wouldn't have the foggiest. How could I? Go, please, and I'll handle it."

They stood there for another three minutes till the owner came back, followed by a woman with a flush-pink face, and a thick bun of golden braids crowning her head. Tall, powerful looking, with the shoulders of a steroid-filled swimmer.

She looked warily at Jaggy, who ignored her. A sheaf of paperwork appeared, an export document, a certified copy of the painting's provenance, three other documents in English. Jaggy inspected them swiftly. She yanked a pen from the hand of the shaken owner, glared at the buxom Valkerie, drew a line through a paragraph disclosing the gallery's limited liability, initialed it, and signed the documents. The owner might've heard something from Braunsweig when he had cleared Jaggy's card for the payment. He stood apart respectfully, his face shaped by the Teutonic deference reserved for the very wealthy.

Eyes still flashing, Jaggy moved a step or two, as if ready to march on the owner again. He bounded several steps away and Thomas could swear the man was shaking.

"You filthy disgusting lout," she half-shouted, her voice unsafe. Then to Thomas, "Our business is over." With the slightest widening of her mouth, she smiled to herself. "It'll look smashing over the dining room fireplace, won't it? We should buy two, but I dislike this bloody peckernose. Take me somewhere, Thomas. If we don't get out of here, I'll vomit…maybe on you, Fraulein Lemonhead," she thrashed out at the blonde woman standing there, pale as a morgue slab.

Jaggy marched out the door; Thomas, with his nerves dancing at a high trot. Briskly, they walked wordlessly for two blocks, no more than two feet apart, when suddenly she half-spun, grabbing for him, missing, then lurched forward and collapsed on the pavement. Writhing, she moaned, unable to sit up. Her face loose, as bluish white as lake ice, a croak rising from deep in her throat. Thomas knelt, wiping away spittle with his thumb. Onlookers gathered and he tried to shoo them off but, curious, they resisted. A hook-nosed woman, bossy, ordered the onlookers to call an ambulance. Mumbles, murmurs, numerous suggestions. Someone headed off for the corner pharmacist, while Jaggy, recovering a little, sat up. "They're trying to locate a doctor," Thomas told her.

"No doctors, tell them, Christ, it'll be everywhere by tomorrow." In succinct Hoch-Deutsch, Thomas told the woman who wanted an ambulance not to bother, thanking her profusely.

Helping Jaggy to her feet, he slung an arm around her waist, walking her to a narrow opening of a walkway separating two storefronts. Leaning her up against a brick wall, he held her there gently while she pulled herself together. Her face drawn now and white-scared, her lips fluttering at times as if she were trying to pronounce a strange word. Dribble reappeared at one corner of her mouth, and once more he wiped it away.

An hour later, at the Kempenski, she reclined against the stuffed pillows of a circular davenport. In her hand, a tumbler of cognac and soda, and she was back to normal or almost so.

"Fell right to my nose," she observed, sheepishly, with a rare self-deprecating look.

"Almost you did."

"Were you embarrassed?"

"Concerned, not embarrassed. What a question. How could I be embarrassed?"

"All those people encircling us, and me upended and blanked out. It's time, I suppose, for the grand confession."

"Confession?"

She waited before saying," I've sickle cell anemia, and if the word gets out to the public I'll be ruined."

"You're saying…you said *sickle cell*?"

"The doctors tell me so. Three of them. Rotten break, eh?"

"But how long have you known?"

"Months."

"Why didn't you say something?"

"I can't talk about it. With the doctors, of course, but who else have I?"

"I'm not exactly a stranger, Jaggy."

"I don't like discussing it. Too terminal a feeling, like having lunch with the mortician. But that's why I'm having my fun when I can and as often as I can. I'm going to live hard as I can and to the *nth* degree. Do it all, do it ten times. They say I've got a year, possibly eighteen months."

"They're not always right, you know."

"One may always hope so, and, well, I'm quite strong for a woman." Looking at him, dispraisingly, she said, "I'm needing you to stand by me."

"Of course, I will. How often does this happen?" he asked. "Passing out?"

"Every fortnight, perhaps. Sometimes, I'm in luck and a whole month goes by."

"We ought to get back to London."

"Not before I'm ready."

"It's nothing to trifle with, Jaggy, if you…if these episodes, are repetitive."

"Fuck it, I'm having my laugh and I deserve one."

"You've got to be looked after."

"I am. You're here."

"Professionally, I meant."

She sighed. "I'm flooded with doctors, all of them I can stand. London, St. Gallen, another from the U.S. who's a fertility expert. You're looking so pensive and I'll wager I know what you're thinking."

"What?"

"That I've one thirty-second worth of the black wog in me, like all Afrikaners. Some are a sixteenth. That's how I inherited the gene for sickle cell disease. The blacks are predisposed, aren't they? I took that biology tutoring, in part, so I could understand more about it. But I don't, not really. You do, don't you?"

"It's genetic, I understand that much. A shot in a million that it would happen to you. Think of that, will you? I don't want to think of it. Still, we must, we must do something. I'll do anything I can."

"I know you will."

"Depend on it."

"I am. Am I ever. Want the other half of my confession?"

"I'm not so sure. I hope it's not any worse."

"I'm trying to have a child, Thomas. Our child. We need an heir. At least, I do."

"You're having a child?"

"Yes, a child. Hawksie knows. Feurenreuth knows, he's in Switzerland, and a woman doctor, a fertility expert at Duke Medical Center. That's in America."

"I know about Duke. Is that where you were before we met in New York?"

"It is, yes. They were checking me. Were they ever checking me."

"But your situation. A child? It's bound to be extremely dangerous."

"Yes, my health, what's left of it. A large piece of my health is my peace of mind. I've precious little of that lately. The doctors are for advice, but I make the decisions. Death is the most dangerous thing to my equanimity, death without a daughter or a son."

"I'm to be the father of a child? You couldn't mean that, Jaggy. You really couldn't."

"Of course. Who else?" she replied, disingenuously, uttering not a word of the recently implanted embryo.

"Don't you still wear anything, take the pill or something?"

"I've wanted you as the father all along."

"We can't do this, Jaggy. You've got to be sensible…"

"We are doing this and I am the one who is being sensible."

"What if you're not around? That could happen. It's going to happen."

"You can have ten nannies. It's a baby, not an international crisis. Anyway, I'm having my troubles having one. I always have. I'm the only one of my friends without children. Besides, there are crucial inheritance issues to deal with, as you know."

"The Trust?"

"No, not the goddamned trust all the time," she replied quickly, artfully. I'm very well off and I have to see to it, attend to it, you see."

"I'm not a fathering type and you—"

"Recall this, if you please. I've assisted you at other times, and am still assisting you. I want you to assist me by giving me a child."

"You should've said something about this long before now, Jaggy."

"I said nothing because I'm not a stupe, that's why. You're too stubborn, Thomas. Too goddamn upright. So righteous and stiff-necked about some things. Just open me up and give me a good barreling and perhaps we'll have a kid. Presto-bango."

"A child who may go through life without a mother?"

"Fancy that, and here we are in the twenty-first century. The child, if ever I have one, will be rich beyond measure. You'll never have to lift a finger."

"I'd want to lift a finger. Lift a lot more than a finger. Why not give your money to something worthwhile?"

"That's another thing we'll never, ever agree upon."

"Why're you looking at me like that? You keep doing it."

"I'm not in the habit of begging anyone for anything. I'm nearly desperate. I *am* desperate. What'll I do? What can I do? Nothing is going right. Not a goddamn thing. If ever you leave me, I'll decimate you. I need you so much, Thomas. Someone to help. You see, don't you…don't you…oh, godammit it all, answer me…"

"I'm here, aren't I?"

"Yes, only after practically kidnapping you."

"I have work, Jaggy. A great deal of work to do and I can't always run off the way you can. Others depend on me, you know."

"And you depend on me, as you seem so easily to forget." She snapped her fingers." You could be gone faster than that," snapping them again, loudly this time.

"I want to help you but not, um, not as a father. We're not even married. We're not.,.it…Jaggy, if we don't get this discussed, it'll haunt us forever and we'll never get it straightened out."

"I see." She had stood, now she sat. "Discuss, yes, let's do our discussing. I want you as a father, as I've told you. Resist me if you wish. Go right ahead. And what I'll do is pick up that phone over there, call the office and your lab will be cut off without a shilling. That's your choice and I must tell you again—too many *agains*—that I don't like begging to get myself shagged." She gave off a thin laugh but he remained stolid-looking. "Anyway, darling, you're the only mate I have and I don't care to scare up another, though I might...I well might...now you come along..."

Whipping off her black turtleneck, she slowly elevated a finger and pointed toward the bedroom door. Later, when she was spread and they were joined, he thought she was nearing climax. It was so, and it wasn't so; she moaned twice before murmuring "Baster, oh Baster..."

He couldn't finish with her, couldn't go on. Like the sojourn in Berlin, it was a dud. It was to be their final lie-down, and final several other things that somehow, when he looked back, seemed connected to this dismal moment.

✴She'd given herself two hormone shots since leaving London, and now, in the bathroom, she took a third. She cleaned herself and then tried to gauge what she was up against. He had resisted her every suggestion. Being a father was apparently a barrier to his sense of propriety. No doubt he'd like the idea even less, if knowing what was already inside her was due to Baster's seed. Baster's and hers, that is. She wouldn't tell him about that end of the equation till all the loose ends were neatly knotted up. With more prodding, with more cornering, he'd see the light.

The lab was his real life and she its paymaster; and the child or children, now, was her life's fullest moment. She was no prayer-maker, never had been, but she would gladly drop to her knees if that's what it took. She'd be ashes in a canister in a year or so. Couldn't he see that, couldn't he help? There were no dynasties in South Africa, but there were a handful of families that had been responsible for its glories; and, in the small parade of doers and shakers, none stood higher than the name of Muldaur. Why wouldn't he help her?

Anyone can marry for that long, even a priest, a priest hiding behind those cockamamie vows at every turn. Not the chastity vow, she'd seen to it that that one was obliterated. But the marriage restriction? He'd called on that excuse once too often, hadn't he?

Hadn't he? He owed her.

St. Curig Fields, Isle of Anglesey, Wales
Geneva, Switzerland

"Pierre, good morning. I'm calling you again about the disposition of The Trust. We're getting nowhere fast on compiling a catalogue of beneficiaries. I'm concerned over the time angle. Almost a year has gone by and we've said nothing to South Africa. I need some help on this, so what's our exact schedule to be?"

"I can't say. We'll give it the once-over at our next meeting."

"That may not be soon enough. We're always delaying. I must make plans with my time and find people to help screen the charities and beneficiaries and so on."

"Why not leave all the screening to us?"

"That was the reason Baster wanted me appointed, to tackle this side of the situation. I owe it to his expectations of what it is I'm supposed to be doing."

"We may be facing a problem or two we hadn't counted on."

"What problem or problems?"

"Thomas, not over the phone. Not this way…"

"You're stalling. Why is that?"

"Complications have arisen."

"I'm a trustee, I've a right to know."

"Not over the phone. We'll discuss it later, next time all three of us are convened."

Down went the phone and up went his disquiet. Dodge 'em tactics, but why? Asking himself, then, if he should go down to London and confer with South Africa's ambassador, and there and then expose the entire story. But then would he be held liable under Swiss bank secrecy statutes? And was the delay in notifying the South Africans so serious that he could justifiably walk away from his confidentiality agreement?

Wishing, then, that he was ignorant of anything and everything to do with The Trust.

London, England

At the dining table sat Lord Richard Searsbey, his wife Mildred Marie, and Sir Harry Maxon-Howard, along with his wife, Pamela; Jaggy and Thomas occupied the chairs at either end of the eighteen-foot table. A night of tumult in the making. If Thomas was not already on his guard, then the evening's proceedings left him without the slightest doubt that Jaggy, like St. Germain, was off on her own tangent, and that he was meant to be among the last to know.

Searsbey was chairman of Anglo-American Line, a preeminent sea-shipper, moving huge tonnages to worldwide ports. Maxon-Howard served as the line's managing director. A robust pair, outgoing, affable, sharp-minded, and, said Jaggy, highly respected in British commercial circles. Thomas recalled seeing Searsbey once at White's, when there with Rhoades McBride, his editor at *Nature*, though was never introduced to him before tonight.

With women present, Jaggy, as a rule, frowned on business talk at her dinners, but did nothing to sidetrack it tonight. Halfway through the main course, Searsbey threw out a teaser to Thomas.

"I say, Thomas, do you know the chaps at Maritime House? The Shipping Conference?"

"Afraid not," Thomas said, shaking his head.

"Come by one day, old boy. They're a good sort, most of them. Always looking for the new thing, new markets and such."

"Yes, I s'pose you would be. However, shipping is far off my track, I'm afraid."

"At Anglo American we historically have kept to the cargo side of shipping. But one of our fellows, a good marketing talent, came by Harry's office"—nodding at Maxon-Howard—"and he had quite a scheme to tell. Harry was there, not me. But when Harry told me, I must say I've hardly enjoyed a wink since. Quite possibly you could fill us in on a dot or two."

"Not I. I know nothing at all about shipping as I said. I like to ocean swim when I can and I see plenty of ships at a distance, but that's about it. I know the names of four or five of those big oil tankers that come by Anglesey at times. Maybe they're yours."

"Possibly." Maxon-Howard broke in, taking over. "From time to time outdated passenger cruise ships are offered on the re-sale market. Attractive prices, we think, that is, if one were able to find a better use for them other than the scrap yard. And if the cost of refitting them is not prohibitive, we think it a manageable proposition to put them to other uses, as I was saying to Jaggy"—looking over at her now, rather benevolently, rather covertly too. "We were wondering about modifying them to...well...I suppose you might say turn them into luxury hospital ships."

"For the military?" Thomas asked.

"For us. For you, as well."

"Me? Why me?"

"You see, we've been advised by our government that this bio-game will be running into new rounds of regulation. Rules and the usual inconveniences as they sort out what's to be what. You'd agree, would you?"

"I'm not sure what you mean by bio-game. Is it biotechnology you're referring to?"

Five minutes went by as Maxon-Howard painted the many strokes of Anglo-American's futuristic idea to invade an untapped and highly promising market...at least to Thomas's ears, as he sat transfixed while the tentative plan was scoped out. He could readily see that considerable spadework had already been done, and, in fairly short order, learned that outside consultants had been engaged.

Maxon-Howard plowed onward; at each pause, and there were not many, Thomas's misgivings soared as the plan unfolded.

Anglo-American would buy up, then reconfigure passenger cruise ships, staffing them with experts on gene therapy; then, cruise the ships in international waters out of the reach of any nation's laws, and compete on even terms with countries—China and others—who had so far placed no stiff restrictions on gene therapy. Patients seeking cures would simultaneously be passengers booked on a top-end cruise, with award-winning chefs, entertainment, gambling, and whatever else the market called for. But the big challenge was to entice Europeans and Americans—where the ready wallets were more easily marketed to—who felt more comfortable with genetic healthcare as invented in the west, not the east. Anglo-American would deliver the full kit-

and caboodle at unmatched prices, the best of service and comfort, and let word-of-mouth carry the message to the marketplace.

Through with his pitch, Maxon-Howard looked at Jaggy twice, almost longingly, or perhaps for approval, before centering his attention on Thomas again.

"Might you have any thoughts?" he asked.

"Very interesting. You might be ahead of the curve. Premature, perhaps. I'd not be a good judge of it."

"Were we to attempt it, the cycle might take three to four years before we can take it to market."

"In that case, you might not be jumping the gun. Hard to say, though. It sounds like gene-tourism or something of that nature."

"Not quite our view, but we're looking to get a jump on the competition," said Maxon-Howard. "Get so far ahead of the others they'd have the devil of a time catching us. We'd like your view on one point. May I ask for it?"

"Sure."

"Will gene therapy be accepted by then?"

"Probably not, or not completely"—and then thinking of The League and NIH— "there'll be plenty of resistance to it, or anything like it, at the start. It'll take time to overcome all of that and then there's the usual bureaucratic red tape. Miles of it. That gene therapy will come to the fore at some point is beyond question. But it's anyone's guess as to when it will happen."

"Our marketing research agrees with that."

"There you are, then. Yours is certainly a different approach. I'll be anxious to hear how it works out."

"Might you join us one day for a more thorough go at our concept?"

Smiling, Thomas returned, "Oh, thanks, but I can't. We've got a full plate as it is. Full to the brim. I'm afraid I couldn't help you there."

Another sidelong glance at Jaggy by Maxon-Howard and then, "What if we were to invest with you?"

"In Muldaur-Courmaine?" Surprised, Thomas's eyes narrowed.

"Exactly. A partnership of sorts," Maxon-Howard replied. "A joint venture you might say."

Thomas's turn now to look at Jaggy, and then back at Maxon-Howard, who was obviously the point-man in a conversation assuming the status of a business conference. Jaggy said nothing. To break the silence, Thomas suggested, "I'm not the one to say, Harry. As for now, I'd be against a partnership arrangement. We're still in a studying stage ourselves, and that's all we can manage at this time."

"We'd want nothing else, Thomas. You would offer technical and scientific advantages we do not have and are unlikely ever to develop internally. We could proceed collectively, could we not? Muldaur has invested in you and that is all the reference and recommendation we require."

"But not necessarily what I would require. I need time to finish a very involved investigation. Even if we're successful, we need even more time to get our bearings as to whatever comes next. You talk of a high-end market of people being gene-treated on ships at sea. People with money. People with advantages and privilege. I'm sort of a mass merchandiser. A low-cost provider, like a used car seller. I don't think I'd fit very well with what you have in mind. Thanks all the same."

"You'd at least consider?"

"Sure, I'll consider anything, as long as I don't have to make any promises."

"Agreed, then, dear fellow. No promises on either side. We can explore the advantages together, is that fair?"

"I hope you're patient because I have to be. We're after a specific chemistry of a specific plant. Very focused, very limited. Applying what we learn to the gamut of gene therapy is somewhere in the far future. I'm trying to be clear with you gentlemen about our efforts, and where we stand and especially where I stand."

"Bravo, and you are. Most assuredly, you are," said Searsbey who, along with the three women, had remained steadfastly quiet.

Again, Maxon-Howard surveyed both Jaggy and Searsbey with a sweeping look. Thomas, picking up on it, wondered if he were the only one who wasn't clued as to what sort of intrigue was in motion. He felt toyed with, condescended to, and resented it.

Conversation sloped off when Jaggy arose, suggesting they move to a drawing room for coffee and a trifle.

An hour or so later, the guests departed and Thomas started in on Jaggy. "Quite a soiree you put together. You might've told me beforehand what was on the agenda. I thought you and I were supposed to be partners."

"Told you what, darling?"

"That your shipping magnates were dropping by for a slice of roast beef and then for a slice of our lab as dessert. We're nowhere near ready for anything like what they're proposing. You could've told me, you know. How hard is that to do? Send me a Post-It note or something."

"I wasn't at all sure it would come up."

"That a fact? Are you saying all that merger of interests talk was a mere coincidence? They meet me for the first time and all of a sudden, with no briefing by me as to what we're doing in Wales; they want to talk about a joint investment? With a couple of ringers like them. That Harry Maxon-Howard is as hard-headed an operator as I've seen in some time. Probably shaves with broken glass. Getting tied up with a couple of smoothies like them ought to be quite some picnic. Like living between spiked bookends. No thanks."

"Ridiculous. You're so exceedingly cynical at times."

"I've seen his type before. He's got the instincts of a wharf rat, smarter maybe but not by much."

Jaggy broke into laughter. "Good, very good. That's exceedingly accurate. Ha!"

"Are they going to name one of the ships after you? The Caviar Comet or something?"

Suddenly glowering, then, she volleyed with, "Watch it, laddie, just you watch it."

"My back, that's what I'll be watching. I'll buy a periscope first chance I get, so I can keep a three-sixty eyeball on what's happening."

"They're dear friends, you know. Very dear."

"Are they? Maxon-Howard's wife is petrified of him. She didn't say ten words all night. Notice how she blinks and blinks whenever he's got the floor, which is most of the time as far as I can tell. A setup, wasn't it?" Thomas complained, his voice sharpening. "A twenty-question contest or whatever it was supposed to be. Well, toots, I didn't like it and if we're supposed to be in the mergers and acquisitions business, I'd like to know ahead of time, so I can start running the other way. Especially so, if you or anyone else is thinking about going into the business of floating clinics disguised as cruise ships."

"Mind, I've the controlling shares of Muldaur-Courmaine."

"Never was it more apparent than tonight. And you ought to mind the fact that some gifted people in Wales are wearing themselves to the nub trying to make a big, big thing happen. If they knew you were about to sell them out, they'd be gone within a week. Don't gamble with my life, or theirs either."

"Oh, you're so huffy. What an old fuss you can be."

"I'd rather be a fuss than a silk-tongued brass-knuckler like him."

"He's an old busybody, that's Harry. But he is imaginative."

"Very. He seemed to be taking his cues from you and I've most definitely learned how imaginative you can be."

"Is that meant as a crack?"

"That, my friend, is a conclusion. A considered conclusion."

"How nice. A compliment. I haven't heard you finding fault with my imagination at certain other times."

"Who would? Not me. I'd only like to get an advisory once in a while about what you're planning for the lab."

"Why not go along, see what comes of it?"

"If I had the time, I might do it out of curiosity. I'm a bench-dog. I run a lab, remember. These are business fellows looking to open up a market. A spurious market from what I can see. They might. But not with me, if I guess what I'll be up against for the next few years, and I don't need those two shoveling any new problems my way."

"Look ahead, always look ahead. That was Baster's forte, and I try to remember it." Unconsciously, she laid a hand against her abdomen. "Why not let's go to Annabel's and see who's there. A nightcap. Be fun."

"At this hour?"

"It's not ten, I shouldn't think."

"Ten is late. Have you had an affair with him? Maxon-Howard?"

"Why would you ever say something as gauche as that?"

"Because of the way he looks at you, that's why? That was tip-off number one and the number two tip-off is the way he never looks at his wife."

"Don't be a bore. Anyway it's none of your *biz*-ness."

"I'm making it my business, because he apparently is making me his business. Or thinks he is. Well, have you...did you? Are you?"

"I shan't answer."

"You just did."

"So damnable clever tonight, aren't we?"

"It's easy to figure out. If his wife hadn't been present, he'd've probably made a hard landing on your lap."

"You can be such an insufferable ass-pain at times. Anyway, shall we be off?"

She ought to get sleep, rest, hold on to herself. She wasn't well and she knew it, flagrantly disregarding any modicum of common sense. She had brimmed with health all her life and now that she was ill, she refused to admit it or take precautions. He could put his foot down, refuse, and she'd as likely as not go out by herself. But not before she kicked up a real row and changed the ambient air into a real steam bath.

"I'll change, and then we go," she abruptly stated.

Hurrying off, she left him sitting alone, resigned to the outing at Annabel's, thinking he ought to go upstairs and change into street clothes. He was too tired to make the effort. He arose, however, and went to an armoire where he poured himself a cognac, thinking once more about the dinner cross-talk. Jaggy had the legal right to bind Muldaur-Courmaine to whatever deal she wished to make, with or without his own assent. Searsbey and Maxon-Howard—both wanting to bend the intent of the law, and, being who they were, might get away with it. Sitting there, dwelling on what he ought to do or not do, he lost track of the time.

A sudden movement caught his eye.

Thomas looked up A second evening was about to commence before the first had drawn to its end. She must be seeking major commotion, he thought. Starkly flamboyant. She looked like a cross between something illegal and what might pass as a screen idol from the 1940s. She had lost weight but plenty of woman was still packed on that frame. She had poured herself into a silvery sheath-like outfit that made every body crevice shout for attention. Her pale blue sequined-frock shimmered, giving an impression she was covered in melting ice. He would wager a good five-hundred thousand dollars of diamonds and pigeon-blood rubies hung around her neck, with one heavy pendant seeming as if it were about to vanish in her unmissable cleavage. On one ring finger was another diamond the size of a grape; ears and wrists also sparkled as if backlighted. She wore nothing underneath her dress, he was certain of it. Tonight what she was wearing was her money, outlandishly.

"Quite a gift-wrap," he said, knowing he was expected to say something. "I think I'll run upstairs and get my sunglasses."

"You like?"

"Startling."

"Oh, pooh to you. I wanted to surprise you."

"You have. You must've had a couple of shots of radium in your coffee."

"Be nice, Tommy."

"I am nice and nicely blinded by your rig."

"Come along, or it'll be late."

"Late for what?"

"We're going out, you promised."

"If I did, then I've changed my mind. I'm not going anywhere. Not even out to sea with Lord Searsbey and Mr. Harry-boy or anyone else trying to make an end run."

"Hell if you aren't, I'm already dressed to go."

"Then undress. I'd give you a hand but my knuckles are still recovering from that last handshake of Harry's."

Their words arm-locked in mid-air. Staring looks, neither of them backing off. Spitting mad, Jaggy paid him a scalding glance, the eyes bearing on him like gun muzzles. Impassively, he sat there and accepted it.

She wheeled and stomped off, the dress shimmering like some indoor waterfall. He let her go without further comment or protest. Several times in the past, he sensed she would cook up a quarrel to purposefully heighten her anger, then, at its height, out of breath, and in some inexplicable shift of mood, she'd want sex. Demand it. Wanted to be taken forcibly, no preliminaries, sometimes hitting him with her fists, taunting him, and she'd unpeel her skirt, wearing nothing else at all, her unwavering eyes taunting and even filling with a smoldering stare. He came to realize how a deep linkage existed between her angers and her desires. He had, in time, and after more instances, acquired this secret about her needs. He never let on, however, thinking it akin to reading a private diary without permission.

When acquiescing, giving her all the sex he could manage, she'd turn blissful, playful, let out with humor and then an abundance of needless generosity. Within a day an expensive great gift would arrive from Asprey's or some other Bond Street emporium. Watches, leather toilet kits with matched silver-backed hairbrushes, sets of cufflinks: one pair belonging to Baster, made originally by Carl Faberge for Czar Nicholas I. They were unique, very valuable, and Thomas had never found a graceful opportunity to return them.

Nothing was mistakable about her mood tonight. She had boiled herself into rage, and he had lit the wick of her temper. First, with his complaints about the maneuvers at dinner, then by refusing to accompany her on the evening's lark to a private club to hobnob with the glitterati and jet-setters.

In the heavy silence of this moment, he began to review his many errors with her. He'd been living in a fool's paradise for too long; hoping he could go along and get along. Be who he was, do his life's calling. He had let her down; no, what he had done was turn his back on her. She was dying and needed support, understanding, even humoring, and a great deal of care.

A few hours dawdling in a night club, what was that? Still, if he didn't make a stand he'd never get the message across: no lap-dogging for him. He had come back from America to follow his faraway star, and day by day it seemed to be shining a little brighter, a little larger. And if she sold her interest to Anglo-America, either by design or out of pique, then what was to become of it all?

Out for a run the next morning in Hyde Park, when returning to the house he discovered Jaggy had gone riding. Mercer, the butler, had no idea when she'd be back. Shaving, showering, and taking his time, he finally went down to the breakfast room, asking the kitchen maid for coffee and reached for the morning paper.

There it was, then, the lead article in the financial section: MULDAUR'S NORTH AMERICAN OPERATONS SLASHED.

Eighty-three years of trading activities, riding out many, many storms in the world markets, and Muldaur had now lost its fabled footing, its commanding edge as African nations, one by one, had begun the confiscation of Muldaur mining properties. In turn, those acts prevented the company from meeting the bulk of its delivery commitments to customers spread across the globe. Forced to turn to the spot markets, unable to buy what it needed in too many instances, staggering losses mounted rapidly, reaching an unsustainable level.

Two quotes from Si Nestor, others from several Muldaur traders; still others from a large competitor, Bachey & Co., its CEO saying, "An era is gone, I guess. We're all having our troubles but we never expected Muldaur to sink. They were the lodestar on this side of the Atlantic."

Waiting on her for another three hours, he finally left for St. Curig at mid-afternoon, thinking Jaggy had become so estranged or perhaps so upset at events, she hadn't cared to share the grim news about New York, especially about Si Nestor.

Dark days, he thought. He had left a note. Not by choice, but never again would he step foot into her lavish Belgravia home. Looking back on the events of the night before, he again realized how small-minded he'd been. That he should've seen to her fun. How many nights did she have on her life-calendar? How big of an ask was that?

And as for Anglo-American, he really had no idea of what Jaggy was thinking? Quite possibly, knowing her days were numbered, she might've been fixing his future; aligning him with trusted friends of the British commercial establishment who could help him, when she couldn't. Perhaps she had chosen not to inform him of the situation beforehand, knowing how touchy he'd become, accusing her more than once of trying to make him into her lap dog.

A sluggish, ponderous trip as the train rolled westerly toward Wales. His sentiments, like his thoughts, were blurry. He was in life's crucible, lamenting his appraisals of himself: who was he? What of his promises to her and to others, direct or implied? What did he owe? What didn't he owe?

She had practically opened her entire life to him and for him. What had he done for her? Not much. In Berlin, she had all but begged him to stand by her, and to father a child to keep the Muldaur lineage intact, yet that too would be outright fakery. The Muldaur bloodline was about as extinct as that of Caesar.

So far, at least within the past day and night, he had miserably fumbled the ball. Worse yet, he was experiencing a piercing fear—that he had jeopardized the lab.

Recalling her warning in Berlin: *"I can close you down with one phone call."*

And she well might, if enough anger strangled her judgment. Unaccountably, she could in quick time fall into a half-rage, as she had at the Berlin art gallery, sending tremors through the owner. Thomas thought he was feeling a tremor or two in himself; perhaps, it was only the lurch of the railcar as it rode westerly. Still, the thought of a shutdown at the lab left him in anguish. At St. Curig, they were making solid headway on *semba*. Though it was only his instincts speaking, he believed with a few more answers to the shrub's cellular riddles, the solution for making Zyme-One, artificially, would pop up suddenly, vividly, unmistakably…the way discoveries often came about.

Clickety-clack, the wheels spinning along, polishing the tracks a thousand-thousand times as the train rolled onward. He hadn't rolled so much as a yard, not in his thoughts. Instead, he remained stuck in his worries, growing older from them. He could not bring himself to cope with another dead-end, another requiem for his hopes, as he experienced with the American foundations. Moreover, the thought of falling into the clutches of men like Searsbey and Maxton-Howard…well no, never, not in this life or any other life.

Still, if Jaggy cut him loose, then what? The feet of that unnerving thought stood directly on his neck for the rest of the trip.

St. Curig Fields, Isle of Anglesey, Wales

A Manchester paper, Sunday edition, carried an op-ed piece. Its sub-head claimed: LABORATORY SECRETLY CLONING HUMANS?

Reading it, he thought—Jaggy will do a flip. He was ready to do some flipping with her.

The name Muldaur-Courmaine had not been mentioned but various other identifiers in the text made it a simple task for any discerning reader to guess the culprit. Cloning humans was strictly forbidden in the U.K. and almost everywhere else. The Human Fertilization and Embryology Authority kept the usual tight rein on bio-experiments, and Muldaur-Courmaine had never filed for any special permits, because its work was largely confined to dissecting and studying a plant. To be sure, a few experiments on rodents and reptiles, but nothing even remotely to do with humans. Still, with all the accusations and insinuations piling up, he expected to be on the receiving end, one day, of a letter of inquiry.

A slowdown then at St. Curig might result until a clearance was issued. But no clearance was likely until the Authority investigators knew everything, and then the cat would be out of the bag. And Pharmus would likely move in to garner whatever it could, and without any way of preventing them.

Whoever the bastards were who were trumping up this media onslaught, they were libeling him; yet, as before, he had no way of identifying them.

Steadily the team worked; steadily they isolated the genes in *semba* that were the creators of Zyme-One. Hours upon hours of harrowing bench work, slugging away. Hours that sometimes seemed to drift aimlessly, but that really wasn't so. Other hours seemed fraught with tension and disappointment, but that was not quite so, either. It was an in-and-out, back-and-forth process with no set rhythm to it.

Above all, they needed a workable concept for reproducing *semba's* active ingredients. The supply at Cyro was dwindling. No *semba*, no Zyme-One. A constant worry, and it furnished the prime reason why Lin-pao spent so many hours with the botanists in Cambridge.

Alexis Hazlett worked on her part of the project, while Lin-pao, with his crystal-ball skills, had his hand in several pots at one time. For over two weeks, a stubborn flu bug had put Timmothe Merrill on the sidelines. Joshua Noyes, the bio-statistician, hung out on the manor's second floor, nailed to his computer, making sure all the data derived from the experiments were accurately collected and recorded. At times, he unearthed abnormalities and curiosities in the welter of data he plowed through. When that happened, then time-consuming experiments were repeated.

Ponsoby did her all to keep the human mechanics running smoothly.

Jaggy had gone to ground. She hadn't been at her London house for weeks; her office would merely say she was abroad, without amplifying. He supposed she was in Switzerland where she'd be living *incognito,* if she were at that clinic she had mentioned.

The schism had occurred. Maybe for the best, he thought. Yet what if she were to perish, then what? And if she were pregnant, well, it was too much to think about.

He slept at the manor, making his own meals, working at his bench till two, three, four in the morning. A monk-like existence but for him it answered. As long as the monthly funding showed up at Braunsweig's London office so that Ponsoby could pay bills and meet payroll, he was reasonably happy.

Working side by side with Lin-pao the rest of one day, they fell into a trough of questions, and they argued. Lin-pao gave him a few new pointers on the fabled female energy-cell that he'd been working on when at Columbia. Another of biology's fascinating facts, the energy cell—mitochondria—was found in female and male genomes alike. But it only passed, generation to generation, from mother to daughter. Inherently a female thing, and it was mitochondria that provided the power grid for creating energy within the trillions of body cells.

At six, they stopped work. It was a Friday, the night of play for the team.

Lin-pao asked, "Will you attend with us at Eight Bells?"

"Later, maybe about eight or so I'll drop in."

"I am the new captain of our darts team. Everyone beats us but I am working on some very excellent tactics. Have you read Sun Tzu's *The Art of War*?"

"Never have, no."

"Dazzling. Strategies for all imaginable situations. A capital work."

"For darts, too?"

"Contests of every category, sir. Stealth, the probing for enemy weakness. It's all there and it's astoundingly fascinating."

"I'll remember. Have fun."

At his desk, weary of eye and bone, Thomas's gaze drifted to the neatly squared stacks of bills, reminders, and envelopes slit at their top edges, left there by Ponsoby. Sorting one stack, he stopped when seeing a letter he had vaguely anticipated for almost a year, though this time it was not what he was hoping for.

> ...not long ago I met with the Holy Father, who directed that I convene our theologians to vet the ever-growing issues posed by your field of science. He seems disappointed over the views of some at the Pontifical Academy of Sciences where there seems to be widespread concern that the Church is fast losing ground in its ability to grasp the meanings (or threats) posed by biotechnology. Indeed, a number in the College of Cardinals echo sentiments of disturbing disquiet.
>
> To this end, I plan to call a meeting in Rome, at our Curia, with our best scholars. I would most certainly want you in attendance, Thomas. You, who have lived this business, who know more than any of us about the new wave slapping at our fragile shores.
>
> Kindly give me a glimpse of your schedule. It will require detailed coordinating to bring the others from far distances, some being in awkward circumstances, as you likely know. I would deeply appreciate an early reply. Meanwhile, my good friend, know you are always missed and many here, were they to know of this letter, would wish to convey their blessings and affections. As do I.
>
> Yours in Christ,
>
> A dM

Refusing the General was an unthinkable response, but that's what he must do. He had nothing to say to Rome until Rome had something to say to him. It was the Vatican's move and apparently they weren't budging on his request for a release from his vows. By now, it was more of a formality than not, and he suspected his old nemesis, Maistinger, was putting up roadblocks. Besides, he had enough to deal with, and getting into a free-for-all with other Jesuits was far, far from his present agenda.

Getting up, he went over to the coat rack, slipping on his Barbour jacket, flicked the light switch and headed for Eight Bells. Life was safer there, or it promised to be more agreeable.

Eight Bells, a popular pub with the locals, was located in Holyhead, a small port only five miles distant from St. Curig Fields. Nearly two-hundred years old, its whereabouts was told by a gilded-red sign stationed over the front door. On a bright day, leaded glass, polished daily, sparkled in the pub's bow-front windows. Inside, smoke-blackened beams crisscrossed the ceiling and the floors were of flagstone, buffed daily till clean as the deck of an admiral's barge. Artifacts, mostly of a nautical bent, were mounted on the white stucco walls; but the centerpiece stood on a cabinet-table; was a glass encased man-of-war four-feet in length with the mainmasts standing a good six-feet. The ship's detail, exquisite; the paint job flawless.

Thomas made his way to the bar for a friendly chat with Ian Woodstel, the proprietor, a retired chief warrant officer of the Royal Navy. Several steps later he halted, surprised at seeing the stranger he had found prowling around the manor at St. Curig early one morning after returning there from a jog. A dark, curly haired man, tall and stocky. A purplish scar, shaped like a crawling worm, ran from one ear straight across the left cheek. Hard to pull one's sight away from that scar, and the man seemed to know it, perhaps wanting it noticed to make some sort of account of himself. On that early morning, when first seeing the man, he had claimed to Thomas he was lost. Lost and hungry. He had looked neither one to Thomas, who had advised the intruder that St. Curig Fields was private property before giving directions to the local constabulary, where the stranger could obtain all the local information he desired. He had then escorted the stranger to his car.

Oddly, no license plate on the Jaguar, a black, mud-spattered vehicle and with a star-shaped hole in one of its side windows.

Tonight the man was flanked by three sullen, long-haired toughs wearing tight-fitting dungarees and black windbreakers. "Cockneys, from the sound of them," Ian Woodstel remarked, stiff-lipped. Hard-eyed, too. "The one with the cut-up face, there…he'll be from the other side of the water. Ulster, is what I'd say. He's been asking about you, Thomas."

"He has? Asking what?"

"Wanting names and the like. Said he was in insurance and looking under every tree and bush for customers. He don't look the sort, not like any insurance man to me. If you was to ask me, that bastard's a troublemaker, Tom. One of them Irish agitators. Come over on the ferry, they do, from Ulster. Rubbish is what they are, not anythin' else but troublin' bastards, the lot of them. Nosin' around here like starved dogs, that's what the like of Tavester does for his coins."

"That's his name? Tavester?"

Woodstel nodded.

"You've never seen him before?"

"Not till fortnight back. About then, I believe."

"Anything else?"

"Not as I can recall, no." said Ian Woodstel. "Maybe there was one thing. He wanted to know about the lady at Curig, out there with you."

"You're referring to Missus Muldaur? We have three ladies plus five other on the domestic staff."

Woodstel shrugged and went back to polishing a tray of ale glasses. Thomas saw why. Tavester was on his way over to the bar where Thomas stood; a smile spread Tavester's face, but nothing else about him seemed light-hearted.

With his back against the bar now, Tavester leveled his gaze, one by one, on the members of the lab's team who stood near the dartboard. Tavester's sidekicks did the same, turning where they stood, staring menacingly at Thomas, as if they had been rehearsed.

Leaving the bar, Thomas went over to Tavester. "I think we met before when you lost your way, as you put it, that morning when you came to St. Curig. I'm told you came there a second time and the gamekeeper shooed you off. Anything I can do to get you straight that the property is private land? What is it you want from us?"

"Tavester," said the man, offering a hand. "Charles Tavester. Insurance."

Thomas ignored the outstretched hand. "What brings you our way? You're not from the isle, I hear."

"Quite true."

"Then what?"

"You see, I'm thinking of taking a place for my family come this summer. The little ones, you see, and my missus. I'm in the insurance line, always looking for a prospect. You know how it goes."

"Where's your home?"

"Ireland. The north, Belfast."

"You're to stay off St. Curig. Permanently, if you please."

"That's a sharp remark, chappie."

"I can always make it sharper."

"You're here with these American ladies and that Chink?"

"Not much of your business, either, is it?"

"Unless the lads and I make it our business. Prospects, as I told you. Don't care to miss a one of them, that's the way I was taught. Even you. Like a little insurance on your life? I'll stand you to an ale; may I do that for you? We can have a chat-up about a policy, a group policy, even, coverin' the whole lot of you."

"Thank you, no, we'll pass."

Tavester looked at Thomas and then over at Alexis Hazlett and her friend, sitting at a nearby table with a couple of the locals, finally, then, he turned his gaze to Woodstel who had his back turned. "Comfy out there, is it? At the place?"

"Quite pleasant."

"Be right chummy, eh, living with all that gash, there? Pussy, you Yanks call it, isn't that right? Nice bit of crumpet, all right. You keep all the women happy, is that it?"

Thomas passed him a hard look. Opening, then closing his right fist. "Your story sounds weak, Tavester. I don't think I like it and I don't think I like you. Stay away, and you'll be happier about life."

"Happier than you, you mean?" The pale blue eyes menacing.

"Happier than you'll be if ever you set foot on the property again. That sort of happy."

"You own a piece of it, do you?"

"What I own and don't own is none of your affair. But I'll bet I'll own a piece of you if you keep sniffing around us."

"They've been tellin' me it belongs to that woman. Rich, that's what I hear."

"Consider me her agent."

A derisive laugh from Tavester who said, "The agent and the go-between man, that's you is it? I'm wonderin' what else of hers that you get between?" Soon as he said it, grinning lasciviously, he snapped his fingers close to Thomas's face; then, raised the middle finger in the well-known insult.

Thomas moved off, joining the others at the dart board, where Lin-pao was being roundly beaten by two islanders, his face hectic with consternation.

Thomas sat. He watched, sipped his ale, cheered when he had reason to, and kept a level eye on Tavester, who raised his glass to Thomas.

During a break in the game of darts, Lin-pao sat beside Thomas. "That gentleman you were talking to at the bar. He was the one who took pictures of my gate house."

"You sure of that?"

"My visions are among the finest in the world."

"Then he went in, into the property? Through the gates? Is that what happened?"

"I did not see that to be so, sir. But he must have been the one found by the gamekeeper near the manor house. Are you going to crown him one?"

Thomas laughed. "No, I'm not going to crown anyone. How go the darts tonight?"

"I dislike this bloody game intensely, but I will learn it. Meanwhile, sir, go over and give that snooper a good shin-kick. I shall be right behind you in the event of a knock-downer skirmish."

Lin-pao got up, rejoining the others at the board. Another game was about to begin and Thomas was left to dwell on his own thoughts.

Why was Tavester nosing around? What earthly reason could he have for staying on Anglesey for days? Just to hunt up a summer place? Taking photos of the gatehouse. Invading the property, for what? Chasing insurance prospects?

Twenty minutes later, Thomas stood as he bid goodnight to Alexis and her artist live-in friend. His back was turned, and, about to say something, when a shocking pain ripped through his kidneys, as if he'd been speared by a spike. Gasping, yet no air seemed to come. Semi-paralyzed, dizzy, he doubled over. The room seemed to have turned red, and bile burned his throat.

Alexis, holding on to him, shrieked. Lin-Pao came up, hovering protective-ly, cursing loudly in Chinese while patting Thomas's back with one hand, and shaking the other at Tavester and his cronies.

"Seems I lost my way again, didn't I?" Tavester taunted. "Did I bump you a bit hard? Sorry, lad." Then, voice hardening, he added, "You'll not want to be threatening me and the lads again, or you'll be looking at what's left of your skull in the gutter. Your little harem here might not like that."

Crouched, waiting for his breathing to return, Thomas gripped the edge of the table for support.

Tavester asked his boys. "Have a look at him, will 'ya? A fookin' priest, is he?"

Priest? How would Tavester know?

Ian Woodstel barged in, brandishing two-feet of a black-briar stick, its club-head an oversized knob. Casually, he swiped the nearest of Tavester's scummers, a direct strike to an elbow, setting off a raging howl from his victim who slumped to the floor after Woodstel stiffed him with a second poke to the plexus. Another of the side-kickers raised his hands in a threatening gesture at Woodstel and Woodstel spun the club in a tricky twirling motion and nailed the hooligan with a sharp rap to the nose. Blood geysered.

Woodstel moved right up, facing Tavester, and telling him, "You're to leave now, all of you, and you'll not be coming back." Slapping the black briar against his open palm, he said, "I'll be putting the next one of these right square to your filthy bollocks. You'll not walk straight for a month. Off you go, while you can...should I see you comin' through my door, I'll not be responsible. Now, run yourselves out of here or you'll get another feel of this stick." He tapped the black-briar club's end against Tavester's chest.

Woodstel, with one meaty hand, bent to the tough still moaning on the floor. Taking him by the collar, he jerked him to his feet with the strength of a circus strongman. He dragged him to the door and booted his rear twice before throwing him out.

A messy, disquieting scene.

His breathing better now, Thomas waited with the others while Woodstel went out to the street to see if Tavester and his side-men were still about. He came back, indicating the all-clear, and Thomas led the others into the night.

The next day's mail brought him a moment of ecstasy; it was a letter he had never expected, but, when opening it, he realized he had waited for it all these months past.

Dear Thomas,

If this isn't out of the blue, then nothing ever shall be blue again, will it? Feeling a bit blue myself the other day, when, after a meeting in Wall Street, I called Si Nestor on the chance we could do a lunch together. We could and we did. What a lovely man. So funny. Your name flew about like a pennant, and slyly (he is sly) he later phoned me your mailing address, which, needless to say, will be kept in confidence.

How, you might ask, did your name get in the way of our lunchtime Bloody Marys? Si had read several articles about your project that have surfaced over here in quite a spectrum of newspapers and periodicals.

Thus, a conversation ensued about the Baltimore-born "whiz kid" as he has tagged you.

That you are being aired, or inked, and with such regularity, makes me wonder a bit. It sounds suspiciously close to a full-scale orchestration, and puts me in mind of that certain organization I once inquired about per your request. The trusty Bazak beak has sniffed the winds, and wonders at what it all bodes.

Here comes my long overdue apology. I reflect sorrowfully on walking out at "21" that night and hope you will be as forgiving as I am contrite. Bad form, indeed. I was upset. I lost it, and escaped while I was intact.

Women do such things. We do not always know why. But I am a friend, a good friend, so let us hope we can still bask in that warming light. Possible, you suppose?

A last word, if I may. Be cautious if you're called for press interviews. It's a sure trip to the hangman.

Fondly,

S.

For the next few hours, he was useless to himself, thinking of little else but her. Twice he saw his hand crawl toward the phone as if the hand belonged to someone else and he was unable to command its movements. Wanting to hear that never-to-be forgotten voice, and then reserve a seat on the next flight to New York. One slip from Shandar to Poppi Nestor, however, and the news of his arrival in New York would ricochet to Jaggy at supersonic speed. Even if Jaggy were nowhere to be found, it wouldn't apply to her communications with Poppy Nestor.

Later, his senses still preoccupied by Shandar, he decided there wasn't the slightest suggestion in the letter that she cared to see him. Still a faint heart never won a kiss from the girl next door.

She had mentioned press interviews, and an idea began to bloom. No longer able to stifle his excitement, he went out for a long walk and a Cohiba.

Days later, when hearing about the woman from *Worldwide Press*, he thought there must be some error. Ponsoby, however, was quick to advise him there apparently was no mistake at all. Appointment or not, the visitor knew exactly who she'd come to see. She knew the business of Muldaur-Courmaine, and she even knew the names of the various team members.

Ponsoby told him, "This woman is insistent. She's the size of a dirigible."

"Have we heard of her?"

"I haven't. Perhaps she's a former lady friend." An eyebrow arose in a perfect arch over Ponsoby's left eye.

"Ah, a sprinkling of Welsh humor, and so early in the day."

"See for yourself. She's in the front hall, says has no intention of leaving till she at least had a preliminary interview with *the…the* Mr. Courmaine."

He thought of sending the woman away. But quickly thought again. Possibly, she was one of the hammers who kept pounding away at the lab. Why not have a look?

"Tell her it's only for five-minutes or she's not to bother waiting around."

Meeting her, he knew instantly he had made the first big mistake of the day. She entered the small office, nearly filling the width of the door frame, heaving after the exertions of climbing the steps to the second floor. A genuine spectacle, he thought, yet unsure of what to make of her.

Maveen Cassidy sat on the other side of his desk. She was like no other reporter he'd ever seen and he'd seen all of them he ever wanted to.

She wore a calf-length flaming red cape, a garment fit for a fortune-teller at a county carnival. She seemed a barrel-like apparition, with festive wooden beads cascading over her gigantic bosom, and with paints, powders and enough cologne to foil a gas mask. When entering, she had walked with the gait of a pack mule, slow, steady, all haunches, as if pulling the weight of a coal car.

That cigarette-scratched voice rasped as she asked her get-acquainted questions. "You see," she said at one point, "I'm so new to your industry and I'm especially interested in what's going on in Europe. Particularly, you American scientists in Europe, and most particularly the Americans in Europe with their names on the front door."

All this time her mind was building images in words she would later use— a stud, she thought, complete with wild-blue yonder eyes, and so blond she wondered if he dyed his hair. Big, too, bigger than she expected, though she hadn't known precisely what to expect. Cassidy almost unconsciously began to dictate to herself an opening for the splashy one-on-one article Murray Raab had been hoping for.

"I've come a long way," she reminded, "all the way across the big pond. And I don't expect to be kissed off. Pissed off, maybe, but no kiss off. Hear me?"

"How far is a long way? I forgot to ask."

"Washington...that's the D.C. Washington, by the way. Mind if I smoke? Care for one?"

"I'd rather you didn't," he said behind a frown.

Ignoring his wishes, Cassidy fished a pack of cigarettes from a leather tote bag that was as scarred as an old catcher's mitt. Tapping the pack against a fleshy palm, she blithely offered a cigarette to Thomas, who declined and was about to remind her there were no ashtrays, when, with a flick of one lavender-tainted fingernail, she snapped a kitchen match into life. The maneuver was not something you see a woman do very often, making him wonder where she'd been raised. On a ranch? By someone from a road gang?

"You're earning yourself quite a reputation, did you know?" A smoke ring the size of a small doughnut sailed out of her mouth.

"I don't have a lot of time to ask, Miss Cassidy, why you're really here. We've got a strong day in operation, so you'll have to make short work of it."

"They say you're something of a shit-shaker, if you'll pardon me. Not my words, by the way, but that's what they're saying."

"They? Who's they?"

"Sources."

"That's not telling me much."

"We protect them, that's why."

"That seems to be the only thing you people do protect. Certainly you don't protect anyone's privacy or pay much homage to the truth either. What I'm protecting is my time. So we'd better get you on your way. Sorry you had to make such a long trip for so little."

An eyebrow, thin as a pencil line, twitched. "You might be as smart as they say. You married? Single? Why don't we get the rest of the dross out of the way, then get down to tacks? Brass tacks."

"You come rolling in here, and I don't know what for. Or who sent you. Or your slant, if any, and why me? Let's get you into a frame, first, Miss or Mrs. Cassidy, then we'll see about your questions."

Thomas was about to continue, when she interrupted, "Look, I may write something, I may not. If I do, the papers may print it, or they may not. Here's some advice for you, Cholly-boy. You're a helluva lot better off helping me than fighting me. This way at least you get to tell your side."

"Side of what?"

"They say you may be on to something. That, if it works, some high-falutin' gene therapy is in the works. You'll be throwing all the quacks out of work, and some who aren't quacks. That's what we call a story. One angle of a story anyway."

"Which is?"

"Just as I said. That you're into something big, big enough to be shrouded in secrecy."

He laughed. "You people in the press really flatten me. Who dreams all this stuff up? There's no story. Around here we're all foam and no beer. Leave your card, and if anything comes up we'll get back to you, that's if we ever decide to hold a press conference."

She passed him a smug, patronizing look. "When I run into a wall, I always look for the first handy bulldozer I can find."

"Let's have a look at your credentials," he said, "and the name of your boss, and his or her phone number. A fax-number will be fine."

Her blood-red lips quivered as she jeered, "I thought you might be smart. You may have just cut your stones off, sonny." Gray faced now and gray from the ash scattering like dandruff over her cape-like dress. Her right hand said everything as it squashed a cigarette butt on the plate-glass top of Thomas's desk. "Hope you don't mind," she said, "your carpet looks flammable." She lumbered out of the chair. "Only because you're so impolite, I'll give you a little tip. The sky's about to fall, and you're in its way. I might give you a break, but not if you keep smart-mouthing me. I know more about you than you might think."

She moved slowly, but all of her moved at one time, like sugar drifting through a glass of iced tea. Cassidy was up now, sliding the loops of her tote bag over an arm thick as a washerwoman's. Half-bending, looking for a stray shoe, her hair falling out of place, gasping from her efforts.

"Okay," he offered. "I'll give you some time, but I want to see those credentials first. I'd also like the general drift of your questions. Those I don't choose to reply to, I won't."

Cassidy handed over a laminated card that was faced in one corner with her squeeze-mouthed picture on it, yet was unmistakably her. The card bore the embossed logo of *Worldwide Press Services*, then an address of where to return the card if found. On its reverse side, her signature and a paragraph of fine print.

He nodded. She sat. The air whooshed out of the chair cushion.

"Let's quit the merry-go-round and get to the reason for your visit, if you please. Before, I was asking you how you found us and somehow in there you mentioned the condition of the sky you said was near to falling."

"I'm here to find out what's so sexy and special about your work that you have to do it outside the U.S. How is it that a Muldaur is in the deal? Are you concocting the Satan-bug or something we ought to know more about? I heard about your trouble in Rome. They say you're quite an accomplished operator. Even something of a crook. Supposing we begin there. Crooks always make such fascinating news."

She kept a surly grin not far from her thickly jowled face, as she asked away, and if the loopy grin wasn't genuine, neither, as far as he could tell, were her questions. Other than generalities, which anyone could pick up within a day's time at a decent library, she didn't know tinker's-all about genetics. What she thought she knew, she faked. She was after him, he figured. She seemed to have a fix on all the articles that had used Thomas Courmaine as a prime example of an expatriate American scientist attempting to skirt U.S. regulations. She knew about the three African women, knew of his skirmishes with the Vatican, knew him to be a member of the National Academy of Sciences, and even knew he had been raised an orphan.

Cassidy came primed with an assortment of facts, a couple of good guesses, and offering a string of innuendos disguised as questions. Other tricks, too, as she asked for more details on the trumped up falsehoods that had been appearing in newspapers.

She had almost made him dumb-eyed as she pounded away like some prosecutor hurling veiled accusations; her shrewish eyes unwavering, the voice brash.

Something here is wrong, he thought, very wrong. He couldn't account for his feelings, but soon he'd had enough of Cassidy; he managed to excavate her from the small office. At the top of the second-floor stairs, neither of them said good-bye but instead exchanged looks of cold contempt.

Cassidy had returned to her lodgings, a small and comfortable inn quaintly named Yr Hendre Guest House. Near Holyhead, only blocks away from The Eight Bells. Her quarters, while not lavish, were furnished in bright cheerful colors, the bedroom large, the bed very large of necessity, and the room's bow-front windows giving out to an expansive view of a nearby forested park.

She had never met the man whose number she was about to dial, as instructed to do by Raab before leaving Washington.

"Is this a Mr. Tavester? Charles Tavester?"

"And who might this be?"

"Maveen Cassidy. I was told to report in and tell a Mr. Tavester of a certain conversation. Are you he?"

"In the skin, love, in the skin."

"You don't mind that I ask you to verify yourself? Give me the name of the person who told you I'd be calling."

"The Beaver is one name. Raab, another."

"You won't need a pencil or pen for what I have to say," Cassidy indicated. "The man I went to see is an iceberg. A cute prick, but a prick all the same. I got nowhere. I'm headed home. That's my very skinny report. Not much, I admit, but there it is."

"Stubborn sodder, ain't he? We'll be taking over from this end. Toodle-de-doo and you'll be hearing about us. Be a lovely little ruckus. Folkloric, you could say. Cute prick, eh? It's what you called him. I like that one, I really do."

"What'll you be doing, what's the next—"

"Leave it to us, my dearest dove. We'll deal with your cute prick. *Au revoir.* Safe trip home and all."

She would never lay eyes on Tavester, but he was about to throw the fear of every known god into her.

St. Curig Fields, Isle of Anglesey, Wales

Thomas had been at his bench examining telomeres, the tiny energy-fuses located at the end of each human chromosome. In youth, a person's telomeres are of a certain length; then, each time a chromosome's genes are called upon to code for the making of specific proteins to re-build body cells, energy is used up. Result: a given telomere gets shorter, then shorter again. As one ages, the telomeres expire, begin to vanish. When this occurs to enough of one's chromosomes, the vital protein-making mechanisms of the human body will no longer function sufficiently.

Life begins to fade; after that, it's your turn with the Reaper.

Using the telomeres of fruit flies, whose entire lives lasted for only ten days or so, but which also offered the advantages of producing as many as thirty-five generations yearly, he was testing and re-testing. By applying Zyme-One, he could splice lengths of telomeres together, inserting them into the flies. And, by doing so, double or triple the lives of batches of fruit flies.

One batch had lived for three full months, extending its life approximately nine times longer than normal. Mutating of genes, quite artificially, and if it worked with the flies, it might do the same in humans. Extending the average human life by a factor of nine, would result in a lifespan of six-hundred years or so.

Quite unthinkable, perhaps, but theoretically possible. The idea of it danced in him for the balance of the day.

At lunch the next day with Alexis Hazlett, he had watched her face slowly tighten as he explained his recent visit to Cambridge.

Telling her, "Last week, I had a drink with an old friend. Balandon Bixby—"

"The ethicist?"

"Right, the philosopher who specializes in human ethics. You know his work?"

"I've read a couple of his books. Penetrating stuff."

"Do you agree with him?"

"On a lot, I think I do."

"Well, he's read some of the slamming against us in the press, so he took me to task. A barrage of questions, and every one of them with an edge. A razored edge. Care to hear what he laid on me?"

"Sure I would."

"He started in with: what do you suppose it would mean if individuals lived for two or three centuries? What would it do to the mind, the ability to persevere, the cycle of human hope, and would it create the likelihood that too many of us would become jaded, bored and indifferent to life? Or would people have to work for all of a century or more to afford retirement. If earth had so many people, when could an individual expect to enter the work force? Who would be awarded jobs, who not? Could a marriage stand up for a century or even two? Would society call for mandatory fertility blocking before the world was overcome by too many of its own? Do you begin your schooling at, say, thirty? Who gets to go to school? Why them? How do you pay for all the social programs, and if you can extend life that long it means then the genes are in great shape and the corollary of that is no one gets very sick…Balandon didn't stop there but I did. So, what do you make of all this? Is he right? An alarmist? On the mark?"

"Frightening to me, that's what I think," Alexis replied." He sounds like he's predicting anarchy. Or a breakdown of society at minimum."

"That's about what I thought."

"Doesn't it worry you?"

"Yes and no. I'm not a sociologist."

"If you're the one who invented the atom bomb and some other guy drops it, it's his fault not yours. That's approximately what you're saying, Thomas. That's a ridiculous position to take."

"Every breakthrough begets a trade-off."

"I do agree, but then I'd not call anthrax much of a breakthrough, would you?"

"Not a relevant comparison, Alexis."

"It is from where I sit. Whether it's gene manipulation or chemicals that cause wipe-outs, all of it has a potential for disaster. Who are we to decide all these questions? We don't decide them, do we; we just make the questions possible?"

"Is that what you think of our work? Your work here?"

"Someone said very, very recently, that every breakthrough begets a trade-off." Smiling at him, but with a voice that had gone flat.

"Touché."

St. Gallen, Switzerland

"How can you be so certain?" Jaggy complained. "So absolute? You'd better be wrong, too."

Caspar Feurenreuth, chief of medicine at Klinik Tönbrin-Foy and classed as one of the top hematologists in Europe, ticked off Jaggy's latest test results for the third time that afternoon. She was in bed and he, sitting in a nearby chair, bent forward, giving her a too-close look at himself. A rail-thin type, his dark hair was combed straight back in glossy strings over his bald, shiny pate. Bony hands hung loosely from the cuffs of his black shirt. On his sharp-tipped nose, a hairy wart protruded; it was the size of a shirt button. He looked too much like a visiting undertaker, arriving for the purpose of sorting out necessary arrangements. Whenever he visited with her, her nerves grew taut, too taut.

"Blood keeps clotting your vessels," Feurenreuth was explaining, a refrain she had heard too any times.

Complicating matters, she was showing symptoms of yet another blood disorder: CML, or chronic myeloid leukemia, a disease as fatal as sickle cell anemia. The risk of a stroke had increased, her vital organs were showing signs of galloping infections. The more transfusions she was given, the greater the iron overload in her blood, yielding other problems to deal with. She was caught up in a cycle, whereby the known treatments were actually worsening the primary causes of her pain and suffering. Fevers. Stabbing pains made her feel as if she were being assaulted by bailing hooks. Shivering cold at times, even when under three layers of blankets. She knew, or had been told, the marrow in her bones was cranking out white cells at a furious rate. All so very depressing. She wished he would go away, leave her be.

"Advisable, Frau Muldaur," Feurenreuth droned, "that the babies be aborted."

"Don't be asinine. I'd rather abort you first."

"I'm trying to help you…"

"Try harder, Herr Doctor. A lot harder."

A second embryo had showed up on a sonogram, elating her when first she heard the news. The second half of the news bore grim tidings, however; she wasn't expected to be alive at the expected delivery date.

Feurenreuth continued, "We must exercise the greatest caution, Frau Muldaur. You are in jeopardy. You are in the—ah—you live as an emergency case. Ah, this is unpleasant discussion, Frau, but we require someone to notify in the—ah—any dreadful event, you see—a family member."

"There isn't any."

"An attorney, perhaps?"

"No, thank you."

"Who would be the other parent? Parent to the second embryo?"

"I'll think on this."

"Please." And with that, Feurenreuth departed.

He had control of her case and she had control of very little when it came to her own health. She disliked him, was even revolted whenever he probed her.

Months earlier, she had bought a one-third interest in the Klinik, agreeing, as part of the buy-in, to build a twenty-bed addition. Glad to be an investor, for she knew she'd be spending lengths of time here, and, other than a side-trip or two, likely would be ending her days here. Switzerland offered sizeable advantages. Zurich lawyers were working on ways to minimize her death taxes. With her comm-sat phone, there was little difficulty in maintaining contact with Muldaur House in London. St. Germain was within hailing distance, and, all in all, she could expect top medical care here.

Yet always asking herself—now what? A child or two, that was *what*! And a more complaisant Thomas Courmaine, that was the other *what*.

Feurenreuth, trying unsuccessfully not to be overly grim or overly specific, was plainly thinking the black veil was about to drop. For one thing, here it was: the question usually posed to the dying—who to notify when she could no longer answer for herself. The Zurich lawyers who had pressed her for similar information, preparing for the day when she was nothing more than a breathing lung. The bio-facts were clear enough: her stepfather, Bastei Muldaur, had parented one embryo. Feurenreuth knew the fullness of that story. He didn't know Thomas Courmaine was the other half of the second embryo. No one knew it, except herself.

The fact of it held large-scale implications for her own estate, to say nothing of The Muldaur Trust. She was in a deadly race against time. She must bear a child, hopefully Baster's, and prove it was Baster's before The Trust's boggling wealth was wasted away. N'jorro, giving that to the Mzura, and the Muldaur-DuPont works to the South African government was sinful enough. That was the end of it! The line must be drawn and she intended to be the one who drew it.

Still, releasing information as to Thomas's involvement wholly unnerved her.

She had had no contact with him since their row that night of the dinner with Searsbey and Maxton-Howard. Three-months had now lapsed. She knew from the servants at St. Curig that he had moved to the old manor house, slept there, ate there, and whatever else there. She'd have to list him, she supposed, as next of kin. He was to be a father, after all. He became one, she supposed, during an afternoon romp before the dinner with Searsbey and Maxton-Howard. Quite a coincidence, almost amusing, given that the situation promised to end up as quite an Annunciation on the day she would inform him his life was about to transform, like it or lump it.

These many years of complications in her efforts to become pregnant, and now this double-hitter. Impossible, yes? Improbable, anyway. Yet here it was, irony of all ironies. Who would look after what she was carrying inside herself? Thomas—for one of them. But what of the other? Each child would one day inherit almost two-billion Euros from her. How would the self-exalted, Mr. Ever-So-Busy Thomas I. Courmaine handle that notion? Indeed, were she to have her way, and she fully intended to, Mr. Go-It-Alone Courmaine would have nothing whatsoever to say about a single ounce of it.

That was final; to her, anyway.

St. Curig Fields, Isle of Anglesey, Wales

A second letter from Augustin deMehlo, this time the tone on the curt side.

"...I had so hoped to have heard from you by now and must assume my earlier letter went astray. May I ask that you call me at the Curia, Thomas. I've heard not a word from you and we are most anxious to proceed with our small conclave..."

Not nearly as anxious as he to avoid a session with deMehlo's varsity, all of the top Jesuit theologians. A wrangle would ensue, one he'd find distasteful. So would they.

That old and tired dispute; science jousting with religious beliefs. He was tired of Rome. He was through with Rome. He only wanted a final, official release from the Vatican. Then he'd talk to them about anything they wanted to talk about. Any hour, any day, any year.

A Man for Others? Not today, he wasn't. He was a man acting solely in his own interests. Still, he spent an hour drafting a cautious, careful, polite letter that he later dictated to Ponsoby. No, he couldn't attend, and the guilt of refusing deMehlo badgered him all of that day.

St. Curig Fields, Isle of Anglesey, Wales
New York, New York

Dusk falling.

Alone in his cubby-hole office, listening to the mutter of thunder, he kept himself confused. After fussing and delaying, he caved, unable to prevent temptation from having its way.

After the call connected, he waited, then there it was, Shandar's voice. No greeting, just, "Should I say, 'As I live and breathe."

"I'm very glad you do. Hello, and tell me how was Australia?"

"Better than I thought it'd be. Lovely people. I'd gladly go back sometime."

"Thanks for your letter, very nice of you."

"I gather things haven't improved on the media-front. Si was talking about it again the other night."

"How're they?"

"He's in the dumps, of course, now that he's no longer the trading kingpin of the Americas. But Poppi is ecstatic now that he's home more. Si probably will call it quits soon. A big maybe, but she's leaning on him with hurricane force."

Listening to her voice, thrilled, drawing pictures of her in his racing mind.

"Please give them my regard. One reason I'm calling is to see if Meric & Morris is available to rescue the innocent and weak."

"Meaning you, I imagine?"

"Yes, and my colleagues. All young, all good, and all of them taking a bad rap by being associated with me. We're getting killed."

"It's not true? Any of those articles?"

"The parts that count aren't true. Far from it," Thomas replied, dismally.

"You sound as though you're speaking from a funeral."

"Well, it makes for plenty of gloom, whenever I think of it. Two feet deep in my own grave. It's getting nastier and nastier and it's going to cost me people, and that'll end up costing a great deal of time and much else besides."

"Whoever it is, they must be on to something or other, Thomas. The media gets used at times, it's part of the business, but you're showing up in reputable papers."

"I'm the one who's getting used. I realize these are mostly op-ed pieces and letters-to-the-editors. But someone ought to check the facts or at least the allegations."

"Have an open house and show the doubters what you're up to."

"I can't afford to. Even a couple of London solicitors have advised me against it."

"If you don't react openly, you'll always be tagged as a false prophet. No explanations of what you're doing obviously will keep raising suspicions. Leaves you wide open, and they know it."

He told her why he couldn't answer a broadside of questions about the lab's work. They had a great deal of know-how to protect and were thus naturally publicity-shy at this time. "On the other hand," he went on, "I realize I can't just turn the other cheek. I know I need help."

"You know the old saying, 'If you don't confront them, you'll never conquer them.'"

"I can't confront whom I can't find. I found out from three of the newspapers that the pieces they ran were written under pseudonyms. I don't get it, that they aren't more careful about what they print. All I get is a bloody nose and I'm tired of it. So, will you help me…please?"

"You mean, *will I?*"

"I don't know anyone else in your line of work, and even if I did I still need someone I can trust. I have to move on this. Sorry if I sound abrupt, but will you or won't you?"

"Right off, I can't say. Pretty sudden of you. I can take it up with our London office and see what they have to say."

"No, you. You, Shandar. A lot of this is happening on your side of the water. I've got to have you…"

"I'm—I couldn't—I haven't the time right now, Thomas."

"I'm desperate, frankly."

"Why isn't your friend lifting her crown?"

"Her people tell her she shouldn't get involved. She is involved, of course, but they prefer she keep a distance. Can't say as I blame her. Shandar, I need you. Please."

"I'll have to talk to Abe Meric. He'll probably suggest our London office. Or Paris. Berlin's a little far, I suppose. He may not suggest anything other than to say no."

"I'll pay whatever it takes. If I can, that is."

"I'll have to get back to you. Nice to hear you, Thomas. Bye."

"Don't hang—"

The click informed him he was now speaking to himself. He leaned back, thinking maybe Shandar was right, that bragging a little now and again couldn't hurt. But bragging to whom? He had no idea how to set up a press conference, and shuddered as he recalled the semi-disaster at Muldaur House when Jaggy announced the formation of Muldaur-Courmaine; and she had known what she was doing, or at least how to go about it. Whom to invite, and why. He was surely not of a mind to mistakenly ask those who could add to the harm.

Late that same afternoon, Shandar dropped in on Abe Meric, summing up her earlier conversation with Thomas. They batted around the question of what could be gained by taking on Muldaur-Courmaine as a client. Abe Meric was disinclined. Lots of start-up work and all for a dicey future. Or no future whatever if the avalanche of derogatory press accounts were credited.

"You see it any differently?" he asked off-handedly

"No, not really. But personally I owe him something. We had a mishap. My fault. I'm off for three days to Brussels near the end of the month. A meeting of the beer barons, no less, and I was intending to stop in London on the way back. I could run up there to Wales and see whatever I can see. Not much to lose, only a day or so. I've got an idea that might work. A tie-in with Haut-Teknik. It's a possibility anyway. They know skin like no one else in the cosmetics industry. I should add this, Abe. He's a natural as a headliner and he told me things that pretty much convince me he's on to something. Whatever the press says to the contrary, I think he's got his hand on the Golden Calf."

Abe Meric's mouth went one way and his shoulders another as he shrugged indifferently. "Do whatever you think best."

"I'll have a look."

"Yes. Don't commit, however, until we talk more."

"No, I wouldn't, of course not."

Thomas, she thought, as she left for her own office. He had sounded like a voice lost in the far wilderness. She owed him one and didn't much like unsettled debts. Haut-Teknik sounded as a good idea to her. Would he buy it though? Has he a choice?

St. Curig Fields, Isle of Anglesey, Wales

Past noon one day, Ponsoby bustled into his office. "Another woman downstairs to see you."

"Not that Goliath again?"

Ponsoby shook her head. "Not unless she shaved off ten stone since last we saw her. This one is quite lovely. A Miss Bazak, she says. She gave me this card." Ponsoby passed it to Thomas who had stood instantly.

"Why didn't you say so?"

"I did. Just. You gone daft, Thomas?"

"Maybe I have. Hold the fort. I may not be back for hours."

"You know who she is, then?"

"An angel-of-enlightenment," he said, scrambling for the door.

"From New York, is she?"

"And Iraq and even heaven maybe," he replied to the perplexed Adele Ponsoby, never having seen him so excited.

He found Shandar sitting in an overstuffed chair near the fireplace in the main room where the Monday staff meetings were held. She smiled, she stood. Then she laughed and he said, "What's so funny?"

"Thomas, hullo."

"Hello, and welcome. What's so funny?" he repeated.

"Your face. The expression when you walked in. You looked like a burglar who just had a flashlight shined in his eyes."

"I admit I am surprised. Am I ever."

"You knew I was coming."

"I got your e-mail but it didn't give me any date. I'm very glad to see you, Shandar. Relief and joy, all at once."

"Thank you. It's nice seeing you, too. And way over here."

'Yes, way over here. Wouldn't matter to me. Here, there, or anywhere. Like something to drink? Eat? Anything? We don't run the Ritz here but the general fare is passable."

"I'm dandy fine, thank you. Show me around, would you. I never expected such a layout. The crown moldings here are fabulous."

"Four-hundred years old. Drafty as a coalmine, as you can see. Or feel. Sure, I'd love to show you around."

Tension had encircled them, as though they were some divorced couple who had unexpectedly reunited. Almost overly polite, but he was set on making things as easy, as friendly as he knew how. He toured her around the lab, introducing her to the team, except for Lin-pao who was away in Cambridge. Then showed her the rest of the manor house. When alone, he asked her how she had found St. Curig on her own.

"I had some business in Brussels, then stopped in London on the way to New York. I hired a car and drove up. Everyone around here knows of St. Curig Fields. A pretty name. I came across a gardener down by the gate. What a gate that is, and then the gardener pointed the way here. You can barely understand the way these people speak."

"In a few days, you'll get used to it."

"Two days, tops. Beautiful, beautiful country, I had no idea, how lucky you are."

"You'll get used to that, too."

"You're staring at me, Thomas."

"I like staring at you, I always have."

He wanted to get closer, have the smell of her, sense the warmth of her. Suffused with want, trying not to show it. She still had that swan-like walk, so gracile, almost like the fluidity of the invisible air. He stood his distance, happy-faced and exhilarated.

"You are the greatest art I've seen in many a month."

"My, oh! my."

"Well, you're like that—like a—like an intelligent orchid. That's art, isn't it? Wait till I tell you what we've been doing with orchids. Lin-pao has…."

"I'm about to melt, mister."

"Melt in this direction."

"Let's—um—I'd like to walk some. I'm stiff after the drive over here. Five hours of it. And then I must find a place to sleep tonight."

"Sleep here at the manor. There're six bedrooms, rarely used. Never used except for one of them and I've only bunked in there lately."

"Thanks all the same. A nice little inn or something of that kind."

She was wearing tan gabardine slacks and a cardigan sweater and had deposited a loden-green duffel coat on a front hall chair. She needed boots, not pumps, for a walk. He found her a pair of hobnailed Wellingtons that were only slightly too large, so fitted her out with a pair of thermal socks, and off they went.

He headed her for the sea, walking a path overgrown at its verges with lolly-pines and tangled gorse and other cover, ideal for the nesting of wild game birds. He pointed out the shooting fields, the pastures for Scottish cattle, the stone barns that housed tractors and other implements, a church for Sunday services—Methodists—who boasted a women's choir of splendid Welsh voices. On they went, the air laden now with a salt-scent and marsh smell, the breeze picking up. Wanting to take her arm, but restraining himself.

Up ahead was the first rise of dunes and he led her to a boardwalk that made the going easier. Her hair, grown longer than he remembered, strayed over her face and she kept brushing it back. He gave her a clean blue bandana he used for a handkerchief to tie around her head. For ten minutes or so, they ambled along the foam-smothered beach but the wind fussed and kicked up the sea into combers, and the sky, as it often did, was showing a telltale gray, auguring a storm.

"I love this," she said. "The air is divine. I never saw so many different birds."

"I should take you to Africa one day. You'd see hundreds of them, all different. Colors that you can hardly imagine."

"You miss it? Africa?"

"Sometimes. I especially miss the sunrises and sunsets. The animals, of course. I miss all of that but not as much as I've missed you."

Hesitant before she replied, "I came here to do a little informal consulting, Thomas."

"And work we shall, but I can still speak my mind, can't I?"

They trudged onward. A gust of wind swayed the shore-side trees, and Shandar lowered her bandana-bound head, covering her eyes against the blowing sand. Steps later, her foot caught by a half-buried log of driftwood; she stumbled headlong just as a wind-pushed wave slapped against the beach, soaking her slacks.

Straddling her with both feet, Thomas pulled her upright. Chest against chest, they clung. What got into him, then, was a force so strong, he submitted to it instantly, pulling her face to his in a kiss—long, moist, lingering.

Flinging her head to one side suddenly, she gasped, then broke apart from him. "No, no more. I—uh—we can't. I won't. We *cannot* do this." She smoothed the front of her duffel coat as if unconsciously wiping him off her body.

"Seeing you and it all comes back. My zones are flooded and I don't mind saying it to you."

"We're not, n-o-t. Please."

"I'm not going to apologize."

Lightning splintered the sky, followed by an ear-shocking blast of thunder. So massive, it seemed atomic in force.

"You suppose that's our message to change the subject?" Shandar asked, lightening the moment.

"Maybe. We'd better leg it. I've been caught in these squalls and they're very moist."

Back at the manor's driveway, he hauled one of her cases from the boot of the rented auto. After she had changed in one of the unoccupied bedrooms, and warmed herself with two cups of tea, he cut right to business, making out-loud guesses about the identity of the flying squad behind the news accounts blasting the lab at bi-weekly intervals. "A mistake," he told her, "choosing the name of Muldaur-Courmaine. We should've used some generic like…well, I dunno, anything but what we decided on. If we had done that, then no one would know she was involved. That'd take some of the pressure off."

"She's upset, I gather."

"Ballistic at times, and I can't say as I blame her."

"Anyone would shriek bloody murder, I suppose."

"Let me give you a general idea of what's been going on here, what we've been up to and have accomplished. Quite a lot and it's quite a lot because we've got a top-notch crew."

He summed up how Lin-pao had done an astounding thing with orchids over at Cambridge, adjusting colors and infusing fragrances totally alien to the orchid family; then Lin-pao and Timmothe Merrill had doubled the growth of hair-fiber on an alpaca, and done it in half the usual growth cycle; Alexis Hazlett had taken a mostly blind hamster and brought back its sight by a series of gene transplants…"and we've done more, too. All of it connected to Zyme-One, and so we know a great deal more now of its capacities. The big trick has been to find precisely how the plant *semba* makes Zyme-One, then learn how to synthesize that process. Without *semba*, the whole thing flops. We've got to have the feedstock to make Zyme-One and we can't depend on getting it out of Africa. Not in the quantities needed. I have a supply at a place called Cyro in Switzerland, but not enough of it to do all we need to get done."

"Sounds like you've a lot to be pleased about."

"Very much so. What we need is to keep steaming ahead to the big break-through. That's why Lin-pao spends so much of his time at Cambridge figuring out the chemistry of *semba*. Seeing if we can replicate the active ingredients that produce Zyme-One."

"Can you?"

"Eventually, I think so. It may call for a bigger effort than we can pull off with our team or our resources."

"What does she say about it? Will she put up more backing?"

"Jaggy and I are on very fragile terms these days. I always have to remember it was she who saved the day for me. We'd never have come this far without her help. More backing, more researchers...I doubt it..."

Shandar held back a moment, weighing his words. Then she offered, "If we do this, and I'm talking of Meric & Morris now, then will you do as we recommend? No end runs that we don't know about? You'll tell us everything?"

"You sound like the prosecutor."

"We need to know more than prosecutors ever do. When the chips are in play, they only deal with twelve people. The jury. Your jury is the majority of the public's opinion. Who you are, why they should care and what it is you do for them. On two continents, if you please. It's a very different arena than any courtroom."

"You'll always know everything I know. That's a promise."

"I want to get straight on something. You told me once you had done some sort of a mouse experiment in Maryland. Human skin genes in a mouse. Was that on the level?"

"Yes, absolutely."

"You're sure."

"The witness works here. Alexis Hazlett. She used to be at NIH, and we used her genes. Hold on, I'll go find her."

When he returned with Alexis, the two women spent a while becoming acquainted. Before long, however, Shandar offered her first question, "And there was no question that that mouse...you said its name was...."

"Peter. There was Peter and another named Paul, but Peter is the important one," Alexis Hazlett replied.

"And it ended up with your skin. Is my memory correct?"

"That's the essence, yes."

"Where's the mouse now?"

"It was stolen."

"Stolen? Stolen?" Shandar repeated. "And you know how that particular experiment was done."

"I didn't then, but I do now."

"Transgenic," Thomas said.

"Spelled like it sounds?"

"Right."

"Is there anything more, Alexis?"

"Not really. We did the same with a hamster here, altering it by using my skin genes again. Worked like a charm. Not only that, but the offspring carried my skin genes, as well. That was remarkable, or remarkably new."

"No one walked off with the hamster, I assume?"

"Safe and sound, in its cage."

"That could help."

"If that's all for now," said Alexis, "I've got something to attend to in the lab. If you need me, I'll be there."

After Alexis Hazlett departed, Shandar said, "Attractive, isn't she? A gamin."

"Good at her game, too. We're very lucky to have her."

"Let's talk about women. Women and their bodies and their faces, especially their faces. Every woman's face is her unique signature. If you knew how much money women spent on their faces, you'd think I was lying. Remember how much press attention there was about those three women in Africa. The reason for it, all the coverage, was that news editors know women everywhere would be curious about it. Didn't you once tell me that you were plagued by other women in that tribe to do the same for them?"

"I think I did tell you."

"You did. And that's a positive that can be built on."

"That, unfortunately, is something that cannot be repeated. In Africa, perhaps, but not here."

"What about another version, done in a different way...names, celebrities, known players. Listen, here's how it might work, so listen...our Berlin office represents a firm in Hamburg known as Haut-Teknik. They specialize in the analyses of compounds and ingredients used in cosmetics. A highly respected name in the trade. Everyone in the industry uses them whenever a new product is underway. They test it for safety, and allergies and color ingredients and pigments, that kind of thing. They know mountains about skin care and what works and what doesn't. Let me tell you what I think we might persuade them to do..."

On she went, infatuating Thomas, who was ready to grasp at most anything.

"Cosmetic change without surgery," she went on. "Live human flesh, real people, given something like the three Mzura women were given—a fresh start. A fresh start on life or at least the way women feel about themselves and their lives. Haut-Teknik could do wonders to validate the work of Muldaur-Courmaine and do it without exposing any of your secrets, especially if they were given a stake in the outcome. Some kind of exclusive for cosmetics only."

"How big are they?"

"I don't know their sales volume. They employ ranks of technicians," said Shandar, "along with at least a dozen dermatologists on staff. Every T is crossed, every dot recorded. Thoroughly German and painstakingly precise…they also have all those high-resolution cameras for before-and-after…Hassen and something…"

"Hassenblad. Those're the best," Thomas said, helping her.

"Those, yes. So, think of this…if we were to persuade them to use your way, the Zyme-One, to alter the skin of, say, twenty volunteers, people with a mess for a skin, having real problems, or even actresses and models who wanted skin makeovers without surgery. Assuming it all worked, you'd have a big, big news story. That story can be tied to the three women in Africa and now we'd have a basis…a platform to launch a counter-campaign against these people who're haranguing you. On top of that, you'd have unassailable corroboration that must be accepted by anyone because the Haut-Teknik reputation is tops. Why do you keep looking at me like that?"

"To please my soul. Go ahead, please, you were extolling Haut-Teknik."

"What I'm saying is they do everyone. Revlon, Mirabelle, L'Oreal and all the French and Italian cosmetic houses. No one, I don't think, is going to doubt Haut-Teknik's endorsement. So, there it is. I've talked to our Berlin people and Berlin thinks it might play. *Might*. That Haut-Teknik could get interested. I can get Berlin to set up a meeting and, after that, it's totally your gig. The question is, can you do it? Make it all happen?"

"We can," Thomas said excitedly. "We've got much better procedures than those I used in Africa. Sounds too good to be true."

"Maybe it is. Think of it from Haut-Teknik's side of the table. Fantastic publicity. No one ever tested anything like it; at least I don't think so."

"What about cost?"

"We'll discuss that after we hear what Haut-Teknik has to say."

"One real snag is the regulating problem. Humans, you know."

"Let the dermatologists deal with it, why not? Germany isn't exactly backwards."

Later, in the lab, Thomas showed Shandar how to take a small journey inside herself. He snipped two-inch lengths of hairs from her head. For the next three hours, he showed her the steps needed to capture a copy of her chromosome-7, and then one of her X-chromosomes that had created her as a female. Using an electro-scope so she could see the process, he cut a piece of DNA segment off her chromo-7 using a restriction enzyme, ran it through a DNA sequencer, then shot pictures with a high-resolution bubble camera. Smearing her DNA residue on a sheet of gel, he denatured it, and then transferred it on to a Mylar membrane, dabbing it with a low-grade radioactive substance, finally exposing it to x-ray film.

"That's you," he told her at one stage, "no one else in the world is exactly like that. Just so you know how exceptional you are."

Peering intently at the gel sheet, what she saw was a series of black bars, hundreds of them—a tiny, tiny bit of her own genome that looked something like a barcode. "Heaven forbid, I'm just a bunch of black blobs," Shandar joked as she looked at another sheet full of bar-bands that spelled out a single gene segment. "I look like rungs on a ladder."

"Any mirror would argue with you."

He showed Shandar how to read herself. Located on her chromo-7 (it looked to Shandar like a tiny hookworm) were ninety-four of her skin genes. They could be used, if she chose, to replace the skin genes of any Haut-Teknik volunteers.

"My color is darker than most German's."

"We can adjust that."

"I'd rather not, thank you very much."

"Afraid we'd fail?"

"Someday you may have to name the gene donors and I would seem less than impartial if I'm a donor as well as your campaigner."

"I see what you mean. We'll, I'll mix your genes with mine, and we can be a cross-breed."

"Don't be silly."

"I might never have to shave again."

"Everyone'll think you're a eunuch."

"I can prove I'm not."

An off-center remark, and for some reason reminding them of who they were and where they were. Polite but firm, adroitly fending him off, she spoke a little tightly. "We have to keep this on a sane level. I came to help you out, if I can. But that's it. I'm not getting involved. You're sleeping with *her*, and you're living on her estate. She bankrolls your operation. Nothing more need be said."

"We kissed and it wasn't exactly casual. I can say that, can't I? I just did say it."

"That's as far as it'll go, too."

"Why?"

"I said so, and that's enough why."

To him, their kiss had been almost life-giving, and he said, "Look at me and tell me you don't feel what I feel. What I've felt since I first saw you at the Nestors. It's never changed and it's never going to change."

"I'm not doing anything with you. I'm not. Please, Thomas—"

"Why? We'll have thrown away something that could be the best thing that ever happened to either of us. All because of a mistake, a miscue, a goof by me or by some bad timing in New York on that night at '21'."

"Let me ask you a question. How about if we leave here tomorrow morning and you can come back to New York with me?"

"You know I can't."

"I do know, and you must know in that whizzy brain of yours that you and I live on different patches. I'm afraid to leave mine. I'm not rich. I cannot do what I please, when I please, where I please. I'm also recovering, like a recovering alcoholic. I'm like someone who's in remission. You know only part of me, of my life. Terrible things happened, Thomas. Terrible…and honestly I don't think I'd ever be up to you."

"What things?"

"I'm not going into that now."

"Try, let's just try."

"Where is she by the way?"

"In Switzerland I think. She's been quite ill. She doesn't even know you're here."

"What're you ever going to tell her, when she finds out?"

"I'll tell her the truth and tell her of your splendid idea with Haut-Teknik. I'd tell her a few other things but that would mean the end of the lab and the end of me and then Haut-Teknik would be a stillborn. A dilemma everywhere I turn, it seems. If I lose you again, I think that'll be the end of my sanity."

In her wonderful face, gone grave, he lost himself. He sought those slightly slanted eyes of the Magyar but she was no Magyar. Her hair, black as ebony, lustrous whenever she passed under overhead lights, and at this moment he was as buoyed as if he'd taken ten straight hits of pure oxygen.

"How very generous of you not to charge us for all the advice," he said at length.

"You're a lucky boy today."

"I've been thinking the same thing." He smiled. "I can pay something. Maybe I can scare up fifty-thousand. I've got a line of credit with Braunsweig."

"Put it toward Germany. You'll need it."

"Well, at least your travel expenses. The bill at the inn, your car—"

"I'll let you take me to dinner somewhere extravagant. Half-extravagant. I'll be a cheap date for once."

"I love you, dear, God, how I love you..."

"There goes the dinner and we're not even there yet. Say that again, and I'm checking out of Wales."

"I love you and you're not going anywhere. I wonder why you came here other than to talk of Germany etcetera. Wasn't part of it to see me?"

Looking away, she said, "Yes, and I can see it's turning into another mistake. I remember a lonesome man in New York with his dinosaur-sized dreams. I remember that look in your eyes, in your face...I still see it. Not everyone has a dream to give help to others the way you do. I hope you succeed. I volunteer at the blind children's hospital and I know what it's like for those kids, never to have any hope of seeing again. Maybe one day you'll be able to give them their sight. Or the hope of it. That's also why I'm here."

"And that's why I love you. Partly why."

"Please don't say it again. Please...please, Thomas."

"Even if I never say it again, I'll always feel it. There's no changing that, nor would I ever want to change it."

But he laid off, then. He dined with her at a seafood house across the bridge on the mainland. Mostly they traded small talk, then he answered more questions about the team, explaining why Lin-pao, the key player, was in Cambridge unraveling various mysteries with their botanists. "Lin-pao has made a sizeable bet with several of the faculty over there that he could, single-handedly, create the world's first black orchid, streaked with pink.

Wholly convinced of his man, Thomas had personally backed Lin-pao's side of the wager.

"I'd like to see it," Shandar said.

"Me, too. And so would those botanists."

"Was it done with your Zyme-One?"

He nodded.

"Wow. Black and pink."

"S'what I'm told. I'll send you one."

"Do, I'd like that."

And something in the way she said the words left him encouraged. Maybe a misplaced hope, and maybe they lived too far distant from each other, but he was a man who fed himself on dreams, even dreams that seemed unreachable.

On a mist-filled morning, she departed Anglesey. Thomas drove to the inn where Shandar had put up for her short stay. They had tea and scones, and, before she could get ahead of him, he paid her bill. Later, he stood on the sidewalk, forlornly watching as Shandar flashed him a magazine-cover smile he was sure he'd never forget even in death, then stood in dazed thought as she threw a quick salute out the window and drove off in her rented Rover.

Instantly unhappy, then.

Seeing her again had soaked him in elation, a feeling he had treasured for almost two days. Most notably than ever—to-be-cherished kiss at the beach. Now, what would it be? His bench, he thought, and little else.

As he drove the road to St.Curig, he realized his behavior toward Shandar had been on the aggressive side, far different that the timidity of the days in New York. He supposed, and rightly, that he viewed the physical charms of women in a vastly different light than he had in the so-called Jesuit days. He could thank Jaggy for that, for it was she, and she alone, who had released him from his cocoon of reticence.

St. Gallen, Switzerland
St. Curig Fields, Isle of Anglesey, Wales

"Oh, you are some rotter, some nervy bastard. Who is it you think you are? You're a foul one and an ingrate," Jaggy retorted to his greeting. She had found out about Shandar's visit from the groundskeeper, later checking on the event with the household staff. Learning that there had been no guests at the lodge, she had phoned the inn in Holyhead where, on occasion, Jaggy parked any overload of her houseguests, and the revenue was not insignificant. Reluctantly, they had provided her with the name of the American visitor.

"It was you who demanded that I do something about these newspaper attacks. Most of it comes from America as I've said to you twenty times. Ergo, I sought help from the one p. r. person who I know there. Why not?"

"You didn't have it off with that Jew of yours, did you? On my property?"

And he was dumbstruck.

"Answer me!"

He waited, she waited.

"I asked you a question…"

"If you refer to her that way again, we'll be at the end of this conversation, if that's what this is supposed to be."

"Who is it you think you're talking to?"

"You. Who else?"

Hearing a sharp intake of breath, he tried to imagine her face, that jaw, those rod-stiff shoulders. He ought to fabricate an excuse, hang up and wait for her to settle down.

But she intervened. "I'd like to know what's going on on my property."

"Why not check with your informants. Or whoever it is who patrols me. Did they happen to mention the other woman who dropped by? Also an American, well, possibly African. A cousin to the hippopotamus at any rate. Charging in here and demanded an interview. She got about one-third of one, and she said she'd been in Rome checking up on me. Maybe she was in Rome, I haven't any idea. I think she might know a lot more than she lets on about all this abuse in the papers. No proof of that, of course, as usual. You will recall that several times I asked for your advice about all this and you preferred to stay out of it. Didn't want any involvement…okay, I understand. Good decision. So I did what I thought I had to do and that is to get someone who knows what might be done to counter these assaults on Muldaur-Courmaine. She's got a great idea that I'll tell you about sometime…the net of it all, Jaggy, is that I'm trying to do something that you insisted I fix and fix fast. It won't be fast, unfortunately. But it will be a genuine attempt…end of report and don't get sore over nothing."

"She's never to set foot on St. Curig again."

"That's fine."

"And if you're to see her again, I shall want to know about it."

"I'm afraid that's not fine."

Another audible intake of breath. "You're looking for trouble. I can see that and I know how to make it, too. You may count on that, Thomas Courmaine."

"I've something else you might care to think about. Why don't I buy out your share of the lab, and we can each take our own fork in the road, and that'll be that. Wouldn't it be better, all around? We can make an announcement that you elected to pull out because you've lost interest. Or whatever you'd like to say. If we can agree on a deal that I can handle, we can set you free and clear. No more worries, no more concerns."

"I might even consider it."

"Do."

"Are we quite through?"

"Definitely."

When hanging up, he re-thought what she had said: *Are we quite through?* Not a word from her in weeks, and the call had come as something of a surprise. Slam-talk. Not a how-are-you, not a here's-how-I am, but instead words rife with protests, bitching and grumbling. Plainly, they had broken apart though neither of them had said so, nor even exchanged written notes. What was there to say? Wreckage had been headed their way for months, their failure all the more poignant now that she dueled with death and he didn't.

Crossing his mind almost weekly was the inescapable speculation as to what awaited the lab when Jaggy was gone. There went the funding. There went St. Curig.

Her shares in Muldaur-Courmaine would end up in her estate and the cost of buying them might well top any sum he could raise, making him wonder again if he'd end up in the claws of Searsbey and Maxon-Howard, adding to his headaches.

Three nights later.

At his bench in the lab, working late, when across the room the phone jangled, interrupting his concentration. Letting it ring. On it went until he gave in and walked over to a desk.

"Hostilities of a high order, sir," said Lin-pao. "Come instantly, we are under heaviest assault."

"What do you mean, hostilities?"

"I see them through the window, though it is dark as the far side of Pluto. At least twenty assaulters. Torches and banging until I'm deaf. A noise to waken Socrates. Two windows downstairs are smashed through. It is the end, the ignominious end. *Christus*, there goes another one, did you hear? The madam will scold us unmercifully. They are devils, dark red devils. Bring all our weapons, sir—"

"Have you been dreaming or something? Drunk on that rice wine?"

"I am drunk on my fears. Hosanna! Sucipiat Dominus Sacrificium. Another stone, another window. I'll be fucked for fair. Didn't you hear the glass smashing to a thousand shards?"

Dropping the phone, Thomas raced down the hall and out the door. A din of distant chanting greeted him. Virtually galloping, he covered the half-mile of rock-strewn grounds to the gatehouse where Lin-pao kept his quarters. Half of the moon showed itself, the night obscure, but he could see flickers of moving flames. Charging on, oblivious to the tree branches that poked at him, some of them scratching his face. Metallic sounds boomed into the night. Yelling, screaming. A great wail pierced the air, like nothing he'd ever heard in Anglesey, a place usually as placid as a nunnery.

He bounded through the back door into more darkness, running into a kitchen chair and banging his shin. A stirring in the corner, then a voice, "If you are here to kill me, if you have no sheriff's warrant, I shall stab you dead—"

"It's me, fr'pete's sakes."

"Sir! You're here, and not a moment too soon."

"What do you make of it?"

"It is the final day, I fear. Crikey! That's genuine Cockney, sir."

"Never goddamn mind."

Thomas made his way to a window, its shattered glass crunching under his shoes. He looked into the night, trying to make something of what appeared to be a mob. Torches burned, the lights waving back and forth. Cries, chants, the banging noises. Carefully watching, carefully considering the situation, then he went for the door.

"Where do you go?"

"I'm headed for that stand of pines that fronts the road. Call the constable. Tell him what's going on. He'll need to know how many people to bring."

"I must be at your side, sir."

"Quickly now, make that call if you please."

Outside, staying within the shadows, he moved toward a thick copse of spruce. Once there, he lowered himself into a crouch, and, silently as he could, pushed through the heavy limbs. Ten steps, twisting this way and that, more branches swatting his face, he was deep into the tall trees. Settling himself behind a hedge, he could see without great worry of being seen.

Perhaps thirty of them. Jumping, hollering, hopping in the guttering light. The torches revealed a face now and again. Young people but who were they? *Thump-thump-brrangg. Thumpa-brrangg,* the clamor from steel lids, clashing like cymbals. Placards were raised and he strained to see what they said: FIGHT MULDAUR-COURMAINE—CLONING BABIES—DEATH STRUGGLE FOR BABIES!

There stood Tavester, yelling and jumping, exhorting the mob. Beside him what looked to be one of Tavester's cronies who'd been with him that night at the Eight Bells. Wearing their customary uniform of black trousers and black windbreakers, both men were wind-milling their arms, egging the demonstrators.

They must be drugged, thought Thomas. Two young men had joined arms with one woman, all three prancing around as bare as the day they had first seen light.

Crack! Crack! Loud popping noises, like firecrackers.

A scream, then a crescendo of screams. Shouts of, "They killed Milly. She's dead. Shot her dead. It's them lab people."

Hurriedly, he scanned for Tavester but Tavester had vanished. Maybe he had gone into the middle of the crowd that now milled about in a squirming huddle. The placards tilted, others of them had dropped to the ground as more banshee-like yells split the night.

Moving out of the trees, he advanced unobtrusively toward the shifting crowd. No one seemed to notice him in the melee of confusion. Shafts of wavering light lit the splayed body of a young woman, her head partly blown away, a thick ooze dripping from a cavernous wound. Thomas pushed closer, seeing the pale hollow blood-smeared cheeks, uneven small teeth in the gaping mouth, hair mangled with blood and brain tissue.

Here, right on the edge of Jaggy's property, a killing.

Down the road a siren bellowed; soon two squad cars pulled up. Uniformed men, and one woman, spilled out the doors, and fast-moving boots smacked against the pavement. They wore flak vests and leather belts holding mace canisters, cuffs, batons, and hand-held radios. Commands, then, and the constables waving flashlights that swung in arcs against the faces of the belligerents. More commands as the mob was separated into three manageable groups, and made to sit on the ground. A woman officer knelt at the side of the dead young woman.

As soon as he'd seen the police, Thomas had beat a retreat into the trees, near to where he had last seen Tavester. No sign of him, and probably well clear of the disaster by now.

Quietly as he could, he headed toward the gatehouse, his heart beating like a pounding mallet. Nearing the gatehouse, he stopped, his mind cart-wheeling. He sat on a stone bench by the rear door, gathering his wits and breath. After a time, calmer, he stood and entered through the back door again.

"Lin-pao?" His voice tremulous. "We've got trouble and we've got work to do. There's been a killing. Turn on a light somewhere and begin to write down everything you recall. All of it. Leave nothing out, including your call to me. Make it very accurate, the police'll want a full statement."

"Let us head now for the manor as if we were never here. Why implicate ourselves?"

"It won't do."

"Why, sir? May I ask why?"

"We have to tell the police what we know. I saw Tavester out there, that lug who was at the Eight Bells. He got away."

"I detest police. I will be in trouble. My life will be over, sir."

"It'll be over for us both if we try fooling the police. They'll want witnesses. That's us. Write that report and don't fudge a word. Not a one, my friend. You do yours first, then I'll write mine."

"I shall be ruined."

Exasperated now. "The report, please. If you please...now, if you please..."

"I have heard you once. It is wholly sufficient, sir."

"Yes, sorry. This, however, is the instant for sitting down, recalling events. They will be coming, I assure you. Off you go."

Lin-pao slunk away like a chastened child. Thomas turned, looking into the grayed dark for a chair, anything to sit on. Still shook, the events still tangling his capacity to make sense of any of it. The day ahead would be dismal, questions from all sides, coming at him like drill-hammers. The police. The press. The team. That misbegotten bastard Tavester. Jaggy in wrath.

Christ, he thought. *Christsakes!*

Thomas had expected the police earlier but not till the next morning did he hear the inevitable knock on the door. He'd been up all night, nervously making notes, drafting a coherent report.

The police had found a pistol, a Smith & Wesson long-barreled .38 caliber. Pending a ballistics test, the weapon was presumed to be the one used in the killing of the young woman, a Mildred Ashcrane, late of Manchester. The serial number on the weapon had been obliterated by acid. The grip, bound with gummy friction tape, prevented the lifting of fingerprints, reminding Thomas of the Beretta that Jaggy had carried in Berlin.

A killer's piece, no doubt, throwing up a spray of suspicion, thankfully none of it directed at the inhabitants of St. Curig Fields.

Yet.

The police believed most of the demonstrators had been jacked up with recreational drugs. A few of the hell-raisers were from Anglesey, the rest were imports, largely from Northern Ireland, having arrived by ferry and posing as tourists. When Thomas mentioned Tavester, he learned it was more than likely a made-up name. Agitators, if indeed he were one, most likely would resort to a *nom de guerre*. The police were still conducting a check, yet a man fitting that description was believed to be a Dutch national, though posing as an Irishman. Interpol was still running it down, a considerable surprise for Thomas that they could move that quickly.

Thomas had handed over his and Lin-pao's written statements. Two hours of questioning elapsed, both thorough and sharp, with heavier attention paid to Lin-pao and his responses. Then, as suddenly as they had appeared, the police departed, showing no signs as to whether they were satisfied or intended a reprise.

Calls by the score came in, fielded by Mrs. Ponsoby. The press were requesting interviews immediately or they'd run the story with what they had, applying the usual implied threat to thwart any opposition to their demands.

Feeling at his unfriendliest, Thomas cut them off cold, an act that did nothing to warm their hearts, or better his relationships with the media.

Within a fortnight of the killing, Ponsoby deposited a letter directly into Thomas's outstretched hand. Written on Crown stationery—from the Home Office (IND)—which, among much else, oversaw immigration matters. The first paragraph, while politely phrased, signified a new round of trouble.

Ponsoby then handed over a similar letter addressed to Lin-pao, who, having already read it, was passing it along to Thomas.

Lin-pao, according to a routine check made by the Home Office through Interpol, had been moving about the world with falsified documents. Interpol, having checked with its 187 participating nations, failed to unearth any record anywhere of a passport issued to a person of that name. Further, Thomas as Managing Director of Muldaur-Courmaine Laboratory, Ltd. was directed to report for an interview at the Home Office, and to arrange an appointment at earliest convenience.

The letters cut like a scythe through his reeling senses. Not possible, he thought; a mistake had been made by someone. He rang Lin-pao's extension and the wizard arrived a few minutes later, a subdued look foreshadowing that trouble was afoot.

Thomas asked, "What's the story on this?" and waved the letter.

"I am the cat run out of its nine lives." Skittish as a caged sparrow, Lin-pao was dissembling and Thomas wanted to go easy but couldn't.

"Be exact with me, brother, I have to know it all. Everything there is."

"It is much too interlaced for a single exposition."

"Unlace it, then. Begin, kindly begin," Thomas urged impatiently.

"Always in propulsion…hurry…and hurry. I must recall the sequence of my various travels with exactitude, sir."

A fantastic story began, so wild and implausible, it seemed like some untold tale from the Arabian Nights. Having escaped China, Lin-pao had made his way to Singapore, lingering there as a fugitive long enough to secure bogus documents that would admit him to neighboring countries. It all began with a stolen passport issued to a Chinese citizen, who had been touring Malaysia. The passport had been expertly doctored to name Lin-pao as its holder of record, with Lin-pao's picture substituted for the original, and, save for an adjustment of the birthdate, the remaining data had been left intact. He had used the tricked-up passport to gain student visas in Indonesia, Thailand,

New Zealand, and eventually the U.S., and finally, of course, a working permit in the U.K.—a long trail of deceit and one difficult to trace. In New Zealand, he'd excelled in his studies at Auckland University of Technology; then, from there, had applied to Harvard for postdoctoral work; refused by Harvard, he had tried Columbia, which welcomed him. Partly, it seemed, Columbia's invitation was due to a series of forged letters from professors of biology at two Chinese universities—Fudan in Shanghai, the other from Beijing University of Technology. Those, however, were accompanied by a genuine letter of glowing praise from a renowned New Zealand professor of advanced microbiology studies. He had taken an evaluation exam as required by Columbia, scoring so brilliantly that he was asked to repeat it. Surpassing the earlier score, he was quickly accorded a Bristol-Myers grant and admitted as a postdoc, automatically qualifying him for a U.S. visa.

A labyrinth of gypsy-like deceit; crimes all, even if victimless crimes.

Incredibly, his peregrinations had worked smoothly for a span of several years. Aside from the single glowing letter of recommendation, Lin-pao's kit of documents included also two faked diplomas from Chinese universities, as well as three other falsified passports, expertly done by yet another "Chinese cousin" who resided in Kuala Lampur. So there it was: posing as a student seeking higher education, Lin-pao had slithered his way undetected through the immigration-wickets of six nations, completely defeating their defenses till now. Likely, his record would've remained unmarred had it not been for the killing that had brought the police at a run, and the subsequent checking of possible suspects, especially foreigners of any stripe.

An astonished Thomas was thinking with one-half of his numbed brain, as he listened with the other half to Lin-pao boasting: "Would you care to inspect my array of passports? They're proper beauties."

"I'd better not. I might get questioned again and I prefer not to lie. My God Almighty, man," Thomas uttered as Lin-pao looked at him quizzically. "Were you in any trouble in China? Something must have started you out."

"I constructed the bomb that wiped out a police station after they tortured and killed my only brother. I thought it better to go amiss."

"Do they know you did it?"

"Of course not, sir. But I couldn't risk that they might find out."

"And you make bombs? On the side? A hobby of yours, is it?"

"I prefer to refer to them as customized explosives. The one that demolished the police station had a two-day delay fuse. Quite hard to do, I rapidly assure you, sir."

"I trust you're not making any customized explosives here. You're not, are you?"

"Never, sir. Unless you are in need of one."

"Christsakes!"

"You will protect me, please, from the authorities."

"How? You're practically a criminal. You *are* a criminal in their eyes."

"As would you be, if you had lived my life." Lin-pao beamed. "It's been quite some tour for an escapist. Are you not impressed?"

Thomas didn't answer, gazing at the imposter in disbelief. What could be done? This was a matter of concern to the British government and he required their goodwill, especially after the senseless killing of a young woman at the gates of St. Curig. Moreover, he still must report to the Home Office himself. Provide answers to them, and probably other answers as yet unknown and as yet indiscernible, if they decided—Muldaur or no Muldaur—to hand him over to the Ministry of Health, with more quizzings about the goings-on at St. Curig.

Such as: "Tell us your side of all that ink you're getting in the newspapers? Take your time; we've all day to listen. Omit nothing. You're the head chap up there, eh?"

At the Eight Bells, the two of them sat at a corner table where they could talk in privacy. "They'll issue a warrant, detain you in some holding tank, hearings and all that kind of thing and demand you consent to extradition, or whatever they do…some of that and possibly even more. I cannot involve Miss Muldaur. I can't even find her. You've got to disappear, Lin-pao. Take the night ferry over to Belfast. Tonight, you've got to go. It's at 10:45, the last one. From Belfast, go straight to Geneva. You won't need a visa to enter Switzerland." He handed over an envelope. "Read it later. There's a man's name and phone number in there. He's an important banker and knows you're on your way. They'll help you as far as Katmandu in Nepal. They've an agent there, an Islamic money-changer. They didn't give me a name but she…it's a woman…can get you into China, the backdoor, if that's what you want. Probably on one of those yak caravans that trade salt. After that, you're on your own. I'm giving you money. Fifty-thousand Euros. It'll be made available to you through…no, no interruptions, just listen…where were we, oh, the money, yes…when you contact the banker, he'll tell you about the delivery of the funds. I think that about covers it…"

In the downlight, Lin-pao's face took on the appearance of a misshapen egg. At one point, Thomas thought he heard a gulp or perhaps it was a soft sob. Maybe it was himself sobbing, for he felt low enough for tears. A sorry, sorry run of events. Everything at the lab going so well, then an uppercut like this one.

"You'll be a consultant to us, or at least to me," Thomas explained. "I don't mind saying you entirely flabbergast me."

"I flabbergast myself, sir. It is how I take joy of this life. It's been wizard being with you."

"I can't believe you've done what you've done."

"At your disposal, sir. Always, sir, we are side by side. Brothers to the end. Lately, I've run into bad synchronicity."

"Bad something, anyway. We'll have to figure out a way for staying in touch."

"I shall be found in Shanghai."

"I'd think you'd want to stay well clear of there."

"That is entirely correct of you, but I must go." Lin-pao nodded to himself. "I suspect the government in Beijing will soon know of my whereabouts. The British will want no problems with China over me, now that I have been globally positioned, as if I were wearing one of those ankle devices. I will go home and my mother will go to the officials and weep for three days. For a week, if she has tears enough. My mother is the champion weeper in all China. Then, when I arrive, I will be splattered with three weeks of questions, then a starvation diet, which I am in need of anyway. I eat like a white shark here, for which I thank you…then they will remand me to the worst, the filthiest, the most scurvy-ridden prison. I will wither and one day they will come to me and offer to make my life a paradise, if only I will toil for them. That is China. My destiny. Those are my stars. Crossed stars. If the Chinese ever contact you, please extol my value." He looked directly at Thomas, almost serenely so. "Most humbling, is it not?"

"Got to be a better answer. Got to be."

"Five-o, five-o."

"Is that code?"

"Fifty-fifty. I proceed halfway, they proceed halfway. An arrangement is struck. It is a very Chinese solution. They will get the better end of it, they always do."

"I wish I knew what else to do."

"I am in debt to you eternally. What honor you've given me. You are a king, sir. A king without a crown but that is the always better sort of king. You will please have someone look after my alpaca."

"Certainly."

"In a month, or close by, my black and pink orchid will bloom in Cambridge. They said it could never be done. Will you arrange someday to send me a petal?"

"Of course. And the wager you'll win, don't forget that. By the way, do the botanists at Cambridge know how you did it?"

"Half-way. They do not know about Zyme-One, only that I had used a secretive agent of change. Should we tell them?"

"One day, perhaps. If you exposed everything now, they'd insist on writing a paper for publication. In which case, they'd claim part of the credit. Would you want that?"

"I suppose not."

"And if you imparted your methods, they'd have to explain it in the paper. We're not ready for that, not yet."

"I see. You are always a leap ahead of me, sir."

"Hardly. I've been wondering, have you a father?"

"He is gone. My father was an acrobat. My mother still trains animals for the Chinese National Circus. A strange family. Circus people are odd. In my family we say some words backwards to confuse outsiders."

"That's interesting. Must be tricky. I guess I would say 'You love I' instead of 'I love you'. The meanings are reversed."

"You must study the technique."

"I'll miss you, Lin-pao. My God Almighty, if I won't miss you."

"I shall always be your brother in all things. No road too rocky, no path to steep." Thomas sat there abashed as Lin-pao volunteered, "Did I tell you one of the technical people at Scotland Yard called me the other morning? She wanted the name of the person in Singapore who dollied up one of my passports. The best one. Matchless quality."

"Maybe she'd like one herself."

"I asked her. She became viciously angry. I told her I might remember the forger if she could arrange to secure U.K. citizenship for me. Hissing at me like a Biblical serpent. A harridan, sir, outright, no other name for her."

Thomas laughed his only laugh of a long, long day. "You can't offer bribes to these people, you know."

"Everyone can be bribed," Lin-pao countered. "One must only detect the other's threshold of temptation. Judas sold out for thirty silver coins. He was very susceptible. A pushover. One does what one does, but bribes likely predate prostitution. Look at you, did you not succumb to a bribe of some sort to obtain our lab."

"Yes, I succumbed. A different kind of whoring, I suppose. Maybe there is no difference now that I think of it."

Finishing the meal, they departed. The moon shone fully on Lin-pao who stood stiffly, his roundish face crestfallen. Or was it from fright that he didn't care to openly display? The mouth drooped, the jaw gone slack, the cheeks set in. Not even a slight trace of the customary ebullience. The clearest sign of life was the shock of black spiked hair that rose straight up as if a power-charge sizzled in its follicles.

"May I hug you, sir? For being my most esteemed friend. No salty tears for us, eh?"

Thomas pulled the genius into his arms. They held for a long moment and then, standing back, he looked deep into Lin-pao's face. "I'll find you again. We'll reconnect somehow, when all this dies down."

"This was my happiest time ever. Thank you, supremely, Thomas. And *mazel*, that is my Yiddish for your best luck. You must report my respects and good wishes to the others."

For the first time, Lin-pao actually called him by name instead of *sir*. They were standing outside near the thinly lighted doorway and suddenly Lin-pao spun, sauntering away, fading into the night as he headed for his bicycle. Thomas saw the bike's lamp flare, and then, like a summer firefly, off it went as if borne away on an air current. He'd not see the likes of him again, so talismanic, so wondrously talented. Staring into the night till there was nothing more to see, knowing a part of himself had also ridden off with the vanishing man who had been like two right arms. Indeed, two of everything.

For a week afterward, Thomas dealt with a swath of queries over the missing Lin-Pao. Alexis wondered if he had deserted the team for Cambridge. Not so, Thomas informed her, though he sensed genuine despondency on her part, and the others who moped for several days. The *igniter* was gone and his inspiring-self had left an obvious gap in the team's dynamics.

Without elaborating, Thomas merely said that their much prized colleague had been summoned to China; there, to see to his mother. The sudden departure had left no time for Lin-Pao to relay his earnest and personal wishes for the team's luck and good fortune, always.

Having pledged Ponsoby to strict silence, he omitted revealing to the others the contents of the letters from the Home Office. Or give forth with Lin-pao's incredible subterfuges meant, at bottom, to save himself and, at the same time, see something of the world. Still, who would necessarily believe the reason behind his zig-zagging path of travels unless knowing he'd blown up a police station in retaliation for the torture and death of his own brother?

Several days lapsed before he gathered the team, giving them the news that the mastermind had departed on shortest notice. Telling them in a way he abhorred, and tried never to do, and mostly didn't: he shaved the truth, at least all of the truth. He conveyed that Lin-pao had left quietly, so as to avoid a fuss, but had left behind his heart-felt good wishes. Were Thomas to lay out the whole of the titillating, color-laden story to the other team members, someone was almost sure to make a slip one night at The Eight Bells, starting a flood of gossip; and the local paper—*The Chronicle*—might pick easily up on it.

The Isle of Anglesey was not small but the natives, a tight-knit bunch, had their ways of passing information as if they had private link-ups with one another.

He had come to agree with the old adage about the "fickle finger of fate", and was in no mood to tempt it. Muldaur-Courmaine had had its bucketful of adverse press, and the idea of a press account, which could be verified, that the lab had been harboring a fugitive, was more than he could stomach.

Washington, D.C.

Cassidy met again with Raab in the lobby bar of the Washington Hilton, a busy place but not so busy of they couldn't find a corner table allowing for some moderate seclusion. She had read an account in the *Mirror* about the killing of the young woman in Wales, refusing to mark it off as a coincidence. Someone had laid death at the doorstep of Muldaur-Courmaine, but who? Worried about the implications, she was up in arms and didn't mind saying so. Anyway she cut it; she was linked or could be linked. She had made her trip to Wales, seen Thomas Courmaine, had been near his lab if not actually in it.

If anyone ever nosed around diligently, they could most likely tie her to the media smear campaign.

Now a killing and now an exit. Hers.

"Don't tell me it's all one great big surprise, Murray." Leveling a beady look at him. "This one's got warts all over it. You'll never admit it, so I'll save you the trouble of lying. I quit. I never bargained for anything like this, buster."

"What's the matter with you? You can't up and quit."

"You're the matter with me, that's what. You and whoever is behind you. I'm out."

"I had nothing to do with that murder business. Nothing, I tell you."

Taking another long look at that unfortunate face, Cassidy said, "I'll give you the benefit of that doubt. But that's all. Someone, somewhere knows what happened and how. I don't want the slightest connection to any of it. So it's so-long Oolong."

"You've undertaken an agreement, remember."

"Past tense."

"You cannot terminate like this," he protested. "On your own." A feral look seized his face as he followed up with, "You stupid bitch, you have no idea at all who you're dealing with."

She was tempted to toss her Old Fashion cocktail at him, a parting shot, something to remember her by. "You make any crummy moves toward me, and remember that I was the one who set up my side of this blitzkrieg. I know who wrote what, everything that muddied up that poor bastard. All my writers used assumed names. You don't have that list, Mur, and you ain't gonna get it either…pay the check…and adios to you, you *furtzer*…that's Yiddish for fart-head. I guess you wouldn't have to be reminded, though."

Raab, gaping, hadn't the quick wit to reply; he'd taken an earful once from Alexis Hazlett, now it was Cassidy pouring wrath on him.

The book on murder never closes and almost fifteen years would pass before Mildred Ashcrane's cousin succeeded to a senior post in Scotland Yard's Special Branch (SO12); aware of the file concerning her unsolved death, dissatisfied that the leads were never followed assiduously, he reopened the case when spotting a brief article in the Liverpool *Echo* reporting that a British free-lance journalist had died, leaving behind a letter indicating his involvement in the cabal to trash Muldaur-Courmaine. The letter presumably written in remorse.

The cousin contacted the FBI in Washington, D.C., calling in a favor.

Cassidy, eventually tracked down, was interviewed by FBI agents. In the peculiar way human events can sometimes unfold, a vetting of The League's operations began, resulting in the convictions of, and heavy fines levied against, 23 Congressmen and women, 71 government bureaucrats (including Murray Raab), along with 91 Pharmus executives, some retired but other still holding down high-level posts. With mill of justice grinding fine, The League was effectively vaporized. As a sidebar, the man bearing the name Charles Tavester was never again seen, or heard of.

Let off with a year's probation for having cooperated with authorities, Cassidy received a stiff judicial warning over her involvement in the cabal intended to ruin Thomas Courmaine. She would never work in journalism again.

Paris, France
St. Curig Fields, Isle of Anglesey, Wales

T ough, mister, it's your turn—ricocheted off the corners of her mind, as
Jaggy listened to Thomas's excuses. "I can't make it to Paris," he claimed.
"We're in the middle of a real push here. Maybe the week after next. I'll let you
know...how about, say, this Thursday and I'll call you back. I'll be able to tell
more by then. I'm glad you're all right, Jaggy. A long time to be out of
touch...sorry for that..."

"Come for the day, or night. You can do that much, can't you?"

"No, I really can't. Where are you?"

"St. Gallen."

"Oh, I thought you said Paris."

"I did."

"I'm confused."

"You're confused about any number of things. I'm going to Paris for a few
days."

"I got it. Well, wait a week, can't you?"

"No. It's now. I'm preggers. You're a father or will be. So a Happy Father's
Day to you in advance. Now, godammit, will you come?" After a lapse, Jaggy
asked, "Are you there?"

"You said you're pregnant."

"I am, finally."

"You're sure."

"You think I wouldn't know?"

"All right, I'll be there tomorrow. No, the day after."

"See that you are."

And she hung up on him. Her hand fell to her soft-hard belly. Somewhere
in there, two fetuses nudged each other. Double jeopardy, perhaps, for herself,
given her weakening body. Yet on the brighter side, and indeed it was bright,

the twin conceptions—one normal, the other not—amounted to god-sent insurance.

Thomas Courmaine, she decided, was about to learn his lessons. He'd sell, she was sure. In the end, if the pickings were sufficiently fat, they always sold.

Paris, France

As commanded, he arrived at the Avenue Foch residence carrying an overnight valise, uncertain how long this pow-wow would last. He had found her in the second-floor salon. Huddled at one end of a long davenport, she was having coffee, and was just replacing a gold-figured Sèvres cup into its saucer as he neared her. Her body's shape was disguised by the way she sat and the flowing black and cream kaftan she wore. Her face, almost the color of egg shell, had lost its fullness. She looked up, rather sharply, as he greeted her. She got this way at times, cold as floe ice, making him speculate if she had a pulse.

"How's the passenger?" he inquired.

"Passenger?"

Thomas pointed at her midriff. "Oh, my baby, you mean," she said. "So far, exceedingly good. Are you glad?"

"I was surprised, naturally. Floored is more like it, thinking of what all this might be like. Motherhood sounds the way it should but fatherhood sounds like an overcoat." He grinned sheepishly. "Sorry, bad joke," not feeling especially light-hearted at this moment.

"This isn't going to be easy."

"Plenty to settle, I'll admit. Where do we start?"

"We're not getting married, if that's of any interest."

Thomas blinked. "How can we not?"

"Simple as it can be. I'm not marrying you and that is that." Her voice haughty, dismissive. "You'll be scot-free, I'll be buying your half out." The startling words issued as if they were a writ. "That's why I asked you to come to Paris, so we could reach an, uh, understanding. And I'm about to let you in on something. I'm carrying two babies and they are not twins."

"How's that again? Two? You say they're not twins, how can that be?"

"Modern science. Your specialty, I believe."

He sat, more puzzled than ever. "You mind explaining this?"

"I just have. I haven't been fucking anyone but you, so obviously you're to be the father of one. The other is an *in vitro*. Baster's progeny."

"*In vitro*? Your eggs, I assume."

"Yes, of course, *mine*. What a silly question. And Baster's sperm. Yours and Baster's, side by side. Something, isn't it?"

Technically possible, he knew, yet still difficult to imagine or accept. How had her doctors allowed this, given her health? "This isn't some oddball joke, I take it. I'd like to—we need to get serious. Really serious."

"I'm exceedingly serious, I assure you I am. Here and now, I'll offer you five-million Euros to give up any rights to the one you fathered. I'm buying you out, you see."

"You make this sound as if we're a couple of camel traders. Buy me out, what exactly do you mean by that?"

"You don't love me. You've not ever loved me. We've been what I suppose passes for lovers, but that's obviously quite a different kettle. So there it is. And we have to admit it to ourselves. I was your experiment in the stratosphere; you were my experiment in changing a priest into a husband. I see that won't work, either. You know I loved you. I told you a hundred times. I can't reshape my life to fit yours. I cannot begin to tell you the problems I'm dealing with, the sodding Africans and a hell of a lot else, I might add. On the telly, all that news over the killing at St. Curig. I signed my life away with the government, swearing you weren't trying to clone humans, or they'd be investigating you right now. All the nasty articles in the papers. The press dislikes you and they despise me. You're damaging me now. Muldaur has taken out a big loan and I've had to make adjustments on the board. They're complaining about Muldaur-Courmaine and the effect the publicity is having on Muldaur Ltd. They've just about given me an ultimatum and I do not particularly care for ultimatums."

"This is going to be a radioactive conversation, isn't it? I thought it was about a child. Let's slow up and—"

She was shaking her head. "Let's speed up. No tears and no cheers. I get the child or the children and you get off the hook. As I've just said, I'll arrange to give you five million in Euros, and I'd say that's a damn handsome settlement. I don't mind telling you that I've wanted a child for years. Ten years, anyway. So I thank you, sir, for your part in it. Oh, yes, another thing. You can have my share in Muldaur-Courmaine. That should do it. Merry Christmas, in advance. So, what do you say?"

"I don't say."

"Meaning?"

"I don't sell children, born or unborn, that's what I'm saying."

"Rubbish."

"You'll soon see."

"You're refusing me, are you?"

"What else? It's an absurd idea."

"You listen to me. I'm sick and tired of being very sick and tired of you all the time. Truly, you're a waste of human blood and bone. Look what else you've done, to Baster for one thing."

"Baster?"

My father...killing him, or getting him killed, which is the same thing." She stood now, after a small struggle, and was shifting from hip to hip, as if making up her mind in which direction to move now that she had the floor to herself. "You seem to excel at that, anyway, getting people killed. One royal cock-up after the next. Baster, killing him, and then that woman at St. Curig."

"Killed Baster! You're cracked, Jaggy. We're going backwards here. Whatever it is that's aching you about me, it can't be Baster. You're sounding as if you're on the verge of hysteria."

"If I do, it's because I'm feeling hysterical. About you, primarily." Squaring her jaw, she snapped, "He adored you, and look what you did to him. Look what you've done to me. Taken over a million pounds of our money, made me feel as if I'm a kitchen rag, so goddamn high and mighty, ruined my name in those foul news rags, and a murder. A murder at St. Curig. Is there anything else waiting for me? Tedious, it's so unutterably, exceedingly tedious. God, how I wanted you, waited for you, dreamt of you. I made you what you are in bed, and I'll give you that...yes...you were miraculous between my legs. Otherwise though, *otherwise*, you're the overriding millstone of this century. Any century. Exceeding all stupidity, how in the name of anything did I get myself into an excursion with you? Muldaur-Courmaine! Who in hell's sweet name do you think you are?" She stopped, out of breath, yet she was only warming up. "Are you ready to accept my offer?"

"No."

"You'll regret it."

"I've regretted many things. What's one more?"

"Have it your way. I want that lab shut. I'm sacking the lot of you. You're to shut it today, and not another shilling either."

Expecting this to happen at some point; still, he recoiled in a jerking motion as if a finger was about to stab his eye. Reminding her, then. "We've a lease on the manor house, don't forget."

"Stay then, but you are to close that operation down."

"We can't. We've employment contracts."

"Pay them off, get rid of them. You, first."

"You'd do that? Close us up?"

"You may consider it done. You're toxic...you are..." Hollering at him, almost, through the razory air.

"If you'll recall, I tried to talk you out of investing at least twice. Maybe you were on one of your opium journeys and forgot."

"Piss off. Just piss off, mister."

"And you calm down. What is it you really want from me? Shall we marry, have a respectable interval, then break it off? I guess some people do it that way. But I'll want time with the child as it grows up. My child, at least, or even both of them now that I think of it."

"I don't want you as my husband. I'm dying. Have you forgotten everything?"

"It's all about The Trust, Jaggy, isn't it? You've been parading as a Muldaur when you are no such thing except by dint of a borrowed name. You've been mongering your way through Africa and got into a jam because you don't know how to compromise, see other viewpoints, appreciate the feelings of others. Even if they are the feelings of the blacks. Especially the blacks. Your Africa and I dare say Baster's Africa is a closed book or will be before long. Why do you care an ounce about The Trust? Let it go...forget about it." Suddenly he stopped, not intending to bring up her anticipated demise again. "Let's try to be friends, let's try—try to reason this thing—"

"Get stuffed, why don't you? That's my reasoning."

He'd been sent for to witness his own execution for past wrongs, real or otherwise. No, he didn't want to marry her but he was aware of the right thing to do and the idea of his child born out of wedlock was unacceptable. Having been born a bastard himself, he refused to sire one.

"Your way or no way at all?" he said. "Five-million. The going market-price when you want to get rid of a man. Husbands or not."

"Damn fucking right it is, chappie," she half-shouted, with another choice selection from the dockworker side of her vocabulary.

"You haven't answered my question. What's supposed to happen when people ask about who the father is?"

Two islands of silence. No words. Just looks, stares, the grimaces of lovers who had lost whatever they once had, if indeed they ever had anything at all to remember or cherish. He should leave. Let her cool off, and cool himself down as well. Yet he wasn't finished and it occurred to him he might never see her again. Her insulting claims gradually drained him of pity for her plight, yet her words were inescapable, building hard anger in him.

"You ought to know that I'm the one supervising the asset distribution list of who gets what in South Africa from The Trust. St. Germain and Claude-Paul Lavalier must vote on it, of course, but I'd bet they'll go along with me. So, I hope your reproductive efforts aren't altogether in vain."

"You give that Trust away and I'll sue...I will... Pierre never mentioned anything like that to me."

"Pierre is not supposed to mention anything at all and neither am I, but I just did."

"It's true, you've started giving it away?"

"In the process of. Too slowly, I see."

"How can that be done? I'm having a genuine Muldaur heir."

"Can you prove it?"

"They won't risk DNA tests on the fetuses, not in my condition."

"So, you don't know? Positively know?"

"I know how to call my solicitors, if I'm forced to."

"And what? Start a lawsuit? This whole mess splashed all over the media. What'll your directors say then?"

"But I'll be dead and gone, won't I?"

"I hope not."

"Why do you think I went through all this? The Swiss doctors, and there was one American too, and they inserted Baster's sperm into my eggs. They can attest to it."

"How can they prove it was Baster's?"

With a triumphant smile, she returned, "The sperm can be matched with his DNA that's kept at Cyro." She reminded him, then, that Baster's remains had been spirited off to Cyro shortly after the funeral in Johannesburg. The casket in his crypt contained only an empty sealed urn and a poem of remembrance written by her.

"You did that? You honestly did something like that?"

"Most certainly I did."

"Didn't miss a trick, I see. Wait'll the newspapers get a load of that minuet. Wait'll the waiting world finds out you had at least one child by your own stepfather, who most seem to think is your real father. That'll be some great favor to a kid who has to live with that label for the rest of its life. I don't know how you can do it, Jaggy. Honestly, I don't."

"Go. Just push off. You're boring me. You're nothing but bloody scut, that's you."

"Oh, I'll go. We should've left each other before we ever began with each other." He stopped, gazing into space, a frown on his face."

"What's bothering you now?" Jaggy asked. "Having second d thoughts?"

"I've got a sort of swirling commotion in my head. I've had this happen before and it tells me something is about to happen. I wonder this time if it's a warning from Baster, telling me of his disappointment that you went right ahead and defied his wishes. Having his child the way you've done it. He'd be disgusted. I recall only too well, and so do you, when he outright refused to have you act as a surrogate mother to the heir he was planning before the accident. He knew, didn't he? He knew you'd try anything you could think of to get control of The Trust. And you think you will now, but you may be as certain as anything you've ever been certain of that you won't come within a thousand miles of it. You really are at the end of the scale, Jaggy...hopeless, I guess...venal for sure... "

Several strides later, he was in the hallway, headed for the stairs. Passing the dining room entry doors, he saw the painting again—the one she'd bought in Berlin—recalling the price she'd paid, using a Braunsweig debit card; a sum that would keep the lab funded for a couple of years at least. One painting!

Turmoil jumbled his thoughts. Something or other was trying to surface. An idea? A plan? Whatever it was, he hoped it would stay in its cocoon a while longer. He had nothing to write with, and when these surges of spinning thoughts arrived, they always arrived in a torrent.

Walking through street after and street of Paris's 16th arrondissement, he passed parks, crossed avenues, went by innumerable alleys and shadowy passageways. Hardly noticing anything at all. Not even the Arc de Triomphe when he footed through its towering archway. The meandering journey had tired his legs. Checking into Hotel George Cinq, a five-star property charging more than he cared to pay, he nonetheless arranged for the concierge to send a bellman to Jaggy's residence for his bag; a handsome pigskin valise she had bought him at Asprey's for his last birthday.

Up in his room, he napped long enough for deep gray twilight to settle across the city. Rousing himself, he showered and was buttoning on a clean shirt, headed downstairs for a quick dinner when his hands suddenly quit on him. Visions flung themselves into chaos. In milliseconds, he knew he was on to an answer for reproducing *semba* infinitely. The idea sank deeper and deeper in him. Pacing the length of the bedroom, he felt levitated, felt that he was riding off somewhere on an airborne balloon. He could not see the smile on his face but inside he had become very warm.

Stupid-faced, he sat on the edge of the bed, as revelations bounded through him. Corn, it was corn…no, maize. That was it—*maize*—how simple. How ridiculously simple. Africa grew untold expanses of the crop and the genes in maize could be modified and tricked into making *semba* by the unlimited tons.

His waking dream unwound itself, spawning a rush of ideas after more ideas. Writing and writing and writing at a small desk the night through, till a faint bar of dawn's light stole silently across the carpet. He looked over to the window, rubbing his grainy red-rimmed eyes, then looked down at the floor littered with small hills of paper. Sifting through them, he spotted various doodlings he couldn't recall the meaning of—squiggly words, math formulae, odd sketches, notes and more notes full of hastily jotted reminders.

But on that dawn of that day, arcane paper scraps be damned, he knew an immense design had been bestowed in him. A vast irony considering what had befallen him the day earlier at Avenue Foch.

London, England
New York, New York

At Heathrow, in a phone booth, he talked hurriedly to Shandar who was saying, "…Then my congratulations to you, Thomas."

"It ought to feel sublime but it doesn't. I'm telling you so you didn't hear it roundabout from Poppi Nestor. The other page of news is that Jaggy and I are in the past. She's run me off her reservation."

"How can you be in the past, when you're having a child?"

"She wants me to give up my rights to any child. Five million pounds, no less, plus her share of the lab."

"Seriously—you—you'd not do that, you wouldn't?"

"I wouldn't, you're right. Maybe it'll turn out that I should. I can't say that either child she's carrying is mine. Maybe but maybe not."

"Either? She has two?"

"Apparently. I'll explain some other time. But she's cutting off the funding for the lab. Wants it shut down tight, so St. Curig is also a piece of history now or soon will be. Facing the team, that'll be a joy to behold. I don't know if I'm up to it."

"Oh, dear…oh, Thomas, I'm so sorry."

"Among much else, there goes the Haut-Teknik foray. Please let them know, or tell me how to do it in the right way."

"I'll handle it. What do you do now?"

"I want to see you as soon as I get things squared up at St. Curig."

"Your lab, I'm so very sorry for you."

"It's disappointing but at least I can salvage our work. She doesn't care about the intellectual rights, but I do."

"You won't even have your colleagues."

"No, I won't and I'll be sorry to see them go. But I'm much further along than I was a year ago, and it's a safer bet. Much safer. When can I see you?"

"Thomas, you need time and much else. I cannot be—"

"There's no *cannot* with us. She wants to do battle, but what I want is a large jar of you. Don't say no, don't ever say no to us or you'll jam our radar…they're announcing my flight to Wales and I've got to run. Keep a closed mind, closed to everyone but us… love you, Shandar, with greatest love…"

Cambridge, England

After the clash with Jaggy in Paris, then the faint re-connect with Shandar from Heathrow, the shut-down at St. Curig, the revelations of the night-long séance with himself at the George Cinq, he realized that what had once been—for not much more than a year—had gone, never to be recovered. He was on his own again, as he had been for most of his life. He had come to Cambridge with reams of papers, logs, other materials, and by dint of old friendships had wangled temporary quarters at the university's Department of Plant Sciences on Downing Street. There, he resumed Lin-pao's impressive studies of *semba* done in this same building; here, he also roughed out computer models to sum up a series of genetic tricks and plant grafts that would make the common maize grow *semba's* key attributes, eventually to be converted into Zyme-One, just as if it had been the genuine *semba* root instead of what it was—ordinary maize, duped.

No botanist himself, still, Thomas caught on well enough. Biology and botany were both limbs on the larger tree of the life sciences. Therefore, many similarities in genetics, cell structures, aspects of biochemistry and more. He dissected the root-plant *semba* more than twenty times, testing methods for switching on-and-off its genes, and then doing the same for similar genes in common maize, learning as he went along. When puzzled, he was given full access to the department's experts. Cheerfully, they pulled him through his wickets of ignorance.

From that regrettable day in Paris to this one, he held to a steady diet of work, and more work, taking meals on the fly, sleeping at odd times in between his investigation. He had never drawn a salary from Muldaur-Courmaine, relying then, as now, on his trustee fees. His needs were modest, living, as he did, in a one-bedroom flat with a sitting room, a small den and a kitchenette. Weekly, sometimes twice in the same week, he called Shandar, catching up with her, conversing for a half hour or so. It came as no surprise to either of them the mud-slinging articles aimed at Muldaur-Courmaine had halted, after the public announcement the lab was shuttering its doors.

A punishing experience when disbanding the team, and bidding goodbye to a tear-soaked Ponsoby.

When wrapping up at St. Curig Fields, he had agreed to cancel the lease on the manor house months before the lease expired, if, in exchange, Jaggy surrendered all rights to Muldaur-Courmaine's intellectual property; in short, everything learned of *semba*—its entirety.

Out of her hair now, and she out of his. So far.

The newer dream, if it could be called one, was miles and miles of African-grown maize fooled into becoming the mother-feedstock for Zyme-One. Which, in turn, would provide hundreds of African villages with the equivalent of their own field-grown pharmacies. No need for elaborately trained western-type doctors. Any decently schooled geneticist could oversee twenty or so natives who, in turn, could be taught technicalities of gene enhancement in low cost hut-schools. They'd be like Ghibwa, only far more advanced in treating ailments and disabilities.

Maybe, Thomas thought at times, that's all Zyme-One would ever be: a more sophisticated bush-cure.

Out of Africa had come the curing ingredients; now back to Africa they would go and in a way never possible till now, never ever imagined till now.

As he began to remake his life, figure its direction, he was never distant from reflecting on those two fetuses, that, in some bizarre way, had supposedly reunited him with Baster. His fetus, allegedly, and Baster's fetus—side by side.

Still, the floating question remained: would either fetus make it, and what of Jaggy—could she possibly withstand the rigors of a double birth? Nor could he help thinking that he would be, or could be, a father. That moreover, he'd be waging a constant fight to assert his rights. Or would he? Suppose, he mused, he was not one of the fathers. If not, other than Baster, then who was?

On he went with the work of the moment, and on he went with his thoughts about Shandar. When thinking of her, intense loneliness set in. Wanting her, needing her, sometimes feeling he'd actually expire without her back in his life.

Shortly after waking one morning and downing two cups of black tea, he notified the Department of Plant Sciences he'd be traveling for the next week or so.

Impelled, he went to her.

New York, New York

At the Westbury, he engaged a small two-room suite, phoned Shandar's office only to learn she was absent from the city. Nothing for it now but to wait and hope she'd get in touch. Though tempted to make himself known to the Nestors, he hadn't any idea of what Shandar may have told them about the impending birth of a child, or children. He didn't care to be quizzed too closely; not at all, in fact, so he left well-enough alone.

On the third day, he heard. She was back, but in a meeting—this, relayed by her secretary—and that Miss Bazak would be delighted to meet him at five-thirty in the Polo Bar at the Westbury. Always a scene worth watching, in she came, looking around, seeing him, and traveling toward him as if moving on an air cushion. He stood as she approached, filled by the sight of her.

"Hi...hullo, hullo" she offered.

"Hi yourself."

"Quite a surprise. You look happy and healthy. You always look so healthy. You must eat quarts of soybeans."

"Seafood, I've been gorging myself for two straight days. Here, have a seat. I've been people-watching for half an hour. Now, I can watch you."

They faced each other across a small table on the window side of the lounge, looking over Madison Avenue. Gripped by joy, seeing her up close, as close as he'd been to her since the kiss on the beach in Wales.

"Like a drink?"

"What's that you're having?"

"A Tusker. I've never seen it outside of Africa before."

"Ah, Africa. Bringing back golden memories? I'd like one of your favorites, a Pellegrino with a slice of lime." He flagged a waiter, ordered, then heard her say, "What's the news?" she asked. "The blessed event must be approaching."

"I'm not in the loop anymore so it's all guesswork for me. Poppi probably knows more than I do."

"She says not. She says she hasn't talked with Jaggy in weeks."

"Incommunicado, all around. I suppose that's Jaggy's preference these days. Maybe it's better, for all I know. She's dying, you know. Or maybe you don't know."

"Dying? You're sure of that? *Dying*!"

"That's what she told me. I'm surprised she hasn't told Poppi Nestor. Yes, she's on her way down, it's from sickle cell anemia and probably a dozen other complications. She's devious but I don't think even she would say a thing like that, that she's terminally ill when it isn't so. She looks ravaged, besides."

"The, um, the child…is in danger?"

"I'd suppose so. It's two children, it seems. Flabbergasting, really. Complicated as the dickens"—and gave her the rundown as it had been relayed to him in Paris. No DNA test as yet, so nothing was certain. Still, Jaggy alleged he had fathered one, the other apparently by Baster Muldaur, an *in vitro*," he said, finishing his brief dissertation.

"I think it's wonderful for you. In some ways, it is."

"I'm trying to get used to the idea and I'm not being very successful, I'm afraid. The estranged father…or father-to-be. She wants to stage a fight over it and that's another story altogether. You're free for dinner, I hope? Say yes."

"I am, yes. I think we'd better skip '21' this time."

"How about if we go up and watch the Yankees mix it up with Boston? Afterward, there's a place I heard about, it's Italian, and we can grab a late dinner. If I can remember the name, I'll call and get us a table."

"Is it Brefano's? That's Italian and in the Bronx. Lots of people I know go there."

"Exactly. That's the name that I couldn't think of. Would you like to go?"

"Love to."

Chatting amiably for a time, they finished their drinks, and outside caught a cab for the Bronx. Luck favored him and he got two box seats on the third-base line, paying skyscraper prices to a ticket-hawker who was scalping the latecomers. He cared not at all. Afloat, gloriously alive. Twice during the early innings, he held her hand; twice, no resistance. At the bottom of the seventh, with Boston slamming the Yankees 11-2, they left early to beat the crowd.

Back in Manhattan after dining at Brefano's, their taxi pulled curbside in front of her building. Thomas slid along the seat behind Shandar, intending to walk her to the front door.

"Coming up, I hope? It's late, getting later."

"Well, I—"

"No arguments."

Hours later, lying next to her, he chose to believe a turn of life had happened, mysteriously carved out of their up-and-down past. Released, joined, crazed, tilted—wrapped in so many bottomless emotions. Tempted to awaken her from her slow, even breathing to make sure he was not dreaming himself. Afraid, too, if he went to sleep again he'd never recover this soaring moment. He had known infatuation with her, but now it had ascended to something more, a rapture entirely fresh to his senses.

Next day, a Friday, Shandar skipped the office and on the following day they left her apartment only once, making a short walk to buy food at Gristedes, a grocery chain that seemed to populate every neighborhood in Manhattan. High fun, laughter, the confection of their mutual turn-on, a waltz of sex but always the creeping realization of an inevitable parting.

Sitting in the kitchen, talking idly, she scrambled eggs while he operated the toaster, keeping a sharp eye so he didn't burn the pita bread.

"You have to go back to England, when?" she asked

"Soon. I've got some experiments underway," and he gave her the gist of what was happening, recounting the night in Paris at the George Cinq when deluged by ideas piled on more ideas, salvaging one now that was undergoing tests at Cambridge.

"Sometimes these weird moments come to me," he said, "and no telling when they'll happen. Something just takes over and that's what happened the night of that day I had the big dust up with Jaggy. I was on my way down to dinner at the George Cinq and my gears started to spin." And he went on with the rest of it till she understood what he was up to in Cambridge: the maize project.

"Sounds big."

"I think it could be."

"I'll be cheering for you."

"I can use all of the sideline rooting I can get, thank you."

"I can tell you're excited."

"I am. But even if it proves out, it'll require pails of money to get something started. I get very tired of money. Raising money. The bane of most scientists, always passing the tin cup to the grant makers."

"Somehow it will happen."

"Aren't you worried about protecting your knowledge-base? Patenting it?"

"Not as much as I once was. The lawyers in London tell me that if there is such a thing as prior knowledge about a something, then no can come along and patent your idea. We've got prior knowledge by the oceanful by now. So, I think we're okay…oh, I've been meaning to tell you something done with Zyme-One by Lin-pao. At Cambridge, he pulled off some sort of botanical miracle by growing two new types of orchids without any plant-grafting process. One type was a black and pink orchid, the other was completely black but with glistening blossoms, as if they'd been painted. I saw them, but it didn't really click with me. The botanists there, however, are scratching their heads. Sort of a stunt, I suppose, but another feather for Zyme-One."

"Wonders that never cease. I'd like to see an orchid like that."

"Come with me and I'll show you."

"I can't, I'm in the middle of something at the office. Speaking of wonders, I'm still wondering about something else," Shandar said, serving up the eggs. "Why is that woman having two children, and one of them by her stepfather? It seems so gruesomely odd, if you ask me."

"It is odd but not unheard of. It's known as superfecundity. Dual paternity when a woman is carrying two fetuses that aren't twins. Two different fathers. In her case it's an outright attempt to upset a huge applecart. A financial juggernaut few people know anything about."

"Like what?"

"I have to be awfully careful in whatever I say, even to you."

Yet he opened up, telling her what he could while trying to stay straight with his confidentiality agreement. "It's a huge, huge agglomeration of assets, accumulating for over four centuries," he said toward the end of his explanation. "Two or three times the size of Gates foundation in Seattle. And Jaggy Muldaur, who isn't entitled to a dime of it, nevertheless wants it all. So, that's why she's done what she's done. She'll be lucky to pull it off in her condition."

"I thought she was very rich in her own right."

"She is. Deep, deep pockets. She's taken some punches in Africa, but she owns bundles of real estate in Europe and Asia. Here in New York, she owns more of it."

"Then she's greedy, I guess?"

"Obsessed. She was in love with her stepfather, and still is. An Electra complex, I guess you call it. She strives to equal his feats but cannot and never will. It drives her almost to destruction. Yet she has a good many qualities and has done a lot of good for others at times. She saved my bacon more than once."

"In that case, we'll forgive her."

"I may not be so generous. If she makes a ruckus over The Trust, then we'll all find ourselves in the newspapers again. I've had enough bad ink for ten lifetimes, and recently I'm worried about something else. Have I ever told you about Pierre St. Germain? He's Swiss."

"Not that I recall, you haven't. Saint-whoosie?"

"Pierre St. Germain," he repeated. "He's a very high-end banker in Europe, a senior partner in Braunsweig und Sohn—"

"I've heard of them, certainly."

"Pierre's one of the trustees of The Muldaur Trust and we see each other four times a year and talk by phone at other times. Usually, I stay at his home when I'm in Geneva. We discuss biotechnology quite a lot, and what I think of this, that, and the other thing. Funny, though, because when I was in Geneva a few weeks ago he didn't invite me to stay with him. He always does but not this last time…and he was…I suppose you could say stand-offish. Very unlike him."

"Maybe he was ill."

"He attended our meeting and seemed fine. I had to make a report on the proposed disposition of trust assets, and he seemed resistant to everything I said but would never say why. Probably nothing to it, but I get a feeling something strange is going on."

"Behind your back, something on that order?"

Thomas nodded. Mopping up the last of his eggs with a slice of the pita toast, he said, "You're a good chef. Delicious, these eggs."

"Grazie. So what do you do about your Swiss friend? Or does it matter?"

"Pretty soon it'll matter plenty. We're running out of time and there's a vaguely named beneficiary to all those billions, and they don't even know it as yet. The money is supposed to go to the citizens of South Africa, but the government there has a say-so in who gets what. That makes for other problems. Big problems."

"Can't you resign? Why not do that?"

"I suppose I could but I wouldn't. Baster Muldaur asked me to stand in, and I'd feel like a louse if I didn't see it through. Besides, I have to live on my trustee fees."

"Oh, in that case, it's much better you stay put." As she started to gather the dishes, she stopped, placing a hand atop one of his. "We've been living together the past couple of days and I relish the thought of a few more. I want you to…well, you see"—a pause and her stoic eyes were operating on him, while he inhaled the fumes of that alluring Baghdad scent she wore. "I've something you ought to know. It's about me. Poppi knows. Si doesn't know. A psycho-therapist in Copenhagen knows, and so does a psychiatrist in Sydney. I'd like you to know, too." A dreaded moment dancing through her as she started in, "When I was there in Australia," saying it slowly, reluctantly, "um, I'm not sure precisely where to begin exactly but I'm afraid not to begin or I might never say it."

"Some sort of difficulty you're in? What is it?"

"You're not going to be upset, or I hope not."

"I wish you'd come out and tell me or I probably will be upset."

"I'm trying. You see I was in therapy some years ago, that was before I came to America. I had a bad experience, really horrifying, and it left me with a serious wound psychologically. You're not going to like this..."

"You mean losing your husband and child?"

"Partly." She nodded. "Partly that and partly something else that happened."

Her eyes darted. Her voice became jerky, then, moments later, it rattled as swiftly as a teletype machine. She related her suffering at the hands of Hezbollah terrorists as she had mindlessly wandered the Syrian-Lebanon border after the bomb blast shredded her husband and daughter. Weeks of terror, misery, treachery, rape. Listening, as intently as ever he had in life, Thomas's face went slack with a mix of fright, sympathetic pain and outright admiration.

"An intense stress disorder got into me," said Shandar, "and I never accepted it, never got away from a state of denial. High angst, unable to cope with men...sometimes unable to cope with myself. Sometimes I met men I liked, men who had made a play, but I rebuffed them. I was fooling both of us that night at "21" when I all but invited you to bed. I'd've flunked. Well, this woman I met in Sydney, a psychiatrist, I saw her every week for five months. She helped pull me out of my tailspin. It's hard to tell you all this. I only hope you understand if you can."

"I wish you'd told me this before," said Thomas. "You should've, you know. You really should have. I cannot tell you how sorry I feel. A terrible, terrible thing."

"Not an easy thing to admit to, let alone discuss. I'm a little surprised I can tell you even now."

"I'm glad you did. Is there more? Tell me, if there is, Shandar."

"Not really. Not unless you want to know what the sessions were like."

"We can skip that, I think. God, darling."

"I know. But it's under control now. I don't have those nightmares anymore."

"If you do, I'll be with you."

"Not always. I thought about telling you when I came to Wales, but I thought it hardly the place or time to shovel up that part of my past. You, well, you were joined at the hips with you-know-whom. Anyway, in Wales we were working on the future, weren't we?"

"Except we weren't working on the other future that matters. That's what we're doing now. Our future. It's the absolutely happiest time ever for me."

"I'm glad it is, so very glad. I love you and will always love you. Now you know my secret side and I hope it'll…I hope everything will always be all right between us."

"I'm going to make sure it is, that it always is. Soon I'll be thirty-eight and you're the only woman I've ever loved. For me it's a large feeling and one I don't ever want to lose."

"And I won't let you lose it. You are my very darling, darling…give me your hands." He did and she said, "Now give me the rest of you."

They left the breakfast table and made love hourlessly. Bliss. He began to grasp the happiness of truly loving someone, and of being loved by her. She was all he wanted; to him, right then, she was what all of earth could offer.

And upon leaving her three days later, they made a pact for a rendezvous as soon as they could manage a breakaway. When he proposed the idea of marriage, she reminded him they needed more time, and it wouldn't be such a bad idea to find out if he truly was about to enter fatherhood, and what it might portend.

Father or not, he was dizzily airborne now that he was emotionally locked with Shandar. He had known men he was immensely fond of, men who had drawn deep feelings from him. But never a woman, not like this, and certainly none like her.

Cambridge, England

He had walked from the Cavendish Laboratory—his other workplace —to Downing, the site of the Plant Sciences Department, there to meet with a group of botanists. Five strong, they sat in a loose semi-circle before a long blackboard, collectively figuring out formulae for estimating how quickly a thousand hectares of scattered African lands could be planted with a newly fangled red-colored maize that housed segments of *semba*'s genes; genes ascertained to be the maker of Zyme-One's active ingredients.

They talked of quantities sufficient to make- barrels of Zyme-One. Indeed, it was the contriving of their hybrid plant—maize plus *semba*—into millions and millions of individual biofactories, eventually able to throw off huge amounts of the tricked-up feedstock that could then be converted into Zyme-One.

Africa was slated to be the proving ground.

Excitement buzzed. Quietly, Thomas basked under the sunny thought of having Cambridge as a partner, and it was just about then when a sharp rap on the door interrupted all the cross-talk. A curly-headed woman poked her face through the doorway. One slender hand fluttered, poising tentatively in mid-air, but then the hand motioned vigorously to Thomas.

Excusing himself, in the hall he was informed an urgent call awaited him. "From Switzerland," said the woman. "Some doctor or other is what I heard him say."

At the phone in a nearby office, "H'lo, this is Courmaine speaking."

"You are the Doktor Cur-maine, *ist so*."

"Yes, this is I. And who are you, may I ask?"

"Feurenreuth, I am Feurenreuth," said the booming voice. "At Klinik Tönbrin-Foy."

"Klinik, say again."

"Tonbrin-Foy, of St. Gallen in Switzerland."

About Jaggy, Thomas thought. "What may I do for you?"

"*Ist* what I be doing for you."

"All right, and what is it you'll be doing for me?"

Feurenreuth stumbled along in broken English. Frau Muldaur, Thomas was told, hovered on the brink, was deathly ill. A sonogram taken only two days earlier indicated that one of the two fetuses she carried had no heartbeat. The prospects for the other were dicey at best. A month yet to go before reaching full term. Decisions must be made promptly. Thomas's name had been listed as a person to be notified in an emergency or if Jaggy herself was incapacitated. She was comatose most of the time, according to Feurenreuth, who warned, "Vot we do ist somezing for you to make the decizhuns. *Verstehen Sie?*"

"Yes, I understand or I think I do. We can speak in German if you prefer. Let's do, because I've some questions and I'd like to be sure I'm understood."

"Bitte."

Thomas did not speak Schweizerdeutch, the Swiss version of the German language, but the two dialects were sufficiently close so he made himself understood. He barraged Feurenreuth, learning more about Jaggy's touch-and-go situation. More, that the paternity of the living fetus was still an unknown; and could be proved only upon being aborted or at birth. In any case, they had no record of Thomas's DNA for a match-up. Possibly, he was the father, possibly not. However, the klinik would not risk a procedure on Jaggy or the remaining fetus, attempting to find out.

"You must come."

"I'm on my way, Herr Doktor. Sometime tomorrow, I'll be there."

St. Gallen, Switzerland

A turreted chateau-like building of three stories, the lowest of them faced with stone and the upper two of white stucco; stained wood friezes with colorful depictions of alpine art, and the rows of shutters painted the patriotic red and white of Switzerland. A roof of gray tile slanted at five angles, impressively so, and, thought Thomas, must've taken considerable skill to lift and place the vast weight of the tile at those heights.

Quite a show, he thought, standing there, surveying the Klinik-Tonbrin-Foy and its surrounds.

Curious to see more, he walked along one side of the edifice, impressed at its size and how it fit so flawlessly in the hollowed out pine forest blanketed by a blue crystal sky. Out to his left, he saw three snow-tipped soaring peaks completing the calendar-art setting.

Two at a time, he went up the front steps, entered the lobby, announced himself to a rosy-cheeked woman buxom enough to pass as the proverbial dairy maid. An hour passed, then another, before he was summoned to Casper Feurenreuth's office.

The meeting—chilly, remote. Thomas's eyes less friendly than when he entered the building. He asked for a fresh rundown on Jaggy's status and to find out whatever he could about the klinik's rulebook. What he himself could do to assist, or not do.

Feurenreuth seemed aloof, resistant, keeping his cards face down. Jaggy, he considered as an untreatable case. Thomas had been summoned to St. Gallen to fulfill a legality and only because, putatively, he might be father to an unborn. Jaggy was unable to talk coherently, and, under the law, her word that he *was* the father, prevailed; indeed, it prevailed even if the remaining fetus was fathered by another who was deceased. Jaggy faced imminent death. Possibly two deaths were in store, the other being the child.

A hard nut, Thomas thought, refining his measure of Feurenreuth who stood tall as a door and with buffalo-sized shoulders, a frame ideally suited to that one-mile voice. His fingers seemed stiff, as if they'd been broken at one time and when talking he frequently chopped the air with the edge of his hand as though practicing karate.

Round and round they sparred, with Thomas made to feel like a nuisance, an interloper who asked too many questions about the course of treatment given Jaggy. At last, however, he agreed to provide a DNA sample for use in establishing paternity, if the fetus could be rescued.

He must know, even if it were a stillborn.

Not till mid-afternoon did he see Jaggy. Shocked, he stared at her liverish face, looking as if it had had been soaked in bluish milk. Her skin waxy, her body flaccid-looking. She had once been strong as most men. The magnificent breasts withered, sagging, and she looked thin as a Dachau refugee. Her belly swelled pitifully in a small dome the size of half a cantaloupe, hardly that of a woman eight months pregnant.

Too little, too late. Time was everything now.

He knelt by her. The closer he got to the shell of her ear, the more he thought she'd already been worked over by the embalmer. Accosted by hundreds of memories, he leaned nearer and whispered, trying to get a rise, speaking of Africa, of Wales and Paris and Berlin. Urging, cajoling, persuading—watching for any signal she heard him. Speaking to her as though she were a child, even humming a little—anything that came to mind—as he held that cool, green-veined hand.

She stirred, calling out for Baster. Listlessly, she moved her arm as if it had a weight chained to it.

Stirring again, her eyelids fluttering. A little tremor in her left hand, then a slight roll of one shoulder, followed by a barely audible gasp. Two quick breaths, her lips making quick sucking noises; he squeezed her hand, feeling a weak response in her damp fingers.

Sounds at the door, feet shuffling, then the parade-ground voice of Feurenreuth. Two nurses stepped in, then Feurenreuth's deputy chief-of-medicine, Artois Lohmann, coming straight at Thomas, waving him aside.

Thomas had been making up his mind ever since seeing Jaggy, instinctively knowing what must be done; indeed, the only thing to be done.

Speaking German, he said to Feurenreuth, "We need to talk privately."

"As to what?"

"I can save her."

"You are being foolish."

"But I can."

"She is irretrievable."

"No, she isn't. I can do it, or I'd not have said so. Privately, please," said Thomas, looking at the others standing nearby. When Feurenreuth had sent them from the room, Thomas explained to Feurenreuth how it was worth an attempt to rescue her. He talked about past experiments, what they indicated, about the innate power of Zyme-One to heal if employed correctly.

Feurenreuth raised a paddle-sized hand, signaling for Thomas to stop. "It is impossible what you suggest. You cannot do this, you are not a medical doctor, you are not licensed in Switzerland…"

"We're talking about life, *Herr Doktor*. Life is not licenses. You are risking two lives by doing nothing."

"We've done everything for her. We can possibly save the child. It is your choice, as I said earlier. No one can save her…I have seen those newspaper articles about you. You are a troublemaker. An impostor."

"Better take a chair. This is going to take some talking. Close that door, if you will. "

Thomas unloaded then, explaining the options. Either to go along, give the alternative treatment a chance, or do nothing and preside over a woman's death. If no attempt was made to save Jaggy and what Jaggy carried, then a lawsuit was a dead-on promise. That he, Thomas, had the right to save what might be his own child; that the klinik was dealing with a famous woman, and her death, and the medical decisions, or lack of them, that abetted a death would create an avalanche of publicity. Its brunt would fall on the klinik, even on Feurenreuth himself. Serious money damages could result and he informed Feurenreuth the best criminal lawyers in Europe would be engaged to pursue a swift, hard remedy; Thomas thinking that if the remaining fetus was sired by Baster, then potentially billions of dollars might go astray if the child's life were wrongly forfeited.

"Make no mistake, Feurenreuth. I mean exactly what I say, all of it. If that child dies, you might be depriving it and depriving the mother of any chance to continue a lineage, and the child's rights to a very considerable inheritance. That's one possibility. That is why she wanted a child, why she's been trying to have one for years. There are medical witnesses in London, one of them a former husband, a doctor, who likely has all sorts of records about this. Not least of it is that I may be the father and, by God, if that child dies needlessly, I'll bend you from your toes to your ears."

"It is extortion, what you're saying."

"And what you're saying is damn foolishness. Let's start over, or half-way over. Presumably, you've got competent doctors who've attended her. I believe one came from America. Why, with all that, did you allow a double pregnancy in her condition?"

"We didn't know. A very strange thing. An *in vitro* had been done, and then"—shrugging—"yet another of her eggs was fertilized naturally."

"Why didn't you check and check again?"

"No one thought it remotely necessary."

"What do you think a lawyer would do with that remark?"

No answer from Feurenreuth, so Thomas answered for him, saying, Rip you to shreds, I'd imagine."

"You're playing at some sort of a cat-and-mouse game."

"I'm playing for keeps, that's what I'm playing for. I'm desperate, Feurenreuth. Think it over. You're getting your one chance to blame everything on me, if Frau Muldaur perishes. I'm going to spend some time here with her. Send me in a sandwich and coffee. If I can get her to talk, I'll convey the results to you. It's all going wrong so far, so don't be a damn fool. Let me be the fool, why not? You think I'm an imposter anyway, right? Another thing. I'll want a copy of the sale document when Frau Muldaur bought her interest in this place. Plus her medical records. All of them. And they had better show that she's carrying a stillborn."

"You have no right, none."

"Lawyers can always subpoena any of it."

"How do you know what she bought? It is a confidential matter."

"You mean it *was* confidential. Is that why you want her to die, so you can reclaim her interest without having to buy it back? Think it over. Think what a lawyer could also do with that information."

"A shameful bastard, that's you. They said so in the newspapers and I say so now." And Feurenreuth got up and lumbered out with his ponderous side-to-side walk, as if wearing moon boots.

Thomas waited by the bedside, a perspiring stretch of time. He lost track of the clock but a nurse came in to hook up another drip-bag of blood and then another one of glucose.

Later, as he ate a knockwurst in a hard roll, Jaggy suddenly opened her eyes. Eyes that seemed drug-dimmed, flattish. At least they were open. Her breathing had eased, and eagerly he asked, "Can you hear me?"

A wan smile, more like a lip-twitch. But he knew that mouth and knew she was smiling. Weakened, floppy as a rag doll, and he realized again he was going to have to do her fighting for her.

"You came," she mumbled, her voice soft as a five-year old's. "Poor old sodder. You—you don't"—gasping—"don't have to tell me I'm dy-i-ing."

"Jaggy...Jaggy, listen to me...this'll go faster if you let me talk. Fast is extremely important right now. They're talking about a Cesarean. That's the only way, the only chance to save the baby, they think. We have to decide. And it's—well, it's possible—you know, anything can happen, you've been terribly sick and there's the anesthesia problem, and—well, I'm terribly sorry to go through all this with you. They have laws when the mother is ill. What I'm saying is that if it's a choice between you and the child, I'm going to tell them it's you who is to be saved. I don't even know why they asked. You have to concur in this as long as you're able to. You, ah, sleep a lot, so we have to tell them soon. Just nod, if you understand me. It's us now—just you and me. We have to decide, if it comes to that, if it's you or the child."

Her head lifted. Jerking it to one side, as if motioning him closer, she repeated the movement, twice, until his ear was only inches away. Her mouth didn't work right, she drooled.

"Save-*uh* the children...the children..."

He hadn't the heart to tell her she had lost one, but his voice hardened. "How could The Trust be more important than your own life?"

"The children, damn you." A resolute command. "I'm so goddamned tired all the time...all the time."

Relapsing again, her head fell away

How to handle Feurenreuth? He didn't care to relay those words he'd just heard. Common sense insisted that he withdraw, let it alone, go away. Whatever was meant to happen would happen without him. Why did he owe her a thing? Paris, in his mind now. She had exploded his world, shutting the lab, accusing him of being responsible for Baster's death.

Yet what of those grim days at the Park Lane Clinic in Jo-burg, when he'd been busted up by the elephant and she'd stood by him all the way, then spirited him out of Africa when he'd had no other way to get out by himself? Got him away, too, from a police inquiry about the Eves, and away from the media's tentacles. He'd been the one in the corner that time; now she was, and while he couldn't fly her off to safety, conceivably he might haul her off the grave-path.

Still, were he to re-engineer her genome, replacing the faulty genes causing the deadly anemia, and then if she still didn't pull through, he'd be cooked. Hawked to the Swiss authorities, ending up as fish bait; and possibly held liable for killing one of the best known women in the world. And another possibly was that his own child, if it were so, would perish, thus doubling his jeopardy. Or tripling it, if the child belonged to Baster Muldaur, and was entitled to billions. The loss would be incalculable, and he would stand first in line when blame was passed out.

St. Gallen, Switzerland
Geneva, Switzerland

"Pierre, I arrived yesterday and I'm in a place they call St. Gallen. She's ...worse than I had imagined but at least she woke up once. I hate to trouble you, asking favors but I need help. You'd know if the Red Cross has facilities near here and if I can access them. Can you intercede for me, get me a lab I can use for a few days? I'd not be a bother to anyone, I promise you."

"What're you wishing to do?'

"Save her life, if I can."

A pause, then: "Substituting yourself for the doctors, you mean?"

"Substantially, yes."

"I think the Red Cross might be wary of getting involved in anything of that kind."

"I've not done anything, not yet."

"They'd want to know what you're up to and they'd resist, I'm sure of it."

"Oh, I see. You mean all my publicity that precedes me? That's twice I've heard that, a daily complaint it seems."

"I'm afraid so, Thomas. Yet I might have a workable thought for you. The army recently took delivery of a half dozen mobile medical treatment units. They're quite complete, at least I'm told so. Mercedes built them. They're goliaths. Huge tractor-trailer rigs. I'm told they have about everything in them. I wouldn't be a judge of that, however."

"What they probably won't have on board is a good electronic scope."

"Would MarocheChem have one?"

"Probably two-hundred of them, I'd suppose."

"I can arrange for one of those, I should think."

"Tremendous. I've got a shopping list if you feel generous and have a pencil handy...the scope I'd like is an Axioscop 2 FS or the equivalent. I also need a PxE Thermal Cycler...that one is for cloning DNA by the millions. See if they have a Stovall shaker, they call them belly dancers...and a hybridization oven would help...okay, I'll slow down, let me know when you're ready...okay, now, if you tell them I'm splicing genetic material, they'll know what else to send. And, I almost forgot, I need a vial of type 43AzGG lab viruses, no, I'll repeat...it's 4-3-A-z-double G...got that?"

"I've got it down, yes. Mind telling me what's really happening here? Or should I ask?"

Thomas held a one-man council with himself, then said, "Never say this till the news is out in the open, if it ever is." And he told St. Germain he intended to manipulate Jaggy's genetic system , hoping to bring her through, but the surviving fetus was anyone's guess; that, more, what he proposed to do was an illegal act, and, in any event, he could fail. He knew the science was solid, but he didn't know if Jaggy could stand the upheaval in her cells, however slight. When he changed her genome, trillions of her cells would be infused with new blood-making genes. "That's what's at stake," Thomas ended.

"You said illegal?"

"I'm not licensed here, or anywhere, to practice medicine. This procedure I'm talking about is not approved anywhere in the world. Yes, illegal."

"I see."

"The klinik will never save her, Pierre. Nor the way they're going about it. She'll die. She's almost there now."

"I'll talk with the army and find you your lab. Where shall I tell them to send it? The St. Gallen area, but where exactly?"

"I'll find a place and phone you back within the hour. I'll have to go looking."

"Anything else?"

"You're a good friend. Not everyone would do this. With all that's been said about me."

"Your reputation is intact with me."

"Thanks, that means something, so thanks."

"Are you sure you can manage this? I refer to Jaggy."

"I think I can or I wouldn't try it. But she's weak. The child is a month or so short of term I'm told. Probably underweight and under everything else, too."

"I'm at your disposal, so don't forget that, Thomas."

Hanging up, Thomas thanked all stars for Pierre. The last time he'd been with Pierre, the air had seemed brittle; now, affable again, standing up and ready to be counted. St. Germaine pushed hidden buttons and things always happened.

Driving up and down various streets, at last on the outskirts of St. Gallen he found a motor hotel, a place travelers would likely choose for a one-night stop. Solid-looking, unpretentious, functional. Driving to the rear of the property, he found what seemed a plausible site for a mobile-lab; the parking lot large, sufficient for a hundred cars or more.

Inside, he introduced himself to the manager, saying he was an American biologist on loan to the Swiss Army, stretching the truth right up to its breaking point. Beginning tomorrow, he would need at least two rooms for a week. Would there be any problem keeping a large trailer truck at the rear of the parking lot, temporarily?

None whatsoever.

Thomas paid in advance, and handed out the only business card he had; it was for Muldaur- Courmaine Laboratory, Ltd. Phoning Pierre's office, he gave details of the motor-hotel's whereabouts.

Just after the noon hour, two days later, he took a call from a Corporal Hannis Gerlaj, who said he was standing in the lobby of the Motor Hotel Möven, awaiting instructions.

Thomas found him within minutes. Gerlaj, a study himself. A great, tall, red-cheeked fellow from the Alpenzeiler mountains, his hair the color of fresh corn, as electrically straight as Lin-pao's. Thomas never saw him take a step less than four feet in length, as if he were climbing an escarpment. His field uniform looked as though he'd slept in it for the past month, hanging on him like a wrinkled sack. Likable, an extrovert, smiling much of the time with the smile revealing wide white teeth.

Out they went to inspect the laboratory on wheels. The size of the tractor awed him, fifty-four feet in length, nine feet wide, painted in camouflage on the exterior, with regimental unit markings on the side panels of the doors and tailgate. It slept three, had a kitchenette, a head, a curtained enclosure for taking a shower, and the rest was a superlative design in the efficient use of space. Impressive craftsmanship and smelling like a new car. Power could be bled off any available line or by firing up a self-contained generator if the cab's engine was turned off to conserve fuel.

"Remarkable," Thomas observed at least twice.

Gerlag asked, "How long will you be requiring me?"

"Several days, maybe four. Or five."

"I was told to stay with you as long as you needed me. I'm on special temporary duty orders."

"What is it you usually do? Your career?"

"Full-time Swiss Army. I drive and I am trained as a medical assistant. Would you mind terribly, if my girl comes to be with me?"

"Sure, bring her on."

"You won't say anything?"

"No."

"I'm a corporal. She's a lieutenant. Against regs, you see."

"Not against my regs. I've got two rooms reserved and paid for. You can take the larger one." Thomas's hand dove into a pocket. "Use this for whatever you need, and let me know if it's not enough." He handed the corporal five-hundred Euros.

Gerlaj thumbed the fold of bills, gave out with another of his roomy grins and said, "I'm liking this already. But you see I'm already on per diem allowances. I cannot accept this."

"You've got your girl to freight. Girls have a way of using up money. Take it. She'll need a corsage or something." Needing no further urging, Gerlaj pocketed the bills. "Let me have a key to this buggy of yours, corporal. Show me how the power works for that generator. Show me everything I need to know."

"I am afraid I can't let you drive it."

"I wouldn't dare try."

"You must be a good friend of the general's." Gerlaj remarked, as he slipped a hand into his pocket, perhaps to reassure himself the money was safely intact.

"Your general? I'll write him a note or is he a she, like your lieutenant? Who is your general, by the way?"

"Brigadier St. Germain. My orders came from his adjutant."

"Huh. I'd forgotten he's an army general. Well, a man like that, it figures. Yes, your general is a friend of mine. Today especially."

Within the hour, he familiarized himself with the innards of the motorized lab. He tinkered with and then adjusted the borrowed electronic scope, the latest model, easy to work with, equipped with a device for attaching a camera.

Later, back at the klinik, he saw a sleeping Jaggy. Sitting on the other side of the room was a nurse, her thick kegs extending from the chair's seat. A formidable-looking customer, her lower lip hung out like a small balcony, pugnaciously, making him think of a prison matron. As he approached Jaggy's bed, the nurse's face hardened with suspicion as she audibly sniffed.

She said nothing, however, as Thomas scraped a small skin sample from Jaggy's toe, intending to use the skin cells to collect her DNA. If only he could obtain cells from the fetus, but it was a useless thought. A hinge-moment had arrived, cutting a deal for someone's life, as he once had done for the Eves.

Now, for Feurenreuth.

"…You've been told and I'll tell you again…utterly, utterly out of the question!" Feurenreuth exploded. "Are you mad? Mad, I say—mad as a Mongolian. You're no doctor. I remind you of that situation for the second or third time."

"But I am a doctor. A different kind than you, to be sure, but a doctor nonetheless."

"It is not the same."

"No, it isn't the same. If it were the same, I'd be like you. Stumped. Unable or unwilling to do anything. Frozen in place while a woman is dying…I do my work with *material medical*. I can replace her faulty genes…I know how and you do not know how and thus cannot. So I'm going to try. I must. You, you're a blood-man, a hematologist. Me, I do genes and I'm good at it. I've changed humans in Africa, and mice and rats, hamsters, fruit flies, alpac-as…well, not the alpaca, but I can remedy Frau Muldaur, so let's get to it…"

Feurenreuth seemed ready to walk away. One shoulder moved, and then an arm moved and from somewhere came a handkerchief. He kneaded it between his hands, asking, "What is it you want from us?"

Thomas outlined his plan. He would do all the work himself, off-site, so that Klinik Tönbrin-St. Foy wouldn't be directly involved. He intended to re-engineer Jaggy's immune system and then wipe out the mutant genes that coded her for sickle cell anemia. That done, he would insert blood-making genes that would eventually make healthy blood. In short, he told Feurenreuth, a gene-therapy procedure. He'd be toiling around the clock, moving at his pace, not theirs. If all went well, then in a month or six weeks she should show signs of a recovery.

"She will never last."

"I disagree. Just don't get in the way, that's what I ask. It's all I ask."

"You are being ridiculous. I never heard of any such foolishness, these genes. This woman suffers from a massive sepsis. The child, too, is probably infected."

"I know but do you have a cure?"

"But—"

"But nothing, Doctor. You're on the verge of making a big mistake. Don't. I'm healthy enough. Your own people know how healthy. They've been all over my bones when I gave up my DNA the day I came here. I'm a pretty safe bet. Genetically, I mean, so I'll use my genes to repair hers."

"It's impossible, what you are asking. This is a reputable clinic."

"Get a lawyer to put the paperwork together. I'll take all the responsibility. I'll exonerate you. Better that you get cracking or I'll have her moved out of here. Were I you, I wouldn't risk her life unnecessarily."

Sensing he was getting nowhere, Thomas performed a fast calculation from memory, toting up his liabilities. He wished he hadn't been so generous to the Society, and then with Lin-pao. He was still guessing at his finances as he said, "Doctor, how would a half-million Euros worth of gold bullion sound? Untraceable gold. You Swiss know all about that, don't you? And if I fail, who's the wiser? You, me, and no one else. You've done all you can, now let me try. Meanwhile, take the gold and have some fun. A little vacation, you've earned it."

He said this last in a mollifying tone, soliciting the other man's sympathy, silently wagering the doctor would genuflect to the well-known Swiss reverence for money. Secretive money, especially gold with no identifying tags on it.

"One other thing," Thomas said. "Have the best obstetric surgeon in Europe standing by. We'll need him or her in about four days. Make it three. Be very sure that they can handle any emergency procedure. Add to that, the best pediatrician. Whoever they are, get them here if you please."

"Who is to pay for all this?"

"Put it on the bill. Pay whatever you must, just get them here."

"You will authorize, I assume?"

Thomas nodded. "I'll call you when I'm ready. The front desk at the clinic has my phone number, if you need me. Follow my instructions and you won't be sorry."

St. Gallen, Switzerland
Geneva, Switzerland

Nervously toothing his lip as he spoke, "...In gold bullion, Pierre, and with no serial numbers on it. Am I good for it?"

"Probably not but you'll have it anyway. Delivered to where?"

"Here. The motel."

"I suppose I shouldn't ask what this is for, should I?"

"If I told you, you'd for certain wish I hadn't."

"No offense meant, but do you really know what you're doing?"

"I'll only know that when it's over. A few days from now it'll be over for me. We won't know anything about Jaggy for several weeks. A month, at least, if she makes it that far."

"You've got me worried, I'll say that. The gold will be sent from our Zurich office. They'll be in touch with you."

"I'll be here. In the truck probably. I've never seen anything like this truck of yours."

"So far we've involved the army, the bank, and probably we've broken five laws we don't yet know about. This is Switzerland and there's a law for everything, even the length of the grass. Have I left anything out? Is there to be more, do you think?"

"No, I think not. Sorry for all the trouble."

"Good luck, then."

One or two bum genes had coded wrongly for an amino acid; that was what had fouled up Jaggy's blood, so the hemoglobin molecules couldn't do their job. Bent like a hook, instead of a roundish normal shape, the molecules ganged up in her arteries, stagnating the blood trying to flow through her vessels, starving her body of oxygen so vital to life.

Yesterday he had journeyed to Winterthur and withdrawn a small supply of *semba*. Milking it down by the usual reduction process, extracting a gob of Zyme-One.

Nerves drove him now. He didn't sleep, he catnapped, his chin slumping against his chest as he sat at a stainless steel bench in the van. Stiff from sitting, jittery from slugs of coffee, tired from over-concentrating, he nevertheless pushed on, fighting the clock. Even if he lucked in, even if he rescued Jaggy, Feurenreuth could always blow the whistle. Were he detained by the authorities, or worse, charged with a crime, it'd cancel out the holiday with Shandar, a thought dropping with its fullest weight to his belly.

He bent to the scope again. Intricate work, splicing and manipulating translucent strings of DNA. His DNA, Jaggy's too. Creating what had never before been naturally created, what was probably never ever meant to be created, and what was definitely missing from Nature's playbook of pre-approved gene combinations.

Gerlaj—disheveled, but happy-voiced and grinning lopsidedly—dropped in to offer his help, and perhaps taking a rest from his lady lieutenant.

The corporal had transformed himself into a *deus ex machina*, a tower of help at every turn. He knew every inch of the lab, excelled as assisting when needed. He had lugged in the metal receptacle, a cubic foot square that held the bullion from Braunsweig. The smallness of the container surprised Thomas, and so did its weight.

A half-million in gold; how to repay it?

After Gerlaj left to rejoin his lieutenant, Thomas returned to the scope his eyes tight to the cups, examining those DNA molecules again, teasing his own genes, the ones for making of blood, coating them with Zyme-One. He'd soon insert them into a harmless virus furnished by MarocheChem; the modified virus would transport the new genes—five-million strong—and, within hours, thrust them into almost every one of Jaggy's trillions of cells. Closely, the procedure resembled the steps taken in Bethesda to move Alexis Hazlett's skin genes into the mouse Peter.

Antibodies, once alerted to the invasion of his genes into Jaggy's genome, would strike furiously, massing themselves against the perceived attack to reject the swarms of foreign genes. If she lived, would she ever know how much she owed to Ghibwa?

At times, resting his eyes and looking around in the van, seeing the metal container holding the gold bullion sent from Braunsweig. He should've offered Feurenreuth half the amount, but no going back on the deal now.

So went that night; that night and the day. Exhausted, his hands trembling at times. Moments came when he was all thumbs, fumbling around, as if trying to thread a needle with a lariat. The inside of the van was a litter of tubes, gel sheets, glass pipettes, chrome trays, and a profane jumble of other paraphernalia—as if a free-for-all had taken place.

One little vial, then, containing a minestrone of genes, bound tight by Zyme-One; bound as tightly as the hydrogen and oxygen that make two gases into water. He gazed at it for what seemed everlasting moments. Had he done it right, hit all the gene markers.

His hand sought the phone.

Ringing and ringing again and again until a sleepy, grumpy voice answered. A maid or housekeeper—with a voice of a Pakistani—took the call, saying the doctor had not yet awakened, and Thomas lied, saying it was an urgent, instant, life-threatening emergency.

Minutes later, Feurenreuth announced himself, his voice impatient, churlish, as Thomas began to roll out his directives.

"…Ease off a moment," Thomas was saying. "Get a hold of yourself and listen very carefully. I'm too tired to repeat myself. Your treasure box is here, you can stop by and…no…you are to listen to me as I said, you are to come here…*here*…I don't operate a delivery service but we'll help you put it in your car. Be here inside the next two hours and you're to call before you arrive. Next, as I've already asked, you're to hand over a full copy of Jaggy Muldaur's medical records from the day she first came to you and add a signed letter that the records are exact and complete…and I still need the copy of her buy-in to the klinik…what?…yes, of course bring them with you…what?….you won't….well, you won't be getting your half-million…what's that?…all right, and there's to be no one, I repeat no one else with you. I'll be in Frau Muldaur's room between nine and midnight tonight, *alone*, no witnesses, not even at the reception desk, and you had better be well away from St. Gallen by then. Next, have you got that obstetric surgeon on standby….yes….yes…he better be the best of the best…all right…I said *all right*…a woman, that's fine…and be sure you do call before coming here…right you are… goodbye…yes, I said goodbye….

Gerlaj could handle the gold. He had the muscle mass of a gorilla, could probably lift the front end of a farm tractor. And then, from nowhere came the memory of his last night with Lin-pao at the Eight Bells, when the subjects of bribes had arisen, and his much missed colleague had so truly advised that anyone could be bribed; that, one need only detect the threshold of temptation.

He had detected Feurenreuth's—the price for getting him lost.

10: 12 p.m.

As Thomas had asked, her room was empty of others; only the two of them now. He was down to the fast heartbeats, a pressure-filled instant as he plunged the needle into Jaggy's inner thigh. Slowly, slowly, and after only seconds, he withdrew it, swabbing her with sterilized gauze. Oddly, he was thinking of plants, of Naruma, then of Shandar and finally of Lin-pao as if each of the images was bearing witness to his acts.

Before leaving her, he leaned over and placed a hand lightly on her belly. He didn't know what to expect, or even why he did it. He only knew he felt nothing there at all. Not a trace. Had the second fetus expired?

Quickly made, quickly born—a Saturday child who met the shock of his new world at 5:37 a.m. Weighing three pounds, four ounces, distributed along his fourteen inches.

Thomas watched every step of it; surprised he didn't faint at the sight of the surgeon doing her job inside five minutes. A nurse had wiped Jaggy's abdomen with an antiseptic solution, then, and quickly, a flash of surgical steel neatly splitting open Jaggy's pouched belly. A probing around, then, a pull and out popped a tiny human handful. Sudden as a lightning bolt.

A squaller, and he was thrashing his extremities as if stung by a bee, shortly to be whisked off to an incubator. Was he the father? The slippery, elusive fact would be known soon, when DNA comparisons were made and reviewed.

By mid-afternoon the facts of parenthood were established; he was the father. The DNA match-up had told its tale. He exalted, a son!—a fabulous, ridiculously lovable blob of a son. Not till the coming day did he learn their son's birth record bore the name of Christopher Magnus Piet Baster Muldaur. Incredible! Paris, revisited. Jaggy claiming an exclusive right to name the child, period. Nowhere in those five names could he find a bare clue of his own identity. To the hilt, start to finish, he was fully named as a Muldaur, albeit a bogus Muldaur.

Like Jaggy herself.

The news was neither good nor bad; mother and son were as before—struggling like a couple of fish trapped in a net, everything still uncertain. Feurenreuth avoided him. Nurses ignored him. The boy he saw twice from behind a glass partition. Jaggy, still comatose, he saw not at all.

Bored now that he had no more to do here. He didn't owe Jaggy an eternal watch and soon he'd be with Shandar. Still, he waited, he waited longer. Would the gene-repair kick in and do its job? Or would Zyme-One fail him?

Was there a single thing he could do for Christopher, a name he was gradually accepting? No, he told himself. The pediatrician had scraped skin cells from the boy's foot for gene screening, determining if the infant had inherited Jaggy's genes that coded for sickle cell anemia. Even so, nothing could be remedied at this stage. The task now was defined and it was singular—keep him breathing. Alive and breathing.

He called Shandar with what news he had, and, in the conversation, she gave him a date, a time, a flight number.

Two days later, he tidied up loose ends and arranged for an extravagant car rental after arriving in Nice. A Ferrari convertible, with a sky-blue exterior and red leather seats. He intended some higher living and knew exactly where and how he would do it.

Baie St. Jean, France

She wore a pale yellow bikini, only its bottom half, as she lay flattened out on a towel. Her knees were spread and raised slightly, as if she were ready to receive him. An urge then to kiss her, and more. Amazing to him, that, barely a year and a half earlier, he had nothing of real value to his name other than a reputation as a good genetics man. Now, he owed a half million Euros; had had unidentified antagonists nailing him in the newspapers, a newborn in Switzerland, no job to count on, no future of any consequence. Instead, here he was with his love dallying in a hugely expensive hideaway on the craggy coast of France just east of the Spanish border. Life is perfect, he thought.

Shandar broke into his reverie. "Are you off in the clouds somewhere?"

"I'm sorting through all the fun it'll be when we're married. I think I'll propose again. Different words this time, I'm working a more sublime Shakespearean approach. Tonight at dinner I'll do it or possibly tomorrow at breakfast. On my knees, naturally. What'll it be, the dinner or the breakfast show?"

"I choose both"

He faked a sigh. "You always win."

For a lengthy moment, in silence, he observed her. He had never known such desire for a woman and it welled deep in him now. "A shekel for your thoughts," he said.

"Save your pesos, lover boy. I'm empty-headed at the moment. Well, almost. I've been tossing an idea about since yesterday. Maybe we should have a little, um, sunshine chat?" She put aside her magazine, then rubbed a dab of lotion along her left leg.

"You bet. Just lie there on your sand-couch and tell old Doctor Thomas C. whatever comes to mind."

"I'd be arrested if I did that. I must also wash my hair, love. It's full of sand. Are you coming up?"

"I'll take another swim and then I'll be up."

"You haven't seen enough bare boobs for one day?"

"I forgot to bring my calipers with me and what's the fun of just looking? Besides, as long as I see yours, I've seen enough for any day on the calendar."

"Ah, my singing heart. Well, come up soon and we'll, ah, see to a little commingling of interests."

"A minute ago, I was just thinking how perfect life is here. And it is, and in thirty minutes it'll get even better."

"It might, at that," Shandar said, smiling. "And I'll tell you what I've been thinking about us, tying the well-known knot that doesn't always stay knotted. So why do people say that?"

"Tell me now."

"When you come up, I shall. We'll resume our per-marital honeymoon sessions, then we can pillow-talk."

"It's a date."

Gathering up her canvas beach bag, sunglasses, the sun lotion, the two magazines she had been leafing through, and then she slipped into her sandals. Stooping to kiss him, off she went and he lay there in a daze. More than two weeks had fled, a shut-off mostly of the outside world, putting off talk of anything and everything but themselves. Days that seemed surreal; easy, soft, and with little allowed to hinder their stream of pleasures, the good food and better wine, lovemaking, the timeless illusion that, when with someone you loved boundlessly, everything else went to the rear of one's existence.

From the day he had picked Shandar up at the airport in Marseilles, her delight at the sky-blue Ferrari convertible he had splurged on, the driving up through the Alps Maritime, this hideaway resort with its twelve beachfront villas, and the little nearby town of Saint-Abbas Sur Mer where he had shopped for a swimsuit, and sometimes dining there, even dancing past midnight on their third evening—all seemed an uninterrupted ride on the mythical magic carpet.

He arose later, dusting off his legs. Wrapping a blue beach towel around his neck, he trudged off the beach. At the outside phone near the main building, he asked the front-desk operator to place a call to Klinik Tönbrin-Foy. Moments later, Feurenreuth was giving him an update, the main part of which was that Jaggy had stabilized, quite amazingly. The intravenous tubes had been withdrawn. She was eating porridge and soft foods.

Then the other news of Christopher.

Choosing to speak in English, Feurenreuth said, "He is ill, very ill. We're making every assistance. Nothing more you see, *ist* nothing more we can do. I alarm you, I am most sure."

"Can you be more precise, at least about the prognosis?"

"Not favorable."

"You told me before of a pediatrician. May I speak with her?"

"Today, she is Zurich. In Zurich."

"What comes next, Doctor?"

"Frau Muldaur cares to speak with you."

So, Feurenreuth had been with Jaggy when the call went through.

"…Thomas…"

"Yes, Jaggy, h'lo."

"Where are you?"

"In France, as the doctor already knows."

"You'll come to St. Gallen, Tommy? Please."

"Do you think it'll really help?"

"We wouldn't ask, otherwise. What if a terrible thing were to happen to Christopher? He's *everything*, you must know that."

Her voice had sounded weak but then when she said *everything*, it came with emphatic force. "You sound like you're getting better," he said. "The old self to the fore." He almost added *unfortunately*, but caught himself.

"They say I am and I feel much better. I'm very indebted."

"If you are, then you can thank the St. Curig team."

"I do thank them, but especially you. Please come. You see, they've removed my fallopians, so Christopher is all there will ever be. I apologize for the things I said In Paris. Unforgiveable…and I'm so very sorry…"

He checked a sigh. "I'll get back to you. If you're incommunicado, I'll leave word with Feurenreuth. Stay well, Jaggy." He replaced the phone in its cradle, quietly but firmly. Thinking of his remaining time here with Shandar, and how the days had traveled so swiftly. Walking through a small forest, he made his way to the villa's bougainvillea-wrapped terrace. He found Shandar on a chaise-lounge, sun-drying her hair.

"What's wrong? Something is, I can tell by your face."

"Jaggy and her doctor."

"Is she dying again?"

He laughed, disdainfully. "No, she seems as resurrected as Lazarus. It's the boy. He's riddled with maladies. Maybe that's overstating things, but Feurenreuth seems very concerned."

"Oh, oh—and they want you to return?"

He nodded.

"You must go. You know you must."

"I suppose I do. He may not last long. Let's have a drink of something or other and talk. See how to handle this. We may have to break camp earlier than planned."

"It's your son."

"Yes, my son. But it's also our time together. Three weeks, a down-payment on Paradise. I'll never forget any of it."

"Neither will I, my darling. But we had to end it all in a week anyhow. Let's have the drink and we'll figure out what to do. I'd like a Campari and soda."

Day merged into night. He awoke after midnight, listening to a nervous wind, then a clattering noise of a flower pot or something that had fallen to the terrace's flagstones; and, farther away, the dull boom of combers slapping against the shore. Unsettling thoughts, then. Why go? What could he do for an infant? Were the boy to expire, he almost didn't care to know. Why not wait, see what happened? The night's dark seemed to go ever darker. Shandar was returning to New York. He could accompany her, marry there, rummage around for a job. Maybe at Rockefeller, or Columbia, NYU. Somewhere he'd find a post; he knew teaching, had been good at it, and highly popular with students.

But then he might never have another child. Not going to St. Gallen would amount to desertion. He had deserted the Society, and knew what that meant: that he'd been a quitter. Anyway he cut it—a quitter.

Outside of Zurich, Switzerland

Not dead, nor alive but groggy, feeble, disoriented. A sliver of light from a slit-window ten feet or so off the floor told him of daylight. Vaguely, Thomas had been tracking the diurnal cycle, guessing his calculations were not off by more than two days. Seventy-nine of them at his last count. Days, however, no longer meant anything; nights, huddled under a threadbare blanket, were so chilly he jittered in spasms till dawn. Dank, the cell teemed with the sickening sewer-smell of methane gas. The toilet cubicle was so shadowed it was barely findable. When the cell's steel door opened, and a food tray was slid in, a shaft of white-yellow light shot across the floor, and he'd turn his head to defend his optic nerves. What he slept on was more a pallet than a cot, inhabited by a colony of bugs that had bored sores into him, almost everywhere on his body except his penis which he covered with a wad of rag made by ripping the bottom off one pant leg.

He ate swill: gruel, lemon rinds, moldy turnips, seeds, some sort of sour ginger drink—food for the dead. His bowels dripped. He was passing blood. He could stand for only two minutes or so at a time, slept poorly, had nothing to read, no one to talk with, his mind breaking up.

Lured into their trap, then salted away.

Arriving in St. Gallen, he had come face to face with an outrageous situation. Jaggy had switched personalities again, not as unctuous as when contacting him in France and breaking into his idyll with Shandar. At the klinik, she had threatened to polish him off if he didn't answer to demands only the insane could dream up.

She had demanded that Christopher be genetically re-tooled; his genome altered by using Baster's DNA stored at Cyro. A half-wit would understand the risks were absurd. Impossibly absurd, and an act so criminal it could finish his career. Finish him, in all ways. Finish Christopher, too.

As Baster had once warned him, Jaggy would stoop to the unimaginable to get her hands on The Trust. It seemed all that mattered to her: plotting, maneuvering, cajoling, and now concocting a plan that put the boy in harm's way.

She had lost the Muldaur *in vitro* heir, artificially created, and now she sought victory by demanding he convert Christopher into a substitute Muldaur, who likely could qualify as a legitimate claimant to The Trust.

She was irked beyond measure, realizing she not only carried Thomas's genes in her DNA makeup, but it was those very genes that had rescued her.

If he could do that, why couldn't he change Christopher? She would hear of nothing else. He recalled only too vividly her previous and persistent questions about cloning, and the startling revelation, in Paris, that she had had Baster's remains moved to Cyro from South Africa. All along, a foul scheme; a scheme of fantastic subterfuge.

He let her have it, very hard and very direct.

What had it cost her to convince Feurenreuth to become the willing accomplice? Feurenreuth, who had been so resistant to Thomas's ideas at first, now seemed a willing convert to the value of gene therapy. How much gold this time?

Wanting nothing to do with it, he had refused outright. "You've left your senses," he had told her and had meant every syllable. "The most dangerous thing I ever heard of. That's our son…that's *my* son, too…"

Rebuking him, snarling, telling him she intended executing an affidavit alleging he had performed medical procedures on her with neither a medical license nor her permission, thus violating a rash of Swiss laws. An echo of Feurenreuth's earlier complaints.

Nothing left but to get out, get away, and worry about Christopher from afar.

He had been about to depart, about to return to Zurich and buy a ticket to New York on the first plane out. On the way out the front door of the klinik, he was met by three men in suits as black as the garb of hangmen. Cuffing his wrists with steel bracelets, they spirited him off in a dark-windowed van to an unknown destination. No outside contact had ever been permitted, no lawyer, no American Counsel No anything except this freezing cave, where he existed side-by-side with silence and deprivation.

For all he knew, he didn't officially exist anymore, as utterly, completely isolated now as the proverbial Prisoner of Chillon.

As if drugged, he stared vacantly into this gray morning. Suddenly a sharp clang and the cell door swung wide. A high-beam light pierced the dimness, then swung in an arc toward him. He blinked, blinked again, shutting his eyes. Eventually he focused, was able to size up the visitor. It was a new man, wearing dark clothing and a white shirt open at the collar.

Saying nothing, the man motioned to Thomas to get up.

He stood, unsteadily, then half-stumbled toward the door. The man led him down a corridor. At its end, he stood still, semi-blinded by daylight, his eyes throbbing. Tired, he folded, sitting on the floor, refusing to get up. Minutes lapsed until his vision righted itself. Sorely tempted to make a run for it, but he hadn't the strength. A stupid idea, he was too weak to harm a housefly. Even so, free of his dungeon, he became coldly desperate, ready to try anything, at least in his mind.

The man, along with yet another one, pulled him to his feet. Looping their arms inside his elbows, they half-dragged him through a maze of hallways.

One floor up, the man cell keyed a metal door that opened to a room several times larger than his cell. Pebble-glass windows were protected by heavy-gauge wire mesh; a steel table ran for a length of ten feet or so; six wooden military field chairs were placed at irregular intervals around the table; the walls a dull, greenish-whitish color. Scabby linoleum covered the floor.

Told to take a seat and shortly the steel door shut with a terminal-sounding slam. A slight tremor of thrill, it was a change, an honest-to-God change, as dramatic as a child's first trip to the circus. The long table, the several chairs suggested someone, perhaps several someones, might speak to him. Voices; humans—at last.

He smelled himself, and with disgust.

Hinges squeaked as the door opened part way, and in came a smiling tanned Pierre St. Germain. Stunned, Thomas pulled himself up, not knowing what to say or even if he could say anything at all. He had not talked to anyone other than to himself in months. He took a step forward, his eyes wet at the sight of a friend, in this God-forgotten sump of a concrete never-never land.

"Pierre…can this really be you?" Thomas wanted to weep. Clearing his throat, clearing his head, he went on, "Good of you—"He began to shake then, choking back a sob.

"Sit, Thomas. See to your own comfort. Here, I brought some of your old favorites along." He handed Thomas a paper-wrapped parcel. "Open it, go ahead."

St. Germain, the ever-present smile wreathing his face, pulled out a chair for himself as Thomas felt the glow of the man's effusive warmth; the native charm there, the eye twinkle, the noticeable expression of concern. The very act of his being here spoke reams.

The package contained two boxes of Cohiba Grande cigars, four small packets of waxed matches and a chrome cutter for snipping the cigar ends. "They—there's no place to smoke here. They'll take them from me."

"I don't think so. I'll see to it that you receive smoking privileges. Let's hope you'll soon be smoking them at your leisure and far away from this place."

"Nothing I'd like more. I can't say thanks to you too many times, Pierre. For coming here and for the Cohibas. Can you get me out of here?" Pleading.

"I'm certainly going to try my best. Sit, please. We've a great deal to discuss. Don't they let you bathe? What's wrong with that eye of yours?"

A yellowish fluid oozed out of Thomas's blood-shot left eye. He had to keep wiping it away, so he could see. It didn't do much good and Pierre handed him a handkerchief.

"Thank you."

"You need attention."

"I need a lot of things. Where am I?"

"Near to Zurich, a facility of the BAP. A detention center." Seeing Thomas's querulous look, Pierre informed him, "Bundesampt für Polizei, the Swiss domestic security agency."

"A criminal, am I?"

"It all depends."

"On what does it depend?"

"On your cooperation. I'm here to fix all this, if I can and if you'll help."

"I'd kiss the backside of every cop in Zurich to get out of this place. At noon, I'd do it. Right there on Bahnhofstrasse."

Pierre chuckled. "You've got yourself quite a beard there."

"I don't have a razor. Regulations, I suppose. Not shaving gives me some-shun…some-shun… to do."

"We've got to get you out of here. Light up a cigar, I'll send for coffee, if you like. I'll fill you in on a couple of things and see if we can make sense of it." St. Germain scanned the room, observing, "They ought to paint this place. Awful looking."

No phone, no intercom, nor had Pierre made a request of anyone. Even so, in several minutes coffee was brought in, along with a metal ashtray advertising Panix-Perle, a popular beer in eastern Switzerland. Listeners were obviously busy, and if they did not disturb Pierre then Thomas decided to ignore them, too. With a shaking hand, he offered a Cohiba to Pierre, who smilingly declined. He lit one for himself, relishing its taste in one deep inhale before a coughing fit doubled him over.

Still, he kept inhaling, unwilling to forego the Cohiba's delicious taste and aroma. He blew an arrogantly circular smoke ring, then indulged in a swallow of the mocha-blend coffee, so vastly different in taste to the watery, acorn-tasting brew they brought him every morning.

"Thomas, I want to ensure I have everything straight as we can make it. It's very complex, what's happened and is still happening. I'll listen carefully to what you say and then I plan to make a proposition to you. Candor would be appreciated. We've got plenty of trouble on several fronts, as you'll soon see."

"It can't be more troublesome than being here...and yes, pleash-ashk away."

"You succeeded in administering some form of gene therapy to Jaggy and because of it she survived. Doing quite well, it seems. Is that the way you appraise it? Am I missing anything at all that is basic?"

"Approximately, that's it. I transplanted some of my genes into her DNA. Blood-making genes and osh-ers for the immune system. Feurenreuth would know more about her progress. Feurenreuth, he's the—"

"I know who he is. I've talked with him several times. "

"Did he men-shun he's a half-million rish-er in unmarked gold bullion? I bribed him so I could treat Jaggy. That's where your gold ended up."

"He said nothing of the kind. Of course, he wouldn't want to admit he's an accomplice for having helped you. Turning a blind eye, and so forth." He watched as Thomas wiped his eye again with the handkerchief, then placed his hands on either side of his face, squeezing it. "Are you following me, Thomas? Are you stable enough to continue?"

"Huh?"

"You look to me like two deaths."

"I'm in fever much of the time and my bowels are ruined. I've two loose teeth. I lose track of things. Where are—were we?"

"Feurenreuth. Feurenreuth swore to an affidavit, and I'll get into that in a moment. He is siding with Jaggy in certain allegations against you."

"They own that klinik together. Probably, she's added to his gold hoard."

"If she did, we'll never know."

"Quite the operator, he coll-esh both ways."

"Feurenreuth can make difficulties for you. He's accusing you, says you're practicing voodoo medicine."

"Voodoo that saved a life."

"Even if it's true, how many others would believe it?

"Don't know and don't care."

"You had better care, Thomas."

"It's horse manure what they're saying."

"Not to the Swiss government."

"Does the government know she was comatose, on her way out, a baby inside her, and Feurenreuth and his people stood by wring-rsh-ing their hand-sh?"

"The government is interpreting the law strictly, and admittedly for its own aims and purposes."

"Then why don't they interpret the one that says I'm entitled to notify the U.S. embassy I've been jailed without charges?"

"We've got a law that covers that situation, too. Listen to me, strictly and carefully listen."

A hacking cough drove Thomas's head to his chest. When he regained himself, Pierre asked, "Can you go on? Is this too much for you?"

"Go ahead."

"Jaggy says if your son is not cut in on The Trust, she'll sue. That would bring everything out in the open. You do grasp what I'm saying? Enormous complications would ensue."

Thomas nodded.

"Second part of this is that our government will not allow this much ownership of prime Swiss properties to fall into the hands of foreigners. Especially when the foreigners get them for free. You do comprehend that point?"

Again, Thomas nodded.

"And third, I've told Bern that you feel strongly The Trust should be dissolved and its assets transferred to South African charities, or the equivalent."

"That's what the covenants say we're supposed to do. We all know that."

"Covenants can be set aside when Swiss security and Swiss national interests are at stake. When you add up all three parts of the situation, it's nothing but an explosive conflict. You see that, I hope?"

"Readily."

"Back to your son. I'm told he has certain genetic maladies. You're quite aware of this?"

"When I came back to St. Gallen, Feurenreuth explained to me that Christopher was screened for faulty genes, es-peshhly sickle cell, and he may beat that one, but he's prone to Mobius Syndrome, Osteogenesis Imperfecta, and another one or two I've forgotten."

"Can you resolve these diseases?"

"I couldn't resolve two plus two. Not from here, I can't."

"Of course, not here. But can you treat him? Make him well? Can you do it?"

"He's too young to try. And I'd never try the way she wants it done. Taking a dead man's genes to rewire my son's genome. It's beneath comment. Can you imagine? I cannot ima-shun a faster way of cutsh-ing my own throat although it's half cut already, it seems."

"Suppose it could be done, theoretically. Where does one start?"

"One starts nowhere. It'd be fantastically complicated." Thomas explained the complexities, and the exertion of the explanation tired him. "It's never been done, or I'd have hear-sh about it," and he nodded off, his jaw gaping. A minute passed. Then another, and then as if jolted by a 200 watt surge, he jerked awake.

"Can you tell me that absolutely, I repeat *absolutely*, it cannot be done?"

"Why would anyone want to?"

"This is why. Again, please pay strict attention," instructed St Germain, worried that Thomas wasn't grasping in full. "Under Swiss banking law it is required of any bank to report to federal authorities any transfer of ownership greater than five-percent of a Swiss-based company listed on the national tractate, which includes the nation's top one-hundred corporations. Braunsweig is compelled by the same law to notify the government that major blocks of ownership in no less than fourteen Swiss corporations, all listed in the "national tractate", are owned by The Trust and are intended to pass to South Africa. One of these Trust's holdings, as you surely know, is MarocheChem. Almost thirty-percent of the company, in fact, has been owned for over a century. A long time and that's why the cost figure of the ownership is so low on The Trust's books. Maroche performs highly confidential work for the Swiss military. Things worsened when I told Bern how much The Trust holds of Nestle and Ciba and Credit Suisse Group and a good many other Swiss concerns. It's sufficient in several cases to elect South Africans to the boards of those companies…that's why you're being kept here…it's not for violations of Swiss medical regulations. That's only a pretense. I hope you see that we're all well advised to find a way out of this. It's that serious. Extremely, extremely serious."

Exceedingly serious, thought Thomas, thinking sourly of Jaggy just then "Anything else?"

"I should say this is quite enough."

Breathing stopped, breathing began. Thomas felt his hands go numb. Yet with a perfect clarity, he said, "I suspect you must've confirmed to Jaggy that The Trust was about to expire and the assets would soon be deeded over to South Africa. That's what caused all this, isn't it?"

"Yes, it is. She might be running a bluff, saying she'll go to a court of law. Yet supposing she did… no one can predict how a court would rule on her complaint. As trustees, we might be forced to turn over all sorts of information. The terms of The Trust would be laid bare. An instrument written in Latin over four-hundred years ago, so who could say how a court would see it in today's world. Being in Switzerland, we could quash it in our courts easily enough. But Jaggy can sue in South Africa, and make a deal with the government to split up The Trust. We could be held liable. You, as well. They could ruin Braunsweig and that is simply intolerable. The Swiss government could be dragged into it, and that, too, is intolerable to them in Bern."

"We'd be doing South Africa out of what belongs to them. I've been saying it for months. I've also been saying that is what Baster wanted. It was his money and we're undermining his intent."

"So you have said. Said it and said it."

"I get it," Thomas observed. "They don't want the blacks in charge of the Swiss crown jewels. Maybe they'd end up ruining one or two of Switzerland's finest, as they're presumably trying to do to Muldaur Ltd."

"That's certainly crossed the minds of Bern and ourselves. It will simply not be permitted."

"It's thievery, Pierre."

"So?"

"What happens to me?"

"At present, you're being held here under a Yellow Z-warrant. Those are issued by a special federal magistrate that gives the government the right to detain you incommunicado and incognito. Without treatment, your son will become very ill at some point, and likely he'll die. And you will die, too, right here and quite ignominiously. You might be signing your son's life away and signing your own death certificate simultaneously, Thomas. Don't, just don't do it to yourself."

"I'm a hostage and you tell me my son is to sh-upposed to be a guinea pig. All of you are nuts."

"You're the one rotting away in jail."

"Pierre, I told you I don't know how to change a large percentage of a genome. And if it ever got around that I did do it, or even tried to, the media would gore me. And you sher-tainly know it."

"I said it could be done legally, and secretively, and it can. Damn it all, man, cooperate with us. Use your head."

"Done how?"

"You'd not be here in Switzerland. It can be done elsewhere. Almost the same as when you apparently skirted the rules when you were in Naruma."

"Where's it to be, then?"

"An ocean-going yacht will be chartered. You'll be in international waters and you'll have the best of everything to work with. I can promise it."

"A somewhat familiar refrain. I'd bet that's Jaggy's idea."

"Why do you say that?"

"Because we had dinner at her house in London with a couple of England's sea barons and they were intending to convert ships so that they could get around the law on the more esh-oterish aspects of bio-engineering by doing it all in international waters. Does it not amaze you she would risk her child this way? You two must've worked hard to spin this idea."

St. Germain reminded, "Someone has to do something at some point. Why not now? Why not get yourself free of here and attend to your son's well-being? You inferred that your boy will have to undergo some sort of gene therapy at some point. That's correct, is it?"

"At some point, yes, he should."

"Then why—if that is what is indicated—why not do a greater makeover?"

"He's my son, that's why. I don't want him made into someone else's."

"You'll be given everything you need, Thomas. Technical assistance and all else. Safe and sound, wholly so."

"You said a yacht? What yacht?"

"In Monte Carlo."

"Have you seen it?"

"I've seen a brochure. A two-hundred and thirty-footer."

"The apex of luxury, I'd bet."

"It's owned by one of the Emirate sheiks. A regular floating palace, I'm told."

"Why not sell all the Swiss shares that The Trust owns? Wouldn't that end the concerns of Bern?"

"If we sold all those billions, it's too many billions and we'd wreak havoc in the market. Prices would be driven down sharply. Most of those companies are clients of Braunsweig and we'll not be the cause of bringing harm to them, I assure you."

"Or harm to Braunsweig, eh? Wouldn't you call that a conflict of interest? Favoring Swiss interests over those of The Trust?"

"I'm favoring you with an opportunity to free yourself. Will you do as asked?"

"Never in my life. What in hell do you take me for?"

"I'd certainly take you for a fool, Thomas. If your son was to die while you rotted in here, then what have you gained?"

"This whole thing is crooked and you know it is."

"We are Swiss. We are small but we are not idiotic."

"You're right on one count, that I'd like to get out of here."

"You'll agree to do it, then?"

"Capital N, capital O."

"You may not get another chance."

Pierre, a piteous look on his face, suspected Thomas was fading again, over-exerting himself, his words slurring every so often, and the stench he gave off was too vile to stand for much longer. Before he could lead the conversation onward, Thomas spoke, "What does Claude-Paul Lavalier have to say? He has the swing voshes...votesh..."

"Claude-Paul is European. He will do what is in France's interest. MarocheChem has sizable operations in the Rhone Valley area and he won't forget that, you may be sure."

"No rock left unturned. Well, thank-shasa for dropping by and for the Cohibas. But for nothing else, I'm afraid...I'ms-sha exhaut..." Slobbering again, his eye draining the yellowish pus, and he hadn't strength to raise the handkerchief.

Pierre went appraisingly silent before saying, "I'm sorry it's come to this. I won't be coming back. Is there anything I can do for you, Thomas? Anything?"

"Help me loc-ash someone. A woman."

He told Pierre what he most wanted, and, when done, his eyelids fluttered and his head thudded against the table.

Retrieving a Cohiba from its cedar box, fumbling, anticipation rising, he undid the wrapper and passed the cigar back and forth under his nose, smelling the inviting fragrance of the Cuban leaf. Patting his pockets twice over but found nothing. Desperately, he rummaged about on the cot. Nothing there, either. He knelt, spreading his hands on the roughened cement floor, making blind sweeping gestures with both hands.

Still nothing.

How could he misplace all four packets of waxed matches? Dimly, then violently, he realized that somehow in the night they'd relieved him of the waxed matches. They left the cigars, he supposed, to torment him. Pierre had promised to obtain smoking privileges, and now Pierre had forsaken him, too.

Feeling his wrists, his fingers then strayed to his carotid artery. Only faint throbs. Life was falling away. Death somehow seemed a gift. He would do the ants soon; the ants were the only energy around him, and he thought of Lin-pao and that his mother was a bear trainer for the circus.

Then, his thoughts whited-out and he descended into a state of nothingness.

Geneva, Switzerland
St. Gallen, Switzerland

"He refused me outright, Jaggy. Good as told me to go to hell."

"He'll come to his senses."

"I think he's losing his senses, frankly. He babbles at times. He's in terrible, terrible shape."

"You wait, Pierre, you'll see. He'll knuckle under."

"He says the whole idea is dangerous in the extreme. I don't profess to understand what he understands. He's not always clear-headed and he smells like a chicken coop. But he talked to the problem of making all these gene replacements and getting things like gene regulators and switches to operate correctly. Hundreds of intricacies. He'd never try, he said, and doesn't care much about securing The Trust for your boy and says it's a criminal act to try gene makeovers like this. He's adamant, Jaggy."

"He can do it, I know he can. That sodder's a genius in some ways."

"He's kept in a medieval cell. We've done a despicable thing to that man."

"Good."

"You can't mean that, you really can't."

"He's an ingrate."

"Who saved your life, it seems. You've got to understand he can only take so much. And it may be that he cannot do what we want for your son."

"I was on death's doorstep, Pierre. I'll admit it and the doctors are still rather astounded. He can do it, if we force him. Maybe we shouldn't have chased that Jew of his out of Switzerland. I wonder. She might have been persuasive. Too late, now, I s'pose."

"He's asked me to try and locate her."

"Did you?"

"We're trying."

"On second thought, I don't want her coming back to Switzerland."

"That's less a worry than the considerable time we're all losing. If he dies in there, all is lost. And I've used up about all the credit I have with the army. They're getting antsy about this matter."

"What's the army have to do with anything."

"That prison falls under their jurisdiction. If Thomas perishes, there'll be some hellacious inquiry—"

"He'll come to heel, you'll see."

"Whatever makes you so sure, Jaggy?"

"He was my fuck for the best part of a year, that is why. You get to know someone, believe me. Tough as they come, that cobber, but he's an egg we can crack."

"I don't want him to crack. We need him, and *you* need him most of all."

"Consider the alternative, Pierre. Braunsweig could get blasted to pieces, never forget. The South Africans could take you straightaway to the poor house, if ever they find out."

"Well, if you sue, they *will* find out."

"You know my conditions. You get what you want, if I get what I want."

And that concluded the business of their ever widening cabal for that day.

Outside of Zurich

He had hidden twelve of the sucrose packets served with the bitter ersatz coffee they brought him with his sparse meals. He emptied some of the white grains on a square of toilet paper, and, using the paper as a sort of sluice, he made four tiny mounds at the corners of a five-foot square he roughed out on the cell floor. Then he sprinkled other grains a foot apart on all sides of the square. When through, he went to the wash basin, bent himself with effort, and near the pipe flange he trapped eight ants that lived behind the wall but came out to forage for food and imbibe water droplets formed by the condensation on the pipe.

His rodeo. His recreation. His newer lease on life.

With intensive acts of seduction, he trained the ants to follow the shape of the five-foot square on the floor, where they could find sustenance for little effort. Obey the rules and win; if not, then needless deprivation; choices, just as he faced his own choices. Within another unknown span of time, possibly ten days, he taught them to ant-march on the sides of a triangle, then a rectangle. Try as he had, he failed to get them to navigate in a circle.

Days merged, as before, one with the next. A leaden-like fog gripped his dungeon; no day, no night. Nothing left to him but his little ant circus. And then one day he ate them in a sheer act of paranoia, fearing he was being watched, fearing they'd take his tiny black friends away, as they had taken the matches.

And all else.

An unmarked manila envelope arrived early one morning on a metal breakfast tray bearing a cup of coffee and a bowl of dry cornmeal. A penlight anchored the envelope. With a rare surge of energy, opening the envelope, he found a single unsigned page of neatly typed text. No letterhead, no date. He suspected there wouldn't be a latent fingerprint, either, other than his own.

Snapping on the penlight, he saw the heading stamped CONFIDENTIAL.

The subject, a woman known as Shandar Bazak, an Iraqi by birth, now a citizen of the U.S., entered Switzerland on the sixteenth of October at Zurich, Swissair Flt. 4099. She reportedly went directly to St. Gallen to the Klinik Tönbrin-Foy and there made inquiries as to the whereabouts of a Mr. Thomas I. Courmaine, also a citizen of the U.S. Allegedly, no information was released and subject, Bazak, was admitted to the klinik by a receptionist, Frau Rena Soellen, and was then referred to a member of the personnel department, a Fraulein Lissa Gendli.

Gaining no assistance in St. Gallen, Bazak next journeyed to Bern where a reliable informant indicates she met with officials of the U.S. Consulate. It is not known what transpired, but subject booked a return Swissair flight to New York, two days later. Presumably, the U.S. Consulate will make further inquiries as to the whereabouts of T.I. Courmaine.

Additional queries disclose that the subject Bazak resigned from Meric & Morris, a public relations firm headquartered in New York City, and her employer for the past eight years, where she served as a vice-president and account executive. Records available in New York County confirm that subject Bazak sold her cooperative apartment in New York City to a Mr. and Mrs. Edwin A. Gillespie, formerly of San Francisco, California.

Bazak's whereabouts, at present, are unknown. Efforts to enlist the cooperation of the U.S. Federal Bureau of Investigation in a further search for the subject have proved unsuccessful to date...

Why had they given him only an extract of what was obviously a larger report? Thinking about it, he decided it must be a ploy; dangling the carrot to make him start thinking of her, relent and give in. It came close to working; he was besotted by fresh thoughts of her after weeks of denying himself any of those tantalizing excursions. He might have been married by now.

In her life, her days, her arms.

Later that day, or was it nighttime, he began to contrive his insanity. Halfway there as it was, and with a little more nudging, and some fakery, he might convince them how rapidly he was going over the edge. His spirits had lifted slightly, learning Shandar had come to find him. Instead of her, prison; instead of her, the specter of insanity, the real thing.

Endurance had fallen to its nadir. He felt disgust with himself. He was lonely, all hope had vanished. Peering at his stiff, swollen wrist, then, rolling his hand over, he was fascinated by the splotchy, purpled bruises. Over the past days, he had pounded on the metal door of the cell, asking, begging, for someone to talk with. Babbling, "I am the second Jesus you filthy bastards. Hear me. Please, please, please, hear me…talk…"

One night, slumped on the floor by the door, he had screamed himself unconscious. No easy thing to do.

And for three days, he ate nothing because he thought—wildly thought—that they had removed his stomach, which, to him, explained why he was never hungry. When they brought his meal tray one morning, he implored them for a Baccarat crystal dish filled with chocolate-covered ants. A pound of them, he had insisted.

Almost sure that he'd insisted; or was it but another dream?

Time froze again. He felt movement, certain he was levitating, ascending into the heavens, like an incarnated Christ. Sinking deeper into torpor, he still saw faces, heard voices, then voices with no faces. Bright piercing light assaulted him. Shuffling sounds, other voices from afar, as he seemed to enter a space that was deeply white and deeply warm, so unlike the Hell he had come to know, and thinking he had truly arrived at the Hereafter; that it wasn't fire-filled and scream-filled, with endless weeping and gnashing, or with countless, vapory souls gathered under fig trees, enjoying the harps of angels, and with endless bounty and joys unparalleled.

It was all a vast pale plain filled with the cacophony of jabbering voices.

Davos, Switzerland

Looking back at his days in prison—that out-of-body nightmare—seemed as something that happened a lifetime ago. Maybe it was, too; at the very least, a very different life, a very different experience than now.

The backside of April had now become the face of May. In the Alps, it was the in-between season: no longer was it winter, but neither was it springtime. For nine weeks he'd been in Davos, in a mountain sanitarium, while they patched him together. For the second time in less than two years, he had round-the-clock relays of doctors and nurses. Mostly nurses, one of whom, a twenty-odd year old, dairy-fed maid of the mountains crept into his bed one night.

Testing? Wanting a performance report? Gearing him up, perhaps, for whatever was to come next? He had lost track, and touch, with everyone he knew. Weekly, however, batches of flowers and a small pack of Cohibas arrived, compliments of Braunsweig und Sohn.

How was it that St. Germain knew of his whereabouts? A puzzling question among several others that had gone unanswered. Still, the man had a wide wingspan, and, of course, was a brigadier of the Swiss Army. Not without his contacts at lofty levels, in a pocket-sized country.

Vision had returned to his infected eye, but he would be wearing a black eye-patch for another month or so. New teeth implants replaced two he'd lost. Muscles had firmed. Hiking in freshest air, his color returning. Hearty fare, usually heavy soups served with a variety of peasant breads and hunks of enriched cheese. Medications cut to a minimum, and sleeping as if he were a hibernating animal. Most afternoons, after the hikes or the mountain biking, he sunned on the south-facing deck outside the suite they had set aside for him.

Thoughts that dwelled on Shandar, then on Christopher. How to deal with those predicaments and his newer ring of foes, the Swiss he had yet to encounter, but knew it was in the offing. No handshaking, not that kind of meeting nor those kinds of Swiss.

Gradually, his scheme was taking shape. He concluded Jaggy must have authored the endeavor to break him down, bend him to her will. Until recently, he hadn't the wit to suspect St. Germain's connivance; but it had to be, for Jaggy by herself could never have arranged to imprison him. Nor Feurenreuth, either. It called for someone of weight, a shot-caller, a finger-snapper. Someone on the order, say, of a top-rated banker, perhaps even a patriot wearing a brigadier's epaulettes.

That visit at the still unnamed prison had revealed that St. Germain put Swiss interests, especially Braunsweig's, above all others. But then why not? What could one expect? St. Germain was Swiss to his toenails. It was the Swiss, after all, who protected—with all their rules of secrecy—institutes such as Braunsweig, which could not prosper without that protection.

Mulling for hours end to end, he calculated a double double-cross. He'd acquiesce to their nefarious scheme, deceive them into believing a Muldaur heir—a defenseless infant—could be re-created with Zyme-One technology. All done against the law of nature, to say nothing of the law of man. A grubby deception had enticed him back to Switzerland from France; he was working up a filthy deception of his own: a Courmaine special.

No day went by, no night either, when he didn't rehearse every step of his dance of the long knives. Another, mostly rainy fortnight went by before he felt himself as ready. Calling, he told Germain to set the meeting. Not an instant to lose, was there?

My turn to spin the wheel, he thought, for he had no intent of going gently into the night.

Or quietly, either.

Bern, Switzerland

Strained, taut, a war footing—upon entering the conference room he immediately picked up on the off-putting atmospherics. Stiff-lipped faces, hard-eyed, voices reducing to whispers as soon as he came through the door.

St. Germain had warned him he'd be attending a meeting that, officially, never took place, would never be on record. Were he to violate the *in camera* nature of the conclave, he could expect an appropriate comeback. "A word to the wise, "St. Germain had said, "now that you are, well, should I say more practiced in our ways." A regrettable remark that was about to travel the path of a boomerang.

Here he sat one mid-morning, dutifully if not appreciatively, with dour-faced Swiss technocrats. A star-chamber, as Thomas sized it up. Much gray: a gray building, a gray room, a funereal gray carpet, gray days—five such days to be had, with the sun showing itself only on the last of them.

Accusations, some true and others not, were ticked off; by day two, he was reminded of the Vatican tribunal presided over by Maistinger and his human hatchets. This time, as it would turn out, the *éminence grise* was no other than that affable, silk-smooth St. Germain, his hands tickling the puppet strings from in and out of the shadows.

Jaggy, it became apparent, had found the Swiss Achilles heel. She had cunningly jockeyed the government into its dilemma: either to acquiesce to her designs so she could gain control of The Trust, or she'd stage an all-out publicity ruckus, charging the Swiss government and Braunsweig, along with Thomas, of a mammoth fraud against the South African government. And as St. Germain had bluntly reminded him, she could easily cut her own deal with the South African government. And as St. Germain had bluntly reminded him, she could easily cut her own deal with the South Africans and settle for half a loaf or even less, ending up with multi-billions for herself.

Her affidavit went so far as to say that Thomas I. Courmaine had know-ingly experimented with genetic therapy on her person. Had done so without permission from herself, or the Klinik Tönbrin-St. Foy, or any Swiss medical authorities. Further, she was prepared to supply materials previously appearing in newspapers, and elsewhere, over the past year, to fortify her claims that Thomas Courmaine and his colleagues had engaged in secretive experiments in Wales, posing hazards to the public. All of this, she alleged, done behind her back as his sole partner in Muldaur-Courmaine Laboratory, Ltd. She also intended to sue him for recovery of her misappropriated assets, for the harm brought against her good name, and sundry lesser charges.

All as threatening as a heaved grenade. She was, most surely, laying groundwork for a lawsuit.

There it was: the government, Braunsweig, himself, all having stakes in the outcome. None more so, however, than did Jaggy Muldaur.

For the Swiss government the risk was both distasteful and unacceptable. She was willful, had the money, had the staying power to make trouble in *extremis*. She most surely had the wherewithal to call a press conference that would draw the most intense interest from the media, saying nothing of the public at large.

Listening to all this, Thomas felt like a calf getting its first look at the slaughter house, in his soul sensing something was about to go terribly wrong. Something he was yet to fully wrap his mind around. He had salvaged Jaggy's life at significant risk to his reputation; now, hell-bent on getting her way, she was about to gore him. Not for the first time, either.

"Is all this clearly understood, Herr Doktor Courmaine?" asked one of the burghers, pointedly adding that Thomas would take the fall, first, before any others met with troubles, should things turn out grimly for the government.

Nodding to them, nodding so frequently he felt like a wind-up toy. "Of course," he kept agreeing knowing his promise to genetically edit Christopher into a Muldaur, at least partly so, could end up annihilating his son, a fifteen-pounder—no more than a big trout!—still not quite eight months of age. Too small and young for any gene therapy, the boy still struggled for his footing in a very tenuous life.

In Davos, he'd fumbled around with Christopher's therapy problems to ready himself for this day: formulating devious ideas, constructing plans no one but himself could decipher.

Others somehow held to the belief he could perform genetic jujitsu. To an extent, they were correct but also incorrect; he couldn't do more than get processes started, processes that could always go awry. The jujitsu, if any, lay, as always, in the inherent clout of Zyme-One. Well, let them go on believing whatever they wished: he had re-engineered three African women and had done the same for Jaggy Muldaur. Why not an infant, who would solve their instant headache.

It was these confused beliefs he must play upon: he, as the supposed shaman, and they the acolytes.

When day three arrived, Thomas began to see the second half of the deck they were dealing from. New cards, new game, but different players.

MarocheChem, not surprisingly, wanted the Zyme-One technology for its own exclusive uses—the patents, the shebang. St. Germain had neglected to say as much as a single syllable about any of it. And to that omission, Thomas went to far internal lengths to check his irritation. The banker was a charlatan, as well?

For most of that day, Thomas traded negatives with the MarocheChem executives, seeing that they, too, had triangulated him, and with on-the-mark targeting. How had they found out so much so quickly? Obviously, St. Germain had put them wise to the successes of Zyme-One; obviously, Thomas, chagrined at himself, had been too loose-lipped over the months. Too full of his own excitement, and much too full of himself, always working a sale, largely out of habit born of defeats in New York, with Jaggy, and elsewhere. He was paying for his mouthings and braggadocio now.

"We can make you rich," they were urging him. "Build you your own lab, the best anywhere." Words that cleared any doubts as to the fullness of their appetite, as they played to his weaknesses. A lab? A MarocheChem lab? A ploy likely fed into the game by St. Germain, who was fast surrendering any guise as a bystander.

Other than Jaggy, outside of this room, who would ever know of a stratagem to royally screw the South Africans out of their clear-cut rights? Or, if they did know, they'd never say, would they? And, to boot, the Swiss wanted to buy what he knew, all of what he knew, about Zyme-One—and very soon, say in an interval with the quickness of a single lightning flash, they'd have it both ways.

Keep The Trust safely in Swiss hands, while gaining control of Zyme-One. Could there, in this entire world, exist another corporate director on the scale of a St. Germain, who was busy saving the hide of Braunsweig und Sohn, while selling out old friend Courmaine?

A gigantic deal: gigantic enough to justify half-killing him in a dungeon.

Listening now and with zeal, as one florid-faced MarocheChem executive delved again into the corporate wallet. "We'll sign you a check for eleven-million Euros. Call if an advance payment against royalties for worldwide rights to Zyme-One…that's eleven, Mr. Courmaine …"

"Not worldwide," Thomas haggled, "all but China and Africa," looking a little too severely at the negotiator, while dancing his side of this minuet on ice so thin he couldn't feel it, let alone see it. Hands stuffed into his pockets, defensive and drawn-faced, he answering them in sparest words, fuming at times, yet moments later adopting a demeanor as contrite as a professional sinner's.

He was many men on that day, the dilettante of ambiguities and of staged repertoire. Advancing, retreating—not quite trigger time, was it? Awaiting his moment to shoot for the end zone, and quite aware he would get only one play, one chance.

Halfway enjoying himself at moments, yet thoughts of Christopher's plight coursed through him, dimming any fleeting thrills, one being: *"This is how the big boys do it…well, well…I say, Chris, let's you and me gather our forces and tell 'em they can jolly well fuck off…"*

Next day, with St. Germain again at the table, full of cheer and bonhomie, pink-shaven, and his eyes fervid as a circuit preacher's. With the banker's re-entry into the proceedings, Thomas sensed the minestrone was about to be warmed and rewarmed; that, in short, the Philistine from Geneva had been re-summoned to glue up a deal.

The cards were face up, his foes having clarified what they required of him. Silence regarding The Trust, that was number one. Abetted by a gene-fix for Christopher, and the added right to the methods used for the fixing, that was number two.

A win-win for the Swiss, naturally.

He tried gauging if he was sending himself to another Hell. Yet, here it was—the fullness of an unforgiving moment. All the toil, all the setbacks, over. With the weight of MarocheChem behind his discovery, proof to the world-at-large was in the bag. Still, and against his ever-long hope, he was under no illusions: they'd milk every opportunity for gain and profit. Behold, he thought! Yet another pact with the devil, matching the one when kneeling to Jaggy in exchange for the St. Curig lab.

Dwelling on it, made the situation no easier to comprehend, and, as before, there seemed no other options. That made no part of it right, of course, but he must somehow get free of these people, including St. Germain. Was there more to had, though?

As discreetly as he could manage, he'd been studying their impatient faces. Hoping his hunch would gain him the ground he sought, Thomas upped the ante, adding some real ballast as he goaded, "No deal of any kind, not unless I am named as sole trustee of The Muldaur Trust. And if and when my son Christopher is declared as heir to The Trust, you must also agree to provide him with Swiss citizenship. He was born here, let us remember. No citizenship, then no deal. And if no sole trusteeship, then ditto on that one, too, for I shall agree to nothing. But consider what I say, gentleman, as your government loses nothing."

The burghers sat there as stilled as mummies. After the MarocheChem executives were shooed out of the room, one of the officials from the FDF (Federal Department of Finance) cut a new path for debate. Practically mowing over Thomas with a bombshell, the words exploded this way: "The Muldaur Trust, as we see it, falls under the Swiss law pertaining to perpetual trusts, which it most obviously is. Four centuries of perpetuity, by our count. But as it has never been brought up to date, it therefore is not in conformity with our laws. The Trust is an illegal instrument. It must undergo alterations to comply with law."

At this, Thomas nearly leaped across the tabletop. "Does that mean its terms and covenants cannot be enforced by anyone?"

"Not here in Switzerland, and that is where The Trust has been domiciled since its inception. The entirety of its life, seemingly."

Glancing sharply at St. Germain, Thomas thought—whatever did this mean? Why was he never informed? Why, even, had these Swiss officials been given access to the controlling trust document: COMPACTUS MULDAURUS? What was flying here?

Another dosage of fat now sizzling away in the fire. Had Braunsweig let the golden calf sleep too long, neglecting its oversight duties? Apparently, they'd been forced to open the books on The Trust to the FDF, when disclosing the threat of prime Swiss assets falling into hands of black foreigners. Braunsweig had somehow broken the rules of good order, the rules that protected Switzerland from *auslanders*; and today, only because he insisted on the sole-trusteeship, the staggering error had revealed itself, because they obviously could not legally condone him as sole trustee to an illegal pact.

How absolutely lovely, he thought, eyeing St. Germain's misery-wracked face. The great money-changer must've been privy, all along. The sonofabitch. But Thomas, wanting to kiss the man from FDF. Well, a friendly hug anyway.

With contrived moral ferocity, Thomas made a pivotal suggestion, "I see it this way, that we've drawn up only half of the blueprint, gentlemen." In his most precise German, he spilled out how to nail down the loose pieces of the deal. "There is much about The Trust that Miss Muldaur doesn't know, unless St. Germain here has done more of his talking than was prudent, perhaps inveigling Missus Muldaur to ignite all this upheaval—"

"See here!" St. Germain half rose, his face seized with white anger.

No one paid the slightest attention to him and so Thomas moved onward, coaxing the others with: "Even so, she knows more than is good for any of us. What prevents her, if she doesn't get her way…" emphasizing it again…"get her way *with you* the way she's already had her many ways with me? I repeat, what keeps her from passing the scandalous news to the South Africans as to how they're being defrauded? Stupendously so. Most surely, they'd believe her, wouldn't they? Being a Muldaur? She might not possess hard evidence about The Trust itself, but Muldaurs, we should note, were among South Africa's greatest benefactors. She despises the blacks, but they'll name an avenue after her when they hear how they're being cut out of all these billions…"

Letting that item swirl in the disquieted air before continuing: "She's a rough bird, you know. Up there in London, some people call her the Stiletto. Look at what she did to me, or got your confreres to do to me. This is all about money and it always will be…do you want her holding the South African axe over the Swiss government for all the years ahead? She can get the South Africans to scream bloody hell and then you'll have the press on you like flies on cow turds. Swiss shenanigans in spades. Your banks accused of filching another nation's assets. Demands by the UN for investigations…that sort of thing. You wouldn't deny it could happen, would you? Not another fracas like the one when Washington went after you fellas for aiding all those rich Americans, helping them to beat their taxes. You'd not want that sort of criminal innuendo reprised all over the papers again…two in a row…be a real killer of a situation, eh? You savvy? Sure you savvy. Let's get together on this and grab the reins and yank her right off her track. She'll never know till it's too late for her to do anything about it. I mean she might even bring down your government. If she ever opens all this up, she'll demolish the idea that it's a safe thing to bank your bucks anymore with the Swiss. You'd have to revamp the entire national sales pitch, right? Butcher your most famous industry. She could, you know, and she might. Up in London, they call her the Stiletto for good reason. Don't let her stab you, too."

And he sat, then, to a bellowing silence; all that he heard was heavy, asthmatic-like breathing. Faces had blanked, one actually turning the color of gray pearl. As if he were some party-crasher, some social leper, Thomas was buffeted by unfriendly frowns, soon dissolving into hardening jaws, a signal that tempers verged on flaring.

"What're you suggesting, Herr Doktor?" asked one of the burghers, testily.

"A simple remedy, that's what've got in mind."

"Which is?"

He proceeded to light up a Cohiba Robusto, drawing on the small brown torpedo till it glowed, his nostrils enthralled by its fragrance. From behind a dense stream of smoke, he paused while considering how to lay out his dealmaker. Or its breaker. And so here goes, thinking, a little unsteadily, it was time to fun things up. Suddenly, and for no specific reason, he felt in his realm, as if he were back in a classroom outlining a concept to the waiting faces.

Let's up the ante one more time, you sonsofbitches, he thought. It was the only shot he had left, and he took it.

Through a curl of smoke, he began, "May I repeat, I need you to make my son a Swiss citizen. That's so we can regularize matters, and so that I can protect my flanks. Who instigated all this turmoil? You know it was Jaggy Muldaur. We must totally isolate her from this situation for it to have the best chance, maybe the only chance of working. Erase every future right she has, or claims to have, over the child. I am to be appointed the legal guardian and the child's sole custodian. The child will remain here in Switzerland after the, um, so-called yacht cruise. You must see to it, somehow, that if she causes troubles she'll lose out on any and all permission for remaining in Switzerland. Deport her, if need be. All the screws tightened down until she gets the idea she can't run Switzerland the way she likes to run everything else. How you do all this juristically is, of course, in your hands. Yet I know she will remain where our son is…and that'll be here…which places her under your authority in case she decides on more combat. This is your turf, why not secure it? If I may say: don't eliminate part of the problem, eliminate it all. It's so much easier…"

Exhaling, a tendril of smoke floating sideways from this mouth, he had hammered in his last rivet, hoping it would square up any out-of-kilter ends.

A symbiotic moment, and then, "Is there more?" a burgher asked.

"Not from me," Thomas replied. "I'm on your side. You be the first responders, then leave the rest to me."

A neatly packaged offer, everything there but the red ribbons. Looking at one another, as if by some undetectable signal, the three burghers arose in unison and left the room. St. Germain also excused himself, hastily departing without so much as a murmur. Thomas reached for a pad from a stack in the center of the table, began making a list of notes. He could feel heartening vibes, an ambient air of tolerance drifting about, and, if not full consent to his stipulations, than a willingness to bend the sails for calmer waters.

When the officials filed in, sat, the burliest of them said, "How do we know you'll comply with your suggestions, Herr Doktor?"

"If I didn't, I imagine you'd have me killed. But if you did that, there'll never be a Muldaur heir, and then you're back to where you started. Only then you'd have a murder to worry about."

"This is not comical. There will be no murder."

"I'm greatly relieved to hear it." Smiling, then, like some father-of-the-bride, anxious to end the party and cut his bills.

"You will make terms with MarocheChem?"

"There'll be no holdup from me. I'll want that eleven-million, naturally. But what is it that we do about the Stiletto?"

"Shall we say it is a matter of concern for the Swiss? The Swiss alone, Herr Doktor."

"Ah, yes, and with all your winning techniques, who could ever refuse you?" Earning himself a bare-toothed, ghoulish scowl.

Two days later, he found himself wading through one-hundred and twenty-four pages of agreements. Offering no surprise whatsoever, the first of them was a three-pager chock full of waivers exonerating the Swiss government of any wrongdoing during his detention. In the mix was a companion document whereby he agreed in substance with Jaggy's affidavit, the one setting forth his multiple evils for having rescued her life.

Folly to disagree, so he signed it: an across-the-board admission of guilt.

No top-heavy winners, though. The government salvaged the sanctity of some of the nation's leading companies, and any potential trouble with South Africa had been snuffed out. So it seemed. Braunsweig dodged serious court troubles. Jaggy would be made to think she had got her way—that The Trust would fall to Christopher one day. Somewhat reluctantly, Thomas signed away the rights to Zyme-One, other than Africa and China, knowing he must either acquiesce or the entire bargain might be forfeited.

With a few more squiggles of the gold-tipped pen, he'd be joining the Philistines as a full-fledged member, and with all of its stiff lessons to remind him of what the club dues cost.

Only one more lap to run now, and it was best left for tomorrow. He would need the time anyway to prepare himself.

You pay and pay forever, he thought. *Never a letup.*

10: 22 a.m.

Taking his leisure at a sun-splashed table on the Bellevue-Palace terrace, having a mocha-coffee fortified by a pony of Hine cognac; at intervals, Thomas Alp-gazed, soaking up the travel-poster day. Yet the day, crystalline as could be, was sullied by his feelings. He'd sold out, taking a low road paved with high crimes, some already committed, and others still in the wings.

Sipping at his cognac, moodily, he set the snifter aside as a traveling shadow appeared at the edge of his healing eye's vision-field. Instinct told him the visitor's identity.

"Thomas," said a slightly winded St. Germain.

He swung his head and saw the banker, then gestured him to the other chair.

"Superb day, wouldn't you say?" observed St. Germain, sitting down.

"Better than the last four, I'd agree."

"You seem to have profited rather regally from the past week. Quite a performance you put on yesterday."

"My Alpine song-and-dance act. Glad you enjoyed yourself."

"Hardly that, I'd say. You inferred you had sensitive matters on your mind. Wouldn't you rather go up to my rooms?"

"I like it right here. Lots of witnesses if things get rough."

"We're not starting off that way, are we?"

"Like a drink?"

"On the early side for me, thanks all the same."

"You might want one before long. I'm having a celebratory cognac. Hine, my favorite. Before I forget…that eleven- million Maroche is wiring to my account? The royalty advance?"

"Yes."

"Take out whatever I owe for the bullion I borrowed to pay off Feuren-reuth. I'll send you an authorization."

"I shall have it attended to as soon as the MarocheChem funds clear."

"I'm curious. How is it that The Trust is valued at over two-hundred forty-billion? Before I was…well, I guess you could say detained…the last valuations of The Trust that I saw pegged its worth at just over sixty-four billion. What jumped it up?"

"The Trust's holdings date back years and years. Over a hundred years in some cases. The holdings are carried on the books at original cost. And those costs are far below current market value. The real estate, some of it, was bought back in the 1800s or even before. Berlin is another example. The Trust bought something like twelve city blocks in 1946 when it was rubble. No one wanted a stick or a brick of it in those days. As I recall we paid for those properties in gold, and so received an even larger discount."

"The best time to buy, I hear. When blood runs in the streets."

"If The Trust hadn't, you may be sure someone else would. We sold the Berlin properties recently for a whopping gain."

"Who bought it from us?"

"A consortium of Saudis, the Emir of Dubai, along with several Hong Kong investors."

"With Braunsweig providing the financing, I imagine?"

"Yes, we did."

"A conflict of interest, wouldn't you say?"

"No one objected."

"I'd bet not, with you and Claude-Paul the only ones voting. What happened to the sales proceeds?"

"For the time being we've invested them in Swiss government bonds. We decided not to do anything, hoping you'd be back to vote on the next stage of asset deployment."

"I'm back."

"Indeed so."

"You're upset about being kicked off the trusteeship, but I've decided to run things my way."

"If you think you can. My partners are decidedly unhappy at the turn of events."

"Needless to say."

"Quite so. Yes, needless to say."

"You've had your four-hundred year ride. Not so bad. I was wondering how much that adds up to in banking fees. A couple of billion, give or take."

"Near enough."

"Not so bad, either. Well, you've done a superior job. Quite incredible, really. Now we've a new chapter to write. Here's how it'll read...I call the overall shots but Braunsweig can keep custody of the assets and oversee...what is we have, about 120 dummy corporations? And Braunsweig can keep those straight, and The Trust will pay for that service and also pay an investment advisory fee."

"Of how much, or dare I ask?"

"Say, twenty-five million annually, all in."

"That's a sheer insult. Not for all the work we do. Fifty at the minimum," St Germain bargained.

"Forty. That's tops. Or I'll go elsewhere."

"Why penalize us?"

"It's forty or nothing."

"You sound…well, quite crusty to be candid…"

"I'm none too eager to please anyone today. I've had my fill of all of you. And you…let's get to you, St. Germain, you violated my confidences, didn't you? Things I've told you over the past year about my work, and you passing them on to your friends at MarocheChem. That's violative and it's unethical. I could tell they knew enough, no, they knew an extreme plenty about what we'd been up to in Wales, and what we had, and what more we can have and probably would've had one day. Got all of it from you, didn't they? No other outsider knew that much. I always thought you were a friend and you turn out to be a ten-cent fucking snitch. Handing away our trade secrets, or the notion of them. You sold me out so you could take care of your Swiss cronies and clients."

"The Swiss government, as you well know by now, would never let Maroche fall into foreign hands. You also well know I'm a director of Maroche and I—"

"So what?"

"I'm merely trying to explain my predicament, Thomas."

"I don't much care about your predicament. I care only about my predicament, my very large, engrossing, fate-making predicament. I've got a very tough junket ahead, where almost anything can go wrong. Murphy's Law and so forth. But that's my business. You tied on to the coattails of the government, didn't you? Wanting to save Braunsweig's backside, right? Then saw your chance to wiggle Maroche into the fray and you took it. I've always known I can't move Zyme-One into world markets by myself. The research isn't even finished yet. They can do it far better and far faster. But you snuck a fast one in behind my back, blabbing away, and you blabbed when you should've respected confidences and kept your teeth glued shut. You told me one night at your own house you'd never pass on the things I was telling you. You reneged and—"

"You'll be wealthy for it."

"Rich is for people like you, St. Germain. Rich to me is my freedom and I'm fast losing that. I've got to consult for five years with Maroche, don't forget. Five…*five*…was that another of your brainchildren, so they could keep me patrolled while they exploited my work? They've got me tied up like a Christmas goose…oh, hell, maybe it won't be so bad, but you used me. I'll not forget that, and I'll make sure you don't forget it, either."

"That's quite a statement you're making."

"And here's its addendum. You conspired with Jaggy to half kill me. More than half. You got in the way of my plans to marry someone. You got in the way of too much. You knew Jaggy Muldaur had pulled the plug on Muldaur-Courmaine, didn't you? I was high and dry. When I needed that gold to pay off Feurenreuth, you never retreated one step, even though you knew I'd have trouble repaying it. But you okayed it anyway, knowing if I succeeded in saving Jaggy, Maroche would have all the more reason to jump in. They'd know almost for sure that I had a winner. And you'd force me to give in, and thus have the wherewithal to repay you. You fixed me up with an army lab and with about anything I needed. What a set-up. I take all the chances while you finagle a big win for your Swiss cronies. Don't deny it…don't lie…you set me up, you sonofabitch…"

"Pure speculation, and that's about all you have," retorted St. Germaine.

"I don't have to prove it, do I? You wanted my head on a pike and you got it. Now, it's off the pike. I'm shortly to be in control of over two-hundred billion dollars of muscle. Like to feel it? My finger is on the trigger and I'm ready to pull. Jaggy is powerful but not so powerful she could get me salted away in a high-security prison. She'd need you for that one, and you went along. Do you deny it? Remember, I've got a full year on the high seas to find out, and, believe me I will find out. Your turn, so go ahead."

But St. Germain made no reply.

But Thomas did. "What I also find of surpassing interest is those gunslingers from Maroche obviously don't know The Trust controls their company. That means me, or may mean me, depending on how things go on our little yacht trip. That means you, too, my friend. My former friend, that is. One day I may wake up and decide to run your butt off the Maroche board," Thomas said, and then asked, "does Braunsweig want the advisory fee I proposed or not?"

"Yes…yes, of course…"

"Send me the paperwork. I'll call your office with my forwarding address. That's it, then. All for today, that is, so I won't hold you. You look to me as if you ought to be in a big hurry."

"What're you going to do when Jaggy Muldaur finds out about all this? That you'll be in charge of The Trust?"

"I'll tell her to gargle with WD-40 or call 9-1-1. The sooner she finds out how the new line-up works, the better for everyone. Come to think of it, I'd rather sail without her. But she's a mother, so we'll let her have a berth as long as she behaves herself, which is none too likely. Let me be expressly clear on one point, I and I alone will be the one to inform her of the overall situation regarding The Trust, and will do so at a time of my own choosing. The Swiss government won't be telling her, we all know that, and if you tell her, or anyone at Braunsweig, that'll be the end of the end."

"You certainly put her in her cage."

"A good place for her."

"Don't be too harsh."

"I may be finding one for you, next."

The air strained now, grim, with St. Germain's mouth looking as if it had been sewn together. After a long pause, he offered, "Let's not leave it this way, Thomas. You needn't have this attitude, you know."

"You're wrong there, brother. As another former friend of mine would say, 'You're damn fucking right' I have an attitude. I've spent a lot of time and a lot of woe honing it to a fine edge. You haven't been where I spent the last few months of my life or you'd know how easy it is to have attitudes. I need my attitude. It's one of the few things I can depend on these days."

"Thomas, fr' godsakes man, don't be so—"

"Beat it. Up and out, and I mean it."

St. Germain arose. "Where do you go from here? That ship?"

"*Palenque* doesn't sail for two weeks they tell me."

"Come to Geneva and we'll sort everything out. I give you my solemn word."

"What is, is. Off you go. Or off I go."

"You forgot a vital point. Everything we all agreed to comes apart if you fail to adjust your son."

"*Conosco mio mestierre.*"

"Beg your pardon?"

"Spanish. It means, 'I know my trade'. I'm about to make or remake the richest boy in history, and I assure you my various agreements will remain intact. Now, for the third time, Monsieur Director, scram. *Marcha!*"

St. Germain's face suddenly became reddish though with a deadpan, aggrieved look Thomas would remember a long, long time. The banker arose, scuttering off as if trying to outrace his shadow.

A most unpleasant parting but Thomas cared little. Surprised at the acidity of his words, the intolerance they expressed; thinking he was becoming another Maistinger, who with his long El Greco face had all the makings of a medieval hangman. Surprised, even more, that the dogma-obsessed, genderless Maistinger had even trespassed into this day. Losing himself, losing control of his better behavior. Only two days earlier he had touched the rung of victory on the ladder of the nameless and the unfamiliar.

For his pains, and there were many—eleven-million Euros. Is this what it did to a man?

He ordered another cognac to anesthetize his bitterness. He was free again perhaps, but knew that as soon as he changed his son, technically, into a Muldaur, as per agreement, he'd thereafter be contending with all the complications and troubles of the super-rich until Christopher came of age, if he lived that long.

A prospect that did nothing to heighten his mood.

Downing the last of the cognac, he dealt with his constant agony. How to find her? Another loss if he couldn't; one too vast to contemplate, and one for adding to his lengthening invoice for the Swiss to pay off one day.

Monaco

He had boarded *Palenque* yesterday just before twilight. The ship—mighty—stood tall-masted against the nervous, white-capped waters; a beautifully raked hull had caught his attention all the way from the quay. Up close, she seemed enormous and stately. Built by Lündistt in Norway for the Emir of Caltaqar, *Palenque,* a motor-sailer, boasted three towering masts spiking up from her decks. At her plimsol line, she ran a full 254 feet in length. Powered by two 12,000 H.P. Caterpillar marine diesels, *Palenque* could make eleven knots hourly in calmed seas. Under sail, she could do no more than six knots if sailing before the wind, but only with all twenty sails set, stem to stern.

A launch, skippered by a Moroccan, al-Mouffa, had been sent to fetch him. On the way through the yacht-clogged harbor to *Palenque*, Thomas, impressed with all he had seen, asked questions about the ship, getting detailed replies.

Came this new morning and he inspected two staterooms in the aft of the ship. Both had been refitted, one as a spacious lab, the other as a small operating theater. Nothing had been spared anywhere. The finest, the very finest. It'd take weeks to outfit this setup so splendidly. So, they knew. They had known all long they could force him into as icy an alliance as an auctioned-off child bride.

Still...

And it was a big *still*, for Christopher would remain who he was always meant to be, his and Jaggy's biological son. Not a single authentic Muldaur gene would ever be active in the boy's genome. He had his ruse laid out as neatly as the rows of a vineyard, feeling not the barest pang of guilt over any of it.

The more he dwelled on it, the more appealing his subterfuge He planned to create two new chromosomes for Christopher, then, taking Baster's DNA, he'd block any if its genetic activity by binding Baster's genes to MicroRNA, a small yet powerful gene found in everyone's genome: all this he would hang on the two artificial chromosomes. Then, he'd park them where they were findable, but disabled, they would be essentially of no use.

Tricky, dicey, tedious, time consuming. Still, he saw no reason why the procedure wouldn't work as planned.

A squad of lab mice would tell the tale, first. If the slightest danger appeared, at any time, he'd kill the project. What then—he didn't know.

Nothing in law said or didn't say that genes had to work or not work in a certain way. Indeed, no one knew all the ins-and-outs of the human genome and the intricacies of its workings. If ever challenged, Baster's DNA could be fished out of Christopher's cells for anyone to see. And in a court of law, or anywhere else, no one could testify with certainty that Baster's genes were inactive in Christopher's life-long, cell-making processes.

Looking at the lab setup, reviewing his intentions, he heard a double knock on the stateroom's door, snapping him out of his reverie. Loudly, Thomas called out, "Come in...come right in," thinking it might be the deck steward with coffee. Day and night they swilled it by the pail on *Palenque*.

The door swung and its opening was fully filled by a man Thomas had seen yesterday, on deck, when boarding *Palenque*. A café-au-lait vision built like Atlas, with the waist of a girl and a neck packed with triangular muscles that bulged his blue-and-white striped sailor's jersey. His arms—thick and roped with standing veins—looked strong enough to toss telephone poles. Hands like grappling hooks. On the easy face was an easy smile showing wide teeth, white as sugar cubes.

"H'lo there," said Thomas after absorbing the giant.

"Good morning. I am Jackson Jellicoe. I beg your leave, sir, to discuss a few points of ship's security. The captain has sent me."

"Have a seat. Take any chair you like, since we've got about eight of them."

"If I may, I'll stand."

"Whatever your pleasure. I saw you yesterday when I boarded. You're not easy to miss."

"I have the deck on second-watch when we're in port. I'm third-officer of *Palenque*. I also serve as the ship's security officer."

"I can see why. How do they call you? Jackson?"

"Most call me Jack. Or Crunch, you might hear that name, too."

"Crunch...Crunch...how'd you get that one?" Now he noticed a tiny ruby stud sparkling on the left side of Jellicoe's nose.

"I do a little stunt with a baseball and that's how the name came about. A silly childish thing. Can't live it down, it seems."

"What's the stunt?"

"Crunching it."

"Crunching it? You can do that with a baseball? I'd like to see it. With your hands, you mean?"

"One hand, actually."

"I'd definitely like to see that done."

"Sometime, perhaps."

"What about now? I've been in here brooding and I can use a little entertainment. Sounds like a circus stunt. "

"Well...I don't know...I came for a chat-up to go over a few procedures." Jellicoe had shifted weight from one foot to the other, his buttocks going flat and then bulking up. Everything about him, the full reach of his six-foot plus frame seemed like a sculpted Olympic statue.

"Where're you from, Crunch? By the way, my name is Thomas."

"By birth, I am Jamaican. My mother is completely a Jamaican. My father was a Scot, a sailor out of Scapa Flow."

"A navy man?"

"Solid, by-the-book. Royal Navy. You can see that I am a two-tone. What they call a *bright* in the Caribbean."

Thomas nodded. "You can't beat being bright. Show me that baseball feat, will you?"

"I'm due on deck to see to a broken winch."

"Can't they leave you alone for ten minutes?"

Jellicoe smiled. "I suspect it'll be all right. A few minutes, I can spare that, surely."

When Jellicoe returned, he was tossing and catching a Rawlings baseball in his right hand; the hand, huge, completely covered the ball when in his palm. Jellicoe posed himself as if he were appearing in a body-building contest, and, suddenly straining, his shoulder grew. His linebacker's neck swelled. Muscle mass rippled down his arm. Both knees bent a little, as if he were about to jump. No jump, but a popping noise and when the giant opened his hand the baseball was compressed to a thick pancake-shaped ellipse.

"I never had reason to doubt you and I never shall in the future. I'm most impressed."

"It is a trick, just a trick, my dear fellow."

"Some trick. Thanks. I'm not going anywhere without you. Okay, back to the security procedures. What is it, I should know?"

Five minutes passed as Jellicoe described special devices on board, and other extraordinary precautions that would apply whenever *Palenque* made port on the voyage. Ending, he asked Thomas for comments.

"Madame Muldaur," said Thomas. "She likes to be called *madame* by strangers. She and the child will board *Palenque* two days from now. A doctor, a couple of nurses…three nurses actually for round-the-clock…and two Swiss technicians are expected to arrive the day after, as I understand it. I'll want half of this second deck secured. Really tight, I mean, so a fly couldn't get through it. I'll want this specific area of the ship battened down, along with the nearest four staterooms. All strictly reserved for my use. Madame Muldaur and her entourage can have the upper deck all to themselves. On no account, ever, is she to be allowed in the lab or anywhere near it." In blank dismay, he added, "You ought to know that this woman is war-loving, so prepare yourself. She'll use intimidating threats. You'll have to use your own ways of ignoring her. But use some care. She can swallow barbed-wire whole."

A visibly perplexed Jellicoe asked, "But is she not paying for this cruise? I heard it to be so."

"Has she said that to someone?"

"I thought it was said in a message to the captain. That she wanted approval of the voyage plan, and a list of all ports of call."

"And has the captain given all that to her?"

"I believe he's awaiting her arrival."

"Thanks for telling me. The ship's charter is actually being paid for by a fund…well, a sort of fund…she's nothing to do with any of it. All the orders come from me except the operation of the ship itself. That's totally the captain's affair."

"Are we to expect difficulties, then?"

"Only from the woman, I'd imagine. When and if that happens, you will please let me know. I'll deal with it. She is to have the child for two hours of every day but only in the presence of a nurse and a security person to be detailed by you. Any communication between madame and me will be in writing. She's to be walled off completely."

Jellicoe blew out a little air, then said, "This child is a…it's a lad?"

"Yes, only eight months old."

"Sick?"

"Very and he will be sicker if we don't take care of him."

"And you are a doctor?"

"I am, but not a medical doctor. I hold a doctorate in biological sciences."

"I see. I ask because a ship, you understand, is like an army barracks. Rumors all the time."

"Ask away, Crunch. Whatever is on your mind, I'd be grateful to know about it."

"And you will be supervising the—." Jellicoe broke off, his hand sweeping in a gesture that indicated the banks of equipment.

"Yes, that's what I do. I run the machines and do other procedures that're made possible by the machines."

"I see."

Thomas regarded the human colossus again, liking what he saw. Jellicoe seemed very together, polite but not obsequious, and possessed of a quiet authority. "Crunch, how'd it be if you worked with me? Only me?"

"I could not, sir. I have ship's duties."

"We both have duties. I'll have a word with the captain and I'm confident we can sort this out. Wuddya say? Would you?"

"I should be most pleased if the captain has no objections…I suppose…"

"Your pay, whatever it is, will be doubled."

"I say now…I say, that'd be an amazing gift."

"We'll figure out your job as we go along."

"Security measures?"

"Largely, yes. Security from the woman and her meddling. I'm sure she'll have someone or maybe two someones who'll accompany her on board. Men, I'd guess. As I mentioned there're two Swiss scientists who're supposed to be coming along. I haven't quite made up my mind about them. Oh, one other thing, have they put in any cameras or listening devices in this area of the ship?"

"Four fish-eye cameras and many listening bugs. One camera is directly overhead; it's that little round fisheye you see up there in the corner of the ceiling. To your right, there. You'd find it easier to go over there and look up."

"I want all of it dismantled. Can you do it?"

"With the captain's agreement, I can."

"Where's the captain now? Or do we know?"

"On the bridge, I believe. I last saw him there with the second-mate."

"All right, I'll add that to my list for the captain."

"I've been wondering why all this spyware was installed." Jellicoe observed. "It's a great much for an area this size."

Quite leery, still, of the Swiss, his newfound bedfellows, he said to Jellicoe: "There are people who're afraid I won't tell them everything I'm supposed to tell them. I don't like being spied upon. I've just decided something. We'll not let these two Swiss board *Palenque* under any circumstances."

"No? How do you suggest we keep them off?"

"I'm trying to figure that out."

"Could it lead to difficulty, should we refuse to board them?"

"Probably so. Definitely so, I imagine. Trouble for me, that is, not for you. That's why I need an angle. Two angles would be better. That fella that runs the launch, al-Mouffa, can you tell him to lose the distributor cap on the engine for a couple of strategic hours? We'll tell him when to do it. And I'll make a request of the skipper to get underway at a certain time when our Swiss friends think we're actually getting ready to pick them up. It might work."

"Likely they'll complain. Stoutly, won't they?"

"The Swiss always complain about something or other. It's endemic. But then we can add to the confusion by saying we didn't expect so many in the Muldaur entourage."

"The *Palenque* is a large vessel. They'd not easily believe that story."

"You're right again. Okay, let's try another tack. We'll say we can't board them unless they're medically certified to be free of any communicable diseases. A sickly child and so on and we can't take the merest chances. No certificate, no coming aboard. How does that one sound?"

"The best yet, I'd say. Very good." Jackson Jellicoe had taken a chair a few minutes earlier. As he stood now, he seemed to grow a foot taller. "I'll handle it for you. Leave them to me."

"I shall…oh, I shall, and with deepest pleasure."

Glancing at a brass-rimmed chronometer on the wall, Thomas checked the time. "I've got to get ashore and do a few errands. Cigars and such. Why don't you come along and we can talk things over at lunch? Besides, we'll need the launch and it's an opportunity to tell al-Mouffa what we want of him. I'll make sure he won't regret it. You'll come ashore with me?"

"Most pleased to accompany you, doctor."

"Thomas…"

"Thomas, I'll remember. Thank you."

"You stand like a military man. Were you?"

"British Army."

"Really? What branch?"

"S.A.S."

"Ah, the special—what's the rest, I forget."

"Special Air Service."

"A commando, were you?"

"You might say."

"And your rank?"

"Sergeant-major. I was wounded in Afghanistan and had had enough, so I chose to muster out."

"I'm liking this better and better. Let's go find the captain and add some woe to his day."

"Would it not be better if you were to see him yourself? I don't want him thinking I dreamed this up."

"Good thought. What's he like?"

"An Aussie, a good bloke. Fine sailor, goes right by the book."

Jellicoe, constantly glancing about the converted stateroom with its banks of equipment, seemed fascinated with the blinking red and blue lights, the gun-metal gray cabinetry, the dials, the levers, and rows of shiny chrome buttons, the electro-scopes, other impressive looking paraphernalia. "Many of them, aren't there? Will you one day show me how these machines work?"

"I'd be pleased to. Right now, I'll see the boss-man and find out if I can cut us a deal. You've put me in a good mood so we're going to find an expensive restaurant and have at it. You know of a good one?"

"They say *Coupole,* that's on avenue Princess Grace. One of the best, I've heard."

"That's the one for us, then."

"I cannot afford that, Thomas. It won't do for me, not at all. Sorry."

"I'm buying the bread today. I'll chase after the skipper now and then I'll pick you up in, say, half an hour and we'll go feast and have a talk about life at sea and other things I cannot yet imagine."

"I'll need your advice on another thing," Crunch said. "Am I to confront those two scientists face to face?"

"I've got their cell-phone numbers. Best to call, first, whenever entering battle. Saves a lot of bloodshed. That's my opinion anyway."

"Right you are. Have you a spare Euro note? A hundred would do nicely. For al-Mouffa, he's Libyan and they thrive on *baksheesh*. Their candy, you see."

"Soon as I get some change, it's yours. How about you, Crunch, have you a susceptibility to *baksheesh*?"

"As long as she's five-feet eight or taller, I do. I'm most susceptible in that case."

Laughing, Thomas said, "You and I will get along famously. I'll be off to find the skipper."

Coupole was as billed by Jellicoe, the meal lavish, the bill outrageous. After lunch, Crunch left for places unknown. Thomas walked a block south and sat on a bench overlooking the Club du Monte Carlo, its beach filled with bronzed loungers and swimmers in scantest swimwear. Slipping a newly acquired cell phone from his pocket, he punched in the numbers for reaching a missing-person investigator—a retired lieutenant from the St. Louis Police Department, a woman with clipped hurried speech, sounding tough as sunbaked saddle leather.

While in Davos, he had engaged the investigator, aided by Braunsweig' New York, to find Shandar. If successful, he meant to bring her aboard *Palenque*, Jaggy or no Jaggy, for he couldn't stand the prospect of another year's separation.

"So far, nothing, a full-blown zero." said the ex-police lieutenant. "She's fully submerged herself. Someday federal records, taxes and so on, might possibly yield clues. A possibility but a year or two away at best. If she's living under an assumed name, finding her could prove very iffy. Or, if she has left U.S. soil, she could be beyond the reach of a domestic investigation."

Done all the time, Thomas was told. People going to ground, leaving no trace, no trail. They obtained false identity papers, just as illegal immigrants do; found out-of-the-way places, tucked their past in mothballs, almost as if they were in a self-styled witness-protection program. Hearing it, he thought of Linpao's ruses and his assortment of bogus passports.

"Is this woman well off?" asked the retired lieutenant.

"I can't say. She lived well but that's about all I know of her finances. Did you try Mrs. Nestor again? A Poppi Nestor living in Brooklyn?"

"I've tried her twice. Mrs. Nestor seems convinced you did something terrible to her friend."

"It so happens I'm in love with her friend. What's so terrible about that?"

"I couldn't say. Anyway, she refuses to cooperate. Nothing there, a flat nothing at all. A fat zero, in fact. She's pretty snotty. Eats horseradish for breakfast, I'd bet."

"She didn't used to be like that. Keep trying whatever you can think of. I'll call you every Wednesday or try to."

"You sure you want to spend all this money? It's going to add up."

"Keep going full bore and forget the expense."

"And what if we find out she's, uh, what I mean is...well, what if she's dead? Any special instructions?"

"I'll want to know exactly how it happened."

"Supposing, I can't find out?"

"Spend whatever it takes...and before I forget, in case you're unsure of getting paid, you'll be receiving your monthly fee and any expenses from a bank in Geneva, Switzerland. Braunsweig und Sohn, that's the name of the bank. It'll come via a check drawn on Bank of America in St. Louis."

"I'm not worried at all. All right, then, I'll keep pressing all the buttons I can find."

"I'll be in touch. Thanks for your help. Find her, and there's an extra hundred-thousand with your name on it."

In hiding? It didn't compute. Dead? A specter so searing it drained the breath out of him. She had been the one perfect thing in his life. Life can be so much better with your eyes and ears closed, he thought. Despondently, he walked a half-mile to the quay, found a stone bench, and, lighting up a Cohiba, he gazed absently at *Palenque* riding at anchor. A year? Would it take that long to re-wire Christopher? Even if it didn't, maybe he should make it appear it required that stretch of time. He needed to be convincing, needed to show the Maroche crowd this was no quick thing.

He could do that, he thought, but then came the prospect of a year at sea with Jaggy Muldaur, seeming to him like more time back in the dungeon. Yet with Crunch on the scene, perhaps she'd be kept at bay. Other questions plagued him. Heading the list was what he'd gotten himself into. He had wanted nothing more, at the outset, than cheap healthcare for everyone needing it. A great thing it would be; yet with MarocheChem in the picture he knew he must shunt that hope aside.

He smoked for a time, pleasurably, watching the movement of boats in the harbor. Watching the aimless drift of clouds and the time-slant of the sun. Three o'clock, he guessed, then checked his watch, noting he was only ten minutes off. Then he watched several pay-for-pay girls laughing and gossiping together, out for a little sun and sea air before plying their nightly trade Monaco. Sandbox for the rich, playground for the wannabes. Well, why not? He was here, wasn't he? But not for any playtime.

Something was pestering him. He lifted a hand to his face, feeling the humidity of his skin, a dampness, he suspected, born of a deepening dread.

Of what though?

That he'd never again see Shandar? That he'd make a mistake when manipulating all those unseeable molecules inside a son for whom he had yet to learn real love? Or that he simply had descended into a state of nagging paranoia?

His thoughts were as tangled as jungle vines.

Looking to one side, he saw Crunch Jellicoe striding down the walkway to the quayside. Thomas snuffed the Cohiba and stood up, waving at his newfound cohort.

Still uneasy, though. Still troubled. A fuzzy impression at best, like the onset of one of his waking dreams where everything was lopsided for a time. Were he a soothsayer, he might have sensed he was bring unnerved: that it was anxiety derived from what he was about to do to save the life of Christopher. Yet it was more, much more—it was a glimmer of the smoking gun-of-the-future, the weapon so rightly feared by deMehlo.

And even if it were a gun invisible, he nonetheless was the one aiming it, firing it—the first ever to remake a genome of a live person

Decades later, looking back on this day, and by then a man torn, he would see he had done what he had done at a cost of everlasting remorse.

To himself and to the world he had hoped to help.

PART III

The Savior said, all nature, all formations,
all creatures exist in and with one another,
and they will be resolved again into their own roots.
—Gospel According to Mary Magdalene, Capitulus 4

Who we were, and what we have Become,
where we were…whither we are hastening;
from what we are being released, what birth
is. And what is Rebirth.
—Theodotus, Asia Minor c. 140-160 AD

Denver, Colorado

Scrolling through a blog, seeing a reference, Sarita Sambinna keyed her way to an article published by a well-known biotech periodical, where she read:

...as this year marks the seventy-second anniversary of Zyme-One, it is worth noting the marvels of genetic therapy, while weighing its frightening abuses. Widely, it is clamed, that Zyme-One was and still is the pivotal force that led to low-cost universal healthcare, and yet it also spawned much of the anxiety we now face as we humans slowly morph into what many see as the post-human or Transhumanism era.

Growing numbers of advocates for a super-species, most notably the *"Gorpos"*, have avidly pressed ahead with their controversial agenda— exhorting the general public to avail itself of gene therapy to lengthen life, enhance memory, achieve exquisitely high intellectual attainments, reach greater peaks of emotional and sexual satisfaction, perfected motor skills, and achieve physical beauty hardly imagined as recently as two or three generations ago. This is accomplished, as many know, by use of Goldilocks gene-paks, an amalgam of genes sold by famous actors, sports stars, intellectuals and other prominent personalities to those wishing to liken themselves to the famous. Or, in some cases, to those who're youth-clinging wannabes who will pay whatever it takes to rejuvenate themselves.

While Goldilocks paks are expensive—upwards of $30-thousand a shot— the cost is no deterrent to the wealthy, who, in their bid to join the genetic gold rush, often charge the treatments to their credit cards, as though it were no more than another trip to a posh resort.

U.S. and European demographers estimate that *Gorpos,* within the next generation or two, will multiply so quickly they'll seriously contend for political control of many of the western world's power centers. Indeed, as one reputable study concludes... "Little stands in their way, they've got the brains and abilities to do whatever they please..."

Perhaps, as the study also points out, *Gorpos* are the in-between stage of a new species of humans, or even some mysterious way station to another sort of mammal-type, whose attributes cannot be accurately predicted at this time. Whatever lies ahead, it appears the human race is headed for a tectonic shift as we morph ourselves into unknown waters of gravest change.

Most worrisome of all is the everyday fear that, to compete effectively, all of society may be forced to follow in the footsteps of the *Gorpos*, meaning, of course, that we only compound the problem accelerating our way to a post-human era.

Nor should we ignore or forget who it was who brought us this quite fantastic, double-edged weapon that, on the one hand, has cured so many maladies, while, on the other, has brought us to the precipice of the unknown. Culprit or savior? Often slandered and as often praised, Thomas Courmaine is the scientist who discovered Zyme-One, the commercial name for an enzyme concoction that allows for limitless gene manipulation. At first, when brought to market, the technology was hailed as one of the great health-giving achievements of our time or of any time. Too soon, however, a spreading sepsis set in when corruption of the processes spawned the morass of troubles we face today.

Lost to history is exactly where this startling chapter of science began. Some say in Africa, others insist it was in Wales. Courmaine won't even discuss it, insisting he has no right to involve other participants, though it is widely known that Lin-pao, the famed Chinese biochemist was in on the ground floor.

Now living a reclusive life on his estate in England, Courmaine is nonetheless often mentioned whenever the topic of gene-fixing comes to the fore. Only a month ago, he was said to have acidly scolded the annual convention of cellular biologists, for, as he put it, "Copping out on your responsibilities to humanity and doing so little to stem the explosive growth of the *Gorpos,* while also failing to persuade the young to get wise to themselves...what I did we might think of as creative destruction of the human race...what you're doing is sitting on your complacent asses..."

Nothing new, nothing Sarita Sambinna didn't already know, quite sure she knew things about Thomas Courmaine few others were aware of, anywhere. Her mood gloomy, she pulled out a sheet of blue vellum stationery, and penned yet another plea.

Done, she inserted a photo of herself standing next to Lin-pao, taken purposely two months earlier in Shanghai. Sealing the envelope, she wrote a notation on the flap, hoping it might draw the notice she intended.

Her fourth attempt, this letter, and he'd better agree to an interview, or she meant to travel to England anyway and become the hot needle in his every day. Courmaine was the linchpin persona of the five biographies she was undertaking over the next decade; personal histories of the most widely acknowledged scientists of the previous century. The Isaac Newtons of their era. The life-changers and game-changers, and none more of a changer than Thomas I. Courmaine, the ex-patriate American called a saint by some, a criminal by others.

At times, she was tempted to plunge ahead without him, relying on hearsay, innuendo, the endless rumors, and volumes of magazine articles, clippings, blogs. She had two filing cabinets groaning under the weight of all the material she'd been collecting for three years or more.

To date, she had scanned over a thousand web pages on the man's doings, many filled with rancorous criticism, curbside gossip, and what-all; others, however, gave out with lavish praise.

She wanted to hear his side of it, wanted to get into his bones, comingle with his mind. The lesser crimes, the greater misdemeanors; what were those all about? Really about? Why had he turned down that Nobel, something most scientists would trade their souls for?

Scientists, she had decided, quested for one golden ring that surmounted all else: wanted to be remembered, wanted their slice of immortality.

Certain she could handle him, if only she could pierce his barricade. More, and with him being none the wiser, she was really after more than his story.

Thoughts kept radiating, even a few budding schemes sprouted, some for the tenth time. Her female antennae notched up into the agitation mode as she considered how her earlier letters had been rebuffed. You could hardly mark it off as a rebuff, for Thomas Courmaine had never once bothered to reply.

Who in the blue hell did he think he was? A resurrected god of some kind?

Atherton Downs
Abington Piggots, England

Cold and blustery, though well into May, a day on which he had reached his one-hundred and ninth year of life. Or so he believed, as no one had ever been certain of his exact day of birth.

A grim way to spend one, Thomas was thinking as he gauged two piles of mail, each nearly a foot-high. Deepening his gray mood was the London newscast he'd watched an hour ago. The *Gorpos* had won another nine seats in Parliament, and were on the brink of taking control of the House in the next election. They vowed to force gene-screening on every British resident, citizen or not, to detect flaws. Refusal to cooperate meant reprisals of one sort or another, including the denial of access to free gene-paks meant to cure maladies; but also hastening the day when humans morph themselves into an ever-growing yet separate sub-species.

The *Gorpos*, a cunning crowd, were maneuvering to force others to become like themselves.

The newscast so riled him, he had turned it off, promising himself to keep it off for a week.

When dressing this morning, reminding himself of the day and his age, he noted little change from when he had turned fifty, the year he had taken possession of Atherton Downs.

Still lithe, still flat-bellied, a full head of blondish hair, though streaked with silver, able to jog five-miles three days of the week and swim fifty laps on most other days. Fit, he had no concerns about his body but his mind was another story: stark worries bombarded him in these waning days of life. The money, Christopher, tidying up his affairs, providing for the staff here at Atherton Downs and others who worked at his lab in Cambridge.

The prospect of a Cohiba had offered its temptations for the past hour, and, a collateral thought was a possible visit to the bar across the library. A snifter of Hine Ancien, a much favored cognac, was steadily climbing with appeal. Still, the hour hand was on the short side of ten in the morning, and, while he might engage in the cigar, any hard drink must await sundown: a rule he had obeyed for decades.

A rule he might soon skirt, however, given the shortage of days left him, a few weeks at best.

Scoping the mail again, he grimaced. Ordinarily, his assistant would cope with it, but in a welter of generosity he'd awarded her an extra fortnight's holiday so she and her husband could tour Tanzania and Kenya with their two children. The thought of Africa, that she was there and he wasn't, elicited envy. He'd like to see it again. In Africa, he was a celebrated hero, and he'd like to feel another wave or two of that gratitude before calling it a day. No, he'd be calling it a life.

Stone-still, he sat in the green-leather, brass-studded Eames chair by the fireplace. A comfortable lair, where he spent lengths of time, liking the pickled pine paneling, the forty shelves of books, the deep and long sofas, the comfort-making ambience. His favorite place to work—a partner's desk he'd bought at a Christie's auction—and some good oils: Constables and Munnings, depicting a long-ago time in the English countryside. Large, friendly and warm, the room held a granite-faced fireplace that burned for eight months of the year. The room's floor was blessed with an elaborately woven rug—a gift of the Afghani government. Often, he took his meals in this room when dining alone.

Walking over to the two-story arched window behind his partners' desk, he gazed into the dull gray thickness hovering above the grounds, letting his thoughts drift like the mist rolling up from the river today.

What had it all meant, these years?

The bell was tolling for men and women like him and tolling, too, for the era of science he had helped to craft. All genes, he thought—those magic-making chemicals that had formed the human race, billions of us, all as individually different as our fingerprints. An astonishing piece of artwork by Nature, now under assault due to his handiwork.

Not a lot of joy to be had, to cherish. Soon enough he could get loose of it. Or try.

He had been plotting his own finish for the greater fraction of five years, beginning with an inspiration that had bounded upon him one afternoon in Geneva, when assessing the suffocating dilemma of what to do about The Trust—that ever expanding money-cow.

Nonetheless, the closer he got to his own ending, the happier his outlook. He simply had run out of usefulness to himself. Four attempts on his life in the past year alone. Twenty-two of them over the past six years, forcing him to live as a loner. So what was the point of going on?

As he thought of it, asking himself now: what was a hundred-and-nine anyway?

Of the dwindling faculty at Cambridge, he knew three who were forty years his senior in age. They had reached 150 age-wise, having availed themselves decades ago of life-lengthening Zyme-One treatments. Likely, they could attain 200 or even 300, if they insisted. Yet they complained of boredom, of too little to do, without any real excitement about what lay ahead. They'd done it all, ten times over. Their health seemed fine but their everyday lives had come to a standstill, fretting them visibly because their minds were as quick and resourceful as others who were far, far younger.

Zyme-One had done them in; now, the prospect was either keep going, searching for fulfillment, or give up by some form of suicide. They were like his Eves in Africa, where it had all started. Genetically refreshed, their appearance belying their true age, they thrived under an illusion: they were what they weren't.

Sometimes they cast disparaging looks his way, as if he alone were responsible for their plight. True, he had cut open the path but they, and they only, had chosen to walk it.

Looking at mail once more, he began to relent. He had been the target of hate mail for too many years, and had come to intensely dislike the sight of it. But he had been expecting a letter from Belgium, and decided he had best sort the piles. Sighing to himself, he started in. Putting some of it aside, the part deserving of an answer, the discards were sailed into a wicker basket; later, the contents would be fodder for a warming fire.

One envelope, headed for an exit to the basket, refused to leave his hand. Postmarked Denver, Colorado, it was of light blue vellum with a laid, cross-hatched finish. Turning over the envelope, he was almost sure he recognized the return address. Similar mail had arrived in each of the past months; mail that his assistant had deposited on his desk. He had replied to none of the earlier letters, nor read them.

Yet this time, on the envelope's flap, the writer had printed: **Lin-pao Inside**.

Tearing it open, he saw a photo-likeness of his old friend, his finest and closest colleague, and watched as the photo fluttered to the floor. Bending, he retrieved it, having a closer look.

There he was, the old self: the spiked hair, the owlish grin, the cherubic face round as a moon, and the narrow shoulders giving way to a bulbous middle, shaping him like an uneven triangle. Next to him, a woman.

He read the letter's four paragraphs. Catching his attention, one brief part mentioned a visit the writer—a Sarita Sambinna—had had with Lin-pao in Shanghai. Lin-pao had never made mention of it, but that meant nothing by itself.

Clever of her, he thought, to have put the tag of **Lin-pao Inside** on the flap, ensuring it would not be idly tossed away.

This woman, whoever she was, asserted she was a biographer, desirous of confirming a number of details linked to the factual essence of his life. She was writing him up for a book, slated, she went on, for submission to her publisher within six months. Striking a note of urgency, she pointed out that if he ignored her, she'd be forced to proceed without him, letting the chips fall where loose chips always fall: helter-skelter.

A veiled threat, was it? The usual journalistic ploy, implying—*help me or I'll skewer you.* Which often happened anyway, help or no help.

He but rarely acceded to requests for interviews. He had been battered for far too long by the media, by authors and pundits and journalists, for whom he attached a privy-like odor in his mind.

Pointless, though, to keep ignoring her. He'd overrule himself, call her or at least send an e-mail.

A thought glimmered. Better, perhaps, to pen her a gracious reply, pleading a mercilessly jammed schedule. Or maybe not, maybe it was time to clean up the record. On a whim, he sat again at a console behind his desk and sent off an e-mail to a woman friend at Cambridge, inquiring about the Colorado woman; all this, as an intriguing idea accosted him.

Within the hour, a reply came from his reliable source, a redoubtable woman herself, his weekly sleep-mate, who, and most helpfully so, served as research-head at the Genetics Library over on Downing Street in Cambridge. She had once worked as an analyst for the British MI-5, was a genuine wizard at ferreting out information from all corners of the globe.

A spot check on the Internet had thrown back forty-seven articles about the American letter-writer and her work. An embedded summary revealed:

Sarita S. Sambinna, divorced, no children. Stillstein Professor of History, Denver University. Ass't. Professor of History University of North Carolina, Research Ass't University of Michigan. Degrees: B.A. University of California; M.A., Stanford University; Ph.D, University of Texas. Author of ten published biographies. McMillan Prize from U.S. Historical Assoc., Pen Award, National Bookseller's First Honor, Tennerwitz Memorial Fellow, nominated for Pulitzer Prize. Hobbies: skiing, fly-fishing, scuba diving, needlepoint, community theater.

Reading it twice, contemplating then: death was doing its door-knocking, his days numbered; thus, this Sambinna woman might have her uses.

Why not leave this world pushed along by the tailwinds of as much of the truth as he could get away with? Time to tell his side, or some of it anyway. Besides, he might get a break and right now he could use one —as the days closed in on him.

A tell-all book; the thought of it purging his earlier mood. As his parting shot from this life, over the past several years he'd masterminded the greatest heist in the annals of history. A monumental scheme, tricked up in ways that left no clues, no traces, no spoor. It had taken him endless, endless hours to set up over three-hundred dummy corporations, then shuffle loads of assets around and re-shuffle them into a complex maze of banks. The identity of the banks and the various account-codes were listed on an encrypted disk squirreled away in a strongbox. Wrapped in four thicknesses of canvas, the box was buried near a dilapidated cairn at the easterly end of the Downs.

He knew exactly where it was, so did Crunch, but no one else knew anything.

A theft beyond imagination. He ranked it as his life's crowning achievement. With this profuse trove, eventually he hoped to make his amends to the humanity he had so misguidedly threatened.

And what of this biographer who was so set on seeing him? What of the very dim prospects of being believed: and that, though trying strenuously, he had failed to get the cogs of his life to fit with the gears he had so assiduously sought. But then who does? And, thinking on it, he asked himself: how many get a shot at having the final word about themselves?

Bring the lady on...

His spirits, by now, had lifted, all because of a letter immersed in a welter of others. A letter he had almost discarded on sight, and would have had he not noticed the reference to his great friend, Lin-pao of Shanghai.

Cambridge, England

Yet another incident at the Downs, putting Thomas in a boiling fury.

Seventy-year old Christopher had assaulted one of the six male nurses hired to keep round-the-clock watch over him. The overseers, all burly types, kept vigil in pairs. Often, it took three of them to contain the unruly Christopher when on one of his rampages. With his abundant guile, he had lured two of the men to the hayloft of a lower-field stable, cold-cocking one, while taking the grossest license with the other. Thinking it a big folly, a laughing matter, the day's very joy, the day's great hilarity—his son, seeing nothing wrong whatsoever in the act, had insisted: "Jolly fun, Daddy. Quite a lovely bum on him, he had. Just good sport, you know…why all the to-do, Daddy? Gave as good as he got…he did, you know…"

Christopher had not the slightest qualm over his behavior. None, not ever. Impervious totally to law, rule, convention and custom. Of another world, he may as well have been from the primeval life of the ancient jungle-peoples.

The abused nurse, enraged, had demanded a payoff or he'd be complaining to the police within the hour. In any event, he had handed in his resignation (finding a replacement was no simple task, initiating other problems); and, with slim choice, Thomas had forked over a sizeable slug of hush-money.

Allegations lodged with the local constabulary would only lead to an official inquiry. Police would arrive, looking for Christopher, making queries that would surely unearth an astonishing roundup of long-buried events and secrets. That'd be the end of his son—who'd admit to anything he thought funny—and that, of itself, once the door was ajar, could blow the lid off a nation shaking story: the seventy-year long cover-up of the greatest double crime of almost any age, known or unknown.

As the paymaster for cleaning up Christopher's dirty linen for fifty-five years of the seventy-years his son had lived, he himself was guilty of obstructing fair-minded justice not fewer than six times.

He was dwelling on this most recent incident when a call came from the lobby-desk of Cavendish Laboratory, where he kept offices and his own small lab at the university. A woman, to see him, he was told by the security guard…"name of Sarita Sambinna, says here on this card she gives us…do we allow her up?"

He had all but forgotten her. Now the remembrance of that Italian name—the biographer-woman from America.

A mis-timed moment—she'd arrived unannounced. Minutes later, a sublime darkness filled the door opening and he heard that faint swishing sound women often make, or their clothes do, and in she came to his presence and his life.

He shaped his face into a half-smile. A rationed reaction, for no full beam was possible today, not after the morning's fiasco.

Better scenery by far stood before him, and she, returning his smile, revealed a ripe mouth, the lips slightly glossed. A quick thought passed through him that he'd seen her somewhere before but knew he hadn't. He stared, fixedly and impolitely.

The Sarita, as he was eventually to think of her, looking forty but was likely in her late sixties, possibly seventy. Everyone looked younger than they should, or had in years past, and he had helped make the fiction of youth possible. Even so, the gene-driven melting away of years sometimes surprised him. Tall, rangy, loose-limbed, with bushy eyebrows arching over deep dark eyes. Ebony hair swept straight back over an oval face with ringlets curling against her brow. With a name like Sambinna, he supposed she might be of Italian extraction if that were her maiden name; maybe not, but she looked Italian or of some other Mediterranean extraction. When moving her shoulders, a thick plaited braid, secured by a silver barrette, shifted across her back. On the middle finger of her right hand a wide-banded silver ring was mounted with a turquoise the size of a cat's eye, flanked by what appeared to be cabochon sapphires.

Collecting his impressions, noting she moved with a slight limp.

Tea was brought in while they sat on stuffed chairs separated by an old rectory bench stacked high with computer print-outs. She talked away, allowing herself to be reviewed, a way of breaking the ice. She seemed cold, judging from the way she gripped her tea mug, relaying its heat into her hands. This was England, also it was Cavendish Lab. Central heat was no part of its amenities. One quickly learned to wear sweaters and tweeds at this season.

"…I gambled I could outlast you," she was telling him, "so I kept asking and asking you until you'd surrender."

"Persistent, hey?"

"Terribly so, and I have to be. I chase facts and you well know how elusive they are. Somewhere I heard you're a stickler for facts."

"Steady diet, yes, I eat them. And you...you just barge right in, without a call or anything?" Repressing, a scolding tone, but not quite soon enough.

"You're about to frazzle my feelings." She spoke so softly, so politely and correctly, always with a hint of a smile.

"I might be intending to," he countered, still out of sorts over Christopher's transgression.

"You're not a curmudgeon, I hope."

"Don't you be so sure, young lady."

"I'll be sixty-nine soon. Hardly that young, I'm afraid. You *did* send me a letter to come ahead to England."

"I didn't hear back, so I assumed you'd changed your mind."

"I did change it. I was diverted to San Francisco for an important meeting with my literary agent. I decided to keep on flying and come here, and, well, surprise you."

"And you have, you have..."

"If I've upset you, I apologize. I tried calling and found you had no public listing. I don't like sat-comm faxing because too many people can read what you send. I thought—um—"and she shrugged—"I suppose I should've done something but I didn't want to be ignored again. I really want to do the book or make a good try at it. You're not thinking of sending me away? Are you? Say no. Please say no. I'm probably saying all the wrong things. I came directly here after landing. I've got to find a sleeping arrangement somewhere, have you a recommendation?"

"Your bags, where're those?"

"In the car. I rented one at the station. A sun-coupe, it's quite nice."

"How'd you know where to find me?"

"I've been looking into you. Where you work and so on. I thought I'd try here first. It's not a military secret you keep a laboratory here at Cavendish."

"No, it isn't but sometimes I wish it were. Well, let's get going. I live several miles up the road. It's a big enough place so you can have two or three rooms to yourself. Staying at the Downs will save us both time and it'll facilitate matters. That suit you?"

"Admirably. Won't I be putting you out?"

"Be no trouble at all. Not on the least."

"Is your wife...wouldn't she want to know? Such short notice."

"Finish up your tea, as you can, and we'll be on our way. You can follow us, or drive with us. I can have your car brought over later this afternoon."

"Who is we, may I ask?"

"My associate, Crunch. His name is Jackson Jefferson Jellico but we call him Crunch. He accompanies me just about everywhere. My sidekick."

"Oh, I thought it might be Mrs. Courmaine. You said we and I just supposed—"

"Actually, who you're referring to is Mrs. Courmaine-Muldaur," he corrected. "But no, she doesn't figure into my commuting. Or very little else, either."

"I see."

"No, you don't. It doesn't matter. A couple of things, Miss Sambinna. Or is it, Mrs.?"

"Miss, I'm single. Is Crunch that big man, dark-skinned? I saw a man like that in the lobby?"

"Probably. Was he wearing dark glasses?"

"I think so. Yes, he was. Like those aviator glasses."

"Sounds like him. While I think of it, if you're on any sort of diet or have food preferences, send word to the kitchen. I say this to you before I forget to say it. We don't eat that pill-food. If you need anything else in particular, tell the upstairs hall maid. Margaret Maisley, that's her name. She'll probably unpack you. She'll insist on it, unless I miss my guess. By the time she finishes, she'll know half your history. She'll be looking after you. Officious, if you know what I mean but she's also as efficient as a hummingbird. Oh, yes, one other thing. I'd like to begin our discourses at nine sharp in the morning. We'll meet in my library on the first floor. I'll allot you a fortnight and that's it. What am I missing? Plenty probably. Will you want a day of rest to settle yourself?"

"Tomorrow is dandy fine with me. A good sleep tonight and I'll be ready to march ahead."

"You're on your own for dinner tonight, I'm afraid. This is a night reserved for my son. Shall we be off?"

"Am I to meet your son?"

"A private sort of person, so no, I don't think you'll be seeing him."

"Oh."

Right away he had a feeling about her, a feeling he couldn't quite place and hadn't a name for. She seemed direct and pleasant enough and yet he had a lingering suspicion or two, but couldn't put a finger on anything specific.

Probably a mistake, having her stay at the Downs but it would save time and time was becoming more precious with every tick of the clock.

Here she was, finally, and he had let himself in for it: she'd be unsealing the past, plumbing aspects of his life as a priest, a father, scientist, a man, the bogus marriage—and other passages of life he had attempted to bury at one of his many private requiems.

How much would he remember accurately? Many things he'd never tell anyone; then again—how much did she already know? He didn't want to lie, certainly, but felt squeamish about opening himself up. More, she said she'd been studying him and he didn't like the sound of that, not one bit.

Yes, here she was, a most useful vehicle for telling things he'd never told anyone. Setting things to rights, finally. Maybe yes, he'd tell her—then again, maybe he'd decide differently tomorrow.

Atherton Downs
Abington Piggots, England

At the agreed hour, they met the next morning and set other rules to govern their routine. Punctually, they'd meet at nine o'clock, have their tea at ten-thirty, break for lunch at noon sharp. Swim, if she chose to, or walk the grounds if her leg permitted. Dinner at eight; a cocktail if she liked at seven or so in the great hall by the fireplace. Everything as regulated as a metronome, the way he wanted it, the way he must have it.

On the second day, taking a breather in the afternoon, he had escorted her, limp and all, along with his two Labradors, on a short walk of the estate. They tarried on a hilltop where she could see the roll of the land all the way down to the river and beyond, nearly 2,000 acres of lush flora and other verdant scenery for which the Downs was famous. When the air was clear of any shrouding weather, as today, the view of the countryside spread for miles and miles. To the rear of where they stood, the old castle, with all its sprawl, was fronted by its circular driveway of crushed white marble, the long center core of the building stretching for seventy yards was flanked by the two L-shaped wings. Five chimneys and two turrets sprouted from the slate roof of each wing. Perhaps, its crowning feature was the series of cathedral-like stained-glass windows that, depending on the sun's angle, constantly changed their hues and shapes, almost like the prisms of a kaleidoscope.

Sarita Sambinna seemed transfixed at the sight of it all, delaying them till he coaxed her along. She finally, reluctantly did, and he marveled at how well she got about with her stiff leg. The soft breezes took to her, blushing up her cheeks, pasting the ebony ringlets fast against her brow.

What he liked most of all was her laugh; low, then rising up the scale, often ending on a note of jubilation. When something struck her as funny, her head flew back, exposing the perfect pink of her neck, and a strong-looking, pulsing throat.

And she was smiling now at something he said, idly, but he was no longer idle as fixated on an aerial ambush. Way up, a good three hundred feet, an assassination was about to take place. A gray-backed falcon, he had come to know, was cutting ever-tightening air-circles while lining up on a flock of plovers flying in a loose formation shaped like an eyebrow. The plovers, intent on finding trees for sanctuary, hadn't noticed their attacker as yet or they'd have dispersed themselves in squawking, crazed fear. Fierce and fearless, the falcon rolled over on its back, then, whipping right side up again, flared its wings, diving straight at its prey, the speed astonishing. In seconds, no more, its razor-talons dug into a plover, the shocking force breaking the plover's back and separating its head from the instantly dead body. Wildly alarmed, the rest of the flock scattered like buckshot.

The fluttering, shrieking commotion raised Sarita's head skyward. As she looked up, several drops of rich red blood spattered her face, though she seemed unmindful.

Pulling a bandana from his pants pocket, Thomas dabbed a corner of it on his tongue, then came to her and told she looked as though she'd been infected by a pox. He wiped her clean, then explained what had happened, the part of it she had missed

"I'm not wounded, am I?"

"Just bloodied a touch."

"Was a bird killed?"

"One directly over us, and another one over by the woods. That falcon lives in a church steeple over in the village and she hunts here all the time. She has young to feed, I'd guess."

"I've seen them in Colorado but I've never seen a killing."

"You missed this one, too."

"I'm not displeased I did."

"Let's head back. I'm expecting a call from Antwerp and I can't miss it."

"What's in Antwerp that can't be missed?"

"A sort of friend of mine. An expert forger. You could write one of your books about him. If you did, though, you'd never live to see it published."

"Why ever not?"

"He's a highly guarded government secret, that's why. Several governments in fact, and they'd be smartly pissed if you let their canary out of its cage."

"So to speak?"

"So to speak, yes."

"Why would a man like you ever need a forger?"

"I'm referring a little business his way."

"Forgery business?"

"Yes, that's what he does. So far as I know it's all he does."

"Is it something you can tell me about?"

"Nope."

"You have a lot of dark secrets, haven't you?"

"A few of them, anyway. Not as many as most women, but we all need one or two. Makes us into better human beings."

Suddenly, she halted. "I might not be able to keep up with you."

He looked down at her leg, then to her breeze-flushed face. "We've got to get that knee fixed, and don't give me another of those looks of yours. It's a simple thing to do and you'd be a helluva lot better off for it."

And so will I, he thought, yet was puzzled at his concern.

Later that night, alone in his quarters, he hit upon an idea that might save time and provide an opportunity to weigh his words, while shaping hers. He'd work up a letter, a sort of diary of the past to explain, amplify, inform. Things he preferred not to say in person out of concern of where they might lead her. Or, that he'd rather not discuss face-to-face because he could easily make a slip and regret it. He'd been a most private man for decades, a hard habit to break he was finding out.

She had already given him a written agenda of topics she wished to cover. Fine. If her story about him were to be fleshed out, and he were to use it, or try to use it, as an expiation of his past, then he realized she'd have to have a grip on his life: how it had traveled, the setbacks, the hard moments when he had to reach for deep gears to keep himself going forward. Most everything, he thought, as he began to see the value of dropping his barriers.

On the evening of their third day, he sat to write what he later termed his letter of elucidation. It would be, as far as he could make it, the truth. Not everything. Of course, not the all of it; he doubted he could recall the all of it.

My dear Miss Sambinna,

I'm composing a running letter for you. I'm thinking of it as my letter to the world, with you as its carrier pigeon.

The letter will, I hope, mortar in some cracks and crevices bound to occur in our conversations. Matters you will no doubt be inquiring about may be topics I cannot answer until I've had some time to reflect on my words. Words about events that happened a long time ago and are now dimmed by time. On your side, you stand to gain greater accuracy this way, and, for my part, I can preserve an illusion of my privacy.

This letter will not answer everything, but then so much in life is never answered at all. If I let you open the gate too widely in certain areas, we'd be days and days getting back on track. I am on the clock, so to speak, and cannot tarry overly long to accommodate your mission as I've one of my own to see to—my death.

This letter, ultimately, will be delivered to you in Denver through the New York offices of Braunsweig und Sohn, private bankers of Geneva, Switzerland. Before we break camp here at the Downs, I will have given you a contact in the bank's New York branch. There, if you wish, you can pose other inquiries to validate my statements. Later on, we shall get to all that.

If you use any of the information I share with you, in your book, I ask that you use a modicum of discretion. Everyone makes mistakes. I've made some classics, thus, I'm hoping you'll call upon your sympathies and see my side of certain matters. I must warn you that if you delve too deeply into what I will be referring to as "The Trust", or even delve at all, you might be risking your life.

Stay far removed from that topic. You'll not want the South Africans after your hide, or the Swiss either. I'm making mention of The Trust only because it has so sorely, so deeply invaded my conscience for seven decades.

Along the way, I shall inform you of some things, and you will quickly and accurately ascertain I am committing a crime of historical ranking. Because I must do it, I shall do it.

Much that I've done in my life must be undone. It will take at least a generation, perhaps two, and I'll need the proceeds of my grand heist to bring matters a full 360-degrees, or make an earnest try.

You will wonder at some point how Genesis, the movement I've founded is so bountifully endowed. Now, reading this, and after our one-on-one sessions, you will know, or can make a pretty solid guess as to where and how they've been blessed or cursed with so much ill-gotten booty. Ill-gotten not by them, but by other scoundrels, of which I count as one.

So, as you might infer from the above, I will be "living on" even after I'm gone. Why not? After all, if the Roman Church can perpetuate its propaganda, then why can't Courmaine?

To establish the authenticity of my handwriting, I shall have Regis Loften Millan of University of Cambridge, a world-renowned forensics expert, attest in a separate document that this letter is written in my hand.

I'm the only single person alive who knows completely of what you're about to learn in our days together. Thus, you will own an indisputable source document, one, of course, that anyone might challenge as to its authenticity. But at least you'll know you have the version from the horse's mouth, and you'll have Millan's statement to go with it.

This letter, therefore, is the best I can do for you. Candidly, it's the best I can do for myself as well.

More, later.

9:03 a.m.

"…and is it a fact that you were excommunicated from the Catholic Church?"

Startled, Thomas replied: "Why are we fiddling around with that, may I ask?"

"We're talking about your life and it's also how I sequenced my questions on the agenda I gave you. Would you prefer I begin elsewhere? What if we start with the Nobel controversy?"

"Do cigars bother you?"

"Not at all. I like the smell, so go right ahead."

"You're a rarity. Most women gag."

He lit up, expelling a stream of smoke, then told her: "I was excommunicated, yes. It took them thirty-seven years to throw their book at me. Canon law, that book. It took them over a thousand years to admit, after all the mudslinging, that our dear old camp-follower Mary Magdalene wasn't the whore they'd always made her out to be. It took them over three-hundred and fifty years to admit they were dead wrong about Galileo, having done all they could to torch him for revealing the truth about our measly little planet. I feel faintly privileged that I didn't have to wait that long to get hung on their clothesline."

"Excuse me, please. I need to adjust my recorder." Sarita picked it up, held the walnut size device near her mouth, then her ear, and proceeded to tap a series of tiny buttons. "There," she said. "It's fussy sometimes…and your excommunication, was it because you founded that new religion? Genesis?"

"It's not a religion, simply a common sense system of belief. It's been with us since the beginning of time, since the beginning of the universe, since the first bacterium settled itself on our planet several billion years ago. All I did was shine a flashlight on what we've forgotten. Forgotten because over the past millennia various religions have done all they knew how to blot it out. Genesis reminds us of what we've always had, and in part why we're here, and that what Nature gave was mostly gotten for free. It is this gift of Nature itself that we've turned out backs on and I'm trying to turn our backs once again, all the way round, so we can see what it is we're ruining, starting with ourselves as human beings."

"The Vatican labeled you a heretic. I was told it was the first such charge levied in over two-hundred years."

"I don't mind what they say about me or call me. I simply say what I think and let whatever it is fall wherever it falls. We have almost five-million members in Genesis and a lot of them are breakaway Catholics. The Vatican gets irritated at that, and they're none too happy with the revenue loss, besides. Our congregate, if I may call it that, is a first-rate crowd. Former medical people, philosophers, ethicists, historians, anthropologists, and many from academia. Very committed, very intelligent, quite like the old Society of Jesus where I got my start."

"Do they, um, badger you? The Vatican?"

"*Au contraire.* I badger them or I did. Now we have an unspoken truce and we leave it at that. I can lay my hands on more money than they can, and the fact of it seems to intimidate them. Not that I'd waste a penny on that sort of fight."

"How fast are you growing?"

"Genesis gets almost a third of a million new members yearly. Just under that figure. We don't advertise and we don't proselytize either. Strictly word of mouth. We've got a good base and soon we'll have a worldwide megaphone. Really go on a roll, maybe."

"Are you the head of—is it a congregation? Is that what you call it, a congregation?"

"There is no single head. A committee of five persons and some administrative housekeepers carry the load. Simplicity. We maintain that every person is his own temple living inside the greater temple of Nature itself. We publish a newsletter and people in various cities and regions have their own get-togethers. Nature walks, outdoor activities, a certain amount of nudism. I hadn't counted on that, but then why not? Lectures, too, from ecologists and astronomers and so on. People seem to like it. They get to re-link with who they are and what they are and where they are. That's about all it is. Belief in yourself. Belief in Nature. After all, she fixed it so we all got here, and without her, earth would be nothing more than a spinning ball of lava rock, like the moon."

"I need more from you. How it began? Who's behind it beside yourself? I may use it and I don't think you want me to make it sound as if it were another secret society like The League?"

"The League? You know about them, do you?"

Sarita nodded.

"Huh."

"Some of it, I do. What I've read. I'd like to ask you about that, too. But now, the other—Genesis."

"I started it with Lin-pao. You know who he is, I see."

Sarita nodded, almost vigorously. "You did get the photo I sent?"

"Yes, thank you. I should have thanked you before now."

"Well, as long as it arrived."

"It definitely arrived. Clever of you to put that notation on the envelope, guessing I would open it, which of course I did and now you're here."

"You were saying about you and Lin-pao and Genesis. Can we go back to that?"

"We got the idea, contacted a hundred or so scientists who're as nervous as we are about the future and we put up some money and we set sail."

"I've read some things about it in the *Denver Post*—"

"Never never believe those goddamn newspapers. As I said, Genesis is not a religion. It's a belief in our own world. All we have, all we know and can see and feel."

"Sorry that I haven't read your Bible, that is, if you have a Bible."

"Our Bible is right out that window behind me. The trees, grass, sky, the water in my lake, the birds that nest near it. Beauty. You just look, enjoy it and love it. You don't need to read anything. That's why it's the perfect catechism. No one ever bullshits you. No myths. You use all five senses you were born with, and Nature shows you the rest. How it clothes you, shelters you, feeds you,' warms you, cools you, waters you. Anyone who needs a better set of beliefs than that is either nuts or they're greedy. Nature is god, or what we call god, and it always was and always is god. Or goddess, if you prefer. There is no more to it and there doesn't have to be. It's kind, it's loving, it made you and one day it'll dissolve you. Meanwhile, you get a life of free birdsong. No one else ever put on a better light-and-sound show than what happens in the sky or offered you a better deal in scenery. It's free, as I said. The air, the sea, the moon, the beaches. Everyone gets a free ticket to it every day. And there's this: no god ever imagined could create the cosmos or the billions of intricacies that happen every day in every living body. You ought to join us. The fee for a lifetime membership is exactly one dollar. I'll gladly pay it for you."

"I might. I'm curious about how many women you have as members?"

"More than half. We're largely run by women. They run everything else, or they want to, so we just said the hell with it and told them to head up the show as long as they don't foul things up. Frankly, they do a wonderful job. My advice is never get on one of those committees, however, or you'll never find time to even pee again. It's endless, the talk, and I do mean endless."

"You're that active? Yourself, I mean?"

"They've got me on the sales side. I do the money part also and sometimes give talks. Wave the flag, so to speak. Matter of fact," and he thumbed through a desk calendar, "yes, there it is, and it says I'm due in Rio de Janeiro a few weeks from now. Samba-land. But I won't be samba-ing."

"Sounds like you have your share of fun."

"I try. Always bet on having fun. Everyone likes fun, that's why it's such a safe bet."

"Is it true that Genesis is opposed to gene therapy? You made your reputation on genetic regeneration of the human body. So, now you're against it. Is that a correct statement?"

"I certainly wasn't against it, at first."

"But you are now? Is Genesis, your act of contrition if I may put it that way?"

"Perhaps, it is...perhaps..."

So it went with them. Flux. In-and-out, cat-and-mouse, calibrating each other, parrying. Intense in her questioning and he, by turns, was often tensing as he either answered or ducked her queries. A relentless interrogator, and she knew far more about him than he'd ever have guessed.

They traveled on their agreed daily track, questions, sometimes replies to the questions, sometimes a drifting silence. Morning tea, then lunch, a walk on the grounds to see the blooming gardens, her glee-filled comments over the black roses—Lin-pao's creation of seven decades earlier—and finally, as day sank away, a cessation as they took to drinks, sometimes dinner together at which all inquiries were off-limits. Relaxing afterward, they often joked, and as often simply looked at each other. On one occasion, he took her to his wine cellar, repository of over six-thousand bottles collected over forty-years.

She found him vital, strong and strict in his views, as times speaking a little too coarsely and vehemently, as though trying to defend some aspects of his life. Obviously, a first-rate mind there and she intrigued herself when attempting to peel its layers, the tickings of it, his weaker sides, plumbing his strengths, or trying to, and what drove him.

Here she was, with the Mahatma of gene-fixing—a high-noon, go-it-alone sort. She had begun to sense his vulnerable side—his worries of the future, its great paradox, and that he had helped, intensely helped, to create what had now come to pass: too many earthlings, great food shortages, water sold at a premium in many places, insufficient jobs, massive boredom and malaise by those in their second century of life, and some approaching their third. And the *Gorpos*, who were his bane.

He clammed up when she wandered near the subject. Yet she was determined to get some kind of telling quote for attribution, something weighty she hoped, even choice enough for a chapter opening.

Yesterday, after taking a call, he canceled an impromptu after-lunch session they had planned. He hadn't explained why, but seemed so preoccupied and in a hurry.

She had taken tea in one of the immense side rooms, hung to its gills with 15th century Gobelin tapestries handsomely displayed against the soaring limestone walls. Sitting idly at a window seat, sipping the tea, she had suddenly seen him with others gathered in the driveway, all engaged in animated conversation. Three vehicles—a gray, a green, a black, all with opaque glass—and Thomas had walked away from the others along with that huge black man who had the musical and courtly island voice, the one they called Crunch. Crunch, the spear-carrier, who was Courmaine's other set of eyes and ears, running interference for him. The others mingling in the driveway, five or six of them, menacing-looking men and…and yes….a woman. All wearing combat boots and khaki field fatigues. Lugging sawed-off shotguns, Uzis, and two of them had orange-sheathed smoke grenades hitched to their jackets.

She could tell the make of most light weapons. She'd served a stint in the U.S. Army, attached to the Center of Military History as a senior historian; three years of it and the Army, in exchange, had generously paid for her postgraduate studies.

The cars were loading.

Courmaine, she saw, climbed into the green auto, in the middle of the armored caravan. Off they went, but to do what? She had no idea, nor did she intend to ask. Yet asked herself if they were about to attack something? Obviously, they were not headed for the picnic grounds.

The clam without his shell, prey to his foes, needing his Praetorian Guard. Living in this fairytale fiefdom, seemingly to keep safe from his assailants, yet she was sure there was more to it.

He did seem a man controlled by fears. Or much else.

More of the letter.

You were asking about women I've known. Quite a question! Simply put, I've had very pleasant times with practically all the women whom I can say I've truly *known*. Blessings, of a sort; though one of them, my present tenant, falls into the category of a curse straight from an angry and unnamed god.

I shall tell you of three who are gone now and beyond any harm from my memories of them. One, a great looker and a mystic, or the next thing to it, was Marie-D'Anne Borgette. A poetess, she lived in Aix-en-Provence on a small and quite gorgeous farm. A cheese-making farm. She died in an auto accident in Marrakech, making for a very gloomy moment in my life. A second and winsome lady was Caramia Buonavatti, a well-known stage actress of Italy. Full of fun and full of zest for life. We parted when circumstances prevented me from marrying her. She then married a Kuwaiti oil mogul and, apparently, or so the story goes, she was murdered for having slept with a Saudi Prince, and, of course, found out. Strangled, brutally, in the Arab manner. A very talented woman but also in great need of regular devotion, like saints and other immortals, and like so many others of the stage or film worlds. So much of life, for them, equals applause. Yet one cannot be expected to clap one's hands day out and day in, cheering on your heart's throb of the moment.

The third is the one I've loved, consumingly, for what seems like forever and an age. Like a myth almost, a fantasy—yet she indeed was real flesh and blood before I lost her. An American via Baghdad and elsewhere. She vanished at a time when I was incapacitated and never was I able to locate her again except in my memories and dreams. I think of her every day, always have...

Casual dalliances—there were those—of a man who's lived for over a hundred years, coping with a man's urges...the biological mandate that is the tyrant of all men, or about all of them.

Of course, in the range of time there's been the Stiletto herself, which, as you've learned, is the media-bestowed sobriquet of Ms. Muldaur-Courmaine. Yet I am disinclined to include her on the list of women who've graced my life.

Though, she's been something of a regular shadow, and still is, I suppose. Ere long, that shall not be the situation, bringing to a close the most symbiotic man-woman thing imaginable.

For me, at least. Goodnight.

"We really ought to fix that leg of yours."

"It's my knee."

"Your knee, then. I've the people who can swing the job for you. Easily. They work for me. The best pit crew in the business."

"I lost my insurance when I left the university. At the Baylor Medical Center in Houston, they wanted over seventy-thousand to do it. I cannot afford that, needless to say."

"At Atherton Downs we have this special out-patient service for guests, and it'll not cost you anything."

"Thanks, but I'm not here as a limping charity case."

"No one said you were. But you don't have to be Patty the peg-leg, either. How did it happen?"

"I was skiing in a club slalom race. I went crashing off the course and cartwheeled, hit a tree and tore the knee to pieces."

"Hurt much, does it?"

"It aches likes anything when wet weather settles in."

"Well, don't be so stiff-necked about it. Let ol' Doc Courmaine send you to the local bone mechanics. Do wonders for you. They can fix anything and it's all done painlessly using nanotechnology techniques. They rearrange a colony of atoms and tissue molecules and shazam! Something not easily imaginable appears right in front of your face. In your case it'll be inside your weeping knee...think it over..."

"You're most kind."

"You caught me on a good day. I like your perfume. What is it?"

She seemed startled, as if he'd just asked her about a strange aphrodisiac, then, evaded him with: "I use several kinds. Variety being the spice of my life. Yours, too, I see."

"Variety? Me?"

"I'll say."

Next day, picking up where they had left off.

"...I will admit I was too certain I was right about my theories on gene-fixing, and in many ways I was. What happens when you *are* right about something important is that you start to think you're right about everything connected to it. A helluva mistake, I will say. Hubris. You don't see everything. You can't, of course. I was a fairly young scientist chasing the platinum pot at rainbow's end. Riveted, overwhelmed, it's as if you're making love every hour of every day but it's the making of love to an idea. Work devoured my life. I never saw the scythe swinging at me, and so I was unprepared for what was to come."

"At some point, you must've known what was coming. You had to."

"I did, you're right. But by then it was too late. The marketing clout of MarocheChem had blasted the message of cheap gene therapy to all four corners and the world came running. The genie had jumped out of the bottle, never to return. You know the old saying, 'You fire the gun, and there's no putting the same bullet back in the chamber of the gun.' It was some firing, I can tell you. MarocheChem had the goods and the power and they pandered to the instincts of every woman with a hundred bucks in her pocketbook. They even put the sex-dysfunction drug-makers out of business. You could fiddle with a few genes and people were sexually boosted all the time. Like taking cocaine. It was ridiculous, dangerous too. But that never stops the fun-seekers. Overnight, it happened, and it was practically pandemonium. People get hooked on such things very easily, and the rest was easy."

"God's gun, you suppose?" A light taunt in her voice.

Startled, he asked, "Where'd you hear that?"

Her hands were folded in her lap. She replied by opening them, a message that could be taken several ways.

He went on, a little more cautiously. "On the other end of it, we conquered and eliminated hundreds of diseases. Over a thousand, actually. Life has doubled, even tripled for some and that's not necessarily a good thing but you can't have it both ways, can you? The good and the not- so-good, and ever it shall be so unless we change the laws and knock off everyone at age two-hundred."

"They'd never do that," she retorted.

"When enough people starve, they might."

Suddenly, as if lapsing into a daydream, he quit talking and started wondering. That phrase again. She had used the full expression—Gun of God—the other day. Strange. Why had she said that? Playing a game or something? Queasiness set in, not for the first time.

"There was a comm-sat show several weeks ago," Sarita said, "and it mentioned you and they interviewed a group of women in San Francisco who practically worshipped you for Zyme-One. Changing their lives, their skin and their bodies. No more need to have boob jobs and they talked about nano-surgery—that was a big thing you did."

"I didn't invent nano-anything. I did help connect it to gene therapy and work out certain problems for manipulating molecules. The media constantly screws up technical stories."

"That's not quite what the documentary said. Anyway, the women were polled and their attitudes were measured. It's sort of love-hate, I'd guess you'd say. So, what is it you say in reply?"

"I say they got what they asked for. Trouble, and a helluva a big bundle of it that they're stupidly perpetuating. Every one of them wanting to look like a ravishing film star, and when they found out they could, then they did. They went for it, or many did, without considering the blowback or the possible consequences. Lots of them ended up looking as if they're cousins. Wanting to do away with their flaws and imperfections, the things that make them human beings. Every second or third woman looks as though she was getting herself ready to audition for a stage part. Bobbsey twins. Sisters under the skin, comrades in arms, genetically speaking. I can tell you've had gene therapy. But you didn't change your body into something it wasn't meant to be. It makes a difference because you're different, and you're different looking and therefore much more interesting as a woman, as a human being too. I commend you for it."

"Thanks."

"You're welcome. How would you like to take a ride in a punt?"

"What's a punt? Not kicking a ball obviously."

"I'll show you tomorrow."

"I still want to ask you more about your days at Maroche."

"I'll think about it. In my letter, maybe."

"Oh, please! Dammit all, I may never see your letter. How will I ever know if you're telling me everything?"

"You won't. And I doubt if I'll tell you everything, but you're getting a lot more than you had any right to expect. Like to go for a swim?"

"I'd rather talk. I want to know about you."

"That's one way of doing it. Water loosens my tongue, like good whiskey. Come along, it's a great tonic for a rebellious knee."

She cut an eye-filling figure in a body-mapping black Speedo-suit, one of the many extras in the lady's dressing room. Exuding health, a skin blooming to a creamy pink, and legs like one might see on the Rockettes at Radio City Music Hall. He found her fetching. Especially, he was taken by her face, with its pearl-gray eyes—deeply inquisitive eyes—and a face, too, with a dozen different smiles.

Diving off the deep end, she pierced the water as if a dart, lapping the twenty-five meter pool forty-odd times, her stroke smooth and strong, and she as sinuous as an otter.

They swam, then talked. As they stood in the shallow end of the pool, he told her: "...I'm very aware of what is said about me, and how I laid waste to the old medical establishment. That was before your time, or mostly was. The average guy was getting chewed alive by medical costs, and if you were poor, you were doomed. I realize millions were put out of work by our discoveries, and I wish it weren't so, but that was the trade-off and there're always trade-offs when you revolutionize. I don't make any apology about what we did to alleviate suffering. Not an ounce. We did great stuff in helping people and even more when we found ways to give everyone a super education for a pittance. I take a certain pride in that...and, no, I don't like it when they go after my scalp, but that's my personal trade-off...that's the invoice I have to pay...so they can say whatever they like. I can show you, if I cared to, bushels of letters I've received over the years. Thank you letters, all of them. They're on microfiche over at the university..."

A half-hour of back-and-forth conversation as they stood chest-deep in that humid air. Aware of him—the male of him—Sarita had crossed her arms over her breasts.

After a time they headed to the sauna, both naked under oversized wrap-around terry-cloth towels; his image of her under the wrap spurred desires and he was quite aware she was conscious of his glances. Twice she reached to tighten her towel, glancing at intervals to inspect how much of herself was still on show.

Thomas set the table when making an overt suggestion: "Would you like to sleep together? Tonight, for instance?"

"I would not. I can't…and I will not. What brought on that?"

"You told me a few days ago that you wanted to know the whole Thomas Courmaine."

"I'm afraid I left you with the wrong impression."

"You didn't actually, but I thought we could create a new impression of me."

"Not that way."

"You could sleep with me but you won't?"

"Never were you more right."

"I don't think we'd be getting an abundance of sleep."

"Let's not talk this way, please. It's impossible what you're suggesting."

"Well, we can always downgrade to a kiss. How about that as a compromise?"

Alarmed, she stood so quickly it was as if a firecracker had suddenly exploded under her bottom. Swift in her movements, her towel slipped and she struggled to cover her derrière, engagingly shaped like an upside down heart. She vanished, then, in a flurry of arms and legs. He supposed he'd be making an apology, but not any too soon. She had some items to answer for, and perhaps an apology or two of her own to offer. He had a feeling, intuitive, and with not a whit of evidence, that she was after more from him than she admitted to. Things she had said twice—Gun of God—for one; how had she heard that one? Where? Then that perfume she wore, though he enjoyed its fragrance whenever she came near.

That was how Christopher often behaved when first meeting someone, smelling them anywhere he felt like, much like a housedog checking out a stranger.

Taking dead aim, Sarita asked: "You sued MarocheChem to get out of a contract?"

"Nope. They sued me when I took a powder after a big row. A real donnybrook," and he laughed as he recalled a verbal fight that lasted for most of a week.

"I've got it backwards then. What brought the fight on?"

"The human egg farms."

"They had another name, though."

"Ova-Ture."

"Yes, thanks. How could I forget that one."

"When they propelled that gambit, well, I had had enough by then. I walked out and they countered, pointing out they held a contract for my services, which they did. And I told them off and went on my way. They withheld over twelve-million Euros of my royalties but I didn't care as long as I had my freedom. Freedom is about the most expensive thing I know of. They got my money and I got my fresh air. A good deal as far as I was concerned."

"And you never had any financial interest in those egg farms?"

"No, though plenty of people somehow thought they were my idea to begin with. I can't imagine anything more discouraging. Making us into chickens. You were supposed to be able to make any kind of human you want. They sold a whole lot of in-vitros and inseminations, abetted by gene-paks so you could custom-order the kid you wanted. That's what got the whole thing going, the illusion you could have any kind of kid you could dream up. Science fiction stuff."

"All made possible by Zyme-One, am I right?"

"The screening part was and the gene-paks were the by-products of Zyme-One technology. I suppose you'll write about that, won't you?"

"You should hope I do, especially if you weren't an owner of those farms. Why do you detest the media so much?"

"I deplore…I don't detest anything anymore. Life's too long to detest anyone or anything."

"How rich are you, by the way?"

"Next question."

"Are you embarrassed by this estate, the castle, all the staff running hither-and-yon?"

"It's been my redoubt when I needed one and I've needed one for fifty years at least."

"Next question. Some of your better press claims you're an original think-er? Would you see it that way?"

"On some things, I might see it that way. On the other hand, everything ever thought of that's useful has a hundred people vying for credit as to who thought it up first. So who can say who did what? One thing I learned about the media, they're good at asking questions but they're terrible when it comes to providing answers."

"Not always."

"Name me one major problem ever solved by the fourth-estate."

"This is my quiz show, if you please. Here comes the next one: you've also been ranked as one of the top five or ten scientists of the past hundred years. How do you account for so much criticism of yourself and your work…it's so…well…the attacks are so vitriolic and rancorous?"

Tapping the ash off his cigar, waiting a long moment, he said: "I told too many bickering scientists and pushy reporters to go fuck themselves. One recrimination led to the next and the scientists who got sore at me began to play ball with the press, and, as a result, I got punched in the nose twice a week for a long time. Courmaine-bashing. Something like that…it happens…at least it did to me and yet I'm still here At least for now. I didn't mind as much as they thought I would. Sometimes it was even useful. Who was it who said 'I don't care what they say about me as long as they keep saying it.'"

"I forget who said it. Mark Twain, I think. I can look it up."

"You needn't bother. You get my point, I'm sure."

"Yes and no. Weren't you frightened at times? I'd be petrified of all that flack."

"I was. But there's nothing to be done about it except go to bed and wait for a better newscast. That, and hope they're no assassins hiding by the front gates. Or the back ones, either."

She pressed him mightily on his years at MarocheChem and he gave to her what he could accurately recall. Not all of it, though. He still had his recollections to plow through. Not till a night later did he pen them into what by now had become a six-page letter, far longer a litany than he had intended.

More on the egg farms.

I left out a few things, so we could move onward yesterday morning. Plus, I needed an interval to recall what I'd so much rather forget, as I append the following:

For me, the egg farms were the final and poisonous straw of my connection to Maroche-Chem. It led, as I said to a bitter blow-up. Still, had it not been that firefight it'd've been some other one, I'm sure. The irony is that if I had wanted to betray a long-held secret, I'd've probably been able to round up enough stockholder votes to control the operations of MarocheChem. I was tempted. I didn't for the sake of prudence. By the time you read and digest this letter, you'll add two and three, and figure out what I'm saying here and what I mean by it.

The reason I got hooked up with MarocheChem is that I'd been confined to a secret Swiss prison until I dissolved and finally consented to rewire my son's genome as part of a plot to defraud the South African government out of many many billions. A long story and one I've already warned you to sidestep. The Swiss forced me to turn over the rights to use the technology that was, early on, known as Zyme-One. MarocheChem got the know-how from me, and I got rich as a Croesus for my troubles. I was getting used, no question there; and, for a time, I didn't mind much. They gave me a laboratory with twenty-eight very able investigators. Paradise regained, for me. But then they wanted work done on the egg farm initiative and I, as they say, blew my cork.

The money was too big, too tempting and MarocheChem still had a patent-lock on Zyme-One in those days. They went all out and they made a killing. People everywhere wanted the perfect baby and, in many cases, I suspect, they got it, or so they thought. In all, there was an avalanche of lawsuits involving product liability issues, and gradually the cost-toll caused a shut-down of the farms. I actually had a hand in the shut-downs, frequently serving, as I did, as a plaintiff's witness. I fought them because I didn't want my life's work sullied by those grubbers.

Ova and sperm farms were situated mostly in the Caribbean where it was legal to fly people in, house them in swanky hotel-clinics, screen their genomes, revise them as wanted or needed, often permanently and dangerously, and you know the rest.

It was nothing short of fantastic. I refer to the number of pregnancies processed to get Gorpo-type infants.

Misfires occurred (that's why the rash of lawsuits) and abortion was rampant for a time, though in many cases MarocheChem quieted the complaints with money settlements, fearing the damaging publicity while the farms were still operating.

But the very idea of taking women who could pass the good looks test, and the health test and show them how to become hens who could sell their unfertilized eggs for a fortune...it bothered me greatly and still does. Actresses, models, pageant winners came out of the closet like swarms of moths to the flame, and it was the flame of very easy money. That was what kicked off the cloning game, the attempts at it anyway. Other secretive clinics for researching were set up in Morocco and Bermuda, there to skirt various legal hurdles. The farms, in their hey-day, were located in a half-dozen time zones and functioned with unbridled success. You could clone the DNA of famous actresses by the score. Twenty, fifty, a hundred copies. The same held true for men. If they had the genetic goods, they were in for a quick fortune. Sperm and the ova were screened and filtered to the point where ten fertilizings would be contracted for, and after the embryos became fetuses just about everything in their respective genomes could be foretold: the hair, eyes, body build, facial characteristics, likely I.Q. range, and as many as eleven other characteristics. One embryo was then chosen. The rest were flushed down a sink or occasionally sold off to pay the high costs of the procedure.

Humans, and our supreme egos. A fearsome combo, I say. And I am a victim of it, I readily admit.

Much of this was started by women, who, bless them all, have this immense urge to age-reverse. Your age is your age. No turning back the clock, right? You can alter the way you look, however, and without using a surgeon's knife. When women found out you only needed a few spurts with a hypodermic, that began the Great Flood.

A despicable use of science and of Zyme-One, as well. The MarocheChem crowd acted like a bunch of fucking Nazis. Master-race apostles and profiteers, no better than Hitler and Himmler and the other thugs who advocated eugenics. Sometimes I wish I'd hung around long enough to dynamite the headquarters and the entire goddamn lot of them. No question of it, Maroche made gene-junkies of a couple billion people. Wreckage that may never be cleared away, as the genes descend, descend, and descend continuously. In the end, the Swiss got rich out of it, and so did I.

So there I was and am...hooked for life it seems...with the truth of the matter twisted out of recognition. Truth, we've all found out, is a much mauled commodity. Always has been. And with that unoriginal comment,

I shall bid you good-night while wondering what path of invasion you will choose tomorrow, pulling apart the ragged seams of my life.

Now you begin to see, perhaps. My life has been a Judas. Another thing I made happen, one way or another. "I've not really had a life; I've only had an existence.

Retiring then, sleeping peaceably. Yet the night kept traveling in other directions, and, what he had quietly worried about, happened—a loose Christopher hunting an unsuspecting, unprepared Sarita Sambinna.

The hall porter had neglected to light the fire and he could see Sarita was chilled, noting the studs of her nipples protruding against a sheer Italian knit pullover. A pleasant slice of scenery to behold on that morning yet he rang for the porter anyway. Pulling out his old friend, a nickel-plated pocket watch, he saw it was also time for tea. Tea and talk and more talk. She'd been at the Downs for over a week. He still had a great deal to take care of before departing for Brazil; many things to tidy up at Cavendish and the university, see his solicitors and a long chat with Braunsweig in London, for which he had scheduled three days. Lastly, he wanted time with Christopher. Never would never see him again after month's end.

Christopher was headed by private charter to where he would be lord of his own kingdom, there, on an island off the southern flank of the Philippines. Happier by far, Thomas hoped; and considerably safer. Safe from the law; safe from himself.

A sad, sad business to contemplate. No one was likely to guess where Christopher had gone to, as the getaway had been entirely finagled through African Heritage, who, in exchange for a weighty gift, would keep their mouths tied, and had better do so if they planned on any more of his largesse.

A tapping at the door, and in came the porter.

Thomas gave him his instructions, then rang for tea, then after a cup or two he'd rendezvous with his morning Cohiba.

Later, he'd have lunch sent in and, afterward, he intended to pass the day with this coltish woman who spared him nothing. She kept digging deep into the silt of his other days, as if she were a river dredge.

Three days earlier, realizing the point was nearing when they would wrap up this ever-long interview, and that Sarita would leave, he had made arrangements to engage a private investigator in Denver. In days to come, while in Rio, he expected to know a great deal more about this enterprising woman.

His guest, yes. But was she his friend?

Moments ago, Sarita had excused herself for a visit to the loo and he had risen, politely, and then he had stepped over to the great leaded-pane window behind his desk, looking across the sweeping lawns, the deep green of the boxwoods, the six circular beds of varietal roses, the climbing rose vines on four tall lattices, then out to a rank of towering three-hundred year old brown oaks—absorbing the impressive beauty on this fairest of days.

He'd miss the Downs, miss much else. But the end was beckoning to him as if it were a court summons, undodgeable.

Sarita returned and lodged herself by the crackling fire.

"I've lost my place," she confessed.

"Are you warm enough?"

"Perfectly, thanks. Or I will be."

"You were about to lead into my life's regrets, I think. The many of them."

"Just the top two or three will suffice."

"That'd be hard. The top two?"

"Try, please."

"Let's try it another time and give me a while to think about it."

"All right. I've been thinking of telling you something, or maybe I shouldn't."

"Go ahead, I'm halfway made of asbestos," said Thomas, unaware at that moment that the incident he most dreaded had come to pass.

"I was asleep; I don't know what time it was. After midnight, I'm sure. And I awoke to this knocking noise. I wasn't sure what it was as it's a huge bedroom and I'm still not used to it. I thought I was in a dream and then I knew it wasn't anything of the kind. The sound came from the window. I got out of bed and sort of pretended I was on my way to the bathroom and I worked my way around in the dark so that I could see what it was…the knocking, you know, and then a light went on. It was outside…the light. A flashlight, I'd guess. Suddenly this beautiful face…an apparition, I thought, I didn't know what to think. I'm up there three stories above ground. How can a face show up at my window? "

She left it there. Waiting until he prodded: "Go on."

"I thought it was a woman at first, but then the light moved and I could tell it was a man. This gorgeous man, grinning, making a motion for me to open the window, and he seemed to step up higher, leering, his mouth working and then, right in front of me he climbed up high and I saw he was fully nude. Pointing to his privates, and he seemed to be trembling. He passed the light all over himself. So powerful looking, with neck muscles looking like they were sculpted from stone," she was saying to Thomas, a look of amazement spreading over her face. "All that curly blond hair, bubbling all over his head. I was spellbound, I suppose. I'd never seen a man like that. Is it—"

"My son. He'd know someone new was in residence and he'd find out just as if he were a dog scenting about. He is immediately aware of strangers. He always knows. I'm sorry if you were frightened. He's supposed to be guarded, but sometimes he gets loose. On your side of the castle, the vines grow all the way to the tower. He climbs them and sometimes hides in them. He wanted to see you and he likely wanted sex with you. It's a combat sport with him and he rarely loses. You were lucky, very lucky. Sorry you had to go through an ordeal like that. I'll have to have a word with his…well, we call them nurses. They're a tough bunch but sometimes they lapse. He's very, very clever and he's fast and can do things others can't keep up with."

"I'd love to meet him. Really, I would."

"You've already met him and I'll be most thankful if you leave this episode out of your book. Christopher is a misfit, a human porridge and a sort of throwback. He's not always responsible for what he does. In fact, rarely responsible. He belongs to another age. A long, long ago age. You'll find more in my letter."

"Is he sick? Mentally sick?"

"He's brilliant. It's just that he doesn't belong to these times and this part of the earth. It's a long story."

"How tragic."

"Wagnerian."

"What about a photo of your son?"

"He's off-limits, all the way. That, my friend, you can take as the final word. No Christopher, period."

"You can't blame a girl for trying. And you were going to tell me about where you went the other day. With those men who looked like commandos."

"In fact, they are commandos. Ex-commandos. Crunch's boys. Where did I go? I went to Cambridge, summoned there on short notice to see a freak. Sometimes, when I leave here, I resort to disguises and then we can use one vehicle to go traveling about. Sometimes we use a decoy vehicle. This time we had to go at a drop of a hat so we had that little motorcade."

"You said a…a freak…."

"I did."

"How freakish?"

"You're squeezing me as if I were the last lemon on earth. I went to my lab to have a look at a beautiful, beautiful young woman. Eighteen, at most. A natural eighteen. She has four ears, full-sized. Two vaginas. She has a penis and testicles that are just above her navel. Had I not seen it, I'd not have believed it possible. Her parents want to know if anything can be done, using nano-surgery. It's possible, I suppose, but no one is sure as yet if we can transform physical defects of that magnitude by atomic surgery. I damn near wept. Rarely do you ever see a face that beautiful. It's still haunting me."

"Why did they come to you?"

"They didn't. They came to my lab and some of my team does work in that area. Nano-genetics. Frankly, we're the best in the business and they'd read about us and they came to the lab without giving us notice. I went because I'm the one who must approve any procedures on unique cases like hers."

"May I see her, please?"

"They've returned to Warsaw, I believe. I doubt if she'd put herself on parade, though. She's understandably bashful. I've seen about fifty others that had deformities and they all came about because of self-administered gene fixing or because of bio-hackers. A goddamn shame..."

"It's not your fault."

"I tell myself that, but I don't always believe myself. You know, I never, never figured on my life turning out the way it has. I only wanted to be a good teacher and a decent priest and see what I could do to alleviate suffering. I won, too, but I lost more than I won."

"You did a great deal of good, though. All the cures and all the disease riddance."

"History will see it differently. History will see it the way it sees Mrs. O'Leary and her cow that burned down Chicago. She probably had nothing to do with it, but it made for a good story and so that's how it got played. And that's what'll happen to me."

"But you're ranked in the top scientists of the past century."

"Genghis Khan was ranked in the top five in his game, as I recall."

"You're so terribly cynical at times."

"And with good reason. Look what happened and is still happening."

"You're not entirely to blame, though."

"You said that. Remember, I was the guy who pried the lid off the can. No one forgets that...and I'll bet you won't either."

She looked off, pensively, and then dropped her head while making a note on her pad. Often, he suspected, she did this so she wouldn't have to speak into her recorder and reveal to him what she was thinking.

Sparing his feelings, perhaps. Waiting for her, he was thinking of Christopher again and then, as if reading his mind, she asked: "You've no other children, have you? Only the one?"

"Only the one."

"You won't relent?"

"Not a ghost of chance, Sarita. If you arouse him, he'll be after you night or day if he thinks you're interested."

"But I'm not going to arouse him."

"That's for him to decide, and I know how he'll decide."

Brazil beckoned, and he had other matters to attend to. Worried about the shortening of time, yet he had more to get off his chest. Weary and stiff from an after-dinner jog around the perimeter of the Downs, he nonetheless took up pen and paper and continued with the letter.

Reading this, you'll recall that frightening night with Christopher rapping at your window, I trust you'll thank all gods you weren't mauled. I'd have been mortified had harm befallen you. We had another close brush with main trouble around here the morning of your arrival in Cambridge. Christopher had sexually assaulted one of his male nurses and the offended party made a credible threat of calling in the authorities.

All I needed was another rape here at the Downs. Damage to you, I could never stand for that, of course, nor for him to be put on trial for a felony so egregious. Given his situation he'd probably be committed to an asylum of some sort, and for principal reasons, I could not let that happen.

A lethal customer—our Christopher.

No raptor ever had anything on him. He swoops out of nowhere and strikes whomever and whenever he wishes. I fear him. His nurses fear him. But they're paid plentifully to answer his strength, be tough, vigilant, and to prevent incidents.

Mostly, but not always, they succeed.

I cannot introduce you to him, as I cannot risk that he'll misinterpret the gesture, thinking I've brought to him a woman to pleasure him, which I've done in the past. I am no longer worried about his sexual escapades with paid-for women, as I personally sterilized Christopher, some years ago. I was forced to. He ruts like a boar, as many as six times daily, according to reports.

What happened to him, and thus to me, is a long, dismal episode. I, the father, was the mechanic, and his mother the witch-crafter. She schemed, won out for a time, and we've all paid and paid hard. None, however, paid harder than Christopher himself. It was done for money. So much money, that, were I to tell you, you'd not believe another thing I said. It was that much money.

As an infant, Christopher was a sickly. I've no doubt he'd have died at a much earlier age had we not elected to replace his flawed genes that programmed him for deadly illnesses. We went, or I went, further though. To survive, and I speak here of myself, I agreed to replace many of Christopher's genes with genes borrowed from his step-grandfather's DNA—the one and only Baster Muldaur. This, to perpetrate a massive fraud against the South Africans, about which I've made an earlier reference and will again discuss elsewhere.

I did all that engineering, personally. On a sea craft bearing the name of *Palenque,* a floating Ritz Hotel. It was this simple of a decision: I chose to live rather than remain in a dungeon till I perished. I came close enough, as it was. In all, however, I mistakenly thought I knew how to take the temperature of the future. What idiocy!

No one ever has, or ever will, outwit the rules of Nature. Indeed, no one knows all her rules to begin with; she's too sharp a dame to reveal all her secrets. Nature is a superb recycling machine, and I fear deep she is close to recycling us humans, if we don't mind our step. Humans, despite what we think are not exempt.

Example: something unforeseen happened when I had altered Christopher's genome. The wrong mix, the wrong approach, and likely even doing it all for the wrong reasons. Saving my own hide...so I believed...

One thing or another is bound to go haywire when you're the first horse, ever, out of the barn and Christopher was that horse: the first human genetically re-wired *en mass*. I was his test-tube jockey, believing I could outsmart the odds, so desperate was I to win and so cocksure I could. Not to be, however.

All of us carry in our DNA thousands of extinct genes. But are they? If we knew how, and probed sufficiently, we'd likely find the genes that diverted us from the apes; even the genes for growing tails. Volcanoes awaken after sleeping for thousands of years, so why not genes that evolution has parked away as no longer needed, so put to sleep? Moreover, genes actually can jump from one location on a chromosome to another. I know his do. And too many of them have. Did I cause that? I don't know. Perhaps I unwittingly turned off too many of his gene regulators or switches. Perhaps genes that should be working together, now, no longer do. I created artificial chromosomes from which to hang portions of Baster Muldaur's genome. Perhaps, Christopher is so surfeited with genes they're confused, and perhaps a hundred other things I shall never know about.

Humans are unique unto themselves. Double that for Christopher. How else to explain that he can copulate as he does? Or that he lopes like a cantering gazelle, at times going for several miles without stopping. Christopher—with all his boyish charm and his incredible physique—feeds, at times, like a grazer does on leaves and grasses. He eats and loves rose petals, especially from the black roses invented by Lin-pao. Insects, too, he eats them, as did I once upon a time while in prison. I've seen him eat scorpions. And he cherishes butterflies slathered in pig-milk butter. I wish I could swing from tree to tree, like a Tarzan, as he also does.

You would know, personally, he hasn't the slightest difficulty climbing vines.

A hybrid. A prehistoric jungle denizen? Or perhaps a post-human? In all events, he is a raging example of what can go wrong when you fiddle with Nature. Once you genetically redesign someone, you're stuck. You cannot reverse the engineering. He is Nature's perfect machine physically yet by our legal standards he is a madman, is without scruple as a python, and is otherwise utterly devoid of acceptable social custom. Sometimes I wonder if he is of an earlier species, say, the breed that knocked off the Cro-Magnons?

That is why I personally sterilized my son. You can imagine what well might happen if he were to procreate. Ultimately, it would be I who was responsible for a throwback sub-species of humankind.

No one can say if he is, or is not. We do know this, however: that he is Beauty and Beast rolled into one, like that lovely but grotesquely deformed young woman from Warsaw. She has no future value to anyone, not even herself. That, pure and simple, is tragedy.

Indirectly, I created this chaos. I'm not strong enough to think about it for very long. Still, I find myself harping on it, to the point that other bioscientists shun me.

Today, and in the past five decades, people have gone nuts on gene-fixes, the same way a teenager takes apart an old car and reassembles it again with new parts. You can reverse the car parts, making the car as it formerly was, but not so with the human gene structure. Once you make a genome you can do fixes to it, but you cannot revolve it to its original design. Too many of the genetic combinations have changed, all the cell rhythms, the switches, the regulators so the genetic music sounds differently, and its original symphony is never replayable. Beethoven has become a Bach and Bach a Mozart, and while Beethoven may assimilate to a combination of Beethoven-Bach-Mozart, whatever made the pure Beethoven at the beginning is forever gone.

Now to the *Gorpos.* In plain English, these so-called *Gorpos* are abjectly fucked now and for always. As will happen to their children, *ad infinitum.* As has happened to my own son.

One of my final missions in this life is to save him from himself. I got him to where he is and I shall get him to where he must be. Free, unable to be harmed and unable to harm others. I shall then rest in the peace of that heretofore elusive space: my death.

You object so, whenever I refer to my death. Be generous, my dear, for I've earned it many times over. You mustn't decry my ultimate freedom.

"For the man who already has everything, what is it you could ever want now?"

"You're mistaken, my dear. I got very little of what I really wanted in life. A lab to work in and do the work in my own way and only working on what I wanted to work on. Also to teach. I like teaching—the life of the mind. Well, before the Edu-chip changed everything. A ration of peace once in a while, I'd've certainly liked more peace. And the only woman I really ever wished for, there at my side, or I at her side and a few other places besides. But now, in the fullness of life's irony, for the first time I am getting what I want. The end of it all, and the best part is that it'll be on my own terms. That ain't so easy to pull off, I'm finding."

"You sound like a member of that Hemlock Society."

"I won't be needing them."

"You make me very sad. Also angry."

"I make myself delighted, and it's my turn for it. I've earned my ticket out. That wasn't so easy, either…feel like heading over to the pool again? Or we could listen to music. I've got some old CDs by Bix Beiderbecke. "Kitten on the Keys," "Bamboula," "Cradle in Carolina"…great stuff, if you like jazz. I'm nuts about it. I'd give anything if I could compose jazz."

"You've composed plenty. Okay. Let's go face the music."

"And dance?"

"Jus-*stt* the music, please."

Later, Sarita passed a copy to him, an extract from a paper written by a faculty member at Brown University of Providence, Rhode Island.

> Spread by the Commo-Net, with over two-billion home devices hooked in, the knowledge of how to make Zyme-One or its equivalent has been publicly available for almost fifty years. The technology, allowing for quick and easy manipulation of DNA molecules in all life forms, has reached a point beyond anything ever imagined. Almost anyone can change anything that lives to anything that has never before lived. It is as impossible to quash this know-how as it is to dry up the Pacific Ocean. Anyone can now engage in so-called bathtub biology. Even small nations can build and have built bio-reactors for a pittance, thereby creating horrific devices for wholesale kill-off of targeted populations, and the world, shrugging, seems resigned to its never dreamed of plight. It is this rogue science, and its ever enlarging cloud of doom that hovers over our lives. Terrorist groups could slaughter anyone, anytime, anywhere.

"No, I'd not seen this one before," he said, handing back the foolscap. "Others like it, plenty of them, but not this one. I'd remember it."

"Any comment?"

"It's the sort of stuff that puts a second hole in my gut."

"And what else?"

"Nothing else. I'd like to send the writer a gold crown."

"He's dead. He was killed in a bio-accident."

"A friend?"

"More than a friend."

"Sorry. Maybe he's lucky. I'll be joining him soon. I'll look him up, what's his name?"

"Stop saying that…please just stop it…"

Had something caught in her eye, or was that womanly mist he saw? He couldn't be sure, but once again she perplexed him. She needed looking into, he thought.

Next day.

"How did you know that Mrs. Courmaine-Muldaur had had sickle anemia? Don't tell me it was a lucky guess."

"Lin-pao mentioned it." Sarita hesitated, then added, "I'm sure he did."

"I see. We haven't gotten around to him, have we?"

"Must we?"

"You didn't like him?"

"He sounds like a waterfall. Very nice, he's that all right but he's also the Picasso of bullshit as far as I'm concerned. I know he's supposed to be brilliant."

Thomas laughed. "Yes, he's fast. Bubbles over like a glass of champagne that's poured too quickly. Also, he has the best mind for science I've ever run into. A one ton brain."

"Have you ever seen his home in Shanghai? Fantastic."

"Many times. I usually visit him every spring when it's not too hot over there. We go cruising on his sailing junk. A pretty incredible sight itself. Long as a city block."

"I didn't get that far. Wasn't urged."

"Another time, perhaps."

"We're off the subject but I think he was gravely disappointed when you didn't accept the Nobel Prize, when you had the chance. I forget the year. But he sort of pulled a face when the subject came up."

"I couldn't accept it. Not by myself. Five of us were involved in what proved to be the breakthrough-work at St. Curig Fields. We didn't know it at the time, but later it became very clear that the work at St. Curig was the lodestar for things to come. They won't award it to five people for the same laureate. So, I passed and am still glad I did."

"I still say he was disappointed."

"He has enough laurels for ten men already. Twenty or so. He won the Japan Prize twice. No one's beat that record."

"Is he your best friend?"

"Right up there."

"And the others?"

"No, you don't. I'm not putting you on any new trails."

"I'm sure they'd treat you well."

"We'll never know, will we? I think I'd like to kiss you right now."

"I'd like to keep this professional, if it's all the same."

"It's only a kiss."

"Not now or any other now."

"A day of disappointments." They'd been on a walk and now they stopped. "Up ahead, you see those ruins. That was once a beautiful barn made out of stone brought up from Devon. Almost two-hundred years old and then it was blown up. Blown straight to hell."

"Who'd do a thing like that?"

"My son would do a thing like that, and he did. He knows a surprising amount about explosives and I've never figured out how he got so acquainted with them."

"Explosives! Really!"

Thomas stood still as he surveyed the wreckage of the outbuilding. "Yes, really," he muttered, echoing Sarita but with a different meaning.

She had gotten him use to thinking in the reverse-mode, his rearview mirror of the past. Today it was SOS. His thoughts had gone awry but were nonetheless vivid; awry because when he linked them he had to admit to so many grave mistakes; vivid because all of them, the ones he'd been describing to her, had been turning points in life. None seemed erasable.

Long ago he had stood before the SOS members, as then constituted, pleading for a chance to show the proof of what Zyme-One could do. Had his concept been accepted, ultimately, then the likelihood was that many governments would have underwritten the needed research. But his proofs, left in the Naruma Station, had been destroyed wantonly. With the destruction had come the next fork in his road. Forced to go elsewhere for help, he had tried America. Defeated there and yet had he not gone there he would never have found the love of his life. Back to Jaggy and her bankrolling Muldaur-Courmaine. Wins and losses, progress and setbacks, pushing the boundaries.

Then Christopher. Then France and Shandar. Then jail and temporary madness. Caving in, selling out to the Swiss. A series of turns in the road of his life, all, more than not, starting with those lost proofs, and never getting his shot at persuading SOS into supporting his breakthrough. What might've happened? Never would he know. Now he could attend tomorrow's session at Cambridge, for he was a member-emeritus, take Sarita along as a guest to observe the proceedings (as she, in turn, would also be closely observed); and, since he was allotted ten minutes of podium time, he'd rant at the audience of elites for not doing more to prevent the misuse of his discoveries.

What irony!

Asking them to help undo what he had once hoped so avidly to get then to shore up and support.

At afternoon tea, that most revered of English ceremonies, he was explaining to her that he'd be bowing out of their next day's session. Giving a short talk at the SOS meeting at Cambridge's Darwin College, he told her. His swan song. He had firm plans in mind to tell them off: that they had shirked even barest efforts to demand that governments prevent degradation of the human race.

"They've become a bunch of lilies," he said, dreary-voiced. "You can tag along if you like. They might lob a few tomatoes at me, if they have the brains to bring any along. You're quite a tomato. They might throw you at me." Seeing her sharp look, he added, "Just kidding."

"I'd love to come if you're certain I won't be in the way?"

"You'll be our star attraction, I assure you."

"Hardly that, I'm sure. I suppose I won't understand half of it. Less maybe."

"No, mam. I don't think you'll have the slightest difficulty. I'll be wearing my preacher's hat but we'll be skipping the Ave Maria's. By the way, don't try to lasso any of them for comments about me. They can get very shirty. Guests are permitted by prior arrangement, which I can take care of. No journalists, however, thanks to every god that ever was imagined. They'll run you out the door, if you crack the rules."

"Are there students still at Cambridge?"

"Some who want to work on history projects and they require practical training in research. The others are mostly gone. Gone for twenty years or so."

"My university is mostly closed. I think we've about five-hundred on what's left of the campus. It used to be in the thousands. It's like that everywhere."

"I think I'm catching on. We're heading into the Edu-Chip, right? It's never just a single discovery, you know. Do you remember a concept called the university-without-walls? You could get a degree from many well-known universities and colleges while doing your academic work at home. It opened the door for a lot of people to higher education. More affordable, for sure. The Edu-Chip was merely an improvement."

"I know scores of professors out of work these days who'd argue it's anything but an improvement. It's been ruinous to us."

"Not to students."

"In America over twelve thousand colleges and universities have ceased educating."

"In the world over nine-billion people have a knowledge base that is measured at five times what could be taught in four years at the old time institutes of higher learning. I consider that more important than the demise of Harvard or Stanford. Wouldn't you?"

"Frankly, I like both ways of educating."

"You're a woman and women always like six options for everything"

"That's unkind."

"The way of the truth, isn't it? Often, so unkind."

The Edu-chip? I didn't fully answer you because I wanted to re-check something.

A dodgy business from the start, the opposition was as if the China Wall had fallen on us. Lin-pao and I found the way to manipulate cognitive and memory genes in certain ways and the nanotechnology boys built an atom-sized engine—the size of a dust speck—and it took about a year to learn how to pack it with as much information as you might find in the Library of Congress.

We taught the chip to be highly interactive with cognitive and memory capacity, well beyond anything known in the past. Inside two decades, a great percentage of the world had knowledge that went far beyond what the old-time doctorate degree called for.

What's wrong with it, I've always wondered?

The gain in knowledge and education for the masses speaks for itself. Half the world can now speak three languages.

Cost per capita for a model A8775 Edu-Chip is $34.00 American, approximately. I checked the price today. Quite a bouquet when stacked against the gargantuan tuitions of earlier times and the fact that today anyone can afford a first-pew education, and we've more highly educated people than ever before. I'm glad I was a part of it but am sorry the Edu-Chip put you out of your career. One reason I put off visiting with you is that of the several attempts made on my life, and thwarted by my great amigo, Crunch, four of the buggers were dispossessed professors bound on revenge.

I had you looked up by a colleague friend of mine. Result: you were another of them of so I thought at the time. I had no way of knowing you wanted an interview so you could lob a grenade at me.

Education, it's our last hope and always has been our first one. That's why I think of the "E-chip" as a version of Gutenberg writ large. He spread it with paper and ink, and I helped re-spread it with atoms taught to connect with genetic pathways in and out of the brain, and then to perform operations that allowed for the free flow of great quantities of knowledge.

All around, a good deal for everyone, except, as you remind me, professional educators.

Someone, somewhere owes us a gold medal. Instead, what I get is attempts on my life. So there you are, and, as they say: "No good deed ever goes unpunished."

Still, I'd bet anything you've got an Edu-chip implant. Am I right? You don't need to answer; I can tell without having you go through a brain-scan.

"…but if I can't meet her, why can't I at least ask about her?"

"A question guaranteed to bring on amnesia."

"Pooh to you."

"Again, if you're going to mention her in your book, you'll want to refer to her as Courmaine-Muldaur. That's the accepted surname and for my son as well. Sure, you can ask about her as long as you understand I may not answer."

"I've read lots, the sort of things you can find in newspaper morgues. What is she like now?"

"Ruthless, generous, shy, niggardly, very rich, outgoing, insecure, devious, a scourge, still sexually wild I'm told, and hard-bitten when she doesn't get her way. Horses, gambling, cussing, there's that, and she shops for a week at a time non-stop on the Internet. Take your pick. Depends on what hour you catch her and truthfully I don't catch her very often. Never a dull moment around the Stiletto. However, she did give me my start in bringing my ideas alive. For that, she still has my thanks and it ought to be mentioned…oh, I almost forgot that she actually graduated from a sex school in Indonesia. A great pastime of hers. You'd think —oh, nothing—"

"Tell me."

"No."

"Are you, ah, estranged? Sounds as though you are."

He laughed harshly, and with contempt. "We've never not been estranged. I take that back. For a time, we were on great terms but it floundered just before the clubhouse turn. We've not been in bed together in seventy-odd years. I stick around here because it suits me. I like to be close to the university. And I worry about my boy. She can't threaten me the way she used to. I own this place, all of it. She's still loaded down with her own real estate, though. I think she has eight homes. Maybe it's down to seven but I think eight. She likes it here, best. She wrote me a letter about it once."

"A letter?"

"Our treaty extends to writing notes to each other. About one per month. Otherwise, we pass messages through our secretaries. Sometimes I feel like one of those Carmelite nuns who never get to speak unless they need a doctor."

"Must be awful," Sarita said in obvious delight, as if happening upon some crucial clue in a mystery.

"It's a blessing, the fullest blessing."

"Back to Mrs. Muldaur-Courmaine—"

"Let's refer to her as M-C only. That way I don't have to hear my own name linked with hers in the same breath."

"Okay, a sort of code, then."

"Yes, good for you. A code."

"Why does she stay on, with all those homes at her disposal?"

"Because of Christopher. She thinks she can get him to sign his birthright away. An artificial birthright, but she's been boxed on that one. She's fanatic about money. Obsessed."

"Are you very rich?"

"You asked that before and frankly it's impertinent."

"You are said to be rich. You must be to own a place like this. I'm trying to confirm facts, that's all."

"I see. Yes, I am what you would call a rich man. Too rich. I can't give it away fast enough. You reach a point where money manages you instead of the other way around. It's very time consuming."

"Would it be in the range of, say, a billion Euros?"

"I will not reply to that."

"All right, sorry." She paused to write a note. "When and where did you marry?"

He looked off, then got up and stepped to the fireplace, rubbing his hands together. "I'll give you some small news. We never did marry. I couldn't stand her and she couldn't abide me. She's like living with a grinding wheel and she thinks I'm worse because I wouldn't agree to be her lap-dog. Ah, well, soon it's over. So, what the hell—"

I sit here in my bedroom thinking about this x-ray job you're doing on me. I'm letting you in on things I've tried to put behind me, if not forget altogether. You're an excellent auditor. You seemed so relieved when I told you that Jaggy Muldaur and I had never married. Why, I wonder?

People, including the public, always took it for granted we were a legally bound couple, because for decades we've lived under the same roof. What an illusion! Every divorce, every man-woman estrangement began in a home somewhere. You may recall that we (or I) were forever in the news and news-hawkers made a fallacious assumption about us, one I never bothered to correct. Easier not to, you see, and we could, at the same time, perpetuate the social conventions of the day. No one seems to care much about marriage in this day and age.

The nutshell is this: Jaggy Muldaur and I were utterly symbiotic, kept together for one reason alone—to protect Christopher from himself and from others who unwittingly wandered into his cross-hairs. Had he ever been found out, publicly, he'd have been committed.

Our thready, unwholesome gluing—that was Christopher's role; he kept us together, though obliviously, we've been living for all these years on dead ground and in deadest air. In all, as I look back, we were both sort of strapped to each other's bomb, neither of us sure whose would detonate first.

To Jaggy, I was never the "good sport". Never measured up. Hadn't the right pedigree, came out of the wrong drawer—that's me. She likes nobility, though I've yet to figure out what so noble about the nobility. For a time, after Christopher's entry into our lives, we were constantly jousting with our various lawyers and such, I tried to bump our compass needle to a more civilized heading, but we had by then lost our magnetic north. I was making large money and my lawyers were equal to hers. As well, I had gained clout with the Swiss who had insisted that if Christopher were to keep his Swiss citizenship, he'd have to reside there for six months for each of the next five years after the birth. We resided in Gstaad, and I commuted to my MarocheChem lab. My work at the lab saved me from an episode of murder—of her.

She did everything imaginable to gain the upper hand over myself, but was foiled. I nearly had to have her run out of Switzerland. When she was so advised by the authorities, the message sunk in and she called off her vendettas. But, like water, peace keeps no constant shape and soon, after moving back to Britain, the flack began to fly again and has not since stopped. One round of sparring after the next, most of it outside the ropes, and no holds barred.

You also seemed startled that over the decades I've managed my communications with her by scribbled notes. But the truth is that there is nothing left between us. Everything had been said and done a long time ago. I do all I can to keep her at a full distance, For one thing, being paranoid, she carries a Beretta pistol, hidden in the folds of those kaftans she favors. I'm giving her no easy chances to pull it on me.

Besides, how could I tell you, face to face, of my bottomless disdain for a woman you've never met? Yes, it is sad and regrettable but it is the truth of the situation and that is what you say you seek—truth.

Here, a fortifying sample of my assertions: One afternoon many years ago, I had caught Jaggy and Christopher in bed together. I had gone out to the guesthouse, where I'd left some papers needed for a conversation with a visiting bio-physicist from Munich. Arriving there, I heard sounds from one of the back bedrooms. Curious, going for a look, I saw them. The door was open, She was naked, straddling Christopher, and with her back to me. Christopher saw me, and suddenly waved, called out: "Dad..." but she kept right on, as If It was all to be expected. A family sex show or the like.

Later, enraged, when I accosted her, she said something like, "He needs his lessons, so sod off...and besides I need to know if he's wild-blooded." A typical comment of hers. I repeat that she and I had terminated all sexual contact since before the cruise of the *Palenque*. I will make this comment: She was some heat pad, equipped with the talents of ten courtesans.

I was certain, then, that one or both of them was insane. I was going insane myself, living in this asylum of my own making. Tragedy incarnate, a son who could not account for himself, a bogus wife-and-mother who at the time was forty-eight trying to look as if she were twenty-five. In fact, she'd become a test-tube woman who was so much of everything—gene-wise—that she has now become a next-to-nothing. Wholly morphed. She exists as human, though only technically. She meets all the criteria I can think of to fill the bill as a world-class, stone-ground *Gorpo*.

Any mother who would bed her son under any circumstances, and, in our case, simply to satisfy her own sexual curiosity is recklessly insane. I no longer hate her for it, yet I shall never forgive her.

One night he crawled into bed with me. I awakened, felt a hand caressing my genitals. An unholy row erupted. I threw the boy to the floor, after which, and how well I remember this, he got to his feet, yanked me off the bed and belted me all the way across the room with punishing body shots—a good twenty-five feet of getting painfully beaten to shreds. Finally, I lifted a chair as a shield and talked calmness into him, who bawled that he had only climbed into my bed wanting to show love, show respect and affection.

Jaggy was of no help. She thought him precious and as singular as the Hope diamond. He is who he is, and that was it for her. I told her I'd kill her if she ever molested him again. So far as I know, she laid off. Is that a pun?

Jaggy spies. She bribes the staff to keep an eye on me. She is never more than a step behind most of my movements, living as she does in mortal fear that I will somehow outfox her and dissolve The Trust. Except it is now The Christopher-blah-blah-blah Trust. (He has many given names). By now, the money is so enormous it's an outrageous embarrassment, even to the sole trustee, who is myself. I made arrangements, secretly, for Christopher to deed The Trust to my care. He has zero interest in money, none whatsoever.

Where he's going he'll not require any of it. Nor will he ever miss it.

Along the rocky way of life, I've discovered that when one sows confusion, one reaps profit. I've created a maze of cross-ownership and sub-ownership that no outsider could hope to figure out. I can barely do it myself. Nothing, absolutely nothing will be traceable when I finish with my grand heist. I must admit I've learned a lot from the gnomes at Braunsweig over the years. They're magicians at obscuring everything, even when *that* everything is in plain sight, right in front of one's face.

Won't the Stiletto be surprised? Christopher will be gone. I'll be gone. The money will be gone and I'm leaving all Downs to Crunch. A black man, well, half of a black man, will be her landlord and she'll scream so loud they'll hear it in Perth. I'd give a lot to hear it myself, I really would. Stiletto, being an Afrikaner, is one-thirty-second black herself though you couldn't get her to admit it short of putting her on the rack. She'd never acknowledge her soon-to-be landlord is also half white.

Now, you've a better glimpse of the person I've "lived with" for seventy years. More, if counting the time before Chris was born. It is as if we all three had been conjured in Hell. Mayhem it is so, and we're just now realizing it.

I leave it for you to decide. Isn't that what biographers do for a living, correct the record?

Cambridge, England

Neatly, successfully executed.

Though the surgery was still in an experimental phase, it was perfectly safe, or he'd not have let Sarita anywhere near it. All of it done with computer-imaging that manipulated a scrupulously detailed picture of her knee joint; all of it also aided by two hook-shaped, hair-thin needles inserted on an x and y axis under the patella of her kneecap.

In the space of only two hours, the bio-engineers constructed a new knee joint made of ceramic nanoparticles that, in their turn, were assembled from millions of atoms shaped to conform identically to Sarita's knee joint before it was damaged. Invisible to the naked eye, the nanoparticles—stronger than steel, flexible as spaghetti—were flooded into her knee and cartilage cells, then thermal coated. The new knee was good for at least a hundred years.

None of the new elements in her knee would be rejected, for they were cemented in place with a version of Zyme-One, assuring they'd stay put. Assuring, too, she'd be better than new when the procedure was complete.

Amazed, delighted, she hardly knew what to say to the nano-techies or to Thomas who'd arranged it all.

With a starlit smile, Sarita hopped about for a full minute on her new knee with its old leg. Doing it out of sheer fun, an act she could not have performed as recently as that morning. Doe-eyed, she turned to him, hugged him, a hug where he felt the full length of her. Thrill warmed him; a very great thrill.

Good for his word, and though he felt the cutting edge of guilt at using her, in any way he could, to tell his story, he sat with Sarita for three hours as they scoured The Trust's core documents. Leafing their way through the collection, here and there, they paused so she could read at length, then inquire if she didn't grasp something.

He kept the documents in a vault at Cavendish, far beyond the reach of Jaggy; taking no chances she might find a way to access them if they were housed at the Downs.

Being an historian by training, Sarita dwelt on the correspondence of Piet Friejjarr-Muldaur I, the Dutch East Indies seafaring trader-merchant cum-crook, who had begun it all. Written in Latin, a language unfamiliar to her, she turned to Thomas for help.

After she finished her inspection of the documents, he handed her a sheaf containing twenty-three of the originals, to use or not, as she saw fit. One more strut of proof that she had gotten to him and his past. He was no longer in need of them; five-hundred years of various forms of secrets had met their demise.

Finally.

Atherton Downs
Abington Piggots, England

Time suddenly had collapsed.

Always it seemed to him that when vibrant people came into his life, they somehow vanished faster than their arrival. Even though he had known and loved Baster, Augustin deMehlo, Lin-pao, and especially, most especially, Shandar Bazak, not one of them had ever seemed a lasting fixture. Almost, as he began to count on them for his sustenance, they left him.

He had not fully realized his feelings for Sarita until she was no longer a part of his daily routine. The hurt, the loss, was not something he would admit to, but that lack did not in any way lessen the sting of learning she had left.

From short-lived habit he had gone to his library, and there waited expectantly for her. Waited till he learned from the day-butler that Sarita had left before six on that morning. No good-byes, no signals or hints that she was about to leave the Downs. It irked him, after all his hospitality.

Later on, an upstairs maid brought him an envelope and a small package wrapped in blue silk and tied with a gilt-flecked ribbon. The note, charming, written with warmth and thanks-giving. Opening the package, he discovered a leather-bound book of Tennyson's poems. Quite old, nearly two centuries, a valuable first edition.

For a time he read from Tennyson, thumbing the pages to find poems he'd studied in high school, back in Baltimore, in days when the Jesuits were shaping him. Opening one page, he saw a card. Hers. A mistake? Or left there on purpose? He let his fingers rest on the open pages, believing she had touched them, imagining the feel of her fingertips.

The card would save time, anyway, for it listed her address, a phone number, and an e-mail locater. He had things to tidy up in London next week: the solicitors, the accountants, get up to date on the taxes, and a long, long session at Braunsweig's.

And leaving the Downs after sixty-five years of life here. Time to let go, he thought, and time, he also thought, to advise that private investigator in Denver a certain woman was headed homeward, so kindly get cracking.

And that night, he put the final strokes to the letter—the last small opus of Thomas Courmaine, now a vetted and revealed man.

Here, comes the wrap-up as I finish exhuming my past and perhaps contribute in some small way to your future, or at least to your book.

I've told you a few things about The Trust, but now what you're about to learn is known only to you and me at present.

Almost three-hundred-billion Euros is soon to be divvied up, and I'm the one in charge of cutting up the butter. Africa will finally get its overdue share. One-half will go to African Heritage so that more can be done to save those splendid animals, one of the profound examples of Nature's glorious plan of evolution and diversity—all of it done without any assistance from Zyme-One. African Heritage will be purchasing over three million acres to be patrolled by top-rated hunters and ex-commandos who, combined, will see to the safety of the herds and flocks and other bio-diverse flora and fauna, doing it all on a scale never before attempted. If we cannot save ourselves, perhaps we can establish a legacy for the wildlife. Dearly, do I hope so and will readily admit that I get very jacked up about that prospect.

The other half of my heist goes to Genesis, in one form or another; in hopes it will reverse, over time, the worldwide catastrophe I wrought. A supreme example of unintended consequences doing its unruly best to maintain the human race in its usual state of confusion.

So, there it is, the dismemberment of a 500-year old money-colossus that has never done anything for anyone. Till now, let us hope.

And to you, my dear one, thanks for stopping by. My only regret is that we didn't find occasion for the soothing bliss of the bed.

By the way, there'll be a lollapalooza of a public announcement about the gift to African Heritage. In, say, two months, the president of African Heritage will accept the gift from an anonymous donor at a reception the Pierre in New York. It'll be quite a show, I think, and stage-managed by Meric & Morris, a public relations firm of the same city. The money is to be handed over via a checque issued by Brown Brothers Harriman & Co., private bankers, also of New York and many elsewheres.

Watch for the fanfare. When it hits the papers and airwaves, you'll at least know I've been on the level with you.

The media will go nutty trying to find out who's behind it all. Tough titty! My final revenge, you might say. Beneath me or not, I mean to serve them a little of their own gruel for a change. I'm sure you'll be on the receiving end of their queries should you elect to show the evidence now in your possession, meaning parts of this letter and copies of historical trust documents I've given you. Happily, I leave that decision up to you. But, as I said before, be careful about the reactions of the Swiss and the South Africans. They're unscrupulous, and their beds are concrete hard, the food unforgettable it's so terrible. You'll find out, sorrowfully so, if they try to milk it out of you where you got what you've got.

So, there it is.

Having stolen the money from the South Africans, I, now, in my position as sole trustee, steal it all over again and this time from my own son. Human nature, as you've learned, is capable of anything. Poor Christopher will never know what a magnificent thing he is responsible for; nor, that his own father is a crime lord of the first quality.

Revoir and best of luck, always. If there exists a Beyond, I shall hope to cross paths there with you, Sarita dear. You are one of the truly value-added dames, I've ever encountered.

TIC

Rio de Janeiro, Brazil

With much still to organize, he had arrived two weeks earlier than anyone had expected. Straight from Brussels, he had flown commercially so his name appeared on the passenger manifest, when the police began their investigation. He had made a short stopover in Belgium to retrieve a forged document, that, was so vitally necessary. To perfect the forgery he must still have certain data entered in the official birth records at the Civil Registry in Montevideo, but that was a task for another day.

Since arriving in Rio, he kept away from his usual haunts, checking into a small hotel in the seaside district of Ponta do Marisco, to the south of the famed Ipanema Beach.

Resting, lazing on the sandy beaches, swimming up to five miles daily in the South Atlantic Ocean, jogging. He was getting his body ready for a swim of at least ten miles of hard stroking.

At the beach, he listened, whenever he could, to the natives talk their Brazilian-accented Portuguese. Tuning his ear, making it easier for his brain to process two languages, each mingling with the other—a vocal disguise of sorts. Also, a necessity for what was in the offing. Eventually, it would become a part of his newer self, his new name and his proclaimed origins as a man who spoke Portuguese yet with an accent that was Uruguayan-type Spanish.

He liked becoming someone else. After years of hibernation, all but isolated at the Downs, he had begun the processes of freeing himself, normalizing, happy to rejoin the milling crowds. He felt so much calmer now that he didn't have to look over his shoulder so much of the time.

The previous night he had ambled along the beachside streets, among the throngs, submerging himself. He loved Rio. Nothing ever worsened here. Not the weather. Not the blue-blue waters. Not the women of the beach gamboling in their revealing thongs. An easy-paced life, as rhythmic as the beat of the samba heard along any of the back streets of Rio's beach communities. The cadence of life here, the tempo and sounds of the *musica popular*—samba and salsa—never failed to polish his mood.

Even so, he was disturbed at seeing Brazilians who had obviously succumbed to the trap of fussing themselves up with gene fixes. Brazilians, a mix of many bloods, were among the most stunning people in the world. A true gift of nature, from thousands of years of natural breeding, and the sight of these remodeled South American he found disturbing. Keeping his distance, though. He still feared he might attract attention. A silvery blond male, white, he'd be tagged an outsider no matter how he talked. Someone, he worried, might recognize him, a risk he could not afford and one that could torpedo his carefully set plans.

Waiting for the right day, he visited a boat dealership and, for cash, bought a thirty-two foot Century-Miramar Cruiser. The cash was dished out from a black satchel he carried; cash that left no traces but in an amount that assured he'd be remembered once the police began their legwork.

Completing the ownership forms, he produced British identity documents that verified his true name and nationality, and now, with smiles all around, he arranged for seven lessons on boat-handling. That, too, was a weighed act. He meant to indelibly establish himself as a seafaring neophyte; a clue to be carefully deposited along his trail of deceit. It was time now to be remembered, part of his ruse, and to leave his true name where he wanted it left.

Next, he negotiated for a berth at a nearby marina, securing a ten-percent discount by paying for a year in advance. Yet another act that would be easy to recollect for the police, but one more subterfuge calculated to add credence to his death.

He took the seven boat-handling sessions, fumbling about, banging the boat twice when docking, fouling a sea-anchor in the propeller by backing over a line when he was supposed to be in forward gear. Making a hash of it, and his instructor shaking his head, growling to himself over this incompetent foreign klutz.

He then left the area, attended a five-day long symposium of the Genesis Society, helping to set membership goals for the coming year, approving budgets, voting three women into key positions, and arranging a donation of a million Euros through a local bank he was becoming interested in.

Not too much money at one time, he decided: it was a note of self-imposed caution, knowing that outsized gifts invited too much curiosity.

Saying his good-byes to his cohorts, he left and an hour later checked out of the Palace Hotel at Copacabana Beach, where he had resided during the weeklong conference of the Genesis Society's council. Now for the make-over. Now for the end of T.I. Courmaine. Excitement sliced through him like a harpoon.

He flew to Montevideo in Uruguay on Varig, the Brazilian airline, using a Uruguayan passport issued to one Raoul Marciara-Quina, the name chosen for the bogus document done up by the Belgium forger. On this flight, the passport's photo was of his true self, one of the changes made to the passport pick pocketed years ago from an unwary tourist while visiting Paris.

Nearly, he was done with himself, with his past, with all else publicly attached to the name of Thomas I. Courmaine. Long, tumultuous, sometimes exciting years, but mostly burdensome times since leaving the Jesuits. Now this abrupt ending. An ethereal, indescribable feeling, as if being reborn without the biological necessity of a mother or father. He had more to do, much more. He had learned something from Sarita Sambinna, or thought he had, and perhaps it would be the most important life-changer of all.

Would it, though? Could he be that lucky again?

Eleven weeks passed while his face was re-worked, allowing him more time to rehearse his accents and speech patterns, to practice a new walking gait, to grow a box-shaped beard. He mended wondrously fast, his face had, the fingers, however, took weeks. Every finger and its print characteristics had been altered, all those little whorls and tiny, tiny ridges. He knew as much as any man living about skin-genes, and, surreptitiously, did a gene-fix on himself to slightly darken his ruddy, white man's complexion. When told his DNA would remain the same, he was unworried. Ten ways from Sunday, he could rework that attribute, if ever he needed to.

He was reinventing himself, almost as surely as he had reinvented Christopher.

Utterly, he had set aside both his qualms and criticisms of others who delved into the fixing game for themselves, by themselves. A hypocritical act on his part, and he admitted to it. Yet survival was uppermost on his mind; that, and parsing of Sarita's artifices.

With every day, came the illusion of new life, reminding him of his three Eves...and what they had been thinking about themselves when he transformed them.

Nearing the time to leave Montevideo, he turned his attentions to the dark business of amending his official but illegally altered Uruguayan passport. He met with a well-known lawyer, who specialized in criminal cases, a man—of useful connections— as described to Thomas during his stopover in Belgium in that other life.

The attorney was a loose end. He'd always know the actuality of the charade. Concerned over it, Thomas had told him, "What you know, you'll have to forget. Only a few people will ever know what I've done to myself. If I'm betrayed, a man named Jellicoe will be looking for you. Let's hope that'll never be necessary. Meanwhile you'll get your million annually for ten years."

After shelling out a memorable fee, three times what he had paid the forger, Thomas was assured all necessary notations would be entered in the official records of the Civil Registry by midnight the following day. If he cared to, Thomas was also told, he could wait around a day or two longer and check the entries for himself.

And he did so.

He went to the Registry offices, and, just as promised, as if by some magical stroke, he had become a bone-fide citizen of Uruguay. The entries had been made, as if recorded many years before: his age, according to the listed date of birth, made him fifty-eight. Looking younger, though, possibly too much younger. He didn't care to be taken for a *Gorpo*.

Next, visiting a public *secretario*, he dictated a letter to the Director-general of Genesis Society, at Rua Xavier de Milveria, 8224, Copacabana, RJ, Brazil, saying he was about to visit that city. While there, he wished to inquire about establishing a Genesis Society chapter in northern Uruguay. Upon arrival, he would—*con su permiso*—phone for an appointment. In the penultimate paragraph, he indicated he was prepared to advance the sum of ten-millions to establish the proposed branch, a juicy carrot dangled to ensure a meeting. Almost foaming with pleasure, for the very first time he signed his new name: Raoul Marciara-Quina.

Entering a new life as one might enter into a new love, swarmed by a heightening sense of adventure, hopes flowing through him in the incalculable shapes of dreams. The future was any future he cared to conjure, its promises gyrating in his head like the spinning Saturn with all its fiery rings.

Yet here he was, hiding again, wasn't he? Same man, new shell. All the shell did was keep his true self in a newly spun cocoon. Otherwise, he had the same memories, had the same brain, was possessed of the same likes and dislikes.

Still, he had gained his second chance, and it was a chance to make his amends. All he could hope for, all he needed if luck and fate would smile upon him.

Returning to Rio de Janeiro, he checked into yet a third hotel, staying three days to collect his wits. Step by step, he processed his movements: the places he'd been since first arriving in South America almost four months previously, the people he'd met with, had conferred with, bought from, and all else he had done to purposely litter the trail with the presence and actions of Thomas Courmaine.

Testing his new self, he visited restaurants, the beach, oceanside cafes. He successfully passed himself off as a visiting Uruguayan, apologizing on occasion for his lame Brazilian-style Portuguese. At two bars, on successive evenings, casual acquaintances treated him to drinks as a fellow South American. At one watering hole, a hip salsa joint with pulsing green and blue lights, a carioca— she, a coffee-skinned, laughing woman—covertly massaged his crotch as they sat side-by-side at a piano-bar listening to a silken-voiced chanteuse with an angel's touch on the ivories. He paid his seat-mate for the night, left her at the piano-bar, returning to his hotel.

Set within himself now, he concocted the final chapter of Thomas Courmaine. He returned to the marina the next day at twilight, untied the recently acquired Miramar Cruiser, fired up the coughing engine and steered a course for Sugar Loaf, some several nautical miles away, north by northeast.

A mile or so distant from the sea-risen Loaf, he throttled down, caught an offshore current, cut the engine, drifting. Stripping to the buff, he donned a blue wet-suit. Stacking his clothes—dungarees, a denim shirt, underwear and sneakers—in a neat pile on the galley table, and leaving his crocodile-skin wallet half out of the side pants pocket so it would be easy to find. The wallet contained a thick wad of Brazilian *cruzieros*, a British driver's license in the name of Thomas I. Courmaine, and sundry other cards bearing his true name. Nearby, he left a folio of notes for a speech he never intended giving, the notes written in long-hand; yet another shred of proof that the soon to be missing man was one and the same Thomas Courmaine, in all probability

Finally, under the wallet he tucked a suicide note in handwriting matching with that of the speech notes. His handwriting style could be easily checked and verified, if needed, by either Interpol or Scotland Yard.

Waiting till nightfall, he slipped quietly over the side and stroked his way through moonlit waters for just over seven miles. The sea fairly quiet, rolling gently, allowed him to body surf at intervals as he headed toward a beach where, two nights earlier, he'd concealed a rubberized bag of clothes.

Clean and final; almost gone for good.

Two days later, he saw the first reports of his disappearance. Strange, seeing the printed word that described him as missing, and a presumed suicide. The note he left aboard the boat was mentioned. That no body was recovered did not pose any ambiguity, since two oceanographers were quoted as saying that, given where a passing fishermen found the drifting boat and its distance out at sea, it was almost a certainty a body would have been carried eastward by prevailing currents. Though speculative, it nevertheless offered a nominal explanation of why his remains had not been recovered.

On the third day, a wire-photo of himself along with an article appeared below the fold on the front page of *Brazil National*, a leading national paper. It brought a grin of satisfaction as he read that he was referred to as "destiny's man" who had made so many remarkable contributions to healthcare and self-education. And the changes his discoveries had brought about in Africa and Central Asia had been nothing short of sensational. In other praising prose, it said "his life had been the story of a genuine change-maker" and a "giant of biology who unleashed the juggernaut of genetic therapy that eventually replaced the traditional medicine of the past century." *Sao Paulo Mata*, yet another popular paper, reported him as widely regarded in international science circles as a "chosen instrument" of his times, but also a man frequently criticized over the past half-century as a maverick who had gone too far, too fast, wreaking widespread havoc…"

Too true, he thought wryly.

For a post-mortem, it was as good as he could expect. Dead, he was treated better than when alive. Garlands and wreaths, almost. Maybe, he thought, he should anonymously donate a monument to himself, the thought building yet another smile on his new face.

Time, a watchful eye on his part, no stupid moves or no wrong-footedness, and he'd be safe and dry before long.

An imposter to be sure, a masquerader for life. Continuing his cover up, he called at Rio's main post office to claim an envelope held *poste restante*—for one Raoul Marciara-Quina. That night, setting up his next move, he read a Denver investigator's six-page report, over and over, till his mind was swollen with its details. Swollen, as well, with remembered desire.

Burning the pages, all but a single photo, he deposited the ashes in the toilet bowl, flushed away the contents. Satisfied, he went down to the terrace-bar and quaffed two Hine cognacs while spending a full half-hour pleasing himself with a Cohiba Robusto.

On the next morning, he walked to the head offices of Genesis Society and there spent over an hour discussing the proposed chapter of the society he wished to open in northern Uruguay. No one showed the slighted hint of recognizing him as his former self. Nor did anyone even hint at a doubt that he was other than who he said he was. When departing, he ranked it as the most triumphant meeting he'd ever attended. Everything so neat and tidy, the talk effervescent, cooperation promised in abundance. Smiles in abundance along with firm and lasting handshakes.

Now for the biggest moment of all. In a few days, he'd know the score, though he thought he knew it already.

Things had gone perfectly, so far.

Santa Fe, New Mexico

A t the airport, he rented a solar-auto, a new-fangled model that practically drove itself. The car came equipped with radar and sonar to avoid obstacles, or other traffic, going or coming. A satellite guidance system guided the car from one point to any other point, as directed by a GPS device; or, if the system was disengaged, one could steer manually.

Checking into an airport inn, he slept till dawn. Waking, hungry, he found an all-night diner still serving old-fashion food. He abhorred the cheap pill-food that was so commonly served; even the more expensive wafers made of compressed nutrients from dried meats; wheat germ, oats, or wheat and grain mixtures were unpalatable. Food was in short supply everywhere, now that the world's population had climbed past eleven-billion.

Later, after dining on outrageously expensive eggs, bacon, rye toast and two cups of coffee, he drove around to get a sense of the surrounds. Feeling free, feeling eased. No one could possibly know him, not here anyway, and he felt as liberated as a ghost.

Slowly, he drove the streets of Santa Fe, a place famous in its time, a place he'd never been before, and, as it was his first return to the U.S. in decades, he had a desire to absorb the scenery. Check out what he'd heard from Sarita who seemed to know Santa Fe quite well; and now he thought he knew why she did.

Driving by Cathedral Place, he slowed to get a better look at the inhabitants. He saw people kneeling to drink from a spewing fire hydrant; over on Grant Avenue, five adults, squatted like birds on a telephone-wire, relieving themselves in a curbside gutter. The hungry stood in long, unruly lines outside what appeared to be a mission-house. Fistfights breaking out, women being knocked to the ground, and man-handled for no understandable reason.

Frustration, perhaps, or indiscriminate anger.

A moody, edgy atmosphere. Litter was scattered everywhere: rotted rinds, dog excrement, curls of old newspapers lifting and blowing about haphazardly.

Store fronts with shutters hanging at an angle; some, driven by the morning breeze, banged noisily. Many windows were painted black, making the streets appear like yawning mouths with missing teeth.

Vagrants loitered on street-corners and by alleyways. Beautiful specimens of humanity; he could see many perfectly chiseled profiles, handsome as idealized statuary.

Cruising slowly, the window open, he smelled foul odors, and from deep in the dark of some alleys the occasional human screams of pain.

Further on, a clutch of *Gorpos* huddled around a fire pit, roasting what appeared to be a large dog skewered on a hand-turned spit. Pulling the solar-auto to a curb, observing. His impolitic stare invited angry glares, sneers, hurled insults. A woman shot him the finger. Solar-autos cost money to use, would be an unattainable extravagance for these street people, and he readily sensed their resentment at his gawking. Seeing a woman picking up a rock, he pressed the forward-button and moved on before she let fly.

A festering field of unrest.

The *Gorpos* had flocked to this refuge, gathering like the hippies of several generations earlier, who had assembled themselves in communes to pursue a life of rejecting the so-called establishment. These were the modern rejects, ostracized by their own kind: the throw-aheads, who demanded the highest genetic standards, thus having created their own caste system. With defects of one sort or another, these outcasts had been exiled as unfit to cohabit with level-one *Gorpos*.

Pursuers of eternal youth, they had sought utopia, chased a dream, and their bodies or the technicians who had injected them with one kind or another of gene-paks had somehow failed them, as perhaps he had failed Christopher seventy years ago.

Products of the push-for-perfection. The women with their Venus-like bodies, the men like versions of Adonis, their brains sharpened by Edu-chips. Second-raters, though, and ostracized now. Nothing to do with their lives, with nowhere else to go. All because, genetically, they had not quite come up to snuff with the higher caste of their fellow *Gorpos*, who were close to reigning in America's power centers.

Inevitably, they'd keep migrating as had the Latinos who forced themselves into the U.S. in the latter years of the twentieth-century. In numbers lay safety, so they had congregated, creating for themselves a ghetto with all of its insular wretchedness.

Here, then was his handiwork. Here, the great blowback. Here, the reason, or part of it, why some had tried to kill him out of raw vengeance for what he had done to cause so much loss, so much havoc.

He touched the solar-engine button, awakening its soft purr and he pushed the steering stick far to its left. The solar-car swung in an abrupt u-turn as he punched in a set of map coordinates. Signals from a satellite would quickly assume control, directing him exactly where he was headed, would even moderate the solar-auto's optimum speeds and handle whatever braking was called for, or speed-ups, on the seventy mile journey up to Taos.

Nerve-gnawed now: next a showdown or a love-up?

Taos, New Mexico

Parked on the street for an hour, he awaited any sign of life from the house. His car would be strange to this neighborhood; himself, equally a stranger. Here, for what? Casing the area? A half-hour earlier, a man had come out the front door of a nearby home, planting himself in the yard, staring for an uncomfortable length of time at the solar- auto.

The last thing Thomas wanted was the police called in, with himself the target of complicating questions; is plan for this day dashed before he could get to its first page.

Suddenly—a woman.

She sauntered down a pathway, wearing a wide-brimmed straw sun hat shadowing her face. Black slacks covered the legs and she wore a pale blue pullover. Over one arm dangled a wicker basket.

Reaching to the adjoining seat, he picked up a large manila envelope and withdrew a glossy black-and-white photo the Denver investigator had taken with a zoom lens. The photo, a close-up, was blurry; as if the lens had moved or perhaps the subject had jerked or had been turning away when the shot was taken.

Glancing then at the woman on the path, then at the photo. Back and forth, he looked at both three times. She moved and then moved more, and when she walked there was not an iota of doubt remaining. Enchantment bounding through him. A stab of fear, then. He was seventy-years different, different in almost everything. In mind, in body, in outlook, in what he wanted, in what he needed.

What would she think?

Was a man in there with her?

The investigator's report made no mention of anyone living with her but detectives didn't know everything. What to say to her? What would she say in reply? Or just shoo him off?

Commanding himself, then, to get moving; he got out of the auto, careful not to slam its door.

Bent over, she was pruning something, placing leafy cuttings in her basket. She was close to a sidewalk gate, her back facing him. He had known that back well enough but it was her face he needed to see.

A pulse-stopping moment. Gazing again, a warmth like none other suffused him. "Hello," he said in a voice sounding as if it belonged to someone else. Looking into her wary face, he went on, "I need to, uh, talk. Can we talk? Will you listen?"

"Listen to what? Who *are* you?"

"I'm about to tell you."

"Is that so?"

"It is so."

Looking him up and down, she asked, "Are you lost?"

"For years I've been lost. About seventy of them."

"You're not making yourself clear. What is it you want?"

"You knew me as Thomas Courmaine. A long time ago. You'll have to let me explain."

"You're not a bit funny. He's dead in case you didn't know. Now leave me be, please."

"How glad I am to hear you say that. That I'm dead. I've gone to a lot of trouble to leave that impression."

Her face took on a different shape, of irritation at being accosted by a pest. In lowered voice, she told him: "Leave, and I'm not kidding."

"Just please listen a moment."

Her face changed appearance several times as he retold parts of the past. How they'd first met at the Nestor's in Brooklyn, that she had made inquiries at his behest about The League, things they did together in New York, then that deplorable, forgettable night at "21", and her going off to Australia. Later, her visit to Wales and the weeks in France before he'd been tricked into returning to St. Gallen, the event that had torn them apart until now.

"I know you came looking for me in Switzerland and I know your real name is Shandar Bazak and not the one you apparently go by. You're listed as Suzanne Burkema. You kept the same first initials. Handy."

Abruptly, her head swiveled in two directions. "Keep your voice down, I've neighbors."

"Not everyone has the ears of you women, and I'm talking about as low as I can."

"You're to leave here. You must've been talking to someone to know all this."

"I talked to my memory of you and my memory of us. Here's something else. You have a small crescent-shaped scar on your upper left thigh. How else would I know about that unless I'd seen it and the way I always saw it was when—"

"How dare you!"

Her big eyes instantly grew bigger just before they became unwavering, and as dangerously hard as a startled gorilla's. "For sweet Christ Jesus sakes!" she muttered. "How do you—I cannot believe all this—"

"I can go on, if you like."

"Thank you, no. Oh, god—" The back of one hand swept her brow, then slid to her neck as if she were protecting herself.

"May I have a glass of water?" he asked, a little hoarsely. "I'm about to perish and you don't want an old friend's death on your hands."

"You look nothing like him. The voice, well, the voice is, oh, I don't know…there's an accent and your eyes. Very blue, the same. But your face is nothing like him."

"But it's me. All the same, it is I. I'll undress if that helps."

She pulled another face at his feeble joke. Her arms lifted, up and down twice, as if she wanted to fly off somewhere more to her liking. "Water, of course you can have some water. I need some, too, I think. How did you possibly ever get here? This is—my god, it's been sixty years."

"More like seventy. Water."

"The water. Yes, right. Come along."

Following her, absorbing as much as he could at that range. Still the gliding swan, still a joy to watch. Happiness lightened his steps. They entered her home through a massive oak door, ten feet in height, with figurines carved in its panels. Like the door to a Spanish mountain chapel he'd once seen, when hiking in the Pyrenees.

Could he do it, connect, get started again? She had already told him to leave, and he'd navigated around that hurdle, but it didn't mean she'd let him stay. Do a catch-up, get a conversation started, cook up a laugh or two?

She directed him to a brightly painted bench, loaded with a medley of cushions, and then suddenly he was alone. Sitting, his gaze probing the large room: its wide windows, its bookshelves, the polished floor tiles, the array of silver artifacts and several large and vibrantly colored paintings. Seeing for himself how she did her living. She loved color, always had. Yet what about the rest of her? What had the years done for her, and done to her?

He had so much to say, and there was even more he wanted to hear. A kiss, for old time's sake? Nothing more—of that he was quite certain. Even the kiss was a long-shot.

Shandar came back carrying a large earthenware jug of water in one hand and a stone-mug in the other, pouring then, and handing him the mug. He pulled in the water as if he had gills. Cool, refreshing, and, thanking her, he tried to contrive a conversation to prolong his stay.

He could tell she'd undergone gene therapy. Probably not more than was needed to extend her years. A faint furrow-line or two on her brow, crow's-feet at the corners of her eyes. Had she had those before? He couldn't recall, but he could see that, overall, time had been her good friend.

He wanted to know more, know everything. "Are you married?" he asked.

"I'm not."

"Someone—a friend?"

"I've my friends, of course"

"Men friends?"

Her mouth softened slightly, and for a bare instant he could see the upper edges of her teeth. She nodded twice, regarding him, even measuring him, or perhaps was simply weighing what she was about to say. And what she said was, "You've a lot of cheek, I'd say, asking things like that."

"Not as much cheek as I once did. They cut some of it away in Uruguay. I had cosmetic surgery."

"I gather."

"Ask any questions you like about our past. I can answer them and, other than you, I'm the only one who can answer them. Like the first time we ever made love, and I'd come to New York and we went to watch the Yankees play. You ate lasagna that night and—"

"If you say so," she broke in, fending him off. "I don't recall, really."

"But I do. I've told you other things, haven't I, and I could tell you more. A lot more. Things only you and I would know of. Shall I start somewhere?"

"I should never have let you through my door."

"It's very, very nice in here. "

"Say good-bye and go. That's what would be the nicest of all."

"I'll go. But we have to get around to talking. I have no real proof but somehow I suspect you sent Sarita Sambinna to see me, or at least got her to thinking about it. I'd like to know why. Then, if you want, I'll leave you be.

Forever, if you wish it that way. I'll have to live on our old memories, but it'd be better by far to create some new ones."

"I'm not trying to be rude, you understand, but this is a little much."

"Much is the right word. Much as you might not believe me, there can't be many days when I haven't thought of you, not knowing whether you were alive or dead. Much to my ultimate surprise and joy, this marvel Sarita arrives out of nowhere, but maybe not quite out of the blue. Not at all. Much as you might not agree, I don't think it's a lot to ask to spend some time talking. What happened to us, and to me. I'd like to explain some of it, if you'll let me."

"Well, you come here out of nowhere, too, and you think you can—"

"I don't think anything of the kind. I'm not presuming. I came because I wanted to come. And because I had to see you for myself if you were alive. I had to know, Shandar, and now I do know."

"I can tell you what I don't believe in, and that is re-living what never was, or what never could be. I'm convinced you are Thomas Courmaine. Shocked, but convinced. I know you had to make your choices and I had to make mine. Why're we even discussing this?"

"Because I really had no choice after our days in France. I was high-jacked and thereafter forced by circumstances to go the way I went."

"Everyone has choices."

"Not always..."

Tempted, then, to remind her of what she had once so painfully, so hesitatingly imparted. Of when her husband and child were killed in a terrorist bombing in Beirut, and, struck dumb, she had lost her bearings and up by the Syrian border had been abducted and ravaged by terrorists posing as nomadic shepherds. Had she a choice in the situation once they captured her? Still, he was on tender ground here, and was not about to open a wound simply to argue a point.

"Come have lunch with me or something. A walk in the village. Anything you like," he suggested.

"I've my work to do, and besides it's better that you go. I'm glad you're not dead. Very confusing...very, well I don't know...very everything. Glancing at a wall clock, she said, "I must go this instant."

"I'll wait."

"Not here, you won't."

"An hour? Two hours? Can't we meet for that long? Not too tough a request, is it? Is your heart on strike?"

"Where're you putting up?"

"At the Adobe and Stars. It's a spiffy bed-and-breakfast. I've even got a hot tub with a view of the mountains," he offered, a ring of hope in his voice.

"I know it or I've seen it. And you could do with a haircut."

"I can?" He felt his head. "Maybe I can. If I get one, will you call me?"

"I don't know. I really can't say. God, how can all this be happening?"

"We're making it happen, that's how. It is my very joy to see you again. My name is now Raoul…Raoul Marciara-Quina. It's how I'm registered at the Adobe in case you were wondering."

"Raoul? *Raoul*? It sounds like a leather tool…you've changed names, too?"

"I had to."

"Spanish?"

"Actually Uruguayan. I speak Spanish with a Portuguese accent and Portuguese with a Spanish accent. Confuses everyone and it confuses the devil out of me sometimes."

"I can't believe—"

"Believe what?'

"Oh, nothing, nothing at all. Seventy years and then *you*…seventy…"

"You were with me every day. In my thoughts."

"You didn't say how you found me."

"I didn't, did I? I'll tell you as soon as we join forces again."

She got up, then sat down again. "I'm in a state of craziness. I've no idea of what to say to you."

"Or do with me?"

"Or do, either. Yes, I'm in a state and I really must excuse myself. And you'll have to be excusing yourself so I'll walk you to the door."

"But I can see you?"

"I need time to think. I'll let you know but probably it's much better if we don't. Raoul…*Raoul*…spare me…what's the rest of it again?"

"Marciara-Quina. With a hyphen."

"A hyphenated mouthful."

"You think I ran out on you, don't you. But it was nothing like that, nothing whatsoever. I got cornered and maneuvered into something and then there was no you to be found. You were the one who pulled the good-bye act, not me. I tried and I tried to find you. I hired detectives. I even tried the Nestors and they'd have told you of that, I'm sure. I had a friend in the British government call in a favor with the FBI here. They couldn't find anything, Shandar, but damn sure there was plenty of effort to find you. All you had to do was get me a message."

"I went twice to Switzerland," Shandar objected.

"I heard. They had me in jail for months but a friend of mine—well, not so much of a friend as I had thought—but an important man in Europe turned some dials. He gave me a copy of a report saying you'd come to Switzerland and on your second trip they barred you from entering."

"Exactly correct. I always thought it so strange."

"All of it was very strange. Some of it still is strange and that's why we must talk."

"I'll let you know, but I'll be late if I don't leave this very moment, Thomas."

"Raoul," he corrected.

"Raoul, yes. The leather-tool man…"

Out the door he went, right through that monastery-like door, the heavy click of its latches sounding so final.

Not knowing where he wanted to go or how to get there, he drove up a climbing switchback for over an hour, taking his time, as he ascended into the Sangre de Christo mountains, the views astonishing him. His thoughts never strayed from her, wondering what she might be thinking, and if, indeed, she would call him. At intervals, he went into reveries as he recaptured their days in New York, when first they had made love, and the halcyon interlude in Baie St. Jean, there in France, when they had lazed for almost three weeks: drowning in each other's currents.

Other than letting her hair go slightly grayish, she hadn't changed all that much: that fascinating Iraqi face still intact, the luminous dark eyes, the perfect teeth were still perfect, and that gossamer-like walk.

Cinderella dreams.

Tiring, he pulled into a rest area designated for viewing the mountains and valleys. He found a teak bench, sat, trying to find his place in the world known as Taos. Thin, cool, clear air flowed over his face. Nearby a small waterfall gurgled, its steady noises eventually calming him.

Not so easy to do, turning back the years, a clock of what seemed like another era. He had an immense future to unfold to her, and he hadn't as yet hopped the first hurdle. He could see his expectations had been wildly off the mark. Soaring hopes had vanquished his common sense. Still, he had come for her, though, and come a long, long way. That was all there was to it—they belonged together. What was seventy years of separation when you could live to age two-hundred, or even three-hundred? Seventy was only twenty-three percent of three-hundred, only a quarter of the years in his probable life-run, if he elected to go that far.

What was the big deal about being among the missing for only seventy years? He had missed her till he was half the time sick from thinking of her.

Didn't that count? Despondent, he thought: *it's like the gold suddenly had gone out of the sun.*

The air at this altitude was cool but the air inside of him burned as if a bush-fire raged. Gazing out at the great brute mass of the Sangre de Cristo Mountains, he watched an eagle circling and veering against the aluminum-colored, cloud-smeared sky. Wishing he could soar, but instead it seemed as if he were plummeting into a dark hole, there to forever disappear. Thinking about it made him low; so low that a sadness crept into him; so much sadness his eyes stung. It was all right, he instructed himself. Women cry over their lost men, so why couldn't he feel that way, too. He did not recall when last he had wept, but no one forgets the feeling when it's his turn to let go.

Something like a trance overtook him, followed by a tremor. Trying to shake off the feeling, it refused him. He felt a quake of something, then, and the back of one hand went to his eyes. But they seemed dry as the mountain air. He knew what it was: those unseeable tears gathering in the backs of your eyes, when there is too little wetness left in you—dry weeping over the found but the lost.

Then, a sudden numbness as his skin went warm and prickly and tight-feeling. His mouth suddenly tasted funny: coppery or was it chalky? His hands wouldn't move when he told them to; neither could he curl his fingers. Moments sailed by as he breathed like a bellows before regaining control of himself. What was that all about? An imminent stroke? The altitude? He was healthy enough, except possibly not so healthy anymore in his head.

A woman, he thought. Was a woman now in charge of his head!

Then he thought: "Fuck it, I'm going loony."

After that, he thought that she had probably crystallized herself the way people do when they've become set, even stagnant, over a stretched span of time. It was foolish to think this, though, because he could not re-know her again within an hour. He'd not been with her for more than an hour at best, and ought to know better than to draw flighty conclusions.

He had a few conclusions to figure out for himself. She hadn't snubbed him, nothing like that; but, and distinctly so, it amounted to a brush-off.

Sitting there, gawping, his mind conferring with the mountains, the start of all his necessary figuring was none to promising at this moment.

Assuredly, she was in no frame of mind to sit under the apple tree and carve a heart with their initials pierced by the well-known arrow.

Yet she was imperative to his future. What would it take to remold her agenda: one that has a certitude, one that included him? Scant choices remained, for he couldn't go back to being Thomas I. Courmaine. Was it all impossible, was it a fruitless chase, even with the largeness of the future he had in mind for them?

Dejected, he stood, and headed for the auto. He still had no place to go other than back to The Adobe. And, nice as it was, it seemed like nothing but a void just then.

After she had shooed him away, the hours and minutes seemed empty of everything else except gloomy complications. She tried to sort them into little imaginary piles, some having to do with her, others with him, and still others she couldn't easily catalogue. All in all, a far more complex situation than ever he could imagine. She hadn't weighed all this before—well, part of it she had—but now it was gathering different angles and proportions.

Until an hour ago, she believed he was dead and gone, never remotely dreaming he would show up at her gate. *Jesus and every Mary!* Right now, she hadn't the time to be thinking about him. Two customers awaited her, errands to run, calls to make. Yet she couldn't keep herself straightened out, while he stood so aggravatingly alive in the center of her thoughts, blotting out everything else.

An invasion, that's what it was, a surprise attack.

Him: So many years ago—a lifetime—she feared counting the time that had elapsed. She had gone to such extreme lengths to forget him, to find her own place, and she had done it without any help from others.

Here he was again, looking like no one she'd ever seen, quite intent on excavating the long buried past. Regrettable. Ridiculous beyond any measure. That little crescent scar on her thigh; only one way he could know of that item, wasn't there? A perfect telltale, and his recollection had really zinged her.

A hand from the grave, that's who he was, though assuredly a great deal more than a hand. Whatever on earth had Sarita said to him, bringing him here like this? Of all places, Taos? How had he pulled that one out of the hat?

It wasn't that he'd behaved badly, was incorrigible or anything like that; still, he had raced into her life like some threatening storm that could dash apart her well-settled life. Of all places, Taos; of all days, today. Or any other day!

This is silly, she thought. And it was silly to waste another three seconds of time over him—in reality, a stranger; a Uruguayan foreigner, probably on the lam now that he had obviously faked his own death.

Wanting what? To pass the peace pipe or something?

If he persisted in being a nuisance, she'd send him packing, as soon as she discovered what Sarita had done. On purpose, had she? One is never done with being a parent until your coffin is ready. She was *en rapport* with her greatly loved Sarita, but now look?

Awakening, blinking the fog out of his eyes, the first thing he saw were embers still glowing in a beehive-shaped fire-box bordered with colorful Mexican tiles. He began to think about how much longer he should stay, hang on, pitch his case. No newer persuasions had occurred to him.

As he pondered that predicament, the call came, sudden as a shooting star. "I'll see you as long as you don't prolong it," she was saying to his lifting heart.

"Would you come here?"

"I've got a perfectly nice place of my own. You can come tomorrow at eleven-thirty. I'll be through with my work then."

"Wonderful. What sort of work do you do, if I may ask?"

"We make silver jewelry. Another woman and I. She's Indian, a Taos."

"Eleven-thirty, I'll be there."

"Yes, eleven."

No goodbye. Just a slightly softened voice and then an abrupt cut off of conversation. He called the front desk, asking where he could get a hair-trim and a shave. Knock off the beard; she might like him better that way. His expectations returning now; she had made the call, hadn't she?

He asked her to do it and she had done it.

Her voice not so serrated, not quite so coolish as she got around to asking: "How did you get here? Find me?"

"I was sightseeing, looking for a view and the view turned out to be you. Serendipity."

"C'mon. It wasn't a coincidence, making your way here to Taos of all places?"

"It was nearer to a coincidence than otherwise. I found an expert navigator in the person of Sarita, the historian-biographer. An old friend of mine in Africa, he's dead now, but he showed me how humans, just like animals, leave distinct trails. It's all in how you observe, he said. As I had no way of personally observing her movements, I had her followed by a private eye and she came to this house a few times. When I finally got a rough description of you, then my bell rang. Really rang. The investigator had also taken a photo of you. It's out in that solar car. It's about all I needed. That, and your address."

"You had her followed? That's what you're saying?"

"I did, yes.

"She's not going to like that. You spying on her, you can bet she'll be peeved."

A thin laugh before he parried, "Have you any notion of the spying she's done on me? She knows more about Thomas Courmaine than I do and I've lived with him all my life."

"Just goes to show that we never know ourselves, do we? Not as well as others do."

"I suppose that's so."

"It is so. And you haven't answered how this all came about. You had a reason to hire your detective. How did that happen?"

"It happened because our comely biographer scattered little clues here and there while she was staying with me. Things she was otherwise unlikely to know about. Things not written down anywhere. Things Jaggy Muldaur knew of, but Sarita had never met with Jaggy. Saw her once in the hallway, but didn't meet her. So, I spun my little deduction wheel and it told me she must've learned things from someone who knew me pretty well...someone, for instance, like you...and elatedly I thanked the world and its stars that you might still be alive somewhere. I made a couple of calls to London and a bank there located a private investigator in Denver to chase after her, after Sarita returned to Colorado. I asked the detective for the usual: where did she go, what did she do, who did she see? At some point, the investigator followed her here to Taos, and at another point the same investigator...she's a woman, by the way...made a descriptive report on you, adding the photo for good measure. Soon as I read the report and saw the picture, I knew it was probably you even if you were using a different name. That makes two of us, doesn't it? New names, new lives, new locations. We could be in a movie together."

"The investigator was a woman? Was she a black woman? I saw a black lady out by the gate one day. Out there on the street. She wasn't a neighbor, I knew that much."

"I've never met her, but I do know she's Afro. I'd guess it was her."

"I don't like being tailed, either."

"How else? I had to know. There was another thing, the clincher. Every so often Sarita would wear a scent. A perfume. I noticed it, thought it familiar, but didn't connect it with you. Not at first, because it's been so long. Then, I did recognize it. It was yours, the same scent anyway. I'd never smelled it on anyone else, other than the two of you. That doesn't prove anything, I admit. But added in with all the other cues, it was too much to be tagged as sheer coincidence. I began to guess that the two of you were somehow linked. That's why the investigator was hired, to connect dots. Or erase them. But the dots fell into place after all."

"I hadn't thought of that…the case of the mysterious perfume. My, my, Sherlock Courmaine to the fore."

"Correction, Sherlock Marciara-Quina. Score one for yours truly."

"I'm not at all sure I can get used to that name of yours."

"It'll have to be my regular moniker from now on. I couldn't re-do all the paperwork now, even if I wanted to. Which I don't. It was damn difficult."

"You're something, you are."

"Meaning?"

"Mm-mm…"

"Meaning?"

"Oh, nothing. Nothing, nothing at all. Did you ever tell Sarita you recognized the perfume?"

"No, I purposefully didn't. I didn't want her to get suspicious and clam up. She's too fast on the draw and she'd catch on and then I'd be catching nothing else from her. No clues. I like having clues to work on. Scientists like clues. Love them, actually."

"I'll be…perfume. Think of that, will you?" Shandar shook her head. "Sarita said she thought you were dying, that you even told her you were dying."

"I led her to believe I was about to die. And I did die. Thomas Courmaine, he's gone, done with."

"Hardly."

"I fooled you, didn't I?"

"I knew who you were after a few minutes. Those things you said, and your eyes. And your height and build. Because of what you know about me and other things about the two of us that I'd never mentioned to anyone else. Your voice, also, I could tell by that. Every voice is different, hadn't you noticed? Like a fingerprint."

"I've never thought about it before. But when you knew who I was, why didn't you say so?"

"I was too—I don't know exactly. Stunned, I suppose. Afraid too. I thought you were dead, Thomas—*Raoul.*"

"Were you sorry I was dead?"

"Sorry? Sure I was sorry, you ninny."

"Sentimentally so, that kind of sorry?"

"I really don't care to talk about our past."

"Is there someone else? Some guy?"

"I don't care to talk about that, either. And it was quite unfair of you to delude Sarita."

"That I was dying? I had to die in order to go on living. Why is that so deluding?"

"It just is. You ask so many questions.'

"Not like her, I don't. She asks more questions than the tax collector."

"I assume you've told her everything? The truth?"

"Of course. What kind of a crack is that?"

"I meant all the truth."

"All the truth? Who can remember all the truth after a hundred years? No one would believe it anyway. She got an earful, an eyeful too," he said, thinking of Christopher's nocturnal visit. "And no part of what I told her was untruthful. I'm not dishonest. Well, most of the time I'm not. I've conducted various deceptions to save my life."

Shandar looked off. He looked right along with her as she stared out the wide bay window to a forever-long sweep of the reddish-hued mountains. Vast, vast country and what seemed like an ever-widening gulf he was trying to bridge with her. He recalled things now; that, when the mood struck, she could be as reserved and skittish as a virgin whose time had come.

Eventually, she returned to him. "What were the other clues? What else did Sarita say that persuaded you to hire an investigator? It had to be more than a few whiffs of perfume."

"References to the past. Other matters she couldn't know by herself or from reading about me. Asking me about the Gun of God, which was a comment Augustin deMehlo made to me a very long time ago. deMehlo's gone to his other world forty-five years ago. So, how did Sarita ever hear that one? Not from me. You knew it, though. I remember telling you about him and his very correct concerns about my science chases. And his phrase, likening biotech pursuits to a gun that would one day turn on its users. One day, Sarita even jumped to the jail incident in Switzerland. That was never in the papers or anywhere else. Almost all the records in Switzerland were destroyed, and for good reason. Well, actually she got that one from Lin-pao. But she knew more than I had ever told him—"

"I told her. At least, what I knew, which wasn't much."

"You couldn't know. I never saw you again until I showed up here."

"The heck I didn't know. Because I did know. Poppi Nestor told me."

Letting that sink in, and making the link-up, he said: "Of course, I can see it now. Poppi got it from Jaggy. And you got it from Poppi."

"I think I did, at that. Probably, yes."

"Sarita made a third misstep. She volunteered, more or less, that she knew Jaggy had had sickle cell anemia. That Lin-pao, when she interviewed him, had told her about it. But then I made a call to Shanghai and found out Lin-pao didn't recall mentioning it. You know him, he's got a memory like flypaper. She couldn't have got it from Jaggy, so then where? It was one more strut to support my growing suspicions. You knew. I had told you all about the St. Gallen episodes at that clinic, when we were in France, and that Jaggy had been close to dying from pernicious anemia…and again it was another clue that pointed towards you." He shrugged, smiling, knowing he had been right, was so self-satisfied now that he was being a little too smug. "I don't mind telling you I jumped ten yards with elation. I really did. I lived on the hope you were still to be found somewhere and that Sarita would be the birddog who'd lead me to you. I lucked in, you might say. And I didn't forget that you came to Switzerland to find me. That was in yet another investigator's report. From Braunsweig, well, through Braunsweig. They had arranged it at my request. I was still in jail when I read it, but that's when I found out you'd been looking for me, and it kept me going, thinking you still cared."

"Many of these investigator types, weren't there?"

"They were needed, too. Especially after you'd turned yourself into the phantom of the Sangre de Cristo Mountains. New name, new life, new many things."

"I can tell you I didn't get here via a yacht. Poppi told me you were out on some palatial yacht. A yacht if you please, and with that wretch of yours. How do you think I felt? All those declarations of undying love. What a laugh that turned out to be. What a chump I was. How could you do it, France and everything—everything we did there and all the other—?

"It was never that way," he protested.

"Oh, that's bushwa. Just a lot of bushwa."

"What's bush-whatever—what's that?"

"Men use a different word."

"Oh, well, it's not bullshit. Nothing like it."

"We were to be married, whatever happened to that? A life together. I believed you because I wanted to believe you." And the next thing he heard was what seventy years of pent-up irritation can do to a woman's voice. Bristling, she let go with: "When I came back from France, I told everyone you and I were headed for the altar. Abe Meric, Poppi and Si, everyone. I ate a half-ton of crow over that one. An indelible memory, I assure you. Very indelible."

"It's possible that's what did it. Got me abducted and imprisoned—"

"Naturally, go right ahead and blame it on me."

"There's no blame, Shandar," he calmly replied. "All I'm saying is if you'd told Poppi we were getting married, as you just said, and she relayed that news to Jaggy, well, it might explain a lot. I was almost the only one at that time who knew the nuts and bolts of Zyme-One for manipulating genes. Jaggy had this reckless, idiotic scheme about our son. A helluva big scheme, too, and halfway it worked. At least, he lived. But she couldn't've made any of it happen without me, and perhaps when she heard you and I were about to get paired up, she might've pulled all the stops to prevent it. I can't be positive, of course, but it sounds like one of her stunts and so it sounds quite plausible to me. She had me padlocked, and I was stuck. Really stuck. She fixed it so I was held and imprisoned where no one could find me. Kept me in the slammer until I gave in. She had help, too. A big time banker got into the act...but that's another story..."

"You don't have to go on. It's so regrettable. You can't unbreak the egg of the past, can you? And I'm not inclined to hatch a new egg, nor cook another omelet. Not after seventy years, I'm not. She's a disease, that woman. A near-death experience or something close to it."

Tight-faced, Shandar left the room, returning a few minutes later. As if the earlier discussion of the long ago past had not been interrupted, she continued right on. "Even if that happened in the way you say, I don't think I'm responsible for any of it."

"No one said you are. Maybe it didn't unroll in exactly the way I suggested, yet it might've. After all, you know how close Poppi and Jaggy are. Or were. Jaggy is ruthless. Less so now because she doesn't wield the power she once had. But she can still be very dicey to handle."

"Made a hash of our lives, hasn't she? I could slay her. I'm Iraqi and we have long memories."

"I'm a transplanted American and we've got memories, too. Mine are still beautiful, the ones of you are. But you needn't worry anymore. Remember, I'm a dead article. Jaggy doesn't know where you are or who Raoul Marciara-Quina is. I bet I could sit at the next table and she wouldn't recognize me. Not if I spoke with my accent. Safe and sound unless you decide to spill the beans."

"I'd not ever talk to her, you may be *very* sure of that."

"But you could talk to someone else and they might let it slip. My life is in your hands in more ways than one."

"I don't particularly care to be accountable for your life, as you put it."

"But you are, you indeed are. Anyway, we don't have to worry about her. She'll be busy trying to find Christopher and she won't be able to. He's perfectly provided for. Living the life of Tarzan by now, I expect. All I have to do is find him a Jane. I've someone looking, except they don't know who it is they're doing the looking for."

"What does that mean?"

"He's in a habitat where he belongs. A very long way away, where he'll be safer and happy. I hope he'll be happy."

"Where is where?"

"I cannot say."

"Another secret?"

"Yes, another secret, that's right."

"Don't you ever blink?" she asked, widening her own eyes.

"Not when I'm entranced and you entrance me."

"Oh, stop. Just stop! It's not going to work; you starting in on me again like this."

"I've never stopped starting in on you, and I never will. How can I? You're the voice in my head that never stops speaking. "

"You shouldn't say things like that. You can't just say that and do whatever—oh, you have to remember I've been on my own for a long, long time and I've learned to do for myself. Make my adjustments and live with my disappointments, trying to make a life, and, well…well, oh, I don't even know how to finish this sentence, so I'm not going to try."

"You don't have to finish. The past is done. It's over. It's been parked on the shelf where they keep everything that's been sent into oblivion. It's the present that matters and the tomorrows that count."

"Tomorrow is our tomorrow, we'll make all the tomorrows our tomorrows."

"Tomorrow you'll probably be in Timbuktu."

"If you'll come with me, I'll give it a go."

"When they gave you a new face, they must've included a dose of amnesia. All that's happened to us, and you disappear like a magician's coin and we're supposed to bate our breath until you reappear. As if you were the Second Coming. I've got a little bulletin for you and it reads like this: sorry, not this girl, I've made the trip before, twice, and that was once too many."

"Thinking you were jilted?"

"Thinking I was abandoned, and with more problems to face than I knew how to face. At the time anyway."

"What problems? Why did you leave New York?"

"I had to."

"But why?"

"It's personal."

"Everything is personal."

"Yes, I suppose it is. But I don't choose to discuss it."

"I had people looking high and low and every place in between. You'd be a good spy, no one knowing who you are or where you are."

"The way I wanted it, too."

"That jig's up, kiddo. Here I am."

"So I see." Shutting her eyes, then.

"What's the matter? Have you a headache?"

"Of a kind, I do. You come back into my life and you expect so much. I went through too much for you and I'm not ready—I can't and I won't—"

"Try, just try. I'm trying, why can't you?"

"I did try. I must go see to something."

She left him.

She'd been hurt, badly so, and by him. Life had turned away from them at a time when all between them was going so nicely. A barely explicable thing. Bad timing, perhaps; it happened. Plainly, she was leery of the slightest prospect that anything equally painful would ever happen again. Who could blame her, he thought? Their pages of living had been so close but never quite bound together. By many standards, they'd had had nothing more than an affair, a few days in New York sleeping together after he had closed the lab at St. Curig Fields, then the glorious romp in southern France. Well, what of it? Not much time together, not a genuine opportunity to create and nourish the faith and trust two people lived on, must live on. They had had their dreams. Only dreams, as it had turned out, but dreams all the same. Yet why couldn't they dream again?

Though they hadn't discussed it, he could tell she had undergone a life-extension treatment. So had he. She didn't look all that much older than when he'd last seen her. They could have a child, even two or three children, if they moved to the right country where no restrictions existed.

He felt like a door-to-door salesman, trying to foil a housewife's objections. He had yet to paint his vision for her, a plan he had in mind that would engage them completely for ten or twenty years. Whatever would she say when he dropped that one on her? He'd have to wait, wait and see, but for how long?

Shandar came back, saying, "I was checking the food. I'm famished. I can offer you chicken burrito and a green salad."

"Wonderful. I can't stand that pill food."

"Neither can I. But I eat it twice in a week to stay within my budget. Sit there and I'll get you something. Iced tea or a beer, either one?"

"Beer'd be fine. This altitude makes me thirsty."

Thirty minutes later he was forking into a spinach salad and asking about Sarita. To one question, Shandar, almost as an aside, casually told him, "Oh, I've known her a long time. Old friends, that's us."

"How'd you meet? Up here?"

"She was born in Taos and raised here."

"She was married, I guess. She told me she was—"

But Shandar intervened with her own question. "Are you planning on staying long?"

"The rest of my life, if you can take it."

She shook her head. "We've been through that, or I have. You didn't come here with that in mind, I hope."

"It is for that exact reason that I came here."

"Because your so-called cruise didn't work out?"

"Some cruise."

"Is that true that Jaggy Muldaur was made a Dame Commander of the British Empire?"

"It is true, yes. And I wouldn't call it a cruise, not the way you mean it. It was no lawn party, believe me."

And he gave Shandar an un-detailed rundown of the eight months spent on the Mediterranean and in the eastern Atlantic, as he tried to fix and regenerate his son's flawed genome. He did not go into his bargain with the Swiss government: the black bargain to create a bona fide heir to The Muldaur Trust. Too complicated to explain and so heavily layered with turns and twists and such an imperceptible, secretive history he couldn't remember it all. Chief among the reasons he couldn't remember it all was that he didn't care to remember any of it. It was the fight for the control of The Trust that had landed him in prison, nearly costing him his life.

Thinking one thing, he was telling her another, "A complex, intense time, that cruise," he finished without finishing anything.

"I'm awfully glad you could save him. And yet you stayed with her? Oh, never mind answering. You don't have to. I've read the letter you sent Sarita."

He verged on starting an argument. His hands tightened, that old habit he'd never shaken, whenever his temper stirred. "That letter was private," he retorted, "meant only for her and for background for her book."

"She thought I should see it, and quite frankly it explained a good deal."

"It certainly did. I may be sorry that I helped her."

"Helped yourself, too, remember. Quite a life you've led and I can readily see why you wanted a turn at explaining some things. Egg farms and whatever."

"It's never been what I wanted out of life," Thomas said. "The old story, I suppose. The cards you get are the only cards you can play. That, or leave the game. I'm not ready to leave it quite yet."

"I'll say, or you wouldn't be sitting here."

"I had to make a clean getaway, and if you read my letter then you know why—"

"The Courmaine gospels, you mean."

"Epistles. Epistles are letters. She got a letter like none other I've ever written."

Uncrossing her legs, alighting from her chair, Shandar changed the subject. "I must pack. I'm leaving for a few days."

"You are? Where to?"

"I've my business calls to make and there's a jewelry showing in Santa Fe."

"Why don't I come with you?"

"Sorry, but nope. No can do."

"Who's left to buy anything there? In Santa Fe it looks like a dead end for the misbegotten."

"You'd be surprised. Back in those gated communities, they still have plenty of wherewithal. I have to do it. All I have left is my government social payments and my little business. My Meric & Morris pension was cut by two-thirds when I resigned. So, me, myself and I—the jeweler now. At least, I'm independent and frankly, I rather like it. Come and go as I wish. Gives me something to do and I have very agreeable clients."

"I'll be a client. What if I buy your inventory out? Would that keep you here?"

"That's absurd and I'd not hear of it."

"Slow up, it was only an idea."

"Not a very good one. If you're not here when I get back to Taos, it was nice seeing you, Thomas."

"I'm Raoul."

"You'll never be a Raoul to me. You don't even look like a Raoul, though I don't know why I'm saying something like that. I've never known a Raoul in my life."

"Now you do. Let me come with you?"

"Totally out of the question. O-u-t."

"Why?"

"It's time for you to skedaddle, that's why. *Tiempo de ir, señor, eh?*"

"Ah, you speak Spanish?"

"Passably, I can. However, I'm no linguist like you. Bye-bye." She fluttered her hands in a shooing-out-the door gesture.

He was beginning to form an intense dislike for the towering oaken doors, for suddenly, when outside, he felt lonely again; a feeling, and a state, he'd been trying to conquer for all of his remembered life. It was not so much a feeling of self-pity, but more like an illness that kept cropping up at awkward times. Like a sucker punch, striking at him when he was unwary and needing to be with someone, and making him acutely aware of the force of loneliness.

Still, it was important that he keep his mind straight, keep it attached to the reason he had come to Taos. The reason was her, and nothing but her. He meant to follow that reason till it was no longer in his way.

She had been rummaging through her clothes, packing for her short trip. In and out of the house, loading her solar-powered van, thinking and thinking, afraid she would forget something. Inside the house again, she sat and tried to stop dividing herself. The past three days had possessed her. They were succeeding and she wasn't succeeding. She was running late. She still had to select the silverwork to fill three large display cases.

She'd never get done, she told herself, irritated.

A damn fool. A fractal, explosive feeling shot through her. Pushy, too, and a big mouth on him. *The nerve*! He was the most persistently stubborn man imaginable. He went where he went, regardless of how high hall the wall, or the odds; the unelected crown prince of bull-headedness.

A long, long time had passed since a man had stirred her. Did he think she'd repeat her mistakes over him for a third time? Who in the hell did he think he was, anyway? Tumult burrowing into her; worries she didn't care to deal with. If he'd only go away.

Uncertainties gnawed. She began to realize her complaints about him were also the same complaints she could, if honest, levy upon herself. She could be as stiff -minded as Thomas Courmaine, if it came down to that; and what it came down to was the tricks of survival when you had no one to count on save for yourself.

Four days passed. From her, not a whisper. Not a breath of encouragement.

Twice he drove by her home to see if could detect signs of her presence, that she was possibly avoiding him. No sign of anyone, however, and he felt silly. Stuck in his own tracks, it seemed, vague as to what to do next.

Every day, he ran two miles or three miles, harder to do up in this thin mountain air. At the Adobe pool, he swam his fifty laps, took to eating expensively at a Tex-Mex diner, where he liked the food and the hospitality of the couple who owned it. He watched more satellite-beamed shows than ever before in his life. The shows began to intrigue him; he had been investigating the possibilities of including this extremely efficient method of communication for his campaign plans. Worldwide reach, round-the-clock, with capability of tapping into all time zones simultaneously.

He thought about the advertising possibilities, time slots, and now he could do what he wanted without worries about cost. Content, what would the messages be, how to keep viewers interested, should he search out the gene-freaks like the wholly ruined beauty from Warsaw—problems inside other problems. The ideas and messages that worked well in America were vastly different than what drew attention and curiosity in Asia, Europe, South America.

Where to do it all?

Liking this town, too. A decent, attractive place with its inspiring scenery. They lived better in Taos than in Santa Fe. He had been reading up on Taos, how, before all the troubles, it was a much frequented winter resort and at all times was filled with artists and crafts-people. Friendly, relaxed, a magnet for a certain type of escapee who shunned big city life and its sordid, dilapidated, depressing scenery.

No one in Taos was more of an escapee than himself. Possibly Shandar—and he wondered how long she'd lived here. He wanted to know everything. Mulling on this, he fussed, searching for a place to anchor his feelings. Trying to get his mind off Shandar, he watched a South African soccer match and then the phone rang. The front-desk receptionist told him she had taken a message by a woman who declined to reveal her name

—Back tomorrow, if you're still here—the receptionist conveyed.

He'd be here. Of course he would, what else? He had more time on his hands than a life-convict. Envisioning her again, the chaos of desire filled him.

Suddenly, as always, one of those odd revelations chipped away, working its way into his consciousness. It labored and scratched for the best part of an hour, before the payoff arrived.

Of course, why in hell not? What was the money for, anyway? A smile creased his face, the first lasting smile in several days. A gamble, to be sure, but worth trying.

Now or never, he thought.

It took four hours to touch all the bases, when returning to Santa Fe. He went to the mission house where he'd seen the *Gorpos* lined up, awaiting their handouts of pill food. There, he cornered the administrative director, and, not wanting to draw too much attention to himself, he lied and said he represented someone who wished to make a substantial donation. Mentioning the figure he had in mind, Thomas was nearly laughed out of the office. He asked for the name of the mission's bank, and, talking in his Latino accent, he handed the director ten-thousand in cash as a good faith gesture.

Afterward, he called his own bank in Rio, and arranged for a transfer of significant funds.

After a few more inquiries, he drove to the city outskirts to find the local comm-sat station—AllAmericaNet—the largest satellite news network in the U.S. For over an hour, he cooled his heels waiting to see the news editor. When finally let in, he told the woman: "I've got an exclusive for you. If you don't wish to break the story, I'll give it to your competitors. It's big and it's local."

"Okay, I'll bite. What's in the works," she replied, "and who're you anyway?"

After giving his new name, he told her, "I'm today's storyteller, doing a little p.r., but what I'm saying is true and I'll tell you exactly how to verify it. Ready?"

"With all ears cocked."

"It's a story about a windfall of thirty-million dollars on its way to Santa Fe to help all those castoff *Gorpos* get a square meal and a clean bed at night. And maybe a future of some sort. Interested?"

"Thirty-million, you said? *Thirty* is it?"

"More, perhaps. Santa Fe is of exceptional interest to a rich friend of a friend of mine. It's up to you whether the rich friend stays interested."

"Why me, may I ask?"

"Satellite news. The power of the cyber-pen. I'm pretty sure your viewers are gonna love this. There's this interesting woman up in Taos and she's got a rich friend. This is really heartwarming. Getting him to hand over the thirty-million, I mean. You'd better get a pencil or pen…"

"I'll record this, instead."

"No recordings, please. My personal words are not for voice-replication."

"Just who are you, anyway," she said, with a protesting tone. But she selected a gold-filled pen from a desk-set, and went on. "I need a name, if you're looking for coverage. Your name, the spelling, and the name of this lady in Taos. And the benefactor, who's the benefactor?"

"The benefactor is anonymous. But the lady in Taos is a Suzanne Burkema. A silversmith. She must have friends everywhere. One of them a Croesus, as I said. I believe he or she is a South American person, and deeply involved in the Genesis movement."

"And you? How do you spell your name? "

"I've a hyphenated surname." And the he spelled it for her.

"Latino? You don't sound it."

"Uruguayan. But my mother was American."

He had been speaking in straight American, with no trumped up accents this time. He had to convince this woman and didn't want her thinking he was an across-the-border Latino up to games and stunts. "The money is being wired to a certain bank in Albuquerque. I've the name of the manager and he'll confirm the transfer if you'll call him in the morning."

It took the better part of an hour to tack down enough details, while persuading the woman to schedule a camera crew and get a reporter or two assigned. Thomas reminded her that the story, at this point, was in the hands of AllAmericaNet. He'd given her enough to get started. Best now that contact be made with Suzanne Burkema, yet to wait a day or so.

"Burkema knows more than she'll ever let on," he said. "You may have to do some digging with her to get the entire story. She'll sound coy, saying she doesn't know what you're talking about and..." he shrugged causally, "well, you people are pros, and you know how to peel the lid off the can, so I'll leave it up to you. By the way, if you'll run this piece at the top of the local news, then possibly we'll have more for you in a month or so. I've a feeling Santa Fe is marked for some real help. A sort of test market, if you follow me. Rehabilitation of the misbegotten and so on. If you really want some inside skinny, put in a plug for Genesis Society. There's talk of a regional office in New Mexico for Genesis and you could be the deciding factor. Well, thanks for your time, mam..."

He'd only shaded a fact or two; the media, having had their way with him for most of a century, he suffered not the slightest remorse at his ploy.

It'd been a long day. Leaving the building, he felt jacked up, happy with himself. Commotion would kick up in a day or two and he knew he'd be on the receiving end of some heavy chatter.

Still, things had been too quiet, drowsy-like; a spurt of action was probably called for, and he had, he thought, planted the seeds.

Hell, it might work, he was thinking, smiling. If not, he'd ratchet things up a notch or two. Not a time for dawdling.

The day after Shandar's return to Taos, late of a morning, he jogged uphill from the Adobe to her home. When he arrived, winded, sweating, it put her in mind of days past when he would sometimes come to her New York apartment, his hair damp, his cheeks pink and moist, a towel wrapped around his neck.

On a deck that looked out to the spread of mountains, they talked; they didn't talk, then talked again, as if they were strangers sitting next to each other on an airplane.

Happy to be with her, Thomas wore his upbeat mood on his new face, the face she kept studying, trying to estimate the meanings of its expressions. Where was the old one, the one she had once been accustomed to? What lay behind this one, other than his declarations that he wanted her back in his life?

After one silence, Shandar went off on a new tack. "You know, I'm extremely surprised you never married. A man like you."

"That's because I was planning on marrying you, if you recall."

"Whatever the reason, I'm still surprised."

"I'm not surprised, not in the least. Marrying Jaggy Muldaur would be akin to marrying a box of steel wool."

A barely perceptible nod from Shandar. "It's why I eventually began to believe you. That you stayed on with her because of your son."

"It was the other way around. She was the one who stayed on with me. I owned the Downs and I had legal control of Christopher. The real control, the only control that counted, and she knew I could make it stick. One day I'll tell you about him."

"I read the letter, remember. You've sort of inferred you won't be seeing him again."

"I won't. He could take it, I suppose, but I couldn't."

"How terribly sad for you."

"We were never that close, frankly. Most of it's in my letter to Sarita that you read. You two must have had quite a tea party together."

"Sarita and I are what you might call—confidants. I might even do her publicity work when she publishes."

"Maybe she won't publish."

"Wanna' bet?"

"No, she will, I know she will. This is perfect, it's really ideal."

"What is?"

"That you'll do a p. r. campaign for her and that'll get you back in the grove so you can do one for me. Well, together...together with me."

"A campaign on what, may I ask? About you? You've been your own campaign ever since I met you."

He unloaded then, explaining his hopes, his resources, more about them than he'd written in the letter for Sarita. The Trust and why he'd taken control of the assets, that he fully expected to use them to save threatened species, including humans. Step-one was to beef up African Heritage and he'd already done so, which he had stated in the letter to Sarita. Next, something that was only mentioned briefly in that letter—Genesis was to be heavily bankrolled for a decade or two or even three decades, in the attempt to reverse the genetic-roulette madness that had overtaken so much of the world. "I think we can kick-start something and make an impact," he appended. "You and I can do it, and I know I couldn't do it without you."

"Me? Why me?"

"Because you're you. You know the ins-and-outs of message-making. And you're the center of everything for me. What I must do, I cannot do without you. Won't you give me that much leeway, at least listen?"

"How long will this take? I've several things I must do."

"So do I. Maybe it'll take an entire day to get everything outlined."

"A day? I can't do a day with you. Not now. I've items to return to Santa Fe. A whole day?"

"When?"

"Tomorrow or the day after. Thursday, perhaps. I'll have to see."

"Tomorrow afternoon," he pressed.

"What is this business you're talking about?"

"Right up your alley. It's that kind of business," he replied. "It's all that's left. I've failed at everything I've ever done. I failed a young woman once, which is half the reason I became a Jesuit. I failed as a Jesuit. I failed you. I failed myself and sold out to the Swiss. I didn't even have the guts to rot in a jail, and I failed my son and I failed the human race when I wouldn't listen to a man who knew more about the great risks of biotechnology than I'd ever know. A man in Rome, a real man for others. I told you about him once. This is all that remains, one chance to undo some of it. And you. Seventy years of waiting for you again. I'm not up to facing another failure—"

"But you haven't, you haven't failed at all. It all happened too fast. But people, we're all people you know and we make mistakes and it's the mistakes that help us to find our way. You need patience. Some faith."

"I'm going to supply that faith."

"Faith in what? In yourself? In god?"

"A faith in Nature, and in ourselves. Genetic discrimination has to be stopped before it worsens. Reversed somehow. It's terribly insidious and getting more so. It's worse than racial discrimination. The so-called *perfects* ranging themselves against ordinary people and, eventually, the way we're going there won't be any ordinary people. We're not that far from the tipping point, when evolution will take over and *Gorpos*, or the equivalent, will rule the roost. Survival of the fittest is an immutable law. We'll all be on this treadmill trying to be perfect and more perfect. Humans aren't perfect, god knows. We're not supposed to be perfect, as you just inferred. But the way they're fixing things, whoever doesn't sign up to be a *Gorpo*, become one of them, will end up as dead meat. We'll all be scuttled, second-classers. Too many gene-adjusted humans won't make the grade. They'll end up like that crowd down in Santa Fe. Nothings. In a ghetto. I find that prospect to be totally unacceptable. We have to fight to be who we are....sorry, I get upset...I..."

"It's all right."

"But it isn't. It's madness and someone has to do something. I started it and I'd like to end it or try to. It'll be very hard, I know that."

"What makes you think I'd do it with you? A crusade, that's what you're proposing."

"The things you fight for are the things that matter."

"To you, you mean."

"I cannot do it by myself, and I can't trust anyone else other than you. Others would want to know too much and then they're liable to say too much. I'm trying to stay alive. I've had eight close calls already and a good friend of mine took one in the shoulder that was meant for my head."

"That's not what I'd call a letter of recommendation to join forces with you. A price on my head. Sounds like a Greek gift..."

"You have to have faith. Like an ex-Jesuit, you know."

She smiled before she laughed.

"Remember how you used to read to blind children in New York," he said. "What I'm talking about is the biggest read ever. A showing of the way. The big, big epiphany. Will you listen to the rest of it?"

"Go on, of course, I will." Something in his face, or in his voice, reminded her of the New York days, in that other life when she had listened raptly to his dreams of bringing gene therapy to the world, the final and great cure-all. Fervent, he was so fervent, and with all those good intentions blinding him to the outcome. That other wouldn't care about the deprivations of Sudan or anywhere else; they'd see one thing only—what was in it for themselves.

"Let's look at our resources," he said. "We have the Genesis Society in place. Then the bucks. The dissolution of The Trust produced assets of hundreds of billion dollars. Much went to African Heritage, as I've said. It was given in Christopher's name and that information will be released to the press about two months from now. The other half remains under my control. That's the funding available to us to get behind Genesis and it's in safe banks all over the world. Many many billions. I can use it all for the campaign, and I mean to do just that."

Eyes widening with disbelief, Shandar exclaimed, "That's insane, that much money in one person's hands. Outlandish."

"I control the purse, but I'm going to use it to undo much of what I made possible over the past. I think it a very good idea. The trick is to keep everything quiet. You and I can figure out what's to be done, and how. But it's Genesis that'll get all the credit. No one in the public will know where the money comes from, and neither will Genesis. Remote control, all the way. Robotic, sort of."

"Incredible."

"I've had years and years to perfect my techniques."

"You really did steal it, didn't you?"

"I stole it all right. It started with thefts on a colossal scale hundreds of years ago. I'm keeping everything consistent. Big-time larceny, but I'll be the one, well, you and I, to end it all. Do something useful with it. The thing I like the most of all is that we can make a great number of mistakes and still succeed beyond anyone's dreams. The yearly interest alone is over five-billions. It's hard to spend even one billion. I've tried and it's no slam-dunk, I assure you."

She shook her head slowly, wistfully. "You're like a one-man crime wave.

"I know this can be done," he went on. "You'd know the p.r. side backwards and forwards and who to hire, though they'd have to be hired, payroll-wise, by the council at Genesis. Mounting a campaign, the themes, the message platforms, that'd be your end. What people will listen to, what they'll buy into. Not all at once maybe, but eventually they'd listen. People would know it was best and we'd go after these gene-hustlers the way people went after the tobacco crowd. It can be done. Look at how The League put the pike into me before they were shut down. We've all the money ever dreamed of to operate a powerful, engrossing campaign. What can stop us? I can buy five commo-sat stations for about two-billion or so. We can be on air anywhere in the world for twenty-four hours every day. Twenty-four-seven. Budget a billion every year and never run out of money. I'll see to that…and if we have to buy politicians, I'll buy them."

"That's crooked."

"Okay, persuade them somehow. Persuade them by buying tables at their fund-raising dinners. That's buying them, isn't it? Any way you cut it, it's buying. Okay, donating. But I know genetics and I know that humans, as we know them, are an endangered species. I know how to make that case technically and make that battle. I expect plenty of trouble from the *Gorpos*."

"I don't want trouble from anyone."

"You won't get it, either. That's one reason the Santa Fe crowd of *Gorpos* are getting thirty-million. We'll have a ringside seat to watch what happens. How they react," he added, testing the waters a little, but leaving out the part about her non-existent role in his massive publicity play. She was about to be heaped with praise, but he was taking no chances on a rebellion, not when things were traveling so nicely.

"How do you expect to keep in the shadows, when you're handing our sums like that?"

"I'm a non-entity. Every decision, every element of any campaign we do, will be executed by the Genesis Council in Rio. We'll be deep in the background, the bag-man with the money but they'll never know who it is. I've gotten very good at hiding money. I learned how from the masters of the game."

"Do you launder it, as well?"

"I can if I have to."

"...god...god'sakes..."

"Think Genesis—the beginning. Smile, please, would you? Everyone looks better when smiling. It's going to be all right, I'll make sure of it. That's what we must do, and that's who we must be. I'm a bench man, that's all and that's over and done with. You're the message-maker and that's the start of everything."

"Everything...what?

'Everything we need to kick off an epidemic of common sense. We've got the key, so let's turn it."

"You're crazy, that's what you are."

"Everyone's a little crazy. That's why they have police. I feel better now than I have in years." He stared. "You're really looking beautiful today. Especially today."

Scowling, she said: "What are you, I wonder? How do you expect to go on, live, if you're giving away all this money?"

"If I said it, it was only a figure of speech. I bought a small bank in Rio. Listen to this, will you—it's located on the Street of Weeping Dreams which is some hell of a poor choice for a bank's address I hope it's not a harbinger of what'll happen to my investment. Guess what the name of the bank is? Give up? Okay, it's Banca Spiritu Santo. That stands for Bank of the Holy Ghost. Not the best choice, I grant you, but it was a sweet buy. The gent who owned it was a Latvian Jewish fella, who'd had a run-in with the Brazilian authorities and they were going to take over his bank until I got an option to buy it. I made the bank an instant success by depositing a large tranche of Swiss-sourced funds, and another fifty-million of my own. The last of my wampum, but enough to get along on for as long as I'll ever need money. At one time, I had well over a billion to my name. You've no idea how free I feel to have given most of it away. Like I'm on roller skates and going through a change of life, so to speak."

"So to speak, what you've got is a built-in magnet for trouble," she said. "And now you want to start a fight with half the world. The next Don Quixote and half a billion windmills to joust with."

"Someone has to try, Shandar. If we fail, we fail. But if we don't try, then we'll never know. We've got years to make a run for the real roses. Seldom do people get a chance like that, fixing what you did wrong and fixing it on such a large scale."

"A chance is right. You said it. A chance for endless troubles."

"Not if we plan things right. I'm pretty good at planning, if I do say so."

"I imagine so. And Sarita, what about her?"

"She's not to be part of this, other than her book. That'll stir up the pot plenty, that book of hers."

"She is part of it, though. She has to be."

He shook his head. "Too risky. She's got a fast head and over time she might add up too many two plus twos. Why should I tell her anything like that? That I'm still alive. What if she put that in her book? Everything I've planned would be demolished, be worthless. I'd be right back to my former self, just with a new face, a new name, and with people chasing me up back alleys."

"If I ask Sarita not to, she'd never mention it."

"Says you."

"Says me, you're right."

"You mean for me to rest my fate on some biographer's whim? I'm not insane, no matter what you may think. I'm amazed you'd even bring it up. And quit giving me the stink-eye."

"I'm not. Stink-eye? Huh! You have to trust someone in this world."

"Not with my life, I don't. I get to do the choosing on that one and I don't choose her, thank you. I choose you and only you. Well, a couple of others—"

"I insist she be told."

"Why ever for? She's—"

"She is my daughter, that's why."

"Oh, she is? She's *your* daughter? You're kidding."

"Why would I joke about something like that? I've got a copy of the birth certificate. "

"I had no idea. Your daughter? You might have told me. But that doesn't alter—"

"She's your daughter, too," Shandar said abruptly, as if she wanted to rid herself of a burdensome sin. "I almost told you the other day when you asked me why I had left New York."

"How can she be my…how is that…why say a thing like that to me?"

"Wow, you should see your face. Where's my camera?"

"How can she ever be my daughter?" he repeated.

"There was France," Shandar reminded him, as if he needed reminding, "as you well recall, having already mentioned it to me about five times. We did what a boy and girl often do and she was the blessed result. She is why I left New York when I'd given up all hope for you, and for us. I thought you'd chosen Jaggy again when I couldn't find you. I had to get away, find a new life. It wasn't going to be in New York, not after what we'd been through and I was carrying Sarita. I had to do what you're doing, and make myself over. Take Sarita and myself to a new place and I did that and I raised her here. She's my daughter but she's also my best friend. We're practically like sisters. Like Poppi and I used to be."

Blushing now as he recalled his erotic longings for Sarita at Atherton Downs. Even making an overture or two. Things he'd written in that lengthy letter, and then—*his own daughter*! Christ, dear Christ! His daughter, and he'd tried to bed her!

Still semi-paralyzed, he sat back, stuttering, "I'm—double damned—I, uh, don't even—what to say. "

"You're lucky. She's a superb gal."

"I compliment you. You raised her wonderfully. I made a pass at her."

"So I hear. Her full-blooded charms evidently weren't entirely lost on you."

"Sorry. I really am sorry but how was I to know? My god."

"There's a lot to Sarita, inside and out. By the way, she told me that she'd certainly have slept with you had you not been her father. But you don't strike me as someone who'd chase after someone half your age."

"I don't or I wouldn't."

"Yet you did."

"I did," he agreed, hoping he hadn't turned scarlet. "I didn't know who she is, that's all," he repeated, shrugging aimlessly, self-consciously. "I wonder why people use that term sleeping with you or sleeping with so-and-so. You're lying down all right, but you're hardly sleeping, are you?"

"The common argot. It's nicer to say I'm sleeping with someone than I'm fucking someone. Anyway, now you know about your daughter and so now she has to be let in on everything that is relevant. I don't hide things from her and you hadn't better if you want her trust."

"Can I think on this?"

"No."

"We'll, we'd both better do some thinking. Sarita is a half-sister to Christopher."

"I'm perfectly aware. What a life, you've led. Is there anything you didn't do?"

"Yes, there is, and I'm looking at her." He shook his head back and forth. "This is an awful lot to gobble at one sitting."

Searching her face for what was to come next, words sticking in his throat, blocked by confusion, as he gathered what remained of his wits. A daughter. He was recalling that night when Christopher had climbed the vines to Sarita's bedroom window and where anything might've happened. A daughter and never an inkling of it, had he not come here. A pair of seemingly disconnected incidents leading him to another stark truth of his past. Seventy years and not the slightest guess as to why Shandar had disappeared, then finding her in Taos, hiding from her own past just as he was hiding from his own.

He crowded her with questions, mainly of Sarita, but others about herself. Why Taos? Why not somewhere else? The Nestors, when they were still alive, how much had they imparted to her of news about him via Jaggy? Had she ever thoughts of living elsewhere? What did she think of the *Gorpos*? On and on, and then on again.

He remarked, after a time, on all that could've been, and what might've happened, but, of course, didn't happen. All these lost years, he was remarking and wistfully.

"You get what you deserve to get…as you've told me before," Shandar said to him.

"Didn't Sarita ever ask you how it was you knew me? She must've done that, um, didn't she, when she was planning to get in touch with me?"

"Oh, yes, I'll say. Kept at me for days on end."

"And what did you say?"

"I told her we met years ago at the Nestors. That we saw each other for a time, and that I even did some consulting work for you when you were living in Wales."

"It went no further than that?"

"I told her she was conceived in France and that you and I were—well, you know. That we'd discussed marriage and it didn't work out."

"Did she think I ran out on you?"

"It never came up. She never knew you, never had any real idea of you as a person in her life until she wanted to do the book on you, and then I told her what I thought she was entitled to know. Closure, if you will. When she was a child, she realized she didn't have a father and most of her little friends did. But it never seemed to bother her that much."

"There's that to be grateful for, I suppose."

"Possibly."

"If you never had a live-in father, you don't really know what it's like, do you? I never had a father, not really."

"Yes, a parallel. I'd not thought of it before."

"And somehow, years later, my name came up and you filled her in? Really filled her in?"

"Yes, of course. She knew things about you, your name. Had read about you. You were in the papers so much of the time twenty or thirty years back. Ten years back...five years even..."

"Why didn't you get in touch with me?"

"When? On the twelfth of never. Ask a woman who knows. You think I wanted more of the same. Come hopping over there and get into a cat fight with your—your—I can't even say her name. I've my pride, too."

"I almost refused Sarita the interview. Almost."

"Been a tragedy if you had."

"This is getting terribly complex, isn't it?"

"It's always been complex. Anyway, she went on with her life. I'm talking about her adolescence and later years and much more, her marriage and schools and more schools...and by the way it was very nice of you to put her up at your, ah, castle is it? A castle, imagine that, with you always being such a socialistic type."

"I told you why I needed the Downs. A great place, really, and the second jail of my life. Much nicer, I will say. You were talking of Sarita, I believe."

"Where was I...Sarita...oh, I remember. She had a bang-up academic career until that business went to hell but she could fall back on her writing.

She's quite a success as a biographer, with prizes and what-all. This is a big series she's doing, the five most notable scientists of the past hundred years, a book for each one of them. Seems like last week, doesn't it? Most of a hundred years going that fast. When she was determined to include you, then I thought I had to tell her about us. She couldn't believe it at first. But she's inquisitive. She wanted to know you and she thinks she does. She says you can be quite wonderful and also a little crusty at times. Oh, I'd like to thank you for having her knee looked after."

"Sure."

"It was very good of you."

"So strange, all this. It's flabbergasting."

"Many things are. Look at the world."

"Yes, look at it. So, all the time," he continued, "she knew who I was and I didn't know who she was. My daughter. You women are damn devious customers. To think that she and Christopher are brother and sister, half way. Rather unbelievable, isn't it?"

"And you'd still want to delude her?"

"There's so much to think about," he said. "What a family. A daughter I never knew I had. And you, the mother. It seems impossible. You know, I can do lots of things for Sarita if she'll ever let me."

"She does quite well on her own."

"I'm sure, but then again she's my...*my kid*. I can't get used to that idea yet."

"Let her decide if and when she ever wants anything from you. I doubt it, though. Why would she ever want anything from Raoul Marciara-Quina, a perfect stranger?"

"I was only thinking that I've got a lot I'd like to make up for. Sure. I guess I can wait. She was married. We didn't discuss it. Who was he and where is he?"

"Erno Sambinna. Handsome as anything you ever saw. He's a Tuscan. A painter and he trained in Florence and Paris, and one day he didn't paint, not around Sarita anyway, and the last anyone heard he was in Tibet learning how to operate a prayer wheel. Burning incense probably wearing one of those saffron robes. No one knows."

"Another disappearing act, like us. I can find out, if he's still alive."

"Don't. It's ancient history. He's better off and Sarita is, too."

"I see. Not a happy time of it, I guess. Where'd the name Sarita come from?"

"My grandmother, it was her middle name. It came down from her paternal grandmother. A hand-me-down."

"I feel like a hand-me-down sometimes."

"A handful, anyway."

"I'm not that bad. Not really."

"Sorry, I don't want to say the wrong thing and I guess I have. It's just that trouble always keeps you dead square in the eye of its periscope. You'll always be a thirty-year old with a long lightning rod in your hand. And now I'd like to take a walk, even though I've a hundred things to do." She shook her head as if to clear it, and said: "Incredible, how much controversy you arouse."

"It's in my manual, the one that tells how to operate my buttons and levers."

"Get yourself a new manual, Señor Marciara-Quina. I've things to do, so I'll see you to the door."

"What for? We were getting somewhere."

"We're getting you to the door, too."

"I don't want to leave." With a look of lament, he told her, "I've missed us."

She went out for a walk after he departed. Often she took to walking in the mountain air when assailed by turmoil. She had plenty of it to deal with just then, and...well, who else was there to talk with, but herself.

Her phone began its trumpeting at the break of dawn. *Ring-a-ling-ring* all morning long, a slight interruption at noon, then resuming for the balance of the afternoon. Sometime after the fifteenth call, the ring of the phone had transformed itself into a semblance of a screeching ambulance siren; a sound for the sick, and it was making her sick, quaking her nerves as to what would come next. The phone had become an instrument for fear-mongering, and she almost decided not to answer anymore. But she was awaiting an important call from her silver supplier and didn't want to chance missing it.

Pandemonium beyond all belief.

News-hawkers by the droves, the mission-head in downtown Santa Fe voicing his profuse thanks, a number of Santa Fe's misfits draping her with praise, an "atta-girl" call from an assistant on the governor's staff, calls from several citizens unknown to her, and still others from a few very surprised friends...all wanting to know if they could help, was she looking for employees, was she planning to do more fundraising in the future? Well-wishers, hangers-on, and instant experts were hers for the taking.

When hearing the sum of money involved from one of the reporters, she instantly knew who to blame, quite obviously so, recalling his claim—that he had all this outlandish wealth at his command, just as he had reported in that long, long but quite enlightening letter to Sarita. He had even said yesterday that money would soon find its way to Santa Fe, exclusively to aid its dead-enders.

It had, just as predicted. The lout!

What had begun as a mist of surprise that morning had quickly converted to a fog-like rage. She had cut off some callers with a flat, abrupt good-bye before they could say much at all. Scorched, livid. Usually, she was even-natured, often gay-hearted, friendly and sociable to most everyone. Yet something seemed to be draining out of her—her composure, that's what it was, sliding away, emptying her so she could make room for ballooning fury

He had boxed her in a paradox. Barely could she afford the life she led; now he had turned her into a one-woman charity, or so it would sound to too many people. Not a single word had been exchanged about involving her publicly in his schemes. In fact, he had talked and talked of operating off-stage, deep behind the scenes. How could he be so crass, so unthoughtful, so reckless, so incorrigible? And now look! How could she ever deny her involvement? She could, she thought, oh yes indeedy, she could. But only by revealing him as an imposter—who he really was, and instantly she knew she'd be paving the way, perhaps, for more attempts on his life.

Betray him? Yet by being truthful with her, and wanting her back in his life, telling her too many times to count, he'd put his life in her hands?

Ring-a-ling-ring.

As the noise jarred her, Shandar's nerves flew. Her teeth snapped shut so violently a sharp pain shot up to the bridge of her nose. Reaching for her cell phone this time, she knocked it off the table and went pawing for it under the bed. Thinning her lips till her mouth looked like a pink slot, reaching into that place where she kept her deepest anger, she punched in the numbers for The Adobe.

He was slipping on his moccasins, when the phone over by the desk rattled. No sooner than picking it up, he braced against the force of an incensed woman. "What've you done, you lunatic bastard? It was you, it had to be *you*, and I'm the one getting all these calls and requests…they want pictures and a statement for print. It's been a madhouse here."

"That comm-sat report, you mean? I'll bet it'll be good publicity for your business and—"

"You and your marbles, I truly wonder if you ever had any marbles in that dumb-brained head. Everyone knows I don't have thirty-million dollars to give out. How silly of you—it's outlandish and—"

"I never said you gave it personally. Neither did the newscast say it, not the one I saw anyway. What I explicitly said to the comm-sat editor was that you personally arranged for the funds to be given. What's wrong with that? A lovely gesture. Kindness and charity. They'll probably erect a statue to you, and I'd like to be the guy who takes the measurements for the sculptor."

"You never...not once...never even had the courtesy to ask me."

"If you'd stick around town for a while, I would ask. Lots of things I'd ask about."

"You've no right...I could hate you, you know..."

"You're the new Santa Fe poster girl. What a country...what a dame. I'm coming by for an autograph."

Cold of voice, she said, "You've put me in a real fix. Everyone'll think I'm rich and that I'm charging too much for my silversmithing. It's calamitous, knowing you."

Cautiously and casually, he said, "Someone else said that to me once. In Paris one very dreary rainy afternoon. Acid rain, as I recall, and it was falling indoors and on me. Out of the mouth of one of your favorite—well, I won't mention the name."

"Why in hell did you do this to me?"

"How do I get you to listen to me?"

"It's preposterous."

"You've got to be a part of this, because I can't win this by myself. I put your name on that gift so that people will know of you, where you stand, that you want to help these jerks who got themselves in such a mess and can't get out of it. You've helped them when no one else has come forward. There'll be talk, lots of it. Eventually, those poor nincompoops will endorse our message. I think they will if you'll do the asking. You'll be a sort of a savior, the fixer of the future. Getting people back to Sane Street...you've got to, you've just got to, Shandar..."

Empty air.

"All the same, you sandbagged me. I'm not forgetting what you did...Raoul-Whatever. Damn you anyway."

"I did implicate you, but all in a good cause."

"You might've asked, you know. You could've asked."

"You said so, already. And I said that half the time I can't find you. You move around like a dust devil. Besides, I did mention it to you the other day."

"I told you I wanted no part in it. Thirty-million…fr'god…"

"I have many thirties at my command, as you know."

"As I've heard, you mean. Yes, the Great Train Robbery or the equivalent. You should be ashamed of yourself. How do you sleep at night, I wonder?"

She sounded as if she were temporizing a bit, easing off; the pitch of her voice had softened. So he returned, "I know how I'd like to sleep at night and it's not alone."

And they talked for a time, some of it disjointedly almost spat-like, but he became slightly more sanguine. He told her he needed some way of illustrating how genuine good could be done for others, investing them with small hopes, or at least a particle of hope, and that money could have its own power for goodness, too. He went on, saying he was showing her in the only immediate way he knew of what was possible and why she was needed, and what he intended to do with his days, and, he hoped, her days.

In her heart she had to know it was right, and he, little by little, could sense it in her words. They settled nothing. Yet at the end she seemed slightly more acquiescent, seemed half-persuaded, as if what he'd been selling her a seat in the realm of the possible.

In the kitchen brewing tea, off-and-on Shandar had been glancing at the comm-sat broadcast, when a local news segment aired. An eruption of jubilation as thousands of milling *Gorpos* at Santa Fe's Old Town Square were waving arms, amid shouting and screaming. The camera lingered on the scene, then panned to the sideliners. She could see rapt looks, as if the awe-struck onlookers were witnessing some benevolent vision descending from the heavens. Zooming in, the camera picked up several tear-streaked faces. People were carried about on the shoulders of the strong. Circles of dancers pirouetted. Horns tooted. Fireworks. Some were making speeches no one could hear, nor cared to. A few nude streakers ran about carrying signs with indecipherable messages.

She poured her tea, squeezing a few lemon drops into the steaming cup. Feeling strange, wondering why, feeling a little light-headed, also wondering why.

Looking at the roaring crowd again, thinking—is this what thirty-million does? Or was it something else? Human caring, perhaps. Human something or other.

Leaning against a kitchen counter, she breathed more heavily than she usually did. Her wits flew everywhere. Her eyes burned. She wiped them clear with a tea towel and the simplicity of the act seemed, oddly, to wash away so many trepidations and unknowns.

She knew, then, that she wasn't finished with him. He was taking some chances himself. Big chances. He was an all or nothing-at-all type. That was the trouble with a man like Thom—like Raoul Marciara-Quina. So much baggage, so much like trudging up a mountain with no top to it. Yet, in all these years, she had yet to meet another man, after the death of her husband, who could keep her interested for more than a week at best.

Why was she so inclined? So molded? Why should she lend herself to the all-or-nothing formula? That's the way of it, the only way it was for him and now, perhaps, for herself. Osmosis or something like it.

Time to get straight with him.

Veni, vidi, vici, she thought, recalling her school-days Latin. Well, balls to that; and double balls to Caesar and all the others who acted like him.

She had no intention, ever, of being conquered. Of being maneuvered into some scheme. Of losing her independence. Of running around with someone raised from the dead.

But as she thought about it, she also thought of those joyfully screaming *Gorpos* she had seen on television. Things change, things always change.

And thinking that, she knew the past seventy years had come to their end. And so had she.

She walked with him along her street—Calle del Cielo—to its end. From there, Shandar led the way on a gravel trail that meandered through a copse of pinion pines, emitting a heavy smell of resin. They footed along till reaching a wide flat opening that gave off to a rock-strewn ledge. Beyond lay a spacious vista of snow-clad mountain peaks sharply etched against a topaz sky. At the center of the opening stood a weather-bleached bench of sturdy timbers, and from out of the northwest, the wind blew in swirling gusts; one moment there, gone the next.

"Pretty stiff breeze," he commented. "I'm glad I don't wear a toupee."

"I'm glad you don't, too. I'm very glad you shaved off that beard, too. I meant to tell you before."

"I was just beginning to get used to it."

"I couldn't ever get used to it. You still have the same chin. It's the same shape."

"That's why I grew the beard."

"I wouldn't worry."

"You haven't been where I have."

They were about to sit when he stopped her so he could clean away bird droppings. He dug up a handful of gravely earth and rubbed it vigorously against the bench seat. When cleaned, they sat and she poured piping hot tea from a thermos.

He sipped, she spoke.

"…you've a bar of iron in you and I don't, or not that much I don't. Lonely courage, that's what Si Nestor used to say about you. Old Si. But you've got to see my side. You arrive here one day at my gate as a total stranger, and then when I was convinced it was you after you began talking and saying everything. France and all. I knew things, a lot of things about you by then. Because, as I told you the other day, I read your letter to Sarita. An unforgettable surprise, you walking into my life like that. I knew you'd told Sarita that you were regretful of so much…and that you said you'd loved only one woman in your life and I didn't have any trouble figuring out that that was *moi*. But seventy years is still seventy years and we all change. I have and so have you, even if you don't admit it although you probably do. All that surgery and whatever. How am I to know how I feel after we had a two-time crackup? Most people don't make it past one. You act as if it's only been a long weekend since we last saw each other and, hey babe, let's ride the magic carpet again. Then you spew all these ideas of how to make war on the biotech people, just like The League once went after you. And some of them went to prison, if I recall, and I'm not recalling too aptly these days, but I think I'm right that they did get jail time. If all of that, all that you're asking, and this life you say you want to follow, if that isn't enough to make someone go off their beam, go crazy, then I don't know what would…and now I'm out of breath completely."

"I went crazy a long time ago. Crazy about you and I intend to stay crazy. That's what's on the table, amigo."

"Why are you always so damn stubborn?"

"It often pays the best dividends. Persistence, I call it."

"…god, you…you *are* something, really you are…didn't you think it rather pompous of you to turn down that Nobel?"

"Pompous? I wouldn't say pompous. I thought I was being fair. Anyway, I've heard of actors who turned down an Oscar. Why can't you refuse whatever you don't want?"

A wisp of her smile, then, heartening him. He wanted to hold her, touch parts of her, connect, finger the fuchsia colored ribbon tying her hair together so the wind wouldn't disarray it.

Pouring more tea, she topped off his plastic mug. She had talked so calmly, so in possession of her thoughts. Sensing she was about to say something terminal, something he could ill afford to hear in his state of feeling, he arose and walked toward the ledge's edge. It seemed as if he were two-stepping on eggshells, that something fragile inside himself was about to crack wide open.

He took perhaps thirty steps, not knowing why he was where he was, and then it seemed he teetered on the edge of earth itself. He looked down, fretfully, into the cavernous abyss and then to the valley floor and its winding strip of river. Standing here, he was unable to think about anything else. Not her, not anything. Be so easy, he was thinking. Why in hell not? *What do I owe anyone?* One leap into space and he could forget all the promises he'd made to himself. Maybe this was the day for the blue suit and a good embalmer, except nothing would be left to embalm. Lights out…like that…a snap of the fingers and he'd be on his way to eternal peace after a life of non-stop tumult.

He heard her calling to him. "What're you doing over there?"

Looking back at her then, ensuring it was Shandar speaking and not a figment of his imagination. "I was calculating some distances. I'd never make it on the high-wire in a circus. You know what? Why don't you marry me and we can cut all this out? Hunt up some good champagne, hustle up a justice of the peace and have a real time of it. If you don't feel like marrying me, okay…that's okay…not really okay but I'll concede you might have a very good argument. I doubt if I'd marry me, either. You can always let things breathe a little, and then decide. I think you're the best piece of art ever done by evolution. The whole corsage. I'm still torqued over you. Imagine getting married. A novelty these days. If you don't care to have a life together, then okay, you don't. I can be a great friend to have. But there'll always be you, and at least I can live on it as long as I can. But damn sure, madam, I'd like to strip you down right to the pink and have some life together starting now. Really pester you. Why don't we take a stroll down Love Lane and see where it goes. Why not try that again? Love, the universal painkiller. Double euphoria. That's what I feel like, and you can always pretend it's the same for you, even if it isn't. Charades, you know…that old game…but you're not a game to me, you're the whole show."

"…Oh, my…oh…" A fresh gust swept the ledge, as she asked stridently, "And what of Sarita?"

"She's invited to the wedding, of course. First on the list. Wouldn't think of not having her."

"That isn't what I meant and you very well know it."

"Yes, I'll tell her. Don't remind me again."

"Promise me."

He gave her a look. "I think I know how Adam felt when Eve tossed him that apple. It's extortion or close to it."

"The wages of sin rise by the day."

"Why don't we lie down together while I'm still recovering?"

"Recovering?"

"Recovering from seeing you again. I'm still thinking how nice it'd be if you and I could go off and invent some newer versions of mortal sin. Dream up commandment eleven and twelve and then break them all to smithereens. We can work on this over lunch tomorrow, but over breakfast would be much better. Early breakfast. Four a.m. or something on that order. In bed and working our way up toward a hundred-and-twenty degree Fahrenheit heatstroke."

Only ten paces away, he heard her say: "You're looking so desperate."

"I probably am desperate. I've had desperate days. And don't laugh, nothing is very funny right now."

"You have these odd looks once in a while. And they are funny."

"I don't feel very funny. Not at all, but my nerves take only so much."

"You've the nerves of a safecracker, and you always have." The wind suddenly picked up and in stronger voice she said: "Come here."

"What?"

Her voice rising, her hand beckoning. "Here, to me. *Here!*"

She stood, and, as she did, a burst of wind ruffled her hair. He came to her, standing directly at her front. Her face with that look that comes to a woman when everything in their eyes has changed, because everything behind their eyes already had changed.

"You meant it about Sarita. You'll tell her?"

"I meant it," he agreed. "I'm also beginning to believe I really am suicidal."

"If it's dangerous for you, it'll be dangerous for me. Anyway, she'd never make a peep. I know my daughter."

"Our daughter, you mean."

"Our daughter, I like that. So much better to hear you say it that way. She'll be thrilled. We'll be a starter-family, won't we?" Shandar laughed.

At first, he didn't catch the gist of her words. But then, when they sunk in, he blurted, "You're with me, then? You'll help?"

"You've always needed a keeper. You're the next thing to a schmegeggy." Saying it, her mouth sculpted into a smile, as alluring to him as a harvest moon."

"A shmegg—what's that again?"

"A schmegeggy. Yiddish, and it means a nincompoop."

"I can't help who I am. Me is only me."

"You needn't remind me."

"I think I do. I know I do. I'm in great need of you, Shandar. I really am, and I love you. I know you know that, whatever you say to the contrary."

She looked off before looking straight at him. "Yes, I'm with you, Raoul...Ra-*ool*. There, you see, I said it without you reminding me, now all I have to do is remember it. Ra-*ool*. I like the name Thomas better, but one can get used to anything, can't they?"

"One hopes."

"Veni, vidi, vici...that's a direct quote from Caesar."

"I remember." Smiling, he said," Meaning what?"

"That I feel silly. I'm going a little crazy. Caesar was crazy, I think, and now I am. And so are you? So there! How do you like that?"

"I'll tell you tomorrow."

"Who knows if there'll be one?"

"We do. You and I do. Remember the lyric, 'All my tomorrows belong to you.'"

"Really? Well, I'm taking you up on that, just to prove to myself I'm crazy."

"About me, you mean?"

"Hush and kiss me. "

Holding her right forearm, he placed a hand against her cheek. In the lifting wind, she swayed slightly, delicately, like an underwater flower. When bending to her, an extreme thing moved in him, and then came a long ago remembrance—*she still tastes like sage and honey.*

END

Acknowlegements

When thinking about this book some years ago, while living in San Diego, I accessed any number of biotech gurus in the area. Some were of the Scripps Research Institute; still others were of the many biotechnology companies scattered throughout that sun-soaked, ocean-side playground of Southern California. One was Kary Mullis, a likeable surfer and biochemist, who won the Nobel and the Japan Prize in 1993, a signal achievement. Never before, or since, replicated.

I was learning things, some of which found their way into this story. It is, after all, a story and not a textbook.

In one of the final drafts of *Gun of God,* Tom Jenks—formerly a senior editor of Scribner's, also a one-time fiction editor for *Esquire*, and the editor/publisher for an impressive list of many well-known American writers—penciled his way through my morass, suggesting many useful and much needed adjustments. Laurie Rosin made other suggestions: Laurie has edited titles that, collectively, have sold over 50-million copies.

From them, other learnings.

In a final dash toward the finish line, a rank of friends (and they know who they are) discovered my proofing flaws, the many of them, and a half-bushel of "illogicals" that peppered the pages.

To my loved wife, Lee, who, with her eagle-eye and Job's patience, I owe plentiful thanks for her many other markings and suggestions.

Indeed, I owe you all, always shall…
DRC

About the Author

DAVID CUDLIP holds a master's degree in business administration from Dartmouth College's Amos Tuck School, and served in Europe with United States Army, in Intelligence duties, before employment with the New York private banking firm of Brown Brothers Harriman & Co. Elected senior vice-president and director of an airline, afterward he went on to became President of Pathfinder Corporation. Later, he co-founded a privately held company—DataMerx—engaged in electronic in-store couponing. He was a member of Fictionaires, a group of well-known California writers. He now lives in Tryon, North Carolina. His first novel, *Comprador*, was published by E.P. Dutton, receiving considerable praise in America and abroad. It is also available as an e-book, accompanied by reviews, at Amazon's Kindle Store. Or, if you're into courtroom dramas, have a look at his *A Moveable Verdict, packed with surprises.*.

ARE YOU A WRITER?

If so, and you would like to collaborate with David Cudlip on added episodes for any of his books, please go to Pen & Pencil Press's website at: **www. Penandpencilpress.com**. Go to the Co-Authoring page. See what's up!

CARE TO POST A REVIEW?

It's easy! If you have an account with Amazon or Kindle Store, follow these steps:
   (1) Go to **www.amazon.com**
   (2) In Search Box select Books from the drop down menu
   (3) In the Search Box, enter, in this case, Gun of God
   (4) When the page loads, scroll down to Customer Reviews and choose the button that says: Create Your Own Review.

If you post a review, and let us know by an email to: **P3@windstream.net**. we'll gladly send you a copy of Georgia Lee Berkley's "picks". You'll find a listing of over 200 memorable books in categories such as Fiction, Biography-Memoir, Mystery-Suspense and Nonfiction. The selections are hers (a top book buyer at Warwick's in La Jolla, CA) but are more fully augmented by other well-known booksellers, college professors, literary agents, numerous book clubs scattered throughout the U.S. and a hefty array of other addicted readers. We encourage you to make your own recommendations, if you wish…

Made in the USA
San Bernardino, CA
09 June 2014